The Baseball Box Prophecy

The Baseball Box Prophecy

Bruce Newbold

Hearthsong

Hearthsong Entertainment, LLC. Salt Lake City, UT

Hearthsong

Text copyright © 2009 Bruce Newbold
Cover art copyright © 2009 David Malan
Illustrations copyright © David Malan
Layout and cover design by M4, Inc.

Published in the United States by Hearthsong Entertainment.
Printed by FC Printing, Salt Lake City, Utah, 2010.

For further information visit:
www.TheBaseballBoxProphecy.com

Library of Congress Cataloging-in-Publication Data
Library of Congress Control Number: 2009908904

ISBN-13: 978-0-9701206-3-2
ISBN-10: 0-9701206-3-X

Second Edition Printing
14 13 12 11 10   6 5 4 3 2

Dedication

There was a boyhood joy in the creation of this story, and I certainly relived early baseball memories time and again. Ed Quinn, you had a large family and a houseful of other priorities, yet you took the time to coach us. Thanks. "Fire in the hole, Ed!" Denny Cockayne, I remember that as the high school star athlete, you took a few moments to play some catch with a lowly ninth-grader there on the pavement of Wake Forest. Thank you. In fact, thanks to all of you who take the time to play with a child in need. And Doug Young, you and I played over-the-line for hours on the playground of Hannah Holbrook. The Weatherby's backyard devoured many a homerun ball. Thanks, Doug, for the memories.

As my time on the planet increases, my profound respect grows for those who never discouraged imagination and the arts. Dale and Barbara Newbold, please know of my love and gratitude for your constant support and guidance. And, Lisa, my beloved—who on the roller-coaster rides of life is the neck that holds the head straight—be confident of my devotion, respect, and fidelity.

Contents

Acknowledgments

About the Author

PROLOGUE

She placed the ancient box reverently upon her brown, burlap skirt and caressed its bronze and wooden panels. The old text engraved on the lid had been translated and memorized long ago. She had voiced it privately thousands of times before, and tonight, in the flutter of candlelight, she responded to the gnawing urge to recite it once again. As she squinted one eye, her craggy, deep voice coughed out the words of the prophecy.

Called by that which he wears upon his feet,
He shall rise with her from the wet earth.
Then shall the powers of the box be revealed,
And to him shall it be delivered.
In that day, comes the searching Traveler.
In the arena of battle, their weapons shall be clubs, orbs, spikes.
The orb shall be driven at his command.
Then, when the heart of the finder fails,
And the son be as the father, the new Traveler shall appear.
In the freezing of time his choice shall be made,
Unsealing the box by the hand of his power.
Then shall the box know him,
For time is red upon his shoulders.

She lifted her eyes to the smooth rocks of the fireplace and inhaled deeply. Her wide nostrils flared.

"How much longer?" she whispered.

Chapter 1

The Discovery

"Let's get it out of the rain and up into the tent," announced Dr. Peter McGuire, looking down at the second body, finally unearthed from the peat that had imprisoned it for nearly a thousand years. "Carry it up and place it on the table next to the other one."

The workers lifted the corpse onto the stretcher and began their ascent up the rock steps that led out of the pit. The light, warm sprinkle that fell upon the archeological site suddenly became a downpour, and the Irish earth swiftly turned soggy, stubbornly clinging to the shoes and boots and pant legs of all who gathered to see the mummified remains.

"Pull those tent flaps down to protect the cadavers!" called McGuire, pointing behind him to the canvas rolls above the tables.

On this dawn of early May 1991, the bog had generously delivered the precious remains of a well-preserved pig and two small children. As McGuire followed the stretcher-bearers into the protection of the canopy, he signaled to the empty space on the long table in front of him.

"There, beside the other body. Let's keep them both a little distance from the pig, however, at least for now."

Carefully, they lifted the small cadaver from the stretcher and placed it on the white sheet that covered the table. McGuire hovered proudly over the corpse.

"Look like boys. Maybe. Hair is shorter. Wearing pants."

Although the years within the muddy tomb had darkened the skin of the tiny bodies, the size, age, and even the facial features of the two children were easily discernable. Both seemed about five or six years old, and each measured approximately three feet in length— one slightly shorter than the other.

From their findings, and by the scientists' calculations, most of the remains unearthed in this area of the bog dated back to near 1000 A.D. Another body, that of a larger man, had been found in this location the previous year. He too had been well preserved by the natural elements of the bog.

"What is that?" McGuire whispered to himself as he leaned over the smaller of the two children. The curious students and workers huddled closer. Pulling a magnifying glass from his pocket, he held it over the neck of the little, blackened cadaver. "Dr. Samuels," he stated, lifting his head away from the corpse. "Will you step over here?"

Bertram Samuels, an expert in Irish history, was studiously bent over the other cadaver. He straightened his bear-like hairy frame, ducked under the center bar that supported the tent's canopy, and lumbered over to McGuire.

"Right there, around the neck," said McGuire, pointing.

Samuels took the magnifying glass and leaned over the corpse.

"Oh, my . . . Look at that." His voice was soft and high; unexpected for a man of his size.

Around the neck of the tiny body, and attached to a finely woven chain, hung an ornament the size of a small cookie. The object lay nestled among the folds of clothing just below the child's chin. With the help of the magnifying glass, Dr. Samuels could discern the sculpted image of a robed man. Next to that image, something else had been imprinted, but only further cleaning and more careful examination would reveal the secret of the tiny, delicate adornment.

"I've never seen the likes of it," announced Samuels, standing up straight. "But step over here to the other child, McGuire. There is something quite unusual you must see."

Samuels led the way back to the larger of the two bodies.

"The lump in the clothing there puzzles me," he said, pointing to a bulge just above the child's armpit. "There, under the top of the vest." He handed the magnifying glass back to his colleague.

McGuire leaned closer, studying the round lump. The object that created the bulge was partially exposed, caught between the skin of the child and the folds of clothing that surrounded it. The child seemed to be protecting the object—its leathery hands cupped and folded near its neck.

Reaching into his coat pocket, McGuire withdrew a flat, metal probe. Carefully, he placed it under the neck of the vest and eased the clothing away from the child's shoulder, further revealing the object. He gasped, hastily straightened, and stepped back.

"That bloody well can't be!" he exclaimed, looking up at Dr. Samuels.

A sudden wind lifted the canopy above them and flapped it twice upon the metal bars that held the tent in place. McGuire sucked in a deep breath and bowed again over the body.

"Come and get as close to the table as you possibly can," he ordered the team without looking up. "I'm not certain what we'll find here, so I need witnesses."

The eyeless child seemed to gaze innocently back up at them, as if wondering if the scientists would rob him of his long-protected treasure.

After Samuels and the students prepared their cameras and focused them on the table where the little body lay, McGuire again probed the clothing near the armpit of the child's vest. Carefully lifting the folds, he exposed the item in question. With a slight nudge and far too little difficulty, the round object fell away from underneath the child's vest, rolled across the table, and settled several inches away from the foot of the smaller corpse.

Cameras flashed and video recorders hummed. Everyone present sensed the awe, the fascination, the incredibility of such a discovery, and none of them would be kept from capturing their fragment of this historical moment. Slipping his callused hand into a latex glove, McGuire grasped the brown orb and lifted it high for all to see.

CHAPTER 2

THE TABLOID
AND THE TEAM

Cletis Dungarvan knew exactly where it was.

A tabloid, he thought. *One of those newspaper-type magazines that always has something really stupid on it.*

He had seen a headline a week or so back that read: "FROG BABY BORN TO FLORIDA COUPLE: MOTHER KEEPS IT IN WATER IN THE KITCHEN SINK AND FEEDS IT FLIES." On the front page was a picture of a baby with a frog's head. Standing beside it, propping it up in the sink, smiled the proud mother. Cletis remembered it well, and he shook his head at the weirdness of the memory.

But this one's different. This one's about baseball, he told himself, as he hurried through the front door of the drug store and passed the checkout counters. When a kid joined the team, it was part of the initiation. Every one of them had to come up with something valuable or unusual or "baseballically" unique.

Baseballically, Cletis mused. *They just made that word up. And* gription *too.*

"Gription," he whispered, tasting the word.

His friend Elston had told him that if a mitt could catch and hold a ball, if your shoes didn't slip when chasing a pop fly, or if you were lucky enough to get a pair of cleats for better running . . . all those things constituted good gription. Hurrying past a row of shopping carts, he thought about this funny new word.

But even after I get this newspaper, I still gotta play good enough to make the team, he reminded himself. His shoes squeaked on the clean tile flooring as he hustled over to the aisle that housed the magazine racks. *And then there might be more to the initiation after that.* He took a deep nervous breath. *One thing at a time.*

As he jogged, his brand new mitt swung at his side, strapped through his belt. He and his dad had bought it just last week and had spent many an hour breaking it in. They had rubbed conditioning oil into the fingers and palm, put a new ball in the pocket, and then rubber-banded the leather fingers to help form it. Cletis even slept with it.

Spying the magazine section, he eased his way down the aisle. Studiously, he searched for the weekly tabloid selection he needed. After a quick glance over all the newspapers, he found it. He paused momentarily, studying its cover, and then reached down and picked it up. The headline read: "THOUSAND-YEAR-OLD BASEBALL FOUND IN THE ARMPIT OF BOG BOY." Below the bold print was a picture of a dark and shriveled tiny body. A scientist-looking man stood next to it, holding up an old brown baseball.

Whoa! Cletis marveled silently. *What if a baseball could really be a thousand years old?*

With the paper tight in his hands, he stepped away from the magazine rack, turned, and rushed down the aisle.

Elston Blanchard was near home plate, eyeing the field. The baseball diamond was located about four hundred yards north of the school grounds in the middle of a large vacant field. Years before, when Greenberg Junction was more of a thriving community, a real baseball diamond had been maintained there, with a nice backstop, a grass infield, two dugouts by the base paths, and a scoreboard in deep right field. But years of neglect had killed the grass and had turned the field ugly, brown, and hard. Though the backstop screen and the scoreboard still stood, concreted into the ground, they now wore a coat of aging rust. The two nicely framed dugouts had long since decayed or, as some reported, had been torn down piece by piece by Mr. Howard, the homeless man who lived behind the grocery store. All that now remained of the dugouts were the two decaying benches bolted to the upright, rusted, steel bars fastened into the concrete slab beneath them.

Elston had been told that in 1986, just before he moved in, the neighborhood boys had cleared the weeds from the infield, dug up the base paths, mowed down the outfield weeds, rebuilt the mound, and formed the Greenberg Junction sandlot baseball team. And since that time, summer after summer, the community kids grouped at the field for any kind of play or practice that resembled baseball.

At eight o'clock that morning, Elston and the team (presently made up of seven boys and one girl) gathered for their first practice of the season. Elston had told Cletis to meet them there. Everything was all planned. Practice would start, Cletis would come with his newspaper, and then decisions would be made. Elston wondered how the players on the field would react to the new kid. As usual, their bikes were deposited haphazardly behind the third base bench, and now, with their mitts and bats and baseballs scattered across the infield, they were huddled around home plate, eager to play some ball.

"So, like Klu's big brother taught us last year," announced Johnny Skinner, the team captain, "every time we're on this field, we gotta be lookin' for some baseball magic. We gotta be makin' it." He lifted his bat onto his shoulder and watched his buddies shuffle anxiously in their places, like horses restless to run. "And that starts right now. Okay, everybody take your positions. Let's get the season started."

Instantly they all scattered.

The baseball *magic* that Johnny referred to came only once in a while during the summer. So it was simply a matter of watching and waiting—waiting for those moments when someone would hit the ball farther than ever before or make some spectacular, diving catch or turn a double play. That was baseball magic.

"Comin' at ya, Elston!" Johnny yelled as he cocked the bat, tossed up the ball, and swatted a grounder to first base.

"So what are we doin' about a ninth player?" questioned Frank Cleveland from third base. He watched as Elston fielded the ball, tagged first base, and tossed the ball to Klu at home plate.

"We're gonna talk about it in a sec," answered Johnny. "Your dad gonna let you play with us this summer, Frank?"

Frank bent down, picked up a couple of dirt clods, and tossed them toward the dugout bench. "Hope so. Depends on the pigs, I guess."

"We need you out here," continued Johnny.

"If I can get the chores done early, I'll be here."

"And you gotta get the ball to my mitt this year," Elston teased from first base, slapping his glove. "I don't wanna go chasin' everything through the weeds out there again." Elston pointed toward the open fields in foul territory behind first base.

"Yeah, yeah," moaned Frank. "You just gotta learn to catch."

Johnny lifted the ball from Klu's mitt, rolled it gently in his hand, and set himself for the next hit.

"Okay, you all know that Ricky moved to Texas," reminded Johnny as he stroked the next grounder to Davey Michaels at second. "So we're a player short. We gotta get a new kid who can play—like in center field."

Davey gobbled up the grounder and fired it to Elston at first. Elston stepped on the bag, spun, and threw the ball back to Klu. Johnny eyed his shortstop—the only girl on the team—and took the ball from his husky catcher.

"Rabbit, here comes!" But Johnny's swing missed, and the ball thudded to the ground. "Sorry. Early in the season." He picked up the ball again and rested his bat on his shoulder. "Just a sec, Rabbit. Okay, back to Frank's question. You guys all know it's tough to come up with a team around here. But Elston knows this new kid." He looked out at Elston. "What's his name again?"

"Cletis Dungarvan," Elston announced.

"Okay, yeah, him. And he's on his way over here this morning."

Johnny tossed up the ball and swatted a hard grounder to Rabbit.

"Hey, I know him from school," she spoke as she backhanded it to her right, set herself, and side-armed a strike to Elston at first. "At least I think I do. He was in the other class—Elston's class."

As Elston took the throw, he couldn't help but admire Rabbit's abilities on the diamond, even after many months of winter. The girl's fielding was poetry. It all came so naturally to her. She was one of the few who could talk and play at the same time. To Roberta Maria de Jesus Vergara Sanchez, baseball was ballet—soft, graceful, fluid, exact. She was the fastest runner at John Adams Elementary School, and she was a better fielder and bunter than any boy in southern Michigan—at least any Elston had seen. Being a girl, Roberta—or Rabbit, as they called her—took her fair share of razzing, but she held her own courageously.

"Yeah, Cletis, he's the one," called Elston as he tossed the ball to Klu.

"If we're gonna ever play in some real league," continued Johnny, "we gotta have nine guys. And so even if this Cletis kid isn't any good, we're still gonna try him out."

"Heck, Timmy's no good, and we still use him," Frank chortled from third, pointing out at Timmy in right field.

Davey, Klu, and Pauly chuckled quietly. They were used to hearing Frank talk with his foot in his mouth.

"Frank's a moron, Timmy Tim," called Rabbit, turning to right field. "Don't listen to him."

"Just jokin', Tim!" hollered Frank, grinning out at the little right fielder. "Nothin' meant by it!"

"But this new guy's gotta earn it," Johnny continued. "He's gotta want it, and he's gotta earn it even though we need another player bad. It's been five years, or so, that there's been guys out here playin' on this field, and no one's ever seen any league play."

"Yeah, it'd be cool to get to play in some real games," agreed Davey, smiling through his freckles.

"So what d'ya know about this kid?" Johnny questioned Elston, while smacking a ground ball to Frank at third.

"I been playin' with him almost every day since school's been out." The throw slapped into Elston's left-handed first baseman's mitt. "And he plays a lot of catch with his dad. He's pretty much as

9

good as we are, maybe. I haven't seen him hit, but he'd make a good outfielder."

Elston looked down at his arms. His dark skin gleamed with sweat as he turned and tossed the ball back in to Klu.

"So can this Cletis kid hit?" called Pauly Allen from left field.

"Elston said he hasn't seen him hit," called Rabbit from short. "Don't you hear nothin' out there?"

"I guess not," Pauly answered, shooing a small buzzing creature away from his white-blond hair.

Johnny tossed the ball up and belted another grounder to Frank. What was supposed to be a shot between short and third turned into a frozen rope over Frank's head. He jumped high for it, but the ball cleared his mitt by a foot. Pauly scurried in from left, picked it up on the run, and fired it in to Davey, who covered second. Davey took the one-bouncer and placed a tag on a make-believe runner.

"He's out!" he called. He pivoted and shot the ball back to Klu.

"Pauly, you got the footlocker, I see," called Johnny, taking the ball from Klu.

Pauly answered by pointing to an assortment of bikes near the third base bench. Pauly Allen, designated as the team treasurer, was in charge of the most important piece of equipment the team owned: the footlocker. The faded-green, splinter-ridden, wooden box that held the baseball memorabilia the boys had donated to the team when they became a part of it. A collection of baseball magazines, pennants, cards, balls, and programs were locked inside.

"Just so you know," announced Klu, handing the ball to Johnny, "I seen this Cletis kid hittin' with his dad—out here. They been playin' together the past few nights. An' he's got a good swing and makes contact."

Johnny tossed up the ball and swatted it to Davey at second.

"How 'bout his arm?" Johnny asked.

"I saw him throw a one-bounce strike from center field to home, like he was puttin' a play on a kid taggin' from third," Rabbit answered.

Davey scooped up the grounder, touched his bag, and fired the ball back across to Elston. The stocky first baseman took the throw and turned and fired the ball to Klu. The throw was wide right, and Klu hustled off to the backstop to retrieve it.

"Sorry, Klu. Yeah, I was the catcher when he did it," agreed Elston. "Last day of school. But it was just field day, and everyone was kinda messin' around."

"Except *he* was real serious about it," Rabbit commented. "Like he really wanted to show everybody he could play."

"Why didn't he come to us and try out last year?" asked Johnny.

"Somethin' was wrong with his eye," Elston answered. "Couldn't see too good. His one eye was always pointin' off to the side."

"*That's* the kid?" questioned Pauly from left. "I saw him at school when I was in sixth grade. He was in fifth. He was the new kid who couldn't see straight. Didn't he have a patch on it for a while?"

"Make it tough to hit a fastball," spouted Frank from shallow third.

"Make it tough to hit *anything*," added Rabbit.

"And he was takin' care of his mom, who was real sick," Elston added. He moved a few steps toward second base to smash a dirt clod. "And she died last summer, or maybe last spring, so don't anyone go sayin' something stupid." He looked across to Frank. "Okay, Frank?!"

"Back off. I won't."

"What's his last name, again?" asked Johnny.

"Dungarvan," answered Elston.

"What kinda name is that?" asked Davey.

"I dunno, but don't go makin' fun of it," warned Pauly. "He's the kid who pounded on Klu's big brother for calling him 'one-eye.'"

"Oh, man," breathed Klu, lifting his facemask. "He's that kid? It was *him*?"

Johnny turned to Klu, surprised. "Is he serious? This Cletis kid went after *your* big brother?"

"Well, yeah, but my brother pounded him right back harder," Klu added with a shrug. "But even though he was gettin' his clock cleaned, that kid didn't back off." Klu went silent for a moment. "It was probably right about the time his mom died, by the sound of it."

Pondering the death of a mother, Elston looked up past the rusty backstop toward the hill behind the school. In the distance, ould see someone running toward them. It was Cletis. His mitt flopped at his side like the ear of a faithful beagle. In his right hand, he gripped what looked to be the rolled-up tabloid he promised he would bring.

"Here he comes," stated Elston. "Looks like he's got it."

Johnny looked out at second base. "Davey, you all set out there?" His voice was quiet.

Davey looked down at the area behind him, right next to the bag at second base. The flies were gathering, and it stunk. He had been careful to avoid the area during the entire fielding drill.

"Yeah, it's ready. Nice layer of dirt over the top of it."

"Gotta check his base-running," chuckled Johnny beneath a sly grin. "We'll see if he can take a joke too."

Elston sighed. He personally didn't think it would be all that funny.

The boys on the field turned and looked up the hill. There, sprinting toward them, came Cletis Dungarvan—the newest wannabe member of the neighborhood sandlot team. Johnny turned back to his teammates.

"Remember, he's gotta earn this," he reminded. "Pauly, get the footlocker!"

Without breaking stride, Cletis lifted his Tigers hat from off his head and shook it beside him to air it out and cool it off. His strawberry blond hair lifted and fell with each stride. *I can catch a fly ball now as good as any of 'em,* he thought, as the excitement grew within him. *I can hit almost as good as any of 'em.*

From his approaching vantage point, Cletis could see the movement on the field, and could hear Johnny calling out orders. He watched Pauly jog over to the pile of bikes, heft a wooden box from underneath a red Huffy, and carry it over to home plate.

The others gathered around the batter's boxes. Their eyes were all on him. A queasy nervous anxiety suddenly churned in the pit of his stomach.

Cletis came to a halt behind the backstop, his breathing labored.

"I got it. Right here," panted Cletis, lifting the newspaper for all to see.

"Bring it over here," responded Johnny.

Cletis came around the third base side of the backstop and crossed to the plate.

"Put it down on top of the locker," directed Pauly, pointing to the newspaper.

Cletis placed the tabloid on the footlocker, unrolled it, and held it in place. The boys and Rabbit leaned low to look at the headline: "THOUSAND-YEAR-OLD BASEBALL FOUND IN THE ARMPIT OF BOG BOY."

There was a moment of silence as it all sunk in. Finally Klu spoke up.

"Boy, that's really weird."

"Yeah, but it's kind of cool, too," added Pauly, studying the accompanying photo of the man holding the ball and the black little bodies in the background.

"That is such a crock," spouted Frank. "They didn't even have baseball back then."

"Open it to the story," demanded Davey. "What does it say about it?"

Cletis pushed past the pages until he came to the actual article. As he held the paper in place, the boys peered in again and pondered the additional photos.

"Look at this," said Rabbit, pointing to a close-up of the ball. "It says they think they can read *Official Little League* written on it!"

Frank was again quick to respond, even in the midst of an eruption of laughter from the other boys.

"That is the stupidest thing I've ever heard! What a pile—"

"Hey, just a minute," spoke Rabbit "It could be true. You never know."

"You think it is?" asked Timmy innocently.

"Do ya think?" responded Klu, elbowing little Timmy in the ribs and pushing him away playfully.

"No, Timmy, it's *not* true," stated Johnny protectively. "They print this stuff for suckers. No offense, Cletis."

Cletis nodded and smiled. He was just happy to be the center of attention for a moment, surrounded by the guys and girl he wanted to play baseball with.

"Yeah, okay, we've seen enough," stated Johnny, taking a big breath. "Into the locker."

Johnny picked up the tabloid and handed it to Pauly. Pauly pulled a little key from his pocket, pushed it into the lock on the side of the box, twisted—the lock fell open with a click—removed the lock from the latch, and opened the box. Cletis curiously peered in. He saw baseball cards, including an old Hank Aaron, a Harmon Killebrew, and a rookie card of the Tiger ace, Denny McClain. He saw an old Tigers program, an autographed baseball—he couldn't make out the names on it—and an unopened pack of Donruss baseball cards. Once the tabloid was resting on top of the other items inside, Pauly lifted the lid, dropped it back down into place, secured the latch, and locked it up. Like marching soldiers, Rabbit and Pauly picked up the footlocker and carried it off to the concrete of the third base dugout.

"Okay, step one is done," Johnny announced. "We got the weird baseball newspaper."

Cletis looked around at the boys, awaiting orders and hoping for some sign of acceptance. He noticed that almost all of them were taller than he was, all but Timmy and Rabbit. He could look Davey straight in the eyes.

"Next, start here," spoke Johnny, pointing at home plate, "and run the bases fast as you can. But slide into second. Hook slide and come up standing."

Those were the leader's orders, given with a straight face. Cletis slipped his mitt off his belt, dropped it at home plate, refastened his belt, and started running.

Taking a wide turn at first, Cletis gathered his thoughts. *Bend one foot under me as I go down. When I hit the base with the front foot, I use the base to stop me, and I lift myself up. Wait a minute, that's not a hook slide. Oh well, too late now. I just hope second base is pegged into the ground or it's gonna go slidin' into left field.*

About eight feet in front of the bag Cletis went down perfectly. But as he hit the ground, he felt the earth give way. A long wall of black, manure-mixed mud flew up around him as he hit the trap. His momentum pushed him to the bottom of the pit, and he came to a complete stop about one foot in front of the bag. Before he could rise, the well-fertilized mud slowly settled in around him. His shoes, pants, and the back of his shirt were covered with the dung-and-dirt mixture. Instantly, he rolled to his left, toward the dry ground of the infield.

A howl of laughter erupted from around home plate. It appeared as if everyone on the team knew exactly what was coming—which seemed to make the success of their practical joke all the sweeter. Elston, whose heart wasn't really in it, raced over the mound toward second.

"You okay?" he asked, leaning toward Cletis.

"Yeah. I'm fine."

Cletis rose slowly. With his arms away from his side, he looked like a stork struggling to rise from an oil slick. At home plate everyone was still relishing the moment, hooting out loud and patting each other on the back. The sight of them all, howling at the joke they had just played on the new boy, brought a smile to Cletis's face. A sudden chuckle escaped through his nose. Cletis stepped a few paces away from Elston and kicked and flipped the mud in all directions, trying to get as much off of him as possible. Then, with Elston at his side, Cletis trudged back over the mound and up to the plate. As the boys continued their laughter, Cletis picked up his mitt, looked up at Johnny, and with a crooked smile asked, "Okay, what's next?"

"Didn't quite make it to third," bellowed Klu, slapping Johnny on the back.

Frank, still laughing, dropped to his knees and rolled onto his side. "Just tuck a baseball under his arm pit, and we got us our *own* bog boy!"

Another round of laughter exploded from the boys. Cletis stood calmly, absorbing the laughter. But from their good-natured taunting, there arose within him a stronger determination to make good on this little try-out.

I'll take this now. They can laugh all they want. But this'll be the last time I'm the butt of their jokes.

Johnny eyed him, still chortling as he gazed down at this mud-drenched newcomer.

"Go out to center field. I'll hit you some."

Cletis turned and ran, a bit stiff-legged, back across the diamond. The mud still flopped away from him with every step, leaving a trail of brown droppings in his wake. The boys roared again as they watched Cletis slosh across the infield.

This isn't gonna stop me, he reminded himself. *This'll help me do better. They'll see.*

Johnny picked up the bat and ball. As Cletis passed second base—the shortstop side of it this time—Johnny called out, "Here it comes!"

He threw the ball upward and belted it. It shot upwards into a high fly that arced toward deep right-center field.

Cletis saw it come off the bat and got a good jump on it. Despite its height and distance, he sensed he had a chance to haul it in. He spotted it over his right shoulder, knowing he'd have to hustle. But there *was* a chance. The muddy manure that clung to his pants made it difficult to run, but Cletis sensed that if he pushed himself to his limit, he could get under it. The sky was blue overhead, which made tracking the ball all the easier. His eyes had never before been able to follow the ball like this. He was again amazed by his renewed vision and depth perception after the surgery.

The ball was coming down now—closer, ever closer—as he hustled after it.

But I'm not under it yet! I'm gonna have to dive! I've never done that before. But if I don't dive, it's gonna just be outta reach!

The moment the ball came over his right shoulder, Cletis lunged, his left hand out-stretched across the front of him. With a gentle thud, he felt the ball enter his mitt, just above the pocket.

Gotta hold it. I'm gonna hit the ground pretty hard.

He landed flat on his chest and slid to a grinding halt. Struggling to find his breath, he looked up into his glove. The ball was still there!

Get it home! Show 'em what you're made of!

He struggled to his feet and turned toward the plate. He knew the play wasn't over yet. *Runner's taggin' from third. Maybe a slow runner.*

He took two steps, and, with all his might, fired the ball back toward the infield. It sailed directly over second, straight as a spear, toward home. His soon-to-be teammates stood in such awe of the catch that they had paid little attention to the incoming toss. Only Klu realized that the throw was sailing directly at him. The big catcher set himself and raised his glove over the plate. The ball hit the ground midway between the mound and home, and on one bounce popped into Klu's mitt, held just slightly to the third base side of home plate and about one foot off the ground. He held his glove in place for all to see, as if framing a good pitch for a slow umpire.

No one spoke. No one breathed.

From deep right center, Cletis glared defiantly in at the plate, still lost in the make-believe moment of the play. He watched as Johnny eyed Klu, studying the location of the catcher's mitt, and then turned and looked back out at the newcomer in the outfield.

Cletis knew it was a great catch and a perfect throw—except for the one bounce. In fact, he had surprised himself! Despite the gathering of flies around his muddy pants, he stayed where he was and watched as the team excitedly huddled over home plate. In the quiet, rural fields outside of Greenberg Junction, sound carried well. Standing still as a scarecrow on a windless day, he listened in on as much of their conversation as he could hear.

"Where did *that* come from?" spoke Pauly, putting his mitt exactly where Klu's had been.

"I dunno," answered Klu, looking out at Cletis. "I haven't even seen Rabbit do that."

"Yeah, but I can," she responded, stepping in front of Klu.

"That's *two* magics in *one* practice, from the same kid, in the same moment!" spouted Johnny. "That ain't never been done before."

Frank said something indiscernible and then laughed. Davey poked at him.

"We haven't seen him hit yet, but we can't pass up an arm like that," declared little Timmy, trying hard to be one of the guys.

"Not to mention that catch," added Pauly.

"Yep," responded Johnny. He took a deep breath, exhaled, and then studied the guys around him. "We need him. But, remember, he's still gotta earn it." He dropped the bat at the plate, and his hands went slowly to his hips.

Cletis then heard him say something about "one more thing to do," but he sensed Johnny had lowered his voice intentionally, attempting to communicate only to those close to him.

The boys and Rabbit fell silent again, and they peered back out at Cletis.

What are they talkin' about? Cletis thought, finally stepping forward to kick mud off his pants.

"We all did it to join this team," Johnny continued seriously. He looked over at Timmy. "All except one. So the new kid's gotta do it too."

"Initiation?" shuddered Timmy.

Johnny nodded. "I don't see why he shouldn't."

Cletis watched curiously. *Initiation? Do they know I can hear almost everything they're saying?*

When Johnny whispered something to the team, everyone peered out at Cletis for a quick moment.

"Yeah, but the initiation is gettin' more dangerous every time," Elston cautioned loudly, his arms lifting from his sides.

"Quiet. We'll just have to see what he's made of," Klu answered.

When all appeared settled, Johnny turned around and eyed Cletis. "Come on in!"

Suddenly a bit concerned, Cletis headed toward the infield. Despite his apprehension, he sensed a measure of respect in their stares as he hustled in and joined the group.

"Nice catch out there and nice throw." Johnny eyed him, as if still sizing him up. "If you wanna play on this team, we want you. But there's still one final part of this try-out."

To Cletis's surprise, there followed an eerie moment of complete silence.

"Okay, what is it?" Cletis slapped his mitt against his thigh.

"Meet us here at midnight tonight," Johnny replied. He eyed the field around them, as if looking to see whether any unwelcome guest had heard his words. "Wear dark clothes," he continued. "Ride your bike. Bring a flashlight. Don't let your mom and dad know. . . . Uh, sorry . . . I mean, your *dad* know. You got it?"

Cletis nodded twice. "Got it."

CHAPTER 3

The Witch

The stars sparkled and danced in the black sky, and a crescent moon smiled knowingly down on the secrets of Greenberg Junction. There was a gentle spring breeze that came in from the north, and the night air was filled with the singing of crickets. At 12:13 a.m., all the boys plus Rabbit were assembled a half-mile north of the ball diamond—all except Timmy. Always protective of his little cousin, Johnny told him not to come.

With their flashlights illuminating the ground in front of them, the kids left their bikes and walked to where Johnny stood. Rabbit, wearing camouflage pants and a black T-shirt, leaned over to Cletis.

"Are you scared?" she asked.

Cletis paused a moment then shook his head. "Not really," he answered. *But that might change here real quick*, he thought.

When Pauly heard Cletis's words, he stepped over to him, wrapped a brotherly arm around his shoulders and whispered in his ear, "You oughtta be, cuz you're gonna feel fear like you've never felt it before. I did this two summers ago. I remember it like it was yesterday."

Inside, Cletis felt his stomach tighten, but he wasn't about to let the others know that. Whatever it was that he was supposed to face, he would do it with courage. Just like his dad had always taught him to do.

Dad . . . His thoughts flew back to the peace of his quiet home and the dependable protection of his father. *What am I doing out here? Dad doesn't even know where I am. He doesn't even know I'm gone. What if something happens to me?*

Cletis had no idea what this "initiation" was to be or what the guys would put him through. What he presently feared was that he would face some challenge that would prove more difficult and scary than he had imagined.

But I really want to play ball with these guys! And if all of them have survived this initiation—even Elston—then I can too. Whatever it is, I'll do it, and I'll get back home, and everything'll be good.

"Gather here in a circle," spoke Johnny softly. The boys grouped in and focused their lights on the ground where they stood. "From here to the edge of the drop-off, we're on our stomachs. When we reach the edge, where we can look down and see her house, we stop. Lights go out just before we get there. Understand? We don't want her to see us or know that we're anywhere close to this place."

Cletis wondered who *her* was.

"At the edge, you're on your own," Johnny added, aiming his flashlight in Cletis's eyes.

Then Johnny turned around and shined his light on the ground behind him. Slowly he lifted the circle of light toward the edge of the drop. The weeds and grass where the boys presently stood were fairly short. But at the drop, Cletis could see that the grass was taller there and that the hillside below was covered with shrubs and giant trees. Some of the trees were probably eighty feet tall and must have been sixty to seventy years old, at least. In the darkness they took on personalities of their own—tall and splendid and watching. Others, leafless and crooked, stood like bony old men and women of the forest with little strength left in them. They too seemed to be watching the boys—watching and waiting. Here and there, silhouetted against the crescent moon, large gray branches like arms and fingers twisted down from the thick trunks that supported them, scratching and clawing the undergrowth at their feet. Even from the tiny plateau where Cletis stood, he could see their shadowy haunting forms swaying lazily in the night breeze.

Cletis could see no lights in any direction around him, and he knew of no one else who lived out in this area. As far as he could figure things, he was about a mile north of his home. He looked into the darkness of the forest before him and wondered what dangers the old trees of the downward declining hillside had conjured for him.

"On your bellies," Johnny whispered to all, dropping to his knees and then to his stomach.

Lizardlike in the weeds, he led the way. Like a platoon of well-trained soldiers, the group crawled forward to the edge of the drop. As Cletis spat a blade of grass off his tongue, he noticed that the crickets nearby were suddenly silent.

Maybe it's cuz we're makin' too much noise.

As he went, he could sense the sideways glances of the others who crawled beside him. Rabbit would look at him briefly and then turn away. Elston, on the other side of him, did the same. But with Elston's dark skin, it was tough to see exactly *what* expression he was wearing. Frank and Pauly were ahead of them and off to the right. Frank shined his light back at Cletis several times and then suddenly grunted when his head hit something hard—maybe the heel of Johnny's shoe.

They're trying to read my face, Cletis sensed. *They wanna know if I'm scared. They know what's goin' on here, and I don't.*

Johnny stopped. "This is far enough," he whispered.

Klu signaled the boys to gather closer into a tight huddle.

"Lights out now," Johnny ordered. All obeyed. "At the bottom of the hill there's a ditch that runs through the woods. Most people around here call it 'the canal.' Two girls and their mother drowned about a half-mile upstream three years ago, out near the bridge. They think maybe the witch got 'em."

The witch? Cletis instantly felt his heart race, and he swallowed nervously.

A sudden movement ahead of them from within shrubs on the hillside caught them all by surprise. Davey gasped and grabbed Elston.

"Don't move," whispered Klu.

In anxious silence, the boys waited. Again the sound of the movement came—as if someone, or something, was walking in the wooded area right in front of them.

"Is that *her*?" breathed Elston. "Is she up *here*?"

"Shhh," ordered Johnny.

Again they heard it. The sound was closer now than before and seemed to be coming from behind the closest shrub on the hillside in front of them.

"I'm outta here," mouthed Davey.

But as he attempted to rise, Klu held him in place.

"Wait."

Whatever it was, it was coming closer in spite of their presence. The boys froze, waiting, watching—their eyes yet adjusting to the darkness. Finally, a shadowy shape moved in front of them, slightly above their eye level and no more than eight or nine feet away. In the blackness of the night and under the cover of the forest, Cletis couldn't make out what it was.

For what seemed to be an eternity, nobody moved. Cletis finally gave into his curiosity, and eyeing the moving shadow, he raised his flashlight, took aim, and turned it on. As Johnny reached back for Cletis's arm, there appeared in the soft yellow glow of the light a slow-moving mother possum. The surprised animal carried two wobbly babies on her back. As the trio froze in the light, an eerie orange color reflected in the eyes of the tiny gray creatures. The animal lifted her nose toward the group and sniffed the air. Then, hopping awkwardly off the broken tree trunk on which she crawled, she waddled back into the forest. Klu instantly sighed in relief. Elston, Rabbit, and Davey all rolled onto their backs and exhaled nervously.

"Oh, man," sighed Frank as he dropped his head onto his arms.

"Cletis, get that light off," Johnny whispered angrily. Cletis obeyed. "What are you doin' turnin' that on? We could've been seen!" Then, referring back to the possum, Johnny whispered intensely, "This close to her house, you never know what that could've been!"

"Sorry," Cletis finally whispered.

Johnny sighed and turned to Elston.

"Elston, you got the tape recorder?"

Elston sat up, lifted the white cloth sack he carried, and pointed to it.

"Batteries good?" asked Johnny.

"Yep."

"It's all set?"

"Yep."

"Hand it over."

Elston leaned forward and gave the bag to Johnny. Johnny untied the knot in the drawstring on the top of the sack, loosened the opening, and pulled out a tape recorder. He handed it to Cletis.

"The witch lives at the bottom of this hill." He paused to allow the thought to sink in. "A real witch. No jokin'. No one has ever really seen her. But she's there. We know it. We've seen her shadow. Sometimes you can see a light in one of the windows. We think it's a candle or somethin'." Johnny turned toward the slope of the hill, rose up on his knees, and peered down through the trees. "Look, you can see it down there now."

They all lifted themselves cautiously and looked down the hill.

"See it?" asked Johnny.

Cletis peered in the same direction, down through the shrubs and trees, toward the old house the boys claimed was there at the base of the hill. Finally, he saw a faint flicker of light far below him.

"Yeah, I see it."

He studied it warily, trying to make out the shape of the house around it, but it was too dark.

Johnny continued.

"It's about fifty yards down the hill. Just before you get to the house, that's where the canal is. Be careful. This time of year it can be up to three feet deep and pretty muddy on the banks. Cross over that ditch and crawl to the house. There's a back porch there. It's covered with old screens. Go through the back door—it's got a handle on it, so it opens easy—and then reach up and tap the chimes hangin' from the ceiling. They'll be right in front of you, just on the other side of the door. Record the chimes with the tape recorder and get out of there as fast as you can. Bring it back to us. We listen to the chimes, and if everything goes right, you're on the team." Johnny pointed to the flashlight in Cletis's hand. "You can take your light if you want, but I wouldn't. She'll see it." He eyed Cletis carefully. "Got it?"

Cletis took a deep breath.

"So I gotta *feel* for the chimes to find them?" he asked.

Johnny nodded his head. "They're there. We come out here on a windy night, and we can hear 'em still. You'll find 'em." Johnny cupped his hand over his flashlight, turned it on, and aimed it at Cletis. "Got your mitt on your pants, I see. Good. This is all about baseball . . . part of the initiation. Oh, one more thing." Johnny allowed a little light to squeeze through his fingers onto Klu's gray sweat-pants. "Show him your leg, Klu."

Klu lifted his pant leg, revealing a long scar on his calf.

"That's where she grabbed me," he stated solemnly. "Just last year. Bled all the way home, but I never showed it to my mom. Just stuck a bunch of Band-Aids on it."

"And I'll tell you something else," whispered Rabbit. "She sharpens her long fingernails just like Ty Cobb sharpened his spikes. Right Klu?"

Klu nodded in agreement.

"Spikes?" asked Cletis, not knowing for sure what Rabbit was talking about.

"You know," answered Johnny. "The cleats on his baseball shoes. Ty Cobb sharpened his cleats so he could slide into people and hurt 'em. The old hag down there sharpens her long fingernails."

"How do you know that?" questioned Cletis, fighting his growing fear.

"Just look at Klu's leg," she answered. "Speaks for itself."

"She tore my new catcher's mitt right off my belt," continued Klu, "and bit off a chunk of it, and ate it right in front of me. Couldn't see her, but I could hear her munchin' it. I finally got away. It's all kind of a blur now. I don't remember much. Never got my mitt back."

Frank spoke up.

"Four years ago one of Johnny's brother's friend's cousin never returned."

Cletis looked to Johnny, who nodded in sad agreement.

"Couldn't find his body," Johnny added. "That's what my brother told me. Cops all over the place the next day, but they never found him."

What am I doing here? Cletis moaned in his mind. *What am I gonna tell dad when he finds me tomorrow morning all torn and broken to pieces in the woods behind a witch's house? I've gotta be outta my mind!* Cletis studied each boy momentarily, and Rabbit too. His heart pounded in his chest. *But I'm doin' it!*

Taking a deep breath and gathering his pluck and courage, he dropped his flashlight at Johnny's feet and took the recorder from Elston's hands. Staying low to the ground, Cletis stepped away from the squad and proceeded down the hill.

Carefully he felt his way through the trees and shrubs, and descended toward the flickering light of the cottage . . . *or haunted house or whatever it is,* he contemplated. Under the darkness of the forest canopy, it was difficult to see tree limbs or roots that were directly in his path.

Great, I'm gonna get poked in the eye and blinded. Dad'll be really happy about that, he thought sarcastically.

Sometimes an unseen dip or a rock under his shoes would trip him or jar his steps, causing him to lose his balance momentarily. He would slide a few feet in the soft earth until he found better footing.

Maybe leavin' that flashlight was a stupid thing to do. I'm makin' so much noise out here headin' down this hill, she's gonna know I'm comin' anyhow. Heck, might as well go up and knock on the back door and ask permission to tape her chimes.

When he reached the bottom of the hill, he paused to listen. The chirping crickets were now accompanied by the percussion of hundreds of frogs. He knew the ditch was close by. Over the natural sounds of the night, he could hear its quiet gurgle. He eased his way carefully forward, spotted the reflection of the yellow moon on the water's rippling surface, and tried to find a place where he could see it clearly enough to jump it. Above and behind him, one of the boys sneezed. It sounded like Elston. Or maybe Frank. Here, too, the sound carried remarkably well.

Great! Just call down to her from up there and let her know I'm on my way!

From where he hid, Cletis could see the dark ragged shape of the house. There were three windows on the back wall. The candle appeared to be placed on the inside sill of the middle window. He could see its quivering glow reflected off the glass. He froze when a shadow passed behind the light. A hunched figure that seemed as if its head were growing out of the front of the shoulders—no neck, only shoulders and a head. He couldn't tell if it was a man or woman.

He could feel his heart race. He squatted, hoping to remain unseen and peered back up the hill.

I gotta show 'em. I gotta do this. If all of them did it, I can do it, too. Wait a minute . . . Maybe all of them didn't do it. Maybe I'm the first one, and this is all a big joke. He thought about that for a moment. *No, they wouldn't do that to me, would they?* His thoughts jumped back and forth as he studied the cottage, the flickering light in the window and the muddy banks of the brook. *No, I saw the scar on Klu's leg. And they talked about this even when I was there at practice. Even Timmy knew about it. Every one of them acted like they knew what was goin' on. So I think this is for real. No trick this time.*

Nervously he moved forward. A twig snapped beneath his shoe, and again he dropped and froze where he was. The croaking and coughing of the nearby frogs instantly stopped, as well as the soft singing of the crickets.

Cletis squatted low by the stream and took a deep, calming breath. With the aid of the moon's pale reflection on the water's surface, he attempted to find the best place to leap. He assumed that on both sides there would be marshy overgrowth. He knew it would be slimy on the banks, and he didn't want to run the risk of losing a shoe in the process of crossing or jumping. He also knew it'd be dangerous to run shoeless up the hill after taping the chimes. He needed sure footing to make a good escape.

Gription. Elston's word. Gotta have some good gription. Gotta keep both shoes on my feet! About six feet across. Cletis reached out and felt the bank with his foot. He could tell where it dropped off into the stream. After walking about ten paces upstream, and finally finding a fairly dry spot of earth, Cletis carefully took three steps back, started a short run, and then made his leap. *Don't drop the tape recorder!* he reminded himself in mid-air.

He cleared the water easily, but the ground on the other side was soft and gooey. Landing on the mud with a slap, he felt his right foot sink into the sludge up to his ankle. Trying desperately to keep the tape recorder off the wet ground, Cletis lost his balance and fell forward. *Don't lose your shoe in the mud!* he warned himself. With a slow and steady tug, his right foot finally sucked free of the mire. As he rolled onto his belly and crawled to dryer ground, he could feel the cold of the mud and water on the legs of his pants.

Staying in the tall grass on the bank of the canal, he inched toward the house. The screened porch was now visible at the far end of the dwelling. Again the figure passed before the window and paused. Cletis flattened himself on the ground behind the house. There he froze and watched. The thin curtain lifted, and he could see the silhouette of the person—or whatever it was—peering through the window. Terrified, he laid rock still, hoping the grasses covered him from sight. The shadow that lingered in the window seemed to be looking right at him. Finally, the curtain fell back down into place, and the figure eased away into the room. Lying on open ground between the house and the canal, Cletis waited. He could feel his heart surging in his chest. He tried to control his rapid breathing. What was only a moment seemed an hour.

The shadow appeared again in the window, and the candle was lifted away from the sill. Within moments, the room went dark. Cletis watched the window. The curtains did not move. He counted off a full minute. He saw no light or movement anywhere in the house. Turning back, he looked over at the stream, sensing the need to secure an escape route if the hunched thing he had seen in the window suddenly came flying out of the house.

Slowly, silently he inched his way forward. The back porch was only a short distance from him. He was close enough to see the outline of the door, and the path before him that led to the porch looked perfectly clear. It would be a matter of only seconds for him to get there, open the door, ring the chimes, record the sound, and make his escape.

Gotta do it now. Things aren't gonna get any better. As a precautionary measure, he turned on the tape recorder and pushed down the "play/record" buttons.

The group at the top of the hill continued to watch and wait. Pauly checked his watch.

"12:28," he whispered. "Cletis has been gone for seven minutes."

"What's takin' him so long?" questioned Frank. "Man, it's only down there and back. That's all of a hundred yards, maybe."

"I dunno," answered Johnny. "It *is* a dark night . . . darker than usual. Just a little bit of a moon. The last times we've done this, there's always been a bigger moon givin' off a little more light."

"You think he fell in the ditch?" whispered Rabbit.

Elston peered over the hill and looked down toward the house.

"Hey, the light just went out in the window."

All rose to look.

"That could be good, or that could be bad," commented Klu. "She works best in the dark, I think. So maybe she's comin' after him."

"You think we should go lookin' for him?" asked Davey. "It shouldn't take him this long."

"Give him another couple of minutes. He'll be coming," answered Johnny.

Though the group calmed a bit upon hearing his words, inside, Johnny knew *he* was getting a bit antsy, too. If something tragic happened, Johnny knew he would be the one responsible.

Cletis sensed the moment was right—he had seen no movement in the house. Rising, he moved stealthily across the back of the lot. He could still feel his heart pounding in his chest, and now there was a shrill ringing in his ears—like it was coming from deep inside his brain. What he crept across wasn't lawn, but neither was it weedy and overgrown like on the hillside above him. The crickets and frogs nearby continued their silent observation, listening to the sloshing and sucking of Cletis's muddy waterlogged shoe. But he didn't dare kick it off. He discovered if he walked crouched on his tiptoes, it made less of a sound.

In a matter of seconds, he closed in on the porch. The steps that led up to the screen door were right in front of him. The sounds of the night suddenly seemed deafening. He took a breath to calm himself and then reached up and grasped the metal handle.

As he pulled, it opened easily and quietly . . . at first. Then, suddenly, it whined out a low groaning sound—as if it were warning the beast inside the house of the young intruder. Cletis froze, holding the door steady. He gritted his teeth in fear, knowing the sound could easily have been heard from inside the old house. Time was crucial now.

I gotta get the job done fast and get outta here.

With the door open just wide enough to squeeze his small body through, carefully he stepped onto the wooden planking of the porch, and holding the screen door in place, he slipped inside. His eyes opened wide as he tried desperately to see through the darkness that surrounded him.

Gotta move fast! Where are the chimes?

His first step landed him on a loose board that moaned under his wet shoe.

Man, now she's heard me for sure! If she came after Klu, she'll come after me!

Reaching up, he found the chimes right above him, just like Johnny said. Cletis lifted the tape recorder and stepped forward. BANG! In the darkness, he kicked something, sending it several inches across the wooden floor, scratching against the porch planks as it slid. It must have been a chair.

I'm a dead man! No time to wait now! Just get the chimes recorded, and get the heck out of here!

With the tape recorder still running, he tapped the metal pipes. They answered with a sweet tender song.

One. Two. Three. There! Got it! Stepping back, he pushed the screen door open, bolted off the porch, and was halfway across the back of the lot when he heard the screen door slam shut.

In only two breaths, he was across the backyard and onto the muddy banks of the ditch. Without pausing, he hit the cold water, high-stepped through the slippery rocks on the bottom of the canal, and was up the opposite bank. Holding the tape recorder over his head, he ascended the hillside—dodging in and out of the shadowy trees and shrubs. This time, he didn't care if they slapped at his face or scratched at his arms or pulled and poked at his shirt. A smile filled his face, as the adrenaline of excitement danced through his veins.

I did it! I out-maneuvered a real witch! I looked death in the face!

Higher and higher on the hillside he climbed, sensing that at any moment he would break clear of the forest, burst happily over the top, and be welcomed into the huddle of the guys who would accept him onto the team with congratulations, high-fives, and manly pats on the back.

At the top of the hill, Cletis heard their voices. Never was there a more welcome sound!

"I hear him. Here he comes," Elston whispered.

"Yep. Sounds like it," agreed Johnny. "Turn your lights on and aim them at the ground, so he can see where we are."

Cletis exploded through the darkness of the forest's edge and sprinted toward the circles of light. Panting, he fell exhausted in the middle of the group and held up the recorder for all to see. Rabbit and the boys gathered around him, shining their flashlights onto his mud-splattered pants and shoes.

Taking the recorder, Johnny dropped to the ground, and, as everyone gathered around him, he pressed "rewind" and waited. When the machine clicked to a stop, Johnny punched the "play" button. Listening for the gentle ring of the chimes, Johnny held it close to his ear.

But nothing came. No sound was heard.

In the silence, everybody leaned in. As they shined their lights upon the recorder, they could see that the tape was still moving, but nothing was playing. Not one sound had been recorded. Johnny pressed "stop," rewound the tape, pressed "play" again, and listened. Still, there was nothing.

"I don't hear anything," he whispered as he held it up in front of his face. "Nothing recorded."

"What d'ya mean nothin' recorded?" spouted Cletis, grabbing the machine. "I was there. I was on her back porch. I lifted it up, rang the chimes, and recorded them." The boys eyed him silently. "Come on guys, I was there! The stream's about three feet deep! The backyard is all weeds and dirt. Look at the mud I got on me! The door squeaks. The floor squeaks. I was there! I did it! I recorded the chimes! You heard the door slam shut, just like I heard somebody sneeze up here."

Everyone looked at Elston and back to the newcomer.

"Shhh, hold it down," Johnny warned Cletis, pushing a finger to his lips. "Just a minute. Let's take a look at this." He took back the recorder and examined it carefully. "Elston, you sure everything was set here?"

"Yeah, new batteries. It was all set."

Johnny turned the machine on its side and shined the light on the volume control. "Nice one, Elston, the volume was turned all the way down to zero."

"What?" gasped Cletis. He looked at Elston with fire in his eyes. "You said everything was all set! I didn't touch a thing!"

"The volume was set on 'seven,' just like the other times. I swear it!"

Cletis was immediately in Elston's face. "I about got killed down there, and you didn't set the volume right?!"

"Look, maybe you bumped it on the way down, or something." Elston reasoned as he leaned away. "That could've happened."

Cletis pushed him backward and was suddenly on the ground over the top of him, pinning him down. "It never touched the ground! It never touched anything. I held it up above me the whole time!"

"Hey, come on," Elston countered. "It was an honest mistake. Really. I didn't mean to sabotage you."

The boys watched in silent surprise as a side of Cletis—a part of his personality they had only heard about—rose to the surface. They were now seeing the Cletis who went after Klu's big brother.

"Yeah, but now I gotta go back!" Cletis barked angrily, pointing a finger in Elston's face.

Johnny and Klu pulled Cletis back.

"Wait a minute," whispered Johnny, attempting to calm the moment. "Don't worry about it, Cletis. We believe you were there. We believe you rang the chimes. In fact, I think I heard 'em. It's okay. You did what you were supposed to do, and we're all cool with that."

"I'm not joinin' this team outta pity," argued Cletis, pushing away from the group. "I'm gonna earn it, fair and square! I'm not gonna have you guys always hangin' this over my head, like you've done me some big favor . . . and in the back of your minds you're gonna be thinkin' I'm not quite as good as you, cuz I didn't get the job done at the witch's house."

"We're not gonna think that," voiced Johnny. "Don't worry about it."

"Well I *am* gonna think that, and I'm gonna do it *right*."

With that, Cletis grabbed the tape recorder out of Johnny's hands and shined a light on the volume control. He set the number to "seven," stood defiantly, and moved away toward the hillside.

"What are you doin'?" asked Klu.

But Cletis didn't answer. Determined and focused, he had a mission to accomplish, and he was going to do it right or not at all. Silently, he disappeared over the hill. As he descended, he heard their whispers.

"Now the witch is gonna be just sittin' down there waitin' for him," warned Elston with real fear in his voice.

"If she comes after him, I'm outta here," added Frank.

"Me too," promised Davey and Pauly both.

"We'll just have to wait and see."

Johnny's were the last words Cletis heard.

At the bottom of the hill, Cletis eyed the shadowy form of the witch's house and listened for the water. He was still soaking from his first visit and chilled by the wet clothes he wore. As he neared the canal, he remembered the slipperiness of the banks and rocks in front of him. He knew he couldn't afford to fall on his face while holding the tape recorder. That would ruin everything. Carefully he approached the edge and slid down into the shallow current. He took two cautious steps, feeling the water fill his shoes and soak his pants up to the knees. Suddenly, with the next step, there was nothing under him. He sank to his waist and felt the cold of the water bite sharply into his thighs and waist. He gasped with the freezing shock as the water soaked into his upper pants and through the bottom part of his T-shirt.

Man, it wasn't this deep the first time I came through here, he thought, as he tried to catch his breath. *Someone could get swept away in this. I must've entered it up closer to the house the first time. Oh, man, my mitt's completely soaked. Dad's gonna kill me.*

Three more steps brought him to the opposite bank, where he squatted low and lifted himself onto the ground above the water. His clothes clung tightly to him, and with a sudden soft breeze, he shivered against the cold.

In the overgrowth of the bank nearest the house, Cletis paused to assess the situation. *No lights. No movement. But I know she's awake cuz I let the screen door slam. There was a heck of a lot of noise last time.* He took a deep breath, pushed the "play/record" buttons down, and put the recorder to his ear. *Yep, it's rollin'.*

Hunching low, he crossed the backyard, sloshing as he went. Within moments he reached the screen door, paused, then pulled it open until it began to squeak. He held the door still, momentarily, listening for any movement from within the house. In the silence, he eased his way through the door and stood below the chimes. *Watch out for the chair.* He felt with his foot, hoping to tap against it. Nothing. *Wait a minute.* He reached his hand out and felt for the chair. *The chair's gone. THE CHAIR'S GONE!* he screamed in his mind. *OH, NO! SHE'S HERE! I'M DEAD! SHE KNOWS RIGHT WHERE I AM! GET THE CHIMES RECORDED AND GET OUT!*

As fast as he could, he reached up and tapped the chimes. Anxiously, he held the recorder to it. The chimes tinkled softly in the night, unaware of his danger. Seconds were hours. *ONE. TWO. THREE. NOW GET*

OUT OF HERE! He quickly lowered the recorder and moved to the door. Then he heard it. Breathing. Something dark to his left brushed against his pant leg. Near to the floor. A shadow. He could hear movement now. Suddenly a strong, wide hand gripped his ankle. He was too late. SHE WAS WITH HIM ON THE PORCH!

"AAUUGHH!" cried Cletis, trying to pull away. In his wet shoes, he slipped and fell to the floor, dropping the recorder next to him. "AAUUGHH!" he cried again, yanking his foot against the hand that grasped him tightly. He could sense a form in front of him—a large round form, moving and grunting and groaning to hold him as he desperately kicked to free himself.

"HELP!" he yelled, fighting against the grip on his ankle. "HELP!"

Suddenly he pulled free—his wet pant leg an advantage. Rolling to his right, he pushed his way through the screen door and tumbled down the steps onto the dirt. He heard the screen tear as he rolled past it. Rising and attempting to sprint, his wet shoes couldn't hold against the ground, and he slipped and went down. He could hear the witch behind him. Her steps thudded heavily across the wooden porch. The screen door screeched open above him. He knew she was right there behind him in the darkness, closing in. He could feel her presence. *GET OUTTA HERE FAST!*

As best he could, Cletis scrambled away—crawling, stumbling, running. But still she was coming after him, gaining ground. He tried to run, but it was like his legs were filled with lead. His waterlogged pants seemed to weigh a hundred pounds. His mind was already up the hill, but his legs were struggling to carry him even across the back lot of the ragged old house.

From the top of the hill, the boys heard the yelling and commotion. Each scrambled to the edge of the drop-off and peered down toward the house. They could see nothing through the trees, but Cletis's cries for help rang through the darkness like a piercing siren.

"The witch's got him!" shouted Rabbit.

"He's dead!" cried Frank. "I'm outta here!"

"Me, too!" yelled Elston.

"Let's move!" moaned Pauly.

Elston, Davey, Frank, and Pauly each dashed away, back toward their bikes.

"Guys! Wait!" Johnny called after them in a loud whisper.

But it was too late. None of them turned back.

For the past two years each of them had heard the haunting tales of the witch's power and evil. They had had the nightmares that accompanied those horrifying thoughts. Each had come close enough to her and her house during their initiations, and now they fled the horrifying reality of experiencing her wrath face to face. In the rapid exit, even Klu arose, caught in the middle of two difficult choices. He stood as if frozen in the spring grass.

"Klu, get down!" whispered Johnny. "Or are you goin' run, too?"

Klu turned, panting. He looked at the fleeing boys, and then back at Johnny and Rabbit. Swallowing hard, he dropped again to the ground.

"Do what you want, Klu, but I'm stickin' this one out."

"M-me, too," Klu mumbled.

"Rabbit, you okay?" questioned Johnny, as he and Klu crawled toward her.

Rabbit peered into the shadows of the forest, her head cocked to one side, listening intently to the commotion below. Unflinching, she nodded her head.

Another cry suddenly echoed through the blackness of the wooded hill.

Cletis darted across the dirt behind the house and headed for the canal. Tears welled up in his eyes, and his heart raced faster than his legs. *Gotta out-distance her! Gotta get past the water and up the hill! Gotta get home! Now!* He could still hear her behind him. But it didn't sound much like a "her." There was nothing female about whatever was chasing him. He heard grunts and moans and heavy breathing that seemed to come from an animal—like a buffalo or a bull—not a person.

Suddenly he was at the ditch. Hitting the bank in stride, he luckily got some good gription and leaped across the water. Landing several feet past the opposite bank, he welcomed the dry ground under his feet and raced up the hill toward the ridge above him. *And I don't even have the recorder!* he lamented, feeling the emptiness in his hands.

Behind him, he could hear the witch approach the water. He felt no need to turn and watch. He didn't want to know how quickly she was moving or what she was doing. He had no idea what magical or evil powers she was hiding or what awaited him if she caught up to him.

Whatever it was that was coming after him, it or she hit the mud hard and landed in the water. He could hear the splashes and the gasps and the moans, and more splashing. Still, he scrambled onward up the hill. His heart was racing, pounding his frightened blood through his cold, exhausted muscles. His only thought was to reach the top of this dark incline and do it in as little time as possible.

Then, to his amazement, a voice was heard through the forest—a deep raspy voice that must have come from the throat of whatever it was that flailed in the water below him.

"Help me! Help me, please!"

His instincts told him to flee, but something in the voice—though craggy and low and sickly as it was—stopped him in his tracks. To his own amazement, he turned and listened. As the splashing continued, the sound came again, sadly.

"Help me!"

Cletis stood silently, still paralyzed with fear. But he remembered his Mom and Dad had always taught him to help people. *But this is different, isn't it?* Still, in the darkness, he waited, unsure of what to do. *If she's a real witch, or something like that, then this could be a trick—a trap! And if I go back, who knows what she might do. But if she isn't really a witch, just some giant, lonely, old lady . . .*

From above, Johnny, Rabbit, and Klu heard everything. It sounded like Cletis was coming toward them, but then his footsteps fell silent. On their bellies, they peered into the darkness, not daring to turn their flashlights on.

"He must be half-way up the hill. That's what it sounded like," Klu whispered anxiously. "What's he doing?"

"I don't know," Johnny responded.

"Was that her, crying down there? Was that the witch?" asked Rabbit.

"I don't know," Johnny breathed. "I've never heard her before. Could be a trick."

Below them, whatever it was or whoever it was, continued to thrash about in the water. They could hear gasps and moans.

"Is that Cletis down there in the water?" Klu questioned.

"Shhh. Don't talk," came Johnny's reply.

"Elston! Johnny!"

It was Cletis calling from the darkness of the woods.

Rabbit was about to speak when Johnny put his hand over her mouth. "Don't answer him. It may be some kind of a trap. You don't know if that's really Cletis."

"We just gonna leave him down there?" mumbled Rabbit through Johnny's hand.

Johnny was silent for too long. He lowered his hand. "We're gonna wait and see what happens," he answered. "Don't move."

"This is wrong," whispered Rabbit. "He needs our help."

"Don't go down there, Rabbit," warned Johnny. "If anything happens to you, I'm dead."

Cletis could hear no response from above him. He waited in the darkness, listening for voices at the top of the hill. But they were either silent or gone. Again, from below, came the pitiful cries.

"Please, someone help me!"

Gradually a strange feeling settled upon Cletis—something like he'd never felt before, except maybe once. It was almost like the feeling he had when his mom died—in that exact moment when he and his dad were with her in the hospital and she passed away. It was a sad moment, and his heart was broken, but at the same time, he felt something wonderful—something inwardly overpowering that spoke a kind of peace to his heart at a time when he felt most alone and sad. Something similar to that was happening to him now. He felt the hair on his arms and neck stand on end as the warm tingling sensation penetrated his entire body.

It's cuz I'm cold. That's all. It's cuz I'm scared. My clothes are wet!

Yet he felt drawn toward the stream even though his racing mind fought against it. *No! She could be evil. You saw the scar on Klu's leg. You heard the guys. Three people died upstream! Don't go down there to that witch!*

Despite the pleadings of his mind, still, his heart spoke differently. He took a step toward the stream. *Wait! You felt her power when she held your leg. You know how strong she is! Maybe there are other powers! Maybe she's not human! You can't go back down there!* Another step toward her followed the first, and then another—like he was being pulled in her direction. Cletis, almost hypnotically, edged his way back down the slope. The strange, tingling sensation continued to surge within him. Though his mind was disagreeing with his heart and arguing violently against his actions, he crept down the hillside.

He could hear her hopeless moaning as he approached the stream. Step by step, he moved carefully down the bank to where he heard her groans.

Suddenly all went silent. He heard nothing. No sounds of movement. No moans or struggles. Cautiously he edged his way to the waterside. *Is this the deep part in front of me? Where did I enter the second time across? Where is she? Did she go under?* He felt his shoe sink into the mud, and he slipped and lost his balance. Landing with a thud, he felt the cold mud ooze out around him. *GET UP! GET AWAY FROM THE MUD! YOU GOT NO CHANCE TO RUN, SLIPPING IN THIS GOO! GET AWAY!*

Without a sound, two unseen hands pushed up out of the water, and with snakelike agility, grasped Cletis's ankles.

"AAUUGGHH!!" he screamed out as he clawed at the muddy banks, trying to twist against the hag's tight grip. Feeling her powerful fingers sink into the flesh of his lower legs, he cried out again. In an instant, he was dragged under, into the dark flow of the canal. Struggling for breath, he fought his way to the surface and gasped for air. Suddenly his legs were free of her grip, but before he could escape, her hands locked onto his upper arms. She was behind him now. Lifting him puppetlike out of the cold chill of the water, she plunged him back down under the surface.

SHE'S GONNA DROWN ME! I CAN'T PULL FREE!

The coldness of the current surrounded him, and he panicked in the underwater darkness. After only a few seconds she hoisted him up into the cool night air. Again, he gasped for breath. He couldn't see her, but he could hear her wheezing and grunting. Her hulking hands clutched him tightly, pinning his arms at his sides. Though he kicked and squirmed against her grip, he was no match for the strength of this being that held him fast.

"If I'm gonna get all wet and muddy, then you're gonna get wet and muddy too, boy."

Her voice—if it *was* that of a woman—was deep, coarse, and masculine, with a touch of a foreign accent. Cletis, still struggling against her, thought it sounded Irish. She cackled out a strange laugh and then coughing up canal water, she spoke into his ear.

"You boys come creeping around my house—breaking things, leaving things—like you had no respect for anything or anybody. Well, maybe you ought to be taught a good lesson."

Visions of torture crept into Cletis's mind—visions of lost bodies never found by grieving parents. He tried to find it in him to call out, but in his fear, his voice was gone. He felt hopeless. He was in her grasp and felt the power of it, and there was no escape now. Whatever he felt on the hillside—that strange feeling that urged him back down to the canal—must have been her conjured black magic.

"Calm yourself, my boy, and help me get us out of this mud." She still held him tightly but allowed Cletis to stand on the bottom of the stream. "Now, I'm gonna release your arm, and let you step toward the other bank, there. Then I want you to turn around and help me out. Not all that squawking you heard from me was nonsense, you know. I could've drowned here, and then you'd have been in a whale o' trouble."

She guided him to the bank and then released one arm. The temptation to pull free and make a run for it was powerful. Yet, with the thought, again, that odd calming sensation flowed gently through his body, filling him with warmth that countered the chill of his wet clothes.

More of her magic? he wondered. *What am I feeling right now? It's like everything seems to be calm again. I should be terrified out of my mind, but that's not what I'm feelin'.*

As if against his best judgment, he cooperated and followed her instructions. *Is she controlling my mind? Maybe she'll just make me walk her to her back porch and apologize for what I did. And then maybe she'll just let me go back up to the guys, and I'll forget all about tonight. Or maybe . . .*

Cletis turned, and against all natural instincts, he gave her his hand and helped pull her from the water. Their feet caught in the mud, and they stumbled a bit, but, despite the terror he should have felt, he supported her in a gentlemanly manner, until they found solid earth beneath their feet.

Even to this point, Cletis had not seen her face. It was too dark. *Klu didn't see it either!* he suddenly realized. *Maybe she doesn't have a face!! Maybe there is just a hole for a mouth! Maybe she has no eyes!*

As he walked next to her, feeling her weight on his arm, he sensed her shape. She was a little taller than he was, but she must have been twice as wide. She moved slowly and steadily, breathing heavily and smelling like canal waterweed and fish.

When they reached the porch, she lifted her club of an arm and motioned him forward. As he stepped up to the screen door, he felt himself begin to shake, and as he moved into the darkness of the back porch, his worst fears began edging their way back into his mind. She hobbled behind him, and they both stood dripping and muddy, leaving little puddles below them on the wooden planks of the flooring.

"There's a light switch just to the side of that door," she groaned. Every sound that came from her throat was fried and heavy and deep.

Cletis felt his way to the door and located the switch on the wall. He flipped it up, and the light of a single bulb that hung above them near the chimes illuminated the little porch. Out of the corner of his eye, he saw the chair and the boxes that filled the small area. Slowly, he turned, not knowing what to expect. *I'm gonna have to see her sooner or later. I think that moment's comin' right now!* He tensed in anticipation. His eyes re-focused with the help of the light, and he brought his head around.

Suddenly she was there, only inches from his face, staring straight into his eyes.

"AUGHH!" Cletis cried out and fell back onto the wall next to the door. She paid little heed to his outburst, as if accustomed to people reacting in such a way.

"Ugly enough for you?" she calmly stated. She reached into a nearby box and pulled out two rags. "Here, my boy. Dry yourself off a bit." She tossed him one. The other she used to dab the mud and water from her face and hair.

Cletis stood mesmerized, frozen by what he saw. He watched the lady—at least he thought she was a lady—dry her arms and clothing. Her hair—a gray matted tangle—was tied and fastened with a simple leather strap behind her shoulders, and it hung down the middle of her back like a wet raccoon's tail. Her neck was thick and almost unseen below the folds of skin that drooped from her chin and jowls.

Heavy bristly eyebrows covered her eyes. Her nose was bulbous and pocked, and the pores on her cheeks were enlarged and spongelike.

Again she looked at him, halting her movement. He had never seen a person that looked as odd and as ugly and as animal-like as she, but when their eyes met, her gaze seemed to speak peace to him, calming his fears. There was an amazing gentle greenness to her eyes. To Cletis it seemed as if someone was looking out at him from beneath a hideous rubber Halloween mask. As he stood dripping before her, he realized he was staring at her and quickly dropped his gaze to the floor.

She and he both spotted the recorder at the same time. Being right on top of it, she bent down and picked it up. It was still running, recording everything that was said and done. She held it up to her face, and using the most witchlike, gravelly voice she could muster, she spoke into the built-in microphone.

"I'll let this one live, but if I catch others, I'll eat them alive. Let this be a lesson to you all!" Then she cackled a bit and turned the recorder off. She looked back to Cletis, who still stood shaking and wet in the corner by the door. She studied his face, and then, to his surprise, she winked at him.

"Ugly people aren't human? Is that what you boys think?" she asked him straight. She extended the recorder in his direction, and he took it. She turned and sat down heavily upon the old cane-back chair that was tucked between two large wooden boxes.

That's probably the one I kicked the first time I was here, Cletis thought.

"Yes it is," she spoke softly, as if knowing his thoughts. "Not much of a detective, are you?" She eyed him and grinned slightly.

Quiet and shivering, Cletis began to wipe the water and mud from his hands and arms.

"Your parents know you're out here at this time of the night?" she asked.

Cletis said nothing, but slowly shook his head.

She looked back to the screen door, still wiping her neck and face. "Last year a boy fell through this screen, kind of like you just did. Probably doing the same thing you were attempting to do tonight. Must've cut his leg pretty badly going through it, because there was blood on the step below it, and blood on the ground all the way to the canal. You know anything about that?"

Cletis immediately thought of Klu. *But that was supposed to be from her fingernails. She was supposed to have sharpened them like claws.*

"Come here, lad." She motioned Cletis toward her.

Cletis stood lifelessly, not knowing what she wanted of him.

"Don't worry, lad. All I'm gonna do is ask you your name."

He took a few steps toward her, but remained silent. *If I tell her my name, then I'm in for big trouble*, he thought.

"Well, you got a name or don't you?"

"It's Thomas. That's my official name. Thomas Dungarvan," he answered. *She'll be callin' the police for sure, now. Maybe I shoulda said Elston or Frank or Davey.* He sighed shamefully. *Nope. I told her the truth. I'll face whatever else is comin' to me, cuz it's all my doin'.*

To his amazement, the old woman straightened a bit and cocked her head. She eyed him seriously, as if he were an old friend she didn't recognize. He thought he noticed a smile begin to form on her enlarged lips, but it quickly disappeared.

"Thomas Dungarvan, eh? . . . Well, Thomas, are you a gentleman?"

Cletis looked at her guiltily, not sure how to respond. "Yes, ma'am," he stated. "Most of the time." He felt frigid water sink deep into his ear, and he shivered abruptly with the tickle. His whole body suddenly reacted, and he shook with cold of the wet, springtime night.

"You come tomorrow and fix this screen for me, and I won't call the police or press charges. Deal?" She studied him a moment and then turned and reached for a small cardboard box. She brushed the dust off it, removed the lid, and then reached inside and pulled out an old, white cloth sack. She opened the drawstrings and pulled out a catcher's mitt. Under the light of the bulb that hung above the door, Cletis could read the name "Kluzuski" on the side of it.

But she was supposed to have eaten a part of that right in front of Klu! That mitt's in perfect condition!

"You know the boy this belongs to?" She held it out to Cletis.

"Yes, ma'am."

He took it from her and breathed deeply, trying to relax his trembling body. He still wasn't sure about all the strange feelings that charged back and forth through his mind, his heart, his being. *First scared to death, then peace, then scared to death again, then peace again.*

"It's a mighty nice glove. A good catcher would be missing this desperately. I've been breaking it in for him for the past year. Thought he'd come back for it, but he never did." The old hag looked down into the cloth sack once again, reached her wet arm into it, and pulled out a new white baseball. She studied it closely and then held it up to her nose and took a deep whiff of it. She smiled with satisfaction and handed it to Cletis. "Gotta keep a ball in that mitt. Helps form the pocket, you know."

Cletis studied her curiously. *She's talkin' baseball here? She's been takin' care of Klu's catcher's mitt? This hag . . . this witch . . . is handin' me a baseball?* As Cletis pondered her words, she rose to her feet and walked stiffly to the porch door. She lifted the screen where it had broken away from the frame.

"Not the first time this has happened. Every spring, it seems, I have to fix this." She pushed the door open and held it for Cletis. "Tomorrow morning, then. Screen door. I'll see you bright and early, won't I?"

Cletis nodded and bowed his head slightly.

"Good night, then, lad."

That's all she said, but Cletis got the point. With the recorder in one hand and Klu's well-conditioned glove on the other, Cletis sheepishly stepped through the door, down the two stairs, and into the blackness of the night. The woman watched him as he plodded over to the canal, slogged across the stream, and began the ascent up the hill. He heard the door of the home shut, and when he turned around to look, the porch was dark.

Johnny, Klu, and Rabbit strained their eyes to see into the darkness. They could hear someone or something coming up through the woods on the slope below them.

"Is that Cletis?" whispered Klu.

"Not sure," answered Johnny. "But get ready to run, if it isn't."

The sound of movement came closer and closer, until Johnny could stand the suspense no longer. "That you, Cletis?"

No answer.

"Turn on your light, but get ready to split."

Klu and Johnny both turned on their flashlights and pointed them down the hill at the same time. Cletis was so close it startled them. He carried the tape recorder in one hand and the catcher's mitt in the other.

"Cletis, why didn't you say anything?" Klu questioned, attempting to hide his fear.

"Man, Cletis, what's goin' on?" questioned Rabbit when he remained silent, just standing there.

"Why didn't you guys come help me?" Cletis finally responded.

The three were instantly quiet as they faced him and then hung their heads in shame.

"I knew we should've," moaned Rabbit, looking back up at Johnny and Klu.

Suddenly Cletis's knees buckled, and he slumped to the ground, exhausted.

"You okay, Clete?" Johnny asked as he shined the flashlight over the muddy wet clothes that draped Cletis's trembling body.

"What happened down there?" whispered Klu, kneeling next to Cletis.

There was admiration in his voice for this new kid who had shown such courage, faced the witch, and lived to tell about it. In the radiance of the small flashlight, Cletis lifted the catcher's mitt. Klu took it and studied it carefully. His mouth slowly dropped open as he read his name on the side and felt the ball in its pocket.

"This is mine!"

"She saved it for you. She took care of it, hopin' you'd come back and get it. She even put a ball in it to help the pocket form right. You cut your leg on her screen door, not her claws."

Klu studied him. "That's what she told you?" he asked suspiciously.

Ignoring the question, Cletis knelt up and handed the tape-recorder to Johnny.

"It's all right there. Listen for yourself."

With a cough, Cletis rose to his feet. As Johnny rewound the tape, Cletis took his glove from his belt. It was soaking and slippery from the several dips in the stream, but Cletis pushed his fingers into the holes, and worked it open and closed with the movement of his hand. He took the ball from Klu's mitt and tossed it into his own. Several times he threw it hard into the soggy pocket of the glove. He picked up his flashlight and still trembling, walked toward his bike. It was time to go home.

CHAPTER 4

A GIFT FROM
THE WITCH

Cletis's father downed a last bite of toast as he listened mutely to the final words of his son's story. With a sigh, he picked up his red nametag from the tile countertop behind the kitchen table and fastened it to his shirt pocket. He looked down and tugged on it to make sure it was straight. The words, "Precision Plumbing" and "Garth Dungarvan," were etched into it in white letters. He swallowed and with his tongue searched his teeth for any stubborn tidbits of breakfast.

"And that's why there's mud in the laundry room," Cletis confessed as he finished the story. "And that's why all my stuff is wet."

"Rewind it and let me listen to it again," insisted his dad, pointing to the recorder. Cletis obeyed.

As the tape rewound, his father looked over at him and then down at his wristwatch. Cletis sensed there were places his father had to be before nine o'clock and that, as usual, he was already behind schedule.

His father was a man with kind eyes, broad shoulders, calloused hands, and muscled forearms. Though his hair was dark and naturally wavy, there was a hint of red in it that became more pronounced in the sunlight. His dark complexion was a strange contrast to the lightness of his son's. He ran a plumbing supply company in Greenberg Junction, and back in 1989, he and his wife, Anna, left their home in Belleville and moved to little Greenberg Junction.

The cassette tape clicked to a halt, and Cletis pushed the play button again. His dad poured himself another glass of orange juice and listened for a second time to the sandpapery voice of the old lady the neighborhood boys called "the witch." Cletis sat shirtless and tired, limply spooning Cheerios into his mouth. His soggy mitt lay a few feet away from him at the end of the table. The new baseball that the old lady had given him rested strategically in the forming pocket. The adventure of last night reflected in his weary blood-shot eyes.

Cletis studied his dad as the recording repeated the strange conversation with the old lady. Cletis was hoping that because all this had to do with baseball, his dad would be lenient on him. In his dad's earlier years he had been a gifted athlete, and now as a father, he longed to see that athleticism passed on to his son. But until recently, the opportunity to play the regular sports with his dad—baseball, basketball, and football, at least—had not existed.

Cletis's vision problem had never allowed him the chance. From Cletis's infancy he had a condition known as strabismus. His right eye functioned perfectly, but his left eye pointed out. So he always saw double. Until two years ago, Cletis had worn large, thick glasses that were supposed to help correct his vision. In his growing-up years, Cletis had yearned to play sports with the other boys his age but struggled with depth perception. No matter what kind of ball was being played with, it was nearly impossible for him to follow the object through the air and into his hands. Often his father would work with him, trying to help him overcome the handicap, but in the process, Cletis took a lot of tosses painfully off his chest, head, and face. But Cletis had remained determined to learn and had forced himself to practice all the harder. Now, two years after the eye surgery, he was finally mastering the mechanics of throwing and catching, hitting and fielding. So in their spare moments together, he and his dad threw baseballs, dribbled and shot basketballs, or tossed footballs back and forth across the yard.

His dad glanced again at his watch and then reached over to the table and turned off the recorder.

"The guys let you keep this tape as a trophy or something?"

Cletis shrugged and nodded. "Johnny brought it to me this morning. He was on his way to the card shop."

"Johnny's thirteen, you say?"

"He's fourteen now."

"And the kid's over workin' with Mr. Sperry after bein' out all night?"

"I guess so."

His dad seemed to ponder that a moment, then steered his attention back to the issue of the old lady in the woods. "You're lucky the woman didn't call the cops on you, being out there at midnight. What were you guys thinkin'? I guess you *weren't*." His dad stepped across the room to the sink, set down his plate and glass, and looked out at the day through the window in front of him. "You could've drowned down there, not to mention what could've happened to the old lady. Then ridin' your bike across the field in the dark of night. That's a whole mile! You could've broken an ankle or a leg. And no one was with you, and I wouldn't have had any idea where you were. Not too smart, eh?"

His father turned on the water, filled up his glass, and raised it to his lips. Taking a mouthful, he swished the water around through his teeth and spit it back into the sink. Then lifting a vitamin lying nearby, he tossed it into his mouth and drank it down.

Mom used to make us good breakfasts, Cletis thought as he watched his father's Adam's apple move up and down with each swallow. *Now Dad just eats vitamins.*

His father set down his glass, opened the briefcase that rested on the countertop next to him, fiddled with some of the papers inside, and then closed it up again. He turned and eyed Cletis, and then crossing back to the table, he lifted Cletis's soggy mitt, pushed his fingers into the holes, and removed the baseball. He threw the ball into the wet mitt several times and eyed the glove.

"Actually, this isn't a bad way to train this leather," he stated, suddenly positive and encouraging. "Some guys would soak their mitt like this and then work it to fit the grip and shape of their hand. Trick is, you gotta keep your hand in it constantly until it dries, or it'll shrink up and tighten on you." He tossed the ball a few more times into the glove and then eyed Cletis curiously. "You really want to play baseball with these guys?" he asked. "They don't sound too responsible."

Cletis nodded wearily. "Yeah, I really do."

His dad pulled out a chair and sat down. He placed his hand on Cletis's bare shoulder. "You seein' the ball okay?" he asked, looking into his son's tired face.

Cletis cupped his hand over his right eye and scanned the room. "Yep. And every day it seems to get better. You know, judgin' the ball and catchin' it and everything."

"Well, you said you made a great catch yesterday. I knew you could do it. It was just a matter of throwing and practicing enough." He patted Cletis's back. "You seeing the pitch well enough to get out of the way if it's gonna hit you?"

Cletis nodded. "I think so. Haven't done much hittin' yet, but I think so."

His dad leaned in, put his face right in front of Cletis's, and studied both of his son's eyes—not really seeing Cletis, just looking at the boy's blue-green eyes. "Your eye's looking great. That's good."

He rose, crossed to the sink, and lifted his briefcase. "Clete, I appreciate you telling me about all this." He pointed to the tape recorder, the mitt, and then the dirty clothes on the floor of the laundry room behind him. "That was a brave and honest thing to do. It was a *manly* thing to do. I don't mean what you *did*—I mean that you had the courage to come and talk to me about it. I still don't approve of what you did last night. I don't think it was in the best judgment.... But I already told you that."

His dad paused a moment. Cletis thought he saw him try to fight back a grin. But he turned, cleared his throat, and continued.

"There's a roll of screen material in the garage. You know how to put it on her door?"

"Staple gun. I think she just wants it pounded onto the wooden door."

"We got staples for the gun?"

Cletis nodded. His dad did likewise and then pointed to another brown vitamin near the sink.

"Take it. That one's yours." He stepped toward the back door. "I don't like leaving you here alone, but I figure if you're twelve you should be—" He paused briefly and looked around the kitchen. "Ah,

I've said all this before. So get your chores done. Be responsible. You know where to find me if you need me."

Cletis nodded again, eyeing his dad's wrinkled work shirt.

"Lots of mud tracked in here yesterday and last night. Make sure you clean it all up before you go runnin' off. Especially soak your shoes. See if you can get that smell out of 'em." He paused a moment and turned back to his son. "You're sure you're doin' okay?"

"Yeah, Dad. Don't worry."

His father smiled, nodded, and then opened the door and stepped out into the morning. Cletis heard the sounds of the van's engine starting up, and he watched the shadow of the vehicle through the kitchen window as it backed down the driveway. But then Cletis became lost in his own thoughts. He took a final spoonful of Cheerios and looked over at the mitt and ball.

One thing is for sure, Dad's a lot different now since Mom died. Kind of gentler, I guess . . . like he's trying to be both a mom and a dad all in one.

It had been a hard thing for both of them to watch Cletis's mom die, especially after she had nursed Cletis back to health following his eye surgery. Her illness came on so hastily—a cancer in her brain, the older people and the doctors had told him. She had always had a lot of headaches, but she had told him it was because of stress and unanswered questions. He never really knew what those "unanswered questions" were, and when he asked about them, she would just smile and say, "Oh, just the regular stuff of life."

Cletis remembered her tone and her whisper. Her caring voice was still fresh in his mind, and he longed to hear it again and soak in her words of encouragement and love. He could still feel her gentle touch and see the smile in her eyes. He could still hear her humming around the house as she went about her daily duties. But now the house was lonely and empty. It would never be the same. Certain wounds would take a while to heal, his dad had told him, but this wound was still bleeding. Though her presence was continuously felt throughout the rooms and halls of their home, she had gone to a different place. Life and death were hard for Cletis to understand, but he dealt with it. He had no choice.

The hag of Greenberg Junction was even uglier in the daylight. The sun seemed to reveal every wrinkle and pore and lump and spot and bulge that covered the poor woman's thick short frame. So Cletis worked hard not to see her. If, by accident, he *did* look at her, he tried to concentrate on her eyes. There was something amazingly youthful about her eyes. They were like two perfect emeralds stuck in the middle of a large sausage pizza. But it was so tough not to see the rest of her, even when he *was* trying to look only at her eyes, that he just decided to keep focused on the business at hand: fixing the screen he had broken the night before.

In his peripheral vision, he noted her clothing. He had never seen anything like her boots before—if they could be called "boots." They were almost a combination of Indian moccasins and riding boots but with an orange-brown hue. They actually looked comfortable, except for the fact that they must have made her hot, especially when the weather got warm in the summer. Her collarless burlaplike dress came down over her tree-stump legs and ended below her knees. The sleeves of the old dress reached her elbows. A tattered gray apron was tied around her neck and waist. Cletis wondered if she had made the boots and dress by hand, but it was obvious there was no concern for being fashionable.

The staple gun was working nicely, and the job was simple. *Just measure the screen, cut it out, hold it up to the door, and staple it on,* Cletis figured. He shooed a fly away from his ear. By the looks of the old screen that was on the door before, she seemed only concerned about keeping bugs out. She didn't seem to be worried about appearances.

As Cletis worked, he snuck a peak at the house, the roof, the back area, and the canal. *In fact, it doesn't seem like she's too worried about how* anything *looks around here.* No grass or flowers adorned the place. Boxes and old chairs cluttered the back porch. He could sense her watching his work as she sat in the shade of the porch on a rickety cane-back chair—the one Cletis had kicked the night before.

As he neared the end of his chore, her scratchy voice broke the silence. She eyed his mitt that was lying in front of her on the flooring of the porch. "Son, didn't you say your name was Thomas?"

He tried not to look at her as he answered. "Yes, ma'am."

"Then why do you have 'Cleats' written on your glove?"

He folded the stapler, jammed it in his pants pocket, and turned to look down at his mitt. "It's a nickname my dad gave me when I was little."

She leaned toward him and studied him intently. "You mean 'Cletis'?"

"Yeah, but I . . . I, uh, spelled it wrong just for fun."

An odd silence followed his comment. Cletis finally lifted his face to study hers, reminding himself again to look only at her eyes. He couldn't help but notice that she was watching him closely—better yet, she was studying him.

He removed his hat and, with the help of his shirt, wiped the trickles of sweat off his nose and chin and forehead. Suddenly self-conscious, he wondered what she was finding so interesting.

She began to mouth some words. Her lips moved but no sound came out at first. Then it was a whisper. Finally, when Cletis could hear what she said, it was like she was talking to some secret unseen companion—maybe someone in her inner mind—as if Cletis were a mile away. He heard two words that sounded an awful lot like "Papa" and "Mama," but he had no idea what she was actually saying.

"I didn't know he called you 'Cletis,'" she finally said in words he could understand. She rubbed her hands up and down on her apron.

"Cletis . . . Cletis . . . Cleats," she mumbled in raspy, deep tones. Then her fingers rose to her chin, and as her mouth dropped open, her eyes widened with wonder. "'Called by that which he wears on his feet,'" she gasped, as if some stunning, new discovery had just settled on her brain. "Yes . . . Yes . . . That's right," she muttered, still studying Cletis. "'He shall rise with her from the wet earth.'" She slapped her wide, husky palms down on her knees. "Dearest heaven, is it finally upon me? Is it finally here?"

Cletis continued to study her eyes. *The nutty old lady's out of her mind. And why is she lookin' at me like this?* Cletis looked away at the forested hillside and then back at the woman.

With her eyes still wide upon him, the seconds passed slowly. She sat back in her chair and exhaled a long guttural sigh. Cletis had never heard such a sound. And then, much to his surprise, she asked him a simple question.

"You like baseball, Thomas Cletis Dungarvan?"

Unsure of what she really meant by it, he slowly nodded his head. "Yeah, I do . . . I, uh . . . yeah, I like baseball."

"And you're playing ball with these boys who raid my back porch each summer?"

Again he nodded his head.

Man, he thought, *she knows exactly what the guys've been doin' down here.*

"You can follow a pitch now? Your eye is healed?"

Cletis froze, and his mouth slightly opened as he pondered her words. *Nobody but my family knows about that. Maybe some of the kids at school . . . and some doctors around here . . . but that's all. How could she know about that?*

He guarded his next words, not knowing for sure whether he was ready for what she would say. "How do you know about my eye?"

She ignored his question and paused to itch just behind her left ear. "Well, Thomas Cletis Dungarvan, *you* have come to *me*. Now I see it clearly. Or at least I hope I do."

With that she arose and bid him to follow her into the house. To his astonishment, and despite his bewilderment, his legs obeyed. *What am I doing? I'm following her into her own house! It's like Hansel and Gretel.* Nevertheless, his feet didn't stop moving, and he stepped forward across the porch.

The back door opened into a dark, narrow hallway. As he followed her, he passed a few closed doors—maybe closets or washrooms. *Or torture chambers. Why am I following this hag? What am I thinkin'?! Klu and Johnny talked about missing boys—bodies the police couldn't find. They talked about her eatin' a part of Klu's catcher's mitt. But, wait a minute, that wasn't true. I gave the mitt to Klu. There was nothing wrong with it. I don't know, but I think I'm only gettin' half the story from them and half the story from her.*

Despite his concerns, he followed her deeper into the house. Then that strange feeling came upon him again—that feeling that had settled upon him the night before as he stood in the dark woods and heard the old woman call for help. Though it was a sensation that had turned his horror into peace, it was still new and different and strange. And in a place like this, he was already getting enough that was *new and different and strange*, and he wasn't sure he wanted more. As he walked slowly on, following the old woman, he looked down at his arms. His hair was standing on end, and he felt an odd, comforting warmth settle across his neck, shoulders, and head. *What is that?* he thought.

They turned to the right and passed an open room on his left that contained an old, worn-out couch. A gray blanket had been tossed over it, as if in an attempt to keep it from wearing out completely. There was an antique lamp standing next to it, and some old books were scattered around on the floor. A window on the opposite wall was so covered with dirt, that only a whisper of light penetrated the pane. Before he could see more, they were past the room. The walls in the hallway held no adorning pictures—no family portraits, no pleasant landscapes. Above him, the ceiling had given birth to hundreds of long cobwebs, some of which hung low enough to gently stroke his hair as he walked under them. The whisper of Cletis's footsteps echoed against the barren walls of the hallway. The woman walked silently on. Cletis felt the moan of the old wooden floors, as if they spoke a warning from below. There were no rugs on the floor, except for the old tattered rag-weave mat by the doorway where they entered. A large hunk of plaster hung from the ceiling in front of them near ready to crash to the floor. He said nothing; he was too afraid to speak.

A sweet smell unexpectedly wafted past him. It seemed oddly out of place in the old house.

What is that smell? Vanilla? Leather? It was a combination he couldn't identify. *It seems to be comin' off the walls!*

Cletis leaned over to sniff the wall, trying to find the source of the fragrance. Suddenly the old woman turned and faced him. With his eyes wide in fear, as if having been caught in a sinful act, he pulled himself upright and stood like a soldier at attention. Before he could attempt to explain his actions, she planted her large hands upon his cheeks and pulled him close to her. She spoke in a hushed tone, but seriously.

"I have known your father for a long time." She paused a moment to let her words sink in. "I know also that when your mother died, you sat at her bedside caring for her until her final breath. I know what a brave young man you have been." She held his face a moment longer and then released him. There was compassion in her eyes, despite the horridly ugly flesh that surrounded them.

Cletis gulped but began to breathe again. "How did you know all that? And about my eye?"

Her face became expressionless. She paused a moment, as if in thought, then turned around and proceeded a few more steps down the hall.

Finally, the old lady stopped in front of a closed door to her left and pulled a long skeleton key from her apron pocket. Cletis kept his distance, not knowing what the room would reveal. She twisted the key and opened the door. A shaft of light danced across the wooden flooring of the hall and up the wall on the opposite side.

"Wait here," she spoke.

She disappeared into the room. Cletis could hear her shuffling about. Within seconds she reappeared with a white envelope in her hand.

"For being a gentleman," she said, extending it to him. "But this is our secret."

Cletis took the envelope. It felt like it contained a piece of cardboard, or two. *Maybe she's paying me for fixing her screen. That's not right. . . . I'm the one who busted it. I was supposed to fix it. . . . Or maybe it's some sort of tracking device so she can always know where I am!*

She closed the door, stepped past him, and silently led him back down the two halls to where they had entered the eerie old home. When they reached the back door, she held the door open for him. He cautiously stepped past her and out onto the wooden planks of the porch. The chimes above him tinkled in the light breeze—as if they were happy to see he had gotten out alive.

"Cletis Dungarvan," she said abruptly. He turned to her. "If you are who I think you are, there is an adventure ahead for both of us. Be ready."

Cletis pondered her words for a moment. He studied her curiously, and then turned and picked up his mitt from off the porch floor. Not quite sure what to say, he kept his mouth shut. In two steps, he was through the screen door and onto the ground below. He didn't look back as he crossed to the canal. Though his knees were a bit unsteady, he found a dry spot on the bank and jumped. Landing safely on the opposite side, he scurried up through the trees. As he pushed his way past branches and undergrowth, he studied the curious envelope he carried.

On his way back from the old lady's house, Cletis approached the ball diamond from center field. Rabbit was the first to spot him as she took practice swings near home plate.

"Hey! There's Cletis!" she called out.

All the boys turned and watched him make his way toward the infield.

In his own world of thought, Cletis pulled the white envelope from the basket on his handlebars and then dropped his bike in deep center field. He removed the two baseball cards from the envelope and studied them as he began a slow jog toward his teammates. His damp mitt, attached to his belt, flapped against his thigh. Being so preoccupied with where he had been that morning, and now concentrating keenly on what the old hag had told him and given him, he was almost completely unaware of the reverence his teammates paid him as he reached the infield. To Cletis, last night's adventure was almost all but forgotten.

"Look at these, guys," Cletis announced as he held up two cards. The team gathered around him as he stepped up near Johnny on the pitcher's mound.

Johnny, who worked at Sperry's Cards & Coins, was the baseball card expert, and everyone looked to him to identify the cards, their worth, and maybe some tidbits of history that would bring magic to the possession. Cletis handed them to Johnny.

"Whoa! Carl Yazstremski and Willie McCovey! Their rookie cards!" Johnny eyed them, studying them for flaws or bends or scratches. "And in mint condition! I've never seen anything like this! Pauly, get the price guide!"

Pauly ran toward the dugout bench, pulled a dog-eared magazine from the old box, and then raced back over to the boys. The magazine was the most recent Beckett price guide Johnny had picked up at the card store, but it was used so often by the boys that it had the appearance of an arithmetic teacher's answer book in a class of math-challenged students.

"Man, Carl Yazstremski," Johnny continued, "the last man to win the Triple Crown!"

"What's the Triple Crown?" questioned Timmy.

"That's when a player leads the league in home runs, batting average, and RBIs," Rabbit rapidly responded.

"How'd you know that?" questioned Frank, looking down at Rabbit with increased respect.

"Mickey Mantle did that once, didn't he?" spouted Davey.

"Yep, Frank Robinson, too," replied Johnny as Pauly arrived with the guide. "And Ted Williams. But no one since Yaz."

"What year's the Yaz card?" asked Pauly, already thumbing through the pages.

"1960. Topps. Number 148."

Cletis was in awe watching Rabbit and the boys go back and forth with the details. His dad had often talked of the baseball card collection he had kept as a boy—the same collection his mom had thrown out while he was away at college.

"It's mint?" asked Pauly.

"Yep."

"Man," sighed Frank, slapping his mitt. "I ain't never seen somethin' like that."

"Says here it's worth $160.00!" announced Pauly.

"You gotta be kiddin'," whispered Elston. "That's almost four months worth of newspaper deliverin'!"

"Now look up Willie McCovey," requested Johnny, still examining the treasures. "Number 316. Giants. Same year."

Pauly ran his finger down the page, searching for the McCovey card.

"They called him 'Stretch,'" continued Johnny, now looking over at Elston. "Played with Willie Mays, Elston. And he played your position. First base."

Elston looked on, admiring the card.

"Yeah, he kinda looks like me, too!"

Pauly found the information and blurted out the announcement. "Same thing! $160.00!"

Again the group voiced their amazement as they squeezed in to get a better look at the famous San Francisco Giant slugger. Johnny continued to hold the cards as if they were delicate insects he was trying to keep alive.

"If I were you, Clete, I'd be careful not to bump the corners. That's gonna be worth a lot of money ten years from now."

He handed them back to Cletis and smiled in awe.

"Where d'ya get 'em anyway?" questioned Davey.

"The old—" Cletis caught himself. He took a quick breath. "An old . . . uh . . . friend of my dad's."

As Cletis carefully placed the cards back in the protective envelope, a silence settled over the group. Cletis lifted his head, and as he studied each face, he realized all eyes were upon him. Instantly, he wondered if everyone had seen through his little fib about the cards and were now demanding the detailed truth.

Johnny looked to Elston and gave him a nod. All the boys dropped their heads at the same time—and even Rabbit too—as if each one of them had been caught cheating on a spelling test.

"Uhh . . . " Elston attempted to speak. "Umm . . . well . . . Klu and Johnny and Rabbit told us what happened last night." He paused again, and looking down at the dirt he kicked away a shiny black beetle that scooted across the ground in front of him.

"He's trying to say we're sorry . . . all of us," added Frank, voicing Elston's thoughts. "We feel bad we ran off."

"Yeah, sorry," mumbled Davey, his face shiny with sunscreen.

Quietly Pauly and Elston each apologized, too.

"Johnny and Klu filled us in on what happened," explained Davey. "About the face-to-face with the witch."

"And the fight in the canal water," added Frank.

"Wish I could've been there," spoke Timmy. "I always miss out on the good stuff."

Johnny patted his cousin's back.

"Yeah, and me and Johnny are sorry too," Klu spoke. "We should've been more help, but we were . . . uh . . . we were kinda scared."

Eyes suddenly went to Johnny, as if no one could believe *he* could *ever* be scared. But a slow nod of his head gave them to know that he was human after all.

"Rabbit was braver than all of us," Johnny declared, looking over at the shortstop.

"Hey, I was scared too," she admitted, slapping her mitt against her thigh. "We couldn't believe you went back there this morning."

"Yeah . . . well . . ." Cletis stammered. "The old lady down there . . . uh . . . she's kinda ugly, and maybe kinda mean, but she might not be a witch like everyone thinks."

All the guys allowed that thought to sink in a bit, as if not certain they wanted to believe him, or *could* believe him. If she wasn't really a witch, it would make all their stories, and their initiations, and their feats of heroism look pretty foolish. If she wasn't a witch, what was she? If her house wasn't haunted, what was it? The whole place around the hag's house was creepy and spooky, and now Cletis was telling them that what they believed to be true might be a misguided fable.

No one moved. No one spoke.

"Maybe she is, maybe she isn't," concluded Cletis.

"Well, at least I got my mitt back." Klu announced, breaking the silence.

"I don't know what the old lady is, but let's play some ball!" Johnny announced. "Cletis, center field!"

No words had ever sounded sweeter to Cletis. He hustled with Pauly over to the wooden box at the bench. Pauly tossed in the price guide, and Cletis gently placed his cards on the top of it. He stepped back and allowed Pauly to lower the lid and lock it into place. Remembering the lump in his pocket, Cletis removed the staple gun and laid it next to the box.

Better not go divin' for any fly balls with that in my pants, he thought as he turned and faced the field.

The breeze was blowing slightly toward left. Two clouds resembling old-time baseball gloves drifted lazily across the sky. Pauly, next to him, covered with sunscreen, smelled like a California beach. A giant smile that hadn't found its way onto Cletis's mouth in over two years gracefully appeared. With no desire to hide his happiness, he pulled his Tigers hat snuggly down over his strawberry blond hair and contemplated the amazing events of the past two days. He pushed his hand into his wet glove and flexed it open and closed. Pauly slapped Cletis on the back as he raced past him toward left field.

"Let's go make some more magic, Clete!" he shouted.

Together the two of them sprinted happily into the solitude of their outfield positions.

Chapter 5

The Baseball Room and The Ancient Box

Several hours later Cletis entered the back door of his home, now sweaty and dust-covered from his first official practice. The house was silent. His dad was still at work. Cletis looked down at the floor—the floor he had cleaned that morning—but muddied pants and socks still lay in a heap in the corner behind the door, and the place smelled like a cow pasture. He'd get to them later, he knew. He left his glove, staple gun, and shoes on the floor, next to the muddy pile, and still carefully holding the envelope with the baseball cards, made his way upstairs to his bedroom. In six jumping strides he covered the twelve steps, and making an immediate right turn at the top of the staircase, he entered the world of his own little room.

There were no fancy electronic toys in Cletis's room, nor was there a TV or stereo. Several books lined the two shelves above the desk behind the open door—mostly grade school required reading. Among his favorites were *Tom Sawyer, Stuart Little, The Chronicles of Narnia,* a book about the Civil War, and a book on baseball sports heroes. A dresser with a large mirror attached to the back of it sat on the opposite side of the room. In front of the mirror rested a prized autographed baseball Cletis's dad had given him for his tenth birthday. The names Dick McAuliffe, Mickey Lolich, and Denny McClain were penned upon it—all Detroit Tigers' heroes from years past—1968 to be exact. 1968 was the year of the Tigers. In that World Series they had beaten the Cardinals in seven exciting games. Cletis's dad and mom had always spoken of those times excitedly. So the baseball was a cherished gift.

Of all the toys and books and games and other stuff with which he filled his room, including the autographed baseball, his prized possession was a family portrait—a picture taken just after Cletis's eye surgery and just before his mom became sick with the cancer. The framed photo, resting next to the baseball, depicted a time when everyone appeared healthy and happy. A friend of his dad's had taken the picture. The three of them had gathered in the backyard on the large gray boulder by the white roses his mom had planted. The boulder had been like a family treasure. It was there when they moved in, and it had been a great place for a boy to play or pretend or think or just be alone. In the photo, the family was seated on the rock—Cletis in the middle, his mom on the left, and his dad on the right. It was a photo that made them look like a family that could happily withstand any challenge life could ever throw at them.

Except maybe not death, thought Cletis.

He lifted the portrait and studied it. Cletis had placed the picture there, next to the autographed baseball, so that every time he entered the room it was the first thing he saw—straight in front of him.

As he considered the autographed baseball and the portrait of his family, Cletis removed the cards from the envelope and placed them in front of the photo, as if showing them to his mother.

"What do you think of these, Mom?" He spoke out loud. "I got 'em from a witch. Well, that's what they call her anyway. Just for fixin' her screen. Of course, I busted that screen last night during my initiation—I think you already know that. Sorry. And she just up and gave 'em to me. Johnny says that together they're worth about $300. Kinda weird, huh? I'm thinkin' about maybe usin' the money for college."

He placed Willie McCovey on the left side of the family photo and Carl Yazstremski on the right. He admired them a moment, then hopped back onto his bed and crawled up to his pillow. He tucked his hands behind his head and stared up at the ceiling, seeing again the two fly balls he had misjudged at today's practice.

The hag sat upon an ancient chair, deep in thought. A ray of light filtered through an opening in the tattered curtains to her right. A fireplace graced the wall directly in front of her, framed by a hearth fashioned from a mixture of rounded, gray and brown stones. The shelf that formed the mantel was covered with dusty knick-knacks—mostly wooden carvings that had a medieval quality to them. In the center of the shelf sat an old wooden box, ornately decorated with shiny, metal plating that covered three of the four sides. It stood on four small wooden legs, each carved to look like an hourglass. It was this box the woman studied. It had been with her now for nearly one hundred years. During that time, it had rested upon a mantel or a shelf or a table, as if in hibernation, awaiting the instance of its awakening.

As she studied the relic, she lost track of time. But then, to the old woman, time was measured differently. She shifted in her chair and gently rubbed her large hands together. For centuries she had awaited a particular moment, but she never knew precisely when that moment would come. She had prepared herself, studying the prophecy that had been mysteriously carved on the box's lid. In the days of her youth, ages ago, the writing was not there. But the box had come to her with the baffling words etched on the top panel. To the best of her ability, she had translated them and attempted to decipher their meaning. Regarding the precise details and fulfillment of the ancient writing, she had hoped the box itself would be her guide, for she remembered its magical powers from earlier in her life. Only time would tell. If she were correct in her hunch regarding the boy—Thomas "Cletis" Dungarvan—the truth would eventually be revealed to her. If she were incorrect, then more years of continued waiting lay ahead—waiting and watching for the coming of another man, young or old, who would match the revealed details of the strange foretelling.

She spoke aloud, contemplating the first three lines of the prophecy:

"Called by that which he wears upon his feet,
He shall rise with her from the wet earth.
Then shall the powers of the box be revealed."

The prophecy rolled musically off her tongue. Within the past day, two of those lines had been fulfilled. At least according to *her* understanding they had been fulfilled. But she had been mistaken before.

Then it happened. For all the long years she had possessed the box she had anticipated this sacred moment. She gasped as she witnessed a soft glow sparkle within the box—a light that grew steadily brighter. She pushed herself upright in the chair and blinked her eyes to focus more clearly. She watched the box in awe, sensing for the first time in her long, worn life that the end of her ordeal was finally beginning. Now the third line of the prophecy with its promise of powers and revelation and secrets was coming to pass before her very eyes.

The ancient wood blushed red, absorbing the mysterious brilliance that came from within. An eerie, warm radiance enveloped the box and cast its light upon the nearby knick-knacks and ornaments that graced the mantel. The long-awaited process—indeed, the fulfillment of the prophecy—had at last begun.

"The powers of the box shall be revealed!" she whispered.

Then it moved—but not from any control or magic she could conjure. Another power was at work here—the original Powers. The Powers she had witnessed as a young woman centuries ago. Invisible hands seemed to caress the box, lift it, and control it. With a smile and a breathy giddy laugh, she welcomed the familiar force, absent far too long from her life. Featherlike, the box floated away from the stone shelf and drifted steadily toward the old woman. Her gnarled heavy hands rose from her lap and reached toward it, awaiting patiently its touch. Her vision clouded with emotion, and she blinked the salty warm tears onto her cheeks, sensing that finally, her real work could begin. Then the box was before her, like a child returning to its mother, accepting the grasp of her plump wide hands and welcoming her loving touch. She held the box reverently, weeping with the feel of the energy that now surged into her arms, shoulders, head, and body.

Magically the lid lifted. Instantly the soft, red glow illuminated the hag's face. She marveled silently, knowing that for as long as she could remember there was never anything within the box that could cause such a wonder.

What is the source of the light?

As suddenly as it had opened, the lid closed back down, and the words of the inscription carved upon the top of the box began to glow a soft blue. Since the day the ancient wooden container had come to her, she had studied the old language of the inscription. Now she pondered the radiant words again, reading each one in a whispered, reverent groan.

Her hands felt the reassuring warmth of the box, and she nested it upon her ample legs. The red light from within gradually diminished while the old letters of the prophecy on the lid retained their comforting blue glow. She sensed a shifting of warmth and light as energy moved from the inside and top of the box to the exterior panels. She lifted the box away from her to better study the magical relic.

Unexpectedly another strange set of markings gradually appeared on the old metal—markings she had never seen before. The etchings appeared in a brilliant, red display, as if being written presently by some unseen hand. The ancient code or text was a series of notches, some perfectly vertical and some carved at a slight angle. An occasional horizontal line connected the odd etchings, as if some ancient accounting were taking place.

The writings of the Travelers, she pondered with a sudden surge of fear. *They know the secrets and Powers of the box.*

The hag slowly turned the relic, watching the etchings appear on the metal panels. When the magical process came to an end, the light slowly faded from the box. Lowering it again to her lap, she reached up to her face and pushed a tear from her cheek.

"The Powers of the box have returned," she whispered. "Yet they are not mine to know."

Cletis and his father sorted through the laundry, tossing the colored items into the washer. As they did, Cletis described in detail his morning with the old woman. The baseball cards the hag had given him lay flat upon the dryer in front of them.

"And then she said she knew you, and she also knew that Mom had died. And she knew about my eye, and she said if I was who she thought I was, then a big adventure was comin' up."

His father eyed him thoughtfully. "She said all that?"

"I was there in her house, after I fixed the screen."

"You went into her house?"

"Yeah, that's where she got the cards . . . outta some room I didn't go into. That's where she told me the stuff about you and Mom and me. I don't know how she knew it, Dad, but it was like she knew all about us."

His father allowed this to soak in for a moment. "That's really strange," he added. He eyed Cletis and then jammed a pair of his son's dirty jeans into the soapy water. "Cletis, I have no idea who this old lady is. She may be completely harmless, but on the other hand, maybe she's not. I just don't know. I don't know how she could have known those things, unless we have some common friend that I don't know about. Maybe I did some plumbing for a friend of hers or something. Or maybe she just reads the newspaper a lot and memorizes details. Mom's obituary was in the paper." He paused briefly. "But that was last year. So, you know what I recommend?"

Cletis eyed him, knowing what he was going to say.

"I recommend you stay away from her. I think that'd be the smartest thing to do. What do you think?"

Cletis looked down at the floor. His father picked up the cards again and studied them.

"When I was a boy," he started thoughtfully, "I had the cards, the old magazines, the pennants." He chuckled through his nose. "Last Yaz card I saw like this had staple holes through the corners of it. A guy named Ricky MacGregory had it. I knew him as a kid. Good shortstop. He stuck it to his bulletin board. Little did he know that the tiny holes from the staples dropped it $100 in value, just like that." He snapped his fingers. "Of course, back in those days we didn't know the treasures we had. We'd chuck 'em around the yard, trade 'em, shuffle 'em. I can remember clothes-pinning a Roger Maris to the fender of my bike. When the spokes went round and round over the edge of the card, it sounded like a little motor. We thought that was pretty cool. I destroyed a '62 Maris that way, and probably a lot of others."

His father smiled and then handed the cards to Cletis. He threw the remaining white clothes into another laundry basket, kicked it over against the wall behind Cletis, and then shut the lid of the washer. The water began to chug and gurgle inside the tub.

"Glad you prewashed those jeans," added his father. "But don't do it in my shower next time, okay? My room smells like one of those pastures east of town."

"Sorry."

"And the old lady... Let's stay away from her, Clete. Safety.... Okay?"

Cletis sighed and nodded, agreeing yet not agreeing. His father turned and left the room. Now alone, Cletis studied the cards. Carefully he placed them into the envelope again. With thoughts of the old woman and the strange events that transpired over the past few days, he walked up to his room and got ready for bed.

It was close to nine o'clock the next morning when Cletis and Elston reached the hillside above the hag's house. The sun had risen in the cloudless blue sky, and the woods below the two boys were filled with the chattering of hundreds of birds. Cletis and Elston stood at the top of the slope, considering the reasons that had led them there that morning.

"I ain't goin' down there. I changed my mind," spoke Elston, squeezing his handlebars tightly. He took his hat off, wiped his brow, put his hat back on, and pulled it snugly down on his head. "And you just said your dad didn't want you down there either, so I don't know why we're even here. I get creeped out when I'm even close to this place."

Cletis stared down at the witch's house, visible through a clearing in the pines, elms, and maples that grew below them.

"But she knows stuff about me, and about my family too. I gotta figure all this out."

From his mitt, Cletis removed the ball the old woman had given him two nights back. He handed it to Elston. Elston eyed it curiously and put it in his first baseman's mitt.

"Tell me you're not goin' down there again," Elston warned.

Cletis ignored him. He studied the slope of the hill.

"Wait here 'til I get back. I need a witness in case I don't come out. She didn't hurt me yesterday. I don't think she will today." He pointed to the ball in Elston's glove. "That's the ball she kept in Klu's catcher's mitt to help form the pocket. If I don't come back, it's yours."

"What am I supposed to do? Just stand here and wait 'til I hear your screams or somethin', then run and tell your dad you're dead?"

"I don't think there'll be any screams." He turned and smiled teasingly at Elston. "But I may vanish into thin air or fall through her floor into a bottomless pit." Elston wasn't amused. "I don't know. It's not like I gotta prove to the guys she's not a witch. That really doesn't matter to me. It's somethin' else. I just gotta do this. It's like I got a mission to do. I know what my dad said, and I'll probably get in trouble, but I need to find out who she is. I been feelin' some strange things lately too, and I gotta know what's goin' on."

With that, Cletis adjusted his Tiger's cap and dropped his mitt on the ground near his bike. Stepping onto the downward slope of the embankment, he maneuvered through the woods of the hillside.

Cletis studied the house as he walked past it. He didn't think there was a basement to the home; he couldn't see any windows below. He looked up. *And there's no second story—no upstairs. Gotta be just one floor as far as I can tell. This place must be a hundred years old. Least it looks that way.*

He cautiously approached the back porch. There was no sign of anyone. He stopped in front of the screen door, opened it, and peered in. A soft moan from the door hinges announced his entrance.

It still squeaks. Should've oiled that when I fixed the screen. She knows I'm here now. From where he stood, he could see that the back door was open. He took two steps forward and was about to call out, when . . .

"Thomas Cletis Dungarvan."

The voice came from his immediate right. He jumped, falling into the wall next to the door. Catching his balance, he turned and saw the old hag sitting on the cane-back chair, hidden behind a pile of large gray wooden boxes. He hadn't seen her at all, yet she was right there next to him, quiet as a serpent. She didn't say hello, nor did she allow him to. Instead she spoke rapidly, staring keenly into his eyes.

"You're in center field. Men on first and third. One out. A one-bouncer is hit to you in the right-center gap. What are you going to do?"

Cletis, caught off-guard by the sudden, strange question coming from this old hag of a woman, swallowed hard and eyed her questioningly. He saw that she was serious. Playing along with it, he asked, "How fast is the runner on third?"

"Real fast," she answered without hesitation.

"I hit the cut-off at second base."

A sudden, happy grin revealed her lack of teeth. Some were broken off, others misshapen, and others completely gone. It was a hideous smile. Yet, behind that grotesque countenance, he sensed an exuberant spirit. She clapped her fleshy hands together, as if congratulating Cletis.

"Ahhh! It's a great game, isn't it?!"

Unsure of himself, he smiled clumsily back at her.

She's talkin' baseball like she knows all about it! Only Dad talks to me that way.

"So you decided to return for a visit, eh?" she questioned, still grinning. Without allowing him to answer, she was up and entering the house. "Follow me." He noticed she was wearing the same thing she had worn the day before.

Cletis followed the old woman down the two creepy hallways they had walked yesterday. The floor creaked again beneath their feet as they approached the door she had opened the last time he was there. Pulling the same odd skeleton key from the pocket on her dress, she inserted it into the lock and twisted it once in her hand.

"Come in Cletis Dungarvan," she spoke in her raspy voice as she pushed the door open. A motion of her hand bid him enter.

Fighting his fears, Cletis stepped toward the doorway. The old woman reached around the wall and clicked on the light. In a moment Cletis scanned the entire room. His jaw dropped. The broken bent house seen from the outside was suddenly left far behind. This—this room—was a different place. A different world! The room was large and clean and carpeted with elegant, long rugs that covered portions of the hardwood floor. But what surprised him most of all was that the space was completely decorated in baseball memorabilia. Pennants and posters and programs filled the walls; old gloves and balls and bats covered the dozens of shelves; and photos and cards were placed carefully upon countertops and cases. Yet, there was a homey feel to the room— as if it were a place where you could come and read a good book, or talk with a friend, or sit and think. Six small lamps lit the room, and a fireplace, created of elegant brown and gray stonework, graced the wall to his left. Upon the mantel and hearth rested autographed photos of baseball's finest.

Cletis wandered, as if in a trance, around and through the furnishings. He reverently touched an old, blackened-with-age, three-fingered glove that must have come from the 1920s or '30s. He studied an old catcher's mitt next to it and noticed the name written on the back of the thumb: *Roy Campanella.*

"Roy Campanella!!" The words exploded from Cletis. "He was on the Brooklyn Dodgers! My dad told me he got in a car accident and was paralyzed—one of the best catcher's in all of baseball!"

The old hag smiled at Cletis, seemingly surprised and pleased by his baseball intelligence.

Cletis continued to wander. He hefted an old Louisville Slugger. *Whose name is this?* he asked himself, looking at the name inscribed at the top of the barrel. He sounded out the letters.

"Rogers Hornsby?!!" Cletis exclaimed. "Is this really his bat?"

She nodded with a grin.

"Man!" He carefully set it down and continued his exploration. Several other bats rested by the Hornsby model.

Mel Ott! Leo Durocher! Willie Mays! Hank Greenberg! He read them all, bowled over by the history and nostalgia contained in the precious items of this one amazing room. Even as young as he was, he sensed the value of what he was seeing.

He continued on. There were old ticket stubs from All-Star games—1949, 1954, 1962—autographed by the likes of Bob Feller, Ted Williams, and Sandy Koufax. Next to them were ticket stubs from World Series: 1939, New York and Cincinnati; 1959, Chicago vs. Los Angeles; and 1971, Baltimore against Pittsburgh.

Man, does Mr. Sperry know she's got all this?! This is amazing!

"Where did you get all these tickets?!"

"I was there," she replied calmly. "I watched all of those games."

"You were *there* at the actual games?" he asked, bewildered. "You were *there?*"

She nodded silently.

His gaze shifted to rows and rows of old baseball cards—some of which dated back to the '30s.

Look at these! Old tobacco box cards. Honus Wagner! Joe Jackson! Old Cracker Jack cards! Bob Feller!

Some cards were autographed. Some were not. He looked down at a Nolan Ryan rookie. Autographed. A George Brett. Autographed, too. Hank Aaron, Willie Mays, Ted Williams—all the greats. Almost every one of them autographed.

"Where did you get all these?! My dad and me have talked about all these guys!"

"I was there. I asked them," she answered nonchalantly.

"This is amazing. This is . . . " He stopped a moment, smiling in thought. "Dad tells me of dreams where he finds this kind of stuff. Like in an old attic he discovers. And now I'm lookin' right at 'em! All here! Right in front of me!"

A pair of shoes—*two* pairs of shoes—caught his eye. He walked over to where they rested in a small glass case below one of the lamps. She stepped up next to him.

"Ty Cobb and Cletis Boyer," she whispered. "You can probably guess whose shoes have the sharpened spikes."

"You got their *shoes*?!" he asked. "Why?"

"That's a long story. I'll tell you—in time."

"But Ty Cobb? Wasn't he way back in the . . . " Cletis didn't even know how early in the 1900s Ty Cobb played. But doing some estimated math in his head, he figured Ty Cobb played before 1920. "That's . . . that's more than seventy years ago!"

She studied him patiently, sensing he was trying to figure her out—her age, her history.

"I've always loved the game since it began," she said. "And I've been around to see most of it." As if diverting his attention from his basic arithmetic, she pointed to the wall above him. "Up there."

He lifted his eyes to look at an old jersey hung above the display of old cleats.

"Whose was that?" asked Cletis.

"What's the team?" she responded.

"St. Louis Cardinals."

"Very good. Can you tell the year?"

"I dunno. It looks pretty old."

"The Gashouse Gang. It was Pepper Martin's. I got it in Detroit back in 1934."

"Wow! Hey, my grandpa lived in Detroit back then. I wonder if he knew much about Pepper Martin?"

He felt her eyes on him as he stared at the old Cardinals uniform.

"The Tigers played the Cardinals in the World Series that year. So your grandpa knew about them. You can count on that. He may have been there for a game or two."

"Think so?"

"And that old three-fingered mitt you touched when you first entered? Know whose that was?"

"Whose?"

"They called him the 'Iron Horse.'"

Cletis knew it instantly.

"Lou Gehrig?! Dad's told me stories about him. Him and Babe Ruth."

"Lou gave it to me after the 1927 World Series."

"1927! Man!" Cletis gasped. "My dad says his grandpa loved the Yankees. They used to live in New York before they moved to Detroit."

"I know," the old lady responded quietly.

Cletis heard her and studied her curiously. There was a serious tone to her voice that captured his attention—like she had something hidden that she wanted to share and was waiting for the right time to do so. She sat with a sigh in the lone leather chair that was placed in the very middle of the room. She took a deep breath.

"We come from families that have loved the game, Cletis. But I've watched it for a different reason." She paused momentarily. "You see, I've been waiting for a player who would be called by what he wears on his feet."

"What does that mean?" Cletis questioned coming around in front of her.

"I didn't know. I tried to figure it out. Shoeless Joe Jackson? Maybe. But he was named for the *lack* of his footwear. Ty Cobb? You *tie* your shoes. But there was no other connection than that. Nothing panned out."

What is she talking about? Cletis wondered.

"Then, years later, Cletis Boyer came along with the Yankees, and I thought I had my man. But he wasn't the one either. Little did I realize that Garth Dungarvan would nickname his son 'Cletis,' right under my nose. I guess I should've been looking there all along, but I didn't think of it."

Cletis frowned in confusion. When she raised her arm and pointed to the mantel of the fireplace, Cletis turned.

"See that wooden box over there?" she asked in her deep, cowlike voice. "Will you bring it to me?"

Cletis walked to the fireplace, lifted the box down, and carried it to the old woman. He noted the strange etchings on the outside panels and the four carved legs that looked like hourglasses—one at each corner of the antique relic.

"Open it," she said.

He knelt before her on the soft rug, feeling like a little pageboy before the queen. He lifted the lid of the old wooden box. Though it was empty of any physical object, he felt a sudden surge of warmth flow through his body. Like electricity. He could feel the hair on his arms and neck stand on end.

There it is again—that same, strange feeling—like I'm covered by some power I can't see.

"Do you feel something?" she asked.

He remained silent. *How does she know if I'm feelin' anything? How can she tell what's goin' on inside of me?* He eyed the old lady, focusing on those strange green eyes.

She eyed him wisely, as if she read his very thoughts. "Do you see the writing on the sides?"

He turned the box. The room's soft light reflected off the old bronze panels that covered the sides.

"It's a type of Old Irish," she said. "Perhaps a form of Runic. The box has been in my family for hundreds of years. I don't know what it means. But the writing on the lid—I understand *that*. Ancient Irish. They are the words of a prophecy."

Cletis looked at the lid, seeing the odd words inscribed in the wood.

"It's a prophecy that will soon be fulfilled. I hope I am right, for I have waited many years to see it come to pass."

As Cletis studied the writing on the lid, again, that odd surge of electricity rushed through his body, his being, his soul. He lifted his eyes to hers, silently questioning the strange power. As she studied him, her gaze dropped to his arms. His hair was still on end.

CHAPTER 6

THE MAGIC OF THE ANCIENT BOX

"**B**oy, took you long enough! I didn't know what happened to you!"

"Sorry," Cletis responded distantly.

Elston eyed him curiously, all the while tossing the ball into the pocket of his mitt.

"What ya got?"

"I dunno. An old box," Cletis stated as he inspected it again—the writing on the top, the bronze panels, and the hourglass-shaped legs—as if seeing it for the first time. "I think she might be crazy," he finally said.

"Why'd she give you an old wooden box?"

Cletis shrugged. "She said she was supposed to. I don't know what she meant by that, but I took it."

"Anything inside?" Elston questioned.

"Nothing."

Cletis opened it to show him. But, to their surprise, the box *wasn't* empty. Inside lay a mint condition, 1958, Topps, *Mickey Mantle*!

"Whoa!" breathed Elston.

"This wasn't in here when she gave it to me!" Cletis's eyes were wide with amazement.

"Have you ever seen that card?" questioned Elston, awe-struck before a Holy Grail of baseball card collecting.

"Never," answered Cletis, reverently.

They studied it in silence for a moment, never lifting it from the box.

"Is it yours?"

"Uhhh...Yeah, I...I guess so," whispered Cletis, still dumbfounded.

They looked into each other's eyes.

"PRICE GUIDE!" they shouted simultaneously.

Cletis closed the lid over the priceless card, held the antique box level in both hands and headed toward the bikes. He and Elston had covered about a dozen steps before they realized they had left their mitts and ball behind.

The hag sat in the leather chair in the middle of the baseball room. Her eyes were open in a fixed stare focused squarely on the fireplace in front of her. Her thoughts were distant—wondering, questioning, doubting. Her breathing was calm and heavy, and her body was relaxed. Her hands lifted slowly to her chin, where she rubbed the bone hidden deep beneath her sagging flesh.

"The box is gone from me now," she spoke aloud. Her eyes remained unblinking, perhaps seeing anew some distant memory or regret. She exhaled, pursed her wrinkled lips, and quoted the words of the prophecy she had long since translated and memorized.

"Then shall the powers of the box be revealed,
And to him shall it be delivered.
In that day, comes the searching Traveler."

She rubbed her cheeks, stretching the skin toward her ears. The house suddenly groaned in the heat of the morning sun—its old timbers expanding with the warmth of a new day.

"If the prophecy be true, now comes the Traveler." She spoke, as if to the house. Her eyes glistened with the thought, and she bowed her head again toward the fireplace. "Do we have the strength, Cletis Dungarvan? Will we have the strength?"

Cletis and Elston plowed through the bedroom door.

"Top drawer on the right side," panted Cletis as he pointed to the desk behind the door.

"I know where it is," Elston reminded him.

When Cletis had first seen the old dog-eared, baseball card price guide in Pauly's footlocker beneath the dugout, he knew he wanted one of his own. His dad readily agreed with the idea and picked one up at Sperry's. Together they had gone through its pages circling the cards his father used to have and figuring out how much his old collection would have been worth. Elston knew right where the book was because he and Cletis had looked at it that very morning before leaving for the old lady's house.

Elston made his way to the desk drawer, opened it, and pulled the price guide off of the pile of sports magazines and comics. At the same time, Cletis sat down on the bed and opened the box. He reverently removed the Mantle card, stood, crossed to the dresser, and leaned the valuable little piece of cardboard on the autographed ball, next to Yaz and Stretch and the family portrait. He then lifted the box off the bed and placed it on the shelf above his desk in an open spot next to *Tom Sawyer*.

"It's gotta be right here in the front," Elston spoke, thumbing through the pages of the price guide. "It was probably one of the first years cards were even out there."

"I think it was 1958," Cletis replied as he walked back to the dresser and lifted the card to look at the backside of it. "Yeah, that's right, '58."

"Man, anybody alive back then?" joked Elston. He found the year in the guidebook and put his finger on the page to mark the spot. "What's the number?"

"150," answered Cletis, still studying the back of the card.

Elston's jaw dropped, and his eyes bulged wide. "$600!" he exclaimed.

"$600?!" shouted Cletis. He rushed over to Elston. Elston's finger marked the place, and Cletis blinked as he followed the numbers from one column to the next. The two boys eyed each other.

"What ya gonna do with it, Clete?"

Cletis stared across the room, pondering the possibilities.

"I dunno," he finally answered. "But I got some ideas."

"Baseballically speakin'," grinned Elston, "a very important decision is about to be made."

It was five blocks of excitement to Sperry's Cards and Coins. As they pedaled away from the Dungarvan house, Cletis and Elston bent low, so the wind would blow down the backs of their shirts and dry the sweat off their backs. If they rode fast enough, their shirts would lift off their skin and puff up big and round with the circulating air—it looked like giant half-pumpkins were tucked up underneath their shirts.

Cletis had placed the Mantle card carefully between two pieces of cereal box cardboard and then stuck it in a business envelope. The envelope had then been placed carefully in the Tom Sawyer book, the book placed in Cletis's mitt, and the mitt was laid in the basket on the front of his bike.

"You know you can't crash," stated Elston, looking down at the mitt in the basket. "A crash is gonna cost you two hundred bucks if you bend the sides of that card."

Cletis nodded. "Yep, no crashes. Safe drivin' all the way there."

Elston's bike screamed out a noisy greeting as the chain scraped against the guard with each revolution of the pedal. The piercing sound could be heard up and down the street for two blocks. The people on the south side of Greenberg Junction, where Elston lived, certainly knew when their newspapers were being delivered each morning, because Elston's bike chain announced his arrival. He'd hop off now and again and fix it, pulling the guard out away from the chain, but after a few seconds of pedaling, the racket would start all over again.

The two boys turned left on Main Street, pedaled south toward the center of town, and as they approached the Wells Fargo bank on the corner of Main and Madison, Cletis wondered what treasures the card would bring. For a block and a half they rode on without saying a word.

"My dad got me this bike before I was born," Elston laughed, patting his handlebars while crossing over to the other side of the road. "He said he waited ten years for me to be big enough to ride this. And he said he knew I was gonna have a paper route, so he was preparin' me for it."

Cletis laughed. "Mine's not much newer." He peered down at the warped front tire under the basket and the metal rods he used for pedals. "At least you got somethin' to put your feet on!"

That was the only thing new about Elston's bike—his pedals, purchased just last week, replacing ones that looked just like Cletis's. Other than that, both bikes were ready for the junkyard. At least that's what the boys thought. The front wheels on both bikes had been bent and then straightened several times. If Elston didn't constantly correct his steering, his bike would veer dangerously off to the left. He used that as an excuse to try to get his folks to buy him a new bike. So far it hadn't worked.

"And my seat's got a big hole now," Elston added, standing up on his pedals and pointing back to show Cletis.

Pausing for traffic on Madison Street, Elston waved to a woman as she strolled her two children down the sidewalk near the bank. "Hey, Mrs. Ketchum!"

"Hey, Elston," she called back, pointing at him.

Cletis looked and smiled but, not knowing the lady, said nothing.

"She's a friend of my mom's," spoke Elston, softly. "She lives close to us. My mom's always takin' her food. Her husband doesn't have work, and I think he's sick or somethin'."

"What's he got?" asked Cletis, waiting for another car.

"I dunno."

Cletis looked back over his shoulder at the woman. She was dressed in well-worn clothes, but they were clean. The stroller she pushed, which held a little boy and girl, was as ragged as Elston's bike.

On their way to the card shop, the boys passed the hardware store, Mr. Pepitoni's bike shop, and the drugstore where Klu's mom worked. East of the hardware store, across Main Street, was John Adams Elementary School. And just south of the school, on the corner of Main and Jefferson, was the city park. The large maple trees there made it a great place for relaxing, picnicking, or unwrapping baseball cards purchased at Sperry's Cards and Coins.

As they rode past the bike shop, they spotted a man lying on the sidewalk near the alley by the drug store. His eyes were closed, and he appeared to be sleeping. He was barefoot and his pants were a ragged brown. An old coat had been wadded up and placed under his head for a pillow.

"You know Mr. Howard?" Elston asked, nodding toward the man.

"Seen him a few times, down here by the stores and over by the library, but not too often."

"His boy died in Vietnam. My dad told me. After that the man's kinda wandered the streets. I seen him out here downtown since I was a kid."

Cletis pondered the words without looking back at the man. "He lives behind the grocery store, doesn't he?" he asked. He slowed as a van passed him on his left.

"Yeah. Mom says he eats the food the store tosses out. He lives in the old railroad hut back there. You seen it?"

"Yeah," Cletis answered, pulling up in front of Mr. Sperry's shop. "Must be a pretty noisy place when the train goes by there."

"If you get close to him, you can smell him," Elston added, slowing to a halt and lifting his bike up over the curb. "He stinks bad. People say he's a nice man, but he won't talk much if you try to say somethin' to him. I don't know why he sleeps on the sidewalk, when he's got a whole park of grass across the street."

Sperry's Cards and Coins was located on the northwest corner of Main and Washington, just south of the drugstore. The boys leaned their bikes against the front wall of the store and carefully retrieved the Mantle card from the basket on Cletis's bike. They entered the main door and approached the glass cases that displayed the cards for sale: a Pete Rose rookie card, a Warren Spahn, a Harmon Killebrew, Don Drysdale, Ted Williams, Johnny Bench, Hank Aaron, Stan Musial, three Willie Mays cards, and many more.

Johnny was behind the counter sorting athletic memorabilia while talking to one of the high school boys there shopping for cards.

"So who should I hang onto?" the boy asked him.

"Hang on to Cal Ripken," answered Johnny, squinting his eyes in thought. "Hang on to Mark McGuire. And hang on to Jose Canseco. They'll be big one day."

Johnny could talk easily about professional baseball and its players, old and new. He knew who held all the records. He knew all the facts and stats from pennant races, World Series, and All-Star games, and his baseball card collection was—until that morning—the best Cletis had seen.

"How about Bonds and Clements?"

"Ahhh, Bonds'll probably turn out like his dad—a good player, but not one of the greats," Johnny responded. "Clements'll probably wear out his arm by '95. All power throwers seem to do that—all except Nolan Ryan. So hang on to your Ryan cards, but Clements will probably be gone in four years."

The boy looked down at the cards in his hand, nodded, then turned and left. "Thanks," he said, without looking back.

"Hey, Johnny," Cletis and Elston called out in unison as they stepped up to the counter.

"Hey, guys. What's goin' on?" Johnny leaned over the glass case and rested on his elbows.

"I got a card here I want Mr. Sperry to take a look at," answered Cletis, a bit unsure of himself. He placed the envelope on the counter and carefully removed the three tiny pieces of cardboard. The middle piece, well protected, was the Mantle card. Cletis carefully slid it away from the cereal-box cardboards and placed it before Johnny.

Johnny's eyeballs came close to falling out of their sockets. He stared in disbelief. "Whoa! Where'd you get this?"

Elston eyed Cletis, waiting for his answer.

Cletis looked down, shuffled his griptionless shoes over the tile floor, and then looked back up to Johnny. "Uhh . . . same friend of my dad's."

It was kind of the truth, and kind of not. *The old lady* could *be considered a friend of dad's,* Cletis thought, trying to justify his fib. *He* does know *of her, and he is friendly to* all *people. So she* is *a friend.* He looked over to Elston, whose face showed no expression at all.

"Man, I know a lot of people who'd like to get their hands on this card."

"We wanna know what it's worth," Cletis stated professionally.

Johnny eyed Cletis. "More than you and me have seen in our lifetimes," he whispered. "Let me get Mr. Sperry."

Johnny disappeared into the back room. Within seconds he returned with Mr. Sperry. Mr. Sperry was tall enough to come within two inches of hitting his head on the doorframe, and he always automatically ducked just to be safe. He must have been about 6' 6" and was probably the tallest man in the community. The rumor was that he played basketball for a junior college somewhere in Arizona and that after his college days he had made some good money investing in gold coins.

"Hi boys," Mr. Sperry announced on his way to the glass counter. He wore a Tigers hat, just like Cletis's, except Mr. Sperry's was a deep, navy blue. "What d'ya got here for me?"

Mr. Sperry leaned down over the card and pushed his dark-rimmed glasses back up onto the bridge of his long, thin nose. To get a better look, he removed his hat, placed it on the glass next to him, and leaned in even closer over the card. From their angle, Cletis and Elston eyed the top of his balding head.

Mr. Sperry pulled a magnifying glass from under the display shelf in front of him and held it over the card. Reverently, he lifted the treasure and checked the front and the back, looking for hidden flaws. Again and again he studied the details of the card—the corners, the photo, the stats on the back—everything. He finally lifted his head and peered over the top of his glasses at the boys.

"That's a darn valuable card, guys. Not many Mantles like this floatin' around. It's in perfect condition, and it's basically as old as me!"

Cletis smiled and nodded but remained silent.

"You tryin' to sell it, or do you just want to know what it's worth?"

"Well, like you said, it's in mint condition," Cletis spoke with sudden confidence. "So we know it's worth about $600. We want to know if you want to buy it off us."

Mr. Sperry eyed them, attempting to cover the beginnings of an off-centered grin. He rubbed his hand across his mouth and scratched his hairless scalp. "Well, let me make a quick phone call, men, and I'll see if I have a buyer. If I do, you're in business. If not, I won't. Fair enough?"

Cletis nodded. He could feel the excitement and anticipation swelling up inside him. He wanted to jump up and down and scream out his delight, but he fought back the impulse.

"But you realize that $100 of that is mine," continued Mr. Sperry, standing up straight and walking away from the counter. "You see, that's how I make my living. If I sell it for you, I get a commission on the sale. You understand? That's how I keep my shop open, and that's how I pay people like Johnny, here."

Cletis nodded. Though he didn't know much about sales and commissions, $500 was still a ton of money.

Mr. Sperry stepped away to the phone and checked a list of numbers posted on the wall next to it.

"I've never seen a card this old in this good of condition," spoke Johnny, leaning again over the card. "Your dad's friend got any more cards like this?"

Cletis just shrugged.

"Pullin' a fast one on your dad? Is that it? Sellin' one of his good cards out from underneath him?" Johnny whispered.

"No."

Johnny winked and stood up straight.

"Hey, I'm tellin' you the truth," Cletis continued. "I'm not pullin' anything on my dad. It's my card. I can do what I want with it."

"Okay, okay. Just teasin'," Johnny stated, lifting both hands in front of him. "I just think you oughta hang on to this one. Not many like this around."

Cletis considered his words but was pretty set on selling the card if he could.

With the phone in his hand, Mr. Sperry stepped forward to the counter and looked down at the card.

"Uh, Ma'am, this is Donald Sperry over at the card shop. Do you remember me? You called over here last summer. . . . Yes. How are you? . . . Good. Say, I've picked up one of those cards from that list you sent me." He paused, listening to the voice on the other end of the line. "Yeah, a Mickey Mantle. 1958 . . . Couple of boys brought it in. . . . Neighborhood kids . . . To me it looks completely mint. It's a beauty . . . $600.00 . . . You sure? I won't move on it unless you give me the thumb's-up. . . . Okay, I'll personally bring it over, carefully. . . . Okay, in the mailbox. . . . You'll have the payment there? . . . Yes, that'll be fine. . . . Yes, I have the address from your note. . . . It's 1:30 now." Mr. Sperry stated, looking at his watch. "I should have it there within the half-hour. . . . Thank you very much, Mrs. A. D. Bye."

He stepped away from the boys and hung up the phone.

"All right boys, you've got a deal. And I can pay you here and now if you'd like."

"Yes, please," Cletis answered, trying to control his excitement.

"Are you the Dungarvan boy?"

"Yes."

"Your dad's in here once in a while, isn't he? He bought a price guide a few days back. I never knew he had cards like this."

"It's not his. This one was given to me."

"Oh," said Mr. Sperry, nodding thoughtfully. He paused a moment and then strode away into the back room, ducking as he entered it. Within seconds he returned with five, one-hundred-dollar bills in his big hand. Cletis coughed as the tall man spread them over the counter next to the Mantle card. Elston gasped. Johnny just laughed.

"Man, I ain't never eyed a hundred-dollar bill," Elston moaned.

"Me neither," Cletis whispered.

"Well, there's five of 'em," proclaimed Mr. Sperry. "Make sure that money gets to where it needs to go, cuz I'd hate to see you lose it on the way home."

Cletis stiffly gathered the bills off the counter, folded them in half, and pushed them down into his pants pocket.

"Do I need to call your dad and let him know you're on your way home with that kind of money?" Mr. Sperry smiled mischievously with the comment.

"No, sir," Cletis responded quickly. "I got it taken care of. Thanks, Mr. Sperry."

"You're welcome, men."

"See you, Johnny."

"Yep. See ya." Johnny answered without looking up. Both he and Mr. Sperry had leaned down over the card again.

Elston and Cletis turned, crossed the tile floor, and made their way out of the store.

As the doors shut behind them, Cletis mumbled through the corner of his mouth. "Save it 'til we get to the park. Nothing unusual. All cool 'til we get to the park."

"I won't do nothin'," repeated Elston through clenched teeth and a plastic smile. "Don't give nothin' away."

They righted their clunker bikes, hopped up onto the seats, and rode off down the sidewalk toward the park. In a matter of seconds they had pedaled across the street—Elston's chain guard screaming out their whereabouts as they covered the block-and-a-half distance.

There were three large maple trees in the northwest corner of the park, directly across from Mr. Pepitoni's bike shop. Elston and Cletis came to a screeching halt under the middle tree. The boys dropped their bikes recklessly, and hook-sliding in under the shade of the large green leaves, they rolled like horses in the grass, slapping high-fives and kicking their arms and legs in the air.

"Can you believe that?" exclaimed Cletis. "Five hundred dollars, just like that! One piece of cardboard with a picture on it for five hundred dollars!" He reached deep into his front pocket, pulled out the bills, and laid them on the grass in front of him.

Over and over the boys silently counted the hundred-dollar bills. Five times Benjamin Franklin smiled back at them, as if congratulating their cleverness.

The seconds ticked by as Cletis pondered his circumstances. *Now what? Now what do I do? Tell Dad? Hide it in my room? Open a savings account? Spend it? Elston's gonna know what I do. Johnny'll ask about it. Mr. Sperry knows I walked out of his store with $500. He's gonna talk to dad about it soon enough. But it's mine. I got it from the box, and the old lady gave* me *the box. I didn't do anything wrong.* Cletis's eyes moved in quick, thoughtful jerks.

"What ya gonna do with it all?" asked Elston.

Cletis eyed the bikes, the money, and then the bikes again. He bit his bottom lip and flared his nostrils inhaling. He looked across the street at Pepitoni's Bike Shop, then over to Elston.

"What are *we,* Elston—the both of us—what are *we* gonna do with it all!"

Within twenty-five minutes, Cletis and Elston were almost a mile from town, following a road that few cars ever traveled—a road shaded by a green archway of spring-infant leaves on tall elm trees. The leaves glistened and shook in the light breeze that eased in from the north. Open pastures flanked the route on both sides, and black cattle and brown horses grazed in the sun. It was freedom at its grandest—freedom and comfort and power. They had left their aged bikes leaning against the brick wall in front of Pepitoni's shop, like two noble but faltering horses hitched in front of a western saloon and then abandoned.

The boys knew exactly what they wanted when they had entered Pepitoni's. They had often dreamed of what they would do if they ever had the extra money. Mr. Pepitoni, the owner of the place, had been only too happy to help deliver his goods to the pair of eager shoppers. Cletis had forked over the money, and the two boys had exited the store laughing and whooping, *and* with $82 of change tucked into Cletis's front pocket. The sleek, polished-green motor-ized scooter Elston stood on cost just over $200, and the new red-and-black mountain bike that Cletis rode was priced at just *under* $200. With tax added to their total, Cletis was still sitting financially pretty and planning what else he could buy with the leftover cash. Mr. Pepitoni was even kind enough to toss in a bit of gas in order to get Elston's scooter started.

On their way out of town, and riding their new toys, the boys decided to take Jefferson Street eastward, past the school and the park, and then out toward the farms and pastures away from town. They really didn't know how far they would eventually ride. What *did* matter was that they were now riding new machines under the warm spring sun with their shirts puffed out behind them and without a care in the world.

Cletis experimented with the brakes and the gears. He rode with one hand and then with no hands, picked up his speed and then slowed down. Elston practiced weaving back and forth across the road, and often turned back and watched the exhaust sputtering out behind him, over the top of the black pavement.

"What are we gonna do with our old bikes?" called Elston, over the putt-putt of the new scooter.

"I dunno. Sell 'em, I guess. Then we could make even *more* money."

The thought never crossed Cletis's mind that anyone would buy the old clunkers. This newly acquired power that came with the cards and the money was a strange and fascinating sensation—one that Cletis quite liked.

I wonder what other cards I'll find in that box? This could be real nice!

Turning to the pasture on the south side of the road, Cletis and Elston spied a man standing alone in the middle of the field of sprouting alfalfa. He was watching them. He stood completely still and offered no wave or greeting. He simply watched them. There were no animals around him—no cows, horses or dogs—and he carried no tools. No vehicle was parked nearby. He was just out there, all by himself.

Suddenly the strangest thing happened. The left handle on the scooter began to crumble under Elston's grip. When he felt it give way, he lifted his hand to see if he could find the cause of the trouble. To his amazement, and right before his eyes, the handle bent and melted away, turning into a fine dust and blowing back onto the road behind him. Next the handlebar cracked, bent, and softened. At the same time, the right handle began to give way, crumbling into dust, exactly as had happened to the other.

"Clete! Hey! What's goin' on here!" Elston cried out.

Riding next to him, Cletis looked on wordlessly and watched the entire little machine crumble underneath Elston, even as he rode it. The motor choked out two or three final coughs and gradually faded into silence. The plate under Elston's feet gave way, dropping him into a quick jog on the pavement below. Astonished, Elston slowed and stopped, and turned back just in time to see the wheels and cables of the scooter dissolve into nothingness in the middle of the road. A film of dust on the asphalt was all that was left of the entire thing. Lighter than air, the remaining powder was carried away southward on the gentle breeze.

Cletis, now looking over his shoulder back at Elston, suddenly felt a strange shudder pass through his new bike. Abruptly the right pedal of the bike dropped to the ground, slid to stop behind him, and dissolved into dust. Pulling on the hand brakes, he attempted to slow the bike, but the handle broke off with the pressure. Studying the shiny metal, which now lay in the palm of his hand, he watched it turn to dust. The front fender was next, dropping onto the tire and dissolving like wet cotton candy within seconds. Cletis instantly felt the seat under him tip to one side, and he fought to keep his balance atop the disintegrating bicycle.

"Hey, what's happening?!" he cried out to Elston. But Elston, stunned by his own situation, offered no response.

Cletis felt himself drop as the crossbars below him melted away. Quickly he put his foot down upon the pavement and dragged his toe to slow his forward momentum. But the bike was literally crumbling beneath him. When the front wheel pulverized and dropped into a thousand dissolving pieces, Cletis was thrown into a sprawling somersault over the top of what remained of the bicycle. With arms and legs flailing, he vaulted over the side of the road and landed in a dry, grass-filled irrigation canal.

"Cletis!" Elston called out. "You okay?"

Cletis rolled back toward the road, hoping to catch a glimpse of what was left of the bike. As he spotted it, the back tire and supporting metal bars crumbled into a fine, light dust.

Out of the corner of his eye, Cletis saw that Elston was standing over the final powdery remains of the scooter. There was no other sign of the brand-new, beautiful, polished-green machine. It was now completely gone.

Back on his feet, Cletis turned again to the ruins of his new mountain bike. The chain mechanism and the remaining gear plates smoldered on the pavement before him, and then abruptly popped into a light powder, like a weak firecracker on a 4th of July evening. Cletis stepped forward and watched in awe as the final eruption floated away on the breeze, dancing over the ditches and pastures on the south side of the road, like yellow pollen off a highland pine tree.

Speechless, the two boys turned and stared at one another. Within thirty seconds, both the bike and the scooter had decayed into complete oblivion. There was literally nothing left of them. In shock, Cletis's hands went to the top of the Tigers cap and he cried out into the air around him, "WHAT IS HAPPENING HERE?"

Instinctively both boys looked out into the south pasture, wondering if the man they saw had witnessed this astonishing phenomenon. To their bewilderment, the stranger was nowhere to be seen. They scanned the entire field, which went in all directions for acres and acres on both sides of the road. But there was no sign of the person. The man had either fallen into a hole or was lying down in the middle of the alfalfa or was gone—vanished with the bicycles.

Almost immediately after the boys had left the store, Mr. Sperry delivered the Mickey Mantle card to the address Mrs. A. D. had given him. He had parked the car on the dirt road in front of her property, and as he approached the mouth of the narrow driveway, he spotted her mailbox. It was an old wooden container, covered inside and out with long vines of ivy and with the white, hairlike webs created by generations of living and deceased spiders. The envelope she told him would be waiting for him, rested inside the box protected by at least three black widows and a large, gray-brown garden spider. Blowing the creatures back, Mr. Sperry reached into the box, cautiously removed the envelope, wiped it off, opened it, and counted the cash.

$500 to cover the boys' purchase and $100 for me, he thought. *Yep, it's all here. She's quick.*

The Mantle card he held in his hand was protected by a hard plastic cover, wrapped in an envelope, and then placed in a small, flat, cardboard container. So Mr. Sperry felt secure in leaving the package there in the box for her. No one else lived on the road. The closest neighbor that he was aware of lived nearly a mile away.

Yeah, the card'll be safe here, he told himself. *It'll be fine.*

What amazed him, though, was that the lady's place was so overgrown and messy. The land was thick with dead and living trees, and the woods were densely filled with undergrowth and fallen timbers that hadn't been cleared away or thinned in years. There was a footpath of flat, gray stones that led back to the old house in which the woman lived. From where he stood, he could barely see portions of the old home.

For someone who has six hundred dollars to dish out for a baseball card, Mr. Sperry thought, *whoever lives here sure doesn't take care of the place. This is a jungle.*

With a grimace and a shudder, Mr. Sperry turned and jogged back to where he had parked his car.

Shortly after the man had left, the hag went to the mailbox and collected the envelope containing the card. She waddled back into the house and went directly to the baseball room. There she removed the card from the box and envelope, and set it tenderly on the mantel of the fireplace in front of her.

"Hello, Mick. It's been a long time. They must've found you in the box." She pondered for a moment. "That's magic beyond my ability. My hunch was right. They're guiding me. I think that means we're finally moving in the right direction. Guess we'll see how the boys do."

She looked at a timepiece on a shelf near the hearth. The old hands of the clock registered 2:00 p.m. She sat down on the soft chair in the middle of the room and simply studied the card in front of her. She cradled her head in her hands and waited. She had nothing better to do. Only twelve minutes had passed away, when the card moved ever so slightly, as if some unseen finger beyond the veil of visibility caressed it respectfully. The old lady leaned forward and smiled, as if being entertained by the magic of some invisible wizard. The card gradually lifted straight up and stood by itself, balancing in place upon the mantel. Several seconds passed before it tipped back into its original position. The wrinkled old lady stood up in front of the chair, concentrating on the card, making certain she missed nothing. Then, again, it lifted into the air and floated softly, mere inches above the mantel. Suspended there, it fluttered as if it were shaken by a light breeze and then abruptly crumbled into a fine, gray dust that floated down upon the stone below it like the feathery ashes of a friendly campfire. What was, only moments before, a mint-conditioned, 1958 Mickey Mantle card, was now a tiny pile of papery powder. The old lady lowered herself back into her favorite chair.

"Yes, that is magic beyond me," she whispered, her eyes wide with wonder. "Someone else is at work here." She rubbed her lips with the back of her hand and sat motionlessly for several seconds. "There are some lessons to be learned, little Cletis. Lessons for both of us, it seems."

About an hour later, the old woman made her way slowly down the dark hallway of her home and out onto the back porch. In the shade of the forest surrounding her house, the day was cool, and the birds and frogs around the canal conversed musically. She sat down on the cane-back chair and patiently waited. He would come. She knew it. She felt it.

As the old woman watched and waited, the crickets, birds, and frogs gradually silenced their concert, and the noises that only humans make echoed off the slope above her. As she peered up the hillside, she could see him work his way through the pines and elms and down toward the house. He jumped the canal at the bottom of the hill and made his way across the stretch of dirt and grass between the water and the home. He paused at the steps in front of the porch. There he pulled his hat off and held it in his hand—his strawberry blond hair was matted with sweat. From behind the porch screens she studied him. She could see by the way he toyed with his hat and eyed the forest around him that he was uneasy and anxious. Though she could hear his concerns already in her mind, she found herself happily anticipating his visit.

Cletis pulled the door open slowly, appearing to gather courage for the visit. He seemed as if he were still wounded and bewildered by the afternoon's experiences. Finally, he stepped up into the porch and suddenly saw her there before him.

The old woman listened intently to the details of the afternoon's events as they flowed from Cletis's mouth. He shared the story from start to finish, unburdening himself in a sort of disorientated, panicked, fascinated confession. When he finished, he sat in front of her on the wooden planks of the porch, studying her eyes, hoping for the answers he himself could not supply.

"He asked us to bring him the pieces, and there weren't any pieces left! He thought we were liars, I'm sure, and now who knows what kinda trouble we're gonna be in."

As his story ended, she sensed that for the first time, her ugliness was not a hindrance. He had spoken to her eyes, or to her soul, and not to the human bulk that covered her so hideously. In response to his concerns, she sat back in the chair, sighed, and looked out into the pines that covered the back hill.

"Cletis, as possessor of the box, you will have to make some very important choices. Some of those choices will probably have nothing to do with the box. But you will come to know *feelings* that precede those choices, for *feelings*, powerfully charged *feelings*, will be a compass to you."

She watched him intently as the words sank in. His head cocked a bit to the right, like a puppy trying to decipher a new sound.

"I know that powerful feelings have been yours over the past couple days," she continued. "And they will be yours in times to come. Sometimes that sensation will simply speak peace to you. At other times it will be a forceful, tangible power flowing through your body." She studied him silently. "That is all I will tell you for now."

She watched him swallow. He straightened and slowly came to his feet. He looked out through the screens at the surrounding forest and then turned to her again.

"I don't mean to ask somethin' I'm not supposed to ask." He appeared to be gathering courage, and he looked into her eyes. "But, uh . . . what . . . what is your name?"

She smiled at his youthful curiosity. "Interesting. . . . So few people have ever cared to know it. But I will tell you." She rocked back and forth and patted her thighs. "I have always been called Abish," she said softly—as softly as her husky voice would allow.

He pondered the name a moment. "What kind of a name is that?" he asked respectfully.

She cleared her throat and put a gentle fist to the fleshy folds of her neck.

"When I was born, my mother and father found a name in the Book of Deeds—an ancient book we used to read. The name was Abishag. She was the wife of a great king from times long past. My mother and father liked the first part of the name—Abish—and gave it to me. Though the last part of the name fits me better now."

Cletis repeated her name, as if tasting it. "Abish." He turned and pushed open the screen door to leave. "No, ma'am, the first part fits you better," he concluded.

A whisper of a breeze cooled the sweat on Cletis's brow as he made his way steadily up the hillside. Elston awaited him at the top, seated in the grass. Cletis wandered over, peered down at him, and then sat beside him. Their old bikes lay on the ground a spit away, a bleak reminder of the afternoon's dispiriting adventure.

"So what'd she say?" Elston asked.

Cletis remained quiet. His thoughts were elsewhere. He didn't mean to ignore the question, but it was like he didn't even hear it.

"You know, if we say anything about this to anyone, no one will believe us," Cletis stated. "Mr. Pepitoni didn't believe us. Who would? If we say anything, we could look like real idiots."

"Or liars," Elston added, as if having thought this through already.

"Or liars . . . or *thieves*," whispered Cletis, emphasizing the last word.

Elston paused a moment, nodding his head. "Yeah, I know. So we better keep our mouths shut, huh?"

They both sat motionlessly.

"What about that man in the field?" Elston asked. "The guy who was there and then just gone."

"I don't know," Cletis shrugged. "I didn't ask her about him."

"This is all super weird, isn't it. This is *scary* weird!"

"Yep. It is." Cletis nodded. "And you know what? Johnny's gonna probably find out about this. At least he knows we sold the card for $500. But he doesn't know what we did with the money, unless Mr. Pepitoni spreads the word and it all comes back to Mr. Sperry."

"I dunno. Maybe he won't. I've never seen him and Mr. Sperry together. And Mr. Pepitoni doesn't know we got the money from selling a card."

"Yeah, that's right," agreed Cletis. He paused again in thought. "I wonder if my dad's gonna hear about it. Maybe they'll *both* call him.

We should've known Mr. Pepitoni wasn't gonna believe a word we said. We shouldn't have gone back there. We should've just kept our mouths shut." Cletis readjusted his hat and sighed. "Yeah, I'll bet he calls my dad."

"What if he *doesn't* call your dad? You gonna tell him about all this anyway?"

"I dunno. Probably. . . . Maybe when I really have to."

"Well, we could just tell Johnny you saved the money for college, or somethin'. Maybe that'd hold him off for now," stated Elston.

"Okay, that's what we'll do. It's not the truth, but for now it's better than the truth."

"Maybe your dad'll never find out. And maybe Mr. Pepitoni'll think we were just messin' around and he'll forget all about it."

Cletis nodded silently, hopefully. The sun was beginning to set, spreading a sweet, golden light through the pines on the hillside. Elston swatted a mosquito that landed on his arm and then flicked it off onto the dirt beside him.

"So we gonna get any of the new stuff back, or is it all gone forever?"

"It's all gone," replied Cletis. He folded his arms and looked up into the sky. "You already got a bike, and I already got a bike. And I guess, for now, they still work, so we'd better be happy."

"So we gotta keep ridin' those old things?" questioned Elston, his shoulders drooping. He nodded toward the bikes. "Man, it was all too good to be true, wasn't it?"

Again Cletis didn't answer. His eyes were focused far away toward the baseball diamond.

"Know where we went wrong in this whole thing, Elston?"

"Where?"

"Let me think about this . . . and I'll talk to ya about it tomorrow."

Quietly Cletis rose and crossed to his bike. With a heave, he pulled it up to him.

"Where you goin'?" asked Elston.

"I better get home. I oughtta be there when Dad comes."

"Yeah," added Elston, "my mom's probably wondering where I am by now."

Tossing their baseball gloves into their baskets, the boys hopped onto their bicycles. Within seconds, the air was soft on their faces, and despite the steady bumps of the earthen path they followed, they were genuinely comfortable on their faithful old machines.

The fluorescent numbers of the clock on the nightstand read 1:00 a.m. Cletis was in a deep sleep when the wooden box above him began to glow, shedding an eerie, soft, red light across the room. Not only did the inscribed letters, etched on the sides and top of the old wood, blush with luster, but the lid of the box lifted, as if yawning to communicate a centuries-old secret that only it could reveal. Cletis rolled in his sleep, as if subconsciously sensing and receiving the message it whispered.

As the glow of the box diminished, a sudden, searing pain shot into Cletis's right shoulder—as if a branding iron were pressed into his flesh. With a groan, he jerked upright and then fell back on the bed, hugging his shoulder toward him. Moaning against the agony that scorched him, Cletis pushed the sheets off his legs, rolled out of bed, and crashed to the floor. Rising up on his knees, he crawled through the doorway and into the hall. The pain took his breath away. His shoulder throbbed with unbearable burning. When the torture only intensified, he finally surrendered to it, curling into a fetal ball and sobbing in agony.

Then, as suddenly and as sharply as the burning had come, to Cletis's amazement the pain disappeared. Though weakened and breathless, he rose to his knees, crawled to the bathroom, and pulled himself up to the sink. With his left hand he flipped the light on. After a few deep breaths, he studied his reflection in the mirror. Concerned for his shoulder, he pulled his T-shirt off and laid it on the counter. He eyed the skin just above his armpit, on the front of his right shoulder. There, to his amazement, appeared the mark of a tiny red hourglass—like a rosy tattoo of an old timepiece imprinted on his skin. It was close to one inch in height and a half-inch wide, and resembled the little hourglass legs located on the bottom of the box

Abish had given him. He rubbed the mark, thinking it might smear, but it did not. He took soap and water to it, trying to wash it off, but with no success. Whatever it was, or whatever it represented, it was on there for good. The spot was permanent.

Cletis, still panting, turned to leave the bathroom but found his dad blocking the doorway. His father rubbed his tired face and studied his son.

"What is goin' on up here? I heard a thud and then you moaning. You okay?"

Cletis had been so focused on the pain and the mark on his shoulder, he hadn't even heard his dad come up the stairs.

"I dunno," he whispered. "I had this burning pain here in my shoulder, and now I got this red mark right where it hurt." He turned to show his father, who, blinking his eyes and wiping his mouth, bent down to inspect the redness.

"Did you fall on something?"

"No."

"Did you get hit by a ball?"

"No."

"Did you burn yourself?"

Cletis shook his head.

His father spoke through a yawn, gently touching the area that appeared inflamed and swollen. "Does it hurt?"

Cletis waited, wondering. "Not like it did."

"What d'ya mean, 'not like it did'?"

"I dunno. It hurt a ton at first. It was killin' me. But now the pain's gone."

His father eyed him questioningly. "Looks like you got branded." He squinted against the bathroom light. "Hurt enough to make you cry?"

"Yeah, it did."

"And now you're okay? That doesn't make sense."

Cletis was silent.

"So . . . you okay, then?"

"I think." Cletis looked back down at his shoulder and touched the mark. "Yeah, I'm okay. I guess . . . I dunno. Doesn't hurt now."

"Hmmm." His dad yawned again. "Well, let's get you back to bed then. We'll check it out in the morning."

Cletis slid his shirt back over him, crossed the hall, and entered his room. He hopped back into bed, took a deep breath, and pulled the sheets up to his waist. His dad studied him for a moment, then crossed back to the bathroom, and turned off the light.

"See ya in the morning."

"Okay."

He listened as his dad moved groggily down the stairs and flipped off the lights he had turned on. The stairway darkened again, and Cletis lay pondering, baffled by what he had just experienced. He touched his right shoulder. *Man, it doesn't hurt now. Not at all. What was that all about?* His eyes gradually adjusted to the darkness surrounding him, and he scanned the room thoughtfully. When his eyes fell upon the wooden box above the desk, he saw that the lid was up.

That's strange. I'm sure that lid was shut when I went to bed.

Suddenly the lid dropped. The sharp slap of wood on wood broke the nighttime silence. Cletis sat up and stared through the darkness at the box. After a few seconds passed, he rose and walked to the shelf on which the box rested. With a finger, he poked it. It shifted slightly.

"Okay, I guess everything's fine," he whispered aloud as he flopped back on the bed.

Within moments he calmed, and despite the night's troubling events, he finally drifted away into a heavy, peaceful slumber.

Precisely two hours later, the box began to glow again. Slowly the lid opened, revealing once more an inward, red radiance. As Cletis slept, a small scroll lifted from within the wooden structure. Hovering several inches above the open box, it quietly unfurled, until the empty parchment lay open and flat. As if sensing the presence of the scroll, the lid of the box eased down into a closed position. Suddenly the prophetic lettering etched upon the ancient wooden lid blazed a hot, bright red, and, as if with the heat of the event, the inscription was replicated letter-by-letter upon the golden parchment above it. As the final word of the prophecy burned onto the open scroll, the glow of the box gradually diminished. Then, as if sensing the completion of the task, the scroll gathered itself from both ends, rolled deliberately back together, and dropped to rest on the lid of the magical box.

The dawn found Cletis and his dad huddled over the kitchen table studying the odd scroll. Spread across the kitchen table, its curled corners were held in place by four soupspoons.

"Man, Clete. I thought I told you not to go over there." His dad lifted his cup and nervously swirled the juice around and around within it. "Didn't I?" Chewing a mouthful of toast, he eyed Cletis and let his words sink in. "Look, I know I may be a bit protective on this, but there are a lot of kooks out there nowadays. And she may be one of 'em." He swallowed hard and then chased down his toast with the juice left in his cup. "Come on, bud. Work with me on this. You're all I got left. You know where I'm comin' from on this, don't you?"

Cletis nodded.

"She gave you this box yesterday?"

"Yeah."

"Is it upstairs now?"

Cletis nodded again. "But Dad, she's just kind of like a grandma, and she just gave me the box. She didn't mean anything bad by it. I think she's just lonely. I think she was happy to have someone visit her."

"Look, Cletis, I know it all seems pretty natural to you, but it doesn't sound good to *me*. You just can never be sure about things like this—*people* like this. After what she's told you?" He paused for a moment. Then pointing to the scroll in front of them, he asked, "This writing came from the box?"

"Yeah, I'm pretty sure."

"And you didn't write this?"

"Nope. I don't know where it came from."

"Cletis, this doesn't make sense. Why would she give you a box with some old writing on it?"

"I don't know. For fixing her screen, I guess."

Taking another bite of toast, his father eyed him suspiciously. "For fixing her screen she gives you something like that?"

Cletis shrugged and toyed with his cereal.

"And then this writing just magically appears out of nowhere? Anything you're not telling me here, pal?"

Cletis inhaled deeply, cleared his throat, and began the confession . . . at least a partial one.

"Well, she told me there was some old prophecy that was supposed to take place . . . you know, be fulfilled, or something like that. And she said that I was supposed to help her . . . kinda like what I already told you she said. I really don't know what she was talkin' about . . . " His voice trailed off.

"Cletis, do you hear yourself?" His father scowled down at him and stepped away from the table. "Man. I tell you to stay away from her, and then you don't." He shook his head in frustration, crossed to the sink, and ran the tap water over his plate. "A prophecy? Cletis, come on! This is exactly what I'm talkin' about. You go visitin' some old lady, and now, before you know it, she's got you—us—wrapped up in some weird talk about who knows what. I don't like that! We don't know who she is or where she's been or whether she's out of her mind or what! Can't you see the danger in that? Can't you trust my judgment on this?" He studied Cletis for several seconds and then bowed his head over the sink, as if considering the dirty dishes below him. "Where's the box?" he finally asked.

Within a moment, the two of them were in Cletis's bedroom studying the old relic. On the bed, Cletis spread the scroll out next to the box. His father opened and closed the lid and examined the text inscribed on the top as well as on the side panels.

"This is amazing," he finally stated, comparing the writings. "This is exactly what is on the scroll here, isn't it. It's like it's been transferred precisely—shapes, spacing, everything. Looks to me like it's Old English or something like that. Maybe Runic."

"Irish," Cletis corrected.

"She tell you that?" asked Garth, still studying the characters on the box and the scroll.

"Yeah. She said it was Old Irish. But even she didn't know some of the stuff on it."

"What, is she some expert on this?"

"I don't know."

His father pondered a moment. "Hmmm.... The land of our fathers."

After examining the objects on the bed for a few silent moments, his father lifted his head and turned to Cletis. He was about to speak when something else caught his eye: the baseball cards that leaned against the family portrait on Cletis's dresser. His father had already seen the Yazstremski and McCovey cards, but now, two more sat regally with them—the Topps rookie cards of both Sandy Koufax and Roger Maris. His father approached them reverently.

"Where did you get *these*?"

"She gave them to me yesterday." Cletis knew that was a lie—at least an *untruth*—but there was hopefully a greater good at stake here. He knew he would fill his dad in on all the truthful details when the time was right. As far as the cards were concerned, he had found them in the box last night before he went to bed.

His father lifted the cards. "She gave you *these*? They're in *mint* condition. Rookies."

"Uh . . . yeah. That's more of my college education, I guess."

Cletis eyed his dad carefully, wondering if word from the bike shop or from Mr. Sperry had passed through the neighborhood and come back around to him. If it had, his father made no comment about it. Still Cletis felt it wise not to tell his father anything about the eerie experiences of yesterday, hoping he could just chalk up the whole strange situation as a learning experience and let it all be forgotten.

His father sighed and then put the cards back on the dresser. "Look, Clete, this is all fun and exciting . . . and you may be having a great adventure with all this. But the reality is, we don't even know who this lady is—what she does, what she's thinking, if she has a criminal record." He looked into his son's eyes and wrapped a hand around the back of his neck. "This is serious. You understand me? I'm not messin' with you. For all we know, she may be tryin' to buy your friendship in order to trick you into some strange trouble."

Finally Cletis nodded his understanding.

"Let me see that mark."

Cletis lifted his shirt. The red hourglass was still there, bright as fresh blood.

CHAPTER 7

MRS. KETCHUM
AND MR. HOWARD

Elston came over that morning, and Cletis talked to him about the scroll. But he didn't mention the red hourglass mark that had appeared on his shoulder. Despite their growing friendship, Cletis decided it was wiser to wait until more was known before sharing that secret. They sat on the bed and eyed the wooden box on the shelf. The Koufax and Maris cards rested on Cletis's pillow to their right.

"There wasn't anything in it when Dad opened it this morning," Cletis announced. "But when *I* opened it last night, I found them both in there." He pointed to the new cards.

"Maybe that's cuz he's a nonbeliever," responded Elston.

"You mean you think the cards only appear when *I* open it?"

"I dunno. Maybe."

The two eyed the box. Cletis rose, lifted it off the shelf, and held it for a moment.

"Should I open it? Is it gonna give us *another* treasure on the same day?"

Elston shrugged. "One way to find out."

Cletis lifted the lid. There lay another astounding find: Hank Aaron—mint condition again—and so old they couldn't recognize the year.

"Wow, look at that!" exclaimed Elston.

"That's Hammerin' Hank . . . when he just started playin'!"

"How old do you think that is?"

"Gotta be the late '50s!" Cletis declared admiringly.

"Man, what d'ya think it's worth?"

"I dunno. At least a couple hundred bucks!"

Cletis lifted the card from the box and placed it on the pillow next to the Koufax and Maris cards. Then his expression changed.

"Okay, Elston, I thought about somethin' all the way home last night. And I thought about it when I went to bed, too."

He suddenly stopped speaking and looked toward the door as if he were seeing things five miles away.

Elston waited. "So . . . you gonna tell me what it is, or you just gonna sit there an' stare?"

Within minutes the boys were in Sperry's Cards and Coins, slapping down a cardboard-protected "Henry Aaron" on the counter in front of Mr. Sperry. Johnny wasn't there yet, so their plan was working so far.

Mr. Sperry made the call again to the same Mrs. A. D. and told her he had a 1957 Henry Aaron card in mint condition. She agreed to pay three hundred dollars for the card, and the deal was done.

"I'll deliver the card to you this afternoon, ma'am," Mr. Sperry spoke into the phone. "Yes, ma'am. . . . I have cash on hand here to pay the seller. Thank you."

The boys waited patiently as he concluded the conversation and hung up the phone.

"Two hundred and fifty dollars is what I can give you. Is that a deal?"

"Yep. That's good," answered Cletis, trying to hide his excitement.

"Where'd you get *this* card? You've been locatin' some beauties lately."

"Uh . . . same friend of the family," Cletis answered, making sure that what he said was consistent with his previous story.

Mr. Sperry nodded his head thoughtfully as he counted out the money—five fifty-dollar bills. "Not sellin' off your dad's private collection, are you?" Mr. Sperry asked teasingly.

"No, sir. His mom threw all his away long ago."

"Oh," Mr. Sperry grimaced, as if in pain. He pushed his glasses back up on his nose and chuckled. "How many times have I heard that sad story?"

Cletis took the money and jammed it into his pocket, still worried that one day his dad and Mr. Sperry would talk about all this. He hoped not.

"Thank you, Mr. Sperry."

As they turned to leave, Mr. Sperry spoke up. "Hey, wait a minute." The two boys gulped, exchanged glances, and slowly turned back. *Here it comes*, thought Cletis. *I'm dead where I stand.*

"Just wanted to ask how practice is going lately?"

Cletis sighed with relief, and Elston spoke right up. "It's goin' great! Cletis is our newest player. We put him in center field!"

"One of these days, if I can get away from the store and everything else, I'm gonna come watch you guys."

The boys nodded, said their good-byes, and dashed out of the store.

They raced to the grocery store and purchased as much food as they felt they could safely hold in the baskets on their bikes—bread, milk, eggs, cereal, fruit, canned goods. Trying hard not to smash things, Cletis squeezed two full sacks into his basket, and Elston did the same. They could ride with one hand, so they carried a third sack under their arm.

"You still got the binoculars and the envelope?" Elston asked as they set off south on Main Street.

"In the bag under my seat. You got the marker and the paper?"

"Back pocket."

Cletis followed Elston left on Washington Street into an area of the neighborhood that was unfamiliar to him.

"Maybe this isn't gonna be any *baseball* magic, but it's gonna be our *own* kind of magic!" Cletis announced.

Elston nodded his agreement as he turned right on Haines Drive and headed for Monroe Street.

When they arrived, they kept their distance and parked their bikes across the street, behind a long line of dense pyracantha shrubs. Absent from their otherwise well-thought-out plan was how to do what they wanted to do without being seen. The homes in this part of town were spread out and had plenty of trees and shrubs for cover, but it still would be a challenge.

"That's the place," Elston said pointing. "That grayish house over there. We can leave the bikes here, outta sight."

"Are they home?"

"Like I said, Mrs. Ketchum's husband's in bed and hardly ever gets up. So he won't see us. I don't know why he can't move. He lays there watchin' TV all day or reading. I hear him callin' to her now and again when I walk by. He's a nice man."

The Ketchum home was missing some shingles from its roof; a kitchen window was cracked—probably from an ill-thrown ball or rock—and the splotchy lawn had been mowed but not edged. From where he squatted behind the shrubs, Cletis could see that the gray paint on the trim of the house was peeling away, revealing the mildew-spotted lumber beneath it. The curtains that fluttered with the breeze in the front window were tattered, as were some of the clothes on the line strung between two trees in the backyard. Two lilac bushes in the front yard still wore their fragrant, white and purple flowers.

"Their oldest kid's eight, and the youngest one's almost two," Elston whispered. "If we see any of them, we can do *this*." Elston put his finger to his lips and made a "shhh" sound. "The two-year-old they named Duke . . . after Duke Ellington."

"Who's that?"

"I think he was a vice-president back about a hundred years ago or so. Somethin' like that."

Cletis nodded. "So they might see us and tell their mom or dad it was us?"

"Well, you got a better plan? Even if they do, that won't hurt too much," Elston countered matter-of-factly as he pulled the note pad and marker from his pocket and handed them to Cletis. "We'll try to be unanimous. . . . But if we can't, no harm done. Here, you write. I'm not too good at makin' it so people can read it."

Anonymous, Cletis corrected him silently as he took the pad and marker and began to write the small note. "I'd still rather do this without anyone seeing us," he said. "How do they spell their last name?"

"Just like *ketchup*, except with an 'm' at the end instead of a 'p.'"

Cletis penned the note, ripped the top paper off the pad, and handed both the pad and paper to Elston. The note simply read:

Dear Mr. and Mrs. Ketchum,
Hope you enjoy these.
Have a nice day.
Your friends.

Elston pulled the rubber band out of his pocket, while Cletis grabbed the envelope from the compartment on his bike. Cletis counted out the $178 left over after the grocery bill, then pulled another $80 from his pocket. Elston's eyes bulged.

"Where'd that come from?"

"Leftover from the *Mantle* card. I figured it was right to throw it in too."

That made $258 in all. He took the note from Elston, placed it on top of the money, and shoved it all into the envelope. On the outside of the envelope he wrote: "To the fine Ketchum family." Cletis wrapped the rubber band around the envelope and placed it on top of the bread in the first bag of groceries.

"Okay. All set. Let's try not to get caught."

With a little finagling, the two of them were able to carry all six bags at once. When the streets were completely clear of cars and people, the duo scurried across the road and ducked behind the foliage of the two lilac bushes. There they paused to catch their breath and study the house and yard. The coast was still clear.

They scrambled to the side of the house near the front porch where they stopped to readjust the groceries and get a better grip. The noise of the bags crumpling and rubbing together urged to the boys to hurry their mission.

"Just around the edge and up to the porch," mouthed Elston with an excited smile as the two squatted together at the side of the house. "Drop 'em and run!"

They again scanned the yard, looking for children, parents, walkers, or anyone. All was still clear. They arose, courageously rounded the side of the house, and crept onto the porch. After placing the sacks on the wooden planks in front of the door, they looked up to see two-year-old, Duke, staring straight at them through the screen. His round tummy protruded from under his breakfast-stained T-shirt, and his full diaper sagged beneath his belly. He occupied himself by licking the dirty screen as he watched the boys. The front door behind Duke was now wide open, and they realized they were in full view of anyone who might pass inside. Just then, footsteps and a voice were heard.

"Duke, where are you?" Mrs. Ketchum called.

The rustle of the paper sacks and the noise of their partially stifled giggles were far from the silence Cletis and Elston had hoped to maintain. They wasted little time in darting off the porch and scurrying away from the house. They hit the ground behind the lilac bushes just as Mrs. Ketchum arrived to the front door.

"There you are, little man."

She hefted the boy and spotted the sacks on the porch. Cautiously she opened the door and stepped out to inspect the situation. The sack containing the envelope addressed to the "fine Ketchum family" was positioned closest to the front door.

Cletis and Elston tried to control their panting as they watched through the dense branches of the lilacs.

Mrs. Ketchum set Duke down and picked up the envelope with the family name written on it. Curiously, she looked inside. Upon discovering the money, she gasped and pressed the envelope against her blouse. In stunned silence she looked around the yard and up and down the street. As she scanned the area, Cletis and Elston remained hidden. Mrs. Ketchum stood momentarily on the porch, then took little Duke's hand, and re-entered the house.

"Now!" whispered Cletis.

At the sound of the screen door against the frame, the boys sprinted across the street and slid in behind the pyracantha bushes where their bikes were hidden.

"Get your binoculars." Elston spoke softly, pointing to Cletis's bike. "We gotta get where we can see what she does."

Cletis pulled the binoculars from the pouch on his bike.

"Where should we go?'

"I know a place."

They raced behind the cover of the hedge to a stand of maple trees some twenty yards from the house on the opposite side of the road. Within moments, both boys were seated on large branches in a well-covered spot, where they could see directly into the Ketchum's kitchen window. They watched through the branches as one-by-one the groceries were brought inside, unbagged, and placed on the kitchen table and counters. As the children gathered around their mother at the table, suddenly Mrs. Ketchum bowed her head and began to rub her eyes.

"I think she's crying," whispered Elston, looking through the glasses.

"Let me see," said Cletis. He took the binoculars and found the kitchen window.

"Do you see her?"

"Yeah, kind of. She's sort of behind one of her kids. Now she just picked up Duke. . . . Yeah, she's cryin'. I can tell by the way her shoulders are movin' up and down."

Cletis watched a moment longer and then lowered the binoculars away from his face and handed them back to Elston. The two boys sat in silence. Perched on the branches, neither spoke. Cletis suddenly remembered riding the shiny, new bike down the open, country roads with Elston beside him on the scooter. He remembered the pride of having lots of money to spend on something he desperately wanted. He remembered the thrill of purchasing something brand new. He remembered the smell, the feel, the colors, the speed, the excitement, the exhilaration. Yet all of those sensations—all of that pleasure— paled in comparison to what he was feeling now.

"You cold?" asked Elston.

"No. Why?"

"You got goose bumps all over your arms."

"Oh . . . yeah." He rubbed his skin thoughtfully and lifted his eyes again toward the Ketchum home. "Does your mom ever cry?" Cletis asked.

"Yeah . . . sometimes she does," Elston whispered.

"My mom cried too . . . sometimes. Her shoulders would move up and down the same way Mrs. Ketchum's did. Not much sound would come out."

Elston turned and studied Cletis respectfully. The two of them had spoken often of Cletis's mom, and the conversations had been natural and healing. Cletis could feel his friend's eyes upon him, but he stared straight forward, still pondering the kitchen scene in the Ketchum house.

"We just made magic, Elston!" Cletis smiled with the thought. "Just like we said we would."

Suddenly Cletis turned to Elston. "Mr. Howard," he said softly. He didn't pause to explain, he just lowered himself down through the branches of the maple.

Garth had come home for lunch to be with Cletis. The topsy-turvy transitions in Cletis's life had introduced his son to challenges most boys would never have to face. Even Garth felt a bit overwhelmed at the prospect of each new day. Since Anna's death nothing had been the same. The house was an empty place now. The kitchen was empty. Life was empty. Yet there *was* Cletis. All he had now was Cletis. Cletis was his only anchor and joy, and he knew he must not allow his tender son to fall through the cracks of his own busy, adult life. So today Garth had made time to be at home for a quick bite to eat, a word of encouragement, and a pat on his son's back. But Cletis was nowhere to be found.

Garth retrieved the scroll from Cletis's bedroom and studied the old manuscript. The parchment stared back at him from the kitchen table as if it were alive, beckoning to him to solve its riddle. He studied the marks and the characters that adorned the old script as he finished off a peanut butter and honey sandwich. Despite his concerns and frustrations, the document had fascinated him, and he wondered how the old lady, a supposed prophecy, the wooden box, this parchment, and now the strange mark on Cletis's shoulder, were all linked together . . . if at all. What was this craziness that was happening in their lives?

A final doughy lump was swallowed as he bent to the cabinet below the telephone and pulled a large phone book from beneath a pile of newspapers. He placed it on the table, licked a lingering drop of honey from his thumb, and opened to the listings under the University of Michigan in Ann Arbor.

I could go into Detroit, or I could go into Ann Arbor, he thought. It was about the same distance either way, but it was more likely he'd find what he wanted in Ann Arbor. His finger pulled down over the names and departments until it came to what he was looking for: "Department of Ancient Languages." After a deep breath, he picked up the phone and dialed the number.

"Uh . . . yes, my name is Garth Dungarvan," he began, still chewing. "Is there someone in the department there who reads ancient European languages—like Old Irish or Gaelic or something like that?" He paused, listening to the response. "Just a minute. Let me write this down." He pulled a pencil out of the drawer next to the phone. "What was that name again? . . . Dr. Canfield? . . . Okay, yes, just like it sounds. Extension 818. . . . Good, I'll give him a try. Thank you." He hung up the phone and studied the note he had just written.

With their last $15, Cletis and Elston had purchased another bag of groceries—bananas, bread, apples, canned drinks—things that were basically healthy and that wouldn't spoil quickly. The large paper sack crinkled as Cletis carried it under his arm toward the old shack behind the grocery store.

Cletis remembered seeing the man sleeping in the alleyway on the concrete next to the hardware store. *To be able to sleep on concrete, you've gotta be drunk or dead tired ... or so downright discouraged that it doesn't matter where you lay your head.*

He remembered the nights he spent with his mom as she lay dying in the hospital. There were times when he'd been so exhausted that he'd fallen asleep on the cold floor of her room. The morning after one of those times, he had awakened on the living room floor at home. He had been so heavily asleep that he hadn't felt his dad take him from the hospital, to the car, and finally, into the house. In fact, when he awoke, his dad was right there on the floor, sleeping next to him.

Dad must have been so tired. . . . Maybe it's kinda the same with Mr. Howard.

The old shack was a run-down railroad hut, where, years ago, passing trains had dropped off goods and mail. The three walls nearest the tracks were made out of old, oil-soaked railroad ties and appeared to be an extension built onto the original wooden frame. Cletis tried to imagine what the shack looked like, or smelled like, inside. The whole place was not much bigger than Cletis's bedroom. Broken wooden crates and cardboard boxes surrounded the dwelling. An old sink, brown with dust and grease, rested on top of the crates piled up next to the grocery store.

"You think there's even a bathroom inside there?" asked Cletis as they inched their way toward the front door.

"Got me," whispered Elston.

The boys froze in their tracks at the sound of movement coming from inside a large cardboard box that lay on the shaded side of the hut near the pile of boards. The side flaps of the box suddenly pushed open, and Mr. Howard slid out and slowly stood. The boys could see a ragged, blue blanket used for bedding still tangled in the box behind him.

Mr. Howard straightened as he eyed the two boys. His face was blackened and streaked with dirt, as if he had just finished a day's work deep in a Pennsylvania coal mine. His hair was long, gray, and matted. His beard, dark in the mustache and white on his chin, brushed against the front of his soiled T-shirt. His dirty and tattered clothes hung loosely about his bony body. He stood nearly six feet tall, and his skin was dark and leathery from years in the sun. He was barefoot as he stood before them, but a pair of worn, laceless Adidas rested next to the open box where he slept. His stench, carried on the midday breeze, wafted past the boys, leaving them breathless.

"What do you boys want?" the man asked in a voice far too gentle and civilized for his scruffy appearance.

Cletis and Elston stood their ground, and taking the bag of groceries out from under his arm, Cletis stepped cautiously forward.

"A friend wanted you to have this," he stated as he stepped forward and extended the bag.

Mr. Howard reached out, took the paper sack, opened it, and looked inside. With no expression distinguishable on his face, he bowed slightly.

"Thank you," he said. He eyed the boys, and then, much to their surprise, spoke again in a dark voice of warning. "But don't you boys ever come here again. You hear me?"

With that, he ducked back into the box, sat down on the bedding, opened the bag, and emptied its contents before him. Hungrily he began to eat and drink.

Cletis considered the poor man's words. Despite his warning, Cletis felt surprisingly cheerful. Rather than sensing fear and concern, a familiar electricity settled upon him again, penetrating his whole being. With a slight grin and a nod toward the occupied refrigerator box, Cletis turned, wrapped an arm around Elston's shoulder, and with his friend, retreated back to the bikes.

The Dungarvan house was empty at a little past two o'clock when the boys arrived. Together Cletis and Elston plopped down at the kitchen table with tall, sweating glasses of orange juice in their hands.

"You could smell him where we stood! He probably hasn't washed in weeks," stated Elston. He blew air down the front of his shirt to cool himself off.

Cletis nodded his agreement and gulped down half the glass of juice.

"Poor guy," Elston continued. "His boy used to play baseball at the high school. Mr. Howard would go and watch every game. My brother said he used to help the coach with the guys on the team—teach stuff like bunting and stealing and fielding."

"He must have had a good home once," Cletis commented. "Wonder why he lives in that run-down shack now?"

There was a pause. The two boys eyed each other. Elston shrugged.

"His boy died in Vietnam?" Cletis continued curiously.

"That's what they say. Long time ago. He had just got outta high school. He was gonna go down to Arizona, or somewhere, to play baseball. But he got sent to Vietnam."

"What about Mr. Howard's wife? What happened to her?" asked Cletis.

"I dunno," Elston shrugged.

Together they lifted their glasses to their mouths and finished off the cool, orange liquid.

"You wanna go see if there's another card in the box?" Cletis asked, taking Elston's empty glass and heading to the sink.

Elston's eyes lit up. "Yeah!"

Cletis rinsed the glasses and then dried his hands on his pants. With Elston on his heels, he raced through the kitchen, up the stairs and into the bedroom. They reverently approached the box. Instantly Cletis thought of the scroll. His eyes scanned the bedroom, but he didn't see it.

Dad must have it, I guess. At least I hope he does, he thought.

He lifted the box off the shelf and carried it back to the bed. "Here goes," he announced, then lifted the lid and peered inside. Detroit Tiger hero, Al Kaline, stared up at him from the bottom panel.

"Wow, look at that," whispered Cletis respectfully. "Al Kaline. That's his rookie card I bet. In mint condition, just like the others. Detroit Tigers." Cletis carefully picked out the card and began to examine it.

"Who's Al Kaline?" asked Elston, seemingly embarrassed for not recognizing the player.

"Al Kaline?" Cletis asked, squinting at Elston with surprise. "You don't know who Al Kaline is? He was an outfielder for the Tigers back in the '50s and '60s. Played about twenty years—the same time as Mantle and Mays and Hank Aaron. He retired a long time ago, though. I thought you, bein' from around here, would know about Al Kaline."

"Nope. Sorry." Elston rubbed his chin across his shoulder, wiping off a bead of sweat. "I wonder what he's doin' now, after playin' all those years?"

"He makes batteries! Didn't you know that?" Cletis rose from the bed and stepped to his desk. "Here, I'll show you." Cletis opened the top drawer and lifted out a pack of AA batteries. "You've seen these everywhere. I know you have." As Cletis leaned back onto the bed, he held the package close to Elston and searched the cardboard wrap. Finally finding the words, he pointed. "Alkaline Batteries. There. See? You use them in your flashlights an' stuff. Al Kaline batteries!"

Cletis stood at the plate taking practice swings and studying the field. Johnny stood on the mound in front of him, but he called timeout to pull up a springtime weed near the mound and toss it off the field.

"We are our own groundskeepers," he announced, kicking dirt over the hole from which the weed was uprooted. "Gotta take care of this place."

Cletis looked up the baselines, out to the scoreboard, and across the outfields. Johnny had told him the story of this field just before practice. According to Johnny, four years ago the boys named the baseball diamond Sperry's Field after their most generous supporter, Donald Sperry. Naturally the neighborhood team changed over time as people grew older or moved in or away, but since there was always a group of interested kids in the community, a sandlot team became customary—even expected. Mr. Sperry loved baseball and over the passing years often watched the boys play. Each year he made his "citizen's contribution" to the cause. The first year he donated five baseballs; the second year, a chest protector, a catcher's mask, and shin guards; the third year, a home plate and a pitching rubber for the mound; the fourth year, three wooden bats. This year, the fifth, he contributed four batting helmets to the team, plus a canvas bag in which to store everything he'd given previously.

Practice that afternoon was a game of over-the-line. In such scrimmages, they always used the old scoreboard behind right field. Johnny had declared the scoreboard to be Rabbit's work and glory. She was the one who brought it back to life. She had repainted the black grid lines across the front so that whoever kept score could post innings, runs, hits and errors. She'd also drawn numbers on thick, cardboard squares and punched round holes through the tops of them so they could be hung from the hooks that still stuck through the tops of the grid squares. The cardboard pieces had so far endured two years of continued summer use. Rabbit made sure that whenever it started raining, they were gathered quickly.

Years back the Coca Cola Company donated the scoreboard to the league that had once played in Greenberg Junction. The big red circle with the words *Coca Cola* written through the middle of it was faded and there was a bullet hole through the first *o* and another just below the *a*, but the pretty girl holding up a glass bottle of the brown, bubbling drink remained unharmed.

"Hey, Rabbit!" called Frank as he hung the fourth inning stats while standing on the rusted, metal folding chair that was continuously stored in the weeds below the scoreboard. "This girl painted on here looks like she could be a grown-up version of you!" He pointed up to the picture above him.

Everyone on the field turned and studied the picture.

"Yeah, the hair and the eyes are kind of the same," called Pauly from left.

"A little bit, I guess," added Davey, standing on second base, "except Rabbit's skin's a little darker."

"We ought to paint a mustache on her!" chimed Klu from center, laughing at his own joke and slapping his mitt with his fist.

From third base, Rabbit studied her likeness a moment before she answered. "Well, I think she's pretty, so thanks for the compliment."

That silenced everyone quickly; everyone except Frank.

"I didn't say she was *pretty*. I just said you looked kinda like her."

Klu laughed for only a second, but then shut his mouth when he saw Rabbit turn her back on the group. Slowly her gaze lifted away toward the hill by the school. Her stillness spoke volumes.

Johnny shook his head and turned to the pig farmer out at the scoreboard. "Frank, you're a moron sometimes."

Frank was silent, as if he knew what was coming.

"You remember that time in fourth grade," Johnny continued, "when you asked Mrs. Baumgartner why her knees rubbed together when she walked?"

Frank bowed his head, puckered his lips, and nodded.

"She was gonna have a baby!" added Pauly. "She was gigantic!"

"Yeah, it was like her fifth or something," quipped Davey.

"When she got all embarrassed, do you know what he said?" Johnny directed the question back to Rabbit.

"You don't have to tell her," called Frank hanging by his fingertips from the frame of the scoreboard.

Heedless, Johnny continued. "He said, 'Oh, don't worry. It's okay. My Grandpa's prized cow has knees like that, but she's the best milker in the county!'"

While everyone laughed, Rabbit smiled.

"Frank, you didn't?" she questioned.

"Hey, it gets better," chuckled Frank, in spite of himself. "If you're goin' that far, you might as well finish the story,"

"Well, that didn't make her feel any better," Johnny continued, "so he said, 'Don't worry, Mrs. Baumgartner. I seen lots of pregnant women who are tons fatter than you are!'"

Again the field filled with laughter.

"I thought I was complimentin' her, and she sent me to the office."

"Frank, you are so stupid!" laughed Klu.

Frank dropped to the ground near the chair and took several steps toward the infield. He pointed back to the sign. "Look . . . all

I'm sayin' is that the girl there kinda looks like Rabbit. That's all. Sorry, Rabbit."

"It's okay," she smiled. "You jerk."

"Okay, let's get back to the game," announced Johnny. "This diamond's for baseball." Holding the ball up in his hand, he turned and eyed the players in the field. "Everybody ready?" Instantly they all set for action. "You okay, Rabbit?" he called, peering out at third base.

She nodded. With the crack of the bat, all was forgotten.

The score on the old metal board stood at 5-2. Cletis's team was losing. Presently Cletis was at the plate with the bases loaded. Elston waited on first, Davey on second, and Rabbit on third. Klu, Pauly, Timmy, and Frank played the outfield. Frank was at the scoreboard this inning—everyone took their turn there, so that only three people played in the outfield at a time. Johnny remained neutral, pitching to both teams.

"Just hit down on the ball, Clete," Johnny coached as Cletis took practice swings at the plate. "You're too worried about hittin' flies. Drive down on the ball, and it'll go. Okay, right over the baseline. Bring the runners home."

"Yeah, Clete! Gotta tie this up!" shouted Rabbit from third.

"Hey, I'm tryin'," called Cletis, frustrated by the fact that he had had no success at the plate so far this practice.

Johnny wound and fired. Cletis connected and drove a fly ball to left field. Pauly came under it, got a bead on it, and caught it easily. With the out, Cletis snatched his helmet from his head and fired it against the backstop. Picking up his bat near home plate, he smacked it hard against the ground and tossed it too against the backstop.

Johnny raced in from the mound and caught Cletis by the arm.

"Hey, knock it off! You play on this team, you stay in control! You got it?" He hesitated briefly to let the words sink in. "Come on! Who cares, anyway? So what if you hit it to left field?"

"Four times in a row!" bellowed Cletis, still fuming. "And runners in scoring position twice! I can't hit the ball to anywhere except left field!"

While Rabbit, Davey, and Elston trotted in from their bases to gather their mitts, Johnny continued to coach.

"Hey, the one who oughtta be mad out there is Elston." Johnny pointed to the scoreboard. "Three outta those five runs up there are cuz he dropped two flies and let another one get by him! He's made three costly errors out there!"

Elston, trotting past to right field, ducked his head, as if Johnny's words were flying daggers.

Johnny looked Cletis square in the face.

"Now cool down and get out there," he challenged. "Everyone's gonna make mistakes now and again. That's what we practice for! To get better! Chuckin' your helmet and smackin' your bat against the ground, just shows everybody you got no self-control."

Hustling in from the outfield, Pauly, Frank, Timmy, and Klu watched Johnny unload on Cletis.

"We'll work on your hittin' each practice. Now cool down, get your mitt, and get out there."

Cletis eyed the incoming boys and felt it best to swallow his pride. He picked up his glove and hustled out to the loneliness of center field. As he settled into his position, he took a deep breath and exhaled.

"I gotta be able to hit," he muttered to himself. "Nobody wants a kid who can only field. That doesn't do the team any good. I gotta be able to drive in some runs."

He faced the field and looked up into the blue sky. The sun was setting behind him, painting the scattered clouds a soft pink. The colors above him and the gentleness of the evening suddenly reminded him of the times he used to sit with his mother on the boulder in their backyard. Together they'd look up into a sky much like this one and watch the sun drop in the west. He remembered the warmth of the boulder underneath him and the feel of his mother's hair that sometimes blew against his face. In times like these—when Cletis was frustrated about something—she had always been a wonderful listener.

He watched Johnny come set on the mound as Klu dug in at the plate and took a final warm-up swing.

"It hurts deep, doesn't it, Mr. Howard?" Cletis whispered.

CHAPTER 8

The Vision

The young woman pulled her cloak tightly around her head, and as she raced through the empty corridors of the village, she held it firmly in place with one hand. In her other arm, she carried the child close to her, shielding it from the vigorous winds that lifted leaves and dust into their faces. As she scurried through the pathways between darkened huts and cabins, she noted that the fires that once blazed with the cooking of evening meals now were black and smoldering in the wind and rain of the oncoming storm. Sobbing as she hurried along, her strands of long, wavy, auburn hair lifted away behind her and tossed in the currents of air. Her eyes were a deep, emerald green and possessed a delicate mixture of wisdom and vulnerability. Her face was perfectly proportioned and exquisitely framed by the flowing hair that whipped about her. Such beauty was beyond that of any woman in the village, except that of her mother.

The toddler in her arms seemed to quietly trust the rush and emotion of the moment, as if knowing that what his mother had to accomplish was needful and right. Tucked safely in her arms, the little boy wore a finely woven, woolen hood, which carried upon it, over the right ear, a green insignia—a family coat of arms; the embroidered image of a scroll, a bear, and a white-robed man. The child was draped in a one-piece, woolen nightshirt and wore expertly crafted, rabbit-skinned booties on his feet and lower legs. The tiny booties were laced up the front with thin, leather straps, holding the soft fur snugly in place.

The young woman's breathing was heavy as she rushed through the village to her cabin. She had little time. Her husband would probably find her there, yet she knew what she must do. The raindrops hissed as they landed upon the glowing embers of nearby fire pits and heated stones. Emotion bathed her cheeks and, with the urging of the strong wind, the tears pushed back across her jawline and disappeared into her exquisite hair.

Her mother and father were gathered in the grand lodge, along with the young woman's father-in-law. There they awaited her return. She had left their presence moments ago with strict and dangerous orders from her father. She was to return to them with the child and the box. Then the Changing would take place. Only her father-in-law could perform that. It *had* to be done . . . for her own good, for the good of the clan, and for the good of her son. These were to be her final moments with the child.

The largest cabin in the complex was hers. She slowed her pace slightly as she approached the dwelling.

He may be within, she thought as she stepped up to the threshold, lifted the latch, and pushed open the wooden door.

Entering cautiously, she stood momentarily in the doorway and scanned the lodge. The room was cold and silent. The fire barely flickered in the corner. It had been a roaring blaze two hours ago when she had prepared a final meal for her and the child. Its dying flames now cast an eerie, dancing light across the shadowed space. She closed the door behind her, and after pausing to watch and listen, she moved to the large, fur-covered bed to her left. Though her senses told her the place was presently empty, she knew he would come.

She sobbed anew as she laid the child down upon the furs and hurried to the fireplace hearth. There she removed two large stones from the lower ledge, revealing a hollowed hiding place from which she lifted a brown, wooden box. With the box in hand, she rose and moved anxiously to the table behind her, where she found a gray, woolen shawl with which she wrapped the box. The little boy rolled over, sat up, and watched her from the bed, as if he understood her task.

Suddenly the woman felt the Power.

The good and the evil together, she gasped, rubbing her arms. *He's here. It has come. The time has come!*

Immediately her son began to cry. Turning protectively toward him, she watched the gray conduit materialize directly in front of the door through which she had entered. Within the conduit, appeared the muscular, handsome man she knew all too well. His long, blond hair cascaded over the sleeveless leather vest that covered his barrel chest. His massive shoulders were bare, revealing on the front of each a tiny red hourglass. He wore dark boots into which he tucked leather pants. As the vibrant energy of the conduit gradually vanished around him, he floated to the flooring of the cabin and faced the young woman. Despite her fear, she grasped the box and rapidly moved between the man and the crying child.

"The box is mine," he declared, his voice deep and resonant. "I will take it and the child, and I will be gone. And you will join us later. For you are mine, and we both well know you haven't the strength to go through with this. If you come with me, we will be together again, and you will see that all I have promised you will come to pass."

She eyed the man bitterly. *It is all just as planned*, she thought. *They are watching me. I know what I must do. And it must be done quickly and thoroughly for the sake of the child and unknown humanity.*

Her mouth was suddenly dry, and she struggled to swallow. Steadily she lifted an arm toward the man, as if fixing her aim upon his chest. His head cocked slightly to the side, surprised by the gesture.

His blue eyes are penetrating and evil now, she thought, *but they were once kind and gentle.*

"Why do you toy with me?" he stated defiantly. "You have no Power. They took it from you. Don't be foolish. Give me the box."

"The decision was made long before this moment," she panted through her tears. "And I will see it through. Even your father agrees with me." She felt the blue Power coursing through her shoulders and arms, knowing that it would be for but a moment. "I once loved you, Ian," she spoke tenderly. "And because of that, I will be gentle with you."

A high-pitched, agonizing cry left her mouth, followed by a flash of blue light that jumped from her fingertips. The light arced across the room, striking the man squarely in the chest, lifting, driving, and pinning him against the wall near the door. Panic and pain painted the man's countenance as he struck the wooden surface behind him. Within seconds his eyes closed, and as the light around him diminished, he sunk to the floor.

The young woman's shoulders heaved as she set the box on the table next to her and crossed again to the fireplace hearth. Her sobs filled the silent cabin as she lifted a large butcher knife from off the stones. She turned and approached the man, and bending over him, lifted the blade to the back of his neck. There she paused, sniffing and weeping as she faced the task before her. She reached down behind him, pulled a large handful of his blond hair toward her, measured the knife against it, and then neatly sawed it off. From a pocket on the front of her skirt, she removed a string of woolen yarn. Carefully she tied the wool around the strands of hair and secured them in place.

"In memory of what we once were," she whispered, pushing the collection of hair into her skirt pocket and rising to her feet above him.

Placing the knife on the table, she turned and hurried to the infant on the bed. As she lifted the little one and held him close, a howl of agony escaped her soul, and she pulled the child to her shoulder and rocked him gently. For one last moment, she absorbed the memories of her beloved home. She inhaled the fragrance of the child's skin and hair, rubbed her chin across his forehead, and kissed his brow and cheeks. The bitter tears that coursed freely down her cheeks gathered at her chin.

At the table, she lifted the wrapped box, tucked it under her arm, and made her way to the heavy, wooden door. Lifting the latch, she paused to pull the blanket around the child. Again she looked down upon the man who lay at her feet. Then, with a groan, she opened the door and raced out into the storm.

In the lodge of the Grand Chamber, the elderly trio awaited the young woman's arrival. Before them, floating in the air, hovered a blue, transparent sphere. Within the sphere, a hologram revealed the actions and whereabouts of the young woman and the child. At present they watched as she made her way from the distant cabin, through the dark and empty village pathways, toward the lodge of the Grand Chamber.

"She used the Power well, did she not?" spoke the woman. With two fingers, she rubbed away a tear that painted her cheek. "This is far too hard on a mother and grandmother," she whispered.

The man next to her wrapped an arm around her shoulder and pulled her close to him.

"Yet, it is just," he replied, kissing her forehead. "We will see her again, and it will all pass in mere moments."

"But she will suffer so long," the woman sobbed.

"Yes, it will be a great test for her. But she is well prepared and wise for her young age."

"And her Power will be magnified if she succeeds," stated the brown-robed man, who stood nearby as he removed his hands from the large pockets at his sides. "A test of this nature has never been observed in the history of mankind. This is unprecedented."

The young woman suddenly burst into the lodge and, clutching the child and the box, rushed toward the trio who stood before her. She extended the box toward her father-in-law and, then panting and weeping, staggered into the open arms of her parents.

Her father-in-law unwrapped the wooden box and lifted the lid. Reverently he held the open relic in front of him next to the floating, blue sphere. As he did so, the hologram within the hovering orb instantly changed, revealing now the young man, who, still in the distant cabin, struggled to his feet.

The old man stroked his long, white beard and then held the open box directly below the transparent orb. As the huddled group studied the hologram, they could see that the young man remained confused and weak from the blast of the Lightfire that was issued from the hand of the young woman.

The old man lifted the open box toward the surface of the blue orb and, raising his arm toward the vision, commanded loudly:

"TIME THAT GAVE DOTH NOW HIS GIFT CON-FOUND!"

A red light instantly rocked the room in which the young man stood, and his mouth opened as if in a painful bellow. With his hands now upon his head, he collapsed to the floor. Immediately there gathered above him a sparkling, blue conduit that descended gradually until it rested upon him and engulfed him. As if in a deep sleep, the young man was lifted from the floor of the cabin and into the confines of the blue conduit.

In silence the young woman, her parents, and the old man studied the hologram. They watched the radiant conduit hover briefly within the distant cabin and then gradually disappear. Instantly the blue orb of the hologram vanished, and as if taking its place, the conduit that encased the young man materialized, suspended over the open box held in the hands of the ancient man.

"Oh, my son, Ian," he whispered as he peered up into the conduit. "It has come to this."

With a gentle motion of his arm, he directed the conduit lower until it glistened and pulsated just above the wooden box. As the energy field descended, it began to swirl rapidly, becoming a minia-ture funnel-cloud that twisted down toward the wooden relic. Inside the whirling energy field, Ian gradually dematerialized, as if disinte-grating into an unseen world.

The young woman gasped and clutched her child to her chest. Wide-eyed she watched as the bright glow of the spinning conduit was pulled steadily into the open box. There the brilliant red rested, spectacular and vibrant, until the lid closed upon it, suffocating its motion and luster. In that precise moment, the old man's hands jerked back, releasing the box. Magically it floated freely in front of him. He studied it a moment and then clasped his hands over his heart and bowed his head.

The young woman pressed her lips against the face of the child and rubbed her cheek gently against his. She felt her mother's caring and steadying arm around her shoulders tighten as the old man turned back to them.

"He who once was a husband, father, and son is now captive to be released only according to the wisdom, time, and prophecy of the Clan and the Travelers."

Reverently the sage turned back to the box that floated before him, closed his eyes, and raised his hand toward it. A beam of light pulsed from his fingers, catching the box and holding it steady in mid-air. As if being touched by an invisible firebrand, characters, letters, and words appeared magically, artfully, one by one, upon the lid of the box. The sweet smell of burnt wood filled the lodge as the smoke of the firing enveloped the small group. When the process ended and the box floated magnetically closer to the old man, he turned to his daughter-in-law.

"The box shall come to you when the time is right. Then you shall study what is written upon it. Its message will guide you toward the final moments of your test." He stepped forward and wrapped his arms around the sobbing young woman and her child. "You and I lose our sons, and your mother and father lose a daughter. Though it be difficult, I will prepare a way for you, and we will be with you until the end. Be wise." He leaned away from her and studied her lovingly. "The hair you cut from his head . . . " He pulled a leather pouch from within his robe and extended it her. "Put it in here and give it to your mother during the Changing. She will return it to you immediately thereafter." Having said that, he stepped back and seized the floating box from the air.

The young woman pulled the hair from her pocket, placed it within the leather pouch, and then handed it to her mother. Facing her father, she took a deep breath and awaited the next horrible step in the plan. Her father touched her cheek and closed his eyes.

"Your Power is hereby taken from you again." His voice was strong.

Still holding the baby, the young lady doubled forward, feeling the sweet energy leave her body once more. With that done, her father wrapped his longs arms around her.

The time for the Changing was upon her.

How she had dreaded it, but she knew it must be. She bowed her head and handed the baby to his grandmother, pausing to kiss, one last time, the chubby face and dimpled hands. Her mother silently took the child, then kissed her daughter's cheeks and forehead.

"I have betrayed the Power of the families," the young woman sobbed. "And I am willing to pay the price needed to regain your trust and your love."

"You will always have our *love*," corrected her mother. "It is the family's *trust* you seek to regain."

She smiled sadly and nodded to her mother. Bowing her head, she turned to her father.

"We shall see you again, and our love for one another will be yet stronger," he whispered in her ear.

She felt his powerful but gentle hands reach around her shoulders and direct her toward her father-in-law—the dear old man who possessed the Power of the Changelings. She pushed her hair away from her eyes. There was an elongated moment of silence in which her life passed before her eyes—the happiness and the misery of it.

The old man placed the wooden box into the hands of the young woman's father and then took the damsel by the wrist. Together they stepped away from the others. Then, when her hand was placed upon the skin of his shoulder and his eyes closed in concentration, she knew the moment was upon her. She took a deep breath and waited. Like a warm flow of blood, the force of the Changeling power passed into her hand, up her arm, and into her entire body. She felt her neck crane backward . . .

With a gasp and a start, Abish sat up in bed. She peered into the blackness that shrouded her. Through the open window of the bedroom, she heard the familiar chirping of the crickets and the gentle gurgle of the canal. Still her heart raced.

Again, she thought. *I see it again and again. So real . . . so real . . .*

She rubbed her eyes with the flat of her hands. Then, with a heavy sigh, she lowered herself back onto her pillow. Like a loathsome intruder, the disturbing revelation had again pushed its way into the private corridors of her mind, haunting the darkest hours of her endless lonely nights.

Chapter 9

The Hourglass Marks

Cletis had lain awake in the blackness of his room for nearly an hour before he finally dozed off. He had thought of the Ketchums—their house, their children, and their voices. He remembered seeing Mrs. Ketchum's face as she wept over the money and the groceries. He had thought of Mr. Howard too. He remembered the look in his eyes—the sadness, the pain—as he received the food. Pondering the memories of the day, Cletis was finally lulled into a sound and perfect sleep.

Until 1:00 a.m.

Abruptly Cletis's eyes opened with the pain of a jolting, searing fire that pierced his left shoulder. The incredible agony was, again, more than he could bear. With a cry, he rolled from bed and landed with a thud on the carpet. He gasped for air against the torture and crawled weeping to the door. Once in the hallway, the walls began to shift and slide. Dizzy and disoriented, Cletis doubled over and tumbled down the stairs.

"Cletis!"

Garth charged out of his room and into the hallway. Cletis lay at the base of the steps, crying in pain and holding his shoulder.

"Clete, what is it?" His dad knelt next to him and placed a gentle hand on his back.

"My shoulder, Dad," Cletis sobbed, curling his body inward toward the agony. "It's the same pain."

His father reached up, turned on the stairway light above them, and then leaning back down, attempted to pry Cletis's hand away from the front of his shoulder. "Hold on, Clete. Let me take a look."

Trusting his father, Cletis finally lifted his hand away from the pain.

There on the left shoulder, in the exact likeness of the mark on his right shoulder, appeared a tiny red hourglass. Blinking against the brightness of the lights around them, Cletis and his father compared the two images. Carefully Cletis touched the second marking.

"Does that hurt you? To touch it like that?"

Cletis looked curiously up at his dad and then back down again at the mark. "Yeah, but . . . but the pain's goin' away. It hurts . . . but not like it did. Maybe a little now."

"A little? You're screamin' in the night and rolling down the stairs, and now you say it hurts 'a little'? Did your fall hurt you? Did you twist an ankle or break an arm or anything?"

"No, I don't think so. I think I'm okay."

His father squinted his tired eyes and rubbed his mouth. "Cletis, what's goin' on here?"

Cletis sat up straighter, not quite sure what to make of the question. "Well, I— " Suddenly Cletis stopped speaking, looked down at the spot on his left shoulder, and rubbed the new hourglass mark. "Dad, it's gone! Totally."

"What's gone?"

"The pain! Just like the last time. It really hurt—like *really* hurt—and now the pain is gone. Like it wasn't ever even there."

His father leaned back against the wall behind him and studied Cletis silently, doubtfully.

"What? Why are you lookin' at me like that?" Cletis questioned.

His father sighed and scratched at his beard stubble. "I don't know. You tell me. You got matching marks on your shoulders. First it hurts enough to make you bawl out loud, and then the pain is gone. Just like that." He snapped his fingers. "First it's on one shoulder, and now you've got the exact same thing on the other? What's goin' on here, Clete?"

"Dad, I'm not makin' somethin' up here. This is real!"

"You know what it looks like to me? I don't wanna say this, but it looks to me like they're burn marks, buddy. Looks to me like you've put matchin' burn marks on your shoulders for some reason, or tattoos of some kind, and you're makin' up a pain story to cover your tracks."

"Dad . . . Dad, they're not burns! They're not tattoos! I promise you. They're not! You think I'm stupid enough to burn myself, and then wake you up in the middle of the night with some weird story?"

"Well, if they're not burns, then what are they?"

"I . . . I don't know. But they're not burns and they're not tattoos, I know that!"

"Cletis, come on. Get serious. Look at them. They're identical! What are you doin' to yourself? Is this some other initiation thing for the team? Are they infected?"

Cletis pulled himself up one step and sat even with his father's eyes.

"Dad, I'm tellin' you the truth! I'm not makin' this up. They just came on my shoulders. They're not burns, and they're not some initiation stuff. I'm tryin' to figure this all out, too, cuz I don't know what's goin' on!"

His father's tired eyes were only half open. "Well, what am I supposed to think, Clete? Come on, you're off visiting this old woman against my orders. She talks about some prophecy. You get this strange box with weird writing on it. Hundreds of dollars of baseball cards show up. And now you wake up in the middle of the night with matching burn marks on your shoulders. I'm not sure what to make of all this, Clete. What's goin' on?"

"They're *not burn marks*, I'm tellin' you!"

"Don't you raise your voice at me."

"You're supposed to *trust* me, Dad!"

"Yes, I *am* supposed to trust you, and you're supposed to earn it—like by obeying me when I tell you not to visit this old woman. In the meantime, I'm left to figure out what's happening to my son, and I don't think I'm gettin' the whole story here."

Fighting his anger, Cletis retorted, "You don't believe me, do you?"

"What's to believe or disbelieve? You haven't done any explainin' about anything yet. And you darn well know I *expect* you to do it—I expect you to explain *exactly* what's goin' on and do it thoroughly."

"But I don't know what's goin' on! I don't know how to explain anything! Cuz I don't know!"

His father leaned toward him, his eyebrows pressed into a frown. "Look, can you blame me for being irritated when I don't seem to be getting all the details? Can you blame me for bein' upset when I ask you not to see this old woman and you go out there anyway?"

Cletis made no comment.

"Son, I think I need to pay this old lady a visit."

"Go right ahead," snapped Cletis. "I'm tellin' you the truth, and you don't believe me!" With that, Cletis struck the wall with his elbow, glared at his father, and turned and marched up the stairs. "Mom would have believed me."

Cletis could tell Elston knew something was wrong. Cletis had said things like "Hi" and "What d'ya wanna do?" but other than that, he hardly paid attention to Elston. And even now—even though Elston sat right across from him on the same bed, in the same room, Cletis was lost in a land of distant thoughts. It was a beautiful spring day outside, but it was gloom and storm inside the Dungarvan home.

"So somethin' is wrong. You gonna tell me about it?" questioned Elston as he tossed a fresh piece of bubble gum into his mouth.

Cletis had already watched him stick two other pieces in his mouth. That made three pieces he was currently chewing. The wad was as big as half a hot dog.

"Ain't nothin' to tell," countered Cletis, looking down at his knees. He got up and walked to the old box on the shelf, where he casually studied the markings on its sides. "How was the paper route this morning?"

"Pre'y good. No dogz. Chain stiw rubz on a guard," Elston mumbled through the giant pink wad. "You sick?"

Cletis shook his head. Now wasn't the time to tell Elston about the events of the past night. Cletis touched his left shoulder where the red mark had appeared. There was no pain. He dropped his hand and watched Elston chew.

Elston studied his silent friend a moment and then puffed out a big bubble. It grew to the size of a cantaloupe before it popped across his lips, nose, and chin. Instantly his tongue labored to bring it all back into his mouth. "Somethin' ba' happen in a famiwy?" he questioned.

"Can't get much worse than what's *already* happened."

Another bubble expanded in front of Elston's nose and eyes, but before it popped, he sucked the air out of it and pushed the wad back into his cheek.

"I go' some extra gum. Wan' some?"

Reaching into his pocket, Elston pulled out a couple of pieces and set them on the bed next to Cletis. Cletis unwrapped them both and stuck one in each cheek.

"May'e we should loo' in the old box and see if you go' anyzing in 'ere. Maybe 'at'll cheer you up."

"I looked earlier this morning and nothing was in there," Cletis answered, sucking on the cubes of gum.

"Maybe we cou' che' again. Never know."

Cletis shrugged. He walked to the desk, picked up the price guide, and tossed it back on the bed. Then he reached up, retrieved the box, and sat down next to Elston. Cletis studied the golden-brown antique he held in his hands, then abruptly passed it to Elston.

"You open it. I'm pro'bly bad luck today."

Elston sucked a bubble back into his mouth. "Me? I've never done it 'fore."

"That doesn't matter," muttered Cletis. "Go ahead."

"Iz 'ere anything I need a know?"

"Nope."

"Jus' open it?"

"That's all *I* ever do."

Elston took the box and studied it. "Open the box, open the guide, check the wuhth, enjoy the ride."

"You just make that up?" Cletis finally smiled.

"Yup."

Reverently Elston opened the lid. There inside lay two cards: Frank Robinson, the outfielder who starred so many years with the Cincinnati Reds and the Baltimore Orioles, and Brooks Robinson, the great Oriole third baseman.

"Hey, looh," marveled Elston, lifting the cards and comparing the names of the players. He pushed his gum into his cheek so he could speak clearly. "The Robinson brothers!"

"Yeah, right," chuckled Cletis, studying the cards. "There's kind of a difference in their skin color."

"Oh," winked Elston, lifting the cards to Cletis. "Well, maybe one was adopted," he joked, happy to see Cletis smile.

Cletis laughed. "You're crazy." He eyed the cards for a moment. "They played on the Baltimore Orioles in the 1960s, but my dad says people used to call them the Robinson brothers, just for fun. So I guess you're kinda right."

"They're just like us!" teased Elston, patting Cletis on the back.

Elston closed the lid and lifted the box back up to the shelf. He then turned and eyed the cards across the room that stared back at him: Yaz, Willie McCovey, Sandy Koufax, Maris, Al Kaline. The Aaron and Mantle cards had been sold.

"Here they are!" Cletis announced, after flipping through the pages of the price guide. "Man, 1957 Topps! These are their rookie cards!"

"So wha' ah they wuhth?"

"Boy . . . uh, both together, in mint condition like they are . . . they're worth at least four hundred dollars!"

Elston coughed, choking on his gum. "Tha' box knows how to pick 'em, doesn't it," he announced, lifting the wad out of his mouth.

The boys darted out of Sperry's Cards and Coins, counting their money. Mrs. A. D., whoever she was, again agreed to purchase the cards from Mr. Sperry. So the sale was made, and Cletis and Elston left the store with close to $325.

"But we can't do this," Elston warned as they pedaled their bikes south past the gas station and the post office. "You heard what he said!"

"I know what he said," replied Cletis.

"You're spending all this money, and who knows, we may end up dead!"

"I don't think anything bad's gonna happen to us." He pedaled faster and looked back at Elston with a knowing grin.

"You're crazy!" bellowed Elston, trying to catch up.

"No. Frank's crazy," called Cletis, looking over his shoulder. "Did you know he ate four hamburgers two nights ago and threw up all over his sister's bed! He planned it that way. His sister screamed for five minutes and passed out. *That's* crazy."

"Yeah, but *we're* riding to our deaths!" Elston responded.

"Not yet. First we gotta do some shoppin'."

Though Elston protested through the whole shopping process, an hour later the boys scurried out of Lindsay's department store with a Tigers sweatshirt and hat, two pairs of men's jeans, a belt, a pair of Nike cross trainers, a razor with replaceable blades, a bottle of Aqua Velva, three T-shirts, three pairs of socks, and a large, wool blanket. As far as the clothing and shoes were concerned, they guessed on the sizes, hoping they were fairly close to a proper fit. They could make changes and do returns later if they needed to.

The next-to-final stop was Burger King, where they ordered three large meals and an extra chocolate shake. Balancing the bags in their baskets, they made their way to the shack behind the grocery store.

It was a fairly warm day, and Cletis and Elston arrived at Mr. Howard's hut during the hours when the sun beat straight down on the place. The train that had just passed created a bit of a pleasant breeze, but it was short-lived. The echo of the locomotive could still be heard down the tracks in the distance. From their bikes, the boys eyed the area around the shack and looked for a place where they could sit and eat, if Mr. Howard was willing. The only shaded place was across the tracks, under the cool shelter of two large maples.

As the boys hopped off their bikes, they saw that the refrigerator box that had once lain at the side of Mr. Howard's place was gone, replaced by a pile of railroad ties. Wondering where the man could be, the boys leaned their bikes against the brick wall of the grocery store and gathered their cargo.

"Do you think he's in there?" whispered Elston, panic in his voice.

Cletis shrugged his shoulders and whispered back, "If he is, he's probably roasting. I guess we'll find out here in two seconds."

"We're dead, you idiot. I don't know why we're even here." Elston took a deep breath, as if it were his last, and allowed the air to hiss slowly out through his lips. Step by step, they approached the frail dwelling.

"We thought the old lady was a witch. We were wrong," whispered Cletis, trying to justify himself in front of Elston.

"We weren't either. She *still might* be a witch. And besides, she never warned us not to come back. Mr. Howard just might shoot us!"

"Elston, relax. If there's a problem, we can outrun him. I'm sure of it."

"You can't outrun bullets," Elston stated flatly.

"Why would a man like him own a gun?"

Suddenly the boys heard shuffling on the west side of the tracks and turned in time to see Mr. Howard rise to his feet and face them.

"What do you boys want?" he called out. "Get away from that place!"

Cletis and Elston hadn't seen him there. He appeared to have just awakened. His eyes were puffy and his hair was matted over his right ear. His old long-underwear top hung loosely over his sweaty chest and was torn and grease-ridden. The suspenders, which were intended to hold up his filthy, baggy pants, hung down to his knees. A tight grip on the top edge of his trousers kept them from falling to the ground. He wore only stockings on his feet, but both were sagging and had large holes at the toes and in the heels.

"I thought I told you boys not to come around here anymore," he called to them harshly. "Can't you leave a body alone?"

Both boys froze in their place. They could smell him where they stood. Finally, Cletis swallowed hard, and then spoke.

"Well, uh, a friend asked us to give you these, and we have a question we wanted to ask you, cuz, um-m, you're probably the only one who knows the answer to it."

With the bags in hand, Cletis walked toward the tracks.

"You're outta your mind!" whispered Elston through clenched teeth. His lips didn't move, except on the "m."

Despite the warning, Cletis continued forward. Fearful, Elston followed him. Together they crossed the tracks and approached the man, but Cletis knew, in his heart of hearts, he was ready to run back for the bike at any moment. He assumed Elston was prepared for the same. Within four feet of Mr. Howard, Cletis extended the bags to him. Cautiously Mr. Howard reached out, took the bags, and peered inside them. Before he could respond, Cletis continued.

"And we also picked you up some lunch." But rather than handing the Burger King bag to Mr. Howard, Cletis stepped over into the shade and sat down in the grass. "Can you help me, Elston, please?" he asked in an over-polite voice as he spread out the food.

Eyes wide with fear, Elston stepped forward, laid down the sacks he carried, and helped Cletis divide up the burgers and fries. Mr. Howard watched, puzzled by what was happening.

"How 'bout we sit here in the shade across from your house and eat together?" Cletis asked as he handed a bag to Mr. Howard.

Immediately both boys sat and began unwrapping their burgers.

"We don't mean no harm, sir," added Elston, sitting down on a black railroad tie. "Oh, and here's an extra chocolate shake for you."

He reached inside the soggy bag, pulled out the shake, and set it on the grass in front of Mr. Howard—who was still standing, shocked by all that was happening. Finally the man bent his skinny body and stiffly sat down across from the boys. Like the boys, he opened his bag and unwrapped his burger.

"My name is Cletis Dungarvan and this is Elston Blanchard," spouted Cletis, pointing to himself and then to Elston. Elston nodded before biting into his burger. "Mr. Howard," continued Cletis, "you know the rules. If a first baseman's holdin' a runner on durin' the pitcher's wind-up, but he's got his foot in foul territory, can the umpire call a balk on the pitcher?"

Suddenly Mr. Howard's eyes lit up with excitement and interest. He studied the boys momentarily and then allowed his gaze to drift back over to their bikes, where the boys' mitts hung on the handlebars. The burger he held in his hands gradually lowered to his lap. A slight smile lifted the corners of his mouth.

It's working, thought Cletis. *There's the real Mr. Howard—the man behind the dirt and stink!*

As soon as that discovery flashed through his mind, a flow of tingly electricity shot through his body once again, standing his hair on end. *I don't know for sure what it means, but it's here again.*

Garth leaned back in his chair and flipped the switch on the wall, turning on the lamps above the kitchen table. With the setting of the sun, the light in the room had gradually dimmed, and not until he had turned on the light did he realize just how dark it had been.

"That's better," he spoke aloud. He peered down at the scroll Cletis had brought him yesterday morning.

Spread out in front of him, it was nearly two feet long. The paper itself was a curiosity. To this point in time, Garth had pondered the etchings on the scroll but not the composition of the material it was written on. That had been a secondary priority. But now, as he felt its texture, it seemed to be a type of a fabric—like an extremely thin cut of leather. It could be torn, he noted, yet it was sturdier than paper and had a sort of organic quality to it.

He sat back in his chair, folded his arms over his chest, and looked out the window in front of him. Sighing, he thought of Cletis and the string of sudden events that had saddled them both over the past few days: the baseball team, the initiation night, the old woman and her prophecy, the wooden box, the cards that seemed to come from nowhere (supposedly gifts from the old woman), and now the marks that appeared on Cletis's shoulders.

And who knows if there's more that I don't know about? That's a possibility, he thought. *What on earth is goin' on with him? What's he gotten us into?*

The lights above Garth momentarily dimmed and brightened, and his gaze lifted curiously to the ceiling. He knew the air conditioner wasn't on.

"Maybe the city's workin' on a power line close by," he muttered aloud. Down the road, a dog barked furiously. The distant racket distracted Garth from the power surge, and he stood and looked through the kitchen window onto the street. Though the barking continued, Garth saw nothing out of the ordinary. He turned back to the table, and itching under his shirt collar, he resumed his study of the parchment.

Cletis's room hummed with supernatural energy as a gray cloud of pulsating, swarming mistlike particles materialized just inside the doorway. The vibrant mass filled the corner of the room, from the ceiling to just above the floor. Within the cloud, a cylindrical conduit appeared, and within that conduit, a large man. Moments later the humming ceased, and as the conduit around the being faded, he floated to the floor.

The man stepped across to the foot of the bed and studied the room curiously, as if finding himself in a world completely unfamiliar to him. The being was lean and muscular, and his hair, thick and blond, hung down his back in a long braid. His pants were made of a dark leathery material, bound at the waist by a white cord. The pant legs were tucked, just below his knees, into dark boots made of rough, thick animal hide. The clothing on his upper body was vestlike. The sleeveless black leather revealed not only his massive biceps and chiseled shoulders, but also the imprint of a tiny, red hourglass mark on the front of each shoulder.

The man scanned the room, his eyes widening as he spied the wooden box on the shelf above Cletis's desk. Reverently he approached it, lifted it to him, and held it in his hands. He stroked the inscriptions on the side panels and breathed deeply with the touch. He studied the curious message etched on the lid, and as he read the words of the ancient language, his eyes squinted into a frown.

Unexpectedly the color of the box in his hands turned a deep, inky black. Amazed at the change, the man's mouth opened in confusion, and he turned the box in his hands to inspect the transformation.

Then, as if overcome by a sudden power beyond his control, his head, neck, and shoulders seized abruptly backward. The man's grip on the box tightened and his teeth clenched into a hideous, agonizing smile. Instantly, the man's bones and flesh pulsed with movement. Throbbing lumps and bulges covered his entire body—as if dozens of molelike animals pushed and stretched within him, moving beneath the surface of his skin and within the dense layers of muscle and tissue. His body groaned as tendons, bones, and joints shifted, pulled and tightened. The muscles that once adorned his strong athletic form knotted painfully, and then thinned, shriveled and deteriorated. His arms, legs, back, and neck constricted and shrunk with the unnatural, shape-shifting alteration. His skin, once healthy and bronzed, stretched, wrinkled, and drooped on his bent and crooked frame. Within moments, the sturdy, youthful being was transformed into a wrinkled, bowed, dying old man. The only physical features that remained unaltered were the two red hourglass marks still visible on the front of each shoulder.

He panted and drooled and attempted to control his breathing and balance. Still clutching the box in his hands, he staggered forward several steps until he caught himself on the dresser and leaned exhausted against it. He lifted his gaze to the mirror before him and gasped at his own reflection. Instead of the handsome, blond braid that once rested on his shoulder, wisps of straggly, white hair now protruded from his scalp just above his ears and fell like cobwebs down upon the black vest. Instead of the youthful, attractive smile, dark, stained, and decaying teeth reflected back at him. His eyes, once blue and energetic, were now dark and vacant. His cheeks were hollow, and the leathery clothing he wore now hung heavily and loosely on his skeleton-like frame. Though there was a slight resemblance to the taller, younger man, the horrible transformation had spawned the haunting, dying being that now gazed back at him. He grimaced, and lifting a hand, he wiped the stream of moisture from his chin.

Despite his near-death appearance, the man's attention focused again on the box in his hands. Desperately he attempted to lift the lid. To his utter frustration, it was sealed to the wood beneath it. With the darkening, the box had become one impenetrable, solid mass. The man studied it, aware of the special magic behind its blackness and the distant being who had the power to conjure it. It were as if the old wooden relic was programmed to recognize the old man and fight against his efforts to exercise its remarkable powers. In frustration the crooked man turned and heaved the box. With a loud CRACK it rebounded off the wall above Cletis's bed, leaving a large indentation in the sheetrock. The box hit the floor and settled at the old man's feet, as if mocking his frustration.

He bent over, lifted the box, and again, studied the blackened relic. His face tightened in a wicked grin, and he turned back to the mirror and studied his reflection. Then, as if in deep concentration, he closed his eyes and pushed his head back toward the ceiling. With a gasp of pain, the man began the Changeling process anew, as if forcing his body to pulse, shift, and mold again into the personage who had first appeared within the conduit. Step by step, his bones, tendons, muscles and skin stretched and groaned, elongated and expanded, gradually reverting back into the form of the young and muscular man. When the supernatural transformation finally ended, when clothing, hair, and countenance were as they had been, he panted with exhaustion and rested against Cletis's bed.

Now satisfied with the reflection that stared back at him, he turned his gaze to the photo of Cletis's family that rested next to the mirror. He lifted the frame close to his face. His hollow eyes conveyed no expression, yet he stood as if pondering the three individuals pictured there.

The distant barking of a dog intrigued him, and he stepped to the window and peered out.

"Dogs are here . . . " he whispered, nodding his head.

Hearing a noise from below, he stepped away from the window.

"Cletis, are you up there?" came the call from downstairs.

With the frame and the box securely in his grasp, the gray energy field gradually materialized around him, enveloping him within the humming cylinder of energy. His body lifted from the floor, and suspended within the power of the conduit, he disappeared.

With his absence, the gray cloud faded into nothingness, and the room was left empty and quiet.

The sound of a thud on the upstairs floor had startled Garth, and he rose from the table, listening. But the incessant barking down the street still concerned him, and, again, he walked to the window and peered out. Seeing no cause for concern, he moved through the kitchen and the living room to the base of the steps below Cletis's room. Again he listened. Another odd sound from above puzzled him.

"Sounds like wind, but there's no wind blowing," Garth whispered.

Again the lights in the house dimmed and brightened, and abruptly the distant barking ended.

Guardedly Garth made his way up to Cletis's room and stepped inside. He eyed the bedroom curiously and scanned the floor for anything that might have fallen. Seeing nothing amiss, he crossed the hall and flipped on the light in the bathroom. Again nothing appeared out of the ordinary. Further down the hall, he opened the door to the study room and peered inside. All was in order.

"Hmmm," Garth frowned. His lips puckered as he turned and checked the hallway one last time. "That's funny. Maybe it was up on the roof." Turning off the lights in the bathroom, he made his way back down the stairs.

Cletis entered the back door, tossed his mitt on the washer, removed his shoes, and crossed the kitchen to where his father was seated. A simple meal of macaroni and cheese, canned pears, and milk was spread on the kitchen table. His dad was busy copying characters from the scroll onto another piece of paper. Cletis paused to check the clock above the window. It registered 8:35 p.m.

"Hey, buddy, what's up?"

"Nothin' much," responded Cletis, pulling up a chair. "We visited Mr. Howard today."

His dad looked up from his copying. "The homeless man we see downtown once in a while?"

"Yeah. Elston's family knows him a little bit. We took him some food."

Cletis purposely omitted all the details, feeling it safer not to talk specifically about another baseball card sale. The Robinson brothers were put to good use, and almost all the money was used to help Mr. Howard. Telling his dad only about the food seemed to be a wise thing to do, at the moment.

"Oh, yeah?" continued his father. "Why would you do that?"

"I dunno. To be nice, I guess. We had a question we wanted to ask him about baseball. Elston said he knows a lot because his son used to play for the high school team. So we asked him, and then he wouldn't shut up. He talked to us straight for about two hours."

"You were probably the first real company that man has had in months. Is he still behind the grocery store in that little shack by the tracks?"

"Yep."

"Well, that was good of you to do that."

Cletis looked down at the parchment. "What're ya doin'?"

"I've got an appointment with a professor at the university tomorrow afternoon. I'm takin' him a copy of these markings. See if he can make heads or tails of all this. I figure I'm not gonna take him the original, in case we need it for something later."

Cletis thought about that a moment, then picked up the bowl of macaroni and scraped a helping onto his plate.

"You may need to heat that up a bit. It's been there a while."

Cletis brought a forkful to his mouth and tested it. It was lukewarm but edible. He began eating but, out of the corner of his eye, watched his father work.

"I've been thinking about last night," his father stated. He turned to Cletis. "I'm sorry. I didn't mean to get so frustrated like I did. And I didn't mean to accuse you of doin' somethin' when I don't have all the details." He paused. "I'm just concerned for you. That's all. I go off to work. I leave you here each day. That's not right. I'm trying to fix that. . . . You see where I'm comin' from?"

Cletis nodded, happy that he could look his dad in the eyes. He didn't know if his dad was expecting a full-blown confession of how the red marks got on his shoulders, but for the moment, Cletis didn't have anything to tell him. He wished he did. He knew the stories of the bike and scooter and the cards were all beyond belief, so he had kept those details to himself. But now the marks on his shoulders were added to that list of strange events—and his dad *knew* about those.

"Yeah," Cletis answered, "I'm sorry too."

He left it at that. If his dad wanted more, Cletis couldn't read it in his face. Instead his dad smiled and then went back to copying.

"Just keep me posted as we try to figure things out, okay? And I'll do the same for you."

Cletis nodded as he chewed. "What d'ya think it all means?" asked Cletis as he watched his dad work.

"Haven't got the foggiest. But if I find out somethin' tomorrow, you're gonna be the first to know."

Comparing his copy to the original manuscript, a look of concern suddenly clouded his father's face.

"Clete, can you run up to your room and bring me the box? I want to make sure I'm gettin' this part right, and I'm not sure I'm seein' this the way it's supposed to be."

Cletis pushed back away from the table and headed through the living room. He bounded up the stairs two at a time, stepped into his room, closed the door behind him, and looked up at the shelf above his desk.

The box was gone!

I must have put it on the nightstand, he told himself as he turned and searched the room.

But the nightstand was empty except for the price guide. A wave of cold dread washed over him. Cletis dropped to his knees and looked under the bed. Nothing. He rose, crossed the room, and looked on, under and behind the dresser. Again nothing. He stood, eyes searching the room around him. He knew that Elston didn't take it. It wasn't with them when they left. They had had it on the bed, and then they had put it back up on the shelf. Cletis remembered that. He turned again to the dresser and shuffled through each drawer, opening and closing them in rapid, panicked succession. Inside his closet, he searched through the shoes and boxes on the floor and then scanned the shelf above his hanging clothes.

"Dad, did you move the box?!" Cletis shouted toward the door of his room

"No. Why?" responded his dad from the kitchen.

Eyes wide with concern, Cletis rescanned every corner of his bedroom. Still, the box was nowhere to be found. He raced out of the room, down the stairs, and back to the kitchen.

"The box is gone!" he called out, hurrying past his father. "It's not in my room!"

"I didn't take it anywhere," responded his dad.

Cletis grabbed his shoes and crammed his feet into them. "I'll be right back."

Immediately he flew through the back door and was gone into the dusk of the late summer evening. As the door slammed shut, his dad rose to follow him.

"Cletis, where are you going? Wait!"

Cletis ran across the open fields between his home and the baseball diamond, knowing he had to get to Abish's house.

What have I done! The box is gone! She's gonna kill me!

It was over a mile to the hill near the canal, but Cletis was determined not to break stride. Sprinting desperately, he made his way across the field behind the baseball diamond and continued down the trail toward the hill above Abish's house. She would know what to do if anything happened to the box. He imagined he heard his father's call from far behind him, but Cletis didn't look back. The whistle of the evening train suddenly roared its distant greeting as it entered the town and passed Main Street, drowning out every other sound.

When Cletis reached the hill above the old house, darkness had fallen over the forest that covered the slope between him and the canal. But now being familiar with the passage down the embankment, Cletis easily reached the bottom, jumped the water, and crossed the grassy flat toward Abish's back porch.

He panted as he eyed the ragged dwelling and pondered unanswered questions. He was still trying to figure out who she was. He knew there was something different about her.

She's like a grandma. . . . Unless she has me under some kind of spell. What if she does, and I don't know it? What if Dad's right, and she's just crazy out of her mind? What if I'm walking right into some strange trap?

He paused to catch his breath. The chimes on the porch sang softly in the light breeze, easing his anxious mind. He opened the screen door, crossed the darkened, box-laden porch, and knocked on the back door.

"Abish!" he called.

A hand touched his wrist. Cletis jumped in fear, not having seen the old lady who was seated to his right in the old cane-back chair.

"I'm here," whispered the craggy voice. "I'm just getting some fresh air and thinking for a moment. I heard the movement through the trees and across the canal, and I wondered if it was you. I'm glad to see that it is. What do you need, Cletis Dungarvan? You're troubled."

Still catching his breath, Cletis knelt in front of her chair. "The box is gone, Abish! It's gone. I've looked everywhere for it, and I can't find it!"

She nodded calmly, as if anticipating the news. "Where did you leave it last?"

"On the shelf by my bed. It was there this morning. I swear it was. That's where we put it!"

"Did anyone else know you had it?" she asked, the old Irish lilt evident in her voice.

"Elston and my dad. But Elston was with me all day. He didn't have it."

"Did your dad move it?"

"He said he didn't touch it. He didn't know it was gone."

Abish paused and looked out into the darkness of the hill behind her home. The water of the canal gurgled peacefully as it passed by. The chimes continued to tinkle overhead in the soft night breeze.

"We talked about *feelings* the other day. You remember?" She patted his hand.

Cletis nodded.

"You've probably sensed some of those sweet feelings lately as you have made wise choices in using what the box has provided you."

Cletis was amazed. *How did she know that? I haven't spoken to anyone about what I've done or what I've felt.*

She spoke softly, as if to herself—as if pondering a new discovery. "In that day comes the searching Traveler." She inhaled deeply and squeezed Cletis's hand. "So it begins, my young Cletis. So it begins. Let us see how we fare." She let his hand drop and she looked away into the woods. "The enemy and the battle may be great." Her head bowed heavily into the cradle of her hands. "What have I done? . . . What have I done?"

"I don't get what you're saying," Cletis said softly.

She looked back up at him. "There is a feeling that comes with good and a feeling that comes with evil. Cletis, you must recognize the difference between the two and where each of those feelings will lead you." She paused, as if allowing her words to sink in. "Thank you for telling me about the box. Go home now, young man. You're father is looking for you."

Though his questions had not been fully answered, Cletis stood and crossed to the door. The chimes rang again above him as he pushed open the screen, stepped out away from the porch, and made his way across to the canal.

At the top of the hill Cletis broke clear of the woods and headed for home. Still puzzled by his little meeting with Abish, Cletis pondered her words. She had told him not to worry about the box. Did that mean she knew where it was?

A feeling that comes with good and a feeling that comes with evil. Okay, I think I know what she's talkin' about. But how does she know what I've been feeling?

At that instant, in the distance, he heard his dad cry out.

"Cletis! Cletis!"

Cletis could sense the panic in his voice.

"I'm over here!" he called back, jogging toward the sound.

Suddenly an eerie, heavy sensation enveloped Cletis—a feeling so unnaturally strange that he froze in his tracks. He stood listening, wondering. Yet nothing was around him. At least nothing he could see. The repulsive sensation lingered and intensified—like a piercing, dark winter fog. Yet this was not like the darkness of a black night. This was something frightfully different and deeper. This was an enshrouding, binding force inside his body, inside his mind, inside his soul.

Someone was near. Someone was watching him. He could feel the presence. The horrific sensation was overpowering. Cletis had never been conscious of anything so ugly and chilling in his entire life—not in the scariest of movies, not during the heaviest of storms, not in the worst of haunting nightmares. Frozen in place and unable to shake free of the gloom that burdened him, his legs buckled beneath him.

"Dad!" he called weakly. "Over here!"

"Cletis! Are you okay? I'm coming! Keep yellin' to me, so I can know where you are!"

"This way . . . " Cletis whispered, fighting against the force that bound him. He dropped to his side, as if pinned against the solid earth.

"I don't want to lose you in the dark. Hang on, I'm coming!"

"Dad . . . " Cletis groaned, covering his head with his arms.

"Where are you?" his father called frantically. "I can't see you anymore!"

"Here . . . " Though he cried with all his might, his voice was weak, stifled by the gloom that cloaked him.

Then at last he heard footsteps, pounding the earth, coming toward him.

Let them be Dad's! Please! Cletis prayed. Though he could hear his father's saving footsteps close to him now, still the ugly coldness pierced his soul. This was fear and darkness and loneliness beyond anything he had ever experienced.

"Cletis!" his dad cried, finally spotting him on the ground.

As his dad came closer, the dark, heavy feeling began to lift—as if whatever or whoever caused it feared the presence of Garth Dungarvan. Yet Cletis was left weak and empty and terrified.

His father knelt down beside him and lifted him into a sitting position. "Clete, are you okay, buddy?"

His dad's cradling arms were never so welcome.

"What did you do?"

Fighting the tears, Cletis rolled in close to his father. "I'm all right," he whispered, his voice trembling.

"You're cold."

His father lifted him in strong arms, held him tightly to his chest, and began the long walk home.

High above Garth and Cletis, from within the conduit of the gray energy that held him afloat, the Traveler looked down on the pair as they crossed the field through the darkness.

The boy felt me. No one has ever felt my presence like that. And the man. There's something strange about him too.

He rubbed the muscles of his arm just below the red hourglass mark on the front of his left shoulder and studied the man and child a moment longer. Methodically he turned his attention to the hill the boy had just climbed. From his lofty vantage point, the old dwelling at the base of the slope was barely discernible despite the darkness of night. The conduit moved gradually toward the home, as if the being sensed the need to explore. Then in a breath the gray conduit vanished into the black of the nighttime sky.

CHAPTER 10

WHAT IS REAL?

Cletis sat shirtless at the breakfast table. He groggily rubbed his eyes as he watched his dad hustle around the kitchen. Usually Cletis slept in a bit longer, but this morning his father needed him up. Cletis tried to keep his eyes open as his dad gathered the copy of the scroll and placed it in his briefcase.

"That one stays here," stated his father, pointing to the original scroll still on the table. "Find a safe place to put it, could you?"

Cletis nodded sleepily and rested his head on his arms.

"How d'ya feel this morning? You look pretty worn out."

"Fine," answered Cletis.

It was another little lie. The darkness of last evening's invisible encounter had haunted him the entire night, and he hadn't slept well at all. But, for the present, he didn't want his dad to know about his fears.

He had quizzed Cletis last night regarding his visit to Abish's house. Cletis had told him that he had gone there to tell her the box was missing and that she had told him not to worry about it. When his dad had asked him why he was lying on the ground groaning, Cletis had told him that he had become sick and then, feeling dizzy, had tripped and fallen to the ground. Those were all the details Cletis had volunteered, but he could tell his dad didn't like the feel of it.

His father closed the briefcase and walked to the sink. "How about your shoulders? They givin' you any trouble?"

"They're fine, I think," Cletis answered.

"I think I'll call the doctor today and have him take a look at 'em."

"I'm not goin' to no doctor," spouted Cletis, instantly defiant.

"That's up to me. If I feel it needs to be done, then we'll do it. No balking about it." His dad tossed a vitamin into his mouth, along with a green herb capsule, and chased them down with a few swallows of juice. "Where you gonna be today, in case there are any problems?"

"Got some cleaning to do here, and then I'll be over at the diamond, I think."

His dad studied him. "Stay close to home. Food's in the fridge. If you need anything extra, head on down to the store and pick it up. The lawn's about due for a cut."

"Okay, I'll take care of things," Cletis answered, yawning through the words.

"Same orders as yesterday. Until I can figure some things out, you stay away from the old woman. You got it? No racin' over there to talk to her."

Cletis sat silently, as if thinking about his father's last command.

"Cletis? We on the same page here?"

"Yeah." Cletis nodded reluctantly.

"I need a commitment."

"Okay," answered Cletis, not wanting to be pressed into a promise.

His father sighed, walked over to him, wrapped an affectionate arm across his shoulders, and patted his bare back.

"You need me, you call me. Got it?"

Again Cletis nodded. His dad turned and walked to the back door. "See you this afternoon. Oh, one more thing," he added, spinning back to Cletis. "We still need to work on hitting to the opposite field?"

"Yep," responded Cletis, his eyes suddenly sparkling with the talk of baseball. "I'm still pullin' everything."

"Maybe we can get to it tonight when I'm home. Save me a few swings."

"Hey, Dad," continued Cletis as his dad turned the knob. "The wall above my bed is banged in. Like something smashed against it. There's a big dent in the sheetrock."

"Oh, yeah? I heard a noise up there yesterday afternoon, but when I went up to check it out, I didn't see anything out of the ordinary. I didn't even notice the wall."

"And you know what else I can't find?"

"What?"

"My picture of us and Mom. It was sittin' on my dresser where I always have it, but it's not there now. That's gone too."

Cletis watched his dad frown.

"That's really weird. Well, maybe they're both together somewhere in your room. Maybe Elston hid them from you when you weren't looking. I dunno."

"Hid our family picture?" asked Cletis doubtfully.

"Got me. I'll look at the wall this afternoon. I'm late now. I'm sure they'll both turn up somewhere. I doubt anyone's taken them. Why would anyone want our family picture?"

With that, his dad was gone, leaving Cletis to ponder the strange events of the past several days.

What will today bring? Cletis thought as he pushed away from the table and made his way to the stairs. *I know one thing for sure, I'm getting out of this house. I don't wanna be alone today.*

Johnny wound up and fired the ball to Klu, who squatted behind the plate. Cletis, who stood in the box, swung hard, connected, and drove the ball to left field. Pauly came under it and made a nice two-handed catch.

"Wait for it," called Johnny, looking in at Cletis. "Swing a little later. Then see if you can drive it up the middle or to the opposite field."

"Yeah," echoed Klu, pulling his mask off and stepping toward Cletis. "You're comin' around too early. Wait just a fraction of a second longer."

In frustration, Cletis eyed the big catcher. Klu was probably the strongest and toughest kid on the team. But despite the outward dirt, grime, sweat, and size, Klu was always quick to help the other boys learn the game of baseball. Like Johnny, he was a born instructor—able to discuss batting grips, base-running, how to place-hit—stuff that Cletis needed to know.

Klu squatted back into position. Standing on the mound, Johnny lifted the ball toward Cletis and then wound and fired. Again Cletis connected and drove a nice fly ball to left field. Pauly moved only two steps, came under it, and watched it drop into his glove.

"Man!" spouted Cletis through clenched teeth. He smacked the bat down with a thud on home plate. "I just can't do it!"

Klu threw off his mask again and walked up behind Cletis. "Let me show you."

"What good is that gonna do him, if he can't do it himself?" cackled Frank from third.

"Klu, I ain't never seen you hit it to the opposite field when you were supposed to," teased Rabbit from shortstop.

He ignored her, and as Cletis stepped back out of the way, Klu called out to Johnny, "Give me somethin' outside."

"Anybody can hit an outside pitch to right field," chimed Frank. "Give him somethin' inside or down the middle, and then see what he can do."

"Don't get your pants in a wad, Frank," called Johnny, kicking a rock off the mound. "One thing at a time."

Johnny wound and delivered. The pitch came in low and outside. Klu, though still dressed in catcher's gear, deftly thrashed a line drive between first and second. Elston, who was playing first, dove for the ball but came up empty. The ball bounced into deep right center, where Timmy finally chased it down, scooped it up, and tossed it back in.

"Nice hit, Klu," offered Johnny as he watched the throw from Timmy come toward him. "See, Cletis, that's the way to do it. Just wait, then it's all in the wrists."

Frank, rubbing in Elston's failed attempt, called out, "A good first baseman would've had that!"

Pauly joined in from shallow left. "Yeah, Elston, you've been lettin' all those past you lately. Come on! Get with it!"

Elston hung his head, and Cletis could see that their words were sharp. "I'm workin' on it," he answered. "At least I dove."

"Hey, back off," called Johnny, addressing the whole group. "Come on. He's on *our* team."

Klu handed the bat back to Cletis and walked back around the plate. "Wait on that outside pitch and then just lean on it. Boom!" He clapped his hand in his mitt and then picked up his mask and pulled it down over his head. "It'll go just where you want it to."

Johnny wound and fired. The pitch came right down the middle of the plate. Sorting through all the new information, Cletis tried to wait that fraction of a second longer before he swung the bat. He attacked the ball and connected solidly. But, despite his best efforts, the hit was just another fly ball—at least to left-center this time. Pauly chased to his left, came under it, and made a nice catch.

"Long fly balls, make for long outs," Rabbit declared from deep short, where she stood to take the throw from Pauly.

Dejected, Cletis threw his bat against the backstop and kicked the dirt with his shoe.

"Hey," called Johnny. "Calm down. It was left-center, not left. We'll work on it."

Rather than heading home for lunch, Cletis and Elston found themselves at the top of the hill overlooking Abish's house. Elston had fought the idea the whole way there, but Cletis had pulled him along, verbally and physically. On the way, Cletis had asked Elston about the box and the missing family picture. Elston assured him he hadn't touched either of them. Cletis knew he was telling the truth. Elston had been with him all that morning and afternoon.

"Didn't your dad say for you to stay away from here?" warned Elston.

"Yeah, he did."

"I don't know about this," moaned Elston, leaning forward over his handlebars. "It's been a lousy day so far already. I can't field and you can't hit. Why do we wanna make it worse?"

"Yeah, you're kinda right, but think of it this way," argued Cletis. "I'm not goin' against my dad. What I'm doin' is gonna answer his questions too. But somethin' bigger than you and me and him is happenin' here, and even my dad wants to get to the bottom of it. So now it's time *you* knew more about this whole thing."

"Why?"

"Because you know about the bike and scooter, and you know about the cards appearing in the box. You're into this almost as deep as me."

"You mean there's more stuff that I don't know about?"

Cletis remained silent, studying the woods in front of them.

"Great," sighed Elston, looking up into the sky. "Look, all this is crazy. So I'll tell ya what . . . I'll just keep my mouth shut about all this stuff, and I'll forget all about it and just get on my bike and head home."

"Elston, don't you wanna find out what's goin' on here?" Cletis pleaded, tugging on Elston's arm. "Why you and me got sucked up into all this? This is magic stuff! This is stuff nobody ever deals with in their entire life! You and me are different, I guess. And I wanna find out why."

"You're the one who got sucked up into it, not me. I just happen to be your friend, and maybe I should quit that."

"Elston, don't say that."

"Look, I just don't want to go back down there. I been to that place once before, and I peed my pants. Goin' back there just seems to be the stupidest thing I could ever do."

"No, it's not. Come on. She's not what you think she is. We'll just stay a few minutes, and then we'll go to my house and eat and do somethin' else. Then we'll be back to the diamond for afternoon practice."

Elston shook his head stubbornly. "This is just gonna get worse. I know it."

"And if it does," Cletis pleaded, "I need *you* with me."

Elston exhaled, eyed Cletis, and then peered down the hill toward the old woman's house.

They left their bikes and mitts in the long grass at the overlook. Elston reluctantly allowed himself to be pulled down the side of the hill, in and out around the trees, and down to the canal.

"What if we find out she *is* a witch," argued Elston, "and you just been tricked the whole time?"

"I don't know. Maybe you're right and maybe you're wrong," reasoned Cletis as they arrived at the edge of the canal. "But I just gotta get to the bottom of all this."

"I'm gonna be regrettin' this for the rest of my life."

"Look, I'll give you a clue—some advice," offered Cletis, ignoring Elston's last statement. "She's uglier than anything you've ever seen. But you just gotta look at her eyes. Study her eyes and forget the rest of her. That way she's not so scary. "

"Yeah, okay," responded Elston nervously. "That's what all witches want you to do. Look deep in their eyes. That's the way they cast their spells on you and get you in their powers." Elston shook his head. "I remember this canal. After I peed my pants on her porch that night, this water helped wash it all away. I'm glad it was here."

"You were *serious*? You really peed your pants tapin' the chimes?"

Elston nodded sheepishly. "That's between you and me, okay? But I can tell you that I ain't never been so scared in my life. And if I'm gonna be here with you, I expect you to keep this a secret too. Favor for favor, okay?"

"I promise," declared Cletis. "You keep my secrets, and I keep yours. Just between you and me. . . . And I'm glad you're here with me." Cletis paused a moment. "I was pretty darn scared that night too."

But last night was scarier than that by far, he thought, still wondering what that ordeal was all about.

"And then you came back here for more," added Elston. "That was brave."

"Maybe. Maybe not."

Cletis thought about Elston's words. Coming back to Abish's house had certainly proven to be the beginning of a weird adventure.

"Hey, look at that," said Cletis suddenly, pointing down into the water. "I've never noticed that before!"

"What?"

"See that? It's like a rock ledge over the water. That's probably three feet deep under there. I'll bet you could swim under that ledge and just lay there, and no one could even see you."

"Why would you want to do that?" questioned Elston.

"I dunno. Just to see if you could." Cletis eyed the rock formation with wonder. "May even be fish under there. And maybe you could even grab one of those reeds there, and hold it in your mouth just right, and lay there under the water and breathe through it."

At that moment, they heard her voice. "Elston Blanchard," was all she said.

Elston froze in place, head down, his eyes bulging with terror. Cletis could see him tense up, so he grabbed his arm to make sure he didn't run in the opposite direction. Elston slowly looked up from the water, until his eyes met the witch—the legendary hag of Greenberg Junction—standing on the other side of the canal.

How she got there, Cletis had no idea. They hadn't heard a thing. But she was standing there right in front of them, in all her hideous glory, staring Elston in the face.

"Well, is that your name?" she croaked, eyeing Elston.

He nodded slightly and swallowed hard. Cletis suddenly felt the weight of Elston's body against his shoulder.

"Elston Blanchard and Cletis Dungarvan, follow me."

With that command, she turned and walked toward the house. They watched as the short, hulking mass of flesh led the way before them.

"We're dead, aren't we Cletis," groaned Elston in a hushed voice.

"No, we're not. Trust me," whispered Cletis, in return.

Elston was still frozen in place, unable to move, when Cletis attempted to pull him forward over the canal.

"Come on. Move your legs. We gotta follow her."

He tugged on Elston's arm.

"You're outta your mind. I'm not doin' this."

"Elston, we'll be fine. I promise."

Elston's legs wouldn't allow him to jump, so he stumbled into the canal and staggered through the water, soaking his shoes, socks, and pants. Cletis managed to clear the canal with a jump, but still holding on to Elston, Cletis lost his balance and was pulled back into the water, drenching himself as well.

Barefoot, with their soggy pants rolled up just below their knees, they stood below the chimes on the back porch of the hag's house.

Silently the grotesque woman led the boys down the hallways of the creepy dwelling. As Cletis continued to hold Elston's arm, he could feel his friend shaking as he walked. Elston was seeing for the first time the cobwebs, the decaying ceiling, and the sagging wallpaper. He was hearing for the first time the groans and creaks that came from deep within the strange house. Elston moved slowly and stiffly—like he had casts on both legs.

There's that smell again, Cletis thought, remembering. *Vanilla? Man, what is it?*

Abish stopped in front of a door, pulled the long skeleton key from the pocket of her burlap dress, and inserted it into the hole below the old knob. Cletis could hear the mechanism inside the door click with the turning of the key. He remembered in exact detail what was inside this room, and he couldn't wait to see Elston's response when his friend discovered what was there. Abish turned the round, metal knob and pushed open the door. Stepping in, she reached up and flicked on the light.

"Elston, it's Christmas morning," whispered Cletis as he escorted his wide-eyed, confused friend into the baseball room.

Though Elston stepped in cautiously, within seconds his jaw dropped, and his arms relaxed at his side. When he finally shut his mouth, a gigantic smile graced his lips. Reverently he stepped toward the center of the room. His huge, brown eyes soaked it all up—the gloves, balls, bats, the cards, the photos, the autographs, the pennants.

Cletis stood back and watched him absorb it. Abish plopped down in the stuffed, leather chair near Elston and simply closed her eyes. Elston wandered the room as if in a trance, methodically studying all he saw. His comments and questions, almost word for word, echoed what Cletis had said during *his* first time in the room. But Elston paused in front of one particular display that Cletis must have overlooked on his first visit.

"Josh Gibson," breathed Elston. Again his jaw dropped.

"Nine hundred sixty-two home runs in a seventeen-year career," reported Abish from the seat in the middle of the room. Her voice was like a giant, human frog. "They say he was a mixture of Babe

Ruth, Jimmie Fox, and Johnny Bench. Rifle arm and quick on the bases. Great fielding catcher. Nothing got by him. Died at just thirty-seven years. A young man."

Elston turned and looked at her. Her ugliness was overpowering, but he remembered that Cletis had said to study her eyes and forget the rest.

"You know about Josh Gibson?" he asked, finally finding his voice. "He was my dad's all-time hero."

"I *knew* him. Not too well, but I knew him. He played for the Homestead Grays when I was acquainted with him, but I was ugly then too, so the players kept their distance. That broken bat you see there I bought from his teammate Buck Leonard after Josh passed away."

Elston looked up at the bat. "My dad taught me about Josh Gibson and Satchel Paige and Don Newcombe and Buck Leonard.... But you *knew* them?"

As he studied her, she smiled, winked, and then, as if reading Elston's thoughts, added, "And your dad has taught you about Jackie Robinson and Larry Doby and Roy Campanella too, hasn't he?"

Elston nodded.

"They're common names in your household, I would imagine." She took a deep breath through her wide nostrils. "Oh, my boys, so many years have come and gone."

With ease beyond her size and appearance, she lifted herself out of the chair and moved to the fireplace. "Come here, both of you. This is why you have come." She pointed to three cards on the mantel. "Come and look at these."

The boys drew near, and as they did, they noticed the cards: Hank Aaron, Frank Robinson, and Brooks Robinson. Beside the cards was a small pile of gray dust that appeared to be the remains of another card, though completely decomposed. Then it dawned on them....

"Hey, those are the cards we sold to—" Elston cut his sentence short and looked at Cletis.

"You're right. They are," responded Abish.

"*You* bought the cards from Mr. Sperry?" questioned Cletis.

She nodded and then pointed to each one of them, identifying the deeds that accompanied each specific sale.

"That one was groceries and cash for Mrs. Ketchum," she said pointing to the Aaron card. "You also used some of that money to buy a meal for Mr. Howard." She pointed to the Robinson cards—Frank and Brooks. "The money from that sale was used to provide food and clothing for Mr. Howard." She then pointed to the pile of gray dust. "That used to be a beautiful card of Mickey Mantle. You used that money to buy a bike and a scooter. They fell apart on you, didn't they?" She studied them as their eyes widened. "So did my Mantle card."

The boys were silent, wondering how the old lady could have known such things. Cletis pointed to the dust of the Mantle card. "That's when I came and talked to you—after that happened," spoke Cletis.

She nodded.

She talked to me about feelings then too, he remembered.

Cletis instantly thought of the dark, powerful feelings that overtook him last night, in the field at the top of the hill. He hoped he could find the chance to talk with her about that too—but not in front of Elston.

"How did you know all that about what we did, Abish?" asked Cletis.

Elston was suddenly dumbfounded. "*Abish*? Is that your name?" he asked.

Again she nodded.

"You never told me she had a name," Elston whispered, looking at Cletis.

With a smile, Abish returned to the chair in the middle of the room and sat down. "What is the greatest talent a baseball player could ever dream of possessing?" she asked, taking the conversation in another direction.

The boys paused in thought, wondering if she really wanted an answer or if she was just thinking out loud.

"Elston?" she asked. "What do you think? What would be most valuable to you?"

His earlier fears having left him, Elston stood comfortably in front of this woman he had once called a witch. "I guess to be able to catch anything anyone hits at me—so nothing gets by me. Cuz it's been a lousy spring at first base for me."

She smiled.

"How about you Cletis?"

"To be able to hit it where they're not. To be able to place-hit wherever I want to."

"Elston wants a Gold Glove, and Cletis wants a batting title," she concluded hoarsely. "What have you been doing to get there?"

"Well, we've been workin' at it, but we haven't been makin' a whole lot of progress," commented Cletis, discouraged by the thought of the morning's practice.

"Yeah, you can say that again," agreed Elston.

The boys eyed Abish, awaiting a follow-up comment. But nothing came. She just sat there looking straight ahead at the mantel. Cletis felt a drip of water run down the side of his leg and onto his foot. Elston's cuffs were dripping, too. Cletis smiled to himself. Luckily, what he was seeing was canal water this time—at least that's what he hoped it was. Their soggy pants were dripping on the tattered, rag-weave rug on which they stood. If it was of any concern to Abish, she didn't let on.

"What if I helped you?" she finally commented, still staring at the mantel.

The boys turned to each other. Cletis's eyebrows lifted. Elston squinted doubtfully.

"Cletis, loosen your grip on the bat," she began. "Don't squeeze it to death. Let your wrists do the work. Line up the knuckles on your hands so that the middle knuckles on the fingers of both hands form one continuous line." She lifted her hands, as if holding a bat, demonstrating what she meant. "That will help. It'll give you more wrist action. Sometimes you've got to slap at the ball, like Rod Carew or Wade Boggs. Give it a try."

Cletis eyed her, pondering. He too held his hands up, mimicking her demonstration and studying his fingers and knuckles. Before he could ask any question, she cocked her head and addressed Elston.

"Elston, you're not lacking speed, you're lacking in judgment. Anticipate the direction the ball will be hit by studying the pitch that's thrown, the stance of the batter, and how he swings the bat— whether he's late, early, or right on time. Use your body to block the ball, whether it's hit or thrown. It won't hurt you. You've got more padding than most. Then nothing gets by you. You see?"

The boys studied her. What she said made sense.

"Do I need to repeat all that, or can you remember it?"

Cletis nodded. "We can remember it."

Abish's eyes darted keenly back and forth from one boy to the other. "So what are you waiting here for? Get back out there and go to work! Change is coming. Always back to basics. See the ball, catch the ball. See the ball, hit the ball."

Still the boys stood frozen in thought. It didn't make sense to be coached by a wrinkled, hideous, old witch-woman. Yet what she said was right. And by the looks of things around them, this hag knew her baseball. Cletis could envision precisely what she suggested, and he imagined Elston was thinking the same. Cletis could feel it in his hands and arms and body—the grip of the bat, the timing of the swing, the anticipation of a hit or a throw.

"So go to work! Nothing will happen if you stand around in here," she barked playfully. "You know where the door is. You know where the field is."

Both boys studied her uncertainly and then turned and left the room and the house.

Cletis was thoughtfully silent as he mounted his bike and sped off across the field. Elston hurried to catch up. Despite the sun-lit sky, the breeze in his face, and the interesting moments with Abish, Cletis remembered the dark moments of last night's horrifying experience. As they approached the spot where it happened—where Cletis had felt the haunting presence, where the weight of the horror had forced him to the ground—he sped off the path and around the place, not wanting to be near it.

"What are you doin'?" Elston called as Cletis left the trail and the gap between their two bicycles widened. "Hey, wait up!"

Right there in that tall grass, Cletis thought as he pedaled by. *That's where I was. That's where I felt it, whatever it was. . . . Man, what woulda happened to me if Dad didn't find me?*

"You okay?" panted Elston as he caught up to Cletis. "What was that all about?"

"Nothin', I guess," Cletis answered. "Just wanted to ride a different way."

"You're crazy, man," frowned Elston. "There's a perfect path, and you wanna ride out in the sticks and weeds." Elston eyed him curiously. "There's stuff you ain't tellin' me, huh."

Cletis remained silent.

As the boys neared the diamond, their paths split. From the area behind center field, one trail headed off to the right and led directly into the back of Cletis's neighborhood, about a half-mile away. But Elston had to ride across the diamond, up the hill, past the school, through the downtown area, and south to Washington Street—almost a mile farther once they parted ways there in center field.

"See ya this afternoon," stated Cletis.

"Hold on a sec," called Elston as he stopped, hopped off his bike, and pulled the chain guard away from the chain. "Stupid bike . . . " he muttered under his breath.

"Know what?" continued Cletis, bringing his bike back around toward Elston. "We gotta keep all this stuff to ourselves, okay?" He watched as Elston pondered and nodded. "It just gets deeper and deeper, doesn't it?"

"First the cards, then the bikes, and now that baseball room," Elston commented, thinking of reasons to agree with Cletis. "And the old lady's talkin' baseball, too."

"Kinda weird, huh?"

"So what's gonna happen next?"

"I dunno," Cletis shrugged. He thought of the marks on his shoulders and of last night's frightening experience, but kept his mouth shut. He watched Elston hop back onto his bike. "Thanks for goin' over there with me."

Elston thought about that for a moment.

"You really got me into somethin' here, didn't ya?" Cletis didn't say anything. "You know, even though this is all kinda cool, it's kinda scary too."

"Yeah, I know," Cletis agreed.

Elston took a deep breath. "Okay, see you later."

He smiled awkwardly, and then pushing off, he pedaled away across the ball field. The chain guard on his bike began to squeak again as soon he passed the dugout bench.

The afternoon passed quickly. Cletis first busied himself with outdoor chores around the yard—trimming roses, mowing the lawn, and sweeping the driveway. He went inside only to eat and change clothes. He felt safer outside. When the work was done, he spent much of the time sitting on the boulder in the backyard, under the shade of the elm tree, practicing his grip on his baseball bat and taking practice swings. From the top of the boulder, he had a direct view of the fields behind his house, and he could see if anyone was on the diamond for practice. As he sat there, passing the afternoon minutes, his mind raced, trying to make order of the turmoil that surrounded him—Abish, the prophecy, the cards, the bikes, the marks on his shoulders, the feelings. And as much as he tried to push last night's experience far from his mind, the horror of those moments still sent a tidal wave of fear through his entire being. That was an event he didn't want to relive. At the same time, he wondered what it was and what power could possibly have had that kind of an influence over him. *And what if it comes again? Like during practice or on the way home or when I'm alone in bed?* And he still wondered about the box and the family picture. He had no idea what could have happened to them. *And the dent in the wall above my bed? How did that get there?*

That afternoon, at about fifteen minutes to 4:00, Cletis spotted Rabbit and Pauly crossing the field toward the diamond. Not wanting to be alone, he gathered his bat and mitt, hopped on his bike, and headed off to join them. Within minutes, Cletis arrived at the third base dugout. After leaning his bike against the backstop, he immediately picked up his bat and continued practicing what Abish advised. *Loosen the grip. Let the wrists do the work. Like Rod Carew or Wade Boggs. Slap the ball.*

Cletis's teammates arrived one by one, ready for afternoon play. Each jogged to their position and tossed balls back and forth among themselves, waiting for Johnny to arrive. He was generally the last one there, but he also brought the equipment bag with all the extra balls and bats and some of the catcher's gear. All that stuff was stored at Sperry's for safekeeping. So until Johnny arrived, practice didn't officially start.

Elston's screaming chain guard announced his arrival. Johnny was close behind, riding his black Huffy and carrying the equipment bag over one shoulder.

"Look what Mr. Sperry gave us!" Johnny announced, rolling the equipment bag off his shoulder and pulling out a new Louisville Slugger.

"Is that painted black," called Pauly, coming in from left field, "or is that what I think it is?"

"Yep," answered Klu, pulling his chest protector from the equipment bag and flipping it over his head. "It's aluminum."

"Aluminum?" retorted Rabbit, jogging in from short. "You don't play baseball with aluminum bats. That's crazy! That's not real baseball."

"It's the thing of the future," responded Johnny as he approached the field. "At least that's what Mr. Sperry thinks."

"I hear they're usin' them in Little Leagues all over the country," blurted Davey.

"The pros'll never use 'em," added Frank, still standing on third. "They say if you hit it right, it'll add about ten to fifteen feet to the distance. Can you think of the pros doin' that? Everyone'd be hittin' homers."

"It's supposed to sting your hands, though, more than a wood bat," commented Elston, walking in from first. "I hear the sporting goods stores are selling a lot more of those golf glove things for baseball players."

"They're called batting gloves," announced Pauly, in an I-know-more-than-you tone. "They're not golf gloves."

"Ahh, that's sissy stuff," called out Klu as he snapped the last buckle on his shin guard and walked out to home plate. "Only golfers wear that crap. You ain't never gonna see me wearin' golf gloves to play baseball in."

"What d'ya mean by *sissy*, round boy," warned Rabbit, tossing a dirt clod against Klu's shin guard.

"Hey, Mike Schmidt wears 'em," Davey spouted. "And so does Ricky Henderson."

"Dale Murphy doesn't," added Cletis.

"Well," concluded Johnny, "it's here if you wanna use it. If not, keep bringin' your wood bats. But I'm gonna give it a try today."

As he walked to the plate, everyone hurried to their positions in the field. Cletis dropped his bat, picked up his mitt, and sprinted toward center.

When everyone was set, Johnny lifted the aluminum bat onto his shoulder and tossed the baseball up in front of him. As it fell, he called out, "Bring it home." The ping of the ball against the metal sounded funny as a grounder was belted to Frank. Bending to his left, Frank vacuumed it up, turned, and fired it back to Klu.

From center, Cletis watched Elston with growing concern, wondering how he would fare when it came his turn to field. Rabbit caught the next hit cleanly and fired it home. Davey took the next one off his chest, but still fielded the ball nicely and threw it home.

Then Johnny turned and faced Elston. "Comin' at you, bud," he called out. "Let's see what you're made of. Line drive!"

"Okay, Elston, concentrate," Cletis whispered, as if coaching from center. "Just like Abish told you. Study the stance. See the hit. Watch it come off the bat. Take it off the body. Nothin' gets by you."

Johnny swung and connected. A rocket roared toward Elston, right down the line. Instinctively he dove to his left, caught the ball over the bag, rolled back onto his knees, and fired a strike to Klu right over the plate. The ball popped solidly into the pocket of the catcher's mitt.

No one moved.

Even Elston remained kneeling—as if in shock. His eyes widened, and he licked his lips and studied the infield. All stood like statues staring at him. He swallowed, brushed himself off, and then came to his feet. Still no one spoke. Not even Frank.

"I think that was luck," Elston called sheepishly to Johnny. "Give me another one."

"Okay," agreed Johnny as he took the ball from Klu. "Here comes another."

"Do it again, Elston!" Cletis shouted, slapping his mitt against his thigh. He watched Elston set himself defensively.

"Same basics," Cletis muttered, acting again as the center field coach. "Study his stance. See the hit. Watch it come off the bat. Guess where it's gonna go."

From his outfield view, it appeared to Cletis that Johnny purposely hit the ball so it would bounce right in front of Elston. Short-hops were almost impossible to catch, especially on this field, where the grass was splotchy at best and far too many clods and rocks still made themselves at home. The ball came fast and hard, landing about two feet in front of Elston and a little to the infield side of first base. Though Elston couldn't quite get his glove around it, he did manage to block it with his body. It bounced weakly back out in front of him. With a quick scoop, he bare-handed the ball, speedily touched the bag to his left, and then fired the ball home. Again everyone looked on in silent amazement.

"You okay? That get you in the neck?" Klu finally asked. He knew it was a tough catch. He had seen it hit Elston.

"No. In the chest," answered Elston, jumping in place as if to shake off the slight hurt. "I'm okay." Wide-eyed, he turned back to center field and stared out at Cletis.

"Way to play it!" shouted Cletis, a grin lifting the corners of his mouth.

"Way to block it, Elston," announced Davey at second. "That was sweet."

"Yeah, Elston," agreed Rabbit. "Two nice plays!"

"Thanks!" Elston's cheeks puckered as he blew through his lips. Around the infield Johnny continued the exercise—grounders and line drives, throws to first, throws to second, double play combinations—working the players around the horn. Elston bobbled the ball once on a tough grounder, and he couldn't catch up with a wild throw from Frank. But other than that, he was perfect. When Elston fielded throws from the outfielders, he was like a human magnet, catching everything in reach.

"Elston ain't never looked this good!" yelled Rabbit, fisting the pocket of her glove. "Let's see how far he can go. Give him about fifteen straight and see how he does!"

"You game for that?" asked Johnny, pulling the ball out of Klu's catcher's mitt.

"Yeah, let's go for it," answered Elston. "I'm feelin' good. See if I can keep it up."

The team gathered around first base. Elston took grounders, line drives, bad bouncers, pop-ups—everything Johnny could crack at him. Only twice did the ball find its way past him. This was new territory for Elston. Never before had he played with such confidence and skill. Four times he took grounders off his body, and in each of those times, he claimed it didn't hurt.

"Boy, get a load of Elston! A new man!" shouted Pauly.

"Maybe we'll move him to short," Johnny quipped teasingly, looking at Rabbit.

"He can't hold my dirty socks," she answered confidently, as if she owned shortstop.

"Don't get your pants in a wad, Roberta," added Frank officially. "There's no such thing as a left-handed shortstop anyway."

"So what's the trick, Elston? What's goin' on?" Rabbit asked suspiciously.

"Yeah, you've never played like this before," added Pauly.

"Timmy, Clete, Pauly," called Johnny, "get in here so you can hear this."

Elston swallowed hard, and as Timmy and the others trotted in, he tried to explain.

"I dunno. I just got some advice lately. Just tryin' to . . . see if it works." He eyed Cletis for a split second and then continued. "I'm tryin' to see where the ball's comin' off the bat. I'm trying to see Johnny's swing—like what's happenin' with his feet and his hands—and then I can kinda guess where the ball's goin'. And I'm tryin' to use my body to block it if I know I'm not gonna catch up to it."

Everyone silently pondered his answer.

Finally Johnny nodded and looked around at his teammates. "Way to go, man. That's the way to do it."

"And he's keepin' his glove down too" added Rabbit. "Did you notice that?"

"And you know what else?" Johnny questioned. "Each hit, he got more and more confident. Like he wanted it. Because nothin' was gonna get by him. That's when it gets fun! Right, Elston?"

"Yeah, I guess so," answered Elston with a smile of self-discovery.

Cletis, excited to see how *he* could apply Abish's direction, stepped away, picked up his bat, and while everyone was making a big, well-deserved, fuss over Elston, he began to take a few cuts, trying hard to keep his hands and wrists loose. He checked the alignment of his knuckles and experimented with the new feeling of the swing.

"We'll see if it lasts until tomorrow," teased Johnny, patting Elston on the back in congratulations. "Okay, everybody in the field. Any position you want. Let's take some pitches." He turned and saw Cletis already holding a bat. "Go ahead, Clete, you're up."

"Ready to shag some?" Pauly called to Timmy as they made their way into left field.

"Might as well get the whole team to stand in left," Timmy ribbed, laughing at his own joke. "That's the only place he hits 'em."

"Oooh, ouch," moaned Rabbit from the infield. "Did y'all hear that? Timmy Tim is trying to be funny."

Cletis smiled weakly at the jab as he stepped to the plate. "Yeah, I heard it too."

"Okay," called Johnny to the whole team. "Name of the game. Hit it where they ain't!"

Those words sound familiar, thought Cletis as Johnny wound up and tossed it home. CRACK! The ball bounded off Cletis's bat, and found its way right into Rabbit's glove at shortstop. She tossed it quickly to Elston at first, who fired it back to Johnny. The second pitch came in. CRACK! A fly ball arched into the afternoon sky and came down into Timmy's glove in shallow left-center.

"Nice catch, Timmy," shouted Elston from first as Timmy tossed the ball to Rabbit.

"Every once in a while he makes one," teased Frank.

Okay, thought Cletis, *everything's still goin' to the left side. Loosen the grip, align the knuckles, wait on the pitch, and slap it. Gotta put all those things together. See if I can go up the middle.*

The third pitch made its way homeward, and Cletis concentrated on each needed detail. He felt the bat loosely in his hands. His wrists were relaxed. The pitch came right down the middle, and he attacked it.

CRACK! The ball jumped off his bat, shot past Johnny, and found its way between short and second. Frank, playing second for the moment, dove for it but came up empty.

"That ball had eyes!" shouted Pauly from left.

"Hey, man," called Frank from behind second, "that was up the middle! Nice hit." Frank picked himself up and looked at the bottom of his shoes.

"Your shoes don't have no gription," shouted Davey from center, retrieving the ball and firing it back to the infield.

"I know," called Frank, taking the throw. "Dad said he's gonna get me some cleats soon as I sell the hog. It's gotta be three hundred pounds before I can sell it."

Pauly, who was good at pig noises, grunted in left.

Johnny wound up and fired another pitch. SMACK! Though Cletis pulled the ball toward left, it was a line drive over third base. Pauly tracked it down on two bounces and threw it in to second, where Frank took the throw and placed a make-believe tag on the invisible runner.

"Two for two," commented Johnny from the mound. "Do you think you can go to the opposite field?"

"I dunno. But I'm gonna try."

"It'll be a first," chided Klu behind him. "Put it right between Frank and Elston. Just wait on the pitch as long as you can."

Cletis closed his stance a bit, putting his front foot slightly closer to the plate. The pitch came in down the middle. Johnny dished up a beauty, and Cletis knew it. Caressing the bat in the palms of his hands, Cletis waited until the last possible moment. *Bat speed's gonna have to be fast and timing's gotta be right on*, he thought as he exploded into the pitch.

SMACK! The ball scooted past Johnny and shot between Frank and Elston—just where he wanted it to go. He watched with pride as it bounced and rolled into an empty right field.

"Man. Maybe I figured it out, Klu," Cletis announced quietly, yet happily.

"Looks like Cletis and Elston been eatin' their Wheaties together," spouted Klu, rising behind the plate.

Cletis's laugh was a bit on the giddy side as he considered what he had just done. *It's all in the hands, like Abish said*, he thought. *I'm feelin' it different.* He stepped back from the plate and took a look at his knuckles and their alignment. *There's* slappin' *the ball, and there's* drivin' *the ball. I think what I just did was* slappin'. He grinned at the thought as he looked back at Johnny on the mound. *See if I can do this again—maybe* drivin' *it this time.*

Johnny wound and called out, "Right center. Line drive."

As Cletis's stroke connected with the pitch, another perfectly placed knock leapt off his bat—this one sailing over Frank's head and into the right-center gap.

"Yes!! I did it! I did it!" shouted Cletis, jumping up and down in the batter's box. "You called it, and I shot it! Give me another one of those quick, before I forget the feel of this!"

Johnny smiled, reached into the bag at the side of the mound, and pulled out another ball. As he did, he called out, "Hey guys, who's in right field? I need those two balls out there."

Davey jogged over from center. "I got 'em."

Johnny faced Cletis again. "Okay, here comes another one, but this one's comin' inside. At least that's what I'm gonna try for. It'll be almost impossible to take it to the opposite field. Just put it in play."

Cletis adjusted his stance, moving his front foot back away from the plate. *This one's goin' right over third base*, Cletis told himself as the pitch flew toward him.

SLAP! The ball rocketed over third base and landed in shallow left field, just foul. Pauly rushed in from deep left, gathered it up, fired it in to Rabbit, and hustled back to his position.

"Nice thought," complimented Klu, pulling his mask off to check Cletis's bat. "A game of inches, it is," he spoke like a sportscaster. "Is that the same bat you've been using lately, cuz this one is sure workin' lots better than the last one."

"First base line," called Johnny from the mound. "See if you can go there. Past Elston."

Klu pulled his mask back on and squatted into position. Elston settled at first, ready for the pitch. Cletis readjusted his stance again and concentrated on the feel of the bat in his hands. *Wait and slap*, he told himself. *Let the wrists do the work. Like Wade Boggs. Like Rod Carew. Like Dale Murphy. Like Hank Aaron.*

Luckily the pitch was a bit outside—perfect for what he wanted. Cletis's timing was exact, and he punched a line drive precisely over the bag at first. Out of nowhere, Elston dove to his left and snagged the ball about a foot off the ground. He rolled, sprang to his feet, touched his bag for good measure, and fired a bullet back to Johnny.

Again silence.

"What the heck is happenin' around here?" called Rabbit from short, eyes wide in disbelief.

Klu spoke up, pulling his mask off his face. "It's what we call *base-ball magic*!"

Arriving at Dr. Canfield's office, Garth approached the grandmotherly secretary who sat at the receptionist's desk.

"He's got about five more minutes in class," she commented, peering up over glasses that rested low on her nose. "If he lets out early, he'll be here any minute."

Garth nodded and took a seat. He settled into the chair, lifted his briefcase onto his lap, opened it, and peeked inside. On top of all the other papers lay the copy of the scroll he brought from home.

About three long minutes passed when Dr. Canfield stepped into the receptionist's area—his arms filled with books and papers presumably from the class he had just taught. He spied Garth.

"You must be the gentleman who called. Please step into the office here."

He pushed open the door next to Garth's chair and entered the room. Garth obediently followed.

Dr. Vincent Canfield was a thin, short man in his mid-'50s with long, black hair pulled into a ponytail behind his head, and a salt-and-pepper beard that was near six inches in length. Flecks of dandruff snowed the shoulders of the brown, loose-fitting jacket he wore, and at the base of his wrinkled gray slacks, Canfield sported an old pair of black, high-top Converse sneakers. Thick-lensed glasses pressed heavily on the bridge of his nose, magnifying the man's eyes.

"Come in. Have a seat. Just leave the door open."

The office was occupied by three large bookcases, which housed hundreds of texts and documents. In the middle of the room, surrounded by the shelves, sat a brown, wooden desk covered with files, papers, memos, and envelopes. Three framed diplomas hung from the wall near the door.

"How can I help you?" Dr. Canfield asked, placing the stack of papers on the cluttered desk.

"I'm Garth Dungarvan," Garth stated, extending his hand toward the man.

Dr. Canfield took it. "Vincent Canfield. Pleased to meet you."

"I've got a copy of a document I'd like you to take a look at," Garth continued, pulling the manuscript from his briefcase. "Maybe you can help me. I copied it from the original. It came off the top of an old wooden box we used to have in our family."

Upon receiving the paper, Dr. Canfield's lips pursed tightly. He placed the copy on top of the papers and folders in front of him, and pulled a large, square, black-handled magnifying glass from a desk drawer. He held it over the paper, and while bouncing gently up and down on his toes, he studied the copy's ancient lines and characters. His beard rubbed against the paper as he examined the etchings.

"It's old Irish. Ancient Irish," he coughed excitedly. "Where did you say you got this?"

"I copied it off... uh... off an old box that has been in the family for... for, uh, some time now," Garth stammered.

Dr. Canfield mumbled a few indecipherable sounds without lifting himself away from the document.

"Do you know what it says?" asked Garth, rubbing his hand across his forehead and leaning down next to the man. "Can you read it?"

"This is amazing," Canfield responded, still bouncing on his toes. "This is fascinating. I've seen markings like this before but not with this kind of flair to them."

Finally, after a moment's thought, he turned to Garth excitedly.

"Even back in that ancient time, each document had its own style and feel to it, depending on who wrote it or copied it—its own personality, if you will. Whoever wrote this was an artist."

He hunched down over the writings again and began to voice sounds unfamiliar to Garth.

"Yes, the characters are clearly copied from the original. I would love to see *that*, if I could," he offered without lifting his eyes back to Garth. "Amazingly ordered and crisp. This lettering dates back to around 900 A.D. So we're looking at a form of writing that's close to a thousand years old. Yes, you have yourself quite a find here, Mr.—" He straightened, frowned, and put his fingers to his lips. "I'm sorry. What was your name again?"

"Dungarvan. Garth Dungarvan."

"Forgive me."

"That's fine."

"You must have a bit of Irish in you as well. Am I correct? *Dungarvan* is Irish."

"Yes, sir, that's right. My family lines go back to a place called Dungarvan on the southern coast."

"Yes, I know the place. The site of a few recent archeological digs. So that makes this manuscript all the more important to you?" Dr. Canfield inquired.

"Well, I'm not sure," Garth shrugged, pulling at the skin on his neck. "Just interested in knowing what the copy says."

"Yes, certainly," agreed the professor.

He turned to a bookshelf behind his chair and removed an old text. Carefully he laid it near the manuscript, licked his fingers, and pushed through its pages. Finally he came to a listing of sorts—a page that contained many of the same characters and marks Garth could see on his copy.

"Let's see here," Dr. Canfield continued, hunching over the book and the paper. "You may want to write all this down as I attempt to translate it. We'll see if any of this makes sense. But I think I can do this for you."

Garth fumbled through his briefcase for paper and pen. Upon finding both, he announced, "I'm ready."

"So am I. This is where the fun begins."

With the magnifying glass in hand, he began speaking a language unfamiliar to Garth, yet interspersed with bits of English.

"Let's see here . . . " the professor began. "This may not be precisely what it means, but we'll give it our best shot. Here goes. . . . *Called by what a person . . . wears on his feet . . .* This is a bit strange, isn't it. But that's what it says. . . . Yes . . . and I think it refers to a man. . . . *Called by that which he wears on his feet . . .* uh, let's see . . . this is something like, *he will rise from the mud, or water, or swamp . . .* with someone . . . so it would be like he will rise from the mud with . . . a woman. That's all a bit odd, isn't it?"

He looked up to Garth, smiled quizzically, then dropped his head and went back to work.

"Now the next phrase . . . hmmm . . . *powers or strength of the box will be understood, or known, or revealed . . .* Yes, that would be right. I think that would be *box*, not *square*." Dr. Canfield looked up again at

Garth. "Is this the box you were referring to, Mr. Dungarvan?"

"Could be. I really don't know."

"Do you still have the box?"

"Uhhh, no. Not anymore."

"Pity."

Clearing his throat, Dr. Canfield dropped down over the document, lifted the magnifying glass, and continued.

"*In that day, or time, one who moves, or travels, or comes and goes* . . . Let me think. How would we say that? . . . *In that time, a person who travels will come* . . . I think that's fairly close." He paused a moment. "Now this next part seems to refer to *an area or arena of battle* . . . a *battlefield*, I would say . . . " He searched the page of the opened text and then looked back to Garth's copy. "Yes, that's correct. *In the battlefield his weapons shall be* . . . *a staff? A club?* Yes. I would say *a club.*" He paused again, reading silently and mumbling occasionally. "Let's see here. Now it's referring to something sharp or pointed, it appears . . . like a *spike or a spear?* So *his weapons will be a club, a spike* . . . Hmmm . . . Now it talks about something round. *An orb? A sphere of sorts?* . . . Yes, I think that's right. . . . *An orb will be controlled by him*—whoever *him* is. The *orb* is a weapon, and *it will be controlled, or driven, by him.* That's what it seems to say."

Garth nodded and continued writing furiously, trying to record every word and idea Canfield communicated. Canfield began again, and line after line, Garth copied, trying to make logic of it all.

But if the old woman claims that this writing is prophetic, Garth pondered, *then I need to get to the bottom of this. At least I need to try to understand what it says. Please, heaven, let it all be an explainable, laughable bad dream.*

Line by line, the translation progressed, until the last phrase was before them. The professor, stroking his beard and checking the book next to him, finally spoke.

"Well, here's another strange one for you," he stated with a grin. "*Time is red upon his shoulders.*"

Despite the ease with which the words were spoken, the strange phrase exploded like a thunderbolt within Garth's reeling brain. He staggered back away from the desk as if struck in the face. Up to this point, the translated document had been pretty much a collection of absurd, nonsensical gibberish. But this last line screamed at him with frightening clarity. Finding the wall behind him, he leaned against it for support. Dr. Canfield looked up at Garth, studied him curiously for a moment, and then continued.

"Now, so that you know, that's not *r-e-a-d*, as in *reading*. According to this, it would be *r-e-d*, as in the color *red*. So this would mean something like a red marking would be seen upon the shoulders of the person to whom it refers. Strange, eh?"

After having made the comment, Canfield bowed back down over his work and, humming a single note, reviewed his findings.

"Yes. That's it," he nodded, agreeing with the translation. "I'm sure of it. *For time is red upon his shoulders.*"

Practice had gone nearly two-and-a-half hours when, toward the end and just for fun, the team started a game of work-up. Everyone took their turn batting and fielding (two people batting at a time, and the rest in the field), and everyone stayed in their same position until a batter got out. When the out was made, that batter went to right field, and everyone else on the field shifted forward one position, working their way up toward home again. When Cletis finally got to the plate, he hit safely time after time after time. Every turn he took at the plate, he was able to place his hit almost exactly where he wanted it to go—left field, right field, in the gaps, down the line. Sometimes he was a little off the mark, but even when he was, the fielder in the area couldn't come up with the ball. Of course, it was easier to hit safely when the defense lacked two fielders.

"You keep hittin' like that," Frank teased him, "and you're never gonna get any fielding practice!"

At the same time, Elston continued to play superb defense, fielding almost everything that came his way—diving, jumping, throwing off balance. It was *baseball magic* for everyone, and everyone was happy to see Elston's and Cletis's successes. To witness such improvement breathed new life into the little team. *Everyone* seemed to be playing better.

"Okay, everybody stop and come in here!" shouted Johnny from shortstop, stepping toward home. "Cletis. Explain this to us. We made Elston talk. Now it's your turn. What's goin' on?"

Cletis tapped the plate with the end of the bat, thinking about his answer. All the teammates gathered around home.

"A friend of my dad's told me not to grip the bat so tight," he began. "She said—"

"*She?*" called Rabbit from behind the plate, yanking the mask up away from her face and standing in closer to Cletis.

"Uhh, yeah," stammered Cletis, suddenly a bit nervous. "*She* was a *she*. And *she* knows a lot about baseball."

"Yes!" Rabbit whispered enthusiastically, pushing a fist into the air. "I'm not alone."

"She talked to me about changing my grip," continued Cletis, ". . . so I did—and letting my wrists do the work. I was holdin' the bat way too tight and tryin' to kill the ball. She said try lettin' the bat kind of rest in my hands. And, uh . . . I dunno . . . She said to try slappin' the ball—let the bat do the work. So . . . I'm just tryin' out some new stuff."

"Seems to be workin'!" spouted Pauly, inspecting Cletis's grip.

"And I've been practicin' changing my stance—closin' it a bit to try to go to the right side."

Johnny pondered a second, studying Cletis. "Okay, so here's the deal. We got a pitcher, a batter, and a first baseman. That's all we need right now. One more play, an' we'll call it a practice. Cletis and Elston, head to head. Rabbit, you pitch."

"All right," she said happily, pulling the catcher's gear over her head and unbuckling the shin protectors.

Johnny turned to Elston, who stood smiling at second base. "Elston, play first, okay? We're gonna have a face-off here." He paused a second. "Sorry to use hockey words on a baseball diamond."

Pauly laughed out loud and slapped his mitt. "Showdown time, first base line."

"We got Mr. Spray Hitter vs. Mr. Gold Glove," added Timmy.

"Here's the test, an' here comes more magic," puffed Frank as he jogged to the mound.

Rabbit grabbed a ball and her regular glove and marched out to the hill. The rest of the boys gathered around the backside of the mound near Frank. Elston jogged over from second and dug in at first base. As he did, Cletis readied himself at the plate, closing his stance, stepping a bit away from the plate, and feeling the bat loose in his hands.

"You both set?" Rabbit called out.

Elston and Cletis nodded, eyeing each other like two western gunslingers ready to draw their pistols.

"Fat pitch comin' in, Clete," she called out, spitting on the dirt in front of the mound. "See what you can do with it!"

"You throw like a girl," teased Frank as he watched her study the plate.

"I *am* a girl," she stated flatly, studying her target. "Or maybe you didn't know that."

"Actually, I did know that," he answered. "Uh . . . I . . . uh . . . "

Turning a slight shade of pink, he decided to shut his mouth. The boys chuckled at the give-and-take, watching Rabbit's graceful movements as she wound up and aimed for home.

"For the first time in your life, Frank, you shut your trap when you should have," she huffed as she released the pitch.

The throw came in, right down the middle and much faster than Cletis expected, coming from Rabbit.

Close the stance a bit and keep the hands loose, he thought. *Let the wrists do the work. Slap it up the first base line. Elston's playing too far away from the bag. He'll never catch up to it if I can put it straight up the line.*

Cletis swung and connected! The ball slapped sharply off his bat and bolted straight up the first base line, bouncing just in front of the bag. Instantly Elston reacted. Lunging to his left, he swung his glove hand across his body in order to make the catch. Back-handing the one-bouncer just behind the bag, Elston landed with a thud on his round stomach. He lifted his mitt high, as if for all to see the prize, and then dropped his glove to the bag and tapped the base twice. It all happened so fast that Cletis was only three steps up the line by the time the play was completed.

The teammates roared their approval with laughter and cheers and high-fives. Cletis eyed his bat and then looked up the first base line at Elston. In return, Elston sat up, looked at the ball in his mitt and stared back down the line at Cletis.

"The baseball magic has just begun!" shouted Johnny, rushing over to first base. Happily he slapped Elston on the back and patted the top of his hat.

For a moment Cletis forgot about the fears that had so recently enveloped his life. Right now the sky was blue and the breeze was cool. Right now the birds were chirping an evening song. Right now he was where he was supposed to be—on the ball diamond surrounded by friends. It was springtime. It was baseball season. All was well and just the way it was supposed to be.

At least for the moment.

After the end of a remarkable, magical practice, Cletis and Elston rode their bikes to the park on Main Street, and picking a patch of green grass in the very center of the grounds, they laid down their bikes and stretched out on the cool carpet of lawn. Mitts under their heads served as pillows as they studied the clouds of the evening that drifted angelically across the heavens above them.

"Man, Elston," started Cletis, "I could hit the ball anywhere! It's like I could guide it. It was like my mind and my hands were . . . I don't know. . . ."

"Yeah, an' I could catch almost anything that came at me," added Elston, excitedly. "It was like I could tell my body which way to go, and it would do it. But, at the same time, it was just like Abish said— study the batter and the stance, and watch the pitcher and the ball."

"Yeah, and you were divin' and jumpin' and rollin' on the ground.

And you were quick too," laughed Cletis, sitting up and slapping Elston's leg. "You've never been *quick* before."

"An' I ain't never seen anyone hit the ball down the line like you did! Especially goin' to the opposite field! That was so cool."

"What's happened to us?" Cletis questioned, pulling up a blade of grass and putting it in the corner of his mouth.

"You think all our practice is finally payin' off?" asked Elston, putting his hands behind his head.

"I dunno. Could be that. Or you thinkin' that it was partly because of what Abish said to us?"

Elston thought a moment. "I don't know."

"She said we had it in us already," Cletis reasoned.

"Yeah, but what we did was . . . uhh, it was like we were doin' things we only *dreamed* of doin' before."

"Ahh, I think it's just practice," Cletis answered as he chewed the blade of grass. "Has to be."

Elston rolled to his side and braced himself up on his elbow. "Man, I dunno, Clete. There's strange, weird stuff goin' on that we can't explain." Elston's eyes widened with the thought, and he sat up quickly. "Cletis, she *just could* be doin' things with witchcraft. . . . That's gotta be it. Cuz you an' me, we don't play like that. We've never done the stuff we were doin' today!"

"Yeah, but maybe we could," Cletis suggested. "But she's not a witch, Elston. I know that."

"Then we just practiced, an' all of a sudden we're playin' like we did out there? That don't make sense to me."

"Well, she *did* give us that advice there in that baseball room, and we *did* try to practice it out there. And, like she said, maybe we had it in us already, and we just had to discover it."

"I dunno. Maybe."

Elston lay back down and put his hands behind his head again. Cletis eyed him, as if on the verge of asking a question, but then turned away.

"What?" Elston asked. "What's the matter? You were lookin' at me weird."

"Nothin'."

"What d'ya mean *nothin'*. You look at me like that, like you're gonna explode, and then you say *nothin'*?"

"Well . . . " Cletis took a deep breath and exhaled slowly. "Can you keep a secret?"

Elston sat up. He saw the serious look on Cletis's face and wondered what else could be happenin' that he didn't already know about.

"Yeah. That's what I been doin' already, isn't it?"

"Well, this is kinda weird, but I gotta show you something."

Cletis looked around him. The park was empty. A few cars rolled past on Main and Jefferson, but he and Elston were alone. Cletis pulled his hat off and set it beside him. Then, with both hands, he yanked his shirt up over his head, exposing the red, hourglass marks he now wore on the front of each shoulder. Elston studied him curiously and then spotted the marks. His eyes widened, and he moved in closer to see the red shapes.

"You got tattoos?"

"No. They're not tattoos."

"Then what are they?"

"I dunno. But they sure hurt when they came."

"They just *came*?"

"Yeah, all of a sudden I got this real bad pain, and I looked and there they were."

Elston thought about that.

"That's weird. So what are they?"

"I don't know."

"Do they still hurt?"

"No. I don't even know they're there."

Elston's gaze shifted thoughtfully from Cletis's face, to his shoulders, and then to Mr. Pepitoni's bike shop across the street.

"Cletis, maybe Abish *is* a witch. Maybe she *is* doin' all this stuff to us. Maybe we just better stay away from her."

"Abish doesn't have anything to do with these marks. At least, I don't think so."

"Hey, you think about it, Clete. All this weird stuff has been goin' on since you went to her house last week on that initiation night. Think about it. The box, the cards we sold, the bikes we bought . . . You and me and Abish are the only ones who know exactly what happened to those bikes. They turned to powder, Clete! How'd that happen? And then there was that guy out in the field who was there one second and then he was gone. Remember? All that's enough to send us both to the loony farm. And that woman is the one who was buyin' the cards from Mr. Sperry. We saw 'em there at her house! She knew exactly what happened. How'd she do that? You answer me that. How'd she know all that stuff?" Elston paused a moment. "You followin' me, man? And now look what's happenin'. You're showin' me these marks on the front of your shoulders, and on top of that, we're magically changed into all-stars!"

Cletis pondered a moment.

"But look at all the good stuff that's happenin' too," Cletis countered. "Like the Ketchums and Mr. Howard. A witch doesn't do good stuff like that."

"Only if she's tryin' to trick ya, she does," stated Elston.

Cletis considered his friend's words, knowing that Elston was aware of only a *part* of it. Elston didn't know about the supposed prophecy. Elston didn't know about the scroll that came out of the box. Elston didn't know about the dark, evil feelings that had just about crushed Cletis in the field last night. Suddenly Cletis felt the heavy burden of all that was happening in his life lately. The joys of the afternoon's baseball practice vanished in this confusing conversation. The park and the community around them were peaceful, but inside, Cletis's gut was being tied in a knot.

All I want to do is play baseball and have friends and live a regular life, he thought. *And I want to sleep in my bed tonight without being afraid. And I want to know who Abish is. I wanna know what these magical, scary things that are happenin' in my life are all about.*

He took a quick breath and studied the grass beneath him and the trees that bordered the park. Off toward the school, a young mother pushed a stroller down the sidewalk.

"I know you keep sayin' she's not a witch," Elston continued, interrupting Cletis's flow of thought, "but there are some weird, creepy things goin' on that you can't just brush under the rug."

"You believe in that stuff, Elston? Witchcraft stuff and evil magic and whatever?"

Elston looked away, not knowing what to say.

"I didn't," he whispered. "Well ... you know what I mean."

Cletis pulled his shirt back on over his head, picked up his Tigers hat, and held it in his hands.

"You're right," admitted Cletis. "There are some strange things goin' on."

The boys sat in silence.

"I think I'd better go home," announced Cletis gravely, shoving his arms through the sleeves of his shirt and pulling it down into place. He lifted his hat and pushed it snugly over his strawberry blond hair.

"Me too," agreed Elston.

Both boys grabbed their mitts and rose to their feet. Quietly they lifted their bikes and pointed them in opposite directions.

Leaving the university, Garth decided to take his translation straight to the old woman. He had no way of knowing the mental or physical stability of this odd lady, but he wanted to see her face to face and try to get to the bottom of this strange prophecy issue. After all, it was a father's duty to protect his son. And if Cletis was ignorant to the dangers connected to this unusual woman, it was Garth's responsibility to recognize them and steer his son clear of any potential peril.

Nearing Greenberg Junction, Garth drove the old Chevy Impala over the wooden bridge that spanned the channel north of town and peered off to his left in an effort to see the old lady's property. *She's gotta be right in there somewhere,* he thought, *because there's the hill that leads up to the field where I found Cletis last night.*

Garth pondered, reliving those moments of searching for his son in the dark. He remembered how frightened and weak Cletis had been when he found him—how like a tiny child he was, clinging to Garth as he lifted him and trembling the entire time he was carried. They had covered a good half-mile before Cletis asked if he could walk on his own. Though Cletis was feeble and weakly hiked the remaining distance, he held tightly to his father's hand.

Cletis hasn't held my hand like that since he was about eight years old, Garth thought. *Something strange . . . something frightening, must have happened to him. But he said he was just dizzy.*

Garth finally spotted what he thought to be the road that led to the old woman's house and made a quick left off the pavement of the state route. The old street sign, which was bent, rusted, and plagued with bullet holes, introduced Garth to a dirt lane lined with elms, maples, and an occasional pine. The evening sun offered little illumination to the path ahead, and Garth turned his lights on to see more clearly.

"Okay, the canal is off to my right," he said out loud, peering through the trees. "And it makes its way through the trees over there, by the side of the hill." He could still see the incline of the hill when a clearing in the woods permitted it.

And above the hill is the field that leads off to the ball diamond. Yeah . . . Okay, this has got to be right.

Finally the road came to an end in front of an old home set far back within the overgrowth of the forest. He stopped the Impala and turned off the motor. He took a deep breath, gathered the copy of the manuscript and the written translation from Dr. Canfield, opened the door, and stepped out into the freshness of the forest's evening air.

By the edge of the road there stood an old, weather-beaten wooden mailbox. It was choked by a tangle of vines and spider webs, and Garth concluded that any postal workers who ventured to insert mail into *that* container took their lives in their hands. Beside the old box, Garth spotted a footpath of gray stones, which bent its way through the undergrowth and led toward the house. Through the stand of trees that surrounded the place, he could faintly hear the soothing murmur of the nearby canal. Despite the natural beauty of the forest around him, Garth was astonished by the cluttered, ramshackle appearance of the home that finally came into view. There was no lawn around the house—no manicured shrubbery, no potted plants, no flowers, no garden—just wild woods and shrubs.

The colorless home was probably close to seventy years old, Garth imagined, and he doubted it had been varnished, stained, or painted since that first coat. The wooden shingles that covered the aged roof were moss-covered and crooked. The windows were unbroken but dirty and dust-covered to the point of being opaque—he could hardly see through them. Every inch of the old place seemed covered by cobwebs, bugs, and decay.

Garth's natural inclination was one of sympathy and concern for the woman. He remembered *his* mother's old age and her inability to do the little things so easily accomplished in her youth—the simple sweeping or weeding or painting. He remembered the pain of Anna's suffering and her helplessness in that final month. A lot of chores didn't get done as the family faced the higher priority of comforting a wife and mother prior to her death. Garth had no idea of the age or physical condition of the woman who lived in this hovel. Perhaps she was completely incapable of caring for the exterior of the home—or the interior, for that matter.

He approached the front door and knocked.

Maybe she's crippled or blind or in pain.

The house was dark, yet Garth heard noise from within—a heavy shuffling that approached the entry. He watched as the latch lowered and the door creaked opened.

Then he saw her.

She stood before him, framed in the arch of the entrance. She was the most hideous woman Garth had ever laid eyes on.

No wonder Cletis screamed when he first saw her, he thought.

He studied her, trying hard not to allow his facial expressions to reveal his mind. Yet, as a ray of last sunlight broke through the branches and softly lit portions of the porch where she stood, Garth noticed the clarity of her green eyes—eyes that appeared to be looking out from under several heavy layers of Hollywood special-effects make-up—*knowing* eyes, comprehending eyes, compassionate eyes.

She studied him closely, looking up into his face and examining him. Then she smiled, revealing the saw-bladed, deformed teeth that inhabited her mouth. Garth involuntarily stepped back. A sudden, sweet smell wafted from the open door—honeysuckle or vanilla—he couldn't tell which.

"Welcome, Garth Dungarvan," she spoke in harsh, raspy tones. "I knew you'd come. Please enter and follow me." She turned and shuffled back into a room close to the front door.

She knows my name, but we've never met, pondered Garth as he stepped into the house.

The woman sat down in a cane-back chair that groaned disapprovingly under its burden. She pointed to the tattered, gray couch next to her.

"Please sit down. Will you?"

"No."

Fighting his instincts to be a gentleman, Garth chose instead to stand. He swallowed and was about to begin his questioning when the woman spoke up.

"I hear your son is quite the ballplayer," she groaned hoarsely. "But more importantly, he is a gentleman. You've raised him well."

Not allowing himself to be derailed from the purpose of his visit, Garth assumed the role of the protective father and, lifting the papers toward her, stepped forward.

"Look, I'll get right to the point," he announced. Turning and situating the papers to reflect the single source of light in the room, he began to read parts of Dr. Canfield's translation. "*'Called by what he wears on his feet, he rises from the wet earth. The powers of the box are revealed. The box is delivered to him. . . . The orb is driven at his command. When the heart of the finder fails. . . . In the freezing of time a choice shall be made. . . . Time is red upon his shoulders. . . . '*" He lowered the paper and faced her again. "What is this trash?!"

Abish sighed calmly. "You have every right to be concerned. Let me explain. The words were written centuries ago by a wise man who had the gift of prophecy. As I understand it, when it comes to pass, only you, I, and two other individuals will feel its immediate impact. Your son is one of those individuals."

Garth was amazed by several factors: first, that she spoke to him as if they were long-time acquaintances; second, that she spoke intelligently and articulately, despite her appearance; third, that she understood the translation of the copy he had taken to Dr. Canfield; and fourth, that she had the audacity to speak of Cletis as if she had some pre-existing connection to him that demanded his involvement in her bizarre scheme.

"Look, I don't have time for this nonsense," Garth continued protectively. "I don't know who you are or what kind of demented state you're in, but you don't go bringing a child into this and think I'm not gonna sit up and take notice—especially *my* child! My son! Cletis and I will not be involved in your demonic little games. Is that understood?! You leave us alone! And you especially leave *him* alone! If you don't, I'll take action against you! You got it! I don't want you near him!"

With that outburst behind him, Garth turned to exit the room.

"Garth Alan Dungarvan," she stated, authoritatively—as authoritative as her voice could sound in its present condition.

Upon hearing his full name, he turned back to her.

"Your father, Alan, was raised in Detroit. A Tigers fan, but too poor to take his family to the games—maybe one or two a summer was all you saw. His father, Angus, grew up in New York, watching the likes of DiMaggio and Gehrig. His father, Arthur, your great-grandfather, worked the docks and was killed when a barrel fell on him and crushed him. His father, Gale Dungarvan, left Ireland in 1870 but drowned off the shores of Maine while his family watched helplessly from a lifeboat. When the Yankees—"

"What is all this about?" Garth interrupted. "Why are you tellin' me all this? What do you want?"

"When the Yankees came to play ball in Detroit," she continued, heedless of his questions, "you used to plead with your father to take you to the stadium. You had saved your money. Others would watch the likes of Mantle and Maris, but you were infatuated with a third baseman named Cletis Boyer. He was a hero to you. Quick, soft hands. Good on his feet. Accurate arm. I watched you. When the little boy, Garth, fell down the stairs and over the railing—" She paused, allowing her words to sink in.

Garth's eyes widened with the memory. It was still vivid in his mind. He had come close to being killed that day. The Tigers were playing the Yankees. Norm Cash was batting. Garth was carrying drinks down the stairs in the upper deck of Tiger stadium when he tripped by the railing near his seat. He was on his way over the edge and would've fallen to his death, but someone grabbed his legs from behind and held him as he teetered on the top of the rail. He was pulled back to safety but was so shaken by the incident that he cried for nearly an hour. His dad held him for three straight innings and told him later that an old lady was there at the right moment and had caught his legs as he was going over. Garth had never seen the lady.

"I was there," she stated with calm assurance. "I was there, Garth Dungarvan." She paused briefly, eyeing him constantly. "Finally the child came that you and Anna thought you could never bear, and though you named him Thomas, after Anna's father, you called him Cletis, after your favorite third baseman. He was your firstborn son, and your sweet wife—"

"Stop it!" Garth spoke abruptly. "Stop all this! This is crazy!"

He paused, eyeing the old hag. He studied her anxiously, wondering who she was and how she had all this information about him and his family.

"I don't know what you want, and I don't know what you're thinking or doing, but you'd better know that I'll have the cops all over you if anything happens to my boy! Get that through your head!" He eyed her angrily. "And just so you know, you're wrong, lady! You're wrong. You missed a fact there!" he added sarcastically. "Better get things straight! He was *not* our firstborn!"

He watched her carefully, noting that she too was studying him, her penetrating green eyes locked on his. Garth and Abish were like two prizefighters, circling the ring, sizing each other up. But he could see in her eyes that her mind was working furiously. Still she remained seated, silently considering him.

"Didn't quite get your homework done there, did you? All the facts not quite in order." He lifted his hand and pointed a finger directly into her face. "And now you're tellin' him about a strange prophecy? You're outta your mind! I don't know who you are or what you're trying to play here, but if you come between me and my boy—" Garth paused, breathing heavily. Nervously he licked his lips. "You stay away from me and my son and my family, you understand me?"

Abish sat dumbfounded and quiet.

"You're insane," was Garth's final statement.

He turned and made his way to the front entry. The heavy door creaked open and then slammed shut with his exit.

Chapter 11

The Traveler

After all he had experienced lately, the last thing Cletis wanted was to be home alone. Still a bit edgy from his conversation with Elston, Cletis had taken a walk around the neighborhood and then had spent about fifteen minutes sitting on the rock in the backyard, looking across the fields, just thinking about things. Finally he had decided it was time to be a man, face up to his worries, and go inside.

He entered his home and immediately called out for his father, knowing there would be no response. He had seen that the Impala was gone. For his own security, he turned on every light in the house and locked all the doors. When he found no note in the kitchen in the usual spot by the toaster, he assumed his dad had stayed late at work. Finally he checked the phone messages and discovered that his father *had* called . . .

"I'll be late, Clete. I've got an errand I need to run after my trip to the university. Get something to eat. Love you."

It was a comfort to hear his voice, even if it was only a recording. He played it twice.

"University?" Cletis questioned. "That's right. He said he was going there."

Nervously he roamed the kitchen, gathering two peanut butter cookies, a granola bar, and a banana. In an effort to calm himself, he turned on the kitchen TV that sat on the counter next to the table. Turning the channels, he tuned in a Tigers game—more for the companionship and noise than for anything else. He pulled some milk from the fridge, poured himself a glass, and sat down. Desperately alone, he dipped and chewed and drank.

Then a noise . . . Was it a thump?

He turned down the volume on the game and listened intently. All was quiet.

"Dad?" he called out weakly. "Is that you?"

No response came. He sat for a moment just listening. Then, courageously, he slid his chair back, rose from the table, and stepped into the front room. From there he had a good view of the entryway by the front door, the stairway leading up to his bedroom, and the hallway outside his father's room. From what he saw, nothing seemed out of order.

"Dad," he called out again, "you home?"

Again there was no response. He waited. The house seemed peaceful.

As he stepped back into the kitchen, he caught a whiff of his own sour shirt. Remembering that he hadn't cleaned up or washed since practice, he decided that, regardless of his concerns about being alone at home, he had to get out of his smelly clothes. Taking a bite of banana and downing another swallow of milk, he hurried out of the kitchen and up the stairs. Despite his efforts to stay calm, he still found himself longing to be back downstairs, close to an exit.

In his room, he pulled off the old, sweaty shirt and tossed it into the hamper in the corner. He paused in front of the mirror and checked the marks on his shoulders. He still had no idea why they were there or how they came or what they meant. He reached up and touched both. As he did, a light, tingling sensation suddenly overcame him. Frightened, he dropped his hands away from the marks. Breathing heavily, he studied his reflection in the mirror. *What was that all about?* Curiously he lifted his hands again and touched the marks. Again the same tingling feeling flowed through him. He dropped his hands to his sides.

Get a shirt on and get downstairs. You've got enough to worry about already.

He took a deep breath and exhaled slowly. Opening the drawer in front of him, he pulled out a clean shirt and threw it over his head.

Though he knew he still needed a shower, he pushed his arms through the short sleeves and tugged it down over him. This would have to do for now. He turned and looked up at the shelf above his desk where the box once rested. It was still gone. He looked back at the empty spot on his dresser where the family picture had been. Still gone. He thought of his mom.

He was turning to the door when it came. He sensed the heaviness—the cold, horrifying emptiness. The ugly, dark sensations that shrouded him last night in the field swiftly encased him again. He felt his stomach knot and his knees buckle. Bracing himself against the chest of drawers behind him, he watched and waited. Something was happening in his room. Facing his bed and desk, he fought to keep his balance. Suddenly a grayish fog appeared in front of his bedroom door. The whirling vapor materialized into a column of energy—a conduit of sorts. Within the conduit—within this mass of swirling, tiny particles—the image of a man appeared.

The darkness and coldness that pressed upon Cletis was suddenly intensified. Overwhelmed by the force, Cletis fell to his knees in front of the dresser. Painfully he lifted his gaze and studied the figure, watching the features of the personage gradually take shape. Finally the conduit disappeared, and the man who now stood above him floated to the floor. Cletis fought the heavy gloom that penetrated him and studied the figure that now stood only a few feet away. Whoever he was, he stared threateningly down at Cletis. In one hand he held a much darker wooden box. In his other hand he held the framed picture of Cletis's family.

He's the one who took them? Why? What would he want with the box and a picture of my family?

The man looked down, and as he stepped even closer, he continued to study Cletis. He was tall with broad shoulders and a muscular frame. He wore a dark, leathery material that Cletis had never seen before. His pants were made of a similar substance, and a white, braided cord tightened around his lean waist. He wore boots made of rough, dark leather, which covered his lower legs up to his knees. His black pants were tucked down into them. A long, blond braid hung over one shoulder—the hair fastened together at the end by a leather tie.

The being leaned down, and as he did, Cletis noticed something that took his breath away. His sleeveless, black vest revealed the same red, hourglass marks that Cletis now wore upon the front of *his* shoulders. They were the exact same marks—the same shape, the same color, and in the same location.

"Were you the keeper of this box?" the man asked in a deep, threatening voice.

Cletis remained silent in fear. He looked into the man's eyes. They were almost completely black—like two giant pupils with no color surrounding them.

"The old woman gave it to you, didn't she?" he continued. "Why? Where did she get it?"

Cletis fought the urge to vomit. Bravely he held back his tears. The man studied him for a moment and then placed the family picture on the floor in front of Cletis. Cletis eyed the photo and then lifted his head again, watching the man's every movement.

"This must be your mother," he said with a sly smile, looking down and pointing to Anna. The being studied the photo. He was close enough now that Cletis could smell the leather of his boots and clothing. "And I suppose this is your father?" He looked at Cletis, eyeing him carefully.

Cletis said nothing.

"I need answers, and I will do what it takes to get them." The man stood straight and looked about the room. "You feel my presence again, don't you?"

Cletis remained quiet. The man stepped closer, reached across to the photo, and with a finger, touched the image of Cletis's father. Then, with a raptor gaze, he peered down at Cletis. Closing his eyes, as if in deep concentration, the man's form gradually began to shift and transform. His flesh, bones, and hair seemed to come alive with movement from within. The veins in the man's hands, neck, and face swelled and pulsed. His muscles flexed and his bones bent and contorted in an eerie shape-shifting dance. His mouth and eyes opened and closed wildly, as if savoring this unnatural metamorphosis. The soft groaning sound of the abnormal pulling and stretching of flesh and bone nauseated Cletis, and he instinctively wrapped his arms around his already queasy stomach. The being moaned slightly as his hands and fingers grasped and tensed, embracing a new appearance and identity.

When Cletis began to recognize the new image, he gasped and pushed back against the dresser behind him. Even the man's clothing pulled, tightened, and bent in this same process. The leathery fabric gradually assumed a new texture, color, and quality. The alteration continued until the person who once stood before Cletis had transformed into the exact likeness of Cletis's father, precisely as he appeared in the family photo. Garth Dungarvan now stood before him—or at least an exact replica. Even the sweatshirt that his dad wore in the picture—the sweatshirt with the cut-off sleeves—was now upon this man. Whoever this being was, he possessed a supernatural power that enabled him to assume the shape of another person.

Cletis trembled as he watched. He wiped a tear away and gazed up at the new being that stood staring down at him. Though the transition seemed totally complete, Cletis noticed one thing that was not altered. The sleeveless sweatshirt revealed the red, hourglass marks still upon the man's shoulders. Though it appeared as if his father squatted down toward him, the marks on his shoulders betrayed the being's true identity. If not for that, Cletis would not have discerned any difference between this man and the real Garth Dungarvan.

But there is still another difference. Cletis shuddered at the thought as the dark, cold sensation lingered, chilling him deep to the bone. *The feelings haven't changed. If what I feel now comes from this man, then I will always know who he is and where he is.*

The man leaned down. Though he looked just like his father, Cletis found no comfort in the man's countenance.

"You and the old woman cannot keep me from finding what I need," he said in a voice that replicated his father's, but in an evil and demanding tone. "Remember that. I'll be watching you."

Cletis's gaze dropped, not wanting to look into the eyes of this being that pretended to be his father. He focused again on the family photo, hoping to draw strength from the images of his mother and father. But to his surprise, he found that the image of his father was gone! Cletis and his mother appeared as it had originally depicted them, but Garth's image was absent. It was as if he had never been there—as if it had been taken only of Cletis and his mother.

"You cannot stand in my way," continued the shape-shifter. "If you try, both you and the old hag will be destroyed. Do you understand that?"

Cletis lifted his eyes to the man. Peering down at Cletis, the being began the changeling process anew. The man's bones jolted, contorted, and then stretched, realigning themselves into the new shape. A groaning seemed to come from deep within him as muscles and tendons tightened and relaxed, allowing the formation of a new body.

Despite his fear, Cletis watched in awe as the shape-shifter performed his fascinating and frightening work. Cletis could have reached out and touched him. Yet, this time, the transformation turned strangely different. As the process continued and Garth's features gradually disappeared, the man suddenly cried out, as if in pain. Slowly and steadily, the frame of the larger, more powerful personage who once stood before Cletis, shrunk and shriveled into that of a bent, failing, twisted old man. It looked as if the being fought to maintain control of the larger, stronger body, but despite his best efforts, his form diminished in size and feature until the frame of a wrinkled, pale-skinned man stood before him.

Cletis cried out in fear as the shriveled figure stooped down and stared into his face. The being's eyes were still an evil dark. Above them, long, white hairs protruded from the place where eyebrows once grew. His lashes were gone, and the pasty-white skin that tightly covered his sockets and cheekbones only magnified the blackness of his deep-set, wicked eyes. His beard was white and sparse, barely covering his sunken cheeks and pointed chin. He was almost completely bald, except for isolated strands of hair that clung to his gray, paper-thin scalp. The heavy, black clothing, which once fit snuggly on the handsome, muscular frame, now hung loosely about his bony, frail body. The old man blinked wearily as he studied a terrified Cletis.

"I fear you will never be the same again," the being spoke in slow, deep, guttural tones. A cackling laugh escaped his lips, and the old man leaned back and rubbed a bony hand across his moist forehead.

Suddenly the gray particles of the conduit surged and gathered around the man. Still eyeing Cletis, he straightened, allowing the swirling cloud to envelop him. In an instant he was gone. The conduit then gradually faded, leaving Cletis alone in the room to ponder the experience. Despite his best efforts to be brave, Cletis collapsed onto his side and sobbed.

Garth's mind raced as he drove home from the old lady's house. *The translation is supposed to be some strange prophecy,* he thought, putting pieces together. *Dr. Canfield must have been fairly accurate in his work because the old woman seemed to know exactly what it was all about. I could have taken the copies to her. She could have translated them. She knew the writing like she'd written it herself.*

As he pulled into his driveway, he continued to ponder the old lady's words. He wondered how she could have known his entire family history. Or how could she have known about his fall at Tiger Stadium? No one but the family knew about that.

And of course, the person who grabbed me when I fell. I told Anna about that a few times, but Anna didn't know this woman. The woman who caught me has to be dead by now! That was thirty years ago! And Dad said that the woman at the stadium must have been seventy or eighty years old back then! That old hag must have found some family journal! But how could she have gotten it? It would be impossible for her to know all that.

He wondered why she would have that kind of information. Did the Dungarvans have something the old hag wanted? Why would she befriend Cletis? She didn't even know about him until the night with the chimes.

Garth shut off the car and opened the door. As he headed toward the back door, he noticed that practically every light in the house had been turned on. That was a bad sign. He charged to the back door and found it locked. Another bad sign. He struggled with his keys, unlocked the door, and bounded into the house.

"Cletis!" he yelled from the laundry room. The only sound came from the TV in the kitchen. Garth stepped to the table where he spied cookies and milk next to a half-eaten banana. He turned the TV off behind him.

"Clete!"

When he heard movement, he hurried through the kitchen and toward the stairs. As he rounded the corner, he spied his young son. There in the hallway, trembling as he stood, Cletis stared silently back at him. The boy was pale. Clutched in his arms was a picture frame.

"Cletis, you okay?" Garth asked, stepping toward him. "What's wrong?"

His son backed away from him. Garth could see his lips quiver and his eyes moisten.

"Cletis? What happened?"

Suddenly Cletis collapsed to the floor, and sitting next to the wall, he pulled his knees up to his chin. Still he stared fearfully up at Garth, as if he didn't know him. Unable to hold back the tears any longer, Cletis wept—never taking his eyes off his father. As Garth approached him, Cletis scooted away, pushing himself along the floor next to the wall.

"No! Don't touch me!" Cletis sobbed. "Stay away from me and my family!"

"Cletis, what is it?" pleaded Garth, kneeling beside his son.

Yet the closer he came, the more Cletis pushed away farther down the hall.

"You stay away from Abish too! She's our friend!" Cletis cried out.

Again Garth attempted to reach out to him.

"Cletis, what's goin' on here?"

His son released the picture frame with his right hand and swung a fist out toward Garth. "Stay away from us!" he sobbed.

Garth leaned back to avoid being struck. He sensed not only the fear in his frightened young son but the anger as well. He knew that when Cletis felt he was wronged or in danger, his temper surfaced and he fought back. It had been that way since he was little. Cletis presently was a cornered cat, afraid of something unknown to Garth.

Garth glanced down at the photo in the frame. It was the picture of the family that Cletis kept in his bedroom.

He must have found it somewhere, Garth thought.

"Clete, it's me. It's me, Dad. Everything's okay."

Again he leaned in and reached toward Cletis, attempting to comfort his boy. Again Cletis withdrew, still afraid of him.

"Cletis, what is it?" Garth asked softly. "Please, come on, buddy. Don't be this way. Tell me what's goin' on here."

Cletis calmed slightly and glanced back down at the family picture in his hands. Garth could see the three members of the family in the photo. He was familiar with it. But Cletis seemed to be studying it cautiously. Slowly his son lifted his gaze back up to Garth.

"What's goin' on here, Clete?" Garth whispered.

Again Cletis looked down at the picture.

"It's me, bud. You can see that. It's your dad."

"Take your shirt off," Cletis suddenly demanded.

"What?" Garth frowned. "Take my shirt off? Cletis, what are you talkin' about?"

"If you're my real dad, you'll take your shirt off."

Cletis's voice trembled, and he fisted a tear from his cheek.

Garth sensed his panic, his dread. With Cletis's best interest in mind, Garth moved away, unbuttoned his shirt, pulled it off, and tossed it back toward the kitchen. Garth turned back again to his son and watched him curiously. Cletis sat up and cautiously crawled toward him. After glancing back and forth, from one shoulder to the other, Cletis looked up into Garth's face. Smiling sadly, Cletis exhaled heavily and melted into sobs on Garth's knees.

The over-the-line game began early in the morning as planned. Not everyone was there though. Timmy, Pauly, and Rabbit formed one team. They were at bat. Klu and Johnny, out in left and center field, made up the other. With Pauly pitching, Timmy dug in at the plate. His skinny arms hefted the bat, and he took a few practice swings.

"Come on now, Timmy," called Pauly from the mound. "The name of the game is *over-the-line*, so that's where you gotta hit it! OVER THE LINE!" Pauly then turned back to Rabbit, who covered the shortstop area behind him. "He's hit everything on the ground, so far. So be ready. Don't let it get past you!"

"Try to give him a higher pitch then!" shouted Rabbit in frustration.

"I'm tryin'!" he called back. Turning again to Timmy, he wound up. "Think line drive this time! Here it comes, right down the middle," he yelled as he fired the ball home.

Again the pitch was low. But Timmy, impatient to hit away, swung with all his might and smacked a grounder that bounded down the third baseline, bounced crookedly past a diving Rabbit and dribbled into left field. Pauly threw his mitt on the ground next to the pitching rubber.

"Man, why didn't you wait for a good pitch?! I coulda gotcha a better one!"

Timmy stood sheepishly at home plate.

"That's three!" shouted Klu from center, as he and Johnny trotted toward the infield.

Rabbit stood up, brushing the dirt and grass off the belly of her shirt. "Ouch, that one hurt," she complained as she rubbed her belt line. "When we gonna get all the rocks outta this infield?"

Picking up his mitt, Pauly sneered at Rabbit. "You call yourself a shortstop?" he teased.

"Hey, it took a bad bounce to the right! You couldn't have gotten to that one! Anyway, get after Timmy! He's the one who can't hit a fly ball!"

"Well, he was pitchin' 'em all too low," called Timmy from home, where he tossed the bat next to the backstop. "I'm sorry!"

"That's okay," teased Klu as he stopped at the pitcher's mound. "You're the best player on *our* team!"

Klu laughed at his own joke.

"Shut up," said Timmy as he picked up his glove and made his way to the outfield.

"Hey, take it easy on Timmy," Johnny warned from the left field foul line. He picked up the ball Timmy had hit, jogged across the infield line, and tossed his mitt by the pitcher's mound. "One day he'll be bigger an' better than all of us." Johnny fired the ball to Klu and headed toward the plate to take his place at bat. "Isn't that the truth, Timmy?"

"Yeah, I guess," Timmy mumbled.

As Johnny took some swings, he peered out into right field. Far behind the scoreboard, out in the field, sat Elston—all by himself—hugging his knees to his chin.

"Hey, guys," Johnny announced, pointing out into deep right field, "that's Elston out there."

"What's he doin' clear over there?" asked Klu.

"Got me," answered Johnny. "Hey, Elston! Get your butt over here! We need to balance the teams!"

Elston lifted his head momentarily, eyed the field and his teammates, and then lowered his chin again onto his knees.

"What's with him?" asked Rabbit from center field.

"I dunno," replied Johnny. "Let's go find out."

Following Johnny's lead, the five of them made their way out to Elston. His posture didn't change as they approached.

"What's the matter?" asked Rabbit. "You okay?"

"You gonna come and play with us?" asked Timmy.

Elston looked up at them all.

"I'm movin'," he stated heavily, as if it were the worst thing that could happen to anyone. "Day after tomorrow."

"You're what?" asked Pauly in disbelief.

"Are you serious?" added Klu.

"Yeah," responded Elston. "Headin' north, closer to the city."

"How come?" asked Timmy.

"Dad got a new job. We got us a home up in Canterbury Heights. It was supposed to be a surprise for us kids. That's why I didn't know about it before."

"Canterbury Heights? Whoa! Isn't that where rich people live?" questioned Rabbit.

Elston was silent.

"So you rich now?" added Timmy.

"Yeah, I guess so," answered Elston.

"So you're not gonna be able to play with us anymore?" asked Johnny. Elston shook his head. No one spoke as the weight of the news sunk in.

"Where's Cletis?" Elston finally asked, looking toward the diamond.

"I dunno," answered Johnny. "We figured *you'd* know. We're still waitin' for him to show. Him and Frank and Davey."

"What are we gonna do about first base if you're gone?" asked Timmy.

Klu threw the ball into his catcher's glove twice, sniffed, and then cleared his throat.

"Man, this is bad," he stated glumly.

"You gonna play ball over there?" questioned Johnny. "At Canterbury Heights?"

"Yeah. Dad says they got organized leagues there. All-Stars and play-offs and stuff like that. Mom's already got me signed up for an All-Star try-out."

Johnny took his hat off and scratched his head. "Mr. Sperry," he began, "was gonna get us uniforms to play in that league. He was gonna surprise us if . . . if we could just come up with the nine players for the team."

Everyone turned to Johnny. No one blinked. Klu's jaw dropped open.

"No kiddin'?" asked Pauly.

"Man, around here it's gonna be tough to come up with someone else to take your place, Elston" Klu stated, opening and closing his catcher's mitt.

"Yeah," added Pauly. "We're lucky Frank's dad lets him play, with all the work on their farm they got goin' on."

"We're lucky we found Cletis," announced Rabbit, "or we'd only have eight."

"And now we gotta find someone else?" questioned Timmy.

"Even if we find someone to take your place, Elston," Klu continued, "it's not gonna be the same. And it's sure gonna be weird if we end up playing *against* you."

Elston's chin, once again, dropped heavily onto his knees.

"Way to make him feel good, Klu," Rabbit chastened, tossing her mitt into the air and letting it drop on the ground behind her.

"Sorry, guys," Elston finally sighed. "Looks like I messed up the team."

Johnny coughed, wiped his mouth, and looked back at the diamond. "Can't do nothin' about it."

Abish hunched over an assortment of ancient books, notes, and pedigrees that covered the massive, circular oak table in the center of the study. The antique table's surface was close to ten feet in diameter and occupied nearly half the room. Under the table, a large, round tree-trunk leg supported the heavy wooden slab. At the very top of the round trunk, wooden branches shot out from the shaft and attached to the underside. At the bottom of the trunk, small shoots like shallow roots spread out across the floor, offering additional support. It looked as if a large tree had grown up right out of the floor but then had been cut off and covered with the enormous, round tabletop.

Surrounding the table were four cane-back, wooden chairs. Covering the walls on both sides of the table were two large bookcases, each about fifteen feet in width. Each bookcase held six shelves, every one of them covered with old documents and records. A shaft of morning light that struggled through the soiled window and tattered curtains illuminated the table and reflected off the parchments she examined. This was Abish's library. As far as she remembered, no one had ever entered this room, nor had anyone ever seen the archives the room protected.

Much of the written material in front of her she had personally compiled, having followed the Dungarvan family in its travels and doings from the days of her youth, all the way up to Garth and Anna Dungarvan. The accuracy of the family record was of greatest importance to her. It had to be precise, or her understanding of the prophecy could prove incorrect. A mistake in her calculations could throw her hopeful plans completely out of balance.

Since her conversation with Garth last night, Abish had pored over the records, following the family lines from centuries past up to the present.

"Yes, it's written correctly," she spoke aloud, as was always her habit. In her years of loneliness, her own voice had become a most welcome companion. "The line begins with my father and my brother, and ends . . . " Her finger traced the pedigree line over several papers, finally coming to rest over the name of *Thomas Dungarvan*. "Yes, right here with Cletis, though that is not his real name. And here is Garth, and here is Anna. Married in 1975, they were." Her short, wide finger continued to trace the names and dates recorded before her. "Born in 1979, Cletis is now twelve years old." She paused thoughtfully and lifted her head to the old, web-ridden chandelier that hung above her. "Then he *was* their firstborn. He *had* to be. They have had no other children besides Cletis. I've watched them carefully."

She thought about what Garth had told her last night.

"He claimed that Cletis wasn't their first child. That doesn't make sense. I have the records right in front of me. Everything I told Garth was true and precise."

But his confidence that that one specific statement was erroneous concerned her. In fact, it frightened her.

She sat down on the chair next to her and stared straight ahead. Then rubbing her face and neck with the flat of her palms, she closed her eyes and took a slow, deep breath. Her head lifted slightly, and her eyes tightened in deep concentration. Suddenly before her, over the top of the table, a tiny blue light appeared. Gradually the light expanded into a perfectly round sphere and hovered like a large, shimmering bubble just a few feet from her face. She opened her eyes and studied it. Inside the floating orb there appeared a tiny hologram and, within the hovering revelation, scenes and characters instantly came into view. The images rapidly passed before her eyes, revealing people from a variety of lands and times. Then the process slowed, and Abish scrutinized the faces and families of the present day Dungarvan family that materialized within the blue ball of light. Finally, Garth and Anna appeared. They were a young married couple at the time. Anna held in their arms a sleeping child, wrapped in a blanket.

"Anna was pregnant," she said aloud. "I saw her in that condition. Beautiful, she was. Then the child came . . . the long-awaited child."

She watched again as the vision continued before her. Images of Cletis appeared—as a toddler, then a young boy, and then the young man of the present.

"I cannot be mistaken. There he is. I see him." She reversed the flow of the images and stopped, again, at the visions of Cletis as a one-year-old. "See! There he is! In the arms of his father! But has something been hidden from me? Could that be? There is no memory here of his months as an infant." Her gaze lifted to the ceiling. "According to what I know, there is no child before Cletis!"

She sat up in her chair, looked back at the hologram and reviewed in her mind the events surrounding the marriage of Garth and Anna, what she knew of Cletis's birth, and the parts of the prophecy that had already been precisely fulfilled.

"We rose from the water together," she spoke. "We were both muddy. He is named by that which he wears upon his feet. Cletis. Cleats. Clete. That's as close as it gets." Her pudgy, squat fingers lifted with each thought, counting and reviewing every specific moment.

"The powers of the box returned. It floated to me, it illuminated before me. The cards appeared within the box. . . . Well, that was not my doing. Neither was the disappearance of the bike and scooter.

That was magic beyond my ability to comprehend. But the Powers have returned. The Powers have been partially revealed. I delivered the box to Cletis. And now the box is gone, and the Traveler will shortly be revealed—if he has not been revealed already. If he has, Cletis hasn't told me about it. It is all in place. Everything is in order. It *has* to be right. I don't know what Garth is talking about . . . 'not his first child.'"

Abruptly the hologram disappeared. Abish sat bolt upright and leaned over the table, her eyes wide. The light of the chandelier flickered slightly—brightened, dimmed, then brightened again. She hurried around the table, moved through the open doorway, and carefully closed and locked the door behind her. She turned the corner and entered her bedroom. Looking around, she saw nothing out of the ordinary. She rushed to the window and looked out. There were no threatening clouds in the sky, nor any sign of wind or storm.

Then she felt it. It had been nearly 1,000 years since that feeling filled her soul, but she could not mistake the heavy, gloomy, hollow sensation. He was loose again and had finally found her.

"'In that day, comes the Traveler,'" she spoke softly to the emptiness around her.

Her eyes moved quickly, back and forth, across the small bedroom. Finally she saw the conduit materialize, with its swirling mass of gray, foglike energy. She had long since forgotten the process of Travel, and she stood mesmerized, watching the force surge and gather before her. The Traveler was visible within the field of energy. She could see his black leather clothing and the boots that covered his lower legs and feet. She saw that he held the wooden box—his box, the box from which the Travelers gained, or *could* gain, the powers unique to their kind. She had always known that he and she would finally meet again, face to face. There was no way of escaping it. The confrontation was inevitable. It was part of the prophecy, and now that moment was upon her. Would he recognize her? She was not certain of that but knew that she could not hide from him forever. Would he come to pry knowledge from her? One thing she knew for sure, he could not be trusted.

He floated a few feet above the green-and-brown, rag-weave rug that covered the wooden planking below him, and as the conduit vanished, he dropped gently to the floor. Abish eyed him, unmoving, unflinching, and unafraid. She saw the familiar long, blond braid that hung over one shoulder. He was handsome and broad-shouldered and muscular—as she remembered him. She spotted the red hourglass marks on his shoulders.

He was always interested in showing those to everyone, she thought to herself as she studied him.

Unsmiling he approached, holding the box out in front of him, as if bringing her a gift. She noticed the darkness of it and wondered what had happened to change its color. He looked her over from head to toe, and upon seeing her green, emerald eyes, he spoke.

"Abish? Is that truly you?"

A sarcastic laugh was followed by a charismatic smile. That smile had once captivated her heart. Indeed it had captivated the hearts of many unsuspecting women. She noted how dark his eyes had become. Where she had once looked into clear, blue eyes, they were now black and hollow.

"Your eyes reveal you," he continued, his voice deep and gentle.

As do yours, she thought, fighting against the cold, dark feelings that accompanied his presence.

"*They only* remained unchanged." He took another step forward. "And I sensed the power of the blue light. It has been a long time. That is all they left you with, I see."

Abish remained silent, waiting and watching.

"The years have been good to you," he sneered, looking around at the ramshackle dwelling. "My, and see how pretty you are!"

Again he laughed. Yet when he noted Abish's confidence in the face of the potential danger he threatened, his tone turned serious and impatient.

"They hid you well. For what purpose, I know not, since I have been imprisoned for most of that time. *Unjustly* imprisoned . . . to rot away my existence." He stepped even closer and peered down at her short, wide frame. "It is difficult to look upon you, ugly as you now are. But the fragrance of vanilla is familiar to me. I'm sure it reminds you of your mother."

He lifted the box toward her. Not only was it darker, but it now appeared to be seamless, with no lid visible.

"I have searched for this since the day you left me. It was mine, and you took it. And then you trapped me, and I have been sealed away ever since. Until now . . . until just recently. With so little time left to live, they finally freed me . . . freed me to play their little game." He spit on the floor and rubbed his boot through it. "Look at you now. We could have had so much together."

Silently he paced the room, eyeing her.

"They have hidden from me my son. And now I cannot open the box. Your family seals it magically. My father must have taught them how. Only the next Traveler can open this—only my firstborn son—and they know it. Only he has the power. They knew this box symbolized my supremacy and my existence, and they have taken it from me and sealed it."

Abish watched his every move. It was difficult to maintain composure in his presence, sensing the evil and hatred that possessed him. Yet she bravely stood her ground.

"So where is he?" he questioned. "Where is my son?"

She knew she didn't have the answer he was looking for.

"In all honesty, I do not know. And if I did, I wouldn't tell you."

"Your voice is as ugly as you are, and I don't believe you," he answered impatiently. He lifted his arm slowly and pointed his fingertips at her head. A bow of light suddenly surged from his hand and arced toward her. In an instant, she recoiled in fear, pulling her arms up to protect her face and body. Yet, as she did, a familiar blue light enveloped her, absorbing the line of Lightfire that exploded about her, shielding her from the impact. The room trembled with the concussion.

Abish was as shocked as the man who stood before her. She studied the Traveler, who, foiled in his attempts to harm her, now leaned against the doorframe, stunned. Feeling her heart racing within her, she pondered the wonder of the moment she had just experienced. Firstly, she was amazed that this man would so quickly attempt to destroy her. Secondly, she was astonished to find that a protective field existed to shield her from this life-threatening danger. Never before had she seen this aura around her. But never before had it been needed.

Father and Padar created this, she thought gratefully, *because they knew this would happen. Padar must have foreseen it from long ago.*

Suddenly the years that separated her from her family vanished away, and she felt their presence, assisting her in this final great test that was upon her—encouraging her to endure through the concluding steps of her homeward journey.

As the blue light faded, she turned angrily to him.

"You come and use the Lightfire on me?!" she demanded.

"You would not have been destroyed, but you would have sensed how serious I am in my efforts to find what I want. And you will not stand in my way like you did before! The presence of my son will be revealed somehow! I will find him!"

Regaining his intensity, he stepped angrily toward her. His approach filled her with fear, not knowing if the same shield would guard her against another assault. To protect herself, she lifted her arms and shifted away behind the bed. But he was instantly next to her and thrust out his hands to grab her arm. Again the blue light engulfed her, protecting her from his attack.

In frustration, he beat against the blue energy, kicking and hitting the shield, as if trying to penetrate the unyielding force. Finally he stepped back, his face tight with anger.

"I vow to find a way to destroy everyone in your family! After what they have done to me, can you expect less? Perhaps then, and only then, will your kin regret withholding the gift of Time from a Traveler!"

"Your father, Padar, was there!" Abish stated bravely as the blue light melted away. "He joined with my father! This is *his* doing too!"

"Brainwashed by your parents, he was!"

The man, again, paced the floor for several seconds and then turned to Abish.

"I have studied the writing your family disrespectfully engraved upon my box. *Perhaps* they have power to create such a prophecy. It *may* be within their potential."

"You blind, stubborn man!" Abish countered, stepping around the bed toward him. "Your *father* had the gift! *He* is the one who pronounced the prophecy! *He* inscribed it upon the box! You know that only a Traveler's magic can be placed upon Time or the box. Padar is the only one who could have done it! I was there! I watched it happen! It was your father!"

"You lie!" he yelled at her. "My father came to me in my imprisonment! He spoke with me! Never did he say anything of a prophecy or a curse upon the box!"

"I gave him the box," Abish explained. "I delivered it to him after I took it from you! He Changed me in preparation for the fulfillment of the prophecy you see engraved there!" She pointed to the box he held. "My father didn't have that Power, and you know it!"

"NO!" he shouted, bringing his hand up again. "Another lie!"

The Lightfire, again, burst toward her. In an instant, the blue shield protected her, absorbing the strange light that exploded from his fingers.

"Know this!" he called out in frustration as the light and the noise faded away. "If I do not find the boy—or the man—wherever he may be in time, I assure you, I will do all in my power to see that this supposed *prophecy* is not fulfilled in your favor! If I do not have your assistance—your family's assistance—to open this box, I swear I will find a way to destroy you all. According to this prophecy, at some point in time a choice is to be made. I assume that choice has to do with you and me. I will counter your efforts with all the strength of my mind and power! And this *new* Traveler—" He pointed to the inscription on the top of the box. "—the one who is prophesied to come—I don't know who or what he's supposed to be, but even he, whomever he is, will not stand in my way. I will open the box some way, and I will live on! The war begins!"

In his anger, he lifted his arm toward the window behind her.

"For old times' sake," he stated in quiet fury.

The Lightfire powerfully leapt from his fingertips and, striking the window and wall behind Abish, blasted away the glass and a large segment of the wall surrounding it. Abish covered her head as the splinters of the mangled wall rained down upon her and her meager furnishings. She turned and looked back through the opening, watching portions of her old house scatter and settle on the ground between her dwelling and the woods by the canal.

No light-shield covered her at the time of the explosion.

Perhaps the blue energy possesses some sort of foreknowledge as to when my life is truly in danger.

She turned back to the man beside her. She could see by the rage on his face that his work was not yet finished. He lifted his arm toward the broken wall, pointing his fingers at the space near the recently created void.

Rabbit and the boys lifted their heads abruptly and looked back toward the sound of the explosion.

"Man, that's comin' from near the witch's house!" announced Rabbit. "That's comin' from the hill!"

"What was it?" questioned Timmy, fearfully.

"I dunno," answered Johnny. "But I'm gonna find out."

The group rose in unison and raced back to the field for their bikes. Elston, whose bike lay behind him, scurried over to it. Within seconds he was on it, racing toward the drop-off above Abish's house.

One by one, Rabbit and the boys mounted their bikes and pedaled across the diamond. Over the outfield and through the fields to the north of the diamond they rode, pushing themselves along at top speed. Another blast sounded as the group caught up to Elston. Feeling the force of the explosion they jumped from their bikes and hit the ground.

"Man!" groaned Pauly. "What is goin' on down there?"

Johnny hopped on his bike again and raced on. Pauly, Klu, Rabbit, Elston, and Timmy were right on his tail.

"Timmy, stay behind me!" called Johnny, looking back over his shoulder. "I don't want you hurt!"

Timmy agreed, falling farther behind and keeping a safe distance.

When they reached the woods, they dropped their bikes and hit the ground. Like a platoon of combat soldiers, they crawled to the overlook and studied the cloud of dust that rose from the witch's house. Suddenly another blast tore through the hag's back wall and roof, shaking the trees across the hillside. They covered their heads for protection and listened to the particles of her house clatter down through the trees, splash into the water, and hit the barren earth beside the canal.

"Man, was that dynamite or somethin'?!" questioned Timmy, his eyes shut tightly and his hands covering his ears.

Cautiously the teammates lifted their heads and tried to see down the hill. From where they lay they had a fairly good view of what was happening below. When the dust settled, they could see the gaping hole in the back of the old house.

"Man, the whole back wall is gone!" whispered Pauly.

"The witch is blowin' up her own house!" declared Rabbit as she peered over the edge of the hill.

"Maybe she's practicin' some spells," added Timmy, "and they went bad on her."

"Maybe . . . maybe not," added Elston, thoughtfully.

"Whoa," moaned Rabbit, "that last one took off part of her roof."

"You think the police or the fire department are gonna be comin'?" asked Timmy, cautiously.

"I think this is too far away from town out here," spoke Johnny.

"I wonder if she got hurt?" questioned Elston.

"Man, how could she *not* get hurt with that kind of blowin' up goin' on around her," answered Pauly.

The dust and particles from the blasts floated above the house, some rising still higher into the air, caught in a gentle, springtime updraft.

"We need to tell Cletis," announced Elston. "He's gotta know about this. He knows her. We've been in her house."

Instantly all eyes were on him.

"Did you say, 'we've been in her house'?" asked Johnny, repeating Elston's words.

"Are you sayin' *you've* been in there, too? You *and* Cletis?" questioned Klu.

"I doubt that," choked Rabbit, shaking her head.

Elston studied their quizzical faces.

"Uh, yeah ... no ... no, I really have," responded Elston. "Honest. You can ask Cletis. He'll even tell you."

No one spoke. This was news to all of them.

"Really. I'm tellin' you the truth," Elston continued, trying to convince them. "We went to her house right before yesterday afternoon's practice."

Uh-oh, thought Elston. *That was probably not the best thing to tell them right now.*

And Elston was right. That little declaration only proved to prolong their stunned silence. Seconds passed. They all stared at him, curiously putting the pieces together.

"You mean that before yesterday afternoon's practice, you and Cletis were in the witch's house?" questioned Klu.

"Wait a minute," Elston proceeded, trying to calm them. "You're not thinkin' she did somethin' to us, are ya? Cuz she didn't. She didn't do nothin'."

Johnny looked back down the hill toward the house, then turned again to Elston. All were still for the moment.

"Look, I don't care what you're thinkin' right now," Elston continued. "I'm goin' to Cletis's house, cuz he needs to know what's goin' on here."

With that, he jumped up and sprinted back to his bike.

"I'm goin' with him," announced Rabbit, springing to her feet and charging after him.

One by one the others followed suit, rushing to their bikes and taking off after Elston and Rabbit.

A disturbing impression that something was wrong awakened Cletis. He sat up, his eyes wide with fear. The cold, ugly feeling that came over him was distant and slight—not nearly as strong as it had been the two previous times. But he could easily identify that familiar, heavy, haunting sensation. The being that had appeared to him yesterday was out there somewhere. For Cletis there was no mistaking the impression, especially now that he knew what and *who* caused it.

His dad's gentle touch calmed him.

"It's all right, Clete. I'm here," he whispered, placing a hand on his son's shoulder.

Cletis had slept in his dad's room during the night on the soft, lamb's wool rug beside his bed. Cletis was tired of trying to be brave through all the recent strange experiences, so when his dad suggested he sleep downstairs, Cletis unhesitatingly agreed. He had wanted his father close to him during the night—he wanted to be able to reach out and touch him, if needed. And after what had happened to Cletis, Garth *wanted* to be nearby.

Last night before going to bed, Cletis had finally confided in his father and told him almost every odd thing that had taken place in the past week—especially the events of the last two days. However, the episode with the bike and the scooter remained Cletis and Elston's secret. Cletis figured it was still all too strange to discuss. He also feared that if he shared it, his dad would probably disbelieve every thing else. On top of that, he feared saying anything about the lost Mantle card. But Cletis *did* discuss with his father the magical appearance of the baseball cards in the box as well as the box's disappearance. And he described in detail the eerie sensation that haunted him in the field when his father found him curled up on the ground, as well as how those same ugly feelings preceded the being's visit to his bedroom. He described the changeling in full, frightening detail, holding nothing back—how the man shifted shapes, how he had turned into Garth, and how Garth's image had disappeared from the family photo. He told his father about the old man's dark, empty eyes and how scared he felt when he was left alone in the house before Garth arrived. He explained to his dad the reasons for asking him to take off his shirt and that even though Cletis had seen his father's image reappear in the family picture and even though the ugly feelings had gone away, he still had to be sure it was him.

Though his dad found the stories hard to believe, he had listened intently without asking critical or judgmental questions. He told Cletis he just wanted him to "lay it all out and get it off your chest," and know that no matter what happened, his dad would be there for him.

Aside from Cletis's concerns, his dad had some stories and questions of his own to share. Together they discussed the trip to the university and the visit with Dr. Canfield. His dad talked about the translation of the manuscript and his subsequent visit to Abish's house. He also expressed his feelings of concern and confusion regarding this whole troubling prophecy and Abish's uncanny familiarity with the Dungarvan family.

Into the early morning hours, Cletis had asked a lot of questions . . . questions his father couldn't answer. "Who was the man that came to me?" "Who is Abish, really?" "Why am I involved in this whole thing?" "Would this man come again?" "What were the marks on the being's shoulders, and what did they have to do with the marks on my shoulders?" With each expressed concern, his dad had only one response: "I don't know."

Frustrated by the uncertainty and physically worn out, they had both finally fallen asleep.

So when Cletis awakened that morning, stirred by a fresh dose of creepy feelings, his dad reached over the side of the bed and placed a gentle hand on his shoulder.

"I'm okay," Cletis answered groggily. "I got that feeling again. It's still with me. But it's like it's far away. It's weird."

"So?" his dad asked, hoping Cletis would supply a few more details.

Cletis thought a moment. "I'm fine . . . I guess." He laid back down, rolled over onto his side, and stared into the open closet in front of him.

As he pondered, he spied the old hat boxes high up on the closet shelf. For as long as Cletis remembered, his mother's hatboxes had been in her bedroom closet—in Belleville and now in Greenberg Junction. He fluffed the pillow under his head.

That's strange, Cletis pondered, *cuz Mom never wore hats.*

An abrupt pounding on the front door startled them both. The faint chattering of boys' voices could be heard outside the house as the beating and knocking continued. Garth and Cletis rose simultaneously and hurried to the front door.

"Cletis!" came the call from the front porch. It was Pauly.

"Come on, Cletis! You gotta be home!" Elston shouted from the same place.

At the door Garth stepped in front of Cletis, pushing his hand away from the knob.

"I'll open it, Clete," his dad advised.

Cletis stepped back silently and allowed his father to unbolt the lock and open the door.

Johnny, Klu, Elston, Rabbit, Pauly, and Timmy greeted them, all speaking at once and all speaking loudly. There was a profound look of concern on each face as each attempted to communicate the fearful events of the morning. Their bikes lay behind them, scattered on the front lawn.

"Wait a minute! Wait a minute!" called Garth, over the top of them, lifting his hands in front of him. "Guys, hold on here."

They calmed a bit.

"Elston, what's happenin'?" Garth asked.

"Cletis, you gotta come!" he urged. "Abish's house is gettin' blown up!"

"What?!" questioned both Cletis and Garth in the same moment.

Klu continued the thought without a pause.

"The whole back wall got blasted out and then the roof got blown away!"

The group nodded in agreement, looking anxiously back and

forth from Cletis to his dad.

"Did you see this happen?" questioned Garth, eyeing the whole group.

"Yeah," stated Johnny quickly, "we were right at the top of the hill, and we looked right down on top of her house, and we saw it happen."

"The whole forest behind her place is covered with plaster an' glass an' pieces of wood," added Rabbit nervously.

"It was three big booms," stated Timmy. "So we rode our bikes over there from the diamond."

"We got there in time for the second and third booms," claimed Pauly.

"Did you guys come straight here?" asked Garth.

"Yeah, we came straight here," answered Elston.

"None of you have told your parents about this yet?"

"Nope. We came straight here, sir," answered Johnny.

"So Cletis, you gotta come with us!" Elston declared with renewed zeal. "We gotta go back there and help her!"

Cletis turned, racing back into the house and up the stairs.

"Cletis, you're not going over there!" called Garth after him.

"I got to, Dad!" Cletis responded, yelling back energetically from the top of the stairs. "I got to!"

Garth paused at the doorway, considering Cletis's words and eyeing the anxious kids on his front porch.

"You all head back over there carefully, but keep your distance. Stay up on the hill. I don't want anybody to get hurt. I'm gonna drive Cletis over there in my car, understand? We'll probably beat you there."

While changing his clothes and listening from his room, Cletis could hear the distant chatter as well as the clatter of bikes as the riders crossed his backyard and rode into the fields behind the house. Below, the front door closed and bolted. Cletis paused only a moment to study his reflection in the mirror. Touching the marks on his shoulders, he wondered what treachery or magic the new day would bring.

After having parked the Impala out by the web-covered mailbox, Cletis and Garth circled the south side of the house following what appeared to be a well-worn deer path. Despite his work repairing the screen door on the back porch, Cletis hadn't seen the path, nor did he know it was there. Even from where they walked, they caught an occasional glimpse of the dust-covered pines and elms that bordered the canal behind the home. Cautiously they made their way to the corner of the house and around to the porch. They halted as they first caught sight of the backside of the dwelling. The water of the near-by canal gurgled heedlessly on, as if completely unconcerned with the destruction that had obliterated the middle third of the back of Abish's house.

A cloud of fine, plaster dust still hovered, foglike, in the air over the gaping hole that exposed the destruction within Abish's bedroom. Pieces of jagged plaster, thin splinters of lumber, shards of broken glass, and puffs of insulation littered the banks of the canal and covered the forest bottoms and the trees behind the house. A portion of the roof was also missing, and support beams that once solidly held the roof and ceiling in place now hung, broken and sagging, over the bed. Garth and Cletis carefully approached the cavernous hole and peered inside.

Above and behind them, Garth and Cletis could hear the muffled sounds of the boys, who, having just arrived at the top of the hill, had begun their descent toward Abish's house.

With his dad right behind him, Cletis stepped up into the open room.

"Abish?" Cletis called gently as the fog of plaster dust settled around them.

All was silent for a moment. Then she spoke.

"I'm here."

Squinting through the dust that filled the room, Cletis spotted her. She was sitting in the hallway, just outside the room, on an old cane-back chair. The doorway framed her squarely and gave her the appearance of a throned queen gazing out over a ruined realm—or a flour-covered baker, taking a moment's rest from the morning's cooking. She eyed them silently as they looked about the room and up into the ceiling. Garth, concerned about the large beams that hung limply above Cletis, guided him out of the way.

"Be careful there," she announced protectively, agreeing with Garth's direction. "They've been trying to decide whether to stay put or to fall for the past fifteen minutes." From where she sat, she didn't appear to be injured, but Garth thought it only polite to ask her.

"Are you all right?"

"Fine enough, thank you," she croaked, blowing a shred of floating insulation away from her face.

Cletis went to her directly and knelt down in front of her. He looked up into her dust-covered face and studied her a moment. Reaching up, he touched her hand that rested upon her knee. She responded by reaching over with her other hand and gently patting his.

"Abish, what happened?"

She eyed him seriously.

"You have met the Traveler, I assume?"

Cletis nodded slightly. Garth stepped closer, frowning at her question.

"Then I should ask you the same question your father asked me," she continued. "Are *you* all right?"

Cletis thought for a moment and then nodded his head.

"I guess so," he whispered.

She could tell by the pain in his eyes that he wasn't being completely truthful.

"See what a kind man he is," she teased, pointing to the yawning hole in the backside of her bedroom. "I now have ventilation. And as I lie in bed each night, I can now look up and see the stars above me."

Cletis smiled weakly at the comment. She patted his hand again.

"Ma'am," spoke Garth, stepping forward and extending his hand. "We're gonna take you to our place, where you can get cleaned up and see if you need any medical attention. Our car's out in front."

She looked up into his face curiously.

"That's a brave thing to do, considering our words last evening. Are you sure you want to do that? I may be 'demented.'"

Garth showed no facial expression.

"For the time being, it's the right thing to do," he simply said.

A powdery cloud lifted from her as she stood. She brushed her clothing gently, attempting to clear away the debris that covered her.

"Why thank you then. Please allow me to gather a few of my things."

Garth eyed her, not quite sure what to make of her comment.

"A change of clothing, perhaps. Nothing dangerous," she stated calmly, noting his uneasiness. "I have no weapons that would concern you."

She turned to her right and waddled down the hall out of sight.

In her absence, Cletis and Garth studied the destruction around them.

"I want us to be very careful," Garth whispered.

He was about to say more, but the boys and Rabbit suddenly gathered outside the opening in the back wall. Garth and Cletis watched them as they hesitantly approached the house. Purposely they kept their distance, ready for a quick getaway if needed.

Abish reappeared in the hallway, holding a small bundle in her dusty arms. With Cletis supporting her right side and Garth on her left, the three of them made their way through the broken bedroom and toward the opening. Gently they helped her through the breach in the wall and down onto the ground below.

"We could have gone out the front door, you know," she whispered to Garth as he released her arm.

He nodded sheepishly in agreement but said nothing.

"But that's alright, because I needed to see these children."

The boys in front of her, as well as Rabbit, almost in complete unison took a few steps back, stunned by the sight of the old woman. She was all they had ever imagined her to be—hideously ugly, short and squat, wrinkled and old—the perfect image of what a witch was supposed to look like. And now, covered in the dust of the wreckage, her appearance was deathlike and menacing. Timmy, standing behind Johnny, suddenly finding himself teetering on the bank of the canal, grabbed his cousin's belt to keep from falling into the cold water.

Cletis watched as the bravado of the entire group seemed to melt before this old hag whom they had always believed to be an evil, child-devouring monster. Even Elston, who had been in her house, peered at her cautiously, still wondering if there was a streak of undiscovered madness in her.

"Johnny," she said, in a low, gravelly tone.

The group jumped, hearing her deep, penetrating voice for the first time. Johnny eyed her uneasily as she stepped forward. He swallowed hard but bravely stood his ground as she took three more steps toward him.

"You have a cousin who lives in Xenia, Ohio," she continued, looking up into his face. He tentatively nodded his agreement. "I sense he will be coming here this week. To stay. He's a southpaw. Pitches and plays first base."

Johnny hesitatingly nodded again. Timmy hid behind him. She then turned, eyed Elston, and took two slow steps in his direction. Elston felt her piercing gaze upon him.

"Welcome back, Elston Blanchard," she stated, her mouth forming a close-lipped smile.

He nodded slightly but said nothing.

Again she eyed the group and then turned and waddled back to Garth and Cletis.

The team watched, fearful and open-mouthed, as the Dungarvans escorted the witch lady around the side of the house and out of sight. Instantly, with the disappearance of the hag, the group let out a collective sigh of relief.

"I thought I was gonna wet my pants when she came out here," whispered Pauly, wiping the sweat off his forehead.

"I ain't never heard a voice like that," confessed Klu. "Sounded like it came from the throat of a cow."

"I don't think her hair's been combed in a year," added Pauly.

"And it was filled with all the dust from the explosion," commented Timmy, stepping bravely from behind Johnny.

"Did you see her eyes?" questioned Rabbit in amazement.

"I wasn't lookin' at her eyes," confessed Pauly. "There was too much other weird stuff to take in."

"I ain't never seen anyone so ugly in my life," pronounced Klu, exhaling heavily. "Did you see her nose?" added Timmy. "It had all those dents in it!"

"And her clothes?!" spouted Klu. "What was that all about? Like she'd been shoppin' in Mr. Howard's closet."

Timmy and Johnny laughed uneasily at Klu's words, as if trying to find something the least bit comical that would ease their tension.

"And Cletis said she had her hand in my catcher's mitt? Gluh! How can Clete and his dad even dare to touch her?"

Elston remained silent, listening. He had thought the very same things at first. But the trip to the baseball room had changed his mind.

"Man, this is what this place looks like in the light of the day," stated Pauly, awestruck by the detail of the old dwelling. "This is scary even with the sun shinin' on it."

"This place gives me the creeps," winced Timmy, releasing Johnny's belt and taking a step back. "She's gotta be a witch."

"I couldn't even look at her," blurted Klu. "She was so ugly, I thought I was gonna be sick."

"You guys are all so stupid!" declared Rabbit emphatically, turning on the entire group. "So if a person is ugly, you don't touch them? If a person is ugly, you stay away from them? You make fun of them? Is that what you're saying?" With her fist suddenly on her hips she eyed the boys. "If a person is ugly, they're not human? That is really stupid!"

"Hey, *I* didn't say that," declared Elston, pierced by her challenge. "I know she's hard to look at, but you didn't hear *me* talkin' bad about her. And neither did Johnny."

"Los ojos verdes?" pleaded Rabbit again. The boys eyed her blankly. "Her green eyes! Didn't anyone notice her eyes?"

"Yeah," responded Elston, "what about 'em?"

"The eyes of the jaguar! The green eyes of the panther! In the country of my grandparents, that is good luck!"

The blank stares of the boys met Rabbit's intense gaze.

"What are you talkin' about," injected Klu.

"It's the truth, I'm tellin' you!" she stressed, her arms stretched out wide.

"The eyes of the panther are good luck!"

The boys studied her doubtfully.

"I think you got that story backward, Rabbit," cautioned Klu. "I think those panther eyes are bad luck. What good luck has ever come from a panther? Man, they eat people!"

With a sudden cry, followed by a large splash, Timmy dropped into the canal. The edge of the bank had given way where he was standing, and in he plunged. Luckily the water wasn't deep there, and within moments Timmy had regained his footing, and spitting water and gasping against the cold, he climbed up the bank to dry land.

"Rabbit, looks like you're wrong," declared Pauly, pointing back to Timmy. "Green eyes are bad luck."

The guys all laughed at the comment as Timmy sloshed, stiff-legged, back toward them.

"Everybody listen to me," announced Johnny with a sudden serious expression on his face. "Guys, every one of us is gonna wanna go home and talk about this to our families. You know what's gonna happen if we do?" He eyed each one of them. "Stories are gonna start spreading, and people are gonna find out about us bein' down here during initiation nights. They might even blame us for this." He pointed to the demolished wall. "Not only is that gonna lead to trouble, but we may lose permission to play together. I don't want that to happen, so we gotta keep our mouths shut, okay?"

The teammates thought about his words for a moment, and every one finally nodded their agreement.

"Elston," Johnny continued, "you know Cletis and his dad the best. Can you ask his dad to keep this quiet . . . so we can keep playin' baseball together?"

Elston nodded.

Behind them, a sagging beam within the house crashed to the floor. The boys jumped with the abrupt noise, and Rabbit bit off a frightened squeal. They turned around cautiously and all faced the house.

"I'm outta here!" declared Pauly. With a quick about-face, he raced back toward the crossing point further up the canal. "We don't know what's in that house!"

"Me too," admitted Johnny. "Come on, Tim. Let's get outta here."

In a rush, the group jumped the canal and made their way up the slope.

Elston remained behind. Stepping cautiously toward the house, he studied the cavity in the back wall. The smell of vanilla pushed past his face as he peered into the mangled, dusty bedroom. The flooring of the broken house was level with his knees, and he leaned into the old room, resting his hands on the floorboards that still remained intact. The bed was broken in pieces and covered with plaster, lumber, and shreds of insulation. The large, gray beam that had just now fallen leaned sleepily on the remains of the tattered mattress.

"Come on, Elston!" called Rabbit from the top of the hill above the house.

"We only got an hour left," yelled Johnny from the same location. "Let's do over-the-line or somethin'. Gotta get our minds off all this!"

"Man, I forgot to tell Cletis I was movin'," Elston spoke out loud, as if Johnny's words had triggered the reminder.

He turned back to the hillside. "I'm comin'," he called out.

Again he paused, listening to the peaceful sounds of the forest and canal that surrounded him. It was so quiet and calm here.

Then he heard them—from somewhere deep within the old dwelling. Steps. Heavy, slow steps. Someone was there, walking in the house. Elston froze, listening to the sounds that seemed to be coming toward the doorway directly in front of him.

"Mr. Dungarvan?" Elston called out, licking his lips and attempting to swallow.

The sound of the steps immediately stopped. Elston remained still, listening and waiting.

Did I really hear somethin'? Did I hear steps?

"Mr. Dungarvan? Is that you in there?" Elston called out with mounting fear in his voice.

No response came.

Elston's heart began to pound within his chest. He knew he had the choice to turn and run away, but it hadn't quite come to that yet. He paused in the silence, wondering if he should courageously step up into the house and explore or hurry back up the hill. He waited, trying to be brave.

Again he heard them. The footsteps ... like boots on the wooden flooring. Leaving his courage in Abish's backyard and feeling a sudden burst of adrenaline rush through his body, Elston jetted toward the canal. He had never sensed such a surge of energy and speed in his life. With one smooth leap he easily cleared the water, and darting in and around trees and shrubs, he dashed up the hillside through the woods.

CHAPTER 12

The Name

Cletis sat near the kitchen window, toying with a baseball in his glove. He watched his dad pace nervously past him, moving from the table, to the kitchen sink, to the laundry room, and then back into the kitchen. Twice he wandered down the hall and into his bedroom. With each visit to the bedroom, Cletis could hear the opening and closing of the closet doors and the shuffling of boxes. The second time, Cletis had risen curiously from the table and had followed his father from a short distance. From the bedroom door Cletis had seen his father bent over his mother's old hatbox. The box was on the bed, the lid was off, and his dad was studying something inside it. Cletis had no idea what he was up to and, feeling it inappropriate to interrupt, returned to the kitchen. Yet even from the kitchen, Cletis heard again the shuffling of cardboard on wood and the closing of the closet doors. Seconds later his dad reappeared in the kitchen, wearing the same troubled expression.

His dad had allowed Abish the time needed to get cleaned up and rest. The bedroom and bathroom directly below Cletis's room had always been empty, and she was invited to make herself at home there—for the time being, at least. His dad had decided to postpone any questions until all three of them could sit down together and discuss details. He had told Cletis privately that though he dreaded the process of pulling answers out of Abish and immersing Cletis in a labyrinth of eerie, unnatural events, he yearned to understand all the details and why he and Cletis had been heaved into this disturbing drama. At the same time, his dad was still uncertain as to the identity of this old woman and whether or not she meant him and Cletis any harm. He had told Cletis he would watch her closely for any telltale signs that would reveal something untruthful or criminal.

Cletis rolled the ball across the table and caught it as it dropped off the edge. *Abish called that man the Traveler*, he pondered. *What does that mean? Where did he come from? Why did he have the box? Why did he have the picture of my family? And last night, before that man came, why did I feel the same scary feelings as I did out in the field two nights ago?* Cletis wondered if the man was near him in the field, somewhere in the darkness. And he had felt the same dark sensation that very morning, but it seemed far away. *Was that because he was at Abish's house?* He tossed the ball into the pocket of his mitt a couple of times and then placed them both on the table.

Finally Abish appeared in the hallway, clean but wearing clothing that resembled what she always wore. She shuffled silently toward the kitchen, but his father intercepted her and directed her through the entryway and into the living room.

The step-down living room had two entries—one from the kitchen and the other near the front door. To the family, this room was a constant reminder of Anna's gentle, maternal influence. She had furnished the room simply but gracefully. There was a cottage feel to it. Lace curtains adorned the large window near the front door as well as the smaller window on the adjoining wall. Their modest, delicate patterns, against the slight yellow tint of the walls, were an indication of the feminine hands that hung them in place. A couch and an overstuffed chair were positioned in the center of the room, facing each other. Both were upholstered in a green, yellow, and white plaid that complimented the walls and curtains surrounding them. A wooden coffee table was positioned between the couch and chair, and a matching end table was placed to the right of the overstuffed chair.

Anna's favorite figurine stood in the center of the coffee table. It was a polished, shiny porcelain couple, about nine inches high. The couple was dressed in clothing of the early 1800s and looked as if they had just stepped out of a Jane Austen novel. The man and woman stood by a white, picket fence, and together they looked off into the distance at something . . . something imagined. A landscape painting hung on the wall to the right of the overstuffed chair, and to Cletis it always seemed as if the porcelain couple was studying it, dreaming of where they wanted to build their home, raise their family, and face their future. Framed portraits donned the wall opposite the largest window—mostly family shots of Garth, Anna, and Cletis. Some of the photos included grandparents and other relatives that Cletis had never known or hadn't seen for a long time.

As the trio stepped down into the room, Abish settled herself in the chair and alertly looked around, studying in particular the family photos on the wall behind her. As she did, Garth wrapped a hand around Cletis neck and directed him back toward the kitchen.

"Could you please bring us some water?" he asked.

Nodding, Cletis stepped back up into the kitchen and crossed toward the cupboard when he heard his father whisper to Abish.

"I still don't know who you are, or what this is all about, but you can be sure I'll be watchin' you like a hawk."

Cletis turned. His father was leaning in close to Abish with his back to Cletis.

Abish answered, "Thank you, Garth. That's precisely what I've been doing to you for the last forty years. I'm pleased to see the roles have reversed."

What's that supposed to mean? Cletis pondered as he opened the freezer.

He dropped ice cubes in each of the glasses and filled them with water. Her words puzzled him, and as he returned with the three glasses, he noted his father was now sitting, still watching her closely. His hand covered his mouth, as if to keep him from speaking. Cletis placed two glasses on the coffee table and one on the end table next to Abish.

"Thank you," she nodded as she picked up the glass and sipped a drink. "Well, this is what you've waited for, Garth Dungarvan. What do you want to know?"

"All of it," he stated stiffly.

Cletis sat down next to his father.

"I want to hear it all. The whole weird story—why you know it, why you know us, who you are, the details of this supposed prophecy—everything. And we'll believe what we choose to believe. When you're finished, I'll decide if I need to go to the authorities. So start when you're ready."

She eyed him patiently and then nodded her agreement.

For the next hour, Abish told and retold her story. Cletis watched and listened as his dad played the role of the interrogator, hounding her for answers, explanations, and clarifications. Abish calmly addressed each question, sometimes two or three different times.

"This part about the box doesn't make any sense," Garth announced in frustration. "It's like this box lives and thinks on its own. That can't be!"

"Then I'll take a different angle," stated Abish, completely controlled despite Garth's aggravation. "The box is a source of the Traveler's powers—at least a key to prolonging a Traveler's life. I don't know why or how exactly, but it has always been so. Each Traveler has had the box at one point in time during his life."

"You mean there's more than one of these guys?"

"Sometimes there can be several. But only one of them will possess and control the box. The box goes with them from one generation to the next." She paused momentarily, watching Garth absorb the thought. "There is something magical within the box that can give each Traveler strength or life. But according to the prophecy . . . and I don't have all the details . . . the box will have to be unsealed. This means that it has to be *sealed* prior to that. When I saw the box in the hands of the Traveler, it had changed. Perhaps now it is sealed. My feeling is that a new Traveler will have something to do with *unsealing* the box."

"But the box was open when I had it," Cletis commented, trying to make a contribution to the conversation. "I could open it and close it easy."

"So could I," responded Abish, "when it was in my possession. It may have been magically sealed when he came to retrieve it—perhaps when he touched it. I think my family, or his father, had something to do with that. For only a Traveler has power over the box."

Cletis looked on as his father continued. "So this 'Traveler,' as you call him, who visited you and Cletis, is supposedly looking for his 'rightful heir'—another 'Traveler'—because he wants to open this box, somehow get the power from it, and be able to live longer?"

Abish nodded. As she did, Garth shook his head in disbelief.

"All this 'magical' stuff doesn't make sense. Come on, this is reality. You can't explain anything to me by claiming magic is the reason. You gotta give me solid answers." He rubbed his forehead in frustration and leaned back against the couch. "This is insane."

"What can I say then, Garth, to help you understand?" Abish continued. "Magic may not be the best word to use. Let me say this instead. It is not magic; it is control of the elements . . . of things, of life around us. Elements and time become subject to certain individuals. They can control those elements because they understand the physical laws that govern them. It was that way in my time and in my family. And, in the case of the Travelers, there is something in their physical and mental make-up that allows them to pass through time and do other phenomenal things."

"Wait, wait, wait," countered Garth, shaking his head again. "Elements. Time. Magic. You're talkin' nonsense. How do you expect me to believe any of this? Look, let's go back to this 'rightful heir' stuff, and this 'searching Traveler' guy looking for his son."

"Alright. This Traveler is looking for his son. And, he thinks I know where his son is."

"Why would he think that?" asked Garth.

"Because when he last saw me, I had the child. But I delivered the child to my parents. From that time on, I was not allowed to be near the child. I assume the little boy grew to manhood, got old, and died just like everyone else. So the Traveler is searching through time, trying to find him. But hoping to save himself valuable moments of life, he came to me first, thinking I might have information to help him."

"And you don't," continued Garth.

"No," she answered.

"And what if he finds his son?"

"He'll try to convince him to open the box so that he can gain whatever power the box will offer him. If he can't persuade his son to help him, he may try to use trickery or force. I don't have all the answers to that question."

Cletis watched as his dad eyed Abish suspiciously.

"You see, Garth," Abish continued, "this Traveler became wicked. Even his father tried to persuade him to mend his evil ways. My family took the boy—his son—from him and locked the Traveler away. Their intent was to protect the child from his father so that the wrong he did would not be passed on to the next generation. I agreed to the plan and was Changed. The Traveler fought the plan, and for that, he was imprisoned."

"So why hasn't this guy come after you before now?"

"My understanding is that he has been bound in Time until just recently. When the powers of the box became active again, it must have sent some sort of command through Time, which released him from his prison and guided him to it. My family and the father of the Traveler jointly planned all these events, being powerful and prophetic as they were. What happened to the child, though, I don't know." She paused. "And I suppose it's better that way."

Cletis sensed a deep sadness in her voice as she paused to ponder her last words.

"They 'changed' you? What does that mean?" his father asked, still skeptical.

"They Changed me into what I look like now," she answered matter-of-factly.

"Why?"

"It was all part of the plan. I was to be hidden from my family and community. They were not to know of the test I was going through. They all thought I was banished for the evil I had done. My duty was to watch over them from a distance and follow them through the generations of time until the test and the prophecy were completed. My Changing was also to teach me other lessons. Only my parents, the father of the Traveler, and I knew of the plan

"So you really don't look like this?" continued Garth doubtfully.

Abish shook her head. "No, I don't."

Cletis and his dad sat silently for a moment.

"There's no way I can believe this," Garth finally stated. "Man . . . so why didn't this guy just go back in time and take out his frustration on the ones who hid the boy?"

"He has no power over them." She allowed her words to sink in. "My family's powers are greater than his. But his own father opposed him. And only a Traveler has the power to confine or imprison another Traveler." She leaned forward a bit. "You see, when he and I joined together—this man and I—we saw that our combined powers were matchless. We could have done anything we wished to do, and for a time, we did. So, despite my family's warnings, I agreed to his plans. With my powers and his, we became a force for evil and tyranny anywhere we chose to live. No one could stop us. But, over a time, my evil deeds became a burden to me, and I knew I needed to make amends for the crimes I committed. And though he was powerfully persuasive, I *felt* . . ."

She halted a moment and studied Cletis, as if hoping to impress the point upon him.

"I *felt*," she continued, "the evil that had replaced the good in him *and* in me. There was an ugliness and darkness to it. I was once good, and so was he. It was because of that goodness that our parents agreed to our marriage. But what I *felt*—the absence of good and the presence of evil—moved me to change the course of my life."

She looked directly at Cletis.

Has she felt it too? Cletis wondered. *Is that what she's trying to tell me? Does she know exactly what I've felt?* He studied her green eyes as she glanced away from him to his father. In the momentary silence, his dad sat up and shifted uncomfortably in his seat.

"Okay, let me get this straight. You say you 'joined' him?"

"He was my husband for a time. I was his wife. The boy he seeks is mine as well as his."

"Oh, my goodness," smiled Garth, slapping his knee. "Okay. That's it . . . The story gets deeper and better as it goes. You're hiding stuff from us." Before she could answer, he continued. "Well, *somewhere* back in time this boy has to be alive. This Traveler guy could just go back and find him, if he's really able to move through time."

"Like I said," continued Abish, patiently. "I suppose he has tried that, once he found the box was sealed. But for some reason, he hasn't been able to find his son. Since both the box and I are in this present time, I think he will search here. If he understands the prophecy, he will remain in the present, close by."

"So how would he *know* his son?" asked Cletis. "How would he recognize him, if he found him?"

"That will be easy. The last line of the prophecy. All Travelers have them."

"Refresh my memory," Garth stated sarcastically.

"'Time is red upon his shoulders,'" Abish stated matter-of-factly.

Cletis and Garth sat motionlessly.

Finally Cletis turned to his father. His dad continued to look straight ahead at Abish, his gaze fixed on her.

"What does that mean, exactly?" he asked, frustration and anger mounting in his voice. "'Time is red upon his shoulders.'"

Abish noted his emotion, yet gently answered, "He will have red, hourglass-shaped marks on the fronts of his shoulders. They are the marks of the Travelers."

Cletis watched his father study the woman for several seconds before his gaze lifted toward a photo of Anna on the wall behind Abish. He sat silently, as if lost in his deep, dreaded thoughts. Cletis could tell by the tightness of his dad's lips that he was doing his best to hide his thoughts and emotions. His hands went to his temples and his eyes closed.

"It's been almost a thousand years. How can that be?" his dad asked in frustration. "That's impossible! No one lives a thousand years!"

"I am Changed," Abish replied calmly. "I can answer nothing further regarding it, because I don't know how it was done. All I know is that I have not died. I am still here, in this awful form and in this awful, lonely state."

"Why? Why did they make you live through all this? What's the purpose?"

"I chose to," she answered, scooting closer to the edge of the chair. "I *chose* to! To prove my heart could change, I *chose* to watch over the family and be with them until the prophecy would be fulfilled and the evil of the Traveler brought to an end. I *chose* to prove my faithfulness to the family, knowing that the reward would be worth it in the end no matter how long the test."

"But a thousand years?" questioned Garth. "What good does it do? What have you gained?"

"The fact that I am still alive proves to me that trusted persons had the power to make the transformation last as long as it was needed. They changed the outside, for my protection, and I, hopefully, change the inside. My family's power reaches across the years of time, and I am confident they will show me what needs to be done to win their trust and pass the test that's before me. I believe the final moments of that test are now upon me."

"So what does this 'family' of yours have to do with me and Cletis? Why are we sucked into this 'test' and 'prophecy'? Why would your family put our lives on the line, if they are truly good and powerful?"

Abish eyed Garth seriously, silently.

"Well, what?" questioned Garth.

Cletis watched Abish, wondering if his father had finally found a weak point in her story—a chink in her armor. Despite Cletis's love for his father, he was hoping Abish would provide answers that would bring them all peace. He felt a great admiration for this lady, even if the strangest of circumstances had brought their lives together.

"Don't you have an answer?" Garth's hands spread out in front of him.

"Yes, I do," she stated. "Yes, I do, Garth. Here is your answer. It is *our* family."

Cletis's hair stood on end as an amazing power coursed through him. He sat up straight and then nonchalantly rubbed his arms, trying to hide the goose flesh.

Garth paused, squinted his eyes into a frown and turned his head, as if trying to absorb the impact of her words. "*Our* family?" he questioned.

"Yes. Our family, Garth Dungarvan. You and I share the same blood."

"What do you mean by that?"

She studied Cletis and his father, as if she knew that her words would carry a heavy and revealing blow.

"My name is Abish…Abish of Dungarvan," she pronounced regally.

Cletis wasn't sure what Abish meant by those words, exactly, but out of the corner of his eye, he saw his dad go rigid.

"Will you excuse us please?" his father stated.

Abish made no gesture. His father rose, escorted Cletis into the bedroom, and shut the door behind him.

His father led him to the bed and then turned and sat down in front of him. He looked up into Cletis's eyes but said nothing. Cletis had never seen such a concerned look on his father's face—not even when his mom was sick. He stood alertly as his father reached out, grabbed him by his arms, and held him steadily.

"Thank you for keeping your thoughts to yourself out there," Garth stated. "I was proud of you. That showed real maturity."

Cletis nodded, but said nothing.

"But there are a lot of other things I need to discuss with her, before we fall into whatever scheme she might be laying for us."

"Scheme?" asked Cletis.

"Some things she says seem kind of true, considering what you've been through lately," his dad answered. "But there are other things I worry about. I mean, if you really think about it, this whole story she's telling us is absurd. It's so fantastical and way out there. But she said some other things that kind of get me wondering . . . and doubting. So I need to get out of her more information that she might, or might not, know before we make any decisions about anything. Got it?"

Cletis nodded again. "But Dad, I need to tell you somethin'."

His dad's shoulders drooped. Cletis could tell by his expression that he was expecting more bad news.

"No, Dad, I think this is good," Cletis said. He took a breath and then began to explain. "The first time I met Abish, even though it was scary, and I was doin' what I wasn't supposed to be doin', I had this strange feeling. It kind of filled my whole body. My hair stood on end—like goose bumps. I was right above the canal, and I could hear her calling for help. It's kinda weird, but it was the same feeling I had at the moment Mom died—at that very moment. Do you remember it? Cuz you said you felt it too."

His father studied him, waiting.

"To me," continued Cletis, "that feeling is the opposite of the feeling I had upstairs in the bedroom or out in the field when that Traveler guy was near me. The exact opposite. But out there in the front room, even Abish talked about those same kind of *feelings*—like what she felt even hundreds of years ago—and what she feels now. Even on her back porch, on the night when I went to her, and I told her I couldn't find the box, she talked about feelings. She said they would guide me. That night was the first time I sensed the Traveler—the bad feelings. But now, when we were talking to her, I felt that same *good* feelings again. Like I had the first time I met her."

His dad studied him. "I know what you're talkin' about, but I don't know what to tell you right now, Clete. I think we gotta go on more than just feelings right now . . . I gotta get some facts too. There's just too much at stake. We really don't know who this woman is."

"Dad, I trust her. I think she's tellin' the truth. It *feels* right to me."

His father paused a moment. "For my sake then—until I can figure some things out—don't talk to anyone, even Abish, about your experiences with that 'being' man, whoever he is. And don't let her know about the marks on your shoulders until I feel it's safe to tell her. Okay?"

"Okay."

"And whatever happens here, it stays between you and me. It doesn't leave our house, until I say so."

Cletis nodded. He took a deep breath in and pulled his shoulders back, as if releasing some pent-up tension.

"And the kids on the team," his dad continued. "They gotta keep their mouths shut about all this. If word gets out about what happened at the woman's house, your team might just fold. We don't want that do we?"

Cletis shook his head. "I'll talk to 'em."

The doorbell rang, jarring their focus away from the conversation. Cletis's dad eyed the clock by the side of the bed.

"Man, it's after 3:00 already?"

They left the bedroom and headed to the front entryway. Garth stepped toward the door and pulled it open. Elston stood there, wearing a troubled expression and balancing in the basket of his bike three full Burger King bags.

"Hi, Elston," spoke Cletis.

"Hey, Clete," he answered. "Mr. Dungarvan."

"Elston," Garth nodded. "You wanna come in?"

"No, sir. But I wanna know if Cletis can take a ride with me."

"Where?" asked Cletis.

"Gotta visit Mr. Howard one last time."

"What d'ya mean, 'one last time'?" Cletis asked.

"Didn't the guys tell ya? I'm movin'."

"What?" questioned Cletis.

"Where?" inquired Garth.

"Up near Canterbury Heights, by the hospital."

"No kiddin'. Well . . . uh, well, that's not too far away," stammered Garth, seemingly still preoccupied with other thoughts.

"Yeah, I guess not. Mom and Dad are pretty happy about it, but not me."

"We're sorry to see you and your family go," stated Garth. "What are the bags all about, Elston? You got a picnic planned?"

"Well, sir, we kinda made friends with Mr. Howard, that's all," answered Elston. "These are for him and us."

Garth nodded a pretended understanding and looked down at Cletis. "I didn't know you had somethin' goin' on with Mr. Howard. Is this pretty important to you, Clete?"

Cletis pondered a moment. "Yeah, it is, Dad. I want to stay here with you, but I need to go with Elston—especially if he thinks this is his last time."

"Will you be safe?" his dad questioned, silently communicating his concerns.

"Yep. We'll be just behind the grocery store. It'll be light for a long time, and I know the quickest way home from anywhere around here."

His father eyed him thoughtfully and then turned to Elston. "Elston, I'm trusting you. Don't let Cletis out of your sight at any time, do you understand me?"

"Yes, sir," answered Elston obediently, though wearing a curious frown.

"We'll probably get a bunch of guys to go with us," added Cletis, attempting to ease his dad's concerns. "You gonna be okay here alone?" Cletis whispered, knowing Abish was right around the corner.

"I think so," nodded Garth. "Don't worry about me."

"Mr. Dungarvan?" questioned Elston hesitantly.

"Yes."

"Uh . . . we . . . on the team think it's probably better not to go talkin' lots about what happened this morning. We don't want trouble, you know, and we want the team to be able to stay together. So if the lady's not hurt or anything . . . we, uh . . . " Elston fumbled with his words, trying to organize his thoughts. "So . . . uh . . . could we ask a favor . . . if you think it's okay?"

"Elston, don't worry about a thing," answered Garth. "The lady is fine. You boys are not in trouble. And I think your decision is wise to keep this quiet and private. This'll be just between us."

Elston nodded gratefully.

"Are you still part of the team, even with your family moving?" asked Garth.

"Uh, no . . . guess not. Still feel like it though."

"I'm sorry. That'll be tough on the team," replied Garth. Putting a hand on Cletis's back, Garth nodded and nudged him forward. "Go take care of Elston and Mr. Howard. Be careful. Get back as quick as you can."

Cletis, happy to be outside and doing something to take his mind off the heaviness of the day's events and discoveries, stepped into the afternoon sun and hurried around the house to where his bike rested against the aluminum siding. He took one of the bags from Elston and placed it in the basket by his handlebars. Cletis hopped on his bike, waved good-bye to his dad, and pedaled off down the street. His father watched them for a moment and then bowed his head and closed the door.

Chapter 13

The Vision In Blue Light

The boys headed toward Main Street, balancing their bikes in order to keep the drinks from spilling. The afternoon was warm, and the heat of the sun felt good on Cletis's shoulders and legs. He had been pent up too long at home. Though he was concerned about being out of the house without his father or Abish, Elston was with him, and the breeze in his face felt liberating. Yet he wondered what his dad would be asking Abish and what she would be telling him.

"I got my shoelace caught in my chain on the way over here," chuckled Elston, breaking Cletis's thoughtful silence. "I just about fell on my face. I had to stop and take my shoe off, so I could get it unstuck. Pretty good balancing. You should've seen me hoppin' around at the end of your street, trying not to dump the bags in the middle of the road."

Cletis laughed at the thought. It felt good to laugh.

"Kinda weird this mornin', eh?" commented Elston, eyeing Cletis over his shoulder.

"Yeah, sure was. And it's gettin' weirder still."

"What d'ya mean?" questioned Elston.

"When I find out what's real and what's not, I'll let you know."

The boys rode quietly for half a block and turned left on Main Street.

"Cletis, I gotta tell you something," stated Elston. "I heard footsteps in Abish's house after everyone left this morning."

"You did?" Cletis sped up next to Elston to hear every word.

"Yeah. Everyone was gone, and I was lookin' back in the house, and I heard footsteps—like boots on her wooden floors."

Cletis knew the Traveler's boots. He had seen them and remembered them well. The thought of that man hanging around in Abish's house after she was gone sent a chill through his bones.

"I called out for your dad," continued Elston, "Cuz I thought he might've come back in through the front door. But no one answered. And then I didn't hear anything. But then, they started up again—just this slow thud, thud—kinda like whoever it was, was gettin' closer. So I ran. I don't think I ever ran so fast in my life!"

Cletis thought about Elston's words, biting his tongue to hold back information he wanted to share, but promised his dad he wouldn't.

"I wonder what it was?" spoke Cletis, pretty well knowing *exactly* what it was. "Kinda weird to see her house all blasted up like that, wasn't it?"

"And did you see the looks on everyone's faces when she came out, all covered with all that dust and stuff?" questioned Elston. "I ain't never seen Johnny lookin' like he was about ready to run for it."

"Me neither," agreed Cletis, panting as he pedaled. "And Timmy was hiding behind Johnny. He was scared too."

"He fell in the canal, after you left."

"Timmy did?"

"Yeah," continued Elston, "Rabbit was talkin' about the witch's green eyes and how they brought good luck. And then Klu was sayin' they brought *bad* luck, and then Timmy stepped back and the edge of the canal caved in, and he fell right into the water. I think that scared everyone even more, and then a beam fell in her house just as Timmy pulled himself out of the water! So they all decided to take off. That's when I looked in her house and heard the steps."

Cletis remained silent, thinking about the footsteps and wondering what power could have blown such a big opening in that back wall. There were just too many unanswered questions and too many things to ponder.

"I rode out to Davey's and Frank's, and I told them everything that happened," reported Elston.

"What'd they say?"

"Nothin' much. They just listened, kinda freaked out."

The boys headed down Main Street. They could see the baseball diamond in the distance, way off to their left behind the school. No one was out there playing. That seemed a sad mistake to Cletis—a great field like that sitting vacant on a beautiful summer day like this. Cletis eyed it longingly, wanting desperately to be out there swinging a bat or chasing fly balls. But today, like it or not, other things were more important.

"You think Johnny's really got a cousin in Ohio?" asked Elston.

"Well, he didn't disagree with her."

"How would she know stuff like that?"

"I don't know. But she knows a bunch of stuff . . . like she sees into the future." Squinting against the sun, Cletis eyed Elston. "You really movin'?" he asked.

"Yeah. Over near Trenton."

"I know where that is. I'll bet I could ride my bike over there. Might take me two or three hours, but I bet I could do it. Maybe Dad would let me."

Elston smiled. "I don't wanna move. But Dad says it'll be good for us."

They followed Main Street past the hardware store and turned right at the bike shop. They both eyed the new bicycles behind the glass and watched their reflections pedal past the shop's large, clear window.

At the back side of the grocery store, they stopped near the train crossing and walked their bikes back to the hut. Still balancing the bags of food, they leaned their bikes carefully against the back wall of the grocery store.

"Do you think he's here?" asked Cletis.

"Hope so. Or we're gonna have to eat all this."

Cletis realized he hadn't eaten all day, but surprisingly he didn't feel all that hungry. His mind had been occupied by so many other important things that eating just didn't seem to be a priority. One of the bags was wet on the bottom, so Cletis cradled it in his hand to make sure the drink didn't fall through.

"You think he's hungry?" asked Cletis.

"Little early for dinner, but I think he's always hungry."

"Well, we better do this fast," Cletis added with a sigh. "This has been a weird day, and I wanna get home."

As soon as the words escaped Cletis's mouth, the sensation was upon him again—the cold, dark, haunting emptiness that had become all too familiar over the past few days. It came abruptly and heavily, suffocating the joy and warmth that accompanied the summer afternoon with a close friend. Cletis struggled to stand and, seeking support, leaned against the wall by his bike. The disturbing eeriness pierced him, sapping his strength and filling him with fear and panic. The being—the Traveler—was close by. Cletis bravely fought the impulse to run, but he didn't want Elston to know what was going on inside him or that he was suddenly afraid. He had to stay strong. He had to face this power, whatever it was, and try to beat it.

"You okay?" questioned Elston when he saw Cletis leaning against the wall.

Cletis nodded, saying nothing. He slowly stood straight again, faced the shack, and plodded forward.

"You sure? You look like you're gonna throw up or somethin'."

Cletis swallowed hard, trying to find the strength to combat the darkness. He looked over at Elston, silently pleading for help.

"Do you feel anything . . . strange?" whispered Cletis, trying to find his voice.

Elston eyed him curiously. "Like what? What d'ya mean?"

Cletis took a shallow breath and continued toward the shack. "Nothin'."

"You sure you're okay?" Elston asked again, frowning at Cletis.

Mr. Howard stepped into the doorframe of the ragged hovel.

"Hi, boys," he said softly, studying them and the Burger King bags they held.

Cletis's knees buckled, and though he struggled to remain upright, he dropped unsteadily to the pavement.

The Traveler was near.

Garth faced Abish across the coffee table, still wanting to doubt everything she said about her past and her connection to the Dungarvan family. Her story was like a fantasy—a tale of an imaginary realm filled with supernatural acts and fairytale people—and, to Garth, all beyond reality. Yet to the old lady it all was so logical and natural.

At the same time, there was information he couldn't dismiss—the marks on Cletis's shoulder, this strange Traveler character, the parts of the prophecy that had already come to pass, and the existence of this box. These were elements of her story that had a ring of truth to them, though he hated to admit it.

Questions and doubts raced through his head. He didn't want any of this to be real, primarily because of the danger into which Cletis would be thrust. At the same time, some of the details of this lady's story were coming awfully close to revealing answers about a moment in time that had always confused and frightened Garth . . . a time that had confused and frightened Anna as well.

There were certain questions he deliberately avoided asking—certain avenues he did not want to explore. If she were able to reveal truths that he had been searching for throughout his married life, then he would have to be accountable for those truths—he would have to admit that this woman's world was indeed real. Perhaps some things were better left unknown. Or were they? As his mind raced, Garth felt as if he were being sucked into a science fiction wormhole.

Abish sat patiently as he continued to question her, attempting to answer every inquiry to the best of her ability. Her eyes were penetrating as usual, and she spoke with expertise about the elements of the unbelievable world from which she had supposedly come. And as he considered her words, he realized that he noted a trace of an Irish accent that, despite her rasping tones, added a bit of family familiarity to the dialogue. That lilt had been heard in the voices of his grandparents and older relatives throughout his boyhood years. But now, after generations of life in the United States, that hint of the old land and family had slowly melted away.

Finally, though he feared her answers, he questioned her about the child born to her and the Traveler.

"Do you remember anything about the child you left behind with your family?" He watched her head bow. *She may have answers I don't want to hear. But it has come to this . . . after so many questions . . . after so many years.*

"Yes," she said, smiling at the thought. "He was about ten months old. His hair was just coming in. It was white when he was born, but it was gradually turning a bit reddish in color. It was much lighter than my auburn hair. His left eye turned out a bit, though, as if it didn't work in tandem with the other. That was a concern to me, and we had tried to heal him, but even my father was unsuccessful."

Garth fidgeted in his seat. "Could he walk yet?" he continued.

"Oh, yes. He was an active little boy. He was a climber and a goer . . . very energetic."

Garth knew he was getting closer to what he needed to know, yet he dreaded asking the question.

She could have collected this information from any number of sources, he told himself. *Medical records, newspaper articles, police reports, local gossip. She's not tellin' me anything that I couldn't have found out for myself.* Yet, in his mind, he stepped closer to the edge of the emotional cliff. *Certain details would be impossible for her to know . . . unless she's telling the truth about all this weird stuff.*

"How did you dress him?" he asked hesitantly.

"Little boys and little girls wore similar clothing," she responded, seemingly familiar with the details. "What I made for him was of wool with a hood. Well, like a hood. It was a separate piece that fit over his head. We knitted a family emblem on the right side of the cap, on the piece that could be folded down to cover his ear. I had long, auburn hair at the time and many strands of my own hair were woven into the emblem. It was a custom." She paused a moment. "Well . . . let me show you what it looked like."

A pencil lay on the end table next to her, and she picked it up. She lifted a piece of scratch paper onto her lap and artistically sketched a detailed drawing of the insignia that would have appeared on the hood flap. The embroidered image was that of a white-robed man with a bear at his side. Before the two images, floating in the air, appeared an opened scroll.

She passed the sketch across the table to Garth and allowed him to study it. "Like that," she said simply. "It would have looked like that."

He tried to keep his face free of expression as he examined the drawing. Her artwork was simple and elegant, and Garth recognized the insignia immediately.

There is no way she could have known that. What she has just drawn and what she has just explained is known only to two people—Anna and me. No one else could've known what this old hag has just put down on paper—unless she speaks the truth! Unless she really knows!

Garth could feel himself falling over the face of that cliff, and he had no idea where he would land. Disciplining his mind and body, he fought back the tears that wanted to surface. Whether they were tears of anger or of joy, he didn't know exactly, but he could not allow this old woman to see him become emotional.

He fired another question her way. "What did he wear on his feet?"

"Rabbit fur," she answered immediately, as if enjoying the memories as she described the details. "The soft lining was inside upon his skin, and the leather side was out. While the children were learning to walk, they would wear them that way. Once they walked, then a different little shoe was made."

Her words penetrated his heart, and Garth rose suddenly and walked around the couch. He stood with his back to her, pretending to look out the window. He knew there was only one possible way left that could explain how she knew all this. And it was his last grasp—his only way out.

If not, then my reality—the reality I've lived in for the past eleven years—is gonna fall apart around me. And I can't let that happen.

Abish went on with her story, as if lost in the pleasant memory. "If I recall, his hair was fly-away, sticking out like soft, downy feathers. Though he was fearless in his physical abilities, I wondered if his depth-perception was flawed because of the problem with his eyes—"

Garth turned on her, abruptly interrupting the flow of her description. "That's enough! Stop talking!" He looked down at the floor and instantly started pacing.

"Did I say something—"

"Stop talking!" He cut her off again. Still avoiding her gaze, he rubbed his face with his hands. "What are you trying to do to us?! Are you tryin' to destroy everything I have left—everything I hold sacred? Are you tryin' to destroy my life? My family? Cletis? Are you?" Finally his raptor gaze drilled her. "Man, who are you really?!"

Surprised by the emotional outburst, Abish sat up straight. "I am who I say I am," she stated emphatically. "Garth, I'm not trying to destroy anything."

"You've really done your homework here, haven't you—claiming to know my family, creating all this prophecy stuff, all this Traveler business. You've probably studied a long time to become familiar with all this stuff you're talkin' about. It took a lot of work, didn't it?" His pacing stopped abruptly. "Look, I don't know what mind games you're playing with us, or how you're doin' it all, but I'm not gonna take it any further!"

Mentally, he searched for a foundation on which he could build the argument he was considering.

"I know what you're up to!" His lips were tight in anger, but he spoke hastily. "I've figured you out—at least a *part* of what you're doing! Nice scheme, lady. Nice set-up. You pulled all this information out of the city files in Belleville, didn't you? You got access to the city files and the police files somehow. Or maybe you stole them! That's the only place you could've gotten what you know.

"What are you tryin' to do to us?! You wanna take him from me?! Well, I can tell you right now, our legal work on him was watertight! We waited two years for that to be final! The adoption was approved through four different levels. And you better believe that nothin's comin' between him and me. Nothing! You understand that? He's my son! Anna and I are his parents! And nothin' you can do is gonna break that up! You got that? And it's gonna stay that way! I don't care how elaborate your scheme is or what kind of illusions you're magically comin' up with, it's not gonna work! I'm keepin' him!"

Abish watched him, frightened and amazed by his outburst.

"I think you really *are* a witch," Garth bellowed. "No one but a *witch* would do what you're tryin' to do to my son and me!"

At that precise moment, Abish sat up straight. Her eyes moved to the window in front of her, as if ignoring Garth's accusations.

"Garth, do you feel that? He's near."

Garth pointed to the door. "Get out of my house!"

Mr. Howard and Elston had helped Cletis up and sat him on an old chair by the side of a large tubing spool Mr. Howard used as a table. Assuming he was ill, they had moved him into the shade and made him sit down. Cletis knew he wasn't sick, but played along with their efforts to help him. The cold, heavy feelings continued to frighten him. Wherever the Traveler was, he was extremely close by. His great fear was that the man who stood before him—the man who looked just like Mr. Howard—was not Mr. Howard at all. But Cletis had no way of knowing that, since the man's clothing covered his shoulders. But there had been no sense of evil coming from *this* Mr. Howard. The gentle, poor man had hovered around the large spool like a nurse around a hospital bed. He had kindly helped Cletis to a chair and, with an expression of sincere distress on his face, had voiced his hope that Cletis's condition would improve. Elston had quickly offered Cletis one of the drinks, thinking that maybe he needed some liquid. But Cletis had rejected it. Mr. Howard had picked up an old crate that lay against the hut and had seated himself next to Cletis. Elston pulled a couple of railroad ties over near the spool and had made himself a chair. There the three sat—two of them doing their best to make sure that Cletis's needs were met.

Elston and Mr. Howard were passing the minutes in light conversation when Cletis felt a change. The heaviness of the icy, dark sensations began to lift away. He sat up straight and took a slow, deep breath. To his surprise, the haunting feelings faded, and he felt his strength returning. He blinked his eyes and shook his head attempting to jog the fogginess from his brain.

Mr. Howard and Elston eyed him curiously.

"You doin' okay?" asked Mr. Howard.

"Yeah . . . yeah, I think I'm okay." *Maybe the feelings haven't gone away. Maybe they're still here around me, and I'm just getting used to them.*

Elston patted his shoulder. "You sure?"

"Yeah, I'll be fine," Cletis answered groggily.

"Are you hungry?" Mr. Howard asked. "You boys were kind enough to bring all this food. I sure hope you can eat it with me."

His concern was sincere, and his eyes were sympathetic. For the first time, it dawned on Cletis that Mr. Howard was wearing the Tigers cap and the jeans and T-shirt they had bought for him. Instead of a dreadful stink, the man smelled of Aqua Velva. Although he was still unshaven and his hair still hung over his shoulders, his countenance was happier and friendlier than Cletis had ever seen before.

Cletis pretended he had an appetite, and he nibbled on his burger and fries. Elston would ask little questions to get Mr. Howard talking, and once Mr. Howard started, they couldn't shut him up. Yet, in spite of the cordial talk, Cletis couldn't help but wonder if Mr. Howard was really the Traveler.

You're not gonna find out unless you yank the man's shirt off, Cletis reckoned. *And that would be pretty stupid if you saw that there weren't any marks on his shoulders.* Still it frightened Cletis to know the Traveler was somewhere close, even if he couldn't be felt.

In the occasional pauses in Mr. Howard's stories, he would ask the boys about their baseball playing. He was especially interested in their desires to be able to hit and field, and how practice had paid off in their efforts in those two areas. Without going into the details, and making sure they said nothing of Abish, the boys described the one practice in which they could do little wrong and where their abilities really began to blossom. They also talked about the team and about how Elston and his family were now moving away to Canterbury Heights.

When Elston mentioned Canterbury Heights, Mr. Howard suddenly stood.

"Just a second," he stated, excusing himself from the spool table. "Gotta tell you something. You'll like this." The old man stepped up into his little home, reached back behind the door, and brought out a baseball bat.

"This is it," he stated, stepping down to them and holding it out reverently.

The bat was a thirty-three inch "Louisville Slugger." Straight, wooden grains stretched from the bottom nub to the rounded top.

"This is the very bat my son used—in Canterbury Heights. Elston, you reminded me of it. There is a ball diamond there by the town hall and the city pool. Gotta tell you about this at-bat. One of the great moments of my life!"

Gripping the bat in his hands and looking out over the tracks as if facing a make-believe diamond, Mr. Howard announced the play-by-play.

"Score was one to nothing. We were losin'. Well, my son, Ted, comes to bat. Runners on second and third. Last inning. Both teams on the edge of their seats. See, that pitcher had always struck Ted out—in all the games they had played against each other. And everyone knew it too . . . Well, *almost* always struck him out. I think he grounded out a few times, but he had never hit this kid. No one could. Darn fast pitcher with good control. He eventually signed in the Pirates organization. So the third-base coach stands there in his box and yells out, 'Fire in the hole!' That meant somethin' excitin' was gonna happen."

There was a glow of enthusiasm in his dark brown eyes. He flipped the bat back and forth with his wrists, as if preparing for an oncoming pitch. Pausing, he lifted the bat for emphasis and pointed it out toward the tracks.

"My son, Ted—he eyes the boy on the mound for a few seconds, then steps into the batter's box. Somethin' great was gonna happen. We could just see it in their eyes as they faced off." Mr. Howard stepped away from the spool. He cocked the bat behind his shoulder, as if he were awaiting the pitch. "Well, the pitcher winds and drills this fastball right over the center of the plate, as if he was saying, 'My best against your best.' And Teddy was waitin' for it." Mr. Howard swung the bat—as if in slow motion—a perfect level swing at the belt.

"CRACK! Right on the sweet spot of this ole Louisville Slugger. That ball leapt off his bat! Just kept risin'." Mr. Howard lifted his hand, as if tracking the flight of a rocket over Cape Kennedy. "Over the center fielder's head it went, and when it finally came down, it landed in the city pool! Luckily no one got pegged by it."

"The pool by the town hall?" questioned Elston, his eyes wide with excitement.

Mr. Howard nodded proudly and smiled—displaying his broken, dark teeth between his parted lips.

"Wow!" continued Elston, as if measuring the distance in his head. "I've been there before. I've been to that field! That's gotta be over four hundred feet from home plate!"

For a moment the trio sat silently, awed by the magical moment Mr. Howard described.

"You're right, Elston. And that's why they raised the fence by the pool," he announced.

Abish should be here for this story, Cletis thought. *She loves the game!*

"Four hundred feet," Elston repeated, lifting his hands behind his head and staring up into the swaying branches of the maples on the other side of the tracks. "'My best against your best.'"

Cletis, caught up in the story, forgot his woes and suddenly laughed out loud. Mr. Howard stroked the bat as if it were a loyal dog.

As the sun set and the mosquitoes began to join the little get-together around the spool, Cletis and Elston excused themselves.

"Thanks, Mr. Howard," spouted Elston. "But my mom and dad are waitin' for me about now, and there's a lot of movin' work to do at my house."

"Well, you boys have a good night, and thanks again for your thoughtfulness." Mr. Howard pushed the brim of his hat up and stood by the side of the spool, still holding the bat in his left hand. With a kind smile, he watched the boys gather their trash and walk away.

"Bye," Cletis called one last time as he hopped on his bike.

Mr. Howard watched the boys disappear around the side of the grocery store. With his bat in hand, he stepped up into the doorframe of the little shack, pushed the door open, and walked inside.

The old hut consisted of three rooms: a small kitchen, a sleeping room, and a tiny bathroom that housed an old porcelain toilet and a small sink. There was running water, but no electricity in the dwelling.

In the diminishing light that filtered through the window on the west side of the little shack, Mr. Howard saw his way through the kitchen area and around to the sleeping room. He stood for a moment in the doorway and then leaned the bat in the corner to his right. There he paused and looked down at the old cot that occupied nearly half of the small room.

He studied the man who slept on the cot.

It was Mr. Howard.

The Traveler removed his cap and tossed it on the sleeping man. A sly grin lifted the corners of his mouth as he stepped away into the room by the front door. He pushed his head back and moved it from side to side, as if stretching the muscles of his neck. Gradually the transformation began. The bones and flesh steadily rippled, contorted and groaned as the image of Mr. Howard faded and the figure of the Traveler began to take shape. His body moaned with the alteration as lumps and bulges pulsed beneath his skin. The clothing also shifted and melded into the boots and black leather worn by the man with the blond braid and the hourglass marks on his shoulders. The Changeling sighed and twisted with the alteration, and then opening his eyes and mouth wide, stretching the muscles of his face, he brought the process to an end. He looked down on the new creation and flexed his muscular arms and legs, as if checking to see that all was functioning as it should.

Again he eyed the sleeping man and smiled confidently. "Ah, Mr. Howard, it is so much easier with a real person than it is with a photograph. You have been of great assistance this evening. If necessary, the boys will be useful to me."

Suddenly a field of dancing particles gathered about him, gradually enveloping him in the conduit of thriving gray energy. Abruptly, the Changeling—the Traveler—disappeared within it.

The setting sun provided sufficient light to see their way to the Dungarvan house, and having promised that he would stay with Cletis the entire time, Elston rode with him all the way home. Turning right off Main Street, they headed into Cletis's neighborhood and made their way down to the end of the street to the Dungarvan home.

"You know what?" stated Cletis, pulling up onto the lawn and hopping off his bike. "If what you say about Mr. Sperry is right, maybe we'll get to play a team from up where you're gonna live." He leaned the bike against him. "And maybe you'll get on a team, and we'll see you in some tournament, or somethin' like that."

"Yeah, maybe," answered Elston, bowing his head. He balanced on his bike momentarily, lifting both feet off the ground. "Well, I'm gonna try to play there if I can get on a team. Maybe I can be good enough to play on an All-Star team. I dunno. We'll just have to wait and see."

"Well, you keep fielding and hittin' the way you do here, and I think they'll sign you right up somewhere." Cletis smiled at him confidently. "And you can be sure I'm gonna figure out how to get to your new place."

Elston kicked at his chain guard. "What happened to you over at Mr. Howard's place? Did you get sick or somethin'? You looked like you were gonna croak, man. You looked gray."

"I dunno," stated Cletis, knowing he was hiding the truth from his best friend. "But, yeah, somethin' hit me, and I felt real lousy. Then it kinda just went away."

"Was it kinda like what you felt when the marks came on your shoulders?"

"No, it was different. This was like all over my body and inside too. Kinda like a real bad flu. The marks just hurt my shoulders. That's all."

Elston nodded, trying to understand.

"Will you do me a favor, Elston?"

"Sure."

"Don't talk about this to anyone? Keep it all to yourself until we get some answers from Abish or we figure out what's happenin'."

"Okay."

"Promise?"

"Promise." Elston smiled and shook his head. "Who's gonna believe me anyway? If I told anyone, they'd think I was crazy. Besides, I can't even explain it, so how am I gonna tell?" Elston lifted his foot back onto a pedal and pushed away onto the driveway. "I'll try to come and see you before I leave, okay?" he added as he coasted out into the street. "But if that doesn't work, I'll call ya."

The streetlights on the road suddenly came on, as if in response to Elston's good-bye.

"Okay. I'll be waitin' for you," agreed Cletis as he watched Elston disappear down the street.

When Cletis entered the house, all was quiet. There was no sign of his father. Nor was there any sign of Abish.

Maybe she's in the guest room, resting, he thought as he closed the front door behind him.

"Dad?" he called, disrupting the stillness of the home.

He waited. There was no reply. He felt a surge of fear spider through his veins, remembering the last time he was home by himself. Cletis crossed through the front room and up into the kitchen. No one was there. The house appeared empty. Cletis froze in the middle of the kitchen floor. He didn't like being in this situation. Again he called out.

"Dad? You home?"

Cletis waited in the dreary silence.

"Yeah," came the response. "I'm in here."

With a thankful sigh of relief, Cletis made his way down the hall toward his father's room. He stopped in the doorway and peered in. His dad sat on the edge of the bed, his shoulders sagging and his head bowed. The old hat box from the closet shelf sat next to him. His arm was draped across it.

"Do I need to take my shirt off?" he asked, lifting his head in greeting.

Cletis paused for a moment. "No."

"Well, just so you can rest assured, I'll do it anyway." His dad unbuttoned his shirt and pulled the edges of it back over one shoulder at a time, so Cletis could see. There were no marks on his shoulders.

Cletis eased his way across the room. "Sorry."

"It's okay."

Cletis sat down on the bed. "Where's Abish?" he asked, trying to sense his father's mood.

His father shifted uncomfortably, ignoring the question. "Were you okay over at Mr. Howard's place?" his father asked. "Everything go okay with you and Elston?"

"Yeah, I guess so," Cletis answered, shrugging his shoulders. Cletis knew it was an untruth, but figured he'd hold back on the details until he found out where Abish was and what was going on with her.

If I tell Dad I had some more of those lousy feelings, he might never let me near Abish or Elston or Mr. Howard again. Anyway, I'll tell him soon enough, but I gotta make sure Abish is okay before I go sharin' more bad news with him.

"We ate the stuff Elston bought," Cletis continued, "and then Mr. Howard talked to us about his son and told us some baseball stories. It was good."

"Good," his father replied, reaching out and taking hold of Cletis's fingers. "I was worried about you. Abish claimed she felt something. I guess she was wrong." He studied Cletis. When Cletis said nothing, he turned away again, bowed his head, and appeared to be lost again in his realm of deep, dark thoughts.

"You all right?" Cletis asked.

His dad nodded, but continued to stare at the floor.

"So is Abish here?"

Without looking up, his dad replied, "I sent her home."

"You mean to *her* home?" Cletis asked.

"Yeah . . . her home." There was a gloom in the bedroom. "I told her to leave, and she left," Garth added, still looking down. He gripped Cletis's fingers a bit more tightly.

"Why?"

"She said some things that made me fear that she might be trying to do something bad to our family. So I felt it wise to ask her to leave."

Cletis paused, trying to think things through. "So she just *walked* home?"

"I didn't drive her."

"Did she go across the field?"

"I don't have any idea how she got home. Maybe she took her broom."

His father lifted his arm off the hatbox, and with both hands, he rubbed his tired face.

Cletis had never heard his dad say anything mean about anyone in his life, especially a woman. "Dad, what's goin' on?"

"I'm sorry." He inhaled deeply. "I shouldn't have said that in front of you. But to be completely honest, I wanted to say it, and it just sorta came out." He turned and studied Cletis. "I just don't know what danger we may be in, Clete, and I can't afford to bring someone into this house who might have a desire to destroy what's sacred to me—what I love. And that's my family. That's *you*."

They sat in silence. His father turned away from him and looked straight ahead into the darkness of the closet. Cletis eyed the hatbox between them.

"Dad, we can't leave her down there—*if* she made it home. The house is wide open to animals and bugs. Everything's covered with dust, and glass, and plaster . . ."

"According to her, she's basically immortal. Nothin's gonna harm her. If she's lived through some thousand years of life, she can figure out how to get home, I'm sure."

"But Dad, you've never treated a lady like this."

"Clete," he answered, looking his son squarely in the eyes, "I don't know whether she's a lady or not." There was a pause. "Let me put it this way, son. I don't know whether she's a good lady or a bad lady. But I get the feeling she's a bad lady, and that she's trying to do something to us I don't want her to do. I don't want her around us, and I especially don't want her around you."

Despite the concern in his voice, Cletis could tell that something was still troubling his father.

"Like what, Dad? What's she tryin' to do to us?"

"I think . . . I don't know if she's telling us the truth . . . and, uh, there's more."

"But Dad, what about the marks on my shoulders?" Cletis reasoned. "What about the man who appeared the other night with the marks on *his* shoulders? What about the feelings that I've had? They're real, Dad. I'm not makin' 'em up. They scare me. And what about the box and the prophecy and the things that have come true so far? A lot of things are real." He paused a moment. "Dad, I think Abish is a good lady. I think she's tellin' the truth. I don't think she's evil."

His dad sat motionlessly, but Cletis knew he was listening, considering.

"And what about the other gifts she gave me and Elston?" he continued. "The cards in the box . . . The cards just appeared, Dad. Sometimes they were there, and sometimes there was nothing. But we sold the cards to Mr. Sperry, and Abish was buying them from him. We didn't know she was, but we found that out later. Remember, I told you about this. And we used the money to buy food and clothes for the Ketchums and for Mr. Howard. Because we did it, she helped us—or at least we think she did . . . Elston and me are a lot better now at fielding and hitting. That's what me and Elston wanted to be able to do more than anything else."

"What?" his father spoke abruptly. "Wait a minute, wait a minute. . . . She *gave* you the abilities to field and hit? What d'ya mean by that?"

"Well, she didn't do anything to us, really, but she coached us. Elston and I sure got a lot better at fielding and hitting . . . like the very same day. She told us some things to do, like with our hands and our concentration, and so we tried 'em out, and now I can hit the ball anywhere I want to, Dad. And Elston—man, he's like a cat out there. Nothin' gets by him now."

"Cletis, I'm . . . I'm not sure what you're saying. What'd she do? Say some magic words, and then you went out and could suddenly hit the ball to all fields?"

"Well, we'd been practicin', you know, tryin' to do better, but then, one afternoon, after we visited her, everything just sort of fell into place. We told her what we wanted to be able to do, and she told us some things to try, and then she said, 'Okay, go and do it.'"

"I thought you weren't goin' over there? I thought I told you to stay away from her. And you guys have been visiting her regularly?"

Cletis said nothing in response. He knew he had told his dad he would stay away from her house, even after he had made his second visit to fix the screen door.

"I dunno, Dad. It's like I'm bein' pulled there. It's like there's something I gotta know and gotta do. Even now, I need to go get her."

"Oh, man, Clete . . ." His father took a deep breath, sensing his son's urgency. He paused, rubbed his face again, and chose not to get angry. "Okay, so you were over there visiting her when I asked you not to . . . Okay . . . What's done is done." He reached over and put a hand on the back of Cletis's neck. "So . . . uh . . . talk to me a second, cuz I just don't understand somethin' here. Talk to me about this hittin' stuff . . . You mean you're not pullin' the ball to the left side anymore?"

"Only when I want to," Cletis grinned. "Dad, remember that part of the prophecy—*'the orb is driven at his command.'* I think the orb is a ball. A baseball. I don't know what else that could mean, and if it's talkin' about *me*, then it's another part of the prophecy that's being fulfilled."

His father studied him speechlessly.

"And the other part, *'Time is red upon his shoulders.'* She knew about that, Dad. She knew what the marks looked like—like she had seen 'em before. She knows the Traveler's son will have the same marks on his shoulders. Those same marks are on me, Dad." He paused, silent for several seconds. "I don't know what that means, Dad."

"I don't know, either, son. I just don't know. That's what I'm tryin' to figure out." His father shifted on the bed, bringing one leg up under him. "This whole thing is gettin' way beyond me, and I'm not quite sure what needs to be done—except I know this . . . I'll protect you whatever comes, and I'm gonna keep our family together!"

Cletis watched him exhale. His dad sat with his shoulders rounded forward. It looked as if he were carrying an eighty-pound bag of gravel.

"Does Abish know about the marks on your shoulders?"

"I haven't told her."

"Good. Don't."

"The man who came to me, Dad, he had the *same* marks on his shoulders," repeated Cletis, emphasizing that crucial, troubling point. "Abish said that Travelers were father and son."

"Yeah, and that scares me. This whole thing scares me. And she knew about some other things too, Clete—things that only your mother and I ever knew." He eyed his son anxiously and then spoke in soft, hushed tones, as if afraid someone might be listening.

"Clete, you've always known you were adopted. We've never hid that fact from you. Your mom miscarried and she was heartbroken. So was I." He eyed the hatbox. "You've always known that we found you in the backyard of the old house in Belleville. You were wandering there. We never found your birth mother. We searched for nearly a year before the actual adoption process began. We've never kept those details from you. But what you were wearing . . . your clothes . . . your mother and I always kept that to ourselves. You've never seen that clothing as far as I know. And I'll tell you about that later . . . but Abish described your clothing perfectly. She described each article you wore—the booties and how they were made. She described the cap. She even drew a picture of the insignia that was over the right earpiece. And years ago, when your mom and I studied the clothing, we noticed that long, auburn hairs were woven into the wool of the earpieces. We could see them there in the fabric, and we always wondered about that. Abish told me that her hair was auburn long ago, and that when she made the baby clothes, she put the strands of hair there purposely. No one could have known that. Then she described the problem with your eye—exactly. She was telling the story of her own child, but she was describing you."

His father paused a moment.

"My fear is that she's trying to take you away from me, Clete . . . that she's found your history in the archives of the court building back in Belleville, and that she's made up this amazing story, and that she's trying to take you away. I don't know how or why, but that's kinda what I feel . . . like she's trying to destroy our family."

Cletis watched his father's lips tighten.

"For the last eleven years, we've wanted to know the story. Your mom and I fell asleep lots of nights tossing ideas back and forth that might explain things. We just never knew where you came from. Always the unanswered question. And we went about life always wondering. We hoped one day the answer would come. And now . . ."

His father let the thought dangle.

"Oh, Cletis, it's not supposed to happen this way. . . . It was all supposed to be happy and simple. . . . As much as I'm fighting it, Cletis, I fear—I truly fear—you're right. And she's right. And that the time has come when I'm gonna have to lay everything out in the open. . . . I just wish I could know for sure what the outcome of all this is gonna be."

His dad made a brave attempt to control his emotions but was unsuccessful. His head dropped into the palms of his hands, and he wept softly. Seeing his father's anguish and sensing the fears of his *own* heart, Cletis too felt the tears come.

Unexpectedly a peculiar, tiny glow began to form between the open closet and the bed. The soft, pinpoint of light expanded into a beaming ball about three feet in diameter that floated about a foot off the ground. The dark room was suddenly infused with the beautiful blue radiance—a delicate light that spoke peace to troubled minds. Garth stood and pulled Cletis to his side. The two watched in awe as images and patterns emerged within this round orb of energy. Suddenly, inside the sphere, there appeared holographic scenes from an old Detroit Tigers baseball game. Garth recognized the stadium, the seats, the field, the uniforms. A young boy was seen carrying refreshments down the steep stairs of the upper deck. As the lad reached the base of the stairs, cheers erupted from the crowd.

Though the perspective of the vision within the orb did not reveal the details of the game on the field, Garth and Cletis could observe, in detail, what had happened on the stairs. The boy looked up to see what caused the roar from the crowd. At that moment, he lost his footing, and went straight forward, toward the railing. The box of food tumbled from his hands—some of it going over the edge, some of it landing on the concrete in front of him.

In that instant, Cletis recognized the circumstances. His dad had told him the story at least a dozen times. But now he was actually seeing the details unfold. The boy, though fighting to catch his balance, went over the edge and teetered there, trying desperately to save himself from the deadly drop to the lower level. They watched as Garth's father frantically reached for him but found himself unable to catch the boy's leg or foot.

In the moment when the child looked as if he were about to go over the railing, an old, short woman reached up from behind, grabbed both his legs tightly in her hands, and pulled him steadily to safety. The frightened boy, once out of danger, ran immediately into his father's open arms without looking back at the woman who saved him. The old woman turned, ascended the stairs, and vanished from the scene. When Garth's father finally turned to thank her, she was gone.

Cletis and his dad saw it plainly. The old woman in the blue vision—the one who had saved Garth—was Abish.

Gradually the images within the orb disappeared, and the blue ball of energy faded into nothingness. In the silence of the darkened room, father and son stood pondering, staring into the open closet in front of them. For several seconds neither spoke. Then his father wrapped an arm around Cletis's waist.

"I hope she's a friend, son," he whispered wearily. "How I hope she's a friend. This is all way beyond me. Let's go bring her home."

CHAPTER 14

COUSIN BERNIE

A pounding on the front door awakened both Cletis and Garth at the same time. Cletis sat up on the lamb's wool rug that lay at the side of his father's bed. For safety, Garth had him sleep close by. Both wondered who could be thumping the door at 7:10 a.m., but Cletis recognized Frank's loud voice.

"I'm coming!" called Cletis. Wearing the old, navy blue shorts and gray T-shirt he liked to sleep in, he hurried out of the bedroom and raced down the hall to the front entryway. "I'm coming!" he called again as the knocking continued.

With Garth close behind, still tying the belt of his robe, Cletis unlocked the door and pulled it open. There stood Rabbit, Frank, Pauly and Klu. Their four bikes rested on the lawn behind them.

"Clete, get your clothes on quick!" announced Rabbit. "We're gonna meet at Sperry's at 7:30! He's got uniforms for us!"

"Really?" questioned Cletis, rubbing the sleep from his tired eyes.

"Yeah. And Johnny's cousin's comin' in from Ohio at ten o'clock this morning," spouted Frank. "Everyone told me that that's what the witch-lady predicted would happen, and now it is! And he's a big guy!"

"Don't call her a witch-lady, moron," corrected Klu, nudging him with an elbow.

"Yeah," added Rabbit. "After what happened yesterday, we decided we gotta find something else to call her—but not 'witch-lady.'"

"How about we call her 'Abish'?" stated Cletis, matter-of-factly. "After all, that's her name. Abish."

They all stood frozen, pondering the logic.

"Man, *she's* got a name?" asked Frank innocently. "I wonder who named *her*?"

"Maybe she had parents, dufus," spurted Klu, giving him another elbow.

"That's hard to believe," chuckled Pauly.

Garth grinned. Sleepily he fought back a yawn.

"What about Johnny's cousin?" asked Cletis.

"He's a southpaw, just like Elston," continued Frank. "So we're gonna practice at 10:30, you know, and see what he can do."

"He pitches too." Rabbit sang the words.

"And we need a lefty in the line-up now that Elston is gone," spouted Pauly.

"Can you come with us?" asked Klu. "We're heading to Sperry's right now."

"Right now?" Cletis looked up at his dad. "Can I go?"

"Okay . . ." he responded thoughtfully, still pondering the family's on-going challenges. "Yeah, go ahead. Just stay with the group and come right back when you're finished there."

Cletis faced his teammates. "Wait for me." He turned, raced past his dad, and dashed up the stairs to his room to change clothes.

Garth left the door open. "He'll be right back," he announced.

Crossing back through the entryway, Garth stepped down into the front room. There on the couch rested the hatbox. He had placed it there late last night after they had returned from Abish's house. And as he studied the box, the events of the previous night, again, passed through his mind. . . . They had driven to Abish's place, and had walked through the semi-darkness, around to the back of her house. They had entered through the gaping hole in the wall and had called her name as they wandered the empty rooms and halls. She had answered with a simple, "I'm here." They had found her in her parlor, just sitting. She had looked up at them, her eyes moist with tears.

Garth had studied her amazingly ugly, funny shape as she sat there alone—all alone in the house, all alone in her life. In that moment, it had struck him how vulnerable she was—how human despite her supposedly "changed" state. He had envisioned in his mind some young lady in her prime, somehow transformed into this rounded, bulbous, deep-voiced hag. Yet her sweet, green eyes revealed the inner woman—a woman of courage, longing to find her former self; a woman of strength, willing to do what needed to be done to meet the demands of this strange prophecy. Garth had knelt in front of her and had looked up into her face. He saw a woman out of place, from a different world, a different realm.

There were still doubts in his mind. It was only natural to disbelieve anything beyond the scope of life's ordinary events. But after having seen the vision in blue, he knew he had to give her a chance.

"I sent it to you," she had simply said. "Did you see it?"

Garth had nodded and looked over at Cletis who stood beside him. "Both of us."

"Then you are Dungarvans. Only they can see the blue visions."

He had studied her thoughtfully, her face, her neck, her straggled hair, her green eyes. "It *was* you, wasn't it? Years ago, you were there. You caught me before I went over."

"Blame it on Norm Cash. It was a double into the left-center gap. Two runs scored. What boy wouldn't have tripped? In fact, I became so caught up in the game that I almost missed the moment."

He had paused, trying to find the right words to explain his fears. "There are a lot of unanswered questions. But I'm willing to try to believe, and if I can, I'm willing to help you. I'm sorry about my mean words. I'm just trying my best to protect my remaining family."

"I understand," was all she had said.

And now, with a new morning, Garth stood by the couch and looked down at the hatbox. He stepped over to the window and peered out onto the beauty of the day, seeing the bikes on the front lawn and their owners all huddled together in excited, quiet conversation. He listened to the shuffling and clunking upstairs as Cletis prepared for the morning's excitement.

Garth crossed over to the couch and sat down next to the hatbox. Lifting it into his lap, he pulled off the lid and peered inside. The faint scent of vanilla wafted up from within it.

Cletis raced down the stairs, zipped past the living room, and darted through the open front door. "Be back in a bit," he announced as he flew by.

"Clete, wait a minute," Garth called.

Cletis came back in, a bit antsy to be off with the team.

"Yeah?"

"Who's the girl out there?"

"Oh, that's Rabbit."

"'Rabbit'? Is that her name?"

"No, her real name is Roberta, but we call her Rabbit. She's plays shortstop."

"So *she* plays with you boys?"

"Yeah, she's one of the best on the team."

Garth grinned.

Cletis turned a bit pink. "Dad, she's one of the guys."

"Oh, I see. . . . Well, be safe. And don't be alone."

"I'll be careful," replied Cletis. "Bye."

With that, he shut the door behind him.

Cletis could smell the excitement all the way to the Cards and Coins shop. When they arrived en masse, they entered the store together and found Mr. Sperry there ready for them.

He had neatly laid out nine baseball uniforms across the glass counters in his shop. He and Johnny had guessed on the sizes of each person on the team and had put the pants, shirts, and belts together on display. On top of each uniform rested a white card that bore the name of the player who was supposed to wear it. The uniforms were simple—white pants with a brown pinstripe pattern; white, pinstriped tops with a large brown "D" inscribed on the front left side; a brown belt; brown stirrups that pulled up over white socks; and a brown hat, with the same letter "D" on the front of it. In other words, Mr. Sperry basically ordered a duplication of the Detroit Tigers' uniform.

As planned, the players had gathered right at 7:30 at the Cards and Coins Shop, alert, thrilled, and eager to hear what Mr. Sperry had to announce. He wandered behind the cases, checking the names and sizes on each uniform, and making sure all the pieces were in order.

"Look around and find your uniform," Mr. Sperry announced, "but don't touch it yet. Just look at it for now while I explain some things. I'm gonna let you take them home and try them on, but only wear them when the tournament games start."

Everyone turned and looked at Mr. Sperry, stunned by the announcement.

"What tournament games?" asked Klu.

"Didn't Johnny tell you?" questioned Mr. Sperry, pushing his glasses back onto the bridge of his nose.

"You were gonna give me the details," answered Johnny, "but then you got busy with some order and you never did."

"Oh, you're right. Sorry. Well, then," continued Mr. Sperry, "let me explain, and then you all need to go back and tell your parents. Gotta get their permission, and we gotta make sure we schedule this right." He smiled and settled his hands on his hips. "I've signed you boys up—" He interrupted himself and looked at the only girl present in the room. "Sorry, Rabbit. No offense."

She smiled and nodded.

"I've signed you up in the Greater Metro Tournament. We're the farthest team away from the center of the action. We're out here in the boondocks. Most of the teams have been playing through the spring in city competition, so it'll be tough goin'. It's single elimination. Seven-inning games. So if we lose the first, that's it . . . or we could play four or five games if we win them all, depending upon how many teams there are in the tourney. So I want you to go home and check with your folks on the dates and times. They're posted on the wall by the door." He pointed to the front door behind them. "I'm tellin' you this because you'll need to supply your own transportation to and from each game.

Okay? So go check the schedule. Hopefully everyone can go. And then go check out your uniforms and make sure everything's there."

Chatter filled the store with talk of sizes and colors and insignias and tournament schedules. Suddenly in the midst of the dull babbling, Johnny shouted out.

"Thanks, Mr. Sperry!"

Instantly, all the team members echoed their agreement.

"You're certainly welcome," he responded. "Just go and have fun, and win some games for Greenberg Junction."

"Hey, who's gonna coach us?" called Rabbit.

There was a momentary silence, until Mr. Sperry spoke up again.

"Oh, yeah . . . uh, well, I . . . I forgot to bring that up. Uhmm . . . a coach has not been found yet, so that has yet to be decided. Check with your parents or your big brothers. Anyone. I can't do it, so we need to find someone willing to help us out. Uh . . . no coach, no tournament. So it's pretty important."

Cletis had an idea.

Cletis burst through the front door of the house, carrying his uniform under his arm. He slammed the door behind him, rounded the corner, and charged into the living room.

"We got uniforms!" he shouted, throwing the pieces of clothing onto the floor beside the couch. "And we're gonna play in a real tournament! Mr. Sperry says!"

Abish sat in the chair by the end table and smiled as Cletis knelt and arranged the uniform into a flat, bodiless baseball player, with every piece of clothing in place except for the shoes.

His dad came in from the kitchen, carrying a small plate and eating a piece of toast. "Looks like the Tigers," he commented through a mouthful of breakfast, looking down at the uniform.

"Yeah! An' right now, over on the diamond, we're trying out a new pitcher!" continued Cletis. "Johnny's cousin. Just like you said, Abish."

She smiled but said nothing.

"He's a southpaw! And Johnny says nobody can hit him, but I'm gonna show 'em how it's done!" Cletis leapt to his feet and hurried back through the kitchen. "Come watch us!" he hollered as he gathered his mitt and hat in the laundry room by the back door. "An' we're not supposed to wear the uniform until the *tournament*, but I'll explain about that later!"

"Tournament?" questioned Abish.

"Yeah!" shouted Cletis as the back door slammed shut.

The team had already gathered at the baseball diamond by the time Cletis arrived. The new guy, Bernie Anderson, was throwing to Pauly, and Pauly was whiffing with each pitch. Davey, Frank, and Rabbit were standing in the outfield, but there wasn't much action. Cletis dropped his bike by the dugout and stepped up behind the backstop next to Johnny and Timmy.

"Come on Pauly," teased Klu from behind the plate. "You haven't touched him yet."

"Wait 'til you try," announced Pauly as he shifted his helmet, dug in at the plate, and awaited the next pitch.

When it came, Pauly swung hard and fouled the ball off toward the scoreboard in right. It was the first time Pauly had made contact, and his smile revealed that he was proud of himself. As Davey tracked it down, Klu tossed another ball back to the mound.

"He's fast, isn't he," stated Cletis quietly as he watched Bernie wind and fire another strike. Pauly tipped it into Klu's glove.

"Tell me if I'm swingin' high or low," Pauly asked Klu.

"Man, I'm just hopin' to catch the darn thing," Klu laughed as he threw the ball back to Bernie.

"Yeah, he *is* fast," answered Johnny excitedly in response to Cletis's comment. "Kinda cool, eh? We got us a ringer from Xenia, Ohio, just in time for that tournament."

Under Bernie's Ohio State Buckeyes hat, Cletis could see a healthy crop of brown, straight hair. He had a fairly light complexion and stood a bit taller and heavier than Johnny. His arms were long, and he seemed to whip the ball toward home. He wore a cocky smile that broadened with each pitch that Pauly missed, and it was obvious that he thought highly of his own abilities.

"Here, try this one," he called from the mound as Pauly awaited the next pitch.

Bernie fired a fastball, even faster than the others. Pauly swung but was way late.

"At least you didn't step in the bucket," announced Klu, congratulating him and tossing the ball back to Bernie. "I think I would've been afraid of that one."

Timmy, who stood on the other side of Johnny, watched the new boy nervously. "He's faster than you, Johnny. I'm never gonna touch him."

"All a matter of catchin' up to him," spoke Johnny, folding his arms. "Just gotta see it. It's all in the timing. Come around a little bit quicker. Don't turn your head. If you're not afraid of it, you'll hit it. The faster it comes in, the farther it goes out."

Pauly fouled another one. This one banged against the backstop, just above where the three boys stood. They jumped back and automatically lifted their arms and hands as if to protect themselves.

"See, little by little, Pauly's catchin' up to him," nodded Johnny, stepping back to the backstop.

"If you call foul balls catchin' up," teased Klu.

Johnny looked down at Timmy. "You can do it too," he nodded, patting him on the back. "Get up there and take your cuts. You'll see. You'll do great."

But Timmy didn't look too convinced.

Just then, Frank, who stood in left field, spotted Mr. Dungarvan coming toward the diamond. At his side walked Abish.

"Hey, Cletis, here comes your dad!" he called from the outfield.

"Who's that with him?" questioned Klu, pulling his mask off.

Cletis and the rest of the boys turned to look.

"Isn't that the old lady we saw yesterday?" asked Johnny as he studied the couple.

"Yeah, it is. It's the witch whose house got blown up," added Timmy.

"Timmy, she's not a witch," Cletis reminded. "Her name is Abish. She stayed at our house last night."

"The witch lady stayed at *your* house?" asked Timmy, staring over at Cletis, astonished by the thought. "Oh, man, we're in for trouble now."

"Timmy! Knock it off!" Johnny reprimanded in a hushed tone, giving him a solid nudge. "Don't say that."

"Because of her, I fell in the canal," Timmy declared.

"You fell in because the bank didn't hold you up. She's not a witch," stated Cletis, annoyed by Timmy's words.

"She sure knows how to condition a catcher's mitt," commented Klu. "Even though it's weird to think of her hand in my mitt, I ain't never seen a catcher's mitt broken in like the way she did it." He popped his fist into his glove. "My dad even said it was the best he'd ever seen."

Everyone on the team paused a moment, looking off to the foul side of left field as the pair approached.

"So who's that?" questioned Bernie from the mound, still unfamiliar with the people and places of this new community.

"Cletis's dad," answered Klu, pointing to Cletis behind the backstop. "And the old lady is . . . uh . . . well . . . she knows Cletis's family. Is that right, Clete?"

"Yeah, that's right. You could say it that way."

"Clete, they're comin' to watch you, so why don't you take the bat and see what you can do," Johnny suggested.

"Yeah," continued Pauly, dropping the helmet at his feet. "I couldn't touch him and neither could Davey and Frank. So knock yourself out."

Cletis waved to his dad and Abish as they came close to the old dugout. "Sit right there on the bench," Cletis called as he swung around the side of the backstop and approached the plate. Johnny and Timmy trotted out onto the diamond and took positions in the infield, while Pauly jogged back out to left field, trading places with Frank.

The team shifted around, preparing for Cletis's at-bat. Even with the new kid on the mound, none of them could take their eyes off Abish—the legendary witch-woman of Greenberg Junction. Though they had finally seen her up close and face-to-face the day before, she was still a mystery to them all, shrouded in the unknown. This was the woman whose back wall was unexplainably blown away. This was the woman who prophesied of Bernie's coming, and now here he was. This was the woman, who, for years, had been the focus of the initiation rituals practiced by every kid who claimed the privilege of playing on this neighborhood sandlot team. The horror stories surrounding this woman and her house still haunted the thoughts and dreams of every boy and girl who lived in the area. And now, here she sat, on their very own dugout bench, watching them play ball.

"Watch out for splinters," laughed Cletis as he picked up his bat.

"Man, Clete," whispered Klu. "You talk to her like she was your grandma or something. How can you do that? She's been the witch of this area for so long."

"I just got to know her a little bit . . . that's all," answered Cletis as he donned his helmet, took some practice swings, and stepped closer to the plate.

"Okay, Clete, show 'em what you can do!" shouted Johnny from second base.

"Yeah, Cletis, show us how it's done!" called Rabbit from center.

"I'll try," he muttered, mostly under his breath.

Bernie wound and fired. His first pitch zipped past Cletis and into Klu's mitt. Cletis purposely didn't swing. He wanted to size this new pitcher up a bit and see how he threw.

"Fast, isn't he?" spouted Klu from behind the plate as he tossed the ball back to the mound.

"None faster that I've seen. Of course, I haven't seen any other pitcher except Johnny or whoever else is throwin' to us."

"Well, I'll tell you then. I ain't never seen anyone our age throw harder than Bernie. An' he throws strikes too. Only four balls outta the strike zone so far. All the rest have been perfect . . . well, kinda perfect. So you can expect it straight down the tube. Just gotta catch up to it."

Klu settled in behind the plate. The second pitch came in, hard and fast and right down the center. Cletis swung and connected, slapping the ball into shallow right field, between first and second. Davey picked it up on one bounce. Bernie followed the hit, seemingly amazed that Cletis had made contact with that one. Turning back to the plate, he eyed Cletis competitively.

"Comin' at ya, Bernie," called Davey, firing the ball back to the mound.

"Nice hit," called Rabbit from center.

"Yeah," added Pauly, "way to catch up to it."

Cletis took a few more practice swings, keeping the bat loose in his hands. As he dug in again at the plate, he spoke softly to Klu. "Gonna have to come around quicker on this boy. But he's throwin' melons."

"Look like BBs to me," confessed Klu.

Bernie continued to eye Cletis from the mound. "Hey, that's not gonna happen again, kid! Nobody hits me like that."

"Cocky, ain't he," whispered Klu, pulling the mask down over his face.

Bernie wound and delivered. The pitch came in hard—high and tight. As it whizzed by Cletis's face, he dropped backward and hit the dirt.

Garth rose from the bench in response to the beanball and took a step toward the diamond. From the mound, Bernie glowered, grinning in at Cletis, who lay flat on his back.

"Hey!" shouted Klu, protectively, rising from behind the plate and pulling off his mask. "*That's* not gonna happen again!"

"Yeah!" called Rabbit from center taking several steps toward the infield. "You don't throw at your own teammates if you wanna play with us!"

"Bernie, knock it off!" warned Johnny from near first base. "Nobody gets hurt here!"

"Just showin' him who's boss," replied Bernie, grinning. "He leans into my territory, I'm gonna brush him back."

"Yeah, but he wasn't in your territory," called Klu as Cletis rose and brushed himself off.

Garth sat down again, everyone settled, and play resumed.

"Initiate him, Clete," whispered Klu as he pulled down the mask. "Right back up the middle."

Bernie wound and fired another fastball right down the tube. Slashing at the ball, Cletis drilled a line drive right back at the mound. Bernie agilely ducked to his left to avoid taking the ball off his forehead. Turning, he watched the ball bound toward Rabbit in center. Then turning again, he looked back at Cletis, eyeing him respectfully. He pulled his hat off, rubbed away the forehead sweat with his shoulder, and then pulled the hat snuggly back down on his head. The sun was rising in the sky above them and so was the temperature. Bernie took the throw from Rabbit and settled in for the next pitch.

"Okay, my best against your best," called Bernie from the mound. "Let's see if you're for real."

Sounds like Mr. Howard's story, Cletis thought, remembering his visit with the old man last night. "Bring it. Let's see if *you're* for real."

Garth chuckled proudly from the dugout bench next to Abish.

Bernie puckered his lips fitfully, prepping himself for the confrontation. He eyed Klu's target and wound and fired. Cletis studied his delivery, watching Bernie's hand and the way his fingers wrapped around the ball. As Bernie's front leg came down, he blasted a fastball toward the plate. Cletis saw it perfectly and brought the bat around quickly. SMACK! The bat and ball collided in sweet, summer music, and the ball leapt off the wood and sailed into the left-center gap.

Bernie watched the ball land and roll, but turned back to Cletis before the fielders gathered it up and fired it in.

"Man, where did you learn to hit like that?" he asked, humbled a bit by Cletis's ability to catch up to his best stuff.

"Where'd you learn to pitch like that?" responded Cletis. "Those are all hard and straight. You need to have Klu give you a target on the edges. If you could paint the corners and throw a change up, nobody'd touch you."

Bernie thought about that a moment as the ball came back in to the mound. "Yeah. Good idea. I'm gonna have to practice that."

One after another, the pitches came across the plate. With each swing, Cletis connected, sending the ball to right field, left field, the gaps, and down the lines. Bernie couldn't put anything past him.

Watching from the bench, Abish spoke up. "Has he always hit like *that*?"

"What d'ya mean?" questioned Garth.

"He's hitting like Roberto Clemente. He's making contact, but his legs are everywhere."

Cletis looked back at her, wondering what she meant, never having had the opportunity to see the great Pirate outfielder play.

He watched her rise from the bench and waddle toward the plate. His dad followed her.

The boys froze as she approached, wondering what the old lady could possibly be doing on the playing field. Klu took a step away from her as she took the bat from Cletis.

"This may seem like a lot to remember," she started, "but I got this tip from Harmon Killebrew himself. The 'Killer.' 'Hammerin' Harmon.' Minnesota Twins. MVP twice. Hit more homeruns than any other player in the 1960s. So listen close. You too Klu."

Klu leaned in to watch. Abish held the bat out in front of her and demonstrated each direction. "Squish the bug with the back foot. Keep your weight back. Pop the hips forward prior to your swing. That way your lower body's doing a lot of the work, not just your arms. Slow feet, quick hands. Extend the arms. Hit the ball out in front of you. And see the contact." She handed the bat back to Cletis. "You got that?"

"I think so." He held the bat out in front of him, pretending to see an incoming pitch. "Uh . . . squish the bug, pop the hips around. Slow feet, quick hands. Extend the arms . . . and, uh, hit the ball out in front of you."

"But you've got to see it to hit it," she reminded

"Yeah," repeated Cletis, "see the contact."

"Do you understand what I'm saying?"

"I guess we'll find out," Cletis answered.

Abish and Garth moved over the edge of the backstop. Behind the plate, Klu squatted back down into position and pulled the mask over his chin.

"You think you can remember all that?" he asked, looking up at Cletis in the batter's box.

"I think so," Cletis stated matter-of-factly as he practiced the motions a few times, eyeing his back foot and checking the movement of his hips.

Cletis dug in and waited for the pitch. Bernie wound and delivered. In that split second, the dance raced through Cletis's mind. *Squish the bug with the back foot. Weight back. Drive the hips through. Extend the arms. Hit the ball out in front of me.*

Cletis swung hard and met the pitch squarely. CRACK! The ball shot off his bat and sailed up and out toward center field. Rabbit took a few running strides back, but then decided just to stop where she was and watch the ball sail past her. When it finally hit the ground, it was some thirty yards behind where she stood.

"Los ojos verdes," she shouted aloud as she watched the ball hit the ground and roll. She turned and looked back at Abish, then slowly jogged after the ball.

Cletis and the rest of the team stood in awe, watching one of the deepest hits they had ever seen on this field. After the glory of the moment, Cletis turned toward Abish—his mouth agape in surprise. She simply winked at him.

"That's the way to give it a ride, kid!!" Garth shouted as he watched Rabbit chase it down and toss it back in to Johnny.

The field was respectfully silent as Johnny scooped up the two-bouncer and tossed it back to Bernie.

Garth folded his arms and turned to Abish. "What are these 'gifts' I hear about that you supposedly gave Cletis and Elston?" he asked.

Klu and Cletis heard the question, and both peered over at the couple by the backstop, anxious for the answer.

"What you just saw was raw, basic talent combined with a lot of good hard practice and natural know-how. I know nothing about any 'gifts.'"

CHAPTER 15

The Hatbox

Cletis stood in front of the bedroom mirror with his dirty shirt in his hand, looking at the marks on his shoulders and pondering the events of the day.

"Clete," came the quiet call from the base of the stairs.

"Yeah?" He stepped to the doorway.

"Can you get cleaned up quick and meet me down here in my room?" his father asked.

Cletis nodded and then stepped back to the dresser and tossed his shirt onto the pile of dirty clothes in his hamper. He felt something significant was going to happen . . . an announcement of some sort from his father. Cletis assumed it had to do with the hatbox. His dad had been carrying it around with him, moving it from the bedroom to the front room. And now he had seen it back in the bedroom again, lying on his dad's bed.

Cletis leaned against the dresser and bent down and pulled off his dirty socks. *I was standing in this very spot when he came to me. I can see his eyes. I can smell his leathery clothes. I can hear his body moving. I can see the marks on his shoulders.*

He took a deep breath, pushed the ugly experience from his mind, and sat down on the edge of the bed next to his new uniform. As he admired it, he thought about the amazing blue light he and his father had seen last night. *Abish said that only Dungarvans can see the blue visions. What does that mean? Could the Traveler man see the blue light? How did Abish make that happen?*

It felt safe to have Abish in the house with them now. She seemed to be comfortable with them and relieved to be under a different roof—a place with people. It felt good to see his dad finally acknowledge that the fantastical events of their lives were real and leading them, inescapably it seemed, toward the fulfillment of the strange prophecy engraved on the box.

Cletis stepped into the bathroom and, splashing water on his hands, face, and armpits, began to wash off the dirt and sweat of the day. Practice had gone well that morning. In fact, it had gone far into the afternoon. Everyone got their chance to hit against Bernie, and Bernie got a chance to hit against Johnny. Cletis smiled to himself as he thought about some of the mammoth hits Bernie belted into deep right-center field. Everyone got a good fielding workout when Bernie stepped to the plate and took his swings. And Bernie was a good fielder too.

There were moments of baseball magic that morning as well. *Pauly made that super catch in left. Knocked the wind right out of him when he landed.* Cletis saw it vividly in his mind. *And he said he would've gotten a quicker jump on the ball if his shoes had better gription. And Rabbit threw Bernie out from second base—from her knees! Bernie didn't think a girl could do that kind of stuff.*

Cletis thought of the hit that he clobbered right after Abish had coached him. Even Bernie's hits didn't travel as far as that one. Cletis smiled. *But it only happened once. Bernie was clobberin' all of 'em! I only got a hold of one.* Again, in his mind's eye, he saw Rabbit watching it soar over her head into deep center field.

He turned off the water, dried his face and arms and ran the towel across his armpits. Back into his room, he threw on a fresh T-shirt, changed into a clean pair of shorts, and then jumped down the stairs. He slowed as he entered his father's room. His dad sat on the edge of the bed with the hatbox next to him. Again his arm rested over the top of it, holding it in position.

"Could you shut the door?" he asked quietly.

Cletis had seen Abish in the front room when he had come down the stairs, and he supposed his dad knew she was there. *This must be something pretty private*, Cletis told himself as he shut the door behind him. His dad's mood was somber, and Cletis could tell that the fun events of this morning's practice were now far from his father's thoughts.

Cletis walked to the bed and sat down.

"I guess the time has come to talk to Abish," his father began, "to lay everything out in the open." He rubbed his mouth with the palm of his hand. "I'll show her some things that even you haven't seen yet. I . . . uh . . . " He paused again, as if trying to select the right words. "I guess your mother and I were a bit protective. There were certain things—circumstances, I guess you could call them—that we always kept to ourselves. We even kept them from you, knowing that eventually, once the answers were in front of us, we'd share them with you, and . . . uh . . . do our best to explain them to you. And we felt it was wise to do it that way. Because it was *our* business—ours *alone*—and no one else's." He paused and looked into the closet. "Those answers we looked for never came, and so what good was it to talk to you about things *we* didn't even know about? The important thing was that you were with us and we were a family." He reached over and patted Cletis's leg. "I hope you'll trust me on this one, and I hope I know what I'm doin'."

His dad lifted his arm off the hatbox. "Let's take the whole story to Abish and see what light she can throw on some old questions that your mom and I have always had. As much as I hate to admit it in our present situation, with all that's going on around us, I just may have to believe her story—her reality. It's still *unreality* to me. But no matter what the outcome, we're still a unit, Clete. You're my son and always will be. Anna is your mother and always will be. You understand?"

Cletis nodded. He ran his fingers through his strawberry blond hair and took in a quick breath through his nose. Not all the pieces of this puzzle were in front of him, but he knew he had to trust his dad. Despite his father's words, he sensed the weight of yet another challenge being tossed onto his shoulders.

"Abish is in the front room," his dad continued. "Let's go to her."
He slowly rose, as if dreading what had to be done.

"Dad?" Cletis asked.

"Yeah." He placed a hand on Cletis's shoulder.

Cletis paused a second and then swallowed. "I'm kinda scared
about all this," he whispered, his eyes clouding with tears.

His dad pulled him close and held him for several moments.

"I know. . . . I know. So am I. I don't like all this strange stuff, and
it worries me to think that we're somehow connected to all Abish
has told us. But I can't deny what we saw in that blue, round thing.
And I can't deny so many other truths that are connected with all
this. We'll just have to ride out this storm together." Garth cupped
his hands around Cletis's neck, stepped back, and looked down into
his son's eyes. "You hear what I said? I said *together*. That means I'm
gonna be with you all the way. Whatever challenges we have to face,
we're gonna do it as a family. Okay? Me and you."

Trusting him, Cletis nodded, wiping back a tear with the side of
his hand. His dad pulled him close once again.

"Okay, let's go do this." His dad kissed his forehead lightly and
then leaned over and lifted the hatbox off the bed. After a smile and
a nod, he wrapped his arm around Cletis's shoulder and led him out
of the bedroom.

In the living room, Abish sat in the chair by the end table. She
looked up at Garth and Cletis as they entered. In her hands she
held the manuscript—the original scroll that had come from the
wooden box.

"Just reviewing it," she groaned as she laid it on the end table
beside her.

Garth stood in front of her as Cletis slid past him over to the
couch. The late-afternoon light filtered through the window behind
them. Abish looked up at Garth meekly, as if she could sense by
his silent, solemn gaze that something significant was coming. He
knelt down at her feet, set the box next to him, and cleared off the

coffee table, setting the books and magazines, along with the figurine couple, onto the floor. Then, looking down at the hatbox, gathered his thoughts.

"Anna and I struggled to have children," Garth began, kneeling back on his heels. "We always wanted children—several in fact—but it didn't happen. Anna was pregnant only once, but she delivered a few weeks early, and the child was stillborn. Shortly after that time, Cletis came to us. So the other night when we spoke at your house, and you told me that Cletis was our firstborn, you were wrong. But, at the same time, you were close to the truth . . . too close for my comfort. So I told you to stay away from my family, and I left. Yesterday when you described other things—other events and other circumstances, I . . . uh . . . I thought you were trying to take Cletis away from Anna and me. I . . . I thought you were trying to destroy my family. I didn't know just how you were gonna do that or why or what you were planning, but . . . uh . . . I was afraid, and so I was protective. You understand that, I'm sure."

Abish watched him, listening.

"Yesterday evening you described your son," Garth continued. "You talked of his hair and his eyes, his age, and his clothing. You knew his clothing in detail. When you described them . . . well, I . . . that was the moment I accused you . . . of . . . uh, trying to take my son from me." He studied her for a moment and then looked down at the box. "Let me show you something . . . then maybe you'll understand why I acted the way I did."

Garth knelt up again, pulled the hatbox close to him, and lifted off the lid. Gently he reached in and removed a pair of small booties. He placed them on the coffee table for Cletis and Abish to see. The little shoes appeared to be made of rabbit skin, with the soft, gray fur lining the inside and the leather side facing out. A thin strip of hide at the top of each bootie appeared to serve as a fastening device—like a shoelace—allowing the bootie to be tied at the ankle, holding it in place on the foot of a small child. Abish studied the booties, leaning forward for a better look. Cletis could see her mind working, yet she remained silent. Cletis too leaned in for a closer examination of the little shoes.

The second item that his father removed appeared to be a woven, woolen shirt, like a toddler's sleeper, with ties in the front to fasten the clothing together. The fashion was nothing Cletis had ever seen, and he eyed Abish curiously, trying to sense what she was thinking of his father's little ritual.

Abish pushed even closer to the table and stared down at the tiny shirt. She reached her hand forward and then stopped and looked at Garth.

"May I touch it?" she asked.

Garth nodded and lifted it toward her. She took the clothing in her hands, and holding it to her face, she studied the weave, the texture, and the workmanship. Her eyes frowned in concentration as she turned the material over in her hands and scrutinized it from several angles. Suddenly she paused and lifted the clothing to her nose. Even from where Cletis sat, he thought he could smell the slight scent of vanilla—something akin to what he smelled in Abish's house.

His dad removed the third and final item—a tiny, woven headpiece with a flap on each side that pulled down to cover the ears of the child that wore it. On the right earpiece was woven a tiny insignia: a man in a white robe with a bear at his side. In front of the man, floating in the air, the image of an opened scroll was embroidered.

Pulled as if from a deep pool of private thoughts, Abish lowered the clothing from her face and looked down at the headpiece Garth held in his hands. Cletis watched Abish's jaw drop. She gasped lightly, laid the tiny shirt in her large lap, and reached for the cap.

"May I?"

Garth placed it into her wide and wrinkled hands. Again she lifted the piece to her face, studying the make, the weave, and the insignia. Cletis and Garth watched her intently as she inspected the cap and rubbed her fingers across the image of the man and the bear.

"Did Anna make these?" Abish finally questioned, lifting her face to Garth.

Garth shook his head. "No, she didn't."

Abish studied him, her eyes unblinking. Cletis looked on, confused and curious. This was all new to him. Yet despite his desire to reach out and touch the clothing, or to ask a hundred questions about where they came from or who made them, he kept his distance and held his tongue. He sensed it important to allow his father and Abish these moments together—these seemingly *sacred* moments— with the strange clothing of the hatbox.

Abish spoke haltingly. "They're exactly like them. The weave and the color . . . like the clothing I made for . . ."

Her voice trailed off, as if she dared not speak further. Tears filled her eyes and overflowed down her round cheeks and onto her chin. Slowly she bowed her head over the cap she held.

Garth leaned forward over the table and touched her arm. "They *are* the clothes, Abish. Look closely and you will see the auburn hairs woven into the earpiece."

She wiped her eyes with her hands and dried her hands on the sides of her dress. As if lifting a newborn, she took the piece from Garth and brought it to her face. She studied the piece in detail. The red hair—*her* red hair—was indeed woven into the emblem. Again she studied the insignia, tracing her fingers along the edge of the weave, endeavoring to be completely certain of what she was seeing. The task complete, she lowered the cap and stared at Garth with what appeared to be an expression of complete confusion—as if she wanted the truth, yet at the same time feared it.

To this point in time, *she* had been the one with all the answers. *She* had controlled the game. *She* had explained the prophecy. But now the tables had turned, and she eyed Garth longingly, as if awaiting words only *he* could deliver.

Garth set the hatbox on the floor beside him and rose to his feet. He stepped around the coffee table and lowered himself onto the open cushion next to Cletis.

"He was in our backyard, behind the house, one Sunday morning," Garth began. "It was late spring and just warming a bit. Anna spotted him and brought him in. Our backyard at the time was fenced off. And the gate on the south side of our house was locked. We checked it twice. We walked the neighborhood, knocking on all the doors, trying to locate his parents, or someone who could tell us where he lived or who he belonged to. And no one knew him. No one recognized him. We went to the police and the city's social services."

Garth looked down at Cletis. "You know about this part, Clete. We've talked about this before." He nodded toward the clothing in Abish's hands and lap. "That was what you were wearing, son. This is what we found you in . . . you were . . . you were just wandering in the backyard, lookin' around at things. We always kept these, thinking that maybe someday they could be kind of a key to help identify your birth mother or family."

Cletis watched Abish lean forward, and still holding the cap in her hand, she rocked twice, as if feeling the child in her arms. She remained silent, with her head bowed. Cletis noted that throughout the entire explanation, Abish had not looked at him. *Is she afraid to? What does all this mean?*

Garth continued. "When no one stepped forward to claim him, and we had no information about who he belonged to, we began the adoption. Everything fell into place pretty easily, and within the year the process was done. He was with us that entire time. We figured our questions about his clothing would be answered sometime in the future. And even if we didn't ever know . . . well, that was fine too. He was ours, and we were a family, and that was all that mattered. When you spoke in such detail about his clothing and his eye, I figured one of two things was happening—either you found the courthouse records and you were trying to take him away, *or* you were speaking the truth. It was Anna who discovered the long, red hairs woven into the cap." Abish looked up at him. "No one else knew of that. But you spoke of it, knowing exactly where they were. Still I had my doubts about you. I didn't know what you were scheming. I didn't know how you found out about all this stuff. I didn't know if the weird things we were seein' take place around us were the result of . . . I don't know . . . some mind game or something. I was afraid of what might happen. I was afraid of the things you knew about . . . " Garth took a deep breath. "I . . . I still am, for that matter. But Cletis and I, we've talked about everything that's been happening, and we decided we needed to trust you. Then the vision in the blue light came last night . . . and I saw . . . " He paused and studied her eyes. "I saw the woman who saved my life."

Fighting to control her emotions, Abish, again, lowered her head and sat silently. Still she did not look up at Cletis.

Cletis turned to his father. "Should I show her, Dad?" he asked quietly. He could tell his father could read the fear in his eyes.

"If you want to," he answered, patting Cletis's leg. "Remember what I said? We're in this together."

Cletis faced Abish. Finally she lifted her gaze toward him. Cletis sat forward on the couch, reached down to the bottom of his shirt, and with both hands, pulled it up over his head. With the shirt in one hand, he rose, edged past his father, and walked around the coffee table until he was standing in front of Abish. He paused there a moment and then knelt before her.

Abish appeared puzzled at first, but then spotted the red, hourglass marks on the front of each shoulder. Instantly she gasped. Her fingers darted up to her lips as she studied the marks. She reached toward his shoulders with unsteady hands but did not touch them. Gradually her eyes met his. She studied Cletis sharply—his eyes, his hair, the shape of his face—as if not having seen him before.

I don't know what to say, Cletis pondered. *What am I supposed to do?* He watched the tears stream down her face.

"I can't cry," she muttered, wiping her cheeks. "I have to be brave. Oh, my . . . But . . . but the weave of this poor world is unraveling around you and your father, my dear boy. Isn't it?" She reached out and took his hands in hers.

Cletis felt a large chasm of emptiness open in his soul as her large hands engulfed his. She had spoken the truth. His world was indeed unraveling around him. It was as if a new life had started at this very moment—a confused life. His mind flooded with questions. *I used to wear the clothes in her lap? Where did I come from? Am I some kind of freak? So who am I? Who would've just left me in the backyard?* She released his hands. *What is happening to me?*

"I wondered," she spoke haltingly. "But I never allowed myself to hope. I saw the strawberry blond hair. I knew you had the surgery on your eye. I saw all that. But . . . but certain things were kept from me, I guess. I thought that Anna gave birth . . . and then you spoke of adoption. . . . I didn't want to . . . " She refolded the clothing on her knees and then looked again at Cletis. "They sent you ahead to us." Her raspy voice quivered. "They sent you forward. That's why I never saw you . . . in the past, I never saw you. I was watching the family, even from the beginning, but you weren't there. I looked for you. They wouldn't speak of you." She fell silent again. "Oh, Cletis, are you really him? Are you really my little son?" She wiped away another tear. "Oh, my . . . What can I say? This is difficult on us all, isn't it? An ugly old woman comes and turns your life on its ear."

Cletis smiled uncertainly. Feeling naked, he threw his shirt over his head and pulled it down over his body. Hesitantly, feeling it the right thing to do, he leaned forward, wrapped his arms around her shoulders, and pulled himself close to her. In return, her arms lifted around his waist, and they held each other. A powerful surge of familiar, sweet energy swept through his body. Cletis looked over her shoulder and saw the hair on his arms rise in goose bumps.

"Do you feel that?" Abish whispered.

Cletis pulled away, looked down at his arms, and rubbed them gently until the gooseflesh disappeared. "Yes, ma'am, I feel it."

"Quite a different feeling compared to the other one, isn't it?"

Cletis looked into her eyes. "You know the other feeling? You know what it's like?"

"All too well," she nodded. "Let me teach you something important, Cletis. I know you have a hundred questions swarming your brain right now, but this is needful. There may come a time when after you have been repeatedly exposed to that other feeling, it will begin to lose it's ugly edge—like getting used to cold water—and you will become familiar with it, accustomed to it, and even comfortable with it, if you are not careful."

Cletis leaned back, shocked by her words.

"How can that be?" he asked. Yet, even as the words escaped his mouth, he remembered last night with Mr. Howard. The horrible feeling came on him fast and strong, but it gradually went away. *Did it go away, or did I get used to it? Is that what she's talkin' about? Did I just get so familiar with it that it went away?*

"It is human nature, Cletis. If we surround ourselves with evil, even evil becomes good to us. If we are not careful, that natural light within us all that teaches us the difference between the two can be snuffed out completely. Even the best of people can fall."

She studied him affectionately and then turned to Garth. "Cletis and Garth, I need to say this." She grasped Cletis's arm, and he watched as her eyes came back to him. "My being here doesn't change anything about your family or your parents, Cletis. Your relationship with your mom and your dad remains the same. It always will. They are your parents. Listen to me closely. They have loved you and raised you, and you are their son and that will never change. Do you hear me? That will never change."

Again she wiped a tear from her cheek and leaned back in the chair, as if allowing herself to bask in the wonder of the moment.

"There are a lot of unanswered questions that we're just going to have to figure out one by one as they come to us. And with your help and your father's help, I'll do my best to answer each one."

Suddenly her eyes opened wide and facing Cletis, she bolted upright.

"Cletis, the man who is the Traveler—has he seen these marks on your shoulders?"

Cletis thought for a moment and then shook his head. "I don't think so. Why?"

She leaned forward and took him by the shoulders. "He must not see them, Cletis. Do you understand me? He must not!"

The warm sun was rising in the eastern sky when the team gathered at the diamond the next morning. As they chatted near the backstop, an occasional crow or starling flapped past them overhead, noising a sunrise greeting. The boys had placed the old memorabilia box on home plate and had set the schedule from Mr. Sperry's store right on top of it. They studied the chart while kneeling in the dirt or standing in the batter's boxes around the plate.

Eight teams were listed on the Greater Metro Single-Elimination Tournament schedule. They recognized only one: the team from Canterbury Heights—the city where Elston had moved.

"We gotta play all those teams?" voiced Rabbit, not understanding how to read the thing.

"If we win every game, we'll play only three," explained Johnny. "That's cuz it's single elimination. That means, with every game that's played, one team goes on and one team drops out."

"So if we lose our first game," added Klu, "we're done. That's it. We come home."

"So we gotta win every game if we're gonna win the tournament?" questioned Davey.

"Yep," answered Pauly. "That's right. All three. That makes us champs."

"And so," added Cletis, "that's why we gotta give my idea a try. It'll work!"

"And so, Mr. Know-It-All," continued Johnny, "you're idea *isn't* gonna work."

"Yeah, it will! It's worth a try! And besides, we don't have a choice. No one has a better idea."

"You're outta your mind, Clete," spouted Frank, "if you're thinkin' *he's* gonna coach us."

"We gotta give him a chance!"

"He can't *possibly* be our coach," continued Johnny. "He can hardly walk down the street, let alone guide us through a tournament."

"He can change," protested Cletis. "He *has* changed."

"Come on, Clete," added Klu. "If we have any hope of winning, we gotta find someone else."

"But none of our dads can do it," pleaded Cletis. "They're all workin'. Even Klu's big brother said no. Mr. Sperry can't do it either. So we got no choice! There's no one else! We gotta give him a chance, Johnny! He knows a lot about baseball!"

"He told you a few baseball stories, Clete," reminded Johnny. "That doesn't mean he knows how to coach."

"And you can smell him a block away," chimed Frank. "And his hair's all matted down and probably full of lice. They'd laugh us off the field!"

"Frank, go easy," warned Rabbit. "You got any better ideas?"

Frank thought for a moment but had nothing to say.

"But he's not even dependable," argued Johnny. "He was supposed to be here ten minutes ago."

"Look, we'll try him one practice," Cletis begged, "and if it doesn't work out good, we'll think of someone else."

The group was silent with the suggestion.

"Who is this guy you're talkin' about anyway?" asked Bernie, still trying to become familiar with the people of his new surroundings.

Suddenly Timmy spoke up. He was looking through the backstop and off toward the hill behind the school. "Hey, guys, don't look now, but here comes someone. And it kinda looks like him. Kinda."

The boys turned in unison and looked up the hill. A man approached the field. He was still at least fifty yards away. He was finely dressed in the clothes Elston and Cletis had bought for him. He moved with new confidence, and he was shaven, washed, and combed. The breeze floating in from the southeast carried a touch of Aqua Velva aftershave. He wore an old mitt on his left hand, and the Louisville Slugger Cletis had seen a few nights back at the old shack, rested over his right shoulder, as if it were a sleeping animal, ready to awaken and attack.

When Mr. Howard saw everyone looking at him, he quickened his pace and finally jogged up to the backstop.

"Sorry I'm late," he announced with a smile. "I've been real tired the past two days, for some reason. Couldn't hardly wake up this morning when Cletis and his dad came to see me." He eyed the silent, gape-mouthed group that stared back at him through the backstop. "Thanks for asking me to come help out this morning. I'm looking forward to it."

Cletis looked up at Johnny and smiled ear to ear. Johnny stood, wide-eyed, gawking at the man who, for as many years as Johnny could remember, had roamed Greenberg Junction dressed in rags and smelling like a New England fish wharf. In fact, not only Johnny but *everyone* on the team wore the same astonished expression.

I didn't feel anything weird this morning when me and Dad visited him, thought Cletis, studying the fresh, new Mr. Howard. *And I don't feel anything strange right now. I hope that means I'm safe.*

"Bernie," spoke Cletis courteously, "this is Mr. Howard. He's our coach for today." Cletis abruptly laughed out loud in happiness. "I think it's time to move this box off home plate and play some ball!"

Mr. Howard took charge and skillfully guided the team through a mountain of drills—teaching one-on-one techniques and strategy. The drills were fun and fluid, and tested the players in ways they had never imagined. He worked with Rabbit, Davey, and Frank on double-play pivots and combinations, reviewing how to stay low on the ground balls, how to keep the ball in front of them, and how to quicken their throws. He worked with Johnny and Bernie on windups, delivery, follow-through, and pitching out of a stretch. He worked with Klu on his throws to second base, teaching him how to read the runner and how to catch a runner off guard or off balance. When the guys were batting, Mr. Howard worked with them on grip, wrist motion, and stance, and how to hit the ball to all fields. In the outfield, he taught Cletis and Timmy and Pauly how to get a good jump on a ball hit to the outfield, how to position themselves under pop-ups, and how to make those hard, over-the-shoulder catches. With each member of the team, he shared tips on baserunning and base stealing, demonstrating how to study a pitcher's motion and how to get a good jump on the pitch. Even Bernie, cocksure as he was, paid close attention when Mr. Howard barked directions at him.

After the two-and-a-half hours of good, hard practice had come and gone, the team gathered with Mr. Howard at home plate. Under Johnny's direction, Pauly and Davey got the memorabilia box out from under the dugout bench and brought it back onto the diamond.

"Mr. Howard," spoke Johnny, pulling the schedule out of the box. "We got a tournament comin' up here in a few days, and if we don't have a coach, we can't play."

Cletis, with the all the teammates, eyed Johnny, sensing the question he was about to ask. Over the past two-and-a-half hours they had all seen Mr. Howard at work, and Cletis could sense they were in awe of the man's abilities. Mr. Howard obviously knew what he was doing on the diamond, and it was exciting for them to get experienced, hands-on instruction.

"Would you be our coach?" Johnny inquired, lifting the schedule toward the man.

Cletis looked on with a knowing, agreeing smile.

Mr. Howard took the schedule and examined the paper from top to bottom. "Is this all paid for?" he asked.

"Mr. Sperry covered the cost," Johnny answered officially. "He even bought us uniforms."

Mr. Howard looked back down at the schedule. "Single elimination, eh?" He whispered to himself as he studied the details. Finally his eyes lifted, and he peered over the paper into the faces of the nine kids who surrounded him. "Well, I, uh . . . If you want me to do this—to be your coach—I would . . . uh . . . I'd be honored."

There were no giant roars of approval, nor any applause or high-fives, but with pleased grins and nods of excitement, the players stepped anxiously forward. As if sensing a new role of confident leadership, Mr. Howard laid the schedule down on the memorabilia box and eyed the group.

"Let's see here. First game's in two days." He spoke, as if he were planning a battle. "And I imagine we'll play one of the better teams first, since the organizers of this tournament probably think we're the weakest in the competition. That's just the way these tournaments are planned. The weak play the strong in the first bracket. That means we're gonna need to play hard and smart every inning of every game." He pursed his lips and rubbed his chin with his hand. "If I do this—if I coach you—it means you're gonna let me direct the strategy on the field. Because if we play as a team and never let up in our concentration, we may turn some heads. I say that because you kids play some mighty fine baseball. Not having been coached, you play mighty fine."

He coughed, then took a deep breath and lifted his hand to his mouth, as if steadying his bottom lip. He looked out over the field, studying the dirt and grass and paths and makeshift bases. He seemed lost in distant thoughts, as if he were seeing the ghostlike images of boys from by-gone years filling the very same field, happily lost in the thrill of an exciting, summer game. Nodding slowly, as if agreeing with a hidden, personal secret, he lifted his face toward the cloudless, blue sky.

"That's it for today," he finally stated. "Nice practice. See you here tomorrow morning at sunrise. Wear your uniforms. Gotta break 'em in." With that, Mr. Howard handed the schedule back to Johnny. "I'll need a copy of this." He bent low, lifted his bat, and turning away from the team, stepped around the edge of the backstop and started up the hill toward the school.

They watched him in silence until Johnny spoke quietly.

"I think we've just seen some more baseball magic."

"It happens when you least expect it," agreed Klu, locking his fingers through the chainlink in front of him.

"Yep, I think you're right," added Cletis under his breath. "Thanks, Mr. Howard," he whispered.

Though Mr. Howard didn't look back, he suddenly tipped his cap and lifted it above him, as if responding to Cletis's remarks. The boys laughed aloud at the odd timing of the moment, knowing he couldn't possibly have heard Cletis, Johnny, or Klu.

It was a coincidence, they all agreed, but Cletis knew that bizarre things were happening all around him—things magical and beyond explanation. Yet, as the practice broke up, Cletis realized that any person around him, including Mr. Howard in the distance, could be the Traveler. He knew he hadn't felt anything cold and scary, but he remembered Abish telling him that the ugly feeling could disappear if he got used to it.

Did I get too used to it when I was at Mr. Howard's? His gaze turned, and he focused on the group of friends that surrounded him—teammates who gathered equipment, chatted playfully, and mounted their bikes. He studied each person, trying not to look suspicious.

"You okay, Clete," asked Rabbit, lifting her bike at the edge of the backstop.

He nodded his head. "Yeah. Why?"

"I dunno. It's like you're frozen. You're just kinda standin' there watchin' everybody."

"I'm okay," he stated, suddenly eyeing her suspiciously.

"Good," she replied. Turning away from him, she walked her bike toward the hill.

Yeah, I'm okay, he repeated to himself.

But he knew his words and thoughts were far from the truth.

CHAPTER 16

The Blue Shield And Travel

Instead of going home, Cletis decided to cross the fields behind the diamond and head the distance to Abish's house. Still troubled by yesterday's events, he felt that time alone would do him good. Besides that, there was plenty to do there in the way of clean-up, and he was concerned about the place being open to whomever or whatever wanted to step inside. Even Abish had expressed that concern. A lot of valuable things were stowed in that baseball room, and Cletis wanted to make sure the place was guarded, at least to some small extent. As he rode his bike away from the diamond, he decided he would make his visit there quick and safe.

Maybe I'll pick up some of the clutter, see how things are, and report back to her when I get home. Who knows? Maybe she's already over there cleanin' the place.

Pedaling on, he thought about the clothing in the hatbox and how Abish had studied each item. He remembered how her eyes had clouded with tears as she held the little cap close to her face. He pondered the look on her face when his dad explained that the articles of clothing were found *on* Cletis—that he was wearing them when he was discovered wandering in the backyard those eleven years ago. He remembered her eyes as she spotted the marks on his shoulders. It was an expression of happiness, fear, pain, and bewilderment all wrapped into one. Finally he remembered the feeling that shot through his soul as he wrapped his arms around the old woman.

Who is she? Who is she really? Is she my real mother? He allowed that thought to sink in, heavy as it was. *Could she really have come from* another time? *Had she really been alive all these years, watching the family? Had she really been changed like she said she was? What did she look like before?* She said she had auburn hair, and Cletis knew there was a bit of red in his. *Not much,* he pondered. *I've always wanted to know who my real mother and father were, and now she's telling me, but how am I supposed to believe all this? She said she was married once to that man who appeared to me? Does that make* him *my real dad?*

The confusing questions raced through Cletis's mind, adding to the frustration he already felt. He wondered if the old woman knew magic and if she was the power behind the cards in the box and the disintegrating bikes and the other supposedly magical moments he had recently experienced. *What can she do that she hasn't shown us yet? And what about me? Who am I really? Can I do magic? Can I travel in time? Who made up this prophecy, anyway, and why do I have to be a part of it? Out of all the boys in the world, how come I'm in the middle of all this?*

Cletis felt discouraged and alone. There was no one really to turn to. His dad didn't know what was going on. Abish had *some* answers, but even she was left in the dark about a lot of things. Even she didn't understand parts of the prophecy. He thought about how easy it would be to wake up each morning like Timmy or Davey or Pauly—do some chores, but then play all day and do what you want. Their families were normal. Their lives were normal.

I guess I don't get a normal life, at least not now. I guess I gotta be different. Not all kids get eye surgery. Not all kids have their mom die. Not all kids have their best friend move away right when they need 'em the most. Not all kids get thrown into the middle of a weird prophecy. Not all kids find an old woman in the forest who is supposed to be their mother. Not all kids have time travelers haunting them night and day.

He took a deep breath, stopped pedaling, and just coasted along for a moment. The gentle bouncing seemed to calm him, and he studied the greens of the field that surrounded him.

So I guess I just gotta face up to this prophecy thing, whatever it is, and battle it out. Cuz the only way out of it is through it—just like mom and dad told me. Yet, again, in spite of his efforts to feel good about himself, the immensity of the situation bore down on him like the dark, threatening clouds of an incoming winter storm. Tears suddenly blurred his vision, but he blinked them away.

When Cletis reached the edge of the hill, he dropped his bike onto its side and gazed down on Abish's house. From where he stood, peering between pines and elms that populated the hillside, Cletis could see the opening in the back wall of the home and the damage to the roof above the broken bedroom. The ceiling was sunken above the gaping hole. As he pondered, the broken rafters of the open roof suddenly groaned—as if knowing Cletis were near and warning him to keep his distance.

I wonder if she's in there. Maybe Dad brought her over here and she's in there cleaning up, or maybe she's getting some things she needs.

He made his way down the hillside and jumped the canal. Once again, he spotted the underwater rock ledge he had discovered earlier. *I still gotta explore that little area,* he thought as he peered down into the flow. Winding his way through the scraps of Abish's house that still lay scattered across the ground, he stepped toward the opening in the bedroom wall and peered inside. Two beams now criss-crossed the length of the room, guarding the door to the hallway.

"Abish?" Cletis called through the haze of still-settling dust. "Are you in here?"

There was no answer. He remembered his conversation with Elston and how Elston had heard footsteps in the house.

"Abish?" he called again.

Hearing nothing, Cletis cautiously lifted himself up through the open wall and stepped into the bedroom. The fallen beams and debris created an obstacle course, but he wound his way to the bedroom door. He peered to his left down the darkened hallway and thought he recognized the door to the baseball room. Straight ahead of him and a little to the right, he could see the front door and the adjacent room where she had been sitting when he and his dad had come for her two nights ago. To Cletis's right, he could see three doors. One was open, and appeared to lead into a large room. He had never been in that area of the house before, and wondering what the open room could contain, he ventured several steps toward it. Suddenly he stopped.

Am I feelin' weird right now, or am I just imaginin' things and puttin' crazy thoughts into my head?

He waited silently. Leaning back against the wall, he listened for any odd sound—anything out of the ordinary. He realized the faint pounding in his ears was his own heart thumping beneath his ribs. He put his hand on his chest, as if to comfort or control the wild beating. The house groaned again, as if suffering the pain of an undeserved injury.

I think I'll just head back to the baseball room, he told himself, trying to tether his courage. He turned and walked back down the shadowy hallway. *If the Traveler guy has come here once already, he may come here again. Maybe I better make this quick.*

The floor creaked and complained as he passed the open, dust-filled bedroom on his left. As he approached the baseball room on his right, another door, on the opposite side of the hall, caught his eye. Its dark, wooden entry was huge—at least a foot wider and a foot higher than the other doorways in the house.

I don't remember this door being here, he thought. *I've walked this hallway twice before, but I don't remember seein' this here. Maybe I was just thinkin' about other stuff at the time. But how could that be? It's so big?*

It was hot and muggy inside the old house, and the air was still filled with dust. Cletis coughed lightly. He pulled his hat from his head and waved it before him, clearing away an old cobweb that floated ghostlike in front of his face. Still pondering the huge door, he wiped his forehead across his shoulder and paused again to listen. Though the house was momentarily tomb silent, Cletis's heart continued to beat wildly.

All the trees around the house must block most of the light, he thought, wishing he could see more clearly. *Cuz it's sure darker than it should be in here. Maybe it's just that my eyes aren't getting used to the change. I've been out in the sun.*

Pushing the cap back down over his head, he studied the large wooden door. *Gotta be somethin' important in there to have a door like this guarding it.* He took a deep breath. *I'm already in this whole thing so deep, I don't think it's gonna hurt if I do some explorin' right now.*

He lifted his hand to the black, round, metal knob in front of him, and folding his fingers around it, he turned it. To his surprise, the giant door opened easily and swung quietly into the room. He stepped forward and then turned and shut the door behind him.

The light of the midday sun filtered though the dirty window on the brown wall straight ahead of him. A pair of yellowed, tattered curtains hung loosely from a simple wooden rod above it. He turned, eyeing every wall, every furnishing, and every nook and cranny in the room. The place was like a giant, medieval library, with bookshelves covering two of the four walls. On the shelves, loosely organized, were rows and heaps of worn ancient texts, frayed books, leather-bound volumes, and piles of rolled-up manuscripts. In the center of the room, directly in front of Cletis, stood a giant, round table, covered with dozens of scattered papers, books, and charts. Near the center of the table, a feather quill rested in a jar of black ink. Crossing the room, Cletis placed his hands on the worn, wooden surface, feeling the texture.

The powerfully sweet sensation he had experienced so often in Abish's presence surrounded him again. The energy entered his head, moved down through his neck, shoulders and arms, and eventually filled his entire body. Happily allowing the surge to flow through him, he breathed in the magic of the amazing rush. He looked down at his arms. His hair was standing almost straight out. He was cold and warm at the same time. The feeling was electrifying, as if he were as weightless as the fibers of dust that floated in the sunbeams before him. He felt as if he were being lifted off the ground, enveloped in a sensation of contentment, love, and joy.

The seconds passed. *Man! This time it's staying with me longer than it ever has! It's never been this strong.* He closed his eyes and rubbed his arms. Gradually the feeling lifted away. *That is so weird. Man, whatever it is, it was like I was on fire!*

The large, thick papers that covered the table were a curiosity to him. The most prominent documents visible were sheet upon sheet of hand-written pedigrees, the names, dates, and histories of which were all recorded painstakingly in beautiful penmanship. He walked around the table and, leaning over the parchments and papers, began to study the written words. Often in the margins surrounding the branches of the charts were tiny notes, also written by hand, containing a varied assortment of dates and locations. Cletis tilted his head to the side, attempting to read the material that, from his perspective, was all upside down.

Man, most of these names are Dungarvans, Cletis realized as he stepped farther around the side of the table for a better look. *Dungarvans everywhere.* From what he could see, each paper recorded a portion of the Dungarvan history, from father to son, and father to son, covering generations that spanned hundreds of years. He carefully lifted several sheets, studying the names written on the documents. Pushing an old wooden chair out of his way, he leaned in for a closer look. One sheet, whiter than the others and seemingly newer, lay by itself, as if Abish had been studying it or writing on it only recently. Cletis lifted the page and read aloud the names, dates, and details.

"Gale Dungarvan, born in Ireland in 1841. Who's that?" He pulled his finger across the chart, following the line of names. "Arthur Dungarvan, born in Boston, 1871. He would be my great-great grandfather. Angus Dungarvan, born in New York City, 1905. My great-grandfather." *Dad talked about him before,* Cletis remembered. *He's the one who loved DiMaggio and Gehrig.* His finger pushed along to the next entry. "Alan Dungarvan, born in 1936 in New York City. That's Grandpa." He smiled with the thought. *He moved to Detroit when he was a boy. He knew Al Kaline and Norm Cash.* Looking down again, he found the next entry and continued reading. "And there's dad. Garth Dungarvan. Born in 1956, in Detroit, Michigan."

Finally, at the very end of the record, Cletis spotted his own name. There it was, inscribed in the same black ink, written with artistic flair and precision. "Thomas Dungarvan." The word "Cletis" was written below it. "Born April 6, 1979, to Anna and Garth Dungarvan, in Belleville, Michigan." *I wonder how she got that date, cuz Mom and Dad always told me they had to guess at it.*

He paused a moment, pondering the fascinating manuscripts that lay before him and the years of diligent workmanship that such a record demanded. Lost in thought, he lifted his head and mechanically reached up and scratched his cheek, wiping away a bead of sweat that trickled down past his ear. At the same time, another drop fell from his chin landing with a tiny splash on the paper below. He wiped the moisture from the page with the side of his finger and rubbed his chin across his shoulder. The last thing he wanted to do was damage Abish's work by dripping sweat on the pedigrees. He studied the sheet below him, hoping the drop of moisture hadn't left a mark. Unexpectedly a short note, written near the place where the drop landed, caught his eye. It was recorded a few inches away from the "Thomas Dungarvan" entry, and the handwriting was slightly different—as if it were written as an afterthought or a reminder. Cletis lifted the paper to his face and turned it toward the light.

Cletis Dungarvan rises from the water.
Cletis Dungarvan is named
    for that which he wears upon his feet.
The powers of the box are renewed in this boy.
The orb is driven at his command.
    Yet is he Anna Dungarvan's son?
Was he not born to Anna?
    At first I thought he was. But now I think not.
        Then who is he?
I hope Time will tell me.
        Soon Ian comes. We must be strong.

"Ian," Cletis spoke aloud. "Who is Ian?" Puzzled, he read the note once more and then set the paper down on the table. *This prophecy is all about me. Why? Who am I? Why am I a part of all this?* The house creaked again and Cletis, startled, looked up at the ceiling.

He lifted his hand to his face and fisted away another stream of sweat that dribbled out from under his hat. At the same time, he tasted the saltiness of beaded perspiration on his upper lip. *How can she live without AC?* he wondered. He stepped over to the window and attempted to open it, but it wouldn't budge. He pulled off his hat, placed it on the table, and looking down at his T-shirt, noticed the whole thing was drenched in sweat. Impulsively he pulled on the front of it and lifted it away from his sticky chest. Releasing it, it immediately sucked back onto his skin, as if the shirt and flesh were magnetized together. *I gotta get this off of me. I'm so hot.* He grabbed the lower hem, lifted it up over his head and removed it, exhaling in relief with the sense of freedom he instantly felt. The sweaty shirt tucked easily through the belt on his pants, and with his hat in hand, he fanned his clammy chest and shoulders.

In a breath, the feeling came again—the icy, empty, haunting sensation. Cletis panicked, knowing the only way out of the large library was through the giant closed door in front of him. He had to get there quickly. He had to get out of the house. He had to run. But his muscles tightened, and his movement became labored and difficult. With the growing nausea, he bent at the waist, coughed several times, but fought the urge to vomit. The air seemed to be sucked from his lungs. Clawing his way around the table, his vision blurred in a dizzy fog. Step by step he moved, leaning on the table for support, but his efforts were slow and strained, and the door was still far away.

In the middle of the room, and blocking Cletis's path, the feared, gray conduit began to take shape, with its teeming mass of tiny, moving particles and its strange, buzzing, supernatural energy. Gradually the vague outline of the Traveler appeared. Despite the foglike substance that surrounded the man, Cletis recognized the blond braid and the black leather clothing, and he watched helplessly as the being materialized within the shaft. As the conduit vanished, the man venomously eyed Cletis and floated to the ground in front of him.

"You again," the man stated. He took a deliberate step forward and studied the boy who squatted in front of the massive wooden table. His arm raised, and he extended his fingers toward Cletis. "What role do you play in this drama, my boy? I intend to find out."

Instantly an arc of light shot from his fingertips and blasted toward Cletis. Cletis crumpled backward onto the floor against a wooden chair and awaited the killing blow.

But the impact never came.

Slowly opening his eyes, Cletis observed a gentle, pulsing blue light, which encircled him. It was exactly the color and substance of the light he had seen in his father's bedroom. The aura shell hovered and shimmered around him, miraculously protecting him from the blasting arc of light that continued to rain from the fingertips of the angry man that stood before him.

Within the encircling ball, Cletis at once felt safe and well. The ugly feelings that had accompanied the presence of this man, and which had flooded the room only moments before, were now gone. They had vanished with the appearance of this strange, glistening shield. Cletis pulled his knees to his chin and watched as the powers of this being were pitted against the force of the stronger, protective blue glow.

The being's eyes widened and his arms dropped to his sides. No sooner had he done this, but the blue shield faded away, leaving Cletis seemingly unprotected in front of the man who had attempted to destroy him. Frightened, Cletis pushed away a wooden chair, rose to his feet, and stepped back between the bookshelf and the table, hoping to use the wide, circular tabletop as a barrier between him and the man.

Puzzled and awe-struck, the Traveler stepped toward Cletis and again lifted his arms, as if preparing to attack. Immediately the blue light returned, shielding Cletis from the potential harm. When the man dropped his arms again, the blue light faded away. The Traveler eyed Cletis curiously. Suddenly the man's mouth opened in a gasp. He leaned forward over the table, as if to get a closer look.

Instantly Cletis realized the man was studying the marks on his shoulders. *Oh, no! Abish said he wasn't supposed to see them! Oh, man . . . what have I done?*

He realized as well that the man's expression and demeanor had abruptly and surprisingly changed. The hatred and anger that had once filled his countenance, both here *and* in Cletis's bedroom, were no longer evident. Instead there appeared to be a sudden unmistakable softening in his eyes as he stepped away from the table and squatted low to the floor.

"Forgive me, please. I have been wrong." He bowed his head and spoke softly. "I had no idea . . . I had no idea."

Still afraid and unsure, Cletis remained silent. The ugly, haunting feelings returned in the absence of the blue light, and leaning on the table, he moved farther away from the man.

"When did they appear on you?"

Cletis did not reply.

"They were painful, weren't they? I remember when they appeared on me. That pain is still imprinted in my mind. I remember it well, even after so much time. And so will you. Throughout the entirety of your life, you will remember it. And no one will understand you, for few others beside yourself, have ever felt it. Do you know who you are?"

The man rose from the squat and stepped away into the middle of the room, giving Cletis his space. "They must have sent you forward," he said thoughtfully, studying the room around him. "Yes, that is what they have done. Father helped them, I'm sure. It all has to do with this strange prophecy, I assume. They *burned* it into my box." He turned again to Cletis. "They took the box from me, and then they imprisoned me. Did you know that?" The man extended his arm again, and immediately, Cletis lifted his hands over his face to protect himself. But the Traveler merely smiled. No shower of light arced from his fingertips this time.

"The Blue knows when you are in danger and when you are not. Fascinating. How did they do that?"

The man closed his eyes and extended both arms out in front of him. Instantly the old box materialized between his outstretched hands. Cletis recognized it in a moment, though the color still seemed darker than when it was in his possession.

Holding it, the man turned and walked toward the wall behind him. An old wooden chair sat next to the large door, and the man sat down upon it with an air of confidence, completely comfortable within the confines of Abish's home—a home he had partially destroyed two days before. Cletis couldn't let himself forget that.

"Whether you realize it or not," he continued, "I gave you life. Abish had a part in that, as you probably know by now, but the blood of the Travelers courses through your veins. You are a Traveler. The marks on your shoulders prove it." He paused a moment, studying Cletis. "Now *you* can give *me* life. All you have to do is open the box. Our family has sealed it against us. They sealed it with the combined powers of the Dungarvan family and my father. You see, my father— your grandfather—was also a Traveler. They used our own powers against us. Interesting. *You* have the power to unseal the work they have purposely done to thwart me, yet you don't realize it." He leaned forward, as if to emphasize the next thought. "This box contains powers that both you and I need. If you open the box, my life is prolonged, and you will then be taught the secrets it possesses—secrets that will extend your powers and the length of your existence."

Cletis eyed him fearfully. The man sat like a king on the chair across the room. This was the man who had haunted him, frightened him, and had, just moments before, tried to destroy him. And now he spoke as if nothing out of the ordinary had happened. Suddenly Cletis noticed that the feelings of darkness and fear that had always accompanied the presence of this being were gradually fading away.

Just like with Mr. Howard. But I can't let myself feel comfortable, and I can't let him into my head.

"You saw me at my worst, I must admit," the man continued, as if reading Cletis's mind. "I sincerely apologize. When I appeared to you in the place where you sleep, my intent was to frighten you, nothing more. The box was in your house. I didn't know why it was there. I assumed you must have taken it from someone or somewhere. But, you see, the box is mine rightfully, and it called to me. It knows me. Its powers will extend my life. That is why I came for it and had to protect it." He crossed his legs and laid the box upon his lap. "You see, my boy, I am an old man now—you know that, don't you. You've seen him." He sat up and leaned forward. "That old man wants to live. *I* want to live. Everything I do now is to ensure my survival. If I can open the box, the old man you saw will disappear, and this young one you see before you will remain. If you will help me, I will live in this, my present form, for nearly one hundred years more." He allowed Cletis to ponder his words.

"When I came to this room, I feared you to be an obstacle to that survival, so I sought to destroy you. But the Dungarvan's have protected you, as we have both seen, and I think I know why. It has to do with their prophecy." He looked down at the box, reading the words etched upon the lid. "'A new Traveler shall appear . . . and unseal the box by the hand of his power.' That new Traveler must be *you*. I assume it is. An interesting prophecy, isn't it? Its outcome appears to be based on *your* decisions." He stood and walked toward the table. Cletis watched him anxiously as he laid the box on the large, wooden slab.

"Like I said, all you have to do is open the box for me. You are a Traveler. You have the ability to do so. I can show you how. I will share with you its powers and secrets. Then, if you wish, I will give you the box, leave, and have nothing more to do with you or Abish or this place. It is your choice."

The man watched Cletis for several seconds, awaiting an answer. "My young man, what do you say?"

The blue light protected me once. Will it do it again? Gathering all the courage he could muster, Cletis forced himself to shake his head. "No," he whispered hoarsely, trying to find his voice.

"'No' what?" the man shrugged. "What do you mean by that?"

"No, I won't help you."

The man eyed him calmly, his face registered no emotion.

"If you choose not to help me, then you and I . . . and Abish will all be destroyed. Do you realize that? Life as you know it will shortly end. 'Freezing of Time' is a part of this prophecy. If Time is frozen, such are the consequences. That is not a lie. You will be taken from the man you think to be your father. You will be taken from Abish. You will be taken from your home and everything that is familiar to you. Abish will be no more, and you will be lost to everything and everyone. That is a reality because you are a Traveler. They are not. I can do nothing about that. I speak the truth."

His words carried no hint of anger or frustration. He simply laid before Cletis a side of this strange story he had neither heard nor considered before.

I can't let him into my mind, Cletis urged himself. *Even though I can't feel him around me anymore, I can't drop my guard. I can't let him in. Maybe what he says is true. Maybe a part of it is. Maybe Abish knows some things she hasn't shared with me yet. Even if that's the way it is, this man destroyed Abish's house. Abish said he is evil.* Cletis fought to control his emotions. He swallowed and rubbed his hand across his moist lips. *But . . . will Abish and Dad really be taken away from me if I don't help him?*

"Don't misunderstand me," the man said calmly. "I *am* happy to see you. More than you will ever know. You are my son." He studied Cletis. "Again, I am sorry that I have treated you poorly or insensitively. It is generally not my nature to act so, but times are difficult for me presently. Forgive me. Under previous circumstances, you would have run to me and embraced me. You did so at one time, long ago, as time measures it. Do you remember? When you first learned to walk, you came to me often in our home, and I held you in my arms. Your name was Torlock then. Did you know that? It means 'one who comes to help.' Now you have the chance to live up to the meaning of your name. You can help me live. You can help Abish live. Your touch will keep me alive. For I *will* survive. I *must* survive. And I will do all that I can do to ensure that." He studied Cletis seriously. "There are two sides to this story, my young boy. In time, you will see that I am right, and I'm sure your mind will change. Think about what I have said. It is all true. We will meet again."

The gray, familiar conduit gathered around the Traveler, swallowing him and the box in the mass of teeming energy. Gradually he disappeared from sight.

Drained of all energy, Cletis closed his eyes and slumped to the wooden flooring beneath him.

Cletis opened his eyes and rolled to his side. With a thud, he dropped off the bench and onto the cold, plastic tiles of the floor. He shook his head, rubbed his eyes, and scanned the room around him. *Where am I?* Naked from the waist up, he yanked his T-shirt out from under his belt, lifted his hat off his head, and pulled the damp shirt over him.

It was a locker room like the boys' dressing room at the high school gym where he had once helped his dad with plumbing work in the shower stalls. But this room was fancier, and the lockers were wider and bigger. He stood, took a step away from the bench, and looked around him. The lockers that filled the room were made of metal, but were separated by small wooden walls, like stalls, that extended out from each one. Within each stall sat a single chair on which a person could sit to change clothes. Above each open stall, placards were fixed, bearing the names of the individuals whose clothing hung in the lockers below them. At least that's what Cletis presumed.

The names were familiar to him, and as he wandered the room and read each placard, his heart began to race. "Berra . . . Skowron . . . Lopez . . . Richardson . . . Kubek . . . Howard . . . I know these names," he spoke excitedly, as if Johnny or Pauly or Elston stood right next to him. "Yankees! I'm in the Yankee clubhouse!" He scratched his chin in thought. "But these names are from the 1960s. How can that be?"

An amazing feeling swept over him gently—dreamlike, in a way—a feeling similar to the giddiness of a Christmas morning or the happy anticipation that comes on the last day of school just before the final bell sounds. He turned to his left and followed the names written above the stalls.

Ford . . . Whitey Ford! His mind raced. *Terry . . . That must be* Ralph *Terry. Maris . . . Oh man, Roger Maris! This is his locker!* He paused a moment, studying the clothing that hung in the locker. As if in a daze, he walked on. *Blanchard . . . Hey, that's Elston's last name . . . Tresh . . .*

Boyer. Cletis Boyer! Man, my dad's favorite infielder. The names and the memories flowed through his mind. He and his dad had often talked about the Yankees of 1960 and 1961 and the great players of those years. He paused for a breath and then studied the name on the placard above the next stall. "Mantle," Cletis spoke aloud.

Just then a cheer erupted from beyond the clubhouse. The sound echoed off the block walls and tiled floors that surrounded him.

They must be playin a game! Cletis decided, still studying the Mantle locker in front of him. *There's a game goin' on out there!*

"Now batting, center fielder, Mickey Mantle," came the announcement over the loud speaker, sounding throughout the stadium and filtering into the locker room. Cletis stopped to listen and think. With the announcement, another cheer erupted all around him.

Looking about, Cletis eyed the four different closed doors on the walls of the locker room and tried to figure out which door would take him toward the playing field.

How did I get here? Man, I've gotta be back in the 1960s!

Then a door opened. Cletis turned quickly.

An elderly gentleman entered the room, carrying a load of towels. "Well, well, we have a visitor," he stated, frowning.

He eyed Cletis curiously as he strode to the lockers. Dutifully he began placing a single towel on each chair in each stall. He was dressed in white overalls and white shoes and wore a white shirt. The white clothing was a perfect match for the thick, white mustache that covered his upper lip. The bristly whiskers hung out over his mouth, and what appeared to be fragments of the day's meals were still suspended within them—ready and waiting to be eaten later. A New York Yankees hat rested gracefully over the man's white hair.

"What ya doin' in here, young man?" he asked, peeking at Cletis out of the corner of his eye. "This is off limits, you know? Who let you in here?" He straightened and studied Cletis for a moment. "Well? You got an answer? How'd you get in here?"

"I'm not sure, sir," Cletis answered haltingly. "I . . . uh . . . I guess I sort of got lost and came in this door."

He pointed to a door to his right, hoping it was a door that led out of the locker room.

"That's a closet," the gentleman replied with a slight chuckle in his voice. "Don't think you woulda come through *that* door."

Cletis stood silently, embarrassed by his answer.

"You ain't in here looting pockets are you?" the man questioned, eyeing Cletis suspiciously. "Because if you are, I'll have you hauled outta here by the stadium police!"

"No sir, I'm not. I promise I'm not." Cletis patted his pockets and lifted his hands.

The man studied Cletis's sweaty shirt and the Tigers cap on his head, and then went about his business of distributing the towels. There was an awkward silence.

"You recognize these names?" the man asked, pointing to the placards above the stalls.

"Yes, sir," Cletis answered. "Most of them."

A cheer sounded off the walls around them—loud and prolonged.

"Mantle must've done something good," the old man said. "Playing hurt, he is. Won't be surprised if it's the only hit he gets in this series. But the Reds are gonna give them their money's worth, though, don't you think? Robinson, Pinson, Post, Maloney, O'Toole. Got some pretty good ball players here in Cincy, don't they?"

Cletis thought for a moment, putting the pieces together. "Reds playing the Yankees?" he asked aloud. "The National League doesn't play the American League . . . unless . . . this is the World Series?" Cletis gasped. "1961?"

The elderly man scowled at him. "Course it is, son," he piped, putting the last towel in Tony Kubek's locker. "Don't you know where you are?"

"Now I do, I guess . . . Can I watch it?" Cletis asked enthusiastically.

"Isn't that why you're here?" the man questioned. "Let me see your ticket, kid."

Cletis knew he had no ticket. Or did he? He quickly started searching through his pockets, in hopes of finding one.

"Now batting," came the muffled voice of the announcer, "catcher, Yogi Berra."

Another cheer sounded from the stands around them. Cletis looked up a moment, as if trying to soak in every detail. Again he continued his search for a ticket.

"Must've fallen out somewhere, sir. I can't find it."

The old gentleman rubbed his mustache. "What's your name, son?"

Cletis took a deep breath. It was all too good to be true. But now he was in trouble. Now he was caught, and how would he get out of it?

"My name's Clete, sir. Short for Cletis."

The man lifted a doubting eyebrow and then suddenly brightened, tipped his head, and grinned a knowing smile. "Tigers fan, are ya?" he questioned, pointing at Clete's hat.

"Uh, yeah . . . I am." Cletis looked up at the brim of the hat on his head. "I'm from Detroit. Well, near there, anyway."

"Wait a minute," the man squeaked, adjusting his cap. "Cletis, eh? That's what you said your name was?"

Cletis nodded.

"Well, there's somethin' here for you. Mr. Maris told me to give it to you." The old man shuffled to the front of Roger Maris's locker and pointed at the dress shoes lying below the hanging pants. "See down there? Those shoes? Check in that shoe on the right."

Cletis was hesitant as he walked to where the man stood. He paused and peered into the locker of the famous Yankee slugger.

"In Roger Maris's shoe?" Cletis questioned.

"You said your name was Cletis, didn't ya?" the man quizzed.

Cletis nodded again.

"I saw him write it myself. Just for you. Must've known you was comin'. Bend down there and check for yourself. You'll find it."

Cletis entered the stall, pushed aside the chair, and knelt in front of the pair of shoes lying at the bottom of the locker. In one shoe rested a baseball. It was brand new, with words written on it. Cletis studied the part of it he could see but didn't touch it. He looked back at the man in white.

"What am I supposed to do with it?"

"Take it out," he urged. "Go ahead. You'll see it's for you."

Clete lifted the ball. Holding it out toward the light, he spun it gently in his fingers until he could see the entire message.

"Well, what does it say?" asked the man as he removed his cap and pushed back the strands of long white hair.

Cletis read it out loud. "'To Cletis, from Roger. 61 in '61.' That's what it says." Below the message was Roger Maris's autograph.

Man, I can't believe this, thought Cletis. He took a deep breath and allowed himself to smile. Just holding the ball sent shivers through him.

Suddenly a doubt surfaced. Something wasn't as right as it should be. "Wait a minute," Cletis reasoned, turning to the man. "Are you sure this wasn't written for Cletis Boyer, the third baseman? Cuz him and me have the same name. We're both named Cletis."

"Let me see that ball," spoke the man, frowning. "I don't think there's a mistake, but maybe I better inspect it."

Cletis handed him the ball. Another cheer erupted from the stands around them. Pulling a chair from Hector Lopez's locker, the man sat down and lifted the ball closer to his eyes. With a puzzled expression he turned the ball over and over, studying the Maris autograph.

"Very clever, Cletis Dungarvan," he spoke, but in a more youthful voice. "You know your baseball." His face lifted, and he smiled.

Cletis eyed him fearfully, sensing what the next moment would bring. Alive with movement, the man's hands, face, and neck began to pulse, shift, and pull, altering their shape and appearance. Cletis at once jumped back away from him as the transformation took place. Though he fought a natural tendency to panic, Cletis forced himself to watch the man's eyes as they closed and opened, dulled then focused, shifting and melding with the Change. He watched as the man's face, arms, chest, and legs expanded and heaved, stretching into their new and larger form. He heard the body groan with the craning and expanding of bones and ligaments. He stared at the man's head and neck as he reared backward and forward with the metamorphosis. The hair and clothing were the last to mold and stretch into their final form. Within moments the Traveler sat before Cletis, grinning snakelike at the concluded production.

Unexpectedly the world went dark.

Cletis's eyes opened, and his head lifted away from the floor. Gathering his bearings and balance, he looked around him. Flat on his back in the old library at Abish's house, he looked up at the underside of the table over the top of him and, then shifting his eyes to the left, studied the tall, packed bookshelves next to the table. Light streamed through the window above him, telling him it was still daytime. But was it the *same* day? Reaching up to the surface of the table, Cletis pulled himself to his feet.

The Traveler sat straight in front of him on the chair by the door. In his hand he held a baseball. He stood and stepped toward the table, tossing the ball up and down in his hand.

"It was not a dream, Cletis," he stated with a grin. "They knew it would not harm you. And they somehow knew that *I* wouldn't harm you. No blue light surrounded you, protecting you from me. It was all quite simple." He tossed the ball up again and caught it easily in the tips of his fingers. "Traveling is all within your power. Allow me to earn your trust, and I will teach you how it is done."

Cletis studied him silently. There was no dark, heavy feeling in the room—nothing disturbing or haunting about being in the presence of this man. And there had been no dreary, scary feelings in the Yankee clubhouse either. Still Cletis remained on the far side of the table.

"Watch this," the man announced, taking several steps back and stopping in front of the huge doorway. He pushed his long, blond braid back off his shoulder, and then he lifted the ball in front of him toward Cletis. As if on an imaginary mound, the Traveler wound up—as easily and as comfortably as any good pitcher—then purposely fired the ball at Cletis.

"Hey!" Cletis cried, lifting his arms and trying to twist out of the way.

Despite the apparent danger, no blue shield materialized around him. It all happened so fast. For a moment Cletis's arms remained high, protecting his face. Then slowly he dropped his hands and looked toward the Traveler. In the split second before the ball had reached Cletis, it slowed almost to a stop. There, hovering in mid-air, not more than a foot from his face floated the baseball, inching its way toward him. Cletis studied the ball in wide-eyed wonder and marveled at the power that could have arrested it in mid-flight. The pitch, which Cletis knew had been thrown hard, now hung in the air—as if it were a humming bird inspecting him, trying to decide if it should reverse direction and fly away, or continue forward. Able to read the Roger Maris autograph written across it, Cletis recognized the ball from the Yankee clubhouse. Mesmerized, he reached up and grabbed it out of the air.

The man laughed out loud as Cletis stared at the ball, which now rested comfortably in his hand. "Think what you could do with a pitch like *that*," he chuckled as the gray particles of the energized conduit filled the air around him. "If you want, you can even make it pick up speed again, *after* it has slowed down. It's untouchable."

Cletis stood at the edge of the table, holding the ball and trying to digest what he had just seen. He said nothing.

The man levitated off the ground and floated within the conduit. He flashed a charismatic smile.

"You will find that Abish is not telling you the complete truth."

With those words, he and the conduit were gone.

CHAPTER 17

The First Game

Cletis was late for practice the next morning. Despite the excitement of wearing a new uniform and practicing the day before the first game of the tournament, Cletis felt exhausted. It had been a tough night with very little rest. Too many confusing thoughts had drilled his weary brain. Before going to bed, he and his dad and Abish had discussed the details of the prophecy, and Abish had tried to explain everything she knew about it. But there were still lots of unanswered questions. At the same time there were certain things Cletis still kept to himself. He didn't talk about the traveling to 1961, and he didn't talk about what the Traveler had discussed with him in the library.

The Traveler had told him his name was "Torlock." *What was that all about?* Cletis pondered. *And he said that Abish and Dad would be destroyed if I didn't help him. What's that supposed to mean? And what about the time travel?* Cletis knew he had been back to the 1961 World Series, but he didn't know how he got there or how the Traveler had power over him to move him from one point to another. *Do I talk to Dad and Abish about all this? The Traveler said that Abish wasn't telling me the whole truth. So who am I supposed to trust? Even the feelings that Abish said would guide me kinda come and go. I didn't even feel anything bad there in the Yankee clubhouse. . . . Did I just get used to him? Will the same bad feelings come back if he appears again?*

By the time Cletis got to the field, everyone was already lined up between home and third. Mr. Howard was walking up the base path, inspecting the new uniforms. Cletis dropped his bike by the dugout bench and hustled to the end of the line near third base. On his way there, he noticed that Rabbit's uniform kind of sagged around her, like a clown's baggy clothing. Cletis couldn't tell if it made her look skinny or fat. But one thing was for certain, she couldn't play ball dressed like that.

"What'd you lookin' at?" she called out to him as he ran past. She was obviously feeling self-conscious about it. But Cletis was too tired to comment.

In spite of his fatigue, it was exciting to see uniforms on this field, and he couldn't help but smile as he took his place in line near third base. Every member of the team seemed to realize they were making baseball history in their little town of Greenberg Junction. Mr. Howard passed each happy player, inspecting what they wore and how they wore it. He approached Rabbit and smiled down at her, eyeing her extra-large uniform.

"Little big, ain't it?"

"Un poquito, no más," she answered sarcastically.

Mr. Howard took a step away from the line and looked down the row. He studied Davey, who stood close to third base, near Cletis. It was clear that Davey's uniform fit him tightly, and from where Mr. Howard stood, it looked like a swap might work.

"Davey," called Mr. Howard, "why don't you trade uniforms with Rabbit. I think you'll both get a better fit that way."

"Okay," answered Davey. He stepped forward and began to unbutton the front of his jersey.

Rabbit looked on, horrified.

"No, Davey," barked Mr. Howard. "Not now. We can wait until after practice. And once you're both changed and the uniforms are washed, you can swap them then. Okay?"

Davey innocently stepped back into line, nodding his head and rebuttoning his jersey.

"Davey, you are such an idiot," chuckled Pauly.

Mr. Howard passed Frank, Johnny, and Timmy. Approaching Klu, he paused for a moment. "Cup?" he whispered.

Klu nodded

"Hard plastic?"

Klu nodded again.

"Gotta wear it every game of the tournament or you and me both get tossed."

"I will," Klu whispered back.

"Good."

Making his way past Pauly, Bernie, and Davey, Mr. Howard finally stopped near third base, in front of Cletis.

"How ya doin', Clete?"

"Fine."

"You look a little tired."

"I am a little. But I'm okay." Cletis took a deep breath. "You look good, sir," he stated, peering up at the man's thin face. He wasn't quite sure how or why the words slipped out of his mouth, but they did.

Mr. Howard smiled down at him and nodded. Then he eyed the row of players, clapped his hands, and walked back toward the plate. "Pauly," he shouted out, "get the box. Put it on home. We got some news to look at."

Good, thought Cletis. *No ugly feelings around here this morning.*

Pauly and Davey ran to the dugout bench, lifted the old memorabilia box and hefted it toward the plate. Dust puffed out beneath the box as they dropped it in the batter's box. Pauly leaned down, removed the opened lock, lifted the hinge, and pulled back the lid. On top of the pile of memorabilia was a fresh newspaper. Pauly reached in and grabbed it. As he did, Cletis noticed the old tabloid he had contributed to the team on the day he first practiced with them. From where Cletis stood, he got a good look at the headline of the crazy article and the picture of the bog boy below it.

All of a sudden, a whole new perspective to that weird story erupted in his brain. Cletis's heart raced. With all that had been happening in his chaotic life and with all that he had recently discovered about himself and Abish, the prophecy, and the Traveler, that once unbelievable headline didn't seem so . . . well, unbelievable. His excited thoughts were interrupted by Mr. Howard's announcement.

"I want you all to look at this," he declared.

He closed the lid and placed the newspaper on the top of the box. All gathered close as Mr. Howard opened to the sports section and that morning's recent scores. A certain box score was circled in red pencil, and Mr. Howard's finger tapped three times on the article above it.

"Read it to us, Johnny," he requested.

Johnny bent close to the print and read the small paragraph above the numbers. "Newcomer Elston Blanchard led Canterbury Heights to a 13 to 2 romping of Metro Golden in the final game of the Tri-City Tournament last night. This new addition to the team, with his spectacular defensive skills, has high school coaches drooling. Blanchard, Hanson, and Stansfield all went 3 for 4, leading the offensive attack. Canterbury Heights looked so polished and talented for such a young team that it will be a surprise if they fail to win the upcoming Greater Metro Tournament."

Johnny lifted his head and looked up at Mr. Howard. "Mr. Sperry said they gave him a tryout at his new place, and right then and there they asked him to play on the Canterbury team."

"Man," sighed Timmy.

"You all know Elston," Mr. Howard nodded casually. "He's a good boy, but he's not superman. Even the best of teams can be beaten." He folded the paper up and slipped it back into the old box. "We can play with any team that enters this new tournament, including Canterbury Heights. Don't you forget that. Now, tomorrow at 4:00 we play a team called Industry. We're the underdogs. They think we're just a bunch of farmers and hicks out here. Maybe we are. But we've got something to prove." He pointed to the diamond. "Out in the field, guys. There's work to be done."

The team broke the huddle and raced out to their positions. Cletis, still feeling exhausted, trotted across the infield toward center.

"Cletis," called Mr. Howard from home plate, "you sure you're okay?"

Cletis looked back at him and nodded and waved. Turning again toward center, he picked up his speed.

Gotta get through this.

The practice had gone nicely that morning, and it had been exciting to see the team play so well together. Bernie's pitching was incredible. Rabbit made three spectacular catches—two at shortstop and one behind second base. Klu and Frank collided down the third base line, chasing down a pop foul, but Klu hung onto the ball, even with Frank lying over the top of him. Neither of them was hurt, and though Mr. Howard said Klu's catch was as good as any catch Johnny Bench or Carlton Fisk had ever made, he wisely took the moment to teach the importance of "calling out" for the ball and "calling off" another fielder. Even Timmy made two good catches in right field and seemed to be learning a lot more about his position with each practice—things like judging a fly ball, knowing what you're supposed to do with the ball once you catch it, and hitting the cut-off. Cletis continued to hit just about everything thrown at him. Mr. Howard would tell him where to place it, Johnny or Bernie would pitch it, and about ninety percent of the time, Cletis would drill it there.

Despite the success of the practice, Cletis couldn't help but be distracted by his recent meeting with the being Abish called the Traveler. Cletis remembered vividly the look of hatred and evil in the eyes of the man who shot fire from his fingers. He wondered about the blue light that protected him from the blast. He remembered the sudden change in the being when he discovered the marks on Cletis's shoulders. Cletis thought about how the evil feelings had faded, only to be followed by the miracle of time travel, the wonder of a World Series locker room thirty years in the past, and a supernatural pitch that floated like a feather.

With such events electrifying his brain, the morning's practice had been an exercise in concentration. He was nearly beaned at second base when Pauly overthrew Rabbit on the cut-off. The ball was sailing straight at Cletis's head, when Johnny yelled at him. Cletis ducked just a split second before impact. Mr. Howard stopped practice, hurried out to second base, and again, asked Cletis if he was okay.

As Cletis rode his bike over the well-worn path across the open field between the diamond and his home, he continued to explore the questions that had occupied his mind. *How did I get there? How did I go back in time? And how did I get back to Abish's house? He was there waiting for me. He had the baseball in his hand. There are two sides to that man. He can be both good and bad. Maybe when he first saw me, he was just trying to protect himself. Maybe he thought I was dangerous to him. Maybe all the ugly feelings I felt in the past were simply his way of protecting himself from the unknown things of* my *world. Maybe he's just as scared and confused as I am. He said he was just trying to survive.*

Cletis aimed for the familiar dirt mound in front of him and sailed over the top of it, lifting his bike four feet into the air and landing not-so-gracefully about ten feet down the path. His tired bike groaned with the impact. *That man can float in the air! That would be amazing to be able to do that! He must have a name. Abish must know his name. Maybe he's the* Ian *who was written on the charts on Abish's table. And how did he make that ball float? He even had good form in his windup. Man, it was like he had played the game before, like he knew how to pitch!* And he had told Cletis he had the power to do the same thing! Cletis sensed how the horror he first felt could easily be replaced by excitement and adventure. And Cletis even caught himself faintly hoping for another encounter with the Traveler man.

Cletis ducked his head down by his handlebars. The breeze on his neck was soothing and cool as he pedaled, and he could feel his new uniform lift off of his back and flap in the breeze. The Maris ball was in his top drawer. His dad didn't know anything about it yet. Neither did Abish. *When should I tell 'em? Or do I keep it to myself?*

In the distance, he could see the back of his house. Abish would be there waiting. *But he tried to hurt Abish,* Cletis reminded himself. *I've got to remember that. He tore up a part of her home. And if the blue light hadn't protected me, he would have hurt me too—maybe even killed me!* Even if the man was trying to protect himself, that was a strange way to go about it. Attack everything that moves? Destroy someone's property? Cletis felt strongly that no good person would do that.

Cletis remembered the blackened box. Even the Traveler spoke about the prophecy. Even he was trying to figure it out—like he didn't know how all the pieces fit together. But he seemed to know about the powers that put the prophecy on the lid. *And he was freaked out by the blue magic that protected me. Way back in time the old family must have had their* own *amazing magic in order to pull something like that off.*

Cletis pulled up in the backyard and hopped off his bike. He leaned it against the aluminum siding and scurried around the back of the house and through the laundry room door. After kicking off his dirty cleats, he walked into the kitchen.

It was cool inside the home. The AC was on, and it felt nice compared to the humid heat of the outdoors. Placing his mitt on the counter near the sink, he paused a second to ponder the stillness of the house. For some reason, he had expected to hear or see activity going on inside. He knew his dad was at work. That was normal. But he thought he'd see Abish somewhere doing something.

"Abish?" he called. "Are you here?"

"In the living room," came the reply.

Cletis crossed through the kitchen. He flapped his uniform top in and out, away from his chest, as he stepped down into the front room.

"Hello," she stated quietly, turning to face him.

"Hi," Cletis answered, crossing behind her and sitting on the floor next to the coffee table.

They eyed each other for a moment.

"Uniform looks good."

"Thanks."

"How are you doing?" she asked, smiling down at him.

"I think I'm fine, but I'm not sure."

She studied him a moment. "Why?"

"Oh, lots of things on my mind," he muttered, shrugging his shoulders slightly. "Lots of questions. Lots of things I don't know about."

"Me too."

She watched him eagerly, as if appreciating and adoring everything about him. He pulled his hat off and combed his fingers through his matted hair. He took a deep breath, lifted his shoulders as if stretching away sore muscles, and then leaned back on his hands.

"The last part of the prophecy," he began, "... the part about time being frozen and a choice being made and unsealing the box ... do you think it's supposed to all happen on a baseball diamond or during a baseball game?"

Abish's bushy eyebrows lifted. "I don't know for sure, but I think you're right."

"How are we supposed to know when all this stuff is finally gonna happen?"

"As far as I understand it, it will happen after the part that says, 'when the heart of the finder fails.' Whenever or whatever that is." She paused a moment. "And I also don't know what it means when it says 'the son is like the father.' Most of the prophecy I think I've figured out, at least to a certain extent, but I still don't understand those parts."

"So we don't know who the 'finder' is?" he asked.

"*I* don't. If you have any ideas, I'll be happy to discuss them with you," she offered. "Is it the finder of the box? Is it the one who finds you? For all I know, the finder could be the Traveler. It could be me. It could be you. I hope not, but it is a possibility. And I don't know if it's literal—like will his or her heart really fail . . . you know, like stop beating? Or is it symbolic—like in talking about courage or desire or determination."

Cletis wondered about the *finder*. *Could I be the finder*, he thought, *or Dad or Mr. Howard or Elston or even the Traveler? The Traveler found me. He found Abish. He found the box. Could that be what the prophecy is referring to?*

Suddenly he remembered the words of the Traveler—words he had spoken at Abish's house.

"Will you or me or the Traveler die if I mess this thing up?" Cletis finally asked.

She seemed to feel the heaviness of his question and the trouble in his heart. "What do you mean, if you mess this thing up?"

"I dunno. It just seems like a lot of what happens depends on the choices I make. I guess I mean, like what if I lose my temper or get scared or get tricked . . . or something like that? What if I do something wrong, whether I know it or not, that messes up the whole prophecy? What will happen to you if this thing doesn't come out the right way? What will happen to me and you and the Traveler?"

She studied him tenderly, as if distressed that such a young man would have to deal with this strange string of inexplicable events.

"Cletis, I don't know how the prophecy will work its way through. I don't know all the details. I never have." She seemed to be choosing her words carefully. "But I do know that somehow a way will be provided. I can't imagine that any life will be at risk, let alone lost. A path will open before us, and we'll see how things are supposed to be worked out. Of course, we will need to *want* to see the prophecy fulfilled in our favor. We will need to work together to that goal. I presume that choice is still yours to make. I know what *I* want to do, and I know what I'm hoping *you'll* do, but when that time actually comes, you will need to make a choice. You, and you alone, will know what choice that will be."

Cletis sighed and bowed his head in thought.

"Clete, when it comes right down to it, though," she continued, "it will be important that you realize this one thing: the man I once married has done much evil. His desires are purely selfish. In times past, his selfishness led to cruelty. But he might do something good or nice before that moment of cruelty. That's called manipulation. He'll manipulate you by doing creative and exciting things for you until he has won your trust, and then he will use you. Don't be fooled by his charm, his smile, his cunning, or his magic. That chain of evil he forged in bygone years ruined countless lives and lands. If he gets his way, I am certain the same thing will happen again for another hundred years. Both of us have seen what he does in his little temper tantrums. He destroys homes and attempts to destroy lives—at least mine anyway."

Mine too, Cletis thought. He sat up and leaned forward, rubbing his hands together.

"His evil must be stopped," she added. "And I am determined to be a part of that effort. I think that is one of the most important aspects of my long test."

Cletis felt her eyes on him as he looked at the porcelain couple on the coffee table.

"Cletis, I know I mentioned this before, but I'll repeat it. You have clearly felt both the good and the evil, and as far as I know, you still do. You can easily distinguish between the two forces. We must stay the course so that both feelings remain obvious to us. That's what will guide us through this process. I'm sure of that. That is how the powers of the family operate. There will be an influence, calm and sure, that will guide us through this test."

Cletis lay back on the carpet. He knew he was sticky and dirty, but that didn't matter at the moment. He was also exhausted. Placing his hands behind his head, he stared blankly up at the ceiling.

"What is his name?" he asked. "The Traveler man. What is his name?"

Abish's eyebrows lifted. "Why do you wish to know his name?" she finally questioned.

"I don't know. I just do."

"In a time long ago," she began carefully, "he was your father. In a time long ago, our family was whole. He was with us, and we loved each other. But my sense is that you do not wish to call him 'Father.'"

Cletis was silent for a moment, then shook his head and sat up again.

"No, I'd *never* think of him as my father," he announced with conviction. He looked up into her green eyes, as if trying to look deep into her soul—to see who she really was. He could tell she welcomed it. She smiled and returned the gaze.

"His name is Ian," she answered. "It is the Irish name for John."

I was right. Cletis remembered the name on the manuscript in Abish's library—written by hand, next to the genealogies. *"Soon Ian comes. Be strong."*

"And what was my name? The name I had back when I was born?"

"Are you sure you want to know?"

He nodded, still studying her eyes.

She paused. "Your name was Torlock. It means, the one who comes to assist, or help. It is a prophetic name."

Then the man—this Traveler man—was right, thought Cletis. *He spoke the truth. He knew my name. It was he and Abish who gave it to me.* His mind was suddenly filled with a storm of unthinkable thoughts. *So is this man—this Traveler—really my father? If he is, Abish is my mother!*

Gradually he pulled his knees up to his chest and wrapped his arms around them.

"I've been with him." It just came out. He surprised himself by saying it. He looked up at Abish. "He saw the marks on my shoulders. He knows who I am."

Abish sat up straighter, as if waiting for details. But Cletis remained silent. With his arms still around his knees, he rolled over onto his side.

"First game's tomorrow afternoon," he spoke gently, with a faraway look on his face. "Can I play under pressure? With each game of the tournament I'll be thinking of the prophecy. I'll be wondering where he is, or who he is, or if I can do what I'm supposed to do."

In a silent stare, he gazed at Abish's boots and the legs of the coffee table. Rolling to his belly, he pushed himself up off the floor. Standing and straightening, he faced the gnarled, ill-shapen, woman in front of him.

"Excuse me," he stated, holding his cap in his hand. "I've got some laundry to do."

He turned away from her, stepped up to the entry hall, and bolted up the stairs.

"Now batting for Sperry's Cards and Coins, number twenty-one, Bernie Anderson," echoed the announcement from the loudspeaker. Bernie swung his bat and eyed the beautifully manicured, grass infield as he strode toward home plate. When the outfielders saw him approach the batter's box, they jogged into a deeper position, settling on the grass just in front of the warning track along the outfield fence. Bernie had already hit one home run back in the second inning, which drove in three runs, so they prepared themselves for anything deep.

Good things were finally happening to the young, inexperienced Sperry's Cards and Coins team. It had been a tough and sloppy game early on. Bernie was the only player on the Sperry team who had ever set foot on a diamond with a grass infield and a warning track. All the other members of the Sperry team had been in awe from the moment they stepped onto the field, which had clouded their focus for the first four innings. Three errors in the first inning had cost them four runs. Pauly and Klu got picked off in the third, and then Johnny's wild pitch in the fifth cost them yet another run.

But now the jitters were gone. The team had settled down and was having fun, and in the top of the seventh, with one out, they found themselves down by two runs. Pauly had grounded out to the second baseman, but Cletis had doubled down the left field line and then had advanced to third on Klu's single to center field.

Now Bernie, with runners on first and third, stood ready to answer the call. He took a quick glance out at the scoreboard behind the fence in center field.

SPERRY'S CARDS 5, INDUSTRY 7.

Unlike the old, beat-up, rusty metal scoreboard back at home, this one was a fancy, new, electronically operated fixture, controlled from the enclosed station above and behind the backstop. Two men sat operating the panel and microphone that rested in front of them. From their lookout booth above the diamond, they called out the names and numbers of the players, recorded the events of the game, and worked the scoreboard.

Below their booth, and farther up the third base line, sat the five Sperry fans that made it to the game. Three of those fans—Mrs. Skinner, Mrs. Kluzuski, and Mrs. Allen—were positioned about ten feet closer to the Sperry dugout than Abish and Garth. It appeared as if the few people who sat near Abish gave the old hag plenty of space. Cletis was sure Abish was aware of that and wondered how it made her feel. At the moment, she was leaning forward, obviously deep into the strategies of the game, and studying Cletis, who took his lead at third.

"One out!" hollered Pauly from the dugout, holding up one finger. "Let's bring 'em around!"

"Gotta happen now, Bernie!" added Johnny from the on-deck circle, balancing his bat against his hip and clapping his hands.

"Here we go, Bernie," called Mrs. Skinner. Mrs. Klu had her hands between her knees, and she rocked nervously forward and back.

Bernie stepped up to the plate, paused before entering the batter's box, and looked down the third base line to get the signals from Mr. Howard.

"Fire in the hole!" yelled Mr. Howard from the coach's box, flashing the signs to Bernie and the base runners. His hand jumped from his hat, to his nose, to his chin, across his belt, and then up to his shoulder.

The first nose-to-chin combination was the "indicator." All the players knew that if that signal were given, the very *next* sign would be the one that would direct their course of action. Immediately following the indicator, Mr. Howard pulled his hand across his belt. That was the steal sign. So Cletis, Klu, Bernie, and every player on their bench, knew Klu was going on the pitch. Cletis would be on his own to decide what he would do, depending on the pitch and what Bernie or the catcher did with it. Then Mr. Howard clapped his hands together enthusiastically making sure Bernie sensed his excitement. No signs were given after the steal sign, so that meant Bernie was to hit away if the pitch was good. Bernie turned and looked across the field, and then eyed the pitcher competitively. Stepping up to the plate, the big left-hander kicked away the unwanted dirt by his cleats and settled into the batter's box.

Cletis, who stood in the base path near Mr. Howard at third, took a few more steps down the line, eyeing and challenging the pitcher. From Cletis's point of view, he watched Klu over at first base. Klu represented the tying run, and for being a fairly slow runner, he had a pretty healthy leadoff. Klu seemed to be daring the pitcher to try to pick him off. But this late in the game, and wanting to protect his lead, the pitcher was being extra cautious . . . and so was Mr. Howard.

"One out, Klu!" Mr. Howard shouted across the field, holding up one finger. "Be careful! You gotta score. Can't get picked off."

With that, Klu took a step back toward first base.

"Watch that pitcher, Clete. Don't get hung out there," reminded Mr. Howard as Cletis crouched and set. The third baseman stepped closer to the bag, as if to warn Cletis a throw could be coming his way.

The pitcher stepped back away from the rubber as the coach in the Industry dugout, in frustration, shouted out instructions to his players. The tall, thin catcher then stepped forward across home plate and flashed some hand signals to his teammates. The infielders immediately stepped forward to the lip of the infield grass and prepared for the next pitch. With the infield in and their defensive strategy in action, Cletis knew they were trying to make a play on him at home plate. Any groundball caught in the infield would be fired to the catcher. Keeping the runner at third base from scoring was certainly their top priority.

As the pitcher eyed his infielders, making sure everyone was ready, Cletis walked back to the bag, and though he already knew the score, he snuck a peak at the scoreboard. He wanted so desperately to win this first game. He bent down, placing his hands on his knees and, again, eyed the infield. Checking the pitcher, Cletis took several cautious steps down the line. Behind by two runs, he felt the pressure of making sure he crossed the plate safely. If their catcher threw down to second, Cletis had to score. He wanted to be ready.

"Watch the fake to first," Mr. Howard warned as the pitcher stepped onto the rubber and looked in at the catcher.

Cletis nodded, digging in on the base line. The third baseman stepped even closer to the base, slapping his mitt with his fist.

The pitcher came set, eyed Cletis, and then looked back over his shoulder to first. His front leg kicked high, and he fired the ball home. Bernie watched the ball zip past him, low and outside. On the pitch, Klu had broken for second and arrived there safely, standing up. With a runner on third, and not wanting to risk the possibility of a wild throw into center field, the catcher didn't even attempt to make a play.

The catcher fired the ball back to the mound as Bernie stepped out of the batter's box to get the signs from Mr. Howard. Cletis and Klu watched carefully too, making certain they knew exactly what to do. But all Mr. Howard did was clap his hands together and then put his fists one on top of the other, as if he were holding and swinging a bat.

"Bring 'em in, Bernie," he shouted from third. "Sittin' ducks. They're all yours! Make contact. You know what to do!"

"Yeah, Bernie!" hollered Timmy from the dugout.

"Find the gap somewhere!" called Davey, who sat next to him.

"Drive it somewhere, Bernie!" called Johnny from the on-deck circle as he swung his bats to warm up.

"A little stroke here, Bernie," barked Garth from the stands near the dugout.

The pitcher came set and eyed Cletis and Klu from the mound. He kicked and fired home. Whether the pitcher meant to or not, no one will ever know, but he rocketed the perfect strike, right down the middle of the plate. Bernie's left-handed swing was a thing of beauty. SMACK! Connecting perfectly, he drilled the ball into deep right-center, over the heads and beyond the reach of the two closest fielders. The ball hit the warning track, bounced off the fence, and rolled back into the outfield. Cletis scampered home and energetically turned and waved Klu in from third. He could hear Abish, his dad, and Mrs. Klu cheering from the stands just behind him. Bernie rounded second and was on his way to third when the throw came in from the right fielder. As Bernie slid into third base, the ball sailed high and wide over the top of him and slammed into the back wall of the Sperry dugout right between Davey and Frank. Rabbit snagged the ball and rolled it back onto the field.

Having landed in the dugout, the ball was instantly ruled out of play, and the umpire awarded Bernie home. With a high five from Mr. Howard as he headed home, Bernie jogged happily to the plate and into the arms and slaps and smiles of three cheering teammates. Cletis and Klu accompanied him enthusiastically back into the noisy, rambunctious, Sperry dugout as Johnny stepped to the plate to take his turn at bat. The scoreboard registered new numbers: SPERRY'S CARDS 8, INDUSTRY 7.

Yet, after Bernie's blast, two quick pitches later the inning came to an end. A spectacular catch in the outfield robbed Johnny of an extra-base hit. And Frank, frustrated that he went after a pitch low and away, fouled out to the right fielder. Now it was simply a matter of playing good defense and holding off Industry's final attempt to take back the lead.

Bernie took the mound in the bottom of the seventh inning, replacing Johnny. Johnny had pitched well until then, allowing only two earned runs out of the seven the other team had recorded. Now it was up to Bernie to hold them off. While he warmed up, the boys in the Industry dugout hung their fingers through the chainlink fencing and watched the kid from Ohio take his tosses. Bernie was big and fast and accurate, and the silence of the team in the Industry dugout loudly communicated their fears.

"Now pitching, number 21, Bernie Anderson," came the announcement.

"Let's go Bernie," shouted Mr. Howard from the dugout. "Mow 'em down."

Bernie smiled at the first Industry batter who stepped up to the plate.

"Right down the tube," called Klu, as if speaking to the batter. "See what you can do with 'em."

Bernie fired three straight fastballs down the center of the plate. The batter watched the first two pitches jet past, almost stepping completely out of the batter's box with each throw.

"You're steppin' in the bucket," called the Industry coach from third base. "Drive that front foot right back at the pitcher!"

Despite the advice, the batter swung feebly at the last pitch and came nowhere near touching it. As the infield fired the ball around the horn, the second batter stepped up to the plate.

"He's throwin' hard and straight," called the Industry coach. "Move back in the batter's box and come around sooner!"

The tall, lanky batter—Industry's catcher—moved back in the box, crowding Klu a bit, and lifted his bat ready for whatever Bernie threw. Klu readjusted his position, eyed the batter's feet and set up a target low-and-away. Bernie's control was right on the mark, and the batter whiffed awkwardly with each throw—three pitches, three strikes, and another out recorded.

Cletis jumped up and down excitedly in center field, laughing out loud at how Bernie blew the last six pitches right past the Industry batters.

One more out, he told himself.

Rabbit, businesslike, turned to the outfield and held up two fingers. She was in her element, remembering details and keeping the fielders on their toes. She turned, bent low to the ground, and readied herself for the next batter.

"Right now, she's probably daring the batter to hit it to her," Cletis chuckled out loud.

The third batter Industry sent to the plate was their leadoff hitter. The kid had reached base safely every time at bat, and he was a mosquito on the bases. He, alone, was accountable for three of their seven runs.

"No two-out rally startin' here!" Pauly called from left.

"Let's get this third!" shouted Mr. Howard, all alone in the dugout. "Finish it here! Everyone concentrates! Timmy, move in!"

Timmy shifted forward several steps in response to Mr. Howard's call.

"Take care of him, Bernie!" barked Johnny from first.

Cletis got down and ready. He could see Abish and his dad standing in the bleachers behind the dugout. Abish had her hands together in front of her chin. Cletis looked briefly back at the scoreboard. *Two outs. Nobody on. Bottom of the seventh. Just where we want 'em,* he thought as he swung his mitt through a flock of gnats that buzzed in front of his face.

On the mound, Bernie wound up and fired. CRACK! Amazingly the kid dished out a lightning line drive to shortstop that surprised everyone except Rabbit. Falling backward and leaning to her right, she dropped to her knees, stabbed the short-hop backhandedly, and miraculously vacuumed it up. Then, still on her knees, she spun and side-armed a strike to Johnny at first. The runner was dead out by three steps.

The field erupted in cheers as the boys and Rabbit ran together to the mound in celebration. Mitts and hats flew excitedly into the summer evening. The little team from far out in the rural pasturelands of southern Michigan jumped and danced and hooted in the middle of the diamond. Game one was now history. Sperry's Cards and Coins had hung on for their first tournament victory ever in the history of Greenberg Junction—at least as far as the boys could remember.

ChAPTER 18

A ChANGE IN ELSTON

Carrying the morning's newspaper, Cletis rushed through the front door and closed it quickly behind him. He raced through the front room and stepped up into the kitchen, opening the paper as he went. He had to find the sports section. Abish and Garth were seated at the kitchen table, eating toast and eggs. Cletis pushed aside their two glasses filled with apple juice and laid down the paper.

"Hey," warned Garth, "watch what you're doin'. Don't spill those."

"I won't," answered Cletis, hardly looking up.

Some things were more important than juice and breakfast, and at the present, finding his box score and reading the news of the tournament was one of those things. Opening the newspaper in front of them, Cletis carefully flattened away the folds.

Turning through the pages, he located the sports. In their little-town newspaper, there were only two basic sections. The sports coverage was usually tucked away somewhere in the back of the second part, next to the farm news, the obituaries, and the comics. As Cletis scanned the articles, he spied the bolder headlines: a column covering Detroit Tigers baseball and another smaller story dealing with some off-season news about the Pistons. Finally, in the bottom right-hand corner of the page, next to an article about a pig disease crossing the border from Canada, Cletis found the coverage he was looking for— the box scores and summaries from the previous day's Greater Metro Tournament.

Feeling the excitement of the search, his dad arose and stepped in behind Cletis, helping him scan the page for the news they hoped to find.

"Here it is!" announced Cletis, pointing to the article.

"Right there," agreed his father at almost the same time. "Look at that," he commented, still chewing a bite of toast. "You were right. They *do* have box scores. That's amazing for a Little League game. I'll bet Mr. Sperry did some calling around to make sure the *Greenberg Flyer* had the information." His dad paused and studied the article. "There you are," he continued, pointing to the exact box score. "Cletis Dungarvan! Big as life, eh?"

"Wow, look at that," exclaimed Cletis, rubbing his hand through his morning hair. He smiled up at Abish. "I got my name in the newspaper! That's a first!"

"Congratulations," she stated. "So what does it say? Give me the stats . . . as if I don't know them already."

"Four for four," stated Garth proudly, patting Cletis on the shoulder. "It was the best game I've ever seen! Beautiful come-from-behind victory! Made it exciting!"

"It was cool, wasn't it?" Cletis smiled up at them both and then focused back down on the paper. "Gotta find Canterbury Heights . . . Elston's team," he announced. "Gotta see how Elston did."

"Don't you have his new phone number?" his father asked, easing down into the empty chair next to Cletis. "Why don't you just call him and talk about it?"

Cletis looked up. "I don't have it yet. He hasn't called."

"Well, you'll probably see him at one of these tourney games— maybe even today—and you can ask him."

Cletis nodded and then went back to the paper. "Here he is!" he barked, leaning down over the news for a better view of the tiny printing. "Man, they beat Jones's Fiberglass 14 to 3! Gee, they crushed 'em. They only played five innings? What's that all about?"

"Skunk rule," groaned Abish, swallowing a mouthful of eggs. "Ten-run rule, probably. I'll bet that's what happened."

"If the team's ahead by ten runs after five innings, they call the game," his dad explained.

"Wow . . . " whispered Cletis, looking back down at the stats. "I heard that Jones's Fiberglass was one of the better teams, and

Canterbury just cuffed 'em." Cletis's eyes widened, imagining the game. Scratching his chin, he continued studying the stats on the page. "It says Elston went two for four with one RBI."

"And look at his," his father added, referring to the paragraph above the box. "It says Canterbury's got this Ty Cobb sort of coach." His dad read silently for a moment, taking in the rest of the article. "They say he's pretty heavy-handed and real strict with the boys. Look . . ." Garth pointed to the words he read. "'A win-at-all-cost type of guy. Some of the parents are upset with him already, saying he didn't *used* to be that way. But they're winning, so they'll keep him.' Hmmm, interesting."

"Those men ruin it for the kids," stated Abish. "It's like they want to live their own frustrated dreams through the lives of the boys. They drive and work those kids until they're either physically worn out or find no more fun in the game. It's a tragedy." She looked directly at Cletis and pointed a finger at him. "Mark my words, Clete. If the adults aren't careful, they'll take the fun right out of the game."

Cletis thought about what she said. "How could baseball stop bein' fun?" he asked.

"Coaches and parents teach failure, if they're not careful," she answered. "I've seen boys your age, Clete, crying on the mound because their dads are yelling at them to throw strikes! Well, do you think the boy is trying to throw balls? Of course not! He's out there doing his best, and the coach or his dad is getting after him for not putting the ball across the plate. Is that fun? No, it's not! Sometimes I think the leagues should just step away and let the boys and girls play by themselves."

Garth and Cletis eyed the old woman with surprise. "You mean just play like we're doin' now?" asked Cletis. "Like findin' a field and just playin'?"

"That's exactly what I mean."

"You may be right," commented Garth. "There's nothin' funner than a quick game of over-the-line or flies-up or work-up. I grew up on those games." He pulled his breakfast plate over to where he was now sitting. "Those boys who want to play in high school or college will find their way to the top."

"Was Dad any good when he played?" asked Cletis, studying Abish.

"She didn't see me play . . . " His dad interrupted his thought and looked over at Abish. "Did you watch me play ball when I was a kid?"

"Once in a while," she answered with a wink.

"Was he good?" Cletis asked, grinning at Abish.

"Darn good," she answered immediately. "None better at diving for a ball."

His dad eyed her momentarily, obviously amazed at the thought that the old lady could have watched him play. "You saw me, eh?"

She nodded slightly. "But I kept my distance."

"I *was* pretty good, at one time, wasn't I?" he finally commented, winking at Cletis. Lifting his empty plate from the table, he carried it to the sink.

"Hey, Dad, Klu's mom said she could drive some of us early to see the Canterbury game this afternoon. Can I go with 'em?"

"His team's playin' again this afternoon?"

"Yeah."

"Then you guys must be right after them?" his dad figured.

"I think so, but maybe on a different diamond."

"So you just gonna dress in your uniforms so you'll be ready to play?"

"Yeah."

His dad paused a moment in thought, rubbing bits of egg off his plate under the stream of warm water. "Yeah, then . . . go and spy on his team. Find out what they're made of. Maybe you can see Elston there and get his number." He looked back at the table. "Just make sure Abish is taken care of, though. Don't just go leavin' her all alone, unless she approves of it. And make sure you guys don't sit in the sun all day. You'll be too weak to play." He wiped his hands on a dishtowel and headed back to his room.

Cletis eyed Abish for a moment as she sipped some juice. "Is that okay with you if I go early?" he asked. "Will you be okay here?"

"I think I'll be just fine. You go ahead and watch them, and your dad and I will catch up to you later this afternoon when your game starts. Will *you* be okay?"

He pondered for a moment. "Yeah, I think so."

They both sat silently, as if reading each other's thoughts.

"How are you doing lately?" Abish finally asked.

Cletis took a quick breath and looked back down at the newspaper. "I dunno." He rubbed his eyes with the palms of his hands. "I'm just tryin' to make this fun. You know, I'm . . . uh . . . I'm just tryin' to play baseball—go out there and have fun and win a game." He paused a moment in thought. "But it's hard to concentrate on the game when I know somethin' might happen—somethin' weird that I won't know how to deal with, or what it'll be, or how it's gonna come, or if anyone's gonna get hurt."

She studied him silently, feeling his pain and confusion. With her finger, she rubbed away the moisture on the side of the glass she held. "I know. It's a hard thing. It could be that when the final moments come, no one but you, me, and the Traveler will even know it's happening. I wonder if that'll be the case during the 'frozen time' thing. It might just be that you and I will be alone with the Traveler, and time will stand still, and we'll have to wait and see what happens."

"Can he do that? Make time stop?"

"Ian can make *objects* stop in time. He can make *people* stop in time. But I really think the details of the prophecy that have to do with time freezing have been created by another Traveler—one more powerful than Ian. His father. A man named Padar." She studied Cletis, not knowing if she should go into detail. "It's an amazing power the Travelers have. They sort of live alone in their own existence, moving through time to different places, creating what they want wherever they want."

"So I have a grandfather named Padar?" Cletis asked. "And he has something to do with this prophecy?"

Abish nodded. "Yes, he was a powerful man. And I assume he is the one who sent you forward. And he and my parents are the ones who created the magic of the prophecy."

Cletis thought about that for a moment. "Man, Abish, I'm just a kid. The Traveler . . . he's a grown man, and he's bigger and stronger and smarter than I am. How am I supposed to know what to do if more of the things of the prophecy start to happen? I don't know how to do all that stuff like Traveling or Changing—all that stuff that he knows how to do. And maybe I don't even have the power to do any of that!"

"Cletis, those powers may not be needed in the fulfilling of the prophecy."

"The prophecy says that in the freezing of time, a new Traveler will appear, and a decision will be made. Is that Traveler *me*? And if it is, what am I supposed to decide?"

She eyed him closely. "If it *is* you, decide to do what is right. Then all will work out."

Cletis paused and thought. "What if this prophecy is supposed to be fulfilled this afternoon at our game . . . What am I gonna do?" In frustration, he closed the newspaper and stared across the room out the window. Slowly his head sunk into his hands. "And to be honest, I'm scared. I just wanna play baseball. But with all this stuff in the back of my mind, it's almost impossible."

In the silence that followed his words he could hear her shallow breathing.

"I noticed you slept in your own room last night," she finally said.

"Yeah. I'm doin' okay now," he answered. "I talked to Dad about it and decided to go upstairs again."

"Two nights ago you were terrified of being alone." She waited until his eyes met hers. "Cletis, something has changed. Are you sure you're okay?"

Cletis pondered the question and then put his head back down into his hands. "Like I said, I've been with him. I've seen him. I've talked with him."

She awaited more details, but Cletis sat silently.

"So what does that mean, Cletis? Are you no longer afraid of him? Is it easy to be with him? Are you no longer feeling the darkness when he comes?"

Cletis sat in turmoil. He heard the questions but wanted to avoid having to answer. He wondered how detailed he needed to be. *Do I tell her everything I know? Or do I keep certain things to myself? Do I tell her that it was exciting to be with him—that it was cool to travel in time? Do I tell her it'd be cool to learn to do the things he can do? Those powers are supposed to be in me too. I want to be with him, but I don't want to be with him. How do I explain that?*

Abish watched him, concerned by his stillness.

"Cletis?" His father interrupted from the hallway as he made his way into the kitchen. "I forgot to mention this baseball." He carried the Maris autographed ball, gently cupped in the palm of his hand. "It was on my dresser this morning . . . So is it a gift, I hope?" He chuckled at his own question. "Or were you just showin' it to me, and now I have to give it back?"

"It's real, Dad," Cletis answered in a serious tone.

His father paused, sensing the somber mood that had filled the kitchen during his absence. "Well . . . yeah . . . it looks real. I'm hoping it is. Maris autograph! Nice . . . So did you pick it up from Mr. Sperry, or something? What'd it cost you?"

Cletis looked up at his dad, then over to Abish. "I went there. I went back to 1961. I was in the Yankee locker room during the World Series against the Reds. I was in Cincinnati."

With a light gasp, Abish's hands went to her mouth. His father shot a look at her and then peered briefly down at the ball he held. Concerned, he stepped closer to the table.

"A man there gave me the baseball," Cletis continued. "It was in Roger Maris' shoe—in his locker in the Yankee clubhouse. I was there! I could hear the crowd. I could hear the announcers! When I held the ball, I told the man that it was probably written to Cletis Boyer, not me. Then he smiled . . . and . . . and he began to morph, to Change." He looked up at his dad's confused frown, then back at Abish. "It was Ian. And I didn't feel anything bad. Not that time. And I forced myself to watch every moment of his Changing. I had to. I wanted to. The next thing I knew, I woke up in your house, Abish, there by the big table." Abish's eyes widened with that announcement. "And then he was there again, in that library room of yours. He gave me the ball. He still had it in his hand."

Cletis ran his fingers through his hair. Looking at their expressions, he felt as if he had done something evil and just confessed to a terrible crime.

"I didn't do any of it on my own. It just happened! I was there in the locker room, and then I was back in Abish's house." He eyed them both for a moment and then announced seriously, "And it was the funnest, coolest thing I've ever done." Cletis studied Abish's green eyes, sensing her concern. "He can't hurt me. A blue light protects me."

Again Abish gasped.

"Like the blue light we saw in the bedroom?" questioned his father.

Cletis nodded and then looked down at the table. "Abish . . . you asked me if I was afraid of him. I was at first, but I'm not anymore. At least I don't think I am. And that's what makes me *more* afraid."

Cletis took his place in the bleachers along side Johnny, Bernie, Klu, Rabbit, and Frank. They had piled in as close to first base as they could, hoping to see Elston and watch his warm-ups. They had figured the stands there near first base would be a good place to heckle him. Besides, there was a large maple tree behind the bleachers on the first base side that shaded that area where they sat. They reckoned it wise to stay out of the sun and save their energy for their late-afternoon game.

Mrs. Kluzuski, who had been kind enough to drive them there, sat down on the bleachers next to Cletis. Once settled in, she immediately pulled a wad of yarn from her large purse. It appeared to be the beginnings of a pink and blue striped blanket. Instantly, the knitting needles started clacking away.

"How are ya doin', Cletis?" she asked in almost a whisper.

Cletis thought for a moment. "Doin' fine, ma'am," he answered looking up at her.

"That's good," was her reply.

Her motherly expression reminded him of the time at the drugstore when he purchased that tabloid newspaper. She was the one behind the counter when he bought it. She was concerned that he was buying a junky tabloid and had asked him if his mother knew about it. Cletis had told her that his mother was dead. From that moment, every time he saw Mrs. Kluzuski, he noticed that she watched him differently—maternally—as if it were her job to keep a nurturing eye on him.

But the headlines and picture and article on the tabloid still haunted Cletis, and he wondered now more than ever if any of it was true. The thought of those bog boys and the old baseball made his heart race. He realized his legs were bouncing up and down nervously as he sat there between Rabbit and Mrs. Klu. He took a breath, and placing his hands on his knees, he exhaled slowly. The steady, gentle clicking of Mrs. Klu's knitting needles seemed to calm him.

The Lock Mall team charged out onto the field and took their positions. In their navy-blue-and-red tops and gray pants, they began their pregame warm-ups. Canterbury's team gathered in the dugout on the third base side of the field. Their bright red-and-white uniforms were a striking contrast against the green lawn of the field, the dark brown of the base paths, and the white powder of the chalk lines.

"They kinda decorate the field over there, don't they," spouted Mrs. Klu, looking in the same direction. "Nice lookin' uniforms."

"Yeah," Cletis agreed, studying the Canterbury players and listening to the Canterbury coach bark out orders and game plans. Cletis could see Elston in the dugout, huddled there with the other boys, and he smiled at the thought of his chubby, calm friend and the exciting times they had had together.

Then Cletis felt it. It seemed distant, but the sensation was the same. It surprised him that the dark, haunting feelings would return after not having experienced them during his last confrontation with the Traveler. He bent over onto his knees and watched and waited. *He's somewhere out there. Could be a mile away, could be closer, but he's somewhere.*

After several minutes on the field, the loud and eager Lock Mall team wrapped up their warm-up drills. One by one, the players took a final grounder or fly ball, made a final throw, and then hustled over to the first base dugout.

Cletis suspiciously eyed the field around him and looked down the row at his teammates. All sat studying the diamond in front of them, unaware of Cletis's dilemma. Tiny sparrows bounced and chirped below the bleachers where they sat, busy cleaning up the particles of leftover popcorn or searching for something edible within the tiny piles of chewed and spewed sunflower shells that had fallen to the ground in previous games. A light breeze tossed the leaves of the maple tree overhead, and the pale blue sky was dotted with cottony clouds. Joggers and walkers moved along the paths on the outskirts of the field, looking in on the boys who prepared for the game. It was a great day at the park and a beautiful day for baseball.

I feel like throwin' up, thought Cletis sadly, resting his forehead on his knees.

Canterbury finally took the field, led by their coach, who carried a long, thin fungo bat on his right shoulder. As Elston scurried out to first base, Klu was the first to greet him.

"Hey, Elston, are you droppin' anything lately?" he teased.

Elston looked up at the group and eyed them strangely. There was something different and distant about him. "No! Nothin' gets by me!" He spied Rabbit sitting in between Frank and Klu. "You losers still got that girl on your team?"

The boys sat dumbfounded, shocked by Elston's words. Rabbit was on her feet instantly, fire shooting from her eyes.

"What'd you say, Elston?" she called out angrily.

"Did I just hear him right?" asked Johnny, almost to himself.

"Did you just call us losers?" hollered Frank, rising to his feet to join Rabbit.

Cletis watched it all in silence.

"Franky, calm down," cautioned Mrs. Kluzuski, still clicking the knitting needles in her lap. "Everybody relax. He didn't mean anything by it."

Elston smiled cockily back up at them, smugly satisfied that he got such a quick rise from this group of old friends.

"Blanchard!" the coach shouted, angrily. He was a small, wiry man, with a shaven head that was revealed only when he lifted his hat and rubbed his scalp. Elston turned to him immediately. "Your eyes are here! You understand me?!" Then calling out to the entire team, he hollered, "No boy on this field turns his attention away from me or this ball! Is that clear?" The team watched obediently, some nodding their heads in submissive agreement. The coach then angrily eyed the Sperry team in the bleachers. "You boys leave my men alone!" he snarled as he commenced his infield drills.

Rabbit sat down, huffing angrily. Frank followed suit, still eyeing Elston.

"What was that all about?" questioned Klu, looking down the bench at his teammates.

"Yeah, that didn't seem like Elston," agreed Johnny.

"He's never talked like that to anyone," added Rabbit, still struggling to calm herself. "Especially not to me."

"So that's the kid who moved?" asked Bernie.

From the stands, Cletis and the others watched as the Canterbury coach drilled grounders around the horn and called out directions as to where the ball should be thrown. He was intense, yelling scolding comments at whoever missed a grounder or a fly or a throw. As Cletis observed the team, gradually the ugly feelings left him, and he slowly sat up straight. Freedom from the frigid, haunting sensation was a sweet relief.

"Boy, that coach sure looks like a fun sort of guy," commented Bernie sarcastically under his breath.

"Sweet as a wet blanket in a blizzard," agreed Frank. "I'll take Mr. Howard anytime over that guy. I don't know how they can play with him bangin' on 'em like that."

As the game began and proceeded into the third and fourth innings, Klu, Johnny, Rabbit, Cletis, Bernie, and Frank all sat wordlessly, stunned by what they saw—not just the outstanding baseball played by the Canterbury team but by the change in Elston. Clearly he was still superb at what he did at first base—snagging a line drive to his left in the first, and digging out and scooping up three bad throws from his infielders in the second. But Elston appeared to be a different boy. He was almost unrecognizable. The humble, happy, complimentary Elston had disappeared. An arrogant, loud-mouthed, disrespectful jerk had taken his place. Even his parents, who sat across the field in the stands and had said hello to the Greenberg Junction boys on their way in, seemed surprised by his attitude and behavior. Cletis watched them as they whispered back and forth after Elston argued a call at first base, spiking the ball to the ground in anger as he ranted. The umpire warned him he'd be thrown out of the game if his unsportsmanlike conduct continued. His coach didn't seem to mind, though. In fact, on that same questionable call at first, the coach ran out onto the field and sided with Elston, yelling at the ump louder than Elston did. The coach received a warning too.

In spite of the intensity and poor sportsmanship of their coach, the Canterbury team was superb in every way. The little squad from tiny Greenberg Junction was stunned by the size and the speed and strength of the boys playing on Elston's team. Their starting pitcher was just as fast as Bernie, and certainly just as big. In the fourth inning, they put in a reliever who was just as fast and as big as the first kid. The Canterbury batters were strong and quick and hit three home runs before three innings of baseball were complete. Their catcher was close to six feet tall and must have weighed 150 pounds. He looked like a man out there, and his throws to second base were bullets—accurate bullets. The infielders, except for a few balls Elston had to dig out of the dirt, played smoothly and confidently. They knew what they were doing. There was no weak link on the team. Everyone hit well, fielded well, and threw well.

At the end of five innings of play, with the score being 12–2, the umpire stepped forward and called the game—the skunk rule, again. Canterbury's players cheered wildly at the announcement and raced to the dugout. From first base, Elston looked up at his old friends, nodded his head defiantly, and as he danced off the field, lifted a fist above him and shook it in the air. His old friends and teammates watched from the bleachers near first base, wondering where their old Elston had gone.

"I wanted to talk to him," spoke Cletis dejectedly as he watched Elston gather with his team in celebration. "But I'm not so sure now after all that trash."

"That was a bit out of the ordinary for Elston, wasn't it?" agreed Mrs. Klu, whose fingers still worked the needles in her lap.

"Would we even stand a chance against Canterbury?" Frank's shoulders sagged a bit as he watched the cheering on the field. "Man, they're good."

"Wait a minute, Franky. First we gotta beat Blackmer Sporting Goods," advised Johnny. "Don't even think about a Canterbury game. Not yet."

After Canterbury's lopsided victory, Cletis, with the others, bought a hot dog and drink from the snack shack below the announcer's booth and, for about an hour, rested under the shade of the maples near the right field fence. Johnny, Bernie, and Klu actually dozed off, lying on their mitts for pillows. As Cletis watched them sleep, he wished he could do the same. But there was just too much on his mind. Mrs. Klu pulled up a lawn chair and continued her knitting as the boys lounged on the grass. Frank wandered off exploring the other ball diamonds, and Rabbit sat next to Cletis, looking out over the diamond as the crew of grounds keepers prepared it for the next game.

"You doin' okay, Cletis?" she asked, repeating her question from a few days back. She tossed a handful of grass into the air in front of her and watched the blades shudder and dance as they floated back to the ground.

He eyed her curiously. "Yeah. Why? Do I look sick or something?"

"No," she answered calmly. "But you look worried. You look like you're off in some far-away, other place again."

"You think I look worried?"

"Yeah," Rabbit nodded, looking back out at the field.

Cletis stared down at the ground next to him and tugged up a long blade of grass. "Just thinkin' of my mom," he answered, knowing his response wasn't too far away from the truth. "I wish she was here to watch all this."

Rabbit smiled. "Don't you worry, Clete. She's watchin'." She pointed heavenward. "An' we're gonna take these guys today," she said, nodding toward the diamond. "For your mom. I can smell it. And besides, we got the luck of the jaguar eyes lady. You just watch." She arose, patted his shoulder, and jogged out onto the outfield lawn.

Cletis watched her go, thinking about what she said. He looked down at his watch. 3:47. Warm-ups would begin in about fifteen minutes. He glanced over at his slumbering teammates. Despite Rabbit's encouraging words, he felt troubled.

A few minutes after four o'clock, the two teams began to gather for the next game. As visitors, Sperry's Cards and Coins laid out their equipment on the first base side of the field, and Blackmer Sporting Goods, being the home team, took the third base dugout. Mr. Howard arrived full of enthusiasm, clapping his hands, talking strategies and encouragement, and calling out the lineup. Since there were only nine players on the team, the batting order didn't change at all from their first game, and the fielding positions basically remained the same too—except Bernie was to start on the mound this time, and Johnny would take over first base.

The dugouts on both sides of this field were situated slightly below the ground level. Each had three concrete steps that led down to a long, wooden bench. Unlike the first field they played on, the front sides of these dugouts were covered with a protective chainlink fence so that no part of the bunkerlike cubicle was exposed to dangerous, line-drive foul balls. The back wall behind the bench was made of solid concrete, blocking the player's view of the stands directly behind it. For added protection, the entrance to each dugout faced the outfield.

As Cletis stood in the Sperry dugout, he removed his watch and patted the thick cement of the back wall. *This is more like a dungeon than a dugout*, he thought. Still feeling uneasy, Cletis placed his watch behind the bench and walked to the home plate end of the dugout. Through chainlink fencing, he scanned the bleachers searching for his dad and Abish. He spied them just as they were sitting down—about three rows up behind home plate and a little toward the first base side. Mrs. Klu sat several feet to the left of Abish, and Johnny's mom and Pauly's parents were seated next to her. There might have been other parents directly behind the dugout, but from Cletis's perspective, he couldn't see them. Timmy's parents usually came with Johnny's mom, but he couldn't find them yet.

On the other side of the stands, the benches were full of families and friends of the Blackmer Sporting Goods team. They filled the bleachers, from the area directly behind the third base dugout to the area behind home plate. Of course, Blackmer Sporting Goods, the company that sponsored the team, was located only a few blocks from the baseball park, so it was only natural that the team would have a great showing from local families and supporters. Cletis took it all in, pacing back and forth in the dugout, studying the baseball field and the stands surrounding it, and remembering the disturbing feelings that had visited him at the beginning of the Canterbury game.

Let's get on with this, he thought restlessly. *Let's get this game goin'.* He looked back up at Abish. *She said that the heart of the finder has not failed yet. And if that's true, nothing weird should happen in this game, cuz that part of the prophecy hasn't been fulfilled. So relax and just play ball.* He put his fingers through the weaving of the chainlink in front of him and took a deep breath. *But maybe it's* me! *What if* I'm *the finder? Maybe* my *heart is failing right now—cuz I'm so nervous and scared. What if that's what it means?*

Standing in front of the bench, he let go of the fence and shook out his legs and wiggled his arms, making sure his muscles were loose. He cast a glance back up at Abish. She and his dad were studying the field and the stands around them. *Just go out and play hard, moment-by-moment,* Cletis ordered himself. *Quit worrying about all the other things. They're out of my hands anyway. Go play and have fun.*

After each team had taken their pregame warm-ups, the umps invited the coaches to a brief meeting at home plate. As Cletis watched them from the dugout, he picked up his watch and checked the time. It was precisely 4:30. He placed the watch back behind the bench and turned toward the field. When the little conference at home came to an end, Mr. Howard scurried back to the team.

"Gather round, guys," he announced as he stepped down into the dugout. "Looks like there's been some poor sportsmanship in the tournament, and the umps want it stopped. That means any kid guilty of questioning calls or being a poor sport is gonna get booted outta the game. That clear?" He studied his players, making certain his statement was heard and understood by all. "You know what happens if one of our team gets kicked out? That means we play with eight. And that also means that every time that kid who got kicked out comes around in the batting order, it's an automatic out. So guys, we gotta keep our cool and be level-headed about everything. We can't toss this game out the window just because we're not concentrating. Gotta think as a team out there. Got it?"

Rabbit and the boys nodded, pondering the weight of his words. At Mr. Howard's lead, they all huddled close, put their hands together in the middle of the group, and hollered a strong, loud "SPERRY'S CARDS!"

Cletis could hear Mrs. Klu in the stands, calling out her encouragement. "Here we go, guys! Let's do it!"

As the team broke the huddle, Mr. Howard called after Roberta. "Rabbit, you're leading off," he reminded her, posting the lineup sheet on the fencing in front of the bench. She knew that and already had her helmet on and her bat in her hand. "Get us started, little lady," he smiled with a wink. "Just do what you always do." With that, he moved past her, climbed out of the dugout, and jogged over to his position in the coach's box at third base.

Despite the pep talk, the huddle, the cheer, and Mr. Howard's words of encouragement, the top of the first inning came and went far too quickly. Rabbit struck out—something she rarely did. Pauly hit a dribbler back to the pitcher and was easily thrown out at first. Cletis lined to right center and ended up on second. But then Klu flew out to shallow left. The stands roared with cheers as the Blackmer squad jogged off the field to the third base dugout.

The bottom half of the first inning was all together different. On the very first toss, the first kid up for Blackmer Sporting Goods cranked a line drive over the left field fence. From where Cletis stood in center, it looked like Bernie's pitch floated carelessly over the heart of the plate, and Cletis wondered what had happened to the usual pop and fire of Bernie's pitching. Pauly had a chance to make a play on it but couldn't quite catch up to it. Though it cleared the short fence by only inches, it was still a home run. Bernie, in frustration, kicked the dirt behind the mound as the batter rounded third and headed for home. The stands erupted in loud cheers again as the Blackmer bench emptied onto the field and gathered around home plate to greet the boy who trotted happily toward them.

Despite Mr. Howard's best efforts to cheer his young team on, after the quick home run, Sperry's Cards and Coins seemed rattled. The next two batters singled, and the following player reached first on an error when Timmy misjudged a high fly ball to right field. Two more runs scored on that blunder, and in the process, the batter eventually ended up on third. As Bernie struggled to maintain his confidence there on the mound, Sperry's Cards and Coins gritted through the rough going. But by the end of the first inning, Blackmer Sporting Goods led 4–0.

"Game's still young," prodded Mr. Howard, clapping his hands and greeting the boys at the dugout. "Bernie, don't worry about it," he spoke optimistically as Bernie wilted onto the bench in front of him. "You'll find your rhythm. You know it's in there. We'll come back. You're better than this, and you know it."

Timmy woefully dragged himself in from right field, arriving last in the dugout. Mr. Howard met him there with his hand extended. "Timmy, chin up. It was a tough fly, yeah, but you gotta pick yourself up and just keep goin'. We'll do fine. You watch."

"Ladies and gentlemen," came the echo of the announcer's voice over the loudspeaker. "As a reminder, the winner of this game will go on to play Canterbury Heights tomorrow evening at 7:30, right here on this diamond, under the lights. Canterbury Heights won their second game here earlier today, beating Loch Mall 12–2, in five innings. We hope you'll join us here at the park tomorrow for the final game of this exciting Greater Metro Tournament."

With the announcement, Cletis remembered vividly the cocky Canterbury squad as they celebrated their crushing victory. He remembered Elston's look of defiance back at his old buddies and his upraised fist. The memory only added to Cletis's nervous energy and uneasiness.

Though Bernie calmed down over the next four innings, striking out a total of seven batters, Sperry's Cards just couldn't seem to manufacture runs. Cletis scored once in the fourth, after having tripled to the right center gap. And Johnny scored in the fifth when Davey singled him in from third. But at the end of five innings, Blackmer still led 4–2.

To start off the top of the sixth inning, Rabbit laid down a perfect bunt up the first base line and beat out the throw. She tagged up and advanced to second when Pauly flew out, in foul territory, to deep left field. Cletis brought her home when he doubled up the first base line. With one out and Cletis at second, Klu flew out to deep center. On the tag, Cletis took third. As Bernie walked to the plate and took signs from Mr. Howard, the score stood at 4–3, still in favor of Blackmer Sporting Goods.

"Fire in the hole," shouted Mr. Howard, clapping his hands excitedly. "It's gonna happen here, Bernie!" Mr. Howard eyed Cletis in front of him, who took a cautious lead from third. "Two down, Clete. You're outta here with the crack of the bat."

Cletis nodded, knowing exactly what to do. He studied the field, relishing the excitement of the moment.

The first two pitches were low and outside, and the catcher made a couple of beautiful defensive blocks to keep the ball in front of him. On the second block, the catcher picked up the ball and still kneeling, fired up the line to the third baseman. Cletis was caught leaning the wrong way.

"BACK!" screamed Mr. Howard as the ball shot up the base path. Instinctively Cletis dove for the bag. He felt the tag come down on the back of his legs just as he touched the base.

"He's SAFE!" hollered the third base umpire, standing directly over the play and spreading his arms wide. Cletis rolled over, blew dirt from his mouth, and raised his arm for time-out.

"TIME!" bellowed the ump.

"He's got an arm, doesn't he?" smiled Mr. Howard as Cletis stood and brushed off the dust. "Left-handed batter makes it easy for him to do that. Be careful. We need your run." Turning again to Bernie, Mr. Howard put his fists together, one on top of the other. "It's your count, Bernie! Drive it somewhere! See it and hit it hard!"

Bernie stepped back into the batter's box and dug his cleats into the dirt. The pitcher took the signs from his catcher, came set, and eyed Cletis over at third. A simple nod of his head faked Cletis back a step toward the bag. Then cocking his leg in front of him, the pitcher reared back and fired the ball home. The pitch was just what Bernie ordered, and as it streaked toward the plate, the new kid from Xenia, Ohio, swung hard and met it squarely.

From his position down the third base line, Cletis watched Bernie's sweet swing. In his mind's eye, he saw it all in slow motion—like the scene from *The Natural*. The ball shot off Bernie's bat and sailed high into the evening sky. The infielders all turned at the same time and craned their necks upward and around, watching the ball soar toward the center field fence. The outfielders followed suit, cocking their heads heavenward and tracing the flight of the ball. They all knew it was a home run the moment it left his bat. The shot cleared the center field fence by at least thirty feet. Sailing over the grassy area behind the fence, the ball crashed into the metal lining at the top of the scoreboard and bounced softly onto the lawn.

When the ball was hit, Cletis had jumped twice in place, as if his motion would help the ball leave the park. Now seeing the ball hit the scoreboard, he danced merrily toward home. With a whoop, Bernie lifted his arms above his head and scampered around the bases. As Cletis crossed the plate, he could hear Abish and his dad cheering from the bleachers behind him, and he turned and smiled back at them. Klu's mom was on her feet too, as were the others. Even Timmy's parents had finally shown up and, standing next to Pauly's parents, grinned and applauded their support. Cletis eyed the scoreboard as the numbers changed. Cletis's run had tied the score at four, and as Bernie crossed the plate, Sperry's Cards and Coins took the lead at 5–4.

When Blackmer Sports relieved their pitcher, the frustrated boy walked dejectedly from the mound to the dugout, despite the ovation from family and friends in the audience. The new pitcher who was asked to step up to the mound—a dark-haired boy they called Orlando—obviously felt the heat and pressure of the moment. Immediately following his warm-up tosses, he promptly gave up a single to Johnny, walked Frank on four straight pitches, and then walked Davey on five. With the bases loaded, Timmy came to the plate. Unfortunately for the little right fielder, the new pitcher finally found his groove, firing five straight bullets past Timmy (he bravely fouled off two of them), striking him out. So despite the opportunity to score again in a big way, Sperry's Cards came up empty, stranding three runners in their top half of the inning.

To lead off the bottom of the sixth, the first Blackmer batter laid down a beautiful bunt up the third base line. Frank made a courageous, barehanded attempt to toss him out, but his throw was wide and careened into the fence behind first base. On the error, the runner took second. The next two batters struck out, but on a passed ball that skipped under Klu's legs and back to the fence, the runner on second advanced to third. The next batter up to the plate was the kid who hammered the home run on the very first pitch of the game. Cletis recognized him immediately. He was at the top of the Blackmer lineup—a spray hitter who had the uncanny knack of being able to hit the ball through the openings and into the gaps. He was the type of player anyone would love to have on their team, and Cletis respected the kid for it. A hit would score a run and tie the game.

"Timmy!" shouted Mr. Howard from the dugout. "To your right!"

Timmy shifted closer to the right-center gap until Mr. Howard stopped him. He then motioned Rabbit back to the lip of the outfield grass and placed Davey in the same location on the right side of the field. With the team set, Bernie eyed the runner at third and began his windup.

Suddenly the cold, dark, haunting sensation, so frighteningly familiar to Cletis, surged through his entire being. Despite his best efforts to stand, he buckled with the heavy, chilling feeling that penetrated his soul. Unable to maintain his balance, Cletis dropped to his knees. Through hazed vision and a queasy dizziness, he watched the first pitch shoot past the batter and land in Klu's mitt. Thankfully the batter didn't make contact. From his hands and knees, Cletis shot a blurry glance towards the stands behind home plate. He could see that Abish was on her feet.

Either she felt the same thing he did, or she happened to see Cletis go down. Mr. Howard, upon seeing Cletis fall, instantly called time-out. Out of the dugout, he raced toward Cletis in center.

As the coach hustled across the outfield grass, Cletis felt the heavy, dark sensation gradually lift away from him. Still clutching his stomach, he attempted to push himself upright. Feebly he lifted his head and scanned the bleachers and the fields around and behind him. *He's watching me. He's watching Abish.*

"Cletis!" called Mr. Howard as he approached. "Are you okay?" He arrived huffing and bent down to look into Cletis's face. Cletis said nothing.

It can't be Mr. Howard. I've been with Mr. Howard all through the game, and I haven't felt like this.

"Cletis, are you all right?" asked Mr. Howard again, lifting Cletis's chin with his hand and studying the boy's ashen face.

"Yes, sir," Cletis whispered, looking up into his eyes. Kneeling up, Cletis feebly attempted to stand. Mr. Howard wrapped an arm around him and helped him come to his feet. Cletis staggered to his left.

"Bend over and put your hands on your knees," Mr. Howard cautioned. "Until you find your balance."

Again Cletis peered in toward the bleachers, trying to focus. He spotted Abish, but his dad was nowhere to be seen.

An umpire hurried out from second base and finally joined the pair. "How's he doing coach?" he asked, observing Cletis's pale complexion.

"Seems to be a little dizzy," Mr. Howard responded, seriously. "Put your head down low, Clete. Get some blood back into your face."

As Cletis obeyed, Pauly, Timmy, and Rabbit hurried over from their positions and joined the circle, anxiously studying their tottering teammate.

"I'm okay," stated Cletis, putting his hands down on his knees and dropping his head. "Just like at your place, Mr. Howard, when me and Elston came over," Cletis added weakly. Mr. Howard eyed him curiously but said nothing.

Cletis lifted his glance to the right side of the field in time to see his dad racing toward him from behind first base. He carried a bottle of water.

"Maybe out in the sun too long," ventured the ump.

"That could be it," agreed Mr. Howard, still holding Cletis's arm.

"I'll be fine," spoke Cletis. "Just gotta catch my breath."

Garth hurried across the field toward the huddled group. Cletis could hear the jangling of keys on his dad's belt as he scurried toward them. He edged in between the ump and Mr. Howard, and offered Cletis the plastic water bottle.

"Take a couple of swallows," ordered Garth, "then lay down a second."

Cletis complied by sipping a bit of water and sitting down on the grass. Garth and Mr. Howard held his arms as he sank to the lawn. Cletis could still see Abish on her feet.

She knows what's happening, he told himself. *But Mr. Howard didn't seem to have any idea what I was talkin' about.*

"Is this what I think it is?" asked Garth, whispering to Cletis.

Cletis nodded. "But it's gone now, and honest, I'm okay. Really."

"How's he doing?" questioned the ump, leaning down over Cletis.

Garth looked up at him and Mr. Howard. "I, uh . . . I think it's under control, sir. Can you give us a second? I'm his dad."

"Absolutely," agreed the ump. "Shall we resume the game here in a few minutes?"

"Yeah," assured Garth as he knelt next to Cletis. "Thanks. He'll be fine."

"Okay, we'll plan on it," spoke the ump. He turned and walked back toward the infield.

"Anything I can do?" asked Mr. Howard, leaning over Cletis.

"You've done plenty already," Garth replied. "Thank you."

"I'm okay, sir," pledged Cletis, looking up at Mr. Howard. "Really, I am. Just got a little dizzy there."

Mr. Howard nodded. "Good. We can't play without you. You've got five seconds to get better." He smiled teasingly down at Cletis and put a hand on his shoulder. Then rising and turning, he headed back toward the dugout. "Okay guys, back to your positions," he called to Rabbit, Timmy, and Pauly.

"Hope you're okay," offered Rabbit as she turned and headed back to short.

"Yeah, Clete," added Pauly.

"Yeah," spoke Timmy. "We need you."

Pauly and Timmy headed off in opposite directions, taking their positions in their respective fields.

Alone with his father, Cletis took a deep breath. "He's here, Dad. He's here somewhere. I didn't think I'd feel this stuff anymore. I thought I was past it. But I guess not."

"Maybe that's good," added his father as he looked around him. "Abish felt it too. Are you doing well enough to continue the game?"

Cletis nodded and picked himself up off the ground. "Yeah, I'm just mad."

His dad steadied him. "Why are you mad?"

"Because I don't know why he's doin' it? Why would he, if he wants me to help him? And I just don't like bein' a puppet. I want this whole thing over with! I don't like these feelings, and I don't want to be used! I wanna be able to concentrate on the game and not have to worry about all this!"

"Okay, calm down. We'll see this through. We're on your side. Do you want to finish the game?"

Cletis took another deep breath. "Yeah, I'm not leavin'," he answered firmly.

"Then, we'll do this. Okay? Just concentrate on one pitch at a time. Except for these feelings, the Traveler can't harm you. You're protected."

"Yeah, I know." Cletis eyed the batter at home, who now sat upon his helmet, waiting for his time at the plate. Cletis shook his arms and legs and then looked back up at his father. "Okay. I'm fine. I'm ready."

"You still mad?"

"Yeah, still mad."

"Well . . . uh . . . at least use it for the good of your team."

Cletis took another swig of water and handed the bottle back to his dad. His father studied him a moment, and then turned and jogged off the field, his keys jangling again from his belt. Cletis watched him as he passed the Sperry dugout and around to the stands. The folks in the stands applauded, leaving Cletis feeling grateful for their concern, but a bit sheepish and embarrassed at the attention paid him.

Cletis turned and studied the scoreboard, making sure he had all the correct information in his brain. *Bottom of six. Two outs. We're still up by one.* He looked back at the infield. *Runner is still on third. The batter's fast and makes contact. Focus on the game . . .* But as hard as he tried, he couldn't. *Man, last time I saw him, he was takin' me back in time, throwin' pitches, and laughing. Why is he doin' this to me now? But maybe he can't control how I feel when he's near. Maybe Abish's family worked it that way to warn me—to know the real him.*

"You ready, Clete?" called Mr. Howard, who stood near the first base dugout.

Cletis lifted his hand and waved. *Okay, get back in the game.*

"Play ball!" called the ump from behind the plate.

Bernie took the signals from Klu, eyed the runner on third, and fired home. The batter jumped on it, cranking a frozen rope past a diving Davey at second base. As the ball made its way into the right-center gap and onto the warning track, Timmy and Cletis charged after it.

"I got it, Timmy! I got it!" called Cletis, catching up to the ball first.

Scooping it up, Cletis turned and eyed the runner. The kid on third base had already scored easily, but his teammate was charging around second and heading for third. Cletis took a step and, with a huff, fired the ball straight at Frank, who was already covering his bag at third base, awaiting the throw. Bernie, having come around from the mound, was set behind him, ready to back up the throw from the outfield. As the runner charged toward the bag, the ball rocketed past him and, without hitting the ground, slapped into Frank's glove, right in front of the base. The runner slid directly into the tag!

"He's OUT!" hollered the ump, jetting his fist into the air.

The boys on the field, as well as the parents and friends on the Sperry side of the bleachers, erupted with cheers.

Frank yelled a loud "YES!" as he rolled the ball back toward the mound and charged across the field to the dugout. "Nice, Cletis!" he called toward center.

"It was PERFECT!" shouted Rabbit, pumping her fist in the air.

"Nice throw, Clete!" yelled Garth, having arrived in his seat just seconds before the hit and the play were made. "Right to the mitt! Right in front of the bag!"

"Oh, my goodness!" roared Abish from the bleachers, despite her concerns about the presence of the Traveler. "I'll remember that throw for a thousand years!" Her voice, oxlike, attracted the attention of all around her, and the fans and families of the Blackmer team looked on in fascinated curiosity as the old hag croaked out her cheers.

"Atta boy!" shouted Mrs. Kluzuski, jumping up and down several feet away from Abish. "Way to mow 'em down!"

The runner at third couldn't believe what had happened. He laid there in the dirt for several seconds. His coach finally pulled him up and, patting his back and wrapping an arm around the boy, escorted him back to the dugout.

"Let's go!" the Blackmer coach shouted out to his team. "All tied up! New game! There's work to be done!"

The kids of Sperry's Cards and Coins celebrated all the way into the dugout and down to the bench. Cletis was greeted with hugs and high-fives as he and Timmy trotted in from the outfield. With the successful inning under their belts and finally playing the type of baseball they knew they were capable of playing, the jitters that had haunted the team through the first part of the game seemed to be gone, and the group was now relaxed and having fun.

"Top of the order," shouted Mr. Howard as he bumped his way through the celebration and up the stairs of the dugout. "Tie game! Let's make somethin' happen! Gotta do it now! Rabbit, get us started!" Clapping his hands, he scurried past the Sperry dugout, around home plate, and jogged out to the coach's box at third.

As Rabbit put on her helmet and eyed the field, Johnny leaned in. "Their third baseman always plays deep. I'll bet you could do it again. First pitch. If he's back, surprise him."

"Do it, Rabbit," added Cletis, nodding his head.

Rabbit smiled and passed a subtle glance up the line at third base. Grabbing her bat, she stepped up and out of the dugout and into the on-deck area.

"Batter up," called the ump.

The seventh and final inning was under way. Rabbit trotted to the plate, and as she was announced, a roar of applause erupted from all the girls and ladies in the seats.

"I think you need to take a step back and bow to your audience," joked the ump. "They've never seen a young lady play like you do."

As if thinking he were serious, she stepped away from the box, faced the audience, and bowed. The applause and laughter increased, in sincere appreciation for the talents of the young girl from Greenberg Junction. Even the Blackmer squad on the field smiled at the notion and relaxed momentarily as the people in the stands applauded and cheered.

With that done, Rabbit stepped back into the batter's box. Cletis watched her cast her eyes across the infield, obviously surveying third base in the process. Sure enough, the third baseman was up in the moment. He was chuckling over at the shortstop, pointing to the crowd, and playing deep in the dirt behind the bag. Even the Blackmer coaches must have been lost in the uniqueness of the circumstances, because they apparently didn't remember that this little girl had laid down a perfect bunt up the first base line earlier in the game.

The pitch came in, and Rabbit squared at the last moment. The third baseman was caught completely off guard. Another flawless bunt crawled up the baseline toward him, staying about six inches inside the chalk line as it bounced and rolled on the infield grass. Rabbit was almost to first base by the time the boy picked it up. Again the ladies in the crowd roared with delight as Rabbit scooted past the bag at first and jogged down the line into the right field foul territory. No throw was even attempted.

"Nice, Rabbit!" called Johnny from the dugout, laughing and clapping his hands.

"Way to be smart!" yelled Bernie, standing next to him.

Mr. Howard applauded from the third base box and yelled out, "Fire in the hole!"

"Now batting, number twenty-three, Paul Allen," echoed the announcement.

Pauly swung the bat as he approached the plate, and eyed Mr. Howard for signs. First and third were defensively shallow, as if they anticipated another bunt, and Mr. Howard recognized that.

Pauly peered down the third base line. Mr. Howard's right hand went to his shoulder, and then to his nose and chin (the indicator), and then to his hat brim—fake bunt then hit away. Turning and stepping up to the plate, Pauly scanned the field and dug in. The pitcher eyed Rabbit carefully, seeing her good lead at first. Every boy on the field knew that the last thing he wanted was to get shown up twice by a girl—let alone the same girl!

Pauly squared to bunt, but as the throw came in, he pulled back and sliced away at a decent pitch. Chipping it off the end of his bat, the ball sailed softly over the second baseman's outstretched glove and bounced into shallow right field—a perfect Texas Leaguer. Not knowing if the second baseman had a chance to make a play on the shallow fly, Rabbit held up about a third of the way between first and second. But as soon as she saw the ball float past him, she scurried on to second, arriving well before the throw from the right fielder. Behind her, scooting down the line, Pauly landed safely at first base and turned the corner there.

The cheers from the Greenberg Junction stands and dugout filled the diamond.

"There we go! Nice hit, Pauly!" shouted Davey from the dugout, clapping his hands.

"Yeah! Way to place it!" agreed Timmy, standing on the bench next to him.

"Okay, Clete, your turn," called Frank, pacing the dugout. "Find an opening somewhere!"

"Now batting, number two, center fielder, Cletis Dungarvan."

Cletis walked to the plate, eyeing the field. The terrifying experience in the outfield still haunted him, and try as he might, he just couldn't seem to chase it from his mind. *Concentrate*, he told himself. *You gotta concentrate. Focus on the game.* Taking a deep breath, he stepped across the plate to the batter's box. Before settling in, he paused outside the chalk to study the positions of the fielders and the runners. *Guys on first and second. No outs. Hit behind the runners. Maybe down first base line. Maybe between first and second.*

"Here we go, Clete," called Davey from the dugout. "Hit us a run!"

"Find a place to drive it, kid," yelled Klu, taking his position in the on-deck circle.

When Mr. Howard gave him the "hit-away" sign, Cletis dug in at home plate. Even though there was no "steal" sign given, he figured that Rabbit would probably head to third at the first opportunity. And by the look of the lead she was taking off second base, that was precisely what she was planning. Cletis eyed the big, dark-haired kid on the mound, took a couple of warm-up swings, and prepared for the pitch. Leaning in, the pitcher took the finger signals from his catcher, nodded, and then came set. He checked second, then first, and then kicked and fired. Out of the corner of his eye, Cletis saw Rabbit break for third. The pitch came in high and inside, and Cletis bent his knees and leaned instantly away. The catcher came up swiftly and stepping in front of the plate, threw hard down the line. But sliding away from the tag on the backside of the bag, Rabbit was into third safely. The third baseman came up ready to throw to second, but Pauly, playing things a bit more cautiously than Rabbit, had remained at first.

Cletis stepped out of the box, and as Rabbit brushed herself off, he studied Mr. Howard. Though he went through a half-dozen motions, none of them meant anything. So, knowing Mr. Howard trusted him to do what he felt best, Cletis turned, faced the pitcher again, and considered his options. *Now with Rabbit on third, that left-center gap looks pretty good*, he figured, and as he dug in again, he set himself for the next offering.

The pitcher came set, studied Rabbit at third, and then peaking over his shoulder, eyed Pauly at first. Focusing once more on the batter, his front leg kicked up, and he pushed away from the rubber, firing the ball toward the plate. Again everything seemed to come at Cletis in slow motion. He could see the ball perfectly. It was a good pitch to hit—down in the strike zone. *Go between short and second with this one*, he thought to himself. *Squish the bug and drive the hips.* The mechanics of hitting shot through his mind and body.

Just before he swung, the icy, dark sensation again flooded his being, and he groaned with the weight and chill of the ugliness. Though his bat came around, Cletis was instantly weak, and his concentration interrupted. As he felt the thud of the ball against the bat, his eyes blurred, and he struggled to see where the hit went. Staggering, he charged down the first base line, striving with all his might to get through the play.

The line drive sailed toward left field, but it was too low. The shortstop deftly dove to his right, snagged the ball out of the air, and landed on his stomach. Quickly rising to his knees, he fired the ball to third. Rabbit, heading for home, was taken by surprise as the kid made the play. Diving back to third, she was too late.

"OUT!" cried the umpire, slicing his fist upwards through the air. Behind him, the third baseman fired the ball across to first.

Cletis, only halfway up the line, staggered, and fell to his knees. He watched Pauly dive safely back to the bag at first, barely avoiding a triple play.

"Time-out, Blue!" called Mr. Howard as he raced across the field and approached his fallen player.

To Mr. Howard's surprise, and to the astonishment of both the teams on the field and the on-lookers in the stands, Cletis regained his balance and strength, pushed his coach away, and stepped toward the dugout. In frustration, he kicked the bats in the on-deck circle, scattering them in several directions. Then, removing his helmet, he fired it hard against the dugout fence. Timmy and Davey, who stood below, next to the chainlink, fell back onto the bench in surprise. Mr. Howard tried to corral an irate Cletis, but was unsuccessful as Cletis pulled away from him twice more.

Suddenly looking up and around him, into the evening sky, Cletis roared, "WHAT DO YOU WANT?! LEAVE ME ALONE!"

The home plate ump, as if responding to what he thought was a tantrum, immediately intervened.

"Young man, you're out of this game!" he called authoritatively, pointing away from the diamond.

Mr. Howard turned to the ump. "Wait a minute, please!" he exclaimed, facing the large, red-faced official. "Give the kid a break. You saw him stagger up the line. He could hardly stand!"

"Yeah," shouted Rabbit, who had followed Mr. Howard in from third. "He's sick! Can't you see that? You can't kick him outta the game!"

"Rabbit, I'll handle this," spoke Mr. Howard, pushing her behind him.

"Well, he seems to be doing fine enough now!" continued the ump, eyeing Cletis suspiciously.

"Come on. Let's rethink this," Mr. Howard spoke, stepping toward the home plate ump. "I've only got nine kids. You saw him go down in center field, and you saw him struggle up the line right now. He may be dehydrated or somethin'. He didn't mean anything by the outburst."

"Coach, you were given fair warning before the game! Don't argue with me. This is the behavior we cannot tolerate on the playing field in this tournament. That boy's well enough to know that," he stated, pointing at Cletis. "Send him off to the designated area! You give me trouble on this and you're gone too!" With that, the umpire pulled his mask down over his face and walked back to the plate.

The people in the stands and the players on the field stood in hushed silence. It seemed as if even the birds and dogs and cars and planes ceased to exist. All was quiet throughout the park. Cletis, still angry, glared out at the field, gazing at, and above, all the players. Turning, he scanned the stands again, looking above and through the people who were seated there staring at him.

Spinning away from the on-deck circle, Cletis stormed down into the dugout. Grabbing his mitt, watch, and hat off the bench, he pushed past his startled, bewildered teammates, and headed back up the steps. At the top of the dugout, Mr. Howard attempted to console him again, but it was useless. Cletis, dropping his head, just walked on by.

"It's right back over—" started Mr. Howard, pointing behind the bleachers.

"I know where to go, coach," Cletis declared sullenly. Accepting his punishment, he left the playing field and disappeared behind the stands on the first base side of the field.

Cletis cast a quick glance toward his dad and Abish. They watched him as he marched dejectedly away, stepped around the bleachers, and entered an enclosed area below the announcer's booth, directly behind the stands where the Greenberg Junction families and friends sat. Looking up through the slats between the benches as he entered the roped-off seclusion, he found his father. He was looking back at him. A hanging canvas on the rear of the bleachers blocked the view of the field and made the area all the more concealed. Cletis sat down gloomily on one of five metal folding chairs. He placed his mitt and watch on the chair next to him and dropped his head into his hands. Gradually the noise from the field and stands resumed.

"Let's play ball!" shouted the home plate ump.

"Now batting," came the announcement, "number sixteen, Theo Kluzuski."

Cletis stood and attempted to see around or over the hanging canvas. When he found it impossible, he picked up his mitt, threw it to the ground in front of him, and sat back down. His head lifted toward the bleachers where Abish and his father sat. There would be consolation in their eyes, he felt. They knew what he was going through.

Suddenly a surge of swimming, gray particles surrounded Cletis. The air around him came alive, popping with radiant power. Cletis stood, anxiously sensing the gathering field of energy that encircled him. Out of the corner of his eye, he saw his father spring up and over the several rows of bleachers above and behind where he and Abish sat. When his dad reached the highest bench, he leaned over the metal railing and looked down. For a moment, their eyes met, communicating the panic they both felt.

"Hold on, Clete!" he called out.

Pulling himself over the top bars, his dad began the climb down the back of the bleachers. As Cletis levitated within the conduit, he watched his father jump the remaining eight feet to the concrete below. He landed awkwardly and fell backward against the metal poles of the stands, yet still he struggled forward and reached for Cletis.

"Dad!" Cletis pleaded, weightlessly rising off the ground.

His father lunged for him, but before their hands could meet, the world around Cletis disappeared.

CHAPTER 19

The Heart Of
The Finder Fails

Cletis immediately recognized the place. It was their old home in Belleville. He and his family used to live there—or if he were back in time, then he and his family still lived there. He studied the house, remembering that he had had his eye surgery in a hospital somewhere near this town. They had brought him back to a special surgeon in a hospital close by. He couldn't remember exactly where it was. The operation had taken place shortly after the time the family had moved to Greenberg Junction.

From the sidewalk where he stood, next to the old, giant maple tree, Cletis studied the red brick home. He recognized the familiar three, white gables on the second floor and the four concrete steps that led up to the front porch. The porch was large and covered half of the front of the house. The wooden rocking chair, where Cletis and his mother had sat so often, was still there. The sweet memories of those moments settled over him like a warm blanket on a cold night, and he took several steps toward the porch in order to get a closer look. He remembered the gentle, back-and-forth motion of the chair and the feel of his mother's arms around him. The smells and sounds and sights of that time came alive again, and in his mind he was, once more, on her lap watching the sunset and the approach of a peaceful evening. He felt her hands on his shoulders as the stars gradually appeared, and he saw the fireflies dart in and out of the darkness over the front lawn. He remembered the feel of his mother's cheek next to his . . . her hair upon his face, the songs she used to sing, and her reassuring laughter.

Cletis took a deep breath and crossed the lawn to the driveway. He eyed the carport straight ahead of him and the thin section of lawn between two stretches of concrete that led to it. The side of the house was lined with red and yellow roses, along with a border of small purple flowers. Cletis couldn't remember what the little flowers were called, but as he thought about it, he figured he probably never knew.

He walked past the kitchen window and cautiously looked up into it. The house next to theirs was reflected in its shiny surface. He remembered the times when he played on this driveway with his little metal trucks and cars. He remembered that when it was time for his dad to come home from work, his mom would stand at the window, open it, and let him know he needed to clean up the driveway.

Didn't want Dad to run over my toys, Cletis thought as he stepped slowly up the thin lane of concrete. *Or me.*

Cletis abruptly stopped in his tracks. As the birds chirped in their nests above and behind him in the giant maple, he pondered his situation.

"What am I doin' here?" he spoke softly, looking around him. He knew the Traveler was responsible for this and that he was probably watching him at this very moment. *But I don't feel him,* he thought. "Why am I here?" he spoke out loud, again.

No answer came.

"Do I still live here?" he whispered. "Why are you doin' this to me?" Cletis waited, looking around him. Again no answer came.

What if I see her? What if I see me? What am I supposed to do then?

The sound of laughter floated down the driveway. He remembered that behind the house there was lawn and a garden. Next to that garden was a huge maple—the "backyard maple," they had called it. He could see the top of it from where he stood. A swing hung from long ropes tied high in the branches of that tree. There was also a sandbox near the garden. Cletis froze, listening. He recognized the voice—the gentle, soothing voice that made the world right. A mixture of fear and joy filled him as he stepped closer to the sounds. Despite the recently healed wounds he knew would open again, he longed to see her.

He stepped around the back of the house and found himself on the cobblestone sidewalk by the green, wooden gate that opened into the backyard. More roses lined the side of the house next to him— white roses here. How his mother loved them, he remembered. In the summer there was always a vase full of them in the middle of the kitchen table. When she wasn't cooking something, the fragrance of the flowers would fill the downstairs level of the home.

Again he heard her voice but couldn't see her yet.

From where he stood by the open gate, he looked out over the yard. It was all just as he remembered. An occasional toy dotted the landscape. The green fence surrounded the backyard—from the carport, to the distant corner behind the maple, to the far side of the house. The entire backyard was enclosed.

This is where they found me. Wandering back here inside the fence.

Now that he had seen the clothing he had worn as a tiny boy and had heard the story once again, his mind was alive with images of the little boy dressed in the woolen overshirt and the rabbit-skin booties.

Then he saw her. She stepped into view from behind the clotheslines at the far side of the house. White shirts, sheets, and other linens flapped gently in the breeze in front of her. A tinier Cletis was at her side, holding on to her pant leg. He must have been about three years old. He was short and round, and carried his favorite yellow truck in his other hand. Anna, wearing a white blouse untucked at the waist, along with casual gray jeans, was speaking to him, laughing at something he must have said or done. She was tall and beautiful and healthy. As she finished pinning a final towel to the clothesline, she clapped her hands together.

"All done," she announced happily. Then, bending down, she lifted the boy into the laundry basket next to her. As Cletis watched from the sidewalk, he remembered the routine and smiled with the thought. The little boy sat down inside of the basket and placed his truck between his short legs. His little hands grasped the side of the basket, and with a dimpled smile, he waited for the game to start.

"Are you ready?" she asked, looking into his chubby, rosy face. His fine, strawberry blond hair tossed and lifted in the light wind.

With an expression of immediate joy, the tiny boy nodded his head and smiled up at her.

"Let's go then," she declared and immediately began to pull the basket across the lawn, making motor noises as she went. Her feet were bare in the green grass. The boy giggled with delight as she tugged him around behind her.

As she came close to the sidewalk by the gate and saw Cletis standing there, she stopped and stood up straight. She studied him as he stood there in his baseball uniform, sweaty and dirty from the game. As if sensing she was in no danger, she smiled and greeted him.

"Hi," she spoke, looking down at him. Cletis could see she was a bit unsure of herself, yet she stepped forward "Can I help you? Are you looking for someone?"

Cletis studied her briefly, not knowing whether to smile or to go to her or to turn and run. In his indecision, he simply stared. The feelings that flooded over him were both painful and wonderful. He studied her eyes, her face, her hands, her clothes. He watched how the breeze toyed with her brown hair, lifting it up and down to match the movement of the clothing that hung from the lines behind her. She reached up and tucked a few strands behind her ear.

"What do you need?" she said with a smile. She studied his uniform. "It looks like you've been playing a good game of baseball?"

Cletis peered down at his clothing. He had forgotten about his uniform.

"Oh, yeah," he whispered, not able to find his voice. He gave her a lopsided smile.

She was as beautiful as he ever remembered. He found himself fighting the emotions he knew would surface, so he turned his attention to the quiet, small boy who looked up at him from inside the laundry basket. Cletis immediately noticed how his left eye drifted to the outside, and how his head turned slightly, favoring his right eye. For a moment he tried to figure out which way the boy was looking. It was all so familiar.

"Uh ... yeah ... we just played." Cletis spoke as he studied the little boy. He chose not to look back up at his mother. "Uh ... I was ... uh ... throwin' the ball with a friend ... and I ... uh ... missed it," he stammered, hurriedly wiping his eye and turning back to the carport. "I thought it came down your driveway." He looked around the area and shrugged, pretending to search for the ball. He still didn't want to look her in the eye. "But I don't see it anywhere ... so ... uh ... so I guess I really didn't see where it went."

"Oh ... well, can we help you look for it?" she asked politely.

"No, ma'am. That's okay. Maybe I'll look over in the neighbor's yard." Cletis nodded and smiled awkwardly, finally looking up at her face. Her blue eyes and her smile were wonderful to see. He studied her as she looked down into his face.

This old world of his—familiar in so many ways—suddenly became strangely odd to him. Though he desperately wanted to stay and be a part of her existence, what would he say? What would he do? Tell her about who he is and what's happening in his life? *Yeah, like she'd really believe me.* He realized that throwing a bunch of new, weird information at her wouldn't accomplish anything. Trying to explain who he was and all the crazy and magical things that were happening to him would be confusing and scary and completely unfair to her. *It wouldn't be fair to little Cletis either. It would be wrong and selfish,* Cletis pondered. *These were her happiest years.* As much as he wanted to see his mother alive—as much as he wanted to feel her embrace and her nearness again—she had passed away. She was gone, and he realized that even if he could travel in time back to see her, things would never be the same. He would always have to love her from a distance, and as he was sensing, that was more painful than not having her at all.

Taking a deep breath, he turned and walked back across the cobblestone sidewalk toward the driveway. As the fragrance of the white roses drifted past him, he realized there was one thing he could tell her that might bring her peace. He knew she was troubled about one thing.

"Uh, ma'am?" he asked, turning back again to her.

"Yes."

Cletis pointed to the smiling boy in the laundry basket. "Uh ... maybe I shouldn't say this cuz it's none of my business ... but ... uh ... I had that same condition with my eye when I was a little boy. It was always stuck off to the left side, kinda like his. But surgery fixed it. I can see perfectly now. I can play ball and hit and catch and throw, just like any kid."

Anna eyed Cletis curiously. His comments caught her by surprise. "Oh . . . yes . . . " she replied gently. "Thank you."

"You're welcome."

Cletis wanted to say more but decided against it. He took his hat off and rubbed his fingers through his wavy, blondish hair—as if he were subconsciously trying to tell her who he was. She tilted her head slightly to the side and smiled courteously back at him. Pulling his hat back down over his head, he nodded and then headed down the driveway. He tried to keep himself from looking back at her, but he just couldn't do it. Near the sidewalk by the street, he turned again, hoping to look at her just once more.

There she was, standing at the end of the driveway in front of the carport. She had followed him out onto the sidewalk. Little Cletis was in her arms. She stood watching him, her weight shifted onto one leg. It made Cletis feel good to see her so healthy and happy. She tucked a few floating strands of shiny, brown hair behind her ear again and observed the boy in the baseball uniform at the other end of the driveway. The younger Cletis tugged at his strawberry blond hair and leaned his head against his mother's neck. Cletis could almost feel her hair on the side of his face.

From the end of the driveway, Cletis waved one last time. Anna lifted her hand and waved back. Turning away from her, Cletis finally allowed his pent-up emotions their liberty. The tears came freely, and he sobbed out loud. Hiding his eyes from her, he jogged into the neighbor's yard, still pretending to search for the lost ball, at least, until he knew he was out of her sight.

Suddenly Cletis felt the gray conduit gather around him. *Good,* he thought, *take me out of here. Anywhere. Just let me go somewhere else.*

Within moments he floated to the floor in front of the round wooden table in Abish's study. His back was to the large door, and he found himself looking over the dozens of manuscripts and pedigrees that still spread across its surface there. He felt an instant twinge in his stomach and buckled again with the cold, dark sensation. Fortunately as rapidly as the feeling came, it faded. That puzzled him. Finding his strength again, he straightened and took in a deep breath. At the same time, though, he found peace in the memory of his mother as her face, form, and presence still lingered in his mind. He sniffed and wiped the tears from his eyes, still feeling her closeness, still seeing her face and hearing her voice. How he had wanted to touch her. How he had wanted to stay with her. How he wanted to hold on to the moments with her.

"An enjoyable trip, I assume," came the voice behind him.

Cletis turned around. The Traveler sat before him in the chair by the large doorframe. He wore his familiar black leather and boots, and his blond braid draped over his left shoulder. Cletis remained silent as the man stood and approached him.

"Some tender moments too, I see," he commented, noting Cletis's eyes. "Well, it is only a beginning. Many adventures await you yet— adventures that will bring you nothing but joy and peace."

You mean pain and longing and broken hopes, thought Cletis in frustration.

Again he had been a puppet, strung out and controlled by someone else's hand—the Traveler's hand. It was wrong and manipulating, and Cletis didn't like it.

Stopping a few steps in front of Cletis, the Traveler extended his arms. Cletis expected the worst, but nothing happened. No light shot from his fingers and no blue shield appeared. Instead the wooden, dark box materialized between his hands. It seemed to be nearly black now, as if it too were dying with him.

"I have shown you only a fraction of the powers you possess," he declared. He brought the box past Cletis and set it down on the table next to him. "You need someone to teach you how to use them— control them." He turned and walked back to the middle of the room. "Think of the great good you could do in the world, taking the secrets and marvels of the future back to the past—sharing them there. Think of the advances in medicine. Think of the discoveries that you could give the world—any world—that would save thousands upon thousands of lives . . . including those most dear to you."

Cletis watched him. He knew he was referring to Anna.

"Placing a textbook secretly upon the desk of a doctor or writing a formula on the blackboard of a struggling professor." The man studied Cletis for a moment. "The world could be changed for the better by your simple acts of kindness. Think of it."

Cletis thought of the game he had been ripped away from, just moments ago, and the frustration and pain he had experienced there on the field.

"What do you want?" Cletis asked, unsure of himself but trying to be as brave as possible.

The man stepped toward him and leaned in. "I need you to open the box. It has been sealed, and only you have the power to reverse that which they have done."

"They must have sealed it for a good reason," Cletis declared, surprising himself with his own boldness.

Ian eyed him suspiciously and began to pace the room. "Abish's family was jealous of my ability to travel through time. They were unaware of what I was doing to benefit mankind. They had no idea that I was accomplishing exactly what I just described to you—blessing the past with the secrets and efforts of the future—saving a child here, rescuing a family there." His hands spread in front of him as he spoke. He looked about the room as if in deep thought and then bowed his head modestly. "Was I going to tell them about my endeavors? Was I to describe the good that was done? Was I going to sing my own praises? Of course not. That would have been arrogant. So when my life became completely misunderstood by that greedy, selfish, close-minded family, they locked me away. Not only did they do *that* great injustice to me, but they poisoned my wife against me, as you can see. Because of their lies, Abish doesn't trust me. But she did once. She loved me once. Though she never Traveled in time, we shared the Powers of the clan . . . until they turned her heart against me. Finally they changed her, imprisoned me, and took from me my son . . . you. That hurts a man. That destroys a man! Without being able to explain myself or defend myself, they locked me away like a wild animal for nearly sixty years!"

Taking a deep breath, he walked back to the chair and sat down. "A Traveler usually lives ninety years," he continued. "I had lived nearly twenty-nine years when I was coldly imprisoned by the Dungarvans in Ireland. I existed in that horrible, captive state, floating in nothingness, until my eighty-ninth year. You have seen the real me. I am an ugly, dying man. I have but moments to live. How kind of them, yes?" He eyed Cletis, then bowed his head in thought. "Once released, I spent months searching throughout time for the box, hoping that upon finding it, its powers would grant me prolonged life— for it has that power, you know. I was finally guided to it, but as I touched it, it was sealed. It was all according to the peculiar prophecy they wrote upon the top of it." "So again I am but a piece upon their board. I am their pawn to be moved at their choosing."

He flipped the braid over his shoulder, rose from the chair, and confidently stepped toward Cletis. "You see, my son, simply by opening that box and breathing in its powers, I will live again—like a second life—with freedom to live and move and bless the lives of humanity! But only Travelers can make operative the powers of the box. Only someone like you or like me can open it and glory in what's inside." He folded his hands behind his back and nodded toward the box. "My father seems to have pronounced a magic upon this box in ages past. Apparently, you are now the only one who can open it. You are the new Traveler. A moment ago you asked me what I want. Well, I'll tell you precisely what I want. I want you to help me open the box. I want to live."

"You mean you want *me* to open the box," Cletis answered. "From what you just said, you don't have any power over it. So actually you want *me* to open the box for you."

The Traveler eyed him. His face registered no expression. "I admit you are correct. But upon opening the box, I will teach you of its powers. No one else can do that. Only I know the workings and the magic of the box."

Cletis took a step away from the box and the man, and stood silently in front of the grand table.

"Cletis, the last time we were together, you enjoyed the moments—the sweet feeling of Time Travel, the Yankee clubhouse, the pitch that floated before you in midair. I sensed within you the happiness and wonder that comes upon a Traveler as he begins to grasp the powers that can be his. I felt that within you. You can't deny it."

He's right. I did experience what he said I did, Cletis thought. He looked into the black eyes of the Traveler. "The heart of the finder hasn't failed . . . at least I don't think it has," Cletis began, trying to choose his words carefully. "Time hasn't been frozen. I haven't made any big choice—not that I know of. According to the prophecy, those three things need to take place before the box is opened, or can be opened."

"Don't be foolish, Cletis," answered the Traveler, quickly. "Those things will only come to pass if you choose to *allow* them to come to pass. Don't you see that if you *choose* to open the box, Time will not be frozen and no one's heart will fail? In choosing to unseal the box, you will avoid the danger of those two prophetic declarations. That part of the prophecy doesn't have to come to pass unless your choices make them come to pass." The man began to pace again, and Cletis sensed his controlled agitation. "Let me tell you what is at stake here, my boy. And I will be clear in my explanation so that you will know exactly where you stand. I want to live. I will do all that I need to do in order to bring that to pass. No one needs to be harmed in that process. You help me open the box, I teach you how to travel, and life goes on. No one is hurt. Everyone is content." He stopped in front of Cletis. There was no anger in his voice. All was logical and matter-of-fact. "But if you choose otherwise—if you choose in Abish's favor—someone's heart *will* fail—which, to me, seems to mean something bad and painful—and Time as you know it will soon freeze and stop. Do you know what that means? It means that you and Abish and I will live in frozen time, until you change your mind and help me open the box—that is, *if* the prophecy allows you to change your mind. And even then, after our frozen moments in Time have ended, we may find ourselves a hundred years in the future, or we may come out five hundred years in the past. Time is that way. You never know where it will take you unless you can control it. Do you see the dilemma? I know how Time Travel works, so that means nothing to me. But you and Abish do not. And if you never learn to Travel in Time, that could be devastating. Think about it: separated from your father because of your unwillingness to help me. Perhaps thrown into a time of evil or corruption or war—a place from which you cannot escape. So it is only wise and considerate and selfless of you to help me unseal the box now and spare your loved ones and yourself unknown suffering." He paused. "Do you understand that? Is that clear?"

Cletis remained silent, pondering his words. *What if he's really telling the truth?* he thought. *If Abish were here, would she tell me anything different? What if he's really right, and by helping him open the box, Abish and Dad won't have to suffer? Because either Dad or Abish might be the Finder. What if Dad's heart fails? What if Abish's heart fails? It would be my fault if they have to go through pain. And how many people will be hurt or in danger if Time freezes? He says Abish and me and him will be frozen in Time forever if I don't help him open the box. What if he's right? What if that frozen Time part means I'll be separated from Dad or Abish when I finally come back to real time? What if I can't find my way through time back to them?*

Observing a thoughtful Cletis, the Traveler stepped closer.

"I'm only trying to be logical here. I'm only trying to lay out both sides of the story so that you understand clearly. Do you see how foolish the old Dungarvan clan was?" he questioned. "This has ceased to be Abish's test. This has become *your* test! But why? Because they misjudged again! This prophecy, so cleverly written and set in motion by the old family, has done little to harm me but has done everything to put you and your loved ones in danger. It's idiotic, isn't it? They think their wisdom will teach Abish a big lesson. Instead a twelve-year-old boy ends up making decisions that will affect and perhaps endanger hundreds, maybe even thousands, of lives! For what? To teach their long-lost daughter that she shouldn't have married a Traveler? It's all absurd, isn't it?! They have put you in grave danger because of their selfishness and their hatred toward *me*!"

Cletis looked up at him and then turned toward the table and the window. Was the man telling him the truth? It all sounded so clear—so cut and dried. If he was right, all Cletis needed to do was help the man open the box and then there would be peace. Or would there be? He would teach Cletis to travel, and then he would go away and leave them all alone. Or would he? No one would get hurt that way, at least according to the Traveler's words. Or would they? And according to Abish, if the prophecy wasn't fulfilled in her favor, she'd stay like she was and she'd never see her family again.

This man would keep doin' bad stuff for another full lifetime . . . clear into the future, pondered Cletis. *But is he really evil? Or is it that the Dungarvan family, way back in time, just didn't understand him? Right now I don't know for sure. But he says he'll do anything he needs to do to live. But if I were in his shoes, and really felt like I was right, wouldn't I fight to live too? Even if it seemed wrong in everyone else's eyes, wouldn't I do all that I could to get my way—to win?*

Cletis looked down at the papers on the table below him. Ian stepped forward and stood next to him. Despite the presence, Cletis concentrated, trying his best to sort through all the heavy details that burdened him.

Abish had always talked to him about feelings. Even if he was confused about who was right or who was wrong, he'd still know the difference between the feelings that had come over him. With Abish, it was peace. With this man, it had always been fear and cold emptiness.

Even coming here, right now, I felt it again—even if it was just for just a little bit. Abish said that in the fulfillment of the prophecy, feelings would guide us. Feelings . . .

Suddenly another thought popped into Cletis's mind. *And what about the blue light that protected me? It saved my life. Both me and Abish were protected by it. And it seemed to know exactly when I was in danger. It knew exactly when that man tried to harm me!*

Cletis turned and faced the Traveler. The marks on his shoulders were pretty much at eye level with Cletis. *I, too, am a Traveler. I wonder if I can learn to travel without his help? Is it something that's natural? I wonder if I can try a few things on my own? Maybe if I can . . .*

Cletis stopped that train of thought. Again he considered the blue ball that surrounded him when the Traveler's arc of light shot toward him. *Even the Traveler, in all his magic and smarts, doesn't have power to match that.* Cletis took several steps around the table, away from the man. *I don't think I'll see that blue light again, unless he gets so desperate that he finally tries to use his powers against me, like he did before. That means I'm pretty much safe, no matter what I tell him. So it looks like whatever I choose right now—to help him or to help Abish—this whole prophecy thing is gonna get set in motion, and there's gonna be no turning back.*

"The powers of the box are beyond your wildest imaginings," the Traveler whispered. "I can teach you how to harness those immense powers. Think of the good that could be done in the world. And it would come because of your noble efforts."

Cletis looked up into the face of the Traveler. *I hope I'm right about this.* He swallowed nervously and took a deep breath. "I'm not gonna help you open the box," Cletis stated firmly, reaching up and tugging his hat snuggly down on his head. "And, uh . . . right now . . . knowing what I know and feeling what I've felt, I don't think I ever will."

Ian squinted and lifted his face to the ceiling. "That's your answer? That is your decision?"

Cletis slowly nodded. "It is." His mouth suddenly went dry, and he felt his heart pounding in his chest.

The Traveler stepped back away from the table. "You're making a grave mistake, my son. I don't think you realize what you're doing."

"Maybe I don't. We'll just have to find out."

The Traveler paced the room silently for a moment. "Cletis, think with me . . . The heart of the Finder will fail . . . We don't know what that means exactly or who that might be. Nor do we understand what the next phrase means—the 'son is as the father.'" He eyed Cletis. "Those are realities that will come to pass. But at what cost? Who will be harmed? And apparently at that instance Time will be frozen . . . for who knows how long. Lives will be in danger and perhaps lost. All to keep me from opening this box and living a renewed life? Cletis, do you know what this means?"

"I probably don't. After all, I'm only twelve," he answered sarcastically.

Ian studied him gravely, his gaze turning raptor sharp. "You choose for the battle to begin? Is that what you're saying? You choose to put lives in danger because of your *feelings* for an old hag when you don't really even know if she's telling you the whole truth?"

Cletis lifted his chin and frowned. "And *you* choose to destroy everything in your path," he retorted angrily, standing his ground, "if you don't get *your* way? It looks to me like you don't care for anyone except yourself. So I could throw that right back in your face and say it's you that chooses to put lives in danger because you're selfish!"

The Traveler was silent for several seconds.

"There's that temper again. It got you in trouble once today. It may get you in trouble again in the future." He folded his arms and turned his back on Cletis. "What does it say in the prophecy? 'In the arena of battle, their weapons shall be clubs, orbs, spikes. The orb shall be driven at his command.'" He peered over his shoulder at Cletis. "That seems to me like a baseball game. Doesn't it to you? So the way things stand at this moment, there will be a game tomorrow evening: Sperry's Cards against the Canterbury team. That seems a likely arena of battle in which the prophecy might be fulfilled."

"But you don't know if we won that game against Blackmer."

Ian folded his arms and frowned at Cletis. "My boy, I'm surprised at you. Am I not a Traveler? Do I not know the outcome of that game? Of course I do. And I was there for most of it, as you well know." He walked over to the table and sat against the edge of it. "But I cannot look into the future to the fulfilling of the prophecy. My father has hidden that from me. The fulfilling of it may come when Time is frozen. I cannot see into frozen Time." Ian closed his eyes. "Cletis, one thing you must consider. Those feelings that have come and gone when I am near—those sensations that have filled you with fear and emptiness. That is none of my doing," he stated calmly.

Cletis eyed him curiously. He felt a bead of sweat run down the back of his ear.

"Again, the Dungarvans cursed me with that. I am like a leper who must always call 'unclean' as I walk through a town. Well, they have done that for me, you see. Almost every member of the

Dungarvan family will feel what you have felt, to warn them of my nearness. Another kind thing they have done for me." He observed Cletis cunningly, as if to see if the thought had any effect on the boy. "I have seen that those feelings impact you heavily. The man you call Garth does not sense my presence. Abish does. But you, especially, are very sensitive to my whereabouts. I have seen how you bend when I am near. So as an experiment I decided to use your weakness to my advantage, to observe how you would react to my presence . . . you know, just in case you didn't see things my way. That decision has proven to be quite revealing.

"This game with the team you call Blackmer, it was all simply a test for you," he continued, opening his arms wide and looking about the room. "A test to see what you would do under pressure. And you did exactly as I thought you would do. Your temper got the best of you, you lost control and were ejected from the game. Because of your immaturity and lack of self-management, your team could have lost. But it appears the fates, or the Dungarvans of old, were guiding you toward the moment we await tomorrow."

He walked to the middle of the room and turned and faced Cletis.

"One last chance, Cletis, my son. I am not the evil man you think I am. Nor is Abish the good woman you think she is." He watched Cletis. "Will you help me?"

Cletis wiped his lips with his sleeve. His knees felt weak, and he wanted to cry.

"Will you?" Ian questioned again. "We could have exciting times beyond your wildest dreams, and you would be wisely protecting countless lives."

Cletis stepped farther around the table and peered down at the pedigrees. Centuries of Abish's work lay in front of him. He leaned against the table for strength.

"No . . . no, I won't help you open the box."

Ian inhaled deeply and turned his back on Cletis. "The battle is on then, my son. And it will be a fight to the death, I'm afraid. We will next meet in that prophesied arena, and you will then see that Abish is no more than a lying, ugly, old hag who has used you like a puppet."

He spoke in a whisper. It troubled Cletis that the man never became angry. Everything he did was so calculated, so rational . . . so cold.

Cletis swallowed hard but said nothing. They faced each other silently, and as the gray conduit materialized and surrounded Cletis, the Traveler simply smiled.

"Just remember this, my son. When Time is frozen, there will be no blue shield to protect you. The Dungarvans have no magic to perform in frozen Time." He lifted his chin and peered at Cletis down his nose. "Any last thoughts or comments?"

Cletis remained silent.

"We could have been a great team together. There is still time to change your mind."

As Cletis fought back the tears, the energy field of gray particles danced around him. Finally he felt himself lift off the floor.

"Then we will play the prophecy and see what comes to pass," Ian stated.

A chilling fear filled Cletis, heart and soul, and as the world of the conduit engulfed him, Abish's library faded from his sight.

His dad and Abish were there alone, in the emptiness of the park, when Cletis reappeared in the conduit. After making sure he was unharmed and able to walk, they escorted the sad, silent boy to the car and made their way back to Greenberg Junction. All the way home, Cletis sat in the back seat looking out the window at the setting sun, at the forests, at the farms, yet seeing nothing. At home, he went straight to his room and lay on his bed. Finally, at ten o'clock, after nearly three hours had passed since leaving the park, he finally asked Abish and his father to gather and hear him.

The three of them sat down around the kitchen table. With difficulty, Cletis described, in detail, the events of the evening—from his final moments of the game to his reappearance in the roped-off area behind the bleachers. But regarding the conversation with the Traveler, he purposely left out several specific details, feeling it wiser to keep certain things to himself—like all that stuff about the Dungarvan family being selfish, and about Abish being a liar, and about the battle to the death. Garth and Abish took it all in, asking occasional questions and listening to the fascinating details of Cletis's time travel.

When the story ended, the three sat quietly for several moments. Cletis felt sure that his dad contemplated Cletis's time in Belleville, at the old house. He sensed that Abish was burdened by the prophetic confrontations yet to come. Cletis watched them as they pondered, wondering how the next day would affect them all. It was then that Cletis asked for details of the Blackmer game.

"We won the game, didn't we," Cletis commented, rubbing his eyes and yawning.

"Yeah, how did you know?" asked his dad.

"He basically told me," Cletis answered. "But he didn't give me any details. And I didn't want to hear 'em from him anyway."

"Well, it was a great finish," answered his dad. "Just after you disappeared, Klu hit a homerun there in the top of the seventh with Pauly on first. That put us up by two. And Bernie held 'em in the bottom of the seventh. So we pulled it out."

"Timmy made two beautiful catches in the outfield in the bottom of the seventh," added Abish. "Basically saved the game."

"Timmy?" questioned Cletis.

"Yeah," continued Abish. "He was playing sort of a right-center with you not there, and one ball was hit to shallow right, and he caught it on the run, coming in. And the other one he caught toward the foul line—last out of the game. Mr. Howard had him placed just right, and when it was hit, he ran under it and grabbed it. Not deep. Just behind first base. Made it look easy."

"We couldn't really enjoy it though, constantly looking down into that pit, hoping you'd return," added his father.

Cletis thought about things for a moment, crookedly grinning at the idea of Timmy making super catches.

Again the three were quiet, and Cletis's smile faded.

"I lost my temper again," he finally said, hanging his head sheepishly.

"We don't blame you," stated Abish kindly. "We saw what you were going through out there. I felt him too."

"But that's exactly what he wanted to see," spoke Cletis. "He wanted to see me break under pressure, and I did."

"Don't worry about it," his father soothed. He reached over and put his hand on Cletis's arm. "The guys on the team wondered where you went. When they saw you weren't there, they thought you had run off somewhere. They waited around for a long time, hopin' you'd get back. When you didn't show, we finally sent them all home and told 'em not to worry about you."

"But we always kept our eye on that area behind the bleachers," added Abish, "figuring... hoping you'd show up there sooner or later. It would've been quite a sight, having you reappear in the middle of all your friends. I'm glad that didn't happen."

"Yeah," agreed Cletis under his breath.

His dad arose, walked to the fridge, and retrieved a pitcher of orange juice. "You had us worried. We didn't know if you were home or if you were stuck somewhere between there and here." Pulling three glasses from the cupboard, he filled them as he spoke. "And then you just materialized. We're glad we stuck around there." His father carried the three glasses to the table and set them before Cletis and Abish. "Do you think she recognized you?" he asked carefully. "Mom?"

Cletis pondered a few seconds. "No, I don't think so," he answered, lifting a glass of juice to his lips and taking several swallows. "I kinda wanted her to say something about it if she did . . . but she didn't. Did she ever say anything to you about a boy in a baseball uniform who walked up the driveway and talked to her?"

"I don't remember her ever mentioning it. She might have."

"Did you ever see anything like that, Abish, as you watched the family?"

"No, I never did," she whispered.

The song of the night crickets chirped through the open kitchen windows.

His dad broke the silence. "So big game tomorrow with Canterbury, eh?"

"Yeah, I guess so," whispered Cletis. "What difference does it make?"

His dad studied him, seemingly considering the weight his son carried on his young shoulders. "Maybe you oughtta get cleaned up and hit the sack. We better wash that uniform tomorrow morning, too."

"Yeah. I'll take care of it," stated Cletis. He finished his juice and pushed away from the table. "Can I sleep downstairs tonight, in your room?"

Abish and Garth passed a glance at one another and then looked back at Cletis. His dad nodded. "Sure. You go right ahead."

"Thanks."

Cletis lifted his glass from the table and headed to the sink. Suddenly the lights in the house dimmed and then brightened. Cletis and Abish froze in place.

Garth paused, looked up at the ceiling, and then about the room. "It can't be the AC," he stated. "I turned it off when we got home. The windows are open."

Placing his glass in the sink, Cletis eyed the room suspiciously. As he stepped back toward the table, the icy, haunting feelings swept over him like a dark, suffocating black shroud. Instantly he buckled over against the counter. With a groan, he lifted his head weakly and scanned the kitchen for any telltale sign of the Traveler.

Abish, feeling the same, turned to Cletis. When their eyes met, she knew he was in pain. "Cletis?" she questioned instantly.

"I'm okay," he responded hoarsely, still watching and waiting.

"What's goin' on?" asked his father as he stood up from the table and moved to Cletis's side. Taking Cletis by the arm, he guided him back to the table. "Both of you talk to me. What's happening?"

Cletis dropped into a chair and put his head down between his knees. "He's here, Dad. He's either in the house or somewhere close."

With that announcement, his father stood up straight. Listening and watching, he stepped into the middle of the kitchen. The seconds ticked away. No one moved.

"What am I lookin' for?" Garth questioned.

Cletis lifted his head and eyed Abish, who sat next to him.

"Do you still feel it?" asked Abish.

"Yes."

"Hey, guys, keep me posted here," Garth commented anxiously. "Am I supposed to know somethin'?"

Again they waited in silence.

Then, a gentle voice spoke from the front room. Cletis and his father recognized it instantly.

"Garth ... Cletis?" it asked, with a hint of fear.

Garth immediately shot a glance at Cletis and Abish. His eyes opened wide in shock and his arms dropped to his sides.

Again the voice came.

"Garth?"

Garth eased his way across the floor toward the front room.

"Dad, don't go out there!" Cletis warned, stepping in behind his father. The lamp in the living room suddenly clicked on, casting its light across the once-darkened entryway, visible from where they stood.

"Sweet heavens, what's happening now?" voiced Garth, sounding totally exhausted. Captivated by the voice, he continued forward toward the living room.

"Dad, wait ... "

"Cletis, what is it?" whispered Abish.

"It's Mom ... "

When Cletis finally took his father's arm, Garth was already in the doorframe, ready to step down into the living room.

"Garth, what's happening here? What's happening to me?" came the voice.

Garth eyed her, gasping at the sight. Anna stood before him, healthy and beautiful as she had ever been. She looked confused and dazed, and stood staring about the room.

"Garth, what am I doing here? How did I get here?"

Garth studied her a moment and then cautiously stepped down toward her. At first Cletis thought it was a trick and that the Traveler would be somewhere behind this evil hoax. But when he saw his mother, so confused at finding herself there in the house, he wondered if she had been brought forward in time—just as Cletis had been taken backward. *Maybe the feeling's still with me because he was the one who brought her here,* Cletis reasoned.

She was dressed in a familiar blue denim dress and wore sandals. She was tall and slender and gorgeous, and his father stepped even closer to her.

Abish moved in behind Cletis, took his hand, and squeezed it tightly. Together at the doorway to the front room they watched as the woman—Anna—studied the room around her, as if seeing it for the first time. She touched the figurines on the coffee table and gazed up to the painting on the wall.

"We were outside," she began, as if explaining a confusing puzzle. "The photographer just finished, and we were by the rock. Then I find myself here. But it's not the same. It's night. It was day." She studied Garth, then noticed Cletis and Abish standing behind him.

"Cletis, is that you?" she asked, looking quizzically at her son.

Cletis nodded toward her.

Quickly gazing back up at Garth, she nervously asked. "Garth what's happening here? It's something strange that I feel."

She reached her arm toward him, and despite his best efforts to question and doubt the whole situation, he automatically took her hand in his. She studied his eyes and stood in closer to him. Still she seemed puzzled and confused.

"Garth, something's not right here, but I'm not sure what it is. . . . Things have changed—they look older." She looked up at him anxiously. "You look older. Cletis is older. And I don't know how I got here."

Fearful, she stepped next to him and wrapped an arm around his waist, as if seeking his protection. Her other hand went to his cheek, and she studied his worried expression.

"Garth, what's wrong? I can feel something's wrong."

Garth was silent, frozen in the moment. But with her touch, and her nearness, he pulled her close and melted into her embrace.

Anna, peering over Garth's shoulder, looked up at Abish. She noticed she was holding Cletis's hand.

"Who are you?" she asked politely, stepping free of Garth, but still holding him around the waist.

No one spoke.

"Garth, speak to me," she stated, turning back to him. "I don't know what's happening here."

With Abish still at his side, Cletis watched the scene unfold—happy for his father, yet knowing in his soul that something was deadly wrong.

The blue denim. She wore it in the family portrait. That's where I remember that dress! The thought ripped through Cletis's mind. *Find the portrait! It's gotta be here in the living room. It's gotta be close by.*

Despite his desires to believe that it really was his mother, he pulled away from Abish and stepped down into the living room. Still feeling the nauseating pangs of the Traveler's presence, Cletis leaned against the chair, scanning the floor, searching. He noted that Anna's gaze followed him as he moved behind the furniture. Finally beside the couch, below the landscape painting, he spied the familiar frame. Kneeling next to it, he studied it where it lay. In silence, the picture screamed out the entire, terrifying story: Anna, his mother, was missing from the photo!

"Dad!" he yelled. "Get away! It's not her!"

The color left Garth's face as he studied the woman, and his eyes opened wide with fear.

Suddenly unsteady, Anna stepped back to the side of the coffee table. With a stunned expression, she smiled wickedly at Garth, and then methodically scanned the room, staring first at Abish and then at Cletis.

"Clever boy," she said, the kindness draining from her face.

Garth's hands went to his chest, and he leaned against the chair for support.

The woman eyed Garth briefly and then put her head back and closed her eyes. Instantly the transformation began. Anna's skin and muscle tissue came alive with the familiar, eerie pulsing movement. Her flesh and bones shifted and pulled, stretching, realigning, and melding into an odd new frame. The woman, who once gracefully stood before them, now yawned and gaped and moaned with the supernatural alteration. Her hair, once dark and shiny, slowly turned wirelike, white, and straggly, as if electrified on a newly sculpted skull. Her flesh, once fresh and youthful, now pulled and sagged on bones that roiled within her as the strange metamorphosis continued. The body whined with the horrifying transfiguration. Even the blue denim darkened and slithered, until the shiny, leathery vest of the Traveler took shape over the bent and crooked form. Finally, when the shifting and moaning halted, a shriveled old man stooped before them.

Deformed and hunched, the Traveler stood in the center of the room and, through eyes of blackness, glared at the three of them. Cletis, now familiar with this being and the Changing process, bravely held his ground and moved protectively across to Abish.

Still clutching his chest, Garth slumped to the floor beside the chair.

As Cletis and Abish rushed to him, the gray conduit gathered around the Traveler, lifting him off the ground.

"It appears that the heart of the Finder has failed, Cletis," he growled. As the old man floated above them the box appeared in his hands. "You had your choice, and you refused me. Now your father lies dying. Your selfishness will be the death of him. Think on that. It may be the death of you and Abish, as well."

Cletis, now kneeling, cradled his father tenderly in his lap. Abish, rising, rushed into the kitchen. As tears gathered in Cletis's eyes, he looked up at the conduit above him.

"I can teach you how to erase this moment in time," the Traveler groaned. "The power to save your father's life is still within your reach." He lifted the box toward Cletis. "Help me open the box, or our war will continue. So many lives depend upon your choice."

Cletis eyed him angrily. "That's exactly why I won't help you!"

From within the conduit the old man stared at him. "Then think of this, my proud, young son. The next part of the prophecy may be more devastating, when 'the son is as the father.' Do you know what that means?" The Traveler grinned through rotting teeth. Again he lifted the box toward Cletis.

Cletis turned away from him and looked down at his suffering father. In the kitchen, Abish spoke nervously to someone on the phone.

"Then we meet tomorrow on the 'arena of battle,'" coughed the old man. "If you change your mind and want to end this conflict before countless lives are endangered, simply think of me. Call my name, and I will come."

The conduit faded. In the distance, the blast of a siren stabbed the stillness of a Greenberg Junction night.

Chapter 20

The Arena Of Battle

The ambulance that roared into the Dungarvan's driveway invited people from near and far to investigate the emergency. So many of the neighbors in the surrounding blocks knew the Dungarvans, and though it was nearly eleven o'clock, the hordes found their way to the heart of the excitement. Cletis was amazed that as the men with the stretcher carried his father to the ambulance, probably a hundred people had gathered on or around his front yard. At least it looked that way. Among the visitors Cletis spied several of his teammates. Johnny, Frank, Bernie, Rabbit, and Davey, all still seated on their bikes, watched in serious reflection as Cletis, Abish, and the stretcher that carried his father's motionless form, passed through the crowd of anxious onlookers. Cletis peered over at his buddies as he marched sadly by. No one said anything, but their concern was communicated even in the silence.

The rear doors of the ambulance opened, and the stretcher was slid into place. Cletis was invited into the back compartment next to the paramedics and his dad. Abish was escorted around to the front of the vehicle, to be seated where there was more room for her ample humanity.

Cletis looked up at the half moon as the rear doors of the ambulance shut, and the siren sounded again over the quiet Greenberg Junction community. As the vehicle pulled away from the house and moved down the street, he looked at his home and its emptiness. It suddenly looked so lonely, standing there by itself. *We were once a whole family in that house*, he thought as his vision blurred. He wiped the back of his hand across his eyes.

The kids on their bikes followed at a distance, but finally faded from view when the ambulance turned right onto Main Street and began its twenty-minute drive to Canterbury Heights, where the closest hospital was located. As the siren sounded through the darkened back streets of Greenberg Junction, Cletis looked sadly down at his dad.

"Like you said, we're together in this," he whispered.

Garth remained unconscious throughout the night and into the next morning. The heart attack had done its damage and the doctors told Cletis and Abish that they would monitor his condition until they knew best what to do. As the hours of the night had passed, Abish and Cletis had watched the flow of nurses and doctors as they entered and exited the room, reading the monitors around Garth's bed and checking the fluids and medication that were going in and out of his body.

From the green hospital chair near the bed, Abish sat forward and looked on hopefully. She had watched throughout the night, pondering the events of the last two weeks and the details of the prophecy, feeling solely responsible for all that had happened, and all that was happening to the Garth Dungarvan family. Where she had once felt so completely in control of the events leading up to the long-awaited fulfillment of the prophecy, now things were slipping from her grasp. She had never dreamed that people would be hurt or families would be broken in the final stages of this, her grand test. But, at present, it seemed there was no way of escaping that reality. This was all her fault, and now, even after a millennium of waiting and suffering, she was still being haunted by decisions she made so long ago as a young lady.

Cletis had finally fallen asleep just before sunup and still lay curled up on the chair next to Abish. A pillow was tucked under his head on the arm of the chair. The old woman watched him sleep, and as she observed his heavy, relaxed breathing, she thought of the days long ago when she held him as an infant in her arms. She remembered the nights that she rocked him and walked him through the cabin until he fell asleep on her shoulder. She remembered the visits from her mother and father, and the happiness of sharing the little child with them. At least, she thought she remembered it all. She knew the memories existed somewhere in her head. But one thing was for certain: after having seen the love that Garth, Anna, and Cletis shared, Abish desperately longed for the chance to be a part of a family again.

A nurse entered the room, studied the monitors, recorded her findings in a folder at the base of Garth's bed, and then turned and exited the room. Abish looked up at the clock on the wall. It was shortly after 11 a.m. Cletis stirred slightly and opened his eyes. He appeared to be immediately deep in thought, as if picking up exactly where he had left off about five hours ago.

"Was that Mr. Howard in the hall earlier?" he asked groggily.

"Yes, I thought you were asleep," she answered quietly.

"I was, but I remember you leaving the room, and I thought I remembered seeing him through the open door . . . but that's about all." He sat up in the chair and stretched his legs out in front of him. "What was he doin' here?"

"He's concerned for you and your dad. He wanted to know how things were going." She watched him stretch his arms above him. "He told me that if it wasn't for you, he'd probably be asleep in some box behind the grocery store."

Cletis looked over at her and then yawned. "It wasn't just me. "

Abish watched him as he folded his arms across the gown that covered his dirty baseball uniform. "Mr. Howard said that Mrs. Kluzuski could take you back home to rest if you needed to. She's downstairs in the lobby, and she said she'd be there as long as you might need her."

"She's down there now?"

"That's what I understand."

"Just waitin' for me?"

"That's what Mr. Howard told me. She's been there all morning." She paused. "Maybe you should take her up on the offer. After all, you were up almost all night." She could sense by his silence that the idea didn't appeal to him. "Maybe Mrs. Klu would let you rest at her house."

Cletis looked down at the floor. "I don't know," he whispered. Turning back to Abish, he studied the wrinkled, round woman. "How are *you* doin'? Are *you* okay?"

She folded her hands in her lap. She didn't answer.

"Cletis, if you don't want to play in this game this evening, you don't have to. I never dreamed people would get hurt or that there would be this kind of danger involved in the fulfillment of the prophecy. My wants are secondary here. Let's just do what we feel is best for the safety of you and your father. Does that seem fair?"

Cletis blinked sleepily. "And what happens if I *don't* play?" he asked, as if already knowing the answer to his question. "Do I just let him win and open the box for him? And then he lives another ninety years, or so . . . and we'll never be free of him . . . and who knows what bad things he's gonna do with those ninety years?" He rubbed his face with his hands. "And then what happens to *you* if I don't play?"

She thought about the question a moment. "You know, I've never really given much consideration to what will happen to me," she whispered, "I guess I've always hoped the family would help see me through this entire test, and then Change me back to my real self, and welcome me home with open arms. I've lived that dream since the time I decided to accept this test. And I've almost paid that price, I guess . . . I hope. But I've never known how it was all to be done." She paused, still watching him. "I just never realized they'd send my own son forward in time to see me through the final moments of this trial. If I am saved in this ordeal and put back in good standing with my family, it will be because of you, Cletis. But I say this in all sincerity, my desires don't amount to anything right now if the life of your father or you or others are at stake." She looked over at Garth, studying his still, resting figure. With her right hand, she pushed a handful of frazzled hair back away from her face. "Mr. Howard said they'd play with eight if they had to."

Cletis dropped his hands to his sides. "I don't see any way around this, Abish. . . . I just gotta face it. We just gotta do it. The only two choices we got are either giving in to him or fighting back. So far the blue light has protected us. Maybe it'll still help us."

"Maybe."

"What if I *do* give in to him, Abish? What if I have to? What if there's no way around it? What if I told him I'd help him open the box? Would I be able to go back in time and change what happened before Dad had his heart attack? Or could I even go way far back and try to change the things that happened with you and . . . and Ian?"

She thought a moment. "I don't know Cletis. Maybe you can't do either without changing critical elements of Time and its balance. I just don't know what happens if you go toying with things like that."

"What happens to *you* if Time is frozen? Will you be hurt?"

"I don't know, Cletis. I don't know what will happen to any of us, if Time freezes. But I assume you and Ian can stay in that pocket of frozen Time until you're able to work out with him what needs to be done."

Cletis paused again, as if weighing all the possibilities before him. "When 'the son is as the father.' I wonder what that's all about?" He studied his father's shallow breathing. "So it seems like I've gotta do something that's 'like my father,' and then time gets frozen. When that happens, he's still gonna want the box opened . . . so there's probably gonna be another little battle of the minds, or somethin' then, before he either wipes me out or I do something to him." He took a quick breath and looked up at the ceiling. "Yeah, right . . . Like what can I do to him?" He put his hands on his forehead and leaned back. "All that is gonna happen . . . and who knows what else . . . unless I call it quits and open his box for him."

She watched his hands drop heavily away from his forehead. He sat in his own quiet space, eyeing his father. He lifted his hand to the front of his shoulder and as if rubbing a sore muscle, began to massage the area where the hourglass mark lay hidden beneath his clothing. Instantly he pulled his hand away, looked down at his shoulder, and sat up. Then, strangely, he lifted his other hand up and rubbed the mark on his opposite shoulder. Again his hand dropped quickly away. His eyes opened wide, and for a moment he stared straight ahead.

"What's the matter?" she asked, seeing the change come over him.

He leaned toward her, intense. "Abish . . . it's in me too, isn't it?" he asked eagerly, as if his mind were sorting battle plans.

"What are you talking about? What's *in you*?"

"I'm a Traveler too, aren't I? It's in me. The ability to travel."

"As far as I know. You have the marks. You were born of a Traveler."

Cletis hastily rose and gathered his few things from off the chair behind him.

"Will you be okay here with Dad if I head back home?"

"Yes. Of course."

"The Traveler told me that when Time's frozen, I'll have no protection from the blue light. Was he tellin' me the truth?"

"I don't know that, Cletis."

Cletis took a deep breath, then paused again to study his father. "I'm gonna play this game tonight, Abish," he stated. "And we'll find a way through all this. And we'll get Dad healthy, and we'll get you changed back to your old self, and we'll find the way to get you back to your family again! We'll figure it all out!" He looked around the room, as if to make sure he had what he needed. "I'm gonna find Mrs. Klu and see if I can get that ride home."

He eyed her a moment, then stepped closer, and kissed her forehead. With a turn, he darted out of the room.

For the final game of the tournament, the ball diamond was decorated with pennants from all the major league teams, and blue-and-white banners hung from the chainlink fences around the field like gathered drapes on outdoor curtain rods. Large red, white, and blue balloons bobbled in the air around the center field scoreboard and near the announcer's booth, fastened in place by ribbons of the same color. The base lines were neatly chalked, and the dirt of the infield was raked and smoothed. A fresh spray of water darkened the brown soil, and the bases were new and white. The lawns of the field had been mowed in the morning and were crisp and well manicured. At seven o'clock, though the sun still graced the field with an evening glow, the overhead lights on the six large electric poles surrounding the diamond had been turned on.

The skies were partly cloudy, but there was little chance of rain. A gentle breeze blew in from the right side of the park, lifting the flags and tossing the balloons slightly toward left field. Sparrows and starlings dipped and dodged about the bleachers, looking for an evening meal.

Sperry's Cards was the home team for the final game of the tournament, but for some unknown reason, the team was assigned the first base side of the diamond. It was the same field they had played on in their previous game of the tournament, but with all the sprucing up done to the grounds and fences, it looked like a totally different place. With play scheduled to begin at 7:30 p.m., all the Sperry team, except for Cletis and Mr. Howard, waited impatiently in the first base dugout.

Cletis, exhausted, stood outside the right field fence, behind first base and several paces up the line from the dugout. There he leaned on the fence and rested under the protection of two tall maples. Behind him several other trees grew—pines and elms combined with the maples to form their own tiny forest. He was ready to join his teammates, but decided on a private, quiet moment to ponder what he had experienced that afternoon, and what was to still come. He studied the field and its decorations, but he was almost oblivious to it all. The opposite dugout was empty. The Canterbury team was nowhere to be seen. From his secluded spot, he could hear his teammates conversing in the dugout. Though they couldn't see each other, he listened in on their chatter.

"They'll make their grand entrance any second now," stated Johnny. He paced as he looked across the field.

"You talkin' about Clete and Mr. Howard, or are you talkin' about the other team?" questioned Timmy.

"Canterbury," answered Johnny, nodding over to the third base dugout.

"Yeah, they'll probably come stormin' onto the field like a foot-ball team," added Bernie.

"Yeah, they'll probably have a band playin' and cheerleaders dancin' in front of 'em, too," added Frank with a laugh. Pauly and Rabbit giggled along with him.

"Where's Mr. Howard, man?" asked Klu in frustration, standing and hanging his fingers through the fence.

"And what about Clete?" asked Rabbit. "Do you think he's gonna play with us with his dad in the hospital?"

Everyone fell silent for a moment.

"I don't know," replied Johnny. "If my dad was dying, would I be here? Probably not."

"My mom took Mr. Howard to the hospital this morning to see Clete and his dad," explained Klu. "But when she brought Cletis back home to Greenberg, Mr. Howard told her he just wanted to stay at the hospital. So he's here in Canterbury Heights somewhere."

"Then he's gotta be in the area, right?" concluded Bernie.

"Well, at least we got the equipment," stated Frank, pointing to the bag at the end of the dugout. Next to it, sitting on the bench, stood a large jug of water with "KLUZUSKI" written on it.

"But if Mr. Howard doesn't show, can we play it without him?" asked Rabbit.

"No coach, no game," answered Johnny, still pacing.

"You gotta be kiddin'," complained Bernie.

They all stared out at the field as the umps measured chalk lines at home plate and inspected the diamond.

"Cletis didn't come back with you, Klu?" asked Rabbit.

"No. He said if he needed a ride he'd call, and he never called. So I don't know how he's getting' here."

Just as Klu finished his comment, Cletis moved quietly through the opening in the fence, around the edge of the dugout wall, and down into the dugout. He took a seat next to Pauly at the end of the bench nearest the steps. Cletis's uniform was still dirty, as were his socks. He laid his mitt down at his side and stared down at the dug-out floor. He felt the eyes of his teammates on him, but no one spoke.

"Sorry about your dad, Clete" stated Pauly finally.

The others in the dugout echoed his concern with moans and mumbles.

Cletis smiled weakly and nodded. "Thanks," he answered, and then sat up straight and stared off into the clouds above center field.

They probably think I'm worried about Dad, he thought. *Man, that's just a part of it. A thousand-year-old prophecy is gonna be fulfilled in the next little while, and I really don't know how that's gonna happen, or what choices I gotta make, or what those choices are gonna lead to.*

Cletis arose and walked past his teammates to the end of the dugout closest to home plate. There he studied the bleachers on the Canterbury side of the field. They were filling with dozens of Canterbury families, fans, and friends. Many wore red shirts and tops, matching the team's colors. Their clothing and strollers and tiny lap dogs were stylish and trendy. Cletis turned around to see the stands directly behind the Sperry dugout. Mrs. Klu, Johnny's mom, and Pauly's parents were the only ones seated on the Sperry side of the field. Timmy's folks and Rabbit's mom approached the bleachers from the Canterbury side of the field, observing the festivities of the park as they came.

No one has any idea what's really goin' on here, thought Cletis as he looked back out at the field. *They have no idea. I guess I don't either. And maybe it's better that way.*

The Canterbury team suddenly burst through the gap in the fence on the left field side of the diamond, and cheering and hooting, jogged down the line toward their dugout. Each boy carried a nice, red equipment bag, and his uniform and cleats were clean and new. Their hats, belts, and socks were red, and their shirts and pants were white with tiny, red pinstripes.

"Are those aluminum bats they're all carrying?" questioned Klu.

"Sure looks like it," answered Johnny distantly.

"And they all got cleats, looks like," added Rabbit, stepping to the dugout fence.

Cletis turned and looked down the line of his teammates. He noted the variety of shoes and cleats worn by his buddies. Timmy,

Rabbit, and Frank still wore their old tennis shoes. He studied the collection of wooden bats that Johnny hung from the fencing by the steps, and the second-hand mitts placed on the bench—probably all handed down from older brothers or even parents. His teammates all looked on, humble and silent as the red Canterbury blitz flooded the opposite side of the field.

The Canterbury players, including Elston, immediately sat down on the dugout bench, as if they had assigned seats. Their cheering abruptly stopped. Their coach instantly began shouting orders that were easily heard in the Sperry dugout.

"Listen to me close!" he barked. "This is killer instinct time! You know how to play ball and you do it well. Now, in this final championship game, we take that to another level! Not only will you execute the game plan as we have discussed it, but you will destroy your opponent! We will say and do things that will bring out the worst in that team over there!" He pointed to the Greenberg Junction dugout. "We will break their minds and their spirits! We will demolish them with our superior skills! That is the way you win! You are winners!" He placed his hands on his hips. "So are you ready to win this game?!"

The team erupted enthusiastically, yelling, shouting, and screaming their agreement. To Cletis they looked like a bunch of pent-up, red dogs in a kennel. Instantly the Canterbury players burst out of the dugout and sprinted onto the field for their warm-ups.

From his vantage point, Cletis watched the umpires gather near the Sperry on-deck circle. The largest of the three men leaned over to the other two men and spoke out a warning.

"Gonna have to keep a tight rein on this game. Gotta control the Canterbury coach and his team. No nonsense from them, okay?"

The two other umps nodded and turned to study the Canterbury coach who approached home plate with the fungo bat resting on his right shoulder.

Elston jogged across the field, took his position at first, and stared cockily into the Sperry dugout.

"What? No coach guys?" he blurted out sarcastically, laughing loudly. "Still waitin' for old man Howard, eh? We may not have a game after all!" He laughed again as he looked down and kicked at the dirt around first base.

"Elston, what's the matter with you lately?" Klu demanded, rising to his feet off the bench and grabbing the chainlink fence in front of him.

Johnny was at his side instantly. "Yeah, you're talkin' like an idiot, Elston! What's goin' on with you?"

"Hey, if that's what it takes to win," winked Elston as he set himself for the warm-up drills. He eyed Cletis for a moment and his countenance softened. He turned back to the playing field, as if concentrating on the upcoming drills.

Again the heavy, ugly feeling settled over Cletis like a fisherman's net. Moving to his seat at the end of the bench, he sat down, leaned over, held his stomach tightly, and pressed his eyes closed. *Someone here is the Traveler*, Cletis told himself. He swallowed hard, trying to maintain control of his balance, focus, and emotions. Opening his eyes, he looked up and down the bench. No one looked suspicious. No one seemed to notice his pained expression. *But no one would,* thought Cletis. *The Traveler wouldn't give himself away that easily*. Leaning his elbows on his knees, he doubled forward, trying to ride out the pain and nausea that accompanied the dark, haunting presence. Not wanting to give the Traveler the satisfaction of seeing him in a weak and sickened state, Cletis grunted and rose slowly to the fence, locked his fingers through the chainlink, and hung feebly against the wall, studying the drills of the infield.

Elston was still as smooth and as agile as he was during the last game Cletis watched. And all the other players on his team were just as gifted. Their throws were accurate, their concentration was intense, and their teamwork was phenomenal. It was both discouraging and exciting at the same time to watch a team play so well together.

To Cletis's right, a sudden a moaning was heard at the top of the steps of the Sperry dugout. Cletis and the others turned just in time to watch a drunken, dizzy Mr. Howard stagger down the concrete stairs, totter past Cletis, and land on the bench next to Pauly. His eyes glazed as he pulled a paper from his pocket and handed it over to Johnny.

"Here's a lineup . . ." he slurred groggily, trying to focus on the young man in front of him.

As Johnny took it, Mr. Howard's eyes rolled, his lids closed, his head bowed, and he collapsed over onto the bench, dead drunk.

The nurse jotted some notes in the folder, closed it, and slid it down into the box that hung at the foot of Garth's bed. Nodding and smiling to Abish, she turned and left the room. Garth remained unconscious. His breathing was shallow and labored, and Abish could hear the discharge of the oxygen as it sprayed into the mask he wore over his mouth and nose. Abish looked up at the clock on the wall. It read 7:30 p.m.

The game is about to start, she thought. *Here we go. Let's see what happens.* It was a moment she had long awaited, and she wondered if her thousand-year-old probation was finally close to an end. She studied Garth's pale complexion and prayed this whole ordeal would conclude swiftly, without further harm to anyone.

I'm sorry, Garth Dungarvan. I didn't mean to drag your family through all this. I didn't ever imagine I would endanger anyone. Forgive me. She reached out and stroked his arm.

Sitting back in her chair, she bowed her head in concentration, and within seconds a blue glow appeared in front of her, just over the top of Garth. The brilliant spot—at first a pinpoint—gradually increased in size and radiance as it shimmered, danced, and expanded above the bed. Abish lifted both hands toward it. Instantly its growth and movement ceased. Light as air, like a gigantic crystal ball, it hovered before her. With the move of a finger, she motioned it toward her. It obeyed, drifting closer to the green chair in which she sat. Again she bowed, as if in thought. Abruptly within the radiant orb, a panorama of the entire ball field materialized before her eyes—the diamond, players, fans, and coaches. She leaned back in the chair and watched intently as Sperry's Cards and Coins finished their warm-up drills and headed to the dugout. Shortly thereafter, the Canterbury coach and Johnny approached home plate for the coaches' pregame meeting with the umpires.

Johnny handed the ump the lineup card, hoping the man could read the chicken-scratching etched upon it. It looked like the writing of a first grader, barely learning to print. The ump eyed it curiously.

"Mr. Howard, our coach," Johnny began, "is . . . uh . . . isn't feeling well. He's in the dugout resting on the bench. I think he'll be okay. If . . . uh . . . if you need me to rewrite that, I'll be happy to. But there's only nine of us, so it shouldn't be too hard to keep track of any player."

The ump nodded. "Why don't you boys take the field, and we'll get this game underway."

"Yes, sir," answered Johnny as he trotted away.

The Canterbury coach handed his lineup card to the ump and hustled off.

"Mr. Martin!" called the ump.

The coach turned. "Yeah?"

"Don't want any trouble outta you or your boys tonight," he called. "You understand that?"

"Sure. I understand."

"I'll pronounce a first warning, but after that, whoever's causin' trouble, they're out of the game. Got it?"

Coach Martin nodded again and drifted back to his dugout.

"That includes you!" the ump barked.

The coach turned again and waved a willing agreement to the ump.

"Okay, guys," Johnny announced as he reached the Sperry dugout. "Out in the field. Let's do this! Let's play this game!"

As the team charged onto the diamond and hustled to their positions, their few fans greeted them with a hearty ovation and supportive cheers.

"Here we go Sperry!" shouted Mrs. Klu.

But Cletis lagged behind in the dugout for a moment. Though the heavy, ugly feeling was gradually fading, still he had work to do, and fast. He bent over the sleeping Mr. Howard and tugged on the bill of the man's cap. Mr. Howard didn't move. Pulling Mr. Howard's shirt back away from his neck, Cletis checked for marks on his shoulders. There were none. With a sigh of relief, Cletis grabbed the Kluzuski's jug of water and hastily unscrewed the lid.

"Sorry Mr. Howard, but we need you." Tipping the jug sideways, Cletis dumped ice water on the sleeping man's face. "Fire in the hole, Mr. Howard!" Cletis yelled.

Mr. Howard woke with a start, gasped for air, stood up straight, and slapped the cold water from his face. With that, Cletis stepped up out of the dugout and jogged unsteadily to center field. Mr. Howard staggered forward to the chainlink fence of the dugout and, grabbing it with his fingers, held himself upright.

The top of the first inning went beautifully for Sperry's Cards and Coins. Bernie struck out the first batter on four pitches. The second batter flied out to Johnny, up the first base line in foul territory. Elston, who batted third, dribbled a grounder back to Bernie in front of the mound. Bernie threw him out easily at first base.

With the applause of the parents in the stands, Sperry's Cards charged back to their dugout. A drenched Mr. Howard met them there, still a bit unstable on his feet.

"Sorry, guys," he stated as the team filed into the dugout and took their seats. Cletis, being the last one to enter the dugout, stood on the steps above Mr. Howard, listening to his somber words. "Sorry I let you all down," he continued. "I didn't mean to come all . . . " He peered down at the concrete floor. "Well, things just kinda get away from me, and . . . uh . . . a lot of crazy memories." He turned and looked out at the field. "Uh . . . my son . . . my son played on this field when he was your age. And . . . uh, I . . . I was his coach." He paused a moment. "So forgive me. I . . . uh . . . I . . . " He wiped his face with both hands. "Well, I'll just leave it at that."

Mr. Howard turned to exit the dugout. He looked up at Cletis and eyed him silently. "Hope your dad's okay, son."

"Thanks for comin' over there this morning," he nodded. He patted Mr. Howard's wet shoulder and stepped down past him. "And thanks for coachin' us."

Mr. Howard bowed and left the dugout. Still teetering a bit, he walked crookedly around home plate and out to his coach's box at third base.

"Get us started, Rabbit!" called Johnny from the far end of the dugout. Rabbit, standing by the steps, pushed her helmet on, grabbed her bat, and scurried out onto the field.

"Okay, here we go, guys!" shouted Bernie, clapping his hands. "Let's see what we're made of!"

To start the bottom half of the first, Rabbit surprised the Canterbury defense by laying down another beautiful bunt up the third base line. She scampered toward first, arriving well before the throw. The Canterbury coaches came unglued, screaming at the third basemen for being late reacting to the play. The kid gloomily took his position again but instantly readied himself for the next batter. Following Rabbit, Pauly went down on strikes for the first out. During his at-bat, the pitcher fired over to Elston at first base three different times. He had a great pick-off move, and Rabbit spent a lot of time on the dirt, diving back to the bag. Elston seemed to enjoy smacking her on the back with his mitt each time he placed the tag. Laughing, he would fire the ball back to the mound.

As Cletis walked to the plate, the tall, redheaded pitcher stepped off the rubber and looked over to Elston at first. Elston stepped forward from his position and waved some hand signals to his infielders. Cletis watched him curiously, never having seen a first baseman deliver signals to the infield—the catcher almost always did that. Elston's teammates watched him studiously, and then, as they set themselves for the next pitch, they smiled eagerly, as if in anticipation of some exciting secret play.

With Rabbit on first, the pitcher came set in his windup and, looking over his shoulder, eyed her at first base. Then before the pitch was thrown, Elston, at first base, broke toward second, and the second baseman broke toward first. The shortstop darted toward second base, and the third baseman scrambled to short. Back and forth they all ran, constantly eyeing Cletis at the plate. When they reached a specified location, they turned and dashed in the opposite direction—sometimes trading places with the other fielder, or sometimes simply faking and returning to their normal places. Though their mad darting to and from their positions created large holes in their defense, it also left Cletis surprised and confused, unable to focus on placing the hit. At the same time, as the pitch came home, Cletis saw something else he had never experienced in his life—a curve ball. It looked good in the beginning, but as Cletis began his swing, the ball dropped in front of the plate. Unable to check his swing, Cletis hammered the top part of the ball and sent a routine grounder toward the left side of second base. The shortstop, coming back from the second base side, scooped it up smoothly, and tossed it back to second. The second baseman took the throw easily, turned, and fired across to Elston at first. What was supposed to be a single up the middle, advancing Rabbit to third, turned out to be a simple, shortstop-to-second-to-first double play.

As Elston held the ball at first, Cletis crossed the bag and dejectedly turned toward the dugout.

"Got your number, buddy," Elston called back to him as he rolled the ball to the mound and trotted across the field.

Outside the Sperry dugout, Mr. Howard, still a bit shaky, counseled his team. "Looks like we got ourselves a ball game here!" he called out. "Okay, Bernie, let's do it!"

As the boys grabbed their mitts from off the bench and headed toward the field, Bernie leaned over to Cletis. "Was that a curve ball he threw you?"

"Yeah, I guess so. Never seen anything drop like that before."

"In Ohio, they wouldn't let us throw 'em, cuz too many kids were hurtin' their elbows," he stated, detectivelike. "But I can throw a curve. One or two won't hurt me. I'll save it for just the right time."

Cletis smiled up at him. "Sounds good to me."

With that, they both charged out onto the field.

The top of the second went quickly and quietly, more or less. Bernie fanned the first two batters for two swift outs. The third boy up stroked a Texas leaguer to left field, but Pauly made a shoestring catch behind third base to rob the kid of a nice hit. Three up, three down.

Finally feeling completely free of the Traveler's presence, Cletis charged in from center. As he did, he wondered about his dad and Abish—how they were doing? *What* they were doing? Was his dad still unconscious? Was Abish able to see the game being played? Did she know where the Traveler was? His stomach tightened a bit in nervousness as he thought about the final points of the prophecy—"time being frozen," and the "son being as the father." As he came to the infield dirt, he scanned the bleachers and field, studying the families, players, coaches, umpires—everyone he could see. He knew the Traveler was somewhere close by.

Klu led off the bottom of the second, smashing a one-bouncer right to Elston, up the first base line. To everyone's surprise, Elston bobbled the ball, taking it off his chest, and then scrambled to pick it up out of the dirt. Regardless of his fumbling, he finally came up with it and stepped on the bag just before Klu got there. To Cletis's amazement, Elston turned and looked into the Sperry dugout, wearing a bit of a panicked, quizzical expression on his face. His eyes met Cletis's, as if he were wondering what had just happened. But Cletis turned away, allowing Elston deal with his *own* challenges.

"Superman Elston's human after all!" cried Frank as he pulled his brown batting helmet over his ears.

"Hit it to first!" hollered Rabbit. "He's losing his touch!"

Their words seemed to have an affect on their old buddy, and he looked down and kicked the dirt in front of him.

With one out, Bernie stepped to the plate. Johnny waited on-deck, swinging two bats at the same time. "Here we go, kid," Johnny called out. "Let's get somethin' goin' here!"

Bernie checked Mr. Howard at third, received a few signs that meant absolutely nothing, and then turned and dug in at the plate. The pitcher wound up and fired the ball home. Chasing the first pitch, Bernie watched the curve ball drop down and in toward his feet. Like Cletis, he couldn't hold back his swing, and as he came around, he touched nothing but air. Canterbury's team and fans cheered loudly, as the lanky, redheaded pitcher smiled from the mound and took the throw back from his catcher.

"Lay off the junk," called Mr. Howard from the coach's box as Bernie stepped away from the plate to get the signs. "Wait for your pitch." As he spoke from third, he gave Bernie the "take" sign twice, as if wanting to make certain Bernie got it. Seemingly surprised at having to hold up and let the next pitch sail past him, Bernie stepped back into the box obediently. The redhead wound and fired. Another curve ball dropped in front of Bernie, hitting the plate in front of the catcher.

"Ball!" shouted the ump. "One and one!"

Bernie stepped out of the box again and looked down the line to Mr. Howard—now with greater respect for his coach's ability to sense what the kid on the mound was going to throw. Again signs came that meant nothing.

"Find something to hit and drive it somewhere," shouted Davey.

"Here we go, Bernie," called Timmy, rocking back and forth on the bench.

Bernie lifted his eyes to the mound. The infield chattered and cheered as the pitcher went into his wind up. The throw came straight down the middle, hard and fast. Bernie kept his weight back, cranked the hips forward, and met the ball solidly. SMACK!! Dancing off his bat, it arced into the right-center gap. The fielders chased after it and watched it hit the bottom of the chainlink fence on the fly. Racing around first and aiming for second, Bernie slid into the bag a split second before the throw from the center fielder hit the shortstop's mitt.

The Sperry bench erupted in cheers, and the parents in the bleachers jumped up and down yelling their congratulations.

"That's it!" shouted Mrs. Klu, bouncing on her toes.

"Nice hit, Bernie!" called Mrs. Skinner. "Way to give it a ride!"

Bernie stood proudly on second base as Johnny walked to the plate. Frank took his place in the on-deck circle.

"Now batting," came the announcement, "number seven, first baseman, Johnny Skinner."

The pitcher, perhaps a bit flustered by Bernie's deep drive to the fence, tossed two straight balls to Johnny (both high and away), and then mistakenly sailed one right across the plate. Johnny came around on it fast and drilled it down the left field line, out to the fence. Bernie, as if sensing that the left fielder had no chance to catch up to it, was off with the crack of the bat. While Johnny floated easily into second, Bernie crossed the plate at home.

Cheers and applause again erupted from the Sperry dugout and stands. Johnny's mom was on her feet ahead of the rest. The kids from Greenberg Junction had scored first, and with only one out, Johnny sat at second in scoring position. As Cletis paced up and down in front of the dugout bench, he couldn't help but hear the shouting in the Canterbury dugout. Their coach was fit to be tied. Hollering and screaming from their bench, he called time, charged up the stairs of the dugout, and hustled out to the baseline. Angrily he called his catcher and the tall, redheaded pitcher over to meet with him. Cletis watched as the man proceeded to chew out his two players, pointing and jabbing his finger toward them as he frowned and yelled and cursed.

When the meeting ended, the coach skulked back to the concrete dugout, and the pitcher and the catcher sprinted back to their positions. Whatever the coach said to them, it seemed to make a difference. The kid on the mound was instantly intense and focused and threw nothing but hard strikes through the remainder of the inning. Frank flew out to right field, and Davey grounded out to second. So after the coach's visit, Canterbury recorded two quick outs, and the inning came to an end. But with the top of the third inning looking them in the face, the scoreboard read: CANTERBURY 0, SPERRY'S CARDS 1.

The next three innings passed with no change in the score. Bernie and the redheaded kid continued to pitch a whale of a game; Coach Martin persisted in his loud and aggressive behavior; Cletis still paced the dugout wondering about his father, Abish, and the prophecy; Mr. Howard sobered up as the game progressed (thanks to aspirin from Mrs. Klu and a Gatorade from Johnny); and the shifting Canterbury infield and a deadly curve ball proved to be the secret weapons that kept Cletis Dungarvan off the bases.

In the top of the sixth inning, Canterbury tied the score on a home run by their left fielder. The ball pinged off the black aluminum bat and easily cleared the right-center fence. Neither Timmy nor Cletis had a chance to make a play on it. Bernie happened to push a pitch over the outside corner, right to the target Klu had set, but the kid caught up with it and hit it nicely to the opposite field. After completing the top of the sixth inning, the scoreboard read CANTERBURY 1, SPERRY'S CARDS 1.

But the bottom of the sixth brought a significant change. Rabbit singled to right field, when the pitch she belted scooted past a diving second baseman. The first pitch thrown to Pauly—a high fastball at his head—caught the bill of his helmet as he ducked away and sent it flying to the backstop. Luckily, Pauly wasn't hurt. His parents were on their feet in a heartbeat. So was Mrs. Klu and Mrs. Skinner. Timmy's parents and Rabbit's mom, who sat closest to the backstop, huddled close, leaning in to look at Pauly, who lay flat on his back in the batter's box.

As Rabbit advanced to second, the catcher leaned over Pauly, as if to apologize. "Right where he was aimin', kid," whispered the catcher. "It's time you guys saw some real baseball."

Pauly rolled over, stood up, and dusted himself off.

"With a runner on base and the score tied?" Pauly questioned smartly. "Doesn't sound like real baseball to me."

"Knock it off you guys," ordered the ump.

"He just told me the pitcher was throwin' at me on purpose!" exclaimed Pauly.

"You okay, Pauly?" called Mr. Howard, making his way toward the plate.

"Yeah, I'm fine," he answered, as he picked up his helmet and jogged off to first.

The ump turned to the Canterbury dugout. "Coach, come here!" he ordered.

Coach Martin, who sat at the edge of the dugout on an upside down, five-gallon, sunflower seed bucket, rose and jogged to home plate.

"You throwin' at these boys on purpose?" the ump asked him privately.

"Of course not," the coach answered with a frown.

"You're catcher's makin' that claim," the ump continued.

"Greg!" Mr. Martin yelled toward his catcher. The kid pulled the mask of his smudged and sweaty face and eyed his coach innocently. "What are you sayin' out there?"

"Nothin', sir," replied the catcher, using his mask to itch the underside of his chin.

"Good. Shut up and play ball!"

The catcher nodded and pulled his mask back over his face.

"Let's have a good, clean game, coach," urged the ump as he turned and lumbered back to the plate.

Coach Martin slipped back over to the edge of the dugout, took a seat again on the bucket, and winked in at his catcher.

"Now batting, number two, Cletis Dungarvan," pronounced the announcer.

With runners on first and second and nobody out, Cletis stepped to the plate. As he approached the box, he scanned the field. Turning to Mr. Howard, he waited for the signs. The coach flashed a series of signals, finally touching his nose and chin. *There's the indicator,* thought Cletis. Mr. Howard's right hand crossed his chest and then rose to the bill of his cap. *Hit and run. Got it.* Cletis stepped into the batter's box.

With Cletis set, the pitcher backed off the mound and faced first base. Again Elston stepped onto the infield grass and sent hand signals to his teammates around him. *Stinkin' shift is back on again*, thought Cletis, as he watched Elston step back to his position at first base. *Just slap it somewhere. Or hit it over their heads. Don't hang Rabbit out to dry.*

The redheaded pitcher took the mound again, looked in for his signs, came set, and eyed the runners on second and first. To Cletis's surprise, no one in the infield shifted! No one moved. They were playing him straight this time! *Okay then, give me something to hit, buddy*, he thought. *Big gaps between short and third, and between first and second.* The pitcher came set and finally, after a couple of head fakes, fired home. The toss was purposely low and away, almost impossible to hit. Coach Martin must have guessed the hit-and-run was on, and had his pitcher throw outside. But when Cletis saw the runners take off, he knew he had to make contact. Lunging for the pitch, he met it on the end of his bat and sent a loping fly ball into shallow right field. He charged toward first, at the same time watching the right fielder who came barreling into view. With a lunge and a grunt, the boy dove forward, extended himself toward the ball and reached desperately to catch it. As the ball came close to hitting the grass, the tip of the fielder's glove slid underneath it just before it touched green. Even as the boy hit the ground and slid another four feet, he held the ball snuggly in the webbing. The fielder rose to his knees and tossed the ball to second, doubling up Rabbit, who now stood on third base. The second baseman fired the ball back to first, hoping to catch another Sperry runner off-guard. But Pauly, as soon as he saw that a catch was possible, put on the brakes midway up the line. Once the out was made, he darted back to first, diving in on his belly.

That's the same thing that happened last game! Cletis reminded himself through clenched teeth. *The same stupid thing! Hittin' into double plays is a game killer!* Flustered and discouraged by his inability to move the runners around, Cletis stopped short of the bag at first base and yanked the helmet from his head. There he eyed Elston. His old friend, who stood but a few feet from him, was holding the ball in the air and grinning broadly.

"You just can't seem to do nothin' right today, can you?" he kidded as he fired the ball back to the pitcher.

As the pressure and frustration grew within Cletis, he fired his helmet against the fence next to the Sperry dugout.

Seeing the unsportsmanlike conduct, the home plate umpire turned to Mr. Howard at third and removed his mask. "Coach, that's one warning against that young man," he stated aloud. "Another display like that and he's out of the game."

Mr. Howard nodded while watching Cletis drop down into the dugout.

Man, what's goin' on, pondered Cletis as he sat on the bench. *This is a mirror image of yesterday's game. Is that what's supposed to happen?*

In that very instant, a group of little boys behind the scoreboard in center field set off a rattle of firecrackers. As they scattered, laughing at their little prank, the popping diverted everyone's attention momentarily from the game. Cletis watched them, but instead of seeing the fireworks, he instantly thought of Abish's library and the light that had blasted from the Traveler's fingertips—the light that had exploded onto the blue shield. He thought of the instant fear he had felt, followed by the sense of wonder and relief as the blue shell absorbed the flow of that strange power.

He said the blue light wouldn't protect me once time is frozen.

"With two outs in the bottom of the sixth inning," came the announcer's voice, "now batting, number sixteen, Theo Kluzuski."

Klu stepped in behind the batter's box and eyed Mr. Howard at third, watching for signs.

"Let's get on base, Klu!" Coach Howard called, bouncing his fists one on top of the other. "Lots of big guns behind you!"

Klu stepped up to the plate and settled in. Behind him, in the on-deck circle, Bernie began swinging a couple of bats. The first two pitches to Klu came in low and inside, forcing Klu out of the box with each toss. The third pitch was on the outside corner and Klu swung away, driving it hard and fast toward first base. With Elston there, everyone in both dugouts must have thought it was a for-sure out. Within the split second needed to make a play on the ball, Elston reacted. But as he extended his glove hand to his right and prepared to catch the line drive, he misjudged the hit and placed his mitt inches too low. The line drive skipped off the thumb of his glove and shot past him into shallow right field.

With Pauly advancing to second, and Klu scurrying past the bag at first, Elston looked down at his mitt. According to what Cletis knew, ever since that showdown time at first base between him and Elston back in Greenberg Junction, Elston had caught at least ninety-nine percent of everything hit or thrown his way. In the tournament games, he had been perfect. And now, twice in the same game—within moments of each other—he had bobbled one hit and completely misplayed another. Seemingly stunned, Elston looked over at the Sperry dugout as if in search of Cletis. At the far end of the bench Cletis stared up at him.

"Blanchard!" yelled Coach Martin from the dugout bucket. "Get back in the game! You gonna stand there lookin' at your mitt all afternoon, or you gonna play ball?!"

Elston turned. Everyone on the field was staring at him. Klu was behind him standing on first base. Pauly was on second. The pitcher, on the mound, already had the ball in his hand. The entire infield was waiting for Elston to get set for the next play. Elston, bowed his head, stepped back to cover the runner, and nodded his readiness to the pitcher.

"Fire in the hole!" hollered Mr. Howard from third, breaking the quiet of the moment.

"Now batting, number twenty-one, the Sperry pitcher, Bernie Anderson," piped the announcer.

Bernie moved forward, pushed down his helmet, checked the signs from third, and then stepped into the batter's box. The pitcher came set in his motion, eyeing Pauly at second and then Klu at first.

"Here we go, Bernie!" shouted Timmy from the dugout.

The pitch came in hard and straight, just above Bernie's knees. Stepping into it, Bernie met it solidly on the sweet spot of his wooden Louisville Slugger. CRACK. Another towering, colossal hit rocketed off of Bernie's smooth, left-handed stroke. Just like in the Blackmer game, the infielders and outfielders simply stood their ground, craned their necks back, and watched the fly ball soar over them into the summer's twilight. Bernie was hurrying around first when the ball finally landed on the lawn behind the scoreboard, fanning the big balloons that floated there as it whizzed past. A picnicking family scattered just in time as the home run hit the earth a few feet in front of their blanket.

The cheers exploded from the dugout and the stands as Bernie chased Pauly and Klu around the bases. The Sperry dugout emptied, and the team moved in excited unison toward home plate. Mrs. Kluzuski, Mrs. Skinner, and Mrs. Allen whooped it up in the bleachers, joyfully watching the three boys race to the plate. Pauly, Klu, and Bernie were greeted wildly at the plate and escorted cheerfully to the dugout.

As Johnny stepped up to the plate, the scoreboard changed: CANTERBURY 1, SPERRY'S CARDS 4.

"Number seven, Johnny Skinner, now batting for Sperry's Cards," came the announcement over the diminishing cheers.

"Okay, here we go Johnny," called his mother loudly from the backstop. "Keep the rally goin'!"

"Let's make some contact," called Mr. Howard from third. "Find a place to park it."

Johnny drove the second pitch deep to left field, giving Canterbury another good scare. But the ball crashed against the fence, six inches below the top metal rail. The left fielder scooped it up and fired it back in to the cutoff. By the time the ball found its way to second base, Johnny was standing on the bag with a double.

As Frank stepped eagerly to the plate, Mr. Howard put two hands out in front of him and gestured for Frank to calm down a bit. Frank nodded and watched Mr. Howard for the signs. The hand motions came, but no offensive play was on. Frank just needed to wait for a good pitch and make contact. A base hit would score Johnny from second. Taking a deep breath, Frank stepped into the batter's box and eyed the pitcher. The redhead wound and threw home. The pitch was far outside and got past the catcher. As he hustled to the backstop after it, Johnny took third.

The catcher fired the ball back to his pitcher as Frank stepped away from the plate and looked down to Mr. Howard for the signs. Again the calming sign came but nothing else. Cletis watched from the dugout as Frank stepped up to the plate, dug in, and studied the pitcher. From the stretch, the kid eyed Johnny at third, faked a motion with his head, and then threw home. This one was hittable, coming in across the ribs, and down the middle. CRACK. Stepping into it, Frank launched a fly ball toward the deepest part of the diamond. The infielders, like choreographed dancers, all turned at the same time and watched the ball sail toward the outfield fence. The center fielder, sensing the fly was playable, drifted underneath it and looked up into the twilight sky. With a bead on it and leaning against the fence, he watched it drop toward him. Raising his glove above his head and shifting to his left, he leaned back over the fence. With a soft thud, the ball landed in his mitt. Carefully he wrapped both hands around it and held it snuggly. Grinning, he hopped twice and then raced toward the dugout. Frank, almost to second when the catch was made, hung his shoulders dejectedly, clapped his hands together, and turned back to the dugout.

With the third out recorded, the Canterbury players scampered to their dugout. At the same time, the Sperry bench emptied to trade places with them. With the top of the seventh inning now looming over the game, Cletis anxiously grabbed his mitt, stepped up out of the dugout, and headed for center. Elston, who had waited a moment near first base, called out to him.

"Hey, Clete?"

Cletis eyed him suspiciously, wondering what he could want.

"I'm losing my gift ... or maybe I've lost it already," Elston admitted.

Cletis walked past first base. "Look, you're gettin' whooped fair and square, so don't go playin' no games with me."

"And I'm sayin' weird things," continued Elston. "And I don't know where they're comin' from. They just come outta my mouth."

Cletis shook his head and then pivoted away and hurried out to center. A glance over his shoulder revealed that Elston still stood near first, looking apologetically out at Cletis. A moment later, Elston turned to his dugout and jogged across the field.

Mr. Martin, who had watched the give-and-take between the two boys, met Elston at the steps of the dugout.

"What are you talkin' to him about?" drilled the coach, gesturing out to the center fielder. Cletis, in the distance, looked on. "You're losing 4–1, and you're talkin' to the opposing team?! What's that all about?!"

Elston looked back toward Cletis and then turned to his coach guiltily. "Nothin', sir," he answered.

"Don't you tell me *nothin'*. I saw you talkin' to him." Coach Martin glared at him. "You used to live out there in Greenberg Junction, didn't you." It was a statement, not a question. "I know that. I also know these guys on this Greenberg team used to be your friends."

Elston looked down nervously. "Yeah, I know 'em all."

"Rumor has it you and him—that center fielder kid out there— were involved with some kind of witch lady. Is that right?"

Elston swallowed. "Where'd you hear somethin' like that?"

Martin pointed to the field. "When those boys were warming up before the Blackmer game. They were talkin' about a witch lady in Greenberg Junction. They said you and that kid used to go to her house. I heard 'em. And they talked about some strange things happening after you and that kid visited her." He smiled at Elston. "You learn a lot about a team listening to their warm-up conversations."

Elston's eyes widened. Anxiously he made his way past the coach and into the dugout. "There ain't no witch, so they got it wrong. That's all. It was an old lady."

"Let's have a batter!" shouted the ump, looking over at the Canterbury dugout.

As their third baseman charged toward the plate to take his turn at bat, Mr. Martin took his place in the third base box.

Cletis took a deep breath in centerfield. The seventh inning began.

Canterbury's first hitter connected solidly on a good pitch thrown by Bernie, punching the ball into the right-center gap. Cletis hurried toward it, picked it up as it rolled, and fired it to Davey at second. The throw came in like a bullet, straight to Davey's mitt above the bag at second. The runner, who was hustling to turn a single into a double, could see that he was clearly out. Davey was there at second base, bending low, ready to make the tag. In an attempt to break up the play, the slide came in hard, and the runner purposely lifted his leg and cranked a dust-hidden kick into Davey's stomach. With a huff, Davey fell backward over the bag. In the collision, the ball came loose from Davey's glove and bounced toward center field. Rabbit, having come in from behind second to cover the play, scooped the ball up.

"HE'S SAFE!" roared the ump as he hustled toward the play. His arms sliced through the dust above the base as he signaled the call.

The runner rose on the bag and glared down at Davey, who, rolling in the dirt below him, struggled to catch his breath.

"What are you talkin' about!" screamed Rabbit. "He made the tag right in front of the base! He had control of the ball when he made the tag! And what about the runner kickin' him? Didn't you see that?!"

"Young man," cautioned the ump. "Do you wanna get tossed outta this game?"

"I'm not a young man!" seethed Rabbit. "I'm a girl!"

The ump eyed Rabbit curiously for a moment, taken aback by her announcement.

"Time, blue!" called Mr. Howard as he crossed the field to attend to his fallen player.

In the hospital room, Abish sat in the chair next to Garth's bed, studying the images that darted in and out of the orb that floated in front of her.

"Come on, ump," she stated aloud, having seen the collision at second base. "That's a dirty play."

The young nurse who stood at the base of Garth's bed looked over at her curiously. "Excuse me?" she asked.

Abish glanced up at her. "Oh, I'm sorry," she groaned. "I didn't see you come in. I was . . . uh . . . just thinking of something. And . . . uh . . . I happened to say it out loud."

The woman nodded politely. A tiny grin lifted the corners of her mouth. "Can I get you anything, ma'am?" she asked as she wrote a few observations on Garth's chart.

Though the giant blue orb floated only inches from the nurse's face, she saw none of it.

"No, thank you," answered Abish, turning her attention back to the emergency on the ball field.

"If we can help you, please let us know," suggested the nurse. She turned and exited the room.

Garth weakly roused and attempted to lift his heavy eyelids. Slowly his head turned toward Abish. Anxiously she leaned forward, right through the blue orb, and studied his countenance. His eyes blinked feebly, trying to focus.

"Blue," he whispered faintly, looking past her into the ball of light.

"You can see it, can you?" she commented. "That means you're a true Dungarvan." She leaned back a bit, taking her lumpy face out of the blue brilliance. "Just so you know, you're in the hospital. You've had a heart attack." He blinked weakly. "Cletis is playing the game. It's 4–1 for us in the top of the seventh inning. And nothing out of the ordinary has happened . . . at least that I know of."

She looked down at him. Despite his best efforts to stay awake and alert, his eyes closed again. Abish watched him helplessly. She sighed as she sat back in her chair and bowed her face into her wide and puffy hands.

"Oh please, dear Papa, see us all through this."

The umps invited both coaches to the plate.

"If there are any attempts to deliberately harm or injure any player in this contest, your team will forfeit the game. Is that understood?"

Mr. Howard nodded. The ump eyed Coach Martin. The Canterbury coach simply shrugged innocently and trotted back to the third base box.

Davey, still pained by the jolt he took, set himself in position. With a runner on second, the Canterbury batter dug in at the plate. Bernie checked the runner's lead at second, and then turning to home and seeing his target, he fired the pitch to Klu. The left-handed batter swung awkwardly at the inside pitch, connecting weakly and sending a gentle fly ball to right field. There Timmy settled under it and waited for it to drop. Which it did, one foot to his left. Having misjudged it, he frantically scrambled after it, picked it up off the grass and threw it in to Davey at second base. By the time the ball arrived in the infield, the runner on second was halfway down the line between third and home. He scored easily. The batter, safe on an error, now stood at second base.

Instead of two outs and nobody on, a whole different situation faced Sperry's Cards. One run had scored, a runner was now on second, and there were no outs. Timmy looked back at the scoreboard and hung his head in frustration.

CANTERBURY 2, SPERRY'S CARDS 4.

"Hey, don't you worry about it, Timmy," hollered Cletis from center. "We'll get it back. Just don't stop concentrating. Every pitch is a new moment!"

"Good try!" shouted Davey from second, still rubbing his sore belly.

"We'll be okay!" called Johnny from first. "Just don't let up!"

Despite their encouragement, Timmy's bottom lip quivered slightly.

The next kid up—the pitcher—took his place at the plate. Bernie looked in at Klu for the signs. Deceptively Rabbit snuck around the runner at second. Klu instantly spotted it and fingered a signal to Bernie. Spinning toward second, Bernie fired the ball back to Rabbit.

Cletis, seeing the play develop right in front of him, charged in to back it up.

"BACK!" yelled Coach Martin from third base.

But it was too late. The runner, caught off guard, was leaning the wrong way. Rabbit took the throw cleanly from Bernie, and bending over the bag at second, she dropped the tag on the runner's outstretched hand, six inches away from the base. By the time Cletis arrived in a back-up position behind second, the play was done.

"He's OUT!" barked the ump, shooting his fist across his body and balancing on one foot.

"Yes!" shouted Cletis. "Nice play, Rabbit! Way to catch him, Bernie!" Happily he slapped his mitt and charged back to center field. "See, Timmy," Cletis called as he eyed their little right fielder. "We got him after all!"

Timmy smiled back at him and then turned and eyed the scoreboard. "One out," he called happily from right field, lifting his index finger above his head.

As the Canterbury runner trudged off the field, he was greeted by the belittling comments of his coach. Hanging his head, he made his way past Coach Martin and down into the dugout.

The next batter swatted the first pitch down the first base line over Johnny's head. Hustling past the bag at first, the kid made a wide turn and looked at second. Timmy, scurrying over to the foul line, picked up the ball and tossed it in to Davey at second base, holding the Canterbury runner to a single.

"Atta boy!" shouted Johnny back at his little cousin. "Way to hold him!"

"Way to be on it, Timmy!" added Davey from second base as he eyed the runner and fired the ball back to Bernie on the mound.

The following batter belted a high fly ball to Pauly in left. He took only one step back, caught it confidently, and firing the ball back in to Frank, yelled, "Two outs!"

One more would finish the game.

Jogging back to his position, Cletis eyed the scoreboard again. *It's gotta happen pretty soon,* he thought. *Something's gonna throw this game upside down, and it's gonna happen right away. I gotta stay in control. I gotta be ready.*

Cletis recognized the next batter—the catcher. He was a solid, square kid kind of like Klu but bigger. Bernie set, eyed the runner at first, and threw home. From where Cletis stood, he watched the ball arc, dip, and fall in front of Klu. *There's that curve ball Bernie promised!* The batter took a big stroke at it and came up empty. But the pitch fooled even Klu, and his attempt to block the ball failed. As it scooted through his legs, the first-base runner alertly darted down to second.

The batter must have guessed fastball on the next pitch, because he jumped on Bernie's second toss like a wolf on a winter mouse. BANG. The ball pinged off the aluminum bat and jetted across the light blue evening sky. Cletis lifted his head and watched it soar over him. The shot cleared the center field fence by at least fifteen feet, landed by the scoreboard, and then bounced and rolled another twenty yards.

The stands and dugout on the Canterbury side roared their support. With two outs in the top of the seventh, their big catcher had tied the game at four. Crossing the plate, he was greeted by a wild, red band of teammates and a screaming, applauding bleacher full of parents and friends.

"Greg Nussbaum has just tied the score, with a towering home run over the center field fence," voiced the announcer, unable to hide his excitement. The numbers on the scoreboard instantly registered the change: CANTERBURY 4, SPERRY'S CARDS 4.

From the steps of the dugout, Mr. Howard watched his dejected pitcher scrape the mound with his cleats.

He pitched a great game yesterday, and now he's in the seventh inning of another tough game, Cletis thought. *We just need one more out, Mr. Howard. What are we gonna do? Johnny's rested. He could finish it up.*

"You okay, Bernie?" called Mr. Howard. Bernie nodded, took a deep breath, and readied himself for the next batter. Mr. Howard studied him. "Here we go then. Let's get this last out! You can do it."

As the next batter settled in at the plate, Bernie wound and threw home. PING. The first pitch was driven over Frank's head into shallow left field. Pauly came up with the ball and fired it to Rabbit covering second base. As the runner turned the corner at first and eyed the infield, in a blink Rabbit fired the ball across to Johnny at first.

"BACK!" yelled Coach Martin from the third base box.

The kid, seeing the in-coming throw, dove headfirst back to the bag. The tag came down on top of him a fraction of a second after he touched the base.

"He's SAFE!" called the umpire, standing right over the play and spreading his arms wide.

"Way to keep him honest there, Rabbit," called Mr. Howard. "Nice throw!"

As the runner stood on the bag and brushed himself off, Johnny tossed the ball back to the mound. Taking the throw, Bernie prepared for the next Canterbury batter.

Five pitches later, that batter trotted to first with a base on balls.

"Time, ump," called Mr. Howard, stepping away from the dugout.

The ump granted it, and Mr. Howard walked toward the first base line and invited Bernie and Klu to join him there. Bernie dropped his head and crossed the short distance to where Mr. Howard waited. Tired and discouraged, he took his hat off and rubbed his forehead on his shoulder. He eyed Mr. Howard as if he knew it was time to be replaced. Klu jogged up the line from behind the plate to join the huddle, pulling his mask off his face and blowing air through puffed-out cheeks. Cletis and Pauley jogged toward the infield, as if in a joint effort to communicate their distant vote of appreciation.

"You've pitched a whale of a game, kiddo," stated Mr. Howard, facing Bernie. "In fact two great games. We couldn't have come this far without you. But I can see you're runnin' outta gas. There's nothin' wrong with that. But I'm gonna bring in Johnny and have you two trade places."

Bernie placed the ball in Mr. Howard's outstretched hand, smiled at Klu, and stepped toward first.

"Johnny," called Mr. Howard, "come take his place."

Johnny passed Bernie on his way toward Mr. Howard. "Nice pitchin'," he stated, slapping him on the shoulder.

"Let's finish 'em off," Bernie answered. "Hold 'em."

Mr. Howard placed the ball in Johnny's hand, patted him on the back, and returned to the dugout.

"Nice pitchin', Bernie," called Cletis.

"Yeah," added Pauly, "way to fire, kid!"

Johnny took the mound and went through his warm-up tosses while Elston stepped into the on-deck circle and awaited his time at the plate.

"Blanchard!" called Coach Martin from the dugout. "Come back here, quick."

Cletis watched Elston return to the dugout. There the team stood huddled around their coach.

Somethin's up, thought Cletis. He looked back at the scoreboard. *All tied up in the top of the seventh.* He began to pace, slapping his mitt on his thigh. There was too much on his mind to relax and wait.

The Canterbury huddle broke up. Some of the players wore silent grins. They nodded and laughed with the words that were communicated. Several of the players, including Elston, looked out at Cletis. Johnny finished his warm-up tosses, and Elston made his way to the plate.

"Let's have a batter," yelled the ump from behind the plate.

Johnny was ready. So was Elston.

"With two outs in the top of the seventh inning," came the announcer's voice, "now pitching for Sperry's Cards, number seven, Johnny Skinner."

The parents on the Sperry side applauded.

"Let's go, Johnny!" called out Mrs. Skinner and Mrs. Allen, both at the same time.

Rabbit turned and faced the outfield. Holding up two fingers, she signaled to her fielders. Cletis, Timmy, and Pauly returned the gesture.

"Here we go, Johnny!" called Cletis. "Let's hold 'em here!"

Cletis continued to eye the field in front of him, wondering when the real trouble would start and when the Traveler would finally show himself. *Runners on first and second. Two outs. Something's gonna happen in the bottom of the seventh or in extra innings. The Traveler is probably doin' his best to control everything in his favor.*

"Now batting for Canterbury," echoed the voice, "number ten, Elston Blanchard."

Elston took the signs from Coach Martin at third and stepped into the batter's box on the left-hand side of the plate. As he scraped the dirt there, Klu greeted him with a sarcastic whisper.

"Scummy little country boys makin' you richies look bad, eh?"

"Klu, I don't know what's goin' on with me. I—"

"I don't even wanna hear it, man." Klu interrupted. "He's never hit you before, Johnny," he called out to the mound as he squatted into position. "And he's not gonna hit you now! He's scared, hidin' behind his tough words and his aluminum bat!"

"Knock it off, catcher," warned the ump. "Let's just play ball!"

"Yeah, Klu," called Pauly from left. "Let's get this done! Here we go Johnny!"

As if determined to fight back against Klu's words, Elston eyed Johnny, knowing his delivery and every pitch the boy could throw. Johnny wound from the stretch, eyed the runners on first and second, and fired the ball home. The toss came in at the knees, on the inside part of the plate. Elston swung and connected. Another PING sounded across the field as the line drive shot off Elston's bat and blasted toward the right-center gap. Hustling across the field, Timmy extended his glove hand across his body, attempting to make the catch. Coming up just inches short, the ball bounded off the top of Timmy's glove and went careening toward center field. Having come in behind Timmy as a backup, Cletis slammed on the brakes and took off in the opposite direction, chasing after the ball.

"I got it Timmy!" shouted Cletis as he chased it down.

The runners on first and second sprinted around the bases ahead of Elston, and Cletis figured, as he reached for the ball, that they would cross the plate no matter how great a throw he could make from center. *Elston is my main focus*, decided Cletis, as he grabbed the ball, rose, and scanned the field in front of him.

Elston was rounding second and heading for third. Mr. Martin was at the coach's box waving him on. But Cletis could see Frank setting at the base, inviting the throw from center. On the run, Cletis leaped and fired. The bullet shot across the outfield grass and straight for its mark in front of the bag at third. On an invisible line, the throw zipped past Elston just as he began his slide. With a slap, it landed in Frank's glove slightly to the outfield side of the base. With a quick pull of the mitt across to the front of the bag, Frank tagged Elston's cleat just before it touched the base.

"OUT!" bellowed the ump, standing right on top of the play, lifting his fist above him.

Frank tagged Elston a second and a third time, just for good measure, and smiled down at him. "Nice hit, Elston, but you forgot who's playin' center."

In the dirt at third, Elston looked up at Coach Martin, but he had already turned to the dugout.

From center, Cletis watched Elston and his coach. He saw Mr. Martin turn away from third base and nod to his outfielders, as if giving them a special signal. Two boys immediately raced past Martin and Elston and out onto the outfield grass, where Cletis made his way back to the dugout.

Uh-oh, thought Cletis. *What's goin' on now?*

"Hey, kid!" one of them yelled.

Though Cletis was now part-way across the outfield, he paused as the two Canterbury boys jogged toward him.

"Come here," waved one of them, signaling to Cletis.

Despite the strange invitation, Cletis stood his ground while they approached.

"We just wanted to say that you've made a couple of real nice throws, that's all."

A kid with freckles spoke—their right fielder. His voice was kind of whiny, and his tone was anything but sincere. He was about three inches taller than Cletis and quite a bit heavier. The other kid—the Canterbury center fielder—was about the same height and had blond hair that stuck out the bottom of his red hat. They gathered close around Cletis, with their backs to the infield.

"You're a witchboy, aren't you," the freckle-faced kid jeered. "Couldn't play ball without some country witchcraft helpin' you, eh?"

They both laughed at the comment.

"Better put a curse on us, witchboy," spoke the blond kid, "because you're gettin' cleaned."

He stepped on the top of Cletis's right foot, pressed down hard, and pushed Cletis backward. With his foot pinned to the ground, Cletis fell back onto the grass in front of them. Quickly he rose again and pushed back at the blond boy, who still stood on his foot.

Instantly the blond kid turned to the infield. "Hey, blue!" he hollered. "This kid's fighting with us! Kick him out of the game!"

The ump that stood at second base turned and looked. Cletis backed off, but there was still fire in his eyes.

"Yeah," claimed the other boy, calling to the ump. "We come out here to tell him he made a good throw, and he starts pushin' us!"

The umpire signaled Cletis to return to his dugout. "Break it up!"

Now with a fresh injury—feeling the pain in his toes and foot, Cletis limped off the field.

"Lucky he didn't kick you out, little witchboy," called the right fielder as he jogged to his position.

On his way to the dugout, Cletis passed first. Elston was there taking throws from his infielders.

"What'd you tell 'em?!" Cletis asked in quiet fury. Elston eyed him guiltily but said nothing. Cletis continued angrily. "Man, I can't believe you lately! I thought we were friends!"

Elston shrugged and bowed his head. "Nice throw from center," was all he said.

"Don't gimme that trash!" Cletis fired back at him. "I don't even know who you are anymore! But I know you're not Elston."

Cletis grimaced with the pain in his foot, and as he limped to the dugout, he thought of how much he hated having said what he just said. *Maybe I'm no different than he is*, Cletis thought. *I'm sayin' stupid things too.*

He tossed his mitt on the bench and looked up at Elston at first base. His old friend looked genuinely crushed. He stood with his head down, staring at the base in front of him. Cletis looked past him, turning his attention to the scoreboard's new numbers: CANTERBURY 6, SPERRY'S CARD 4.

On the field, a new pitcher walked to the mound. He was a good-looking kid, with short, brown hair. Just about as tall as the redhead who pitched before him, he threw hard and stood serious and confident on the hill.

"Davey's leadin' off," shouted Mr. Howard, calling out the lineup. "Then Timmy, Rabbit, and Pauly. We can do this, guys! We've played with and beaten the best of 'em." He clapped his hands energetically. "Gotta believe you can do it! Two runs to tie, three to win!"

"Now batting for Sperry, number ten, Davey Michaels."

The new pitcher blew three straight strikes past Davey. He fouled the last pitch off, but it stayed in the catcher's glove. Discouraged, Davey trudged back to the dugout.

"He's fast," he spoke quietly as he passed Timmy by the on-deck circle. "Keep us alive, kid."

"Now batting for Sperry, right-fielder, Timmy Russell."

From the mound, the new pitcher measured the little batter carefully. Timmy was a smaller target, and for most pitchers, the tighter strike zone was a challenge. Amazingly Mr. Howard gave Timmy the "take" sign on the first three pitches. All were balls, just barely outside the zone. On the fourth pitch, Mr. Howard signaled for Timmy to fake a bunt. As the pitch came in, Timmy squared around, and then pulled his bat back at the last moment. The toss came in right over the plate, for the first strike. On a three-and-one count, Timmy studied Mr. Howard once more to get the signs. Again the "take" sign was given. Timmy dug in, waited, and watched the next pitch sail by his chin.

"Ball four!" called the ump. "Take your base."

Timmy smiled, tossed his bat aside, and sprinted excitedly down the line to the first base bag.

"One down," called Mr. Howard over to Timmy, lifting a finger. "Watch the line drive! Be movin' on a grounder! Halfway on a fly ball!"

Timmy nodded and vigilantly took a step away from the base. Elston stood silently in front of him, ready for the throw from the pitcher.

Rabbit took the signs from Mr. Howard and stepped up to the plate. She set herself deep in the box and waited. The first pitch came in low and on the outside corner of the plate. A quick swing and solid contact drilled the ball to Elston. With a catlike dive to his right, he snagged the line drive and landed on his belly. Timmy, who was moving with the pitch, slammed on the brakes when the ball was caught and, before Elston could get to his feet, scurried safely back to first base, avoiding a game-ending double play.

Maybe Elston isn't *losing his gift*, thought Cletis as he paced the dugout searching for his helmet. *That was a super catch. Maybe there was never any gift to lose. Maybe he's a natural, and it just took a little encouragement to open his eyes.* He watched Rabbit return to the dugout. She was fighting back the tears.

"Hey, that was a great hit, Rabbit," complimented Cletis as she stepped down to the bench.

"Yeah, Rabbit," agreed Johnny and Bernie at the same time.

"Sometimes it just don't fall where you want it to," advised Frank, speaking from experience.

Despite the words of support, she sat morosely, staring out at the field.

"We got two down, Timmy," barked Mr. Howard from the third base box. "You're goin' on anything hit. Got that?" Timmy nodded from first base, taking a careful lead.

The drama unfolding in front of him, Cletis stepped out of the dugout and into the on-deck circle.

"Now batting for Sperry, left fielder, Pauly Allen."

"Here we go, Pauly!" called Cletis from the circle. "Pick a pretty one and give it a ride."

As Cletis considered the present situation on the field, he suddenly felt the pressure of his upcoming at-bat. If Pauly reached base safely, Cletis knew he'd be stepping up to the plate with the game on the line. He eyed the field and the stands intently, knowing still that the Traveler was somewhere out there.

Man, I wish Abish and Dad were here, he thought as he adjusted his helmet and began swinging his bat. *I don't wanna do this all by myself . . . what*ever *it is that I have to do. I'll bet Abish is watchin' from the hospital somehow. But a lotta good that does me here.*

The first pitch flew by Pauly, high and away. The catcher came up to snag it and faked a throw up to first.

"BACK!" yelled the teammates from the Sperry dugout bench. Timmy was on his face in the dirt immediately, but no throw was made.

Cletis studied the field around him and pondered all the details he was supposed to be keeping track of. It all seemed so overwhelming. Suddenly lost in his thoughts, everything before him became dream-like, as if all were passing in front of his eyes in slow motion: Elston's quick glance over to the pitcher, Mr. Howard's calls from third, Pauly's swinging of the bat at home plate, the pitcher's concentration toward the plate. Cletis took it all in as if he were sitting in a theater, watching actors on a stage. Though he stood in the on-deck circle, though he continued to swing his bat, and though the game was going on around him, worries about the fulfillment of the prophecy flooded his mind.

How will it all happen? The game . . . Dad's health . . . Abish's changing back to who she was . . . the final moments with the Traveler . . . time being frozen. All of it was heavy on his shoulders—too heavy. He took a deep breath and continued to swing the bat. *One thing at a time,* he cautioned himself. *You'll be guided. Trust Abish. Trust her family. No matter what happens here on this field, something bigger than life is gonna follow.*

"Be careful, Timmy!" shouted Johnny from the dugout, snatching Cletis from his dreamlike stupor. "Two down! We need your run!"

The pitcher wound and fired home. CRACK! Pauly swung hard, connected, and launched a line drive into the gap in shallow right field. As he charged for first, the ball found its way nearly to the fence. Timmy, smartly running with the hit, eyed third base as he rounded the corner at second. There Mr. Howard stood, frantically waving his arm clockwise in the air. With a burst of speed, Timmy sprinted down the line and slid safely into the bag. Pauly, turning the corner at first and seeing an easy double ahead of him, charged on to second base, arriving well ahead of the cut-off throw from the right fielder.

The players in the Sperry dugout and the families behind them in the bleachers, exploded in cheers and applause! With runners on second and third, the little country team from Greenberg Junction still had hope.

Klu replaced Cletis in the on-deck circle, and Cletis limped to the batter's box.

"Here we go, Clete," called Klu. "Just do what you do!"

"Here we go, kid!" shouted Frank from the dugout. "Base hit ties the game!"

"He's yours!" yelled Rabbit, clapping energetically and jumping up and down in front of the bench. "Squish the bug. See the contact. Hit it where they ain't!"

Cletis stepped to the plate. His foot hurt, and the tremendous pressure of both the game and the prophecy made him feel slow and tired.

"With two outs, now batting for Sperry's Cards and Coins is center fielder, Cletis Dungarvan."

The announcement echoed across the diamond.

In the hospital, Garth groaned again, rolled his head to the side, and opened his eyes. The blue orb shimmered above him, still filled with the images of the game and its players. He blinked his eyes slowly, fighting against the pain and fatigue that beleaguered him. The oxygen mask still covered his nose and mouth. His body seemed a solid, unresponsive mass, despite his limited ability to move his head and face.

Abish leaned forward and touched his hand. "Can you hear me?" she asked.

He blinked slowly, as if answering her question.

Despite Garth's attention, she looked back up into the blue ball of light, knowing Cletis was stepping up to the plate. "Bottom of the seventh," she announced. "We're down 6 to 4. Two outs. Runners on second and third, and Cletis is in the batter's box."

Garth's eyes widened a bit, and he fought to maintain focus on the images that moved within the orb.

"No sign of the Traveler yet," she continued, hoarsely. "But if there was ever a moment to show himself, this would be it. The kids on the Canterbury team are starting to give Cletis trouble about something. I don't know what they're saying to him. But they're provoking him to fight. They pushed him down in the outfield. Cletis has talked with Elston a couple of times, and so far, it looks like none of it has been friendly." She looked back down at Garth and patted his hand. "So things are happening under the surface. It's like a volcano out there, and I think we'll see it all erupt here soon."

Garth studied the blue orb, fighting to keep his eyes open.

"Time-out," called Coach Martin from the lip of the Canterbury dugout. The umpire granted it, and the wiry coach stepped away from his bucket to the foul line and invited his infielders to huddle around him.

Cletis limped out of the batter's box and took a few more practice swings, doing his best to work the heaviness out of his limbs. He sensed that their scheming against him was, in itself, a backhanded compliment.

But now is not the time to get cocky, he reminded himself. *There's more at stake here than just a game. Now is the time to think. Remember what happened this afternoon. Remember the instructions.*

Though the huddle was a beehive of sounds, Cletis could make out a sentence or two. Maybe that was the coach's intent. " . . . on the lip of the grass this time," and " . . . goin' home with it," were spoken loud enough for Cletis to understand.

Coach Martin grabbed the jersey of the pitcher, pulled him close, and whispered more directions. He then turned to Elston and pointed at him. Though what he said was indecipherable, Elston's response was much too loud for secrets.

"Coach, there are two outs and a runner on third. He's not gonna bunt."

"Am I the coach here or are you?!" Martin shouted back at him.

He whispered something else to Elston and then turned to his catcher.

"Do just as we discussed. Tell him everything I told you to. We're gonna win this right here!"

The boys, all except Elston, nodded their agreement. The huddle broke, and the players returned to their positions. The catcher, passing by Cletis at the batter's box, baited him immediately.

"You're never gonna touch this guy, witchboy," he whispered, knowing the ump was out of earshot.

Cletis pretended to ignore him. He looked suspiciously out at Elston. Their eyes met for a moment, but then Elston turned away.

"Fire in the hole!" yelled Mr. Howard from third.

Cletis stepped back to get the signs. The coach's two fists came together again, one on top of the other. Cletis got the message. As he stepped to the plate, the infield shift began again. The Canterbury infielders came in to the edge of the lawn and darted back and forth and in and out of their positions, faking one way, and then slanting off in the opposite direction. The outfielders were also in constant motion, scurrying into the gaps and then back into position. It was a strange dance to watch, and it worked again. Cletis was slightly out of his comfort zone.

If I can hit the gaps, Cletis told himself, *that'll score two runs. But he's probably gonna try to pitch me low for the grounder. Gotta make contact and drive it past 'em.*

As Timmy and Pauly took their leads, and as Elston moved closer to the plate for the bunt, the infielders suddenly began to chant, "Witchboy! Witchboy!"

Cletis studied the puzzling tactics Canterbury was using. *Elston is playin' in for the bunt? What's that all about? They think I'm buntin' with two outs and the game on the line? That's stupid.*

As if baffled by the strange strategy, even the umpires looked back and forth, from one to the other. The kids on the Sperry bench did the same thing, eyeing each other curiously as they leaned against the chainlink fence of the dugout.

"What are they sayin' ump?" called Frank from the Sperry bench.

"Come on, blue!" shouted Mrs. Klu from the stands. "Name calling? What's that all about?!"

The first pitch came in high and tight. The catcher rose to snag it, took several steps forward past the plate and fired it again to the pitcher. On the way back to his position, and making sure the ump wasn't looking, the catcher deliberately stepped on Cletis's foot—the right foot again. Viciously the catcher bore down, twisted, and then passed innocently by. When Cletis flinched and dropped to his knees with the pain, the catcher turned around and apologized.

"Oh, I'm so sorry," he said quietly. "I didn't mean to do that, witchboy." Politely he extended his hand.

The umpire turned around just in time to see Cletis slap away the catcher's hand. But the Greenberg Junction parents rose in the stands, having clearly seen the dirty play.

"Come on ump!" shouted Mrs. Kluzuski. "That was intentional. He walked right over his foot! Couldn't you see that?"

Rabbit's mom shouted something angrily in Spanish.

Cletis turned to Elston. "What'd you tell 'em?! Everything?"

"I don't know what's happenin' to me, Clete!" responded Elston, pleadingly. "Honest!"

"I trusted you!" shouted Cletis. "Man, you used to be my best friend!"

The umpire hastily intervened, stepping out in front of the plate. "That's enough, boys! Let's check the tempers and play ball."

Mr. Howard made his way toward the plate and helped Cletis to his feet. "You okay?" he questioned.

Cletis nodded and pulled away. His mind was racing.

"Drive it somewhere Clete. You can do it. Watch the outfielders and put it where they're not." With those words, Mr. Howard returned to the coach's box.

Cletis limped around home plate for a moment, catching his breath and trying to work off the pain. Finally he paused, checked the signs from third, and took his place at the plate. The "witchboy" chant began again and echoed eerily across the park. At the same time, the shifting process commenced among the infielders. Like darting flies under the diamond's lights, they criss-crossed back and forth between their positions. Elston moved up the line again, as if in preparation for the possible bunt. With such antics happening around him, the pitcher eyed the plate, checked his runners, and then fired home. The pitch came in low and outside.

"Stee-rike ONE!" bellowed the ump.

"That was outside!" Cletis yelled back at him, still feeling the pain in his foot as well as the frustration and the pressure of the whole situation.

"Young fellow, you wanna get tossed?" warned the ump.

Cletis exhaled, limped out of the box, took a few practice swings, and again eyed the field. His foot hurt badly. He was tired. He was afraid. He was alone. He wondered about his dad. He wondered about Abish. He wondered how he could face the Traveler alone. Swallowing hard, he took a deep breath and turned to Mr. Howard for the signs.

I've gotta focus on the moment. Just play the game pitch by pitch. Answers will come.

Mr. Howard simply clapped his hands and nodded his head. Turning back to the plate, Cletis studied the outfield gaps and limped into the batter's box. The infielders came in shallow, awaiting the pitch, and Elston was still way up the line from first.

There's no bunt comin'. Their coach should know that. Why's Elston still playin' so shallow? Cletis wondered. *What's that all about?*

When Cletis dug in at the plate, the chant began again.

"Witchboy! Witchboy! Witchboy!"

The shifting infielders darted back and forth again as the pitcher came set and eyed the plate. Rearing back and pushing forward, he threw home.

"Abish is dead," the catcher suddenly whispered.

Cletis, fearing truth in his words, dropped his concentration and instantly turned back to him. The pitch came in right down the middle and across the belt. Cletis saw where the catcher caught it. The boy didn't have to move his mitt at all.

That was the pitch to hit, and I let it go by!

"Stee-rike two!" bellowed the ump. "And catcher, that's your last warning! Anything more outta you, and the game's called!" Pulling his mask from his face, the ump lumbered over to the Canterbury dugout and faced Coach Martin. "Did you hear what I just told your catcher?"

"Yes, I did."

"And call the wolves off, Coach! No more chanting!"

"Come on, blue! All they're saying is 'which boy.' Which boy is gonna get this kid out?' That's all! There's nothing bad about that!"

"Change your chatter!" the ump demanded. "Or you forfeit the game!"

Nodding, Martin called out to his players. "Regular chatter guys. But loud as you can!" He spit a few sunflower seed shells onto the dirt in front of him and resumed his seat on the upside down bucket. "And Greg!" Coach Martin called to his catcher, "I said nothing over the plate!"

While the umpire plodded back to home plate, Cletis glared at the catcher. The kid smiled, winked, and fired the ball back to his pitcher. Still wondering about the last thing the catcher had said to him, Cletis turned to Elston. When their eyes met, Elston turned and made a rapid escape back toward the bag.

Was Abish dead? Was she hurt? How would Elston know that? Who would have told him? Was it a lie, or was it true? He turned and eyed the Canterbury bench. *Someone over there is pullin' information outta Elston . . . or givin' him some that I don't know about. And they're usin' it against me now. But I don't know if it's true or not.*

"Blanchard!" came the heated voice of Coach Martin. "Get up that line, like I told you!"

"There're two strikes, Coach!" Elston yelled back in frustration. "He's not gonna bunt now!"

"Play it my way or sit! Now get up there!" shouted Mr. Martin from the edge of the dugout. Snakelike, he turned to his catcher. "Give him the target! Where I told you! Nothin' gets by Elston! Challenge the batter!"

During the give-and-take, the Canterbury catcher leaned toward Cletis. "We know everything," he whispered, smoothing the dirt in front of him and then dropping back down into position.

Despite the anger he felt rising within him, Cletis didn't look at the catcher. Instead he studied Elston. *Everything I did with him, he's told 'em—the whole Canterbury team knows about what we did together? He promised me he'd keep our stuff secret! They probably think I'm outta my mind.* Cletis watched as Elston came up into position close to the batter's box. *And it's all to break my concentration, isn't it. It's all to make me mad at Elston and lose my temper at a really important time in the game.* Cletis looked at the bat, checked his grip, and eyed the pitcher. *Like right now . . .*

Suddenly, the reality of the situation struck him. *Oh, my gosh! That's why he's playin' him in for the bunt. It's all a set-up! I see it now . . . It's all according to his plan! I have to let him think they're gettin' to me. He's somehow playing Elston against me! I'm supposed to let him think I'm getting mad at Elston. I have to let it all happen. I think it's the only way this is all gonna come to a close! I have to let it all happen . . . for Abish. I have to do this for Abish and Dad. It's wrong, but it's right! I think this is the beginning of the end. And it has to happen right now!*

Instantly that amazing, familiar, wonderful feeling swept over Cletis. The sensation settled upon him like the warmth of a fire on a cold winter's day. It lifted his confused spirit and whispered peace to his heart.

Feelings will guide us, Abish said. Trust it. Trust them.

Cletis took a deep breath, exhaled, and stepped into the batter's box. Elston moved hesitantly further up the line. The Canterbury chatter began again— deafeningly. The bench and the outfield joined in. The players shouted and hollered, saying nothing in particular, but yelling at the top of their lungs. The infield began their frenzied, crazy shift again, darting back and forth on the edge of the grass as the pitcher eyed Timmy and Pauly, and came set.

Cletis watched it all again, as if it were all happening in slow motion. *I think this is the time,* he said to himself, swallowing nervously. *It's gotta be! I think everything is in place the way it should be.* "The son is as the father." *Allow your temper to get the best of you, Cletis Dungarvan! It's supposed to happen this way! This is where it has to end!*

"Pink tattoos on your shoulders," voiced the catcher, over the commotion of the infield.

Cletis allowed the words to pierce his soul. That's what they were meant to do.

He knew what had to be done. At last the final details were a clear reality to him.

Gotta let my anger build. It seems wrong! All wrong! But answers will come later. I know what to do, and I have to do it now! It'll be okay. Let 'em see it! Control your temper by losing it! It has to happen this way!

His thoughts screamed at him.

The pitcher fired the ball homeward. In a fraction of a second, Cletis eyed Elston. He stood a mere twelve feet up the line. The pitch came in high and away, perfect for what Cletis needed to do. *Let them see the anger!*

Suddenly Cletis heard himself yell.

"EAT THIS, YOU TRAITOR!!"

CRACK. With all his might he met the ball, slamming it directly at Elston. The ball crashed into the first baseman's forehead with a loud WHACK, dropping him where he stood. Bouncing off Elston's face, the ball rolled innocently across the grass and came to a delicate stop near the base line. Cletis dropped his bat and raced toward first. He looked down at his dear friend, who lay crumpled on his side, unconscious. Blood gushed from his nose onto the white chalk of the base line.

Abish looked on, horrified. Her hands shot to her mouth as she gasped. The wild anger in Cletis's eyes and the manner in which he drove the baseball with precise accuracy into Elston's face sent a shudder through her soul.

"How could he have done such a thing?" she called out, her mind racing in confusion. "What is he thinking?"

Garth looked on helplessly, studying the blue sphere above him but making no sound.

"It has come," stated Abish, dropping her hand from her mouth. "The final stages of the fulfillment are finally upon us. But at what cost?" Her eyes closed and she took a deep breath. "And here I sit in a hospital room while that dear boy faces the enemy alone." Nervously she rubbed her wide hands over her wrinkled, puffy face, pushing the loose skin up and down as she thought.

Abish glanced at the clock on the wall above Garth's bed. Though it currently read 8:51, the second hand was no longer moving. Her eyes drifted over to the monitors next to the bed. Their lights had stopped flashing, and the numbers were locked on the same pattern and readings. She looked out through the slightly open door to the room and spotted two nurses in the hallway. They appeared to be in conversation, but both were frozen and unmoving. With sudden panic, she glanced down at Garth and then back to the images within the blue vision.

"Garth," she spoke softly, "Garth . . . Cletis is the only one who is moving on the field." She turned and raced to the window. "Oh, no . . ."

Despite the fading light of day, she could clearly see what was happening on the street and in the parking lot below her. Nothing was in motion. People were in mid-stride crossing the street or walking on the sidewalks. One little boy who had jumped off the curb floated in mid-air, while his mother, at his side, looked down on him with a motionless smile. Drivers sat in their cars, staring straight ahead or out their side windows, frozen in position. Trucks, motorcycles, and other vehicles passing through the middle of the intersection were locked in their locations, still and unmoving. Even a bird that floated above the tree below their hospital window hung suspended in the moment—its wings pointing downward, its face looking up at the hospital wall in front of it.

Garth moaned painfully.

"Garth!" Abish called. "The monitors!" She turned from the window and raced back to his bed.

It was as she had figured. The machinery around his bed had ceased to function. The medicines and fluids that his body so desperately needed no longer flowed through the several tubes visible on his bed. Everything had come to a complete stop!

Garth's eyes slowly closed.

All of a sudden, another pinpoint of blue light appeared above Garth and expanded over him until it covered his entire body. The protective glow then dropped down upon him, enclosing him in a cocoon of shimmering soft light. Immediately Garth sucked in a deep breath, and his eyes opened wide. A look of surprise filled his countenance.

"Are you all right?" groaned Abish, bending toward him.

"Yes, I think so," he sighed through the radiant shield.

Abish studied the light curiously. "They have prepared all. They have provided all." She eyed him tenderly, and reaching through the light, she touched his hand. "Time is frozen," she whispered.

CHAPTER 21

TIME IS FROZEN

Standing on first base, Cletis surveyed the field curiously. In the time it took him to run there from home plate, all action—all life as he knew it—had come to an abrupt halt. As far as his eye could see, nothing moved. No one breathed. All was silent. Stepping cautiously back down the base path toward home, Cletis studied the frozen forms. Timmy, who was charging in from third base, hung in midair and mid-stride, his eyes riveted on the Canterbury first baseman who lay on the lawn near home plate. Pauly, running from second to third, had his back foot planted in the dirt while his front foot floated ten inches off the ground. He too was looking at Elston. In fact, as Cletis scanned the field and the stands, every single person—umps, players, scorekeepers, families, and fans—wore an expression of horror as they stared out at Elston. Coach Martin, too, was frozen in position. From his bucket-top seat next to the dugout steps, even he looked over at his young first baseman with panic and concern.

Fearfully Cletis walked back down the chalk line toward his fallen friend. He knelt down on the dirt next to him and reached out and touched Elston's hand. To his utter amazement, the hand was as solid as concrete. Cletis eyed his buddy curiously.

Placing his hand on the lawn near Elston's shoulder, Cletis yipped in pain and pulled his hand away.

"Ouch! Man, what is that?" The blades of grass were sharp and brittle, and when he lifted his palm to his face he discovered the grass had punctured his skin. Tiny droplets of blood formed red polka dots on his hand. "Man, what is that all about?" Cletis voiced curiously, shaking his hand and eyeing the grass next to Elston. Cautiously he rose and stepped onto the lawn. To his surprise, he found that the green blades crunched beneath his feet like shards of tiny icicles. His cleats left footprints on the broken lawn wherever he stepped.

In awe of his new surroundings, Cletis eyed Elston's hat lying nearby and bent to pick it up. To his surprise, the hat was as solid as Elston. Putting both hands under the brim, he lifted with all his might. Finally the hat budged. *It might as well be a hundred-pound anvil,* Cletis thought.

Again on his feet, Cletis eyed the field and the players, pondering the eerie strangeness of this new world.

He's gotta be around here somewhere. I can't feel him now, but I know he's here. Will the blue light protect me now?

He pulled his helmet off, wiped his brow with his sleeve, and walked cautiously back to home plate. He placed his helmet on the dirt in the batter's box next to his bat, as if saving his place there . . . as if hoping he'd eventually come back to this last at bat. *I'll find a way to get us all out of this,* Cletis thought as he anxiously studied the players on both teams, the umps, and even the people picnicking out by the scoreboard.

He took a deep breath and exhaled. *I gotta stay calm,* he told himself. For several moments he stood completely still and waited. Slowly turning toward the bleachers behind him, he studied the people in the stands. All remained hauntingly frozen, looking out on the field.

Cletis took several uneasy steps toward the backstop, taking special note of the drinking fountain directly in front of him, on the other side of the fence. Above the spout, little balls of water floated—arcing up into the air and then dropping down again toward the drain. The flowing of the water was caught in mid-movement, and the shining droplets were suspended in flight. Curious, Cletis decided to make the trip around the backstop and visit the fountain.

Keeping an eye out for any movement, Cletis walked past the dugout and onto the sidewalk behind it. As he stepped past the back of the dugout—in front of the people in the bleachers—Cletis had the creepy feeling that he was being watched. He shot a quick glance over at the Canterbury dugout. All was still. He studied Mrs. Klu, Johnny's mom, and Rabbit's mom where they stood. He eyed the Canterbury side of the stands—the children, the dogs, the parents. All were mannequins. *They're alive*, he thought, *and yet they're completely still—not breathing, not moving—like they're all seeing me, but they're not.*

He came to the fountain and bent closer to the water. Curiously he reached out a finger and touched the droplet closest to the drain. To his amazement, he could put his finger right through it. The shape of the shining little ball of water shifted and changed, yet the little drop remained there. Cletis noticed that his finger was a tiny bit wet, and lifting it toward his mouth, he touched his tongue to it.

I taste the wet, he told himself. *It still tastes like water, and it still feels like water. I can probably still drink it.*

Curious, he bent forward, and, doglike, lapped a droplet onto his tongue. Though it was solid at first, it finally dissolved in his mouth, like a piece of wiggling gelatin—water that had to be chewed. Swallowing it down, Cletis reached forward for more, and chewed and drank it all, until there were no more balls of water remaining in the air above the spout.

"That's weird," he said out loud, again breaking the cemetery silence that surrounded him. He immediately thought of the canal behind Abish's house, and how it would be to stand down into the middle of the running water—water that was kind of solid and gelatinlike—water that was locked in place by the freezing of time but was basically still water.

Cletis made his way back onto the field and walked over to where the baseball rested in fair territory on the lawn, about five feet in front of the plate. Tapping it with his foot, he was surprised to find that it rolled away. He took a few steps toward it and tapped it with his foot again. Once more, it rolled easily, this time toward home, stopping in the batter's box on the first base side of plate. Walking to it, he bent down, picked it up, and studied it curiously. For some reason, the present conditions that surrounded him—that made Elston's hat immovable and Elston's hand feel like granite—had no power over this little baseball. He tapped the bat with his foot. It too moved. *The ball, the helmet, and the bat,* Cletis reasoned. *Everything that was connected to me.* Warily he set the ball back in its place, and watched and waited and wondered.

A slight shuffling sound came from behind him. Startled, Cletis turned toward third base. Nothing moved. Feeling his heart beating in his chest, Cletis scanned the field. All was lifeless, frozen. *I know I heard something.* Again the sound came. Again from the third base side.

Slowly Coach Martin came to life. He tossed a few sunflower seeds into his mouth and began breaking the shells with his teeth.

"Well, well . . . I must say that I'm pleasantly surprised at you." Casually he rose from the bucket and walked toward Cletis. "I wasn't sure you'd make that choice," he continued, pointing toward Elston. "But you did. When the 'son is as the father.' Isn't that what the prophecy says? And now Time is frozen." He spit a seed shell from between his lips, and it floated to the grass near the third base line. "You deliberately hurt that boy—a boy who was once your friend. And now two other elements of the prophecy are fulfilled. Only a few other details remain. But it appears the time has come to make a choice."

Cletis eyed him silently, suddenly wondering again if the blue light would protect him in this new world. His heart raced within his chest, but he tried to act like all was under control.

"We're both in the middle of this prophecy thing, trying to see it fulfilled how we want," Coach Martin continued. "Some things you can't control, and some things I can't control." He spit another sunflower seed shell onto the dirt and tossed a few more fresh ones into his mouth. "So, for the present, I'll deal with the things that are within my control. For example, you can help me open the box, and we'll all get on with our lives." He spread his hands in front of him and the dark, wooden box materialized.

Cletis took a few steps back to the batter's box and sat down on the top of his helmet. His mind was racing, but he didn't want the Traveler to know he had no idea what he was supposed to do. More importantly, he didn't want the Traveler to know he was afraid. He swallowed and looked out over the playing field.

"You set things up here to trick me into making a choice . . . because I said I wouldn't help you. It was part of your plan. But it was part of my plan too. So now, you and me, we need to compromise," Cletis said.

Martin took several intense steps toward Cletis and extended his hand. An arc of light shot from his fingers toward the boy. Instantly the blue light encircled a suddenly cowering Cletis, protecting him from the rays of the destructive force. Immediately the Traveler dropped his hand, the arc of light disappeared, and the blue protective shell vanished from around Cletis. Clearly shaken by the attack, Cletis lowered his arms away from his head, sprang to his feet.

"That was a stupid thing to do!" shouted Cletis.

"My, look at that temper," Martin stated, pacing like a principal in front of a wayward student. "It keeps landing you in real trouble, doesn't it."

"If that light didn't protect me, you wouldn't have had anyone here to help you open the box!"

"You underestimate me, my son. It would have only stunned you and burned you a bit. I didn't give you a full force. What I did was basically a test—a test to find out if higher powers are still at work here. And they are. We're still being watched." He eyed the darkening sky above the lights. "Yes, in some strange Dungarvan way, we're being watched."

"You lied to me!" Despite his fear, Cletis bravely protested. With clenched fists, he eyed the Traveler. "Either that, or you just don't know what you're talking about. You said I wouldn't be protected once Time was frozen. And I am!"

"Actually, that surprised me," Martin responded thoughtfully. "That means my father had something to do with this specific moment of magic. Only a Traveler could create powers that operate within a realm of unmoving Time . . . an amazing trick."

Cletis took several defiant steps toward the Traveler. "I'm gonna tell you something right now, so you know exactly how I feel. Even though you did some nice things for me, I hate you for what you did to my dad! And I hate you for what you've done to Abish! You're a manipulating, old coward. If you didn't have that light stuff comin' out of your fingers, and if you didn't have power over Time, you'd be nothing but a dying, wrinkled old man."

"You know nothing about Abish. Her present situation is all her *own* doing."

For the first time, Cletis saw anger in the man.

"Did I make her as she is? No. That was *her* choice. Did she have to put herself in this bind? No. That was her choice too. And on top of all that, she has dragged your whole family into this, and it gets more dangerous as the prophecy is fulfilled. Is that my doing? No. That was hers! So don't blame *me* for your dilemma. Blame Abish!" The man turned away heatedly from Cletis. "I grow impatient. We will now play this game according to my rules."

The Traveler faced Timmy near third base and extended his arm. A blazing arc of red light flashed away from his fingertips, blasting into Timmy's frozen form. With a loud explosion and a shower of pink and white particles, Timmy was gone.

Cletis watched in horror, covering his face from the blast.

"WHAT ARE YOU DOING?" he shouted through the dust, taking several quick steps toward third base.

"I'm simply showing you that I'm not to be reckoned with. You help me open this box now, or one by one, these people on this field will be obliterated."

Cletis's hands went to the top of his head, and his eyes opened wide in panic. "WAIT! Wait a minute!" he yelled. "You gotta let me think about this! This is all too fast!" Tears began to well up in Cletis's eyes as he watched the dusty cloud settle around third base.

Martin eyed Cletis with pretended pity, then slowly lifted his head back and closed his eyes. Instantly the transformation began again. Although Cletis had witnessed the eerie alteration three different times now, the chilling, unnatural process still troubled him. The stretching and contracting of bones and tendons, and the groaning sounds made within the body frightened Cletis. The twisting and morphing was abnormal and creepy. The Traveler clutched the box firmly in his hands as his body shifted and pulled and moaned around it. Gradually the sagging, hunched form of the wrinkled and dying man took shape—the black leather hanging loosely from his skeleton-like frame. The black holes of Ian's eyes focused on Cletis, and as he faced him, he stepped closer.

"Here is the dying, crumpled old man you spoke of," the Traveler stated angrily. "But that is about to change."

Still holding the box, he turned and lifted his arm toward Pauly, at second base.

"NO!!" cried Cletis.

An arc of light shot from the Traveler's fingers and rocketed across the field, striking Pauly and the Canterbury shortstop, who stood behind Pauly. Both figures exploded at the same time, sending a cloud of particles high into the stillness of the frozen night.

"WHAT ARE YOU DOING?!" cried Cletis again as he watched in disbelief. His hands covered his face, and he dropped to his knees in the dirt. "What are you doing? Those are people! Those are my friends!"

"I told you, Cletis of Dungarvan, I mean to live! You have the power to help me do that. So I will do whatever it takes to convince you that this box must be opened!"

"What are you?! You just gonna wipe out everyone on this field?!"

"Perhaps. And if you are not able to restore Time to a moment just prior to this happening, these people will not be alive when Time resumes."

"But I can't do that!" Cletis pleaded. "I don't know how to do that!"

"Precisely why you need me," stated the Traveler.

Cletis knelt silently on the ground, frantically racking his brain for the ideas he needed—for the direction he had to take. *What am I supposed to do? I had an idea of what I needed to do, but now I'm lost. Do I let him destroy everyone here? I can't do that, cuz I don't know if I'll ever be able to have control over Time. I don't know if I can put things together again, so that Timmy and Pauly and that other boy will be alive again when Time comes back. This isn't the way this was supposed to turn out!*

In his desperate confusion, he shouted at the Traveler. "But how can I trust that you'll help me, if I decide to help you?"

"You can't. You see, that's why I said we're now playing by my rules."

"So if I help you, how do I get out of this frozen Time? How can I get things put back the way they were? How can I save my friends?"

"That's your problem. The Dungarvan clan, with the help of my father, learned how to travel. They sent you forward, didn't they? That was the work of my father and Abish's parents. They're controlling all of this. Or at least they think they are. And you can be sure they're watching us even as we speak. So you'll have to ask *them*." The Traveler lifted the box toward Cletis. "Open it! Now!"

"First, I want to know about Abish and my father. I want to know if—"

Before Cletis could finish, the Traveler stepped toward Klu, who stood frozen in the on-deck circle behind them, and lifted his hand toward the Sperry catcher.

"NO!" screamed Cletis, charging toward him and jumping between Klu and Traveler. "Don't! Please! He's my friend!" Cletis stood panting in front of the dark eyes of the intense, evil old being. "Okay, I'll help you!"

"Don't test my patience again!"

"What do you want me to do?" shouted Cletis back at him. "I don't know how to open that box!"

The Traveler extended it toward Cletis. "Touch the corners of it where it's sealed," he commanded, glaring at Cletis. "Just reach your finger out and touch the corner of it."

"What'll that do?"

"I imagine your touch will break the seals," he stated angrily, through clenched and broken teeth. "I don't know why or how. All I know is that only another Traveler—you, the 'new Traveler'—can break the magic."

Cletis took a deep breath. Still his mind was reeling, trying to figure out how to do what he had been instructed to do. Slowly he reached out his finger and touched a corner of the blackened box. Instantly the seal disappeared from that area, and the original brownish-golden color of the wood returned. The Traveler smiled, turned the box, and extended the next corner. Cletis touched it, and again the golden color was restored.

Cletis's mind continued to race, knowing he still had to find a way to accomplish what the man and woman told him must be done—a man and a woman he had never seen before until this afternoon—a man and woman whom he had met under the strangest of circumstances and in a place he did not recognize. Yet their instructions were sternly specific: get the box from the Traveler and learn to Transform. Learn to Change. Hesitating, Cletis reached his finger toward the third corner of the box. With his touch, again, the seal disappeared, and the true color returned. Only one corner of the box remained to be unsealed. Once it was touched, all four corners would be freed and the lid could be opened. If that were to come to pass, Cletis had no idea what would happen or how the powers of the box could renew the life of the old man that stood in front of him.

Suddenly a conduit formed around the Traveler, and he lifted off the ground within it. Floating freely, he turned the box again and extended the fourth corner toward Cletis.

It's like he's preparing for a getaway, thought Cletis, *and I can't let that happen.*

Cletis reached up through the conduit to touch the box, not knowing what exactly would happen. *But I gotta learn how to Change, and I gotta get the box! And I don't know how I'm gonna do that, but I gotta try somethin'!* At the same time, he realized that if he were unsuccessful, he would be lost in this frozen moment of Time, Abish would never be able to change back, and the Traveler would be set free with the box to renew his life and to continue his evil ways. As he pondered the consequences of his choices, his heart pounded in his ears.

Cletis extended his finger toward the fourth and final corner of the box. But inches before touching it, he pulled his hand quickly away.

"What are you doing?" demanded the Traveler.

"You teach me to Change first—to morph the way you do—and then I touch the last corner." Cletis stepped away defiantly.

"You foolish boy!"

Cletis looked up into the conduit, staring straight into the dark eyes of the Traveler. Though his knees shook and he felt as if he would drop to the dirt at any moment, he desperately and boldly stood his ground.

"NO!" cried the Traveler. "We are playing by my rules now!!" In his anger, the man raised his hand toward Cletis and released the flaming arc of fire and light. Again the protective blue shield pulsed into existence around Cletis, absorbing the blast.

Attempting to control the fear and emotions that welled up inside him, Cletis clenched his teeth and took a deep breath. With a roar, the fire danced against the shiny, blue orb. From within the safety of its shield, Cletis could see the hatred and desperation in the man's face, and he wondered if the blast was meant to kill.

"I will destroy all of these!" the Traveler cried furiously, pointing back to the boys on the field.

"Then go ahead! Destroy 'em!" shouted Cletis as the blue light faded around him. He stepped toward the old man. "You could've killed me right there! And if you did, you woulda rotted away in this frozen place with that stupid box still in your hands! So I guess it really doesn't matter now either way! Three dead or twenty dead, it really doesn't make any difference! If I can't get things put back together and right with Time, we're all goners anyway. So you go ahead and fire away!" Cletis, unflinching, looked up at the man in the conduit.

The two of them faced off. Cletis pretended to be brave, seeing that his comments silenced the withered, old man. Several seconds passed. "Teach me to morph—to Change—and I'll touch the final corner."

"And if I don't?"

"I don't know. I guess then, we wait around here until one of us dies. I don't know how long that'd be or how long I'd last. But I'll last at least as long as the blue light protects me. But *you* don't have much time left."

The Traveler eyed the boy heatedly. "You fool, you don't know what you ask. You want to be a Changeling? Is that what you're saying?"

Cletis swallowed. "Yes."

The old man glared at him. "Do you realize what that would mean?"

Cletis tried to be brave. "No . . . I don't."

"It would mean that you would have to be unprotected from the blue light in order to be taught. It would mean that from that point in Time onward, you would become a pure Traveler, and there would be no Dungarvan shield to baby-sit you. It would mean that I could kill you easily after that, if I chose to."

"How am I supposed to believe you? You lied to me before."

"It will have to be your choice. But this I know, you will be un-protected. For you will cease to be a Dungarvan. It means your mind will possess a portion of the knowledge of whomever you become. It means you will become as I am! You will feel a portion of what I feel. You will know some of what I know!" He cackled out an evil laugh. "Do you want that?"

Cletis studied him cautiously and nodded his head. "If I'm a Traveler, I want to learn what Traveler's can do," he stated with pretended confidence.

If he's willing to teach me, thought Cletis, *maybe it means he won't hurt me . . . or kill me. Or maybe not. I don't know. I gotta trust that man and woman. Then maybe I'll figure out what I need to do after that happens.*

The Traveler squinted, as if weighing his options. "'When the son is as the father' . . . perhaps there is more to that fulfillment than what has already taken place. After all, you *are* my son." The Traveler continued to float within the conduit, about a foot off the ground. Rubbing the top of the box as if it were a beloved pet, his dark eyes peered down at Cletis. With a cunning smile he extended his hand. "Come into the conduit with me."

"Not with the box in there with you," answered Cletis, swallow-ing against the dryness in his mouth. "You put the box away from us on the field, and then I'll come into the conduit."

"You know that I can make the box materialize in my hands whenever I want to."

"Yeah, I guess I do know that, but at least this way I can see it."

"Very well," the man replied, allowing the conduit to disappear around him. Holding the box, he floated to the ground. "You are certain you want to do this?" he asked again.

Cletis remained silent, trying to keep his legs steady.

The Traveler turned and walked toward the Canterbury dugout. At the steps, he bent down and placed the box on the dirt near the upside down seed bucket. "Does that satisfy you?" the man asked, turning to Cletis.

Cletis nodded nervously.

Again a conduit materialized around the Traveler, and he lifted off the ground within it. With a movement of his hand, the field of energy widened, as if in preparation to receive a second person. The man extended his arm to Cletis and invited him to enter. Completely unsure of what would happen next or how he could get out of his present dilemma, Cletis wiped his eyes and nose with the backside of his bloody hand and stepped fearfully into the conduit.

The second blue shield still surrounded Garth, and as he lay within it, he seemed to be more alert and comfortable. From their room in the hospital, Abish and Garth looked on, studying the scenes and images that moved within the blue sphere before them. Abish had watched Cletis's activity in frightened astonishment from the instant Elston was struck by the ball. In horror, she felt as if her world were crumbling to pieces around her. In her mind, Cletis should have controlled his temper, emotions, and frustrations. In her mind, the prophecy should have been fulfilled through the choices that Cletis made on the field—choices that represented his faithfulness to Abish, to good, and to the feelings that had guided him to that point. Her expectations of seeing the prophecy fulfilled in her favor seemed now a distant dream—almost a hopeless wish. She had watched in shock as the Traveler appeared before Cletis. She was horrified when the Traveler cold-bloodedly destroyed the three frozen forms of the boys on the field. In sadness, she had watched the heated confrontations between Cletis and the old man, until Cletis finally had given in before the cunning and power of the wicked man who had once been her husband. Grief-stricken, she looked on as Cletis touched the three corners of the box, giving new life to the old, blackened relic held in the hands of the Traveler.

And now her uneasiness and dread were magnified as she watched the Traveler pull Cletis up into the conduit.

"What is he doing now?" she pleaded, her eyes wide with panic and confusion. As if answering her own question, she continued, "He's either learning to Travel, or he's being taught how to Change." She stood and leaned closer to the blue sphere. "Garth," she added softly, "if he is taught the Changeling process, he will soon be out of the bounds of the family's protection. I fear that when that time comes, he will no longer be protected by the blue light, and we will no longer be able to see him within this orb."

Abish and Garth watched as Cletis lifted his hand to the hourglass mark on the Traveler's shoulder. Within the conduit, a sudden radiant surge seemed to shake Cletis, and Abish could see fear etched upon his wide-eyed countenance.

"No, Cletis!" moaned Abish, taking a step away from the light. Her hand went to her mouth. "If he is Changing, then his mind will become one with Ian's. Garth, he won't be able to bear it!"

Suddenly the blue orb of visions fragmented before their eyes, like a balloon bursting with the prick of a pin—only silently. Abish lifted her arms in front of her, as if to shield herself from the soundless explosion. To her amazement, the orb was gone.

"What's happening?" whispered Garth.

Abish turned to him sadly. "He is no longer a Dungarvan. He has become one with the family of the Travelers."

Within the conduit, Cletis's left hand pressed against the hourglass mark on the front of Traveler's right shoulder. The painless, yet forceful, jolt of power from the Traveler had surprised Cletis. There was a feeling of strength that had accompanied it, yet at the same time, a familiar sense of lightness coursed through him.

"You feel that power that surges through the bodies of two Travelers?" questioned the old man.

Cletis nodded, his eyes alert with the shock of the new experience. He felt small and weak, now clearly at the mercies of the evil man in front of him.

"That surge used to be much stronger," stated the Traveler, holding Cletis's hand in position next to the black leather. "Keep your hand there. You'll get used to it." Taking Cletis's right hand, he lifted it up into position over the hourglass mark on his opposite shoulder. The old man seemed instantly excited to be teaching Cletis what he knew. Again Cletis felt a surge of power, this one entering his right hand.

Cletis watched in wonder as the Traveler lifted his head back and closed his eyes tightly. Through his contact on the old man's shoulder, Cletis instantly felt a renewed rush of power that filled every fiber of his being and seemed to dismember him from the inside, out. Something strange and fascinating was happening within him, and he felt his eyes close and his neck crane backward.

An image of the young Traveler fired into Cletis's mind, placed there by a power beyond his control. Astonishingly, yet painlessly, he felt bursts of motion inside his body. It began deep within him, as if his internal organs stirred with independent life. Then, with another surge of energy, he felt his bones soften. His skeleton, muscles, tendons, and flesh were instantly alive with movement. Unable to control the contortions and shifting, Cletis felt his body meld and bend and twist, taking upon itself an entirely new shape. A slight groaning seemed to come from within him as his entire being engaged in this unique Changeling metamorphosis. Even his hair and teeth and eyes seemed to shift and alter with the physical transition. Still there was no pain. It all happened as if Cletis were watching it from inside himself. He felt as if he had stepped on board a strange, awful ride, with no idea of when, where, or how the trip would end.

Within the deepest recesses of Cletis's brain, images gradually began to flutter into view. The lush, springtime greens of an Irish landscape appeared, within the roll and dip of gentle hills, lofty mountains, and valley forests. Faces and places and dwellings cascaded before him, with warm fires and cozy huts, the smell of roasted boar, and the sounds of laughter. The images of families and festivals and rosy-cheeked children spun and flitted through his mind's eye, building one upon another—as if gracefully illustrating the story of a charmed life. A ruddy and rugged young man appeared, muscular and athletic, intelligent and resourceful, leading friends in play— leading armies and peoples into battle. It was Ian, beloved of the clan, village, and kingdom. Cletis identified him immediately. He was a hero and a friend to all.

A beautiful young lady with flowing auburn hair suddenly emerged within the portrait Cletis absorbed, appearing in a thousand graceful images, becoming a central character on the rich, mental landscape. A child was carried tenderly in the young lady's arms—a child with white hair and one eye fixed to the side. They called him Torlock, "he who comes to help." Cletis could see that the little one brought joy and hope to the family. There was a goodness to this young couple—nobility and graciousness. Their powers were admired. Cletis felt it. *Felt it.*

But then, a gradual change. Powerful images of evil and hatred, selfishness and pain, materialized in the panorama. Places and people Cletis had never seen before passed rapidly before his view. Drums, armies, forces of battle, vistas of warfare ravaged the peaceful portrait. Scenes of pointless death, torture, tears, and broken hearts violated the earlier images of unique goodness. Devastating fire and destruction, cities destroyed, and bodies lifeless, now littered the landscape of Cletis's mind. A vapor of darkness steadily clouded the vision—the fog of betrayal, the haze of hopelessness. The woman with the auburn hair wept within a lodge, the baby in her arms. A gray conduit dissolved in front of her. Then sudden blackness.

Cletis's head throbbed. The haunting images filled his mind with horror. The despair of dashed hopes tore at his heart. In his increasing anguish, the familiar darkness—the ugly, cold, horrible feelings that had accompanied the presence of the Traveler—intensified as never before. In nauseating pain, Cletis felt his hands pull from the Traveler's shoulders and instantly clutch at the sides of his head. Despite his agony, Cletis sensed the difference in his being—his body. His hands were bigger and stronger. His hair was long and thick. Though fighting the staggering pain of the sickening, disabling feelings, Cletis kept his eyes tightly shut.

Gradually, within his mind, despite the horror he both saw and felt, there came a clear understanding of how the Changeling process took place. It were as if two different parts of his brain were working simultaneously through the odd morphing—one part striving to cope with the overwhelming agonies that tormented him, the other sorting through the details of physical transformation. With focused concentration on the Changeling act—the physical transformation—he saw the process clearly, and he understood the source of the mental power used to channel that gift through the entire course of an alteration. Not only that, but he instantly understood the processes of transporting and how the powers of the conduit, along with personal concentration, could assist in the Traveling from one location to another. Yet he noted that he had not received from Ian any understanding of the Lightfire power that he had used against Cletis. Nor did the old man reveal the secrets of Time travel or the control of Time. It was like he had blocked those processes.

With this limited grasp of his newfound gifts tucked stealthily away in his brain, the horror of the Traveler's dark deeds returned in full force. The countless images of destruction, for which the Traveler had been selfishly and deliberately responsible, wracked Cletis's brain. Still holding his head, he felt the pain rise to a final intolerable level.

"AUGHHHH!!" Cletis screamed.

He pushed through the wall of the conduit, fell to the ground below, and rolled on the dirt in front of the dugout. His mind was on fire.

"NOOOO!" he cried, in torment. "AUGHHH! I CAN'T DO THIS! IT'S KILLING ME!!" he roared, in a voice different from his own.

He forced himself to stand but staggered to keep his balance. Still holding his head, he leaned against the dugout fence. His eyes opened slowly, and he looked down upon himself. A long, blond braid hung over his right shoulder. The baseball uniform that had once covered his body was now replaced by black, leathery clothing and dark boots. He recognized the muscular frame at once. Taking a deep breath, he sensed the strength and power of this large, masculine body.

Laughter roared from the conduit above him.

"Now you and I are one! You know the ways and secrets of the Travelers—at least those that I chose to share with you. And now, the 'son is as the father,' in a very real way! The prophecy was correct again!" Once more he laughed. "That is but a taste of the power you possess. Yet I have given you only enough knowledge to confuse you. You will never be a threat to me, dear boy. Other mysteries are locked within the box, but they will never be revealed to you. No one will ever teach you!" He laughed again, as the gray conduit gradually disappeared around him. The old man floated to the ground, walked to the box, and magically summoned it into his hands.

The final corner was yet to be touched.

With a forced concentration, Cletis began the transformation back into his real self. The process took less time than he thought it would, and it almost felt natural and comfortable. When the act was done and Cletis opened his eyes again, he looked down at his twelve-year-old frame—at the Cletis Dungarvan who still wore the Sperry baseball uniform and the rubber cleats. He slowly lifted his head and looked up at the Traveler. The old man, hawklike, studied him.

"Oh, it is so rapid when you are young!" the Traveler hissed. "It is magic to behold. You have learned it well for one so young—as if you have done it before. But coming out of a shape is one thing . . . assuming a shape, and holding it is a more difficult task. I helped you with the first time, but you will be on your own in the future."

Cletis sensed that one step in the course he was directed to follow was now completed. He eyed the box in the Traveler's hands and wondered how he could take it from him.

"I saw where I was born," began Cletis, stepping unsteadily toward the old man. Though the nauseating, haunting feelings faded, his head pounded painfully with the horrors of the revolting scenes that holed up in his brain. The images sickened him, yet with all his mental might, he was unsuccessful in pushing them from the trenches of his mind.

"I saw you and the lady with the red hair," Cletis spoke, fighting through the pain. "She was beautiful."

"You know who that was," the old man spoke coldly.

"Yes . . . and I saw that you were once good."

"My young boy, you will soon learn that there is no good or evil. There is only attaining what you want. There is only survival."

A blue conduit unexpectedly materialized around Cletis, surprising both him and the Traveler. The old man's eyes opened wide in wonder as he watched the energy gather. With the coming of the conduit, Cletis was instantly filled with that familiar, warm and wonderful sensation.

I must be doin' something right, he thought. *But I still gotta get the box, and I don't know how I'm gonna do it.*

Engulfed by the conduit and new, refreshing feelings, a portion of the prophecy abruptly burst into his mind: " . . . unsealing the box by the hand of his power. Then shall the box know him." Cletis gasped with the idea. *Maybe that's it! The prophecy knows!* With a sense of what had to be done, and hoping he was right, Cletis stepped toward the man who was once his father. With the energy of this new conduit still surrounding him, Cletis reached toward the sealed corner of the box. The old man watched him suspiciously, as if concerned by the emergence of the humming, blue field that encompassed the boy.

"Did you conjure that?" asked the Traveler, eyeing the blue conduit.

"What do you think?" answered Cletis, pretending to know exactly what he was doing, at the same time attempting to hide the pain of the continuous pounding in his head. He reached for the box. "My part of the bargain," he stated, matter-of-factly.

"Yes, it is," the Traveler replied, looking on anxiously.

Cletis's finger touched the fourth corner of the wooden relic. The seal disappeared instantly, and the blackness of the remaining area changed to a golden brown.

The old man smiled adoringly down on it. "At last!" he breathed. "The powers of the box are mine again!" He held it reverently in his grasp and allowed a gray conduit to gather around him. "And now there is no need for you."

He lifted his arm toward Cletis.

Suddenly the box glowed with a red light, trembled slightly under the Traveler's arm, and then disappeared from his grasp. Instantly it reappeared within the blue light of Cletis's conduit and floated, light as a bubble, in front of him. Cletis gasped, then lifted his face to the Traveler. The old man was awestruck. His eyes and mouth were opened wide, confused by what had happened.

"'Then shall the box know him,'" Cletis recited, wrapping his arms around the box. Concentrating on the ancient village, Cletis watched the blue conduit surge magically around him.

"IT SHALL KNOW *ME*!" screamed the Traveler, raising his arms toward Cletis. "IT IS MINE!"

Fire shot from the outstretched fingers of the Traveler, but the glowing stream of power passed harmlessly through the disappearing blue conduit.

"I WILL FOLLOW YOU! . . . " were the last words that Cletis heard as the field, the game, the frozen figures, and the Traveler, faded into oblivion.

CHAPTER 22

FACING DEATH

Cletis had experienced the weightlessness of the energy field twice before, at least that he could remember. He could recall nothing of the time he was sent forward as a tiny child, nor could he remember anything about the trip to Cincinnati. But the travel back to Belleville, where he saw his mom at his old house, was still vivid in his memory.

The second time was today just before the game. It was somewhat accidental, but it taught him things the Traveler didn't realize he knew. Cletis hadn't yet had the chance to share the experience with Abish or his Dad, but now, within the protection of the blue conduit, the details of the afternoon's experience raced through his mind.

Mrs. Klu had dropped him off at his home, where he had hurried to his room. Still with his hat and cleats on and his mitt latched through his belt, he had pressed the marks on his shoulders, just as he had done in the hospital room. He had wondered about the sensation of energy and lightness he had felt, and he had questioned if the red images were somehow connected to the power hidden within him. When he pressed on the marks, he had sensed an amazing energy and weightlessness flow through him. He remembered how the blue aura of the conduit had gathered around him. Then, within the conduit, a power beyond his control had taken him, as if with the speed of thought, to a different time and place. There, in a large, cabinlike lodge, he found himself standing before two people—a man and a woman. They were alone, as if awaiting his coming. The man had introduced himself as Mahon and had given Cletis instructions.

"You must learn to Change," he had said. "And you must return with the box."

Who the two people were or how they knew him, Cletis had no idea, but the *feelings* that accompanied his visit there were overpoweringly sweet, and the two persons seemed to know all about his situation and the details that surrounded the prophecy. And then, in complete fear, filled with near hopelessness but following their direction, Cletis had allowed the blue light to gather around him again. Focusing his thoughts on the baseball park and the upcoming game—as he was instructed to do—Cletis found himself, almost instantaneously, softly dropping to the ground in the grove of trees near the right field, foul-line fence. With all of those events in his mind, Cletis had walked unsteadily over to the dugout near first base and had joined his team there just prior to the game.

As the blue light of the conduit dissolved around him, Cletis floated to the ground and found himself standing, again, in the large, round, open lodge he had visited that afternoon before the game. The floor was of dirt, seemingly packed in place by the feet of those who had often used the structure. The walls that surrounded him appeared to have been made from upright, cut logs that had been dropped into the ground, one next to the other, and then set soundly in position deep within the earth. Three large wooden pillars, in the middle of the open space, also set similarly into the ground, supported the ceiling, which must have been close to fifteen feet high. In the middle of the three pillars was a rock firepit and, above it all, an opening in the roof, through which Cletis assumed smoke could ascend. Shafts of light entered the lodge through the opening above him, as well as through the three open doorways that led to the outside village. From where he stood, he could see men, women, and children passing by the lodge, busy with their daily activities. Several small wooden and block dwellings were also visible through the doorway, each surrounded by colorful flowers and vegetable gardens.

Cletis's body and brain demanded a moment's rest, so he simply stood and breathed and looked around him. Though his head still pounded with the dismal visions of Ian's former life, and his body

ached, he found a quiet tranquility in this place, as well as a remarkable sense of protection.

He turned and wandered toward the middle of the lodge. Several
meters away to his right stood two people near a table by the far wall.
He studied them as they walked toward him. With their approach,
the peaceful feeling that had filled him when the blue conduit had
formed was suddenly magnified. His flesh tingled and his hair stood
on end as they stepped closer. He recognized them instantly. He
had been with them earlier. He inhaled deeply as the warm sensation
bathed him. Whatever the impression was, it filled him with a confidence that what he was doing was good and right, no matter how
frightening and odd it happened to be. Now more than ever he wanted
that calm security to stay with him.

The man and the woman were taller than Cletis. By the way they
held hands and leaned in to one another as they walked, he figured they
were probably husband and wife. When they stepped into the light of
the opening in the ceiling, Cletis could see they both wore beige, woolen,
belted robes. Below their robes were dark, leathery boots, similar to those
worn by Abish. The man had a neatly trimmed, white beard that was
close to two inches in length, and his wavy, long, white hair hung close to
his shoulders and rested upon the hood that draped down his back. The
woman was slender, tall, and though partially hooded, Cletis could see
that her hair was as white as the man's. She appeared to have been weeping, for she wiped both cheeks with a quick, graceful pass of her hand.
Yet she wore a smile as she and the man stepped closer to Cletis.

Though Cletis had seen the woman in his earlier meeting, she
hadn't spoken to him. The man had done all the talking. *His name is
Mahon,* Cletis reminded himself, thinking back on their first moments
together. Cletis studied the man submissively, knowing that he was the
one who had given him specific instructions about the circumstances
relating to the baseball game and how he could recognize and prepare
for the difficult decisions that had to be made in order to set in motion
the fulfillment of the prophecy.

Mahon stepped closer. His manner was soothing and reassuring.
He is the one who told me I had to learn to Change. He told me I had

to return with the box. With that thought, Cletis looked down at the golden square in his hands. *I don't want this old thing. I hope he takes it and throws it away.*

In Mahon's right hand, he carried what appeared to be a deep, rounded, wooden spoon. He kept it level as he lifted it to Cletis.

"It's water," he simply said. "If you'd like, drink it." The man's voice was deep and resonant, and his way of speaking was similar to Abish's, with a music and lilt to his words. It was sweet to the ear and left Cletis wanting to hear more.

Still dizzy with the throbbing in his head, Cletis tucked the box under his arm, took the spoon, and swallowed down the water. He handed the spoon back to the man and wiped a few drops from his chin.

"Thank you."

"Cletis, Torlock of Dungarvan, you are welcome." The man spoke reverently.

Puzzled by the tone of his words, Cletis took the box from under his arm and lifted it to the bearded man. But to his surprise, the man raised his hand in front of him, rejecting it.

"The box is yours, Cletis," he said softly. "You must keep it. There is still a great work to be done, and the box will assist you in that effort."

"But I've done everything you told me to do," Cletis stated, squinting his eyes against the pain in his head. "Time has stopped where I live. My friends and everyone else—they're all frozen, hard as rocks. I've learned to Change—but I'm still not very good at it. And I have the box." He held it up again. "Did I miss anything?"

"You have done well."

"So is Abish free? Has she changed back?"

"No, she has not. That will not take place until the Traveler is confined."

"You mean like put back in prison?"

Mahon nodded.

"When is that gonna happen?" Cletis asked.

"Soon, we hope."

"Yeah," agreed Cletis, "the sooner the better, I think." Cletis brought his hand to his forehead and massaged his skin above his eyes. "How's that gonna happen?"

The man took a breath, glanced at the woman, and then turned back to Cletis. "That, my brave boy, is your job."

Cletis's hand dropped heavily back to his side. "What?"

Mahon reached out and touched Cletis's shoulder. "Yes. You are the one to do it."

Cletis stepped back away from him. "Me? Why? I can't do that."

"You are a Traveler, Cletis . . . and you are the only one the box will recognize. No one else but you can do what needs to be done. You are the one to confine him."

"But . . . how? I'm just a kid! I don't know anything about this world of yours and all this stuff about powers and magic."

Cletis stepped back again. He was exhausted. He eyed the two of them questioningly. He felt the sudden heaviness of the box in his hands and looked down at the writing inscribed on the lid.

The woman began to weep. She turned her back to Cletis and leaned her head against the man's shoulder. The lady reminded him of his mother—tall, graceful, sensitive.

They know about Dad and Abish. They know about the Traveler. But he says I'm the only one who . . . Who am I? . . . He looked back down at the box. His head throbbed. *But so far every part of the prophecy has been fulfilled. So far the feelings have guided me. But do I trust these people? I don't even know them, and I don't know where all this is gonna end . . . and I'm scared.* He looked up at the tall man in front of him.

Mahon studied him, allowing him his quiet moment of thought.

They must know what they're doing. And I know for sure that the old man back at home is my enemy . . . so I guess that puts me on the same team with these two people, whoever they are.

There was a long pause.

"How am I supposed to do what I have to do?" Cletis finally asked.

Mahon pointed to the box in Cletis's hands. "The Traveler's box will guide you," he answered solemnly. He leaned in closer. "The box must be opened. When it is, you will see words appear— a phrase. Those exact words must be recited with the box open toward the Traveler."

"Wait . . . I . . . That means I gotta get close to him," trembled Cletis, frightened by the thought of facing the Traveler again. "He'll kill me. That's what he was tryin' to do when I got away!"

"He needs the powers of the box in order to continue living, and he knows that. But now the box will recognize only you," Mahon continued. "You are the new Keeper. But the box can still be used to his advantage, and he will strive to take its magic. You now have powers to match his. He grows weaker, but he is still forceful. Be careful."

"What powers? I don't have any powers!"

"You can transport. You are now a Changeling. Time is also now your tool."

Cletis felt his knees buckle, and he dropped into a sitting position on the dirt in front of Mahon. "What about Abish and my dad?" Cletis questioned, lifting his hand to steady his quivering bottom lip.

"All is well with them, for the moment," stated Mahon. "As I said, what you have to do can only be done by a Traveler. We had power to confine him for a time, but your power is unique. Your power will banish him completely. His banishment will literally save the world from the evil he plans. And you have witnessed the evil he is capable of committing. That will continue if he goes on."

Cletis sat thoughtfully in front of the couple.

"One other thing, Cletis," stated Mahon, squatting in front of him. "The blue light will not protect you now. Ian spoke the truth. In the realm of two Travelers—two Changelings—there is nothing that can protect either of them from one another. You will have to rely on your speed and your wits."

"Cletis," the woman spoke gently, stepping forward. "We know you are concerned. We know you have doubts and questions. We know it is dangerous." She paused and again wiped tears from her eyes. "But there is much at stake."

"Do you know where he is right now?" Cletis whispered. He studied her pretty face and her white hair. "I heard him say, 'I will follow you.' Does that mean he will he come here?"

"No, he will not come here. He will wait for you there. When you return to your home, your land, he will sense where you are, and he will find you. But you can do the same with him. You will know where he is."

Cletis thought about that for a moment.

"Remember another important detail," added the white-haired man. "You cannot Change into another person unless you have something that *is* that person. Any likeness will do . . . or a hair or a fingernail or a tooth. That may sound strange, but it is the reality of the Changeling. Did Ian teach you this?"

"I don't think so."

Cletis eyed the man, then allowed his gaze to drift again to the woman. She smiled wearily back at him, stepped forward, and knelt gracefully in front of him. She took his free hand in hers and looked up into his face.

"My name is Teagan. I am Abish's mother," she whispered. She was a beautiful woman, with soft, white skin and clear, green eyes. Cletis thought of Abish, for their eyes were almost exactly the same. She lifted her hand toward the bearded man next to her, and added, "And Mahon, my husband, is her father." The old man put his hand lovingly on Teagan's shoulder, yet kept his eyes keenly locked on Cletis. "What you do for us," she continued, "will save our daughter and many others too. And only *you* can do it. You are a Traveler. So, you see, you are a savior to our family, and we will always be grateful to you for your brave efforts."

"You're Abish's mom and dad?" Cletis squinted.

"Yes, we are," she responded.

Cletis studied her. *Man . . . What is happening to me? . . .* He took a deep breath and scratched his head through his cap. *Yeah, but what if I can't do it? What if I don't win this battle? What if I can't figure out a way to beat him?* He looked back up at Mahon.

"We know you have doubts, my son," spoke Mahon, as if reading Cletis's mind. "But we will try to help you in any way we can."

"But it's pretty much up to me?"

They studied him seriously and both nodded at the same time.

A thousand questions pounded through his aching head, but he voiced only one of them. "So are you my real grandparents?"

Teagan looked up into his eyes. "Yes, we are, Torlock."

He gradually smiled at the thought and at the way she pronounced his old name. The woman began to weep again, and the sight of her tender tears brought more of the same to Cletis's eyes. Bravely he tried to fight them back but was unsuccessful. She reached toward him and, with a featherlike touch, wiped them away as they rolled down his cheeks.

Still fearful, Cletis stood up. By the power of thought, he allowed the blue light to gather around him, and as he pictured in his mind the time and destination he needed, he wrapped the box between his arms and pressed on the hourglass marks on his shoulders. Mahon, Teagan, and the lodge vanished instantly from his sight.

Abish stood at the window of the hospital room, studying the frozen forms on the street and lawns below. She and Garth still moved and lived within this lonely moment of suspended Time, but she had no idea how long it would last. Soon food and water would be an issue of concern—more for Garth than for her. But with the blue light that still hovered around Garth, she at least knew that the Dungarvan family was looking on from some distant perspective, still protecting them as much as they could.

She walked back to the bed, wondering about Cletis—where he was, *how* he was. The last she had seen of the boy, he was with the Traveler in the conduit. *If I cannot see the boy,* she asked herself, *is it the same with my family? Can they see him? If my blue vision disappears here, has the same thing happened in their time and place?*

She sat thoughtfully, eyeing the frozen monitors next to Garth's bed, when she heard him moan slightly. She rose and stood over him, seeing him through the film of blue that shrouded his injured body. His eyes were focused over her shoulder, toward the center of the room.

"Light . . . " he whispered hoarsely.

She turned quickly, hoping to see what he was seeing.

There, above the bed, a pinpoint, blue dot hung brilliantly in the air and hovered momentarily, growing brighter as it floated. Gradually the orb expanded, tossing its blue light in all directions, filling the room with a soft radiance. Abish's eyes squinted momentarily, as the beaming ball transformed into the round, familiar, visionary sphere through which she had so often watched the endeavors of the Dungarvan family.

"What have they done to bring it back?" she asked aloud. "If he is a Traveler, I shouldn't be able to find him or see him through the power of the orb."

Cletis appeared behind the center field fence and allowed the conduit to hover about him. Cautiously he searched the field for the Traveler as he floated to the ground. *This was a bad place to land. I gotta get better at controllin' where I show up. He can see me too easily here.* He opened the box and directed it toward the diamond in front of him. With each step forward, the grass fractured noisily under his cleats. He remembered touching the grass by Elston and looked down at the dark, dried blood on his palm.

The Traveler appeared suddenly behind second base, and as the gray conduit dematerialized, he floated to the ground and walked across the outfield lawn toward Cletis. The crunching of the grass under each step filled the park with a strange, unseasonal sound. Cletis held his position and watched the man as he drew nearer—at the same time constantly checking the inside of the box for the words he was told would appear.

Man, I'm out here in the middle of nowhere where there's no place to hide. There's no protection here! This fence isn't gonna do nothin' for me if he fires.

Slowly, a red inscription began to form and glow on the inside, bottom panel of the box. Letter-by-letter and word-by-word, a message appeared on the ancient wood.

TIME THAT GAVE . . .

The Traveler stepped ever closer, eyeing the opened box in Cletis's hands.

"What will you do now, Cletis of Dungarvan, my son?" he called, as he approached the frozen figure of the Canterbury centerfielder.

Cletis lifted his eyes to the Traveler. Instantly the cold, dark feelings overwhelmed him. Bending at the middle, his vision blurred. Fighting to maintain his balance, Cletis grabbed the fence and placed the opened box on the bar in front of him. His eyes darted back and forth between the box and the Traveler, as the message slowly appeared.

Come on! Hurry! I'm dead standin' here!

TIME THAT GAVE DOTH . . .

Is that all there is, or is there more? Step by step the Traveler came closer. Cletis's stomach ached, and he coughed with nausea. *I don't' think that's all of what it's supposed to say, but I gotta try it. He's too close!*

Cletis frantically called out the words: "Time that gave doth now . . . !"

A bright light shot from the Traveler's hands and crashed with a roar into the chainlink fence in front of Cletis, instantly burning the pennants and banners that hung there. The force of the explosion threw Cletis backward onto the lawn behind him. As he landed, the tiny blades of grass, like dozens of sharpened pins, stabbed into the flesh of his arms and legs. With a cry of pain, he rolled to his side and rose to a low squat. His hands were empty.

The box!! Where is it?!

Frantically, through the smoke and the burning metal, Cletis searched the lawns around him. *Where is it? I can't lose it!!* Before him, the entire metal barring of the fence where he had stood glowed red-hot. The finer chainlink below it blackened and crumbled where it had been struck by the Lightfire.

Now close to the centerfield scoreboard and only feet away from the frozen family that was picnicking there, Cletis was still unprotected except for the shroud of smoke. Through the destruction of the smoldering fence, he scanned the field in search of the box. He could hear the crunch of the grass as the Traveler came on. Finally, Cletis spotted it—on the outfield grass in front of the charred fence about fifteen feet away from where he now squatted.

After all that work, I lose the box! No!! There's no way I can reach it now before he fires at me again. If I try, I'm dead!

"THEY TAUGHT YOU!" the Traveler cried out, stepping onto the warning track by the smoking fence. "THEY TAUGHT YOU, DIDN'T THEY?"

More fire roared from his fingertips, and as it shot through the remains of the scorched fence, Cletis watched the protective blue light of the Dungarvan conduit envelop him. The lawn, where he once crouched, erupted in flames and crackled with the heat that seared it to stubble.

Guiding the blue energy, Cletis dropped down behind the stands in back of home plate. From there, he could still see the Traveler. He knew he had to get the box back, and until he could, he realized he had no power to stop the old man's attacks. Now, through the mannequin-like legs of the people in the bleachers, Cletis anxiously watched the Traveler kick down the charred, center field fence and approached the wooden relic.

Cletis watched him bend low to study the box. It was still open, and as he looked in, Cletis was sure he was reading the partial phrase that had appeared on the bottom panel. "Time that gave doth now . . ." Those were the last words Cletis had seen.

The Traveler arose and studied the field.

He knows I'm close. Why doesn't he pick up the box?

The old man scanned the Sperry dugout and the fence on the right field foul line. "Here's your box, Cletis of Dungarvan!" he cried over the quiet of the park. "But you'll have to go through me to get it! And you don't have the powers to battle me yet. You're incapable of it!" He turned suddenly toward the stands behind home plate and looked straight in Cletis's direction. "We can stay in this predicament until we die. And certainly, if the man you call your father isn't dead already, he soon will be! It's time you faced your battle!"

Why doesn't he pick it up? Does he think it will come to me again if he touches it? Just like last time?

Cletis's head and heart still pounded. He looked down at his arms and hands and saw that they were bleeding from the dozens of tiny incisions made by the blades of grass. He glanced back out at the Traveler, knowing that the man knew right where he was.

What if Dad is dying . . . or dead? Cletis pondered. *With time stopped, what happens in the hospital to all that stuff around Dad? What if the Traveler's tellin' the truth this time? I gotta get to the box and finish this whole thing.*

The words of Mahon coursed through his brain. *Your wits and your speed,* remembered Cletis. *That's what he told me—but how?*

An idea came to mind. He stepped beside the snack shack, and as the conduit closed around him, Cletis disappeared in the flow of blue energy.

Abish studied the sphere of visions that floated in front of her, revealing the images of Cletis and the Traveler as they battled for possession of the box. She watched with fear as the Lightfire of the Traveler blasted the fence where Cletis stood, sending the box flying from the boy's hands. She trembled to think of the box in the Traveler's possession and wondered why the old man left it lying on the grass. She watched with concern as Cletis appeared and then disappeared behind the bleachers by home plate.

"He's gone," she whispered to Garth. "I don't see him anymore. He's lost the box, and now I'm not certain what he's doing or where he is."

As she pondered, another blue light suddenly appeared behind her, filling the room with its soft glow. Abish turned and gasped as she watched it materialize. Instantly Cletis was there with them, surrounded in the radiance of the conduit. He dropped to the floor and, at once, ran to the fleshy embrace of the large, old woman with the beautiful green eyes. He held her tightly for a moment, panting, exhausted, and scared.

As she looked down at him, she noticed the bleeding on his arms. "Oh, Cletis, what have you done!"

"My head hurts a lot worse than my arms."

He immediately pulled away and went to his father's bedside where he reached through the blue shell, took his father's hand and gently squeezed it.

Garth smiled weakly back at him. "Hi," he whispered from under the oxygen mask.

"You're alive," Cletis whispered, trying to control his panting.

"I think I still am," his dad responded.

"I didn't know. How are you doin'?"

"Been better."

Cletis studied him for a moment and then turned back to Abish, as if knowing his time was short. "I don't think the Traveler will come here, but he might. So I gotta work fast."

"Cletis," she started, "this isn't what I had imagined . . ."

"Abish, are you the one who taught Ian your family powers?"

She paused, startled by the question. "Yes, some of them."

"Like what he's doin' to me, with the light out of his hands? Did you teach him that?"

"Yes," she answered apologetically.

"How do you do it?"

She slowly extended her arm. "I don't know exactly how it works. It's just always been there. Well, not always, but since I was a young lady. It's a sense of force, I guess, that comes from your head, and you feel it move down your shoulders and arms until it reaches your hands. It's kind of like opening your mouth and pushing out a sound or a cry. It requires a bit of thought control, but it just comes. And you can control how strong a force it will be."

"And you just taught him how to use it?"

"Yes, he learned it with my help . . . but there was a bit more to it than that."

"Could I do it now, by myself . . . as Cletis?"

"No, you're too young. Your body has to be mature—like seventeen or eighteen-years-old.

"Does that power get weaker as a person gets older?"

"A little bit, I think. Why?"

Cletis studied her a moment. "Well, when he taught me to Change—to transform—I became him . . . the younger him. So I felt what it was like to—"

"Wait!" She interrupted him. "You know how to Change now?"

He paused. "Yeah, I guess I do. But I don't know how good I am at it. I've never done it by myself, and he told me if I tried it on my own, I might not be able to hold my shape." Cletis paced the room from the chairs to the windows and back again. "What I'm thinkin' is, I need to turn into him, and I need to face him, and get the box back. If I could turn into him again, then maybe I could use the powers—like the Lightfire—the way he did against me, and somehow get the box back. I'm thinkin' about tryin' that. They told me to use my wits and my speed and my gifts." He spoke quickly as he paced, trying to figure out a plan. "But the only real gift I have now that could help me is to be able to Change and somehow trick him."

"Wait a minute. Who is *they*?" she asked quickly.

He studied her anxious face a moment, not sure if he should explain it all to her.

"Abish, who Changed you? When the whole thing got started a thousand years ago, who was it that Changed you?"

"It was Padar, my father-in-law . . . Ian's father. Why?"

He paused. "I'm just thinkin', that's all. Tryin' to figure things out."

Again he paced to the window and looked thoughtfully out across the front of the building.

"Cletis, what's happening out there," Abish questioned anxiously. "This isn't coming to pass like I thought it would. What's going on with the box?"

"It recognizes me . . . You know, 'Then shall the box know him . . .' That part. So he can't touch it. At least that's what I'm thinking. Last time he did, it vanished out of his hands and appeared in front of me. So I think he's gonna let it stay there on the grass until I come and get it."

"Why are you bleeding? What's happened to your arms?"

"My legs, too. With Time frozen, the grass is like little razor blades. You roll on it, it cuts you up . . . Abish, I don't think I can explain everything right now. But I'll tell you this, we're in trouble." He crossed the room toward her. "I got an idea, but I don't know if I can do it. But it's the only idea I can think of right now." He studied her a moment, deep in thought. "I need something that will allow me to Change into the younger Ian."

"What are you talking about?"

"I gotta have something of his to be able to Change into him. Do you have anything from him? Like, uh . . . this may sound weird, but . . . like a drawing of him or a tooth from him or . . . or something?"

She thought for a moment, puzzled by the question. "Cletis . . . " her eyes opened wide. "Yes, I have some of his hair! I cut a lock of his hair the day I was Changed. Padar told me to do it. That's why! He knew it would last through the years until now." She remembered the moment clearly. "It's in a brown leather pouch with a string tie on the top of it."

"Where is it?" asked Cletis anxiously, stepping closer to her.

"It's in my library . . . somewhere on a shelf on top of some old books, on the right side of the table, I think . . . on the top shelf. Up high. I haven't seen it in years, though, but I think I put it there—on the shelves on the south wall next to the table. But will you be able to move the pouch with time frozen as it is?"

"Oh, man, I didn't think of that." He remembered how tough it was to move Elston's hat. Now he had to find a pouch with a wad of hair in it. "And it's gonna be pretty dark, too." He rubbed his face with his hands. His head still throbbed, and he just wanted to rest. "I can't think of anything else. I gotta give it a try."

His mind was racing, worrying that he wouldn't be able to find the pouch, let alone lift it or open it. He also wondered if he'd be able to make the Change and hold the shape long enough to get the box back. He had to get going. He rubbed his bloody arm on his pants and leaned over to his father again. Reaching through blue light, he took his hand once more.

"I gotta go," he whispered. "I don't want him to come here."

Garth smiled back at him, nodded slightly, and squeezed Cletis's fingers.

Cletis rose and walked to the center of the room where the conduit had space to gather around him.

"Cletis?" asked Abish, grabbing his arm. "You didn't answer my question. Who are *they*? Who instructed you? Who did you speak with?"

The boy studied her, yet remained silent. He peered into her green eyes, as if seeing them for the first time.

"My grandparents," he finally stated. "I spoke with my grandparents."

The blue of the conduit gathered around the boy and swallowed him up. Abish stood, looking up into the empty air where Cletis once stood. Her eyes closed.

"Oh, Papa . . . Mama . . . " she whispered as her eyes filled with tears. "What have I done?"

Within seconds, Cletis touched down in Abish's library. He quickly maneuvered around the table and began searching the shelves. The house was dark to begin with, but with the trees now blocking the late-evening sun, Cletis was forced to feel with his hands as much as see with his eyes. He pushed his fingertips over the top of the dust-covered books and manuscripts, scanning contents he figured hadn't seen the light of day in years, He pondered the warning from Mahon. *The Traveler will know where you are. But you will be able to sense him too.* With that in mind, Cletis worked all the faster, occasionally pausing to listen for any strange sounds or awaiting the feelings that always accompanied the old man's presence.

As he searched for the pouch, he still tried to figure things out. *If he touches the box, he might lose it. Because then it might come back to me, just like it did when I was in the conduit. Mahon said the box only recognizes me. But I don't think the Traveler's gonna leave it there to try to come after me.*

A wooden, cane-back chair next to the bookcase provided a step for him, and he climbed higher to get a closer look at the top shelf. He reached back to the far panel of the bookcase and slid his hand across the volumes, hoping to feel something that resembled leather. He worked his way to his right, stepped up onto the round slab of the wooden table, felt his way along the top of the books, and then stepped back down onto another chair on the front side of the table. Shelf after shelf and row after row, he searched with no success. Finally, in the far corner of the case on the south wall, on the highest shelf, lying on top of two large books, Cletis felt a small leather bag. His heart jumped.

"This has gotta be it," he voiced out loud.

He reached up to his far right, tucked his fingers behind the pouch and began to pull it forward. Though it required strenuous effort, the little bag gradually slid along the top surface of the volumes. When it came to rest at the very edge of the book-tops, Cletis stopped.

Don't let that thing fall on your foot, he thought to himself, pondering its heaviness. To be safe, Cletis stood on the table and, with his right hand, reached out and over to the shelf. Setting his fingers behind the pouch, again, he pulled it toward him. Finally the pouch teetered and fell forward, plunging down past four rows of papers and documents, and landing with a dull thud on top of the chair where Cletis had been standing.

Hopping off the table, Cletis could feel the pulse of his heart through every vein of his body. In the dimming light, he felt for the tie on the top of the pouch. To his good fortune, the top of the leather pouch had broken off with the fall, revealing an opening about the size of a quarter. Carefully he pushed his finger into the cavity of the stiff leather bag. At the very end of his reach, he felt the strands of hair. Working his finger around them, he dragged the stiff, brittle hairs toward the opening.

I don't think it matters if they break, he thought. *Just gotta get a bunch of 'em.*

With several hairs now close to the opening, Cletis was able to pinch them between his fingers and thumb. Carefully he pulled them away from the bag, placed a strand in the palm of his hand, squeezed it, and concentrated.

The image of a young Ian instantly appeared in his mind. The Changeling portion of his brain came alive, opening a channel of focus and power that detailed the entire transformation process. The alteration began. Cletis felt his body shift and meld and hum with the Change. Bones, sinews, muscles, and skin pulled and stretched to match the mental image of the young Traveler. Cletis's head craned back, and his eyes closed tightly as he felt strength and power course through his new body. At the same time, the ugly images and feelings from the earlier Changing flooded again through his mind. His headache throbbed more viciously, and he reeled with the pain.

As soon as the morphing process was complete, Cletis allowed the conduit to gather around him. He pictured in his mind the canal behind the house and found himself instantly there. As the blue energy faded, he dropped to the ground and staggered toward the stream.

The water instantly captivated him. Panting, he bent down next to it and studied it curiously. He thrust his Ian-like hand down into it and found it to be like the water of the drinking fountain—gelatin-like and firm, yet still water.

I wonder if the fire from the Traveler can go through this.

He stood, again amazed at the strength of the massive body he now possessed, yet sensing an internal imbalance caused by the ravaging headache that throbbed behind his eyes. He focused his attention to the woods on the opposite side of the canal, and lifting his arm to one of the fallen trees, he tried to summon the Lightfire power Abish had spoken of. Suddenly, a surge of energy flowed down his arms, electrifying his entire being. The power of the Lightfire coursed through his hands, released through his fingertips, flew across the canal, and blasted an old tree that stood on the opposite bank. To his surprise, the decaying trunk exploded into a million pieces, clouding the forest with the spray of dust and particles.

Stunned by the experience, Cletis staggered backward away from the canal. Quickly he regained his balance, and desiring to test the effort a second time, he stepped forward to the water's edge, lifted his arm to another dead tree, and concentrated once more on the flow of energy. Again the power pulled down through his arm, but much weaker this time. The blast arced across the canal, struck the rotting trunk, and shattered it away from the healthy maple it leaned against. The decaying shaft collapsed through the limbs and crashed onto the forest floor.

He can make his burn. Mine just makes things explode. What's the difference? And now I'm getting weaker. He sighed and shook his head. *Man, I've only got one good shot*, he thought, dejectedly. *Maybe one and a half. I don't stand a chance.*

As he worried, he pointed his hand at the water and concentrated hard. Another surge moved weakly down through his arm and fizzled out onto the water. To his surprise, it bounced off the glazed surface and ricocheted up into the weeds and grasses on the far side of the bank. The plants sizzled and collapsed with the Lightfire, but that was basically all that happened—no thundering explosion was repeated; no deafening burst of power. At the same moment, Cletis felt his body Changing. Slowly he was reverting back to his old self.

No! I've gotta hold the shape! But he couldn't. *Changing shapes isn't gonna do me much good if I can't hold the new body. Maybe it's because this body is so big compared to my real one. Or maybe it's just that I'm tired. Or maybe I just need practice.* He continued to feel the shifting within him and sensed the return of Cletis Dungarvan.

Discouraged, he closed his eyes and allowed the retransformation. Within seconds, the young Traveler was gone completely, and the twelve-year-old Cletis stood gloomily on the banks of the canal. He looked down at the blood that had soaked through his baseball pants and through the sleeve on his left arm. He was too busy and too tired to feel the pain there. He studied the wad of hair fibers held in his left hand and shoved them into his back pocket. *These still might be useful,* he thought.

His mind began to race. Somehow he had to get the box back. Somehow he had to get the Traveler into a situation where the box could be opened toward him, and where Cletis could recite the words. *The words,* thought Cletis. *I don't even know what they all are. If they would've come quicker in the box, I could've finished the job by now!*

Instantly, a scary thought struck Cletis. *What if he is able to transform into me! What if he can get some of my hair, or a picture of me, or somethin'? Then he could Change into me, and maybe the box would recognize him, and he could use the box to help him stay alive?! But wait a minute . . . everything in my house is frozen in place. But if he went to the house, he could pry out pieces of hair from the brushes, or maybe he'd find them on the floor.*

Suddenly Cletis's mind shifted to the photos of him and his family that lay on counters and dressers all over his house. *He could touch 'em, just like he did with Mom and Dad's picture! That's all he needs to do! But would he leave the box unprotected and go to my house? I don't think he'd chance that. He's probably gonna stay right there with it and wait for me.*

At that same moment, another idea burst into his mind. He thought of Abish—of the young Abish. *Her hair is woven into the baby clothes! And Abish used the Lightfire back when she was young. And she's smaller. Maybe I could hold her shape!*

His head throbbing, the blue conduit gathered about him. He needed to go home.

The only light visible in the house came from the main bathroom at the end of the hallway. Cletis moved swiftly through the kitchen of the darkened home. He knew the Traveler could sense where he was.

Concentrate on the task, he ordered himself. He remembered having seen Abish with the baby clothing on her lap as she sat in the living room. He raced into the front room and found the clothing lying neatly in a pile on the floor by the side of the chair. The cap rested on top of the folded stack. He knelt down next to the clothing and tried to lift the little cap. But it was as heavy as Elston's baseball hat.

There's got to be a better way, thought Cletis. Eyeing the clothing in front of him, he decided to experiment. Finding the auburn hair interwoven in the earpiece, he pressed his fingers down on the delicately woven cap. *If this works, I've gotta move fast. Abish, if this is wrong, don't be mad at me . . . but I gotta do* something.

An image of the young Abish materialized in his mind. It was as he had thought. The young woman seen so often in the mind of the Traveler *was* Abish. And now, seeing her from her *own* perspective, from inside her *own* world, he knew that what he had concluded was true. Gradually his body began to morph. With the Change, Cletis witnessed the scenes and reflections of her life—her youth and family and the homes and communities in which she had lived and grown. He sensed her hopes, fears, and joys. Mahon and Teagan, full of youth and vitality, were there, guiding her through the stages of her delightful young life. Cletis saw how she was educated in the knowledge of the powers of the Dungarvan clan and how the family united in love and harmony around her. He saw the young man Ian, full of strength and vigor, enter her life. He saw their marriage and the happiness it brought the society in which they lived.

Cletis's neck craned back and his eyes closed as the final stages of the transformation took place. Still the visions of Abish's years of contentment floated delicately, one upon another, through the galleries of his mind. And then there was a change—not physical, but spiritual. Following her marriage with Ian, doom and shadows gradually shrouded the previous joys. Their combined gifts were used for gain and power. Lives were broken, families torn apart, and communities crumbled. Heartache replaced happiness, and a spirit of betrayal suffocated the bliss that had once been a constant companion. Mahon and Teagan wept with her as she finally sensed the breadth and impact of her misdeeds. In her misery, Ian departed. A cloud of gloom shrouded her as she wandered in her own empty world, trying to make right that which was wrong. Then finally the Time of Changing and testing came. Her parents and father-in-law gathered privately with the young and beautiful Abish. The tiny boy Torlock was taken from her to be raised by one she knew not. Suddenly hundreds of years were ahead of her—hundreds of years in which to again earn the trust she had forfeited. Padar pronounced the physical Change upon Abish, and with that declaration, the visions in Cletis's mind, as well as the transformation he underwent, abruptly ended.

Jolted back into reality, he inhaled and opened his eyes. Catching his breath, he felt the lightness, vitality, and strength of this new body. He explored the unique sensations of a different form. He sensed he was about five inches taller than his normal self. He moved his toes against the soft inside of the leather boots that covered his feet and lower legs. He lifted his arms and felt the woolen garment on his shoulders and upper body. He sucked in a deep breath and sensed the grip of the leather belt that wrapped around his waist.

This is what Mahon and Teagan wore, he thought to himself. *Or at least something like this.*

Not daring to look down on himself yet, he stepped carefully up and out of the living room and moved steadily down the hallway to the bathroom. The large wall mirror was there, and he knew the light was still on. When he reached the room, he closed his eyes and felt his way across the counter to the sink. His heart—his new heart—beat rapidly. He knew the mirror was right in front of him. Cletis swallowed nervously and then opened his eyes. He gasped instantly. There in the light—there in the mirror, the image of the beautiful young Abish stared back at him. Here was the true Abish, the woman who was his tender mother—the charming, elegant daughter of Teagan and Mahon. His vision blurred as he peered into the vibrant, green eyes of the woman who, for centuries, had been hidden beneath the hideous flesh now worn by the beloved old hag of Greenberg Junction.

"Hello, Abish," Cletis whispered. He stood reverently and re-spectfully before the reflection, awed by the grace of the lady who smiled back at him.

Her hands came to her cheeks, and Abish stood slowly, studying the images that floated within the orb before her. Garth too, though weak, stared eagerly at the drama that had unfolded in front of them. Together they had seen Cletis appear in the Dungarvan home, find the old cloth-ing, and undergo the transformation. And now they watched as the boy stood in front of the mirror, studying the reflection before him.

Garth's gaze drifted over to Abish, and he watched her as she remained riveted to the scene before her. She stood perfectly still, staring at her former self, seemingly lost in the memories of a bygone century. Unblinking, she studied the young woman in front of the mirror—pondering, wondering, dreaming—until the blue light of Cletis's conduit swallowed the image away.

Safe within the conduit, Cletis felt the power surge through his head, neck, and shoulders. He knew he had a couple of good shots of Lightfire within him. *As long as I can hold her form, I've got a chance. But what if the box doesn't recognize me? Maybe the box will think I'm Abish and not Cletis! If the box doesn't know me, then I've gotta wait until . . .*

Cletis's blue conduit appeared above the frozen Canterbury cen-terfielder. In the image of Abish, Cletis floated softly to the ground.

He knew the Traveler was near, and keeping his eyes open wide as the conduit above him faded away, he made his way toward the open box. Precisely as anticipated, the Traveler's conduit appeared directly in front of Cletis, and the old man turned within it to face him. But upon seeing the young Abish before him, he seemed momentarily shocked.

Instantly Cletis let the Lightfire fly. The surge blasted the grass in front of the Traveler, knocking him off his feet and sending him sprawling across the ground. He lay groaning on the frozen lawn for several seconds.

"A moment's weakness, I see," Cletis called out to him in Abish's voice—his arm still raised to fire again.

Ian rolled over and looked up into the face of the young Abish.

"Look at you." Cletis stated, stepping toward the box. "You continue to destroy everything in your path. How dare you treat our son as you have!" Keeping his hand outstretched and his eye on the old man, Cletis kicked the box away from the Traveler.

"I don't believe you are Abish," spoke the Traveler as he lifted himself to his knees. The blades of grass cut into the flesh of his legs, and the old man winced with the pain. "I taught you well, and now you use the power against me."

Again Cletis blasted the ground next to him, sending him rolling away, dazed by the Lightfire. Quickly Cletis leaned down and scooped up the box. The lid was open, and he shot a glance at the words inscribed on the bottom panel.

TIME THAT GAVE DOTH NOW . . .

Still the phrase was incomplete. Hoping the box would react to his touch, Cletis waited a few seconds, watching and hoping for some addition to the message. But none came. *The box doesn't recognize me! I gotta change back.*

"If you are who I think you are," moaned Ian, "why don't you destroy me now? You have your chance." The old man rolled to his side and stared at the young Abish.

The pounding in Cletis's head suddenly intensified. His eyes blurred, and his stomach lurched. The familiar darkness that accompanied the presence of the Traveler rapidly enveloped him once more. *Am I Changing back into Cletis? I didn't feel this when I first saw him. This wasn't supposed to happen!* The haunting, cold sensation shot through his bones, and he bent slowly forward.

It was the sign the Traveler needed. The dazed old man raised his hands at Cletis. The Lightfire shot from his fingers and arced through the air toward the staggering boy. Falling to his side and rolling away, Cletis dodged the bolt that exploded past him. Though he was amazed at the lightness and agility of Abish's young body, he was still unprotected from the sharp blades of grass that penetrated the flesh of his arms, shoulders and legs. He rose to his knees and aimed at the old man's feet and fired back. The blast struck the ground directly in front of the Traveler, hoisting him into the air and hurling him backward at least ten feet. He hit the earth with a thud and lay motionlessly as fiery bits of grass and dirt sprinkled down around him.

Cletis rose to his feet, panting. *If I can Change back into my real self before he comes to, then maybe the box'll know me and the words'll be there.* Cletis stepped forward and studied the Traveler. *Do I finish him here? He's trying to kill me. He's trying to kill Abish and Dad too. Would I be wrong in doing it?* Slowly the old Traveler began to move and moan. *No . . . no . . . I can't do that. That's not my mission.*

Cletis concentrated, allowing the Change to begin. Not knowing how long it would take, he knew he needed to put a safe distance between him and the old man. With the grass crunching under his feet, step by step, Cletis moved away from the Traveler. At the same time, he sensed his hold on Abish's form slipping away. Cletis's head went back, and he felt the muscles and bones within him reverting again to their true form. At the same time, he tried to keep an eye on the man before him, preparing himself for any attack the Traveler might attempt. He discovered that while the Changing process took place, it was almost impossible to focus on anything else. *Man, I have no control over this. And it's not happenin' fast enough! He could turn and fire at me any second! And as Cletis, I don't have any way to defend myself.*

The old man rolled to his side and attempted to come to his knees. Though unstable, he was determined. He groaned as he pushed down against the brutal blades of grass and lifted himself into a kneeling position. Droplets of blood formed on his face, neck, and arms.

Though the seconds seemed an eternity to Cletis, the transition finally ended. The twelve-year-old, exhausted Cletis now stood the short distance from the Traveler. Instantly he peered down into the box hoping to see new words.

TIME THAT GAVE DOTH NOW . . .

Back and forth his eyes darted, from the wooden relic to the Traveler, waiting for the wording to change and, at the same time, preparing an escape. Cletis knew that within a matter of seconds, he would need the protection of the conduit. In frustration, he sensed the opportunity to catch the Traveler slipping through his fingers. *Where are the words! I'm losing my chance! Come on, box! You gotta work for me!!*

As the old man attempted to stand, another word to the phrase finally appeared, first glowing red and then fading to black.

TIME THAT GAVE DOTH NOW HIS . . .

Not knowing if the sentence was complete, Cletis raised the box to the Traveler and shouted out the words: "TIME THAT GAVE DOTH NOW HIS—!"

Staggering to his left, the old man released the Lightfire toward Cletis. But his aim was high and wide, and Cletis easily ducked away from it.

"THEY WON'T TAKE ME LIKE THAT AGAIN!" Ian screamed hoarsely, attempting to rise. "You could have killed me when

I was down and been done with the whole mess! But you're a coward!" Again the Lightfire shot from his fingertips and blasted toward Cletis. Again Cletis dodged it, moving farther away from the Traveler.

"I don't kill!!" he screamed at the old man. "I am *not* as the father!"

Gradually another word glowed red on the bottom panel of the box.

Time that gave doth now his gift . . .

Cletis hurriedly raised the box to the Traveler, and hoping the phrase was complete, he cried out again. "TIME THAT GAVE DOTH NOW HIS GIFT—!"

But the crooked man was finally stable on his feet again and, though dazed, lifted his arms toward Cletis. The Lightfire exploded from his hands and shot toward Cletis. As if avoiding a fastball, Cletis stepped back and spun away. But the bolt of energy, well aimed this time, whipped past Cletis close enough to scorch the sleeve of his uniform and burn the skin of his upper right arm. With a cry of agony, Cletis went down on the sharp blades of right-center field. The razor points of grass penetrated his skin, and Cletis howled in pain. He rolled to his side, came to his knees, and welcomed the blue light of his conduit. Another bolt of raging Lightfire burst from the hands of the Traveler and roared directly at Cletis. It was the last thing Cletis saw before vanishing safely into the night.

Cletis appeared at the south side of his house, near his bike that rested against the aluminum siding. *He's gonna be right behind me. Can't stop.* He leaned against the wall next to the old bike. Exhausted and panting, he looked around him and above him, searching for signs of the Traveler. In the dim light, he studied his arms, legs, and sides. All were bleeding afresh from his latest roll on the grass. But what pained him most was the Lightfire burn on his arm. Though his upper arm pulsed with agony, he was grateful he was still alive.

He lifted his sleeve and studied the raw, dark, and oozing flesh. The pain from the burn almost put him to his knees. He fought against the longing to give up or give in, and forced himself to gather his thoughts and think through his possible options.

I can't transform into anyone or the box won't work for me, he reasoned quickly. *And I gotta be holding the box toward him so that all this will work. At least that's what I think I remember them tellin' me. And the Traveler seemed to recognize the danger of what I was doing, cuz that's when he fought back the most.*

Cletis looked down at the old box in his hands and cautiously lifted the lid. New letters instantly began to appear on the bottom panel, slowly forming another word. C-O-N were the first three letters. *Come on! Can't they hurry this up!* The letters F-O-U-N-D followed, each one glowing a bright and radiant red.

TIME THAT GAVE DOTH NOW HIS GIFT CONFOUND.

"'Time that gave doth now his gift confound'? Is that all?" Cletis whispered.

Nothing more came. The message was complete. He repeated it over and over in his mind until it was memorized. When he was confident that it was permanently set in his brain, he closed the lid.

Now I just gotta stay ahead of him, he thought. *I don't have any Lightfire now. All I got is the box.* He thought of the trees and canal around Abish's home. *If I go there, at least I got some cover. There are a lot of places to hide. I know the woods around her house. And her house could be a good hiding place too, now that it has that big opening in the back of it.*

Suddenly Cletis sensed the old man's presence. The Traveler was close. The ugly feelings that always followed the wicked man shot through Cletis's body and soul again, and like a dried sponge, he absorbed the nauseating, weakening sensation. He had to act fast.

He bent down to the lawn at the bottom of the siding and searched the concrete base of his house. *I know it's gotta be here somewhere*, he thought, *cuz I tossed it here.* He leaned low, attempting to recognize the shadowy shapes in the lawn below him. Finally he spotted it—the old, green hose. He squatted down and worked his fingers under the end of it, trying not to cut himself on the pointed blades of grass. With all his strength, he lifted. When the long, thin, hose budged, he stepped over the top of it and slammed his heel down on it. CRACK. The hose snapped off about a foot from the end of it.

His head throbbed, his body ached, and his arm was on fire with pain. He could feel himself weakening. *Gotta try this. It might work for me.* With all his might, he attempted to lift the broken piece of hose. *It's too heavy! I can hardly budge it, let alone use it in the water!* He rose feebly, and holding the box securely in his hands, he prepared the conduit. Suddenly a flash of light from above him thundered down on the corner of the house. Cletis felt the impact of the explosion rock him to the bone just as he disappeared into the protective realm of the conduit.

Frightened and shaken, Cletis appeared by the canal behind Abish's house and floated to the ground. *He knew right where I was!* Cletis thought as he staggered to the water's edge. *How can I hide from him?* Quickly Cletis eyed the water near the slab of rock that jutted out into the canal. *It might still work if I need to try it . . . if I can figure out how to stay under the water. The hose would've worked nice if I could've lifted it.* He took a final, wishful look at the stone in the water, and then jumped the canal, darted up into the forest, and ducked behind the fallen trunk of a dead maple tree. There he watched and waited.

With Time frozen as it was, the forest was a cruel place. The plants and trees had no bend and give anymore. The grasses were not soft underneath him. Their brittle stalks and stems cracked and splintered as he attempted to find a comfortable place to settle. Finally he realized there would be none. The fresh growth of springtime plants was like an army of upturned knife blades slicing at his legs. The forest would be his enemy until the conflict was finished—whatever the outcome.

He panted and trembled as he opened the box and studied the words again.

TIME THAT GAVE DOTH NOW HIS GIFT CONFOUND.

It's in my mind. I know it by heart. He studied the forest around him, trying to figure out the best way to run or where to hide if his situation became life threatening. The woods were completely still around him. Not a sound was heard. He listened for any telltale sign of the Traveler's presence, but his thoughts turned to Abish and his father at the hospital; to Elston, lying on the grass at the baseball diamond . . . and to Timmy and Pauly. *Can I bring them back? Can I put everything right again? Timmy and Pauly are gone! And even if I do get out of this alive, how do I make Time obey me? How do I get it to start once more, and how do I start it where I want it to start?*

Again he studied the burn below his right shoulder, the box in his hand, and the gaping hole in the back of Abish's house. He blew on his painful bleeding arms and lifted his sleeve carefully away from the burn. On top of the pain, he felt dead weary—the near-sleepless night in the hospital; not having eaten much during the day; and now this whole ordeal of Changing and Traveling were all taking their toll on him. He wiped at his eyes with dirty fingers.

All he has to do is find me and blast away. How can I stop him? Whatever I do, I gotta think ahead and not give in. With that determination in mind, Cletis suddenly sensed the presence of the Traveler. Silently opening the box, he prepared for the old man's coming.

The forest suddenly illuminated with the flash of Lightfire. The bright flow of the deadly energy cascaded down upon the tops of the trees above Cletis. Leaves, branches, and trunks high in the canopy exploded into powder and flames.

He's above me!!

Under a shower of rocklike particles, Cletis leapt to his feet and charged across the hillside, away from Abish's house. On the run, and turning toward the emptiness of the dark sky above him, Cletis held up the open box and called out the words.

"TIME THAT GAVE DOTH NOW HIS GIFT CONFOUND!"

Nothing happened. He kept moving. The sound of his own footsteps was all he could hear. Ducking under the protection of a large pine, he stopped and listened.

Though all was quiet around him, his heart beat wildly in his chest, and he was unable to control the heaviness of his breathing.

"I'm right here, boy!"

Directly behind him came the Traveler's gritty voice.

Cletis dove instinctively to his right. The stream of Lightfire shot past him and exploded through the evergreens. Instantly Cletis was on his feet running down the hill. A second blast hit the ground to his left, knocking Cletis to the forest floor and showering the area with dust and burning branches. Cletis hit the ground with a cry, landing directly on the burn of his upper right arm and driving the Time-frozen sticks and grasses into his scorched and tender flesh. He gasped in agony as the pain stabbed through his entire body. But he didn't dare stop. Still he held the box tightly in his hands, and pushing himself to his feet, he was again on the run—jumping fallen logs and sprinting down the hillside through the trees toward the canal.

Another streak of Lightfire coursed past him, barely missing his head. The line of bright energy struck the ground on the far side of the canal below him, just to the north of Abish's home, blowing earth and rocks and grass high into the air. He ducked directly into the cover of the oncoming barrage of particles, and jumping the canal, he sprinted past the gaping hole in the ground where the Lightfire had struck only seconds before.

Hurrying to the north side of Abish's house, Cletis peered through the dust back up the hill. Another bolt of Lightfire flashed toward him. He dove to the ground and rolled to his stomach, protecting the box with his arms and body. The blast, which struck several meters past him, lifted Cletis off the ground and sent him flying into the wall of Abish's house. Again a rain of rocks and dirt showered over him, covering him with earth and debris. Dazed and dizzy, Cletis realized he no longer held the box. Instantly he was on his hands and knees, scrambling across the ground, blindly pawing at the earth. Several feet to his left, next to the house, he finally found it. He pulled it close, cradled in his arms, and opened the lid. Frantically he pointed it in the direction of the Traveler's last fire.

"TIME THAT GAVE DOTH NOW HIS GIFT CONFOUND!" His voice was weak and tired, and he coughed with the dust.

Again silence. *Did anything happen?* He sat motionlessly against the wall, breathing heavily. His mouth was dry. His head pounded furiously. He peered out into the vapor of black that surrounded the house, trying to see any movement. *I've gotta get outta here! He's still out there somewhere!* The blue conduit instantly encircled him, and he disappeared through the haze of dust that fell like volcanic ash around him.

Cletis placed himself at the top of the rise overlooking Abish's home. As the bluish hue disappeared from around him, he dropped to the ground and slumped forward. The instant his elbows hit the dirt, an explosion rocked the house below him, destroying much of the north wall of Abish's dwelling. He watched and listened for a moment and then closed his eyes dejectedly, fighting against the pain and exhaustion that so weakened him. He wracked his mind, trying to think of a way to get into position near the Traveler.

But he knows where I am! He follows me! He tried to catch his breath. His head still pounded and the burn throbbed agonizingly. His arms and legs were sore and bleeding from his falls, and his whole body ached dreadfully. He peered down the hill, and spitting dirt from his mouth, he listened again. All was silent as a tomb.

Slowly he bowed his head to the earth and rolled onto his side. *I'm so tired. I can't do this.* The ground was barren at the top of the hill, with no piercing plant life to be concerned about. *But I gotta keep movin'. I can't stop. I can't just lay here. I gotta keep tryin'.* He felt something warm on his ear and reached up to wipe it away. He studied his hand, which he held close to his face, and could see it was blood. The wound was somewhere hidden in his scalp, but with all the dirt in his hair and on his hands, he couldn't feel it. Wherever it was, it was bleeding heavily. He thought of the blast that knocked him into the wall of Abish's house. It must have happened then. He took a deep breath and pushed himself to his knees. *Can't give up!*

A mental picture of the canal below him came to mind. Again the blue conduit eased around him. *I gotta give it a try. It might work. If I can get into the water fast—under that rock, maybe the reeds will help hide me. I can come up for air there.* He knew the effort would be near impossible, but he was determined to give it a try. *Maybe I can lift up outta the water and open the box.*

Cletis appeared at the edge of the canal, dropped to the ground, and moving under the cover of floating debris, hastily crawled toward the stream. He was close to reaching the water when another burst of light illuminated the forest and canal. With a thunderous explosion, a shower of dirt and stone pummeled his face and body, throwing him backward toward Abish's porch. The jarring force seemed to turn Cletis inside out. His bones and muscles and organs quivered with the impact.

And then, another blast.

In a black daze, Cletis felt his whole body leave the ground. Aware of his own weightlessness, he watched the tops of the trees float by against the twilight sky. While in midair, the box escaped his grasp. To his left, he caught a shadowy glimpse of it as it flew toward the steps behind Abish's house. Finally, with a dull thud, he hit the ground some fifteen feet farther up the canal. With the impact, the air shot from his lungs, and as he struck the unyielding earth, he heard a loud crunch in his upper right arm. Tossed over the rock-hard plants that grew on the bank of the ditch, he heard the snapping of the stems and stalks as they broke under the weight of his tumbling body. With a gasp, he plunged into the solid, chilly water. Dazed and broken, his body sunk below the surface and slowly dropped the four feet to the bottom of the canal. The world around him gradually grew dark and cold.

Don't give in! he suddenly screamed in his mind. *Don't let yourself go! You're under water! Get up! Breathe!*

The taste of the water was confusing to him, as he sucked it into his mouth while gasping for air. He struggled against the heavy murkiness of the solid liquid and fought to push himself up through the gooey substance. Another snap in his right shoulder shot unbearable pain through his entire body, and he found his right arm instantly useless. Despite the horrifying agony, still he fought to stand. Desperate for oxygen, he finally forced his aching, trembling legs underneath him, and pushed his head above the surface. Coughing and spurting, he lunged forward toward the bank and collapsed against it. His chest heaved as he struggled to find his breathe, and he clawed and kicked his way up the solid mud.

His stomach and chest now resting on dry earth, Cletis looked down at his right shoulder above the burn. His uniform clung tightly to his body with the heaviness of the moisture, revealing a gruesome bulge just below the shoulder joint. Fresh blood ran out from under his sleeve, soaking the ground where he lay. His vision gradually blurred, and his eyelids closed.

Cletis, stay awake! You've got to fight it! You've got to get the box!

But thoughts and actions were two different things.

Struggling to focus on the world around him and wrestling against the agonizing pain that ravaged his body, he weakly lifted his head and rested his chin on the ground. Despite the heavy fog of dirt and debris that fell from above, he forced his eyes open to search for the box. At last he spotted it near the porch and pointlessly reached toward it with his left arm. Again the dizzying darkness engulfed him. He heard footsteps, but they seemed far distant. His eyes glazed, his focus blurred, and he fought to remain conscious. A final hope, he strained to generate the blue light of the conduit. But he couldn't conjure it. Cletis's head slumped over onto the dirt, and his eyes closed. The footsteps came closer now. He knew there would be no escape this time. He felt the coldness on his legs and wondered if they were still in the water. Silently his world turned midnight black.

"NO!" cried Abish as she leaned over the blue orb in the hospital room. Both of her hands lifted desperately to the top of her head, and her fingers combed restlessly through her nest of gray-and-white hair. She and Garth stared helplessly into the floating sphere, riveted on the motionless body that lay sprawled on the canal bank behind her house.

"Garth, there must be something we can do!" she cried out. She scurried over to the door again and tried to open it. Solid as a stone, it wouldn't budge. Even if she *could* get out into the hall, she knew there was no place to go after that. Doors to the elevators and stair-wells all through the hospital would be sealed like bank vaults. There would be no way to get to her home from the hospital. She raced back to the blue light and looked into it again, wringing her old and puffy hands together as she concentrated.

Garth attempted to rise but fell back weakly on his bed. Abish's hand immediately darted through the protective blue skin that surrounded him, and she grasped his hand.

"He'll do it, Garth." She was uncertain despite her encouraging words. "He'll find a way. We'll see." She turned back again to the sphere of light. "Cletis!" she pleaded again, as if he could hear her, "you've got to fight it! You've got to stay alert! Please!"

Within the blue vision, they watched the Traveler approach the seemingly lifeless boy.

"Oh, Papa. Please, Mama," Abish wept aloud. "We can't let him fail! He can't die there!"

Abish and Garth watched as the Traveler, panting heavily, bent low to study Cletis. He seemed to take special note of the ugly bulge below the boy's shoulder. Abish could see the stream of blood that flowed from beneath his uniform sleeve and reasoned that Ian obviously saw it. The old man placed his foot on the lump and pressed down hard.

"No!" cried Abish.

She could see the bone shift below the Traveler's weight. But Cletis didn't respond. The slight rising and falling of the boy's ribs revealed he was yet alive.

"I'm getting weaker, child, thanks to you," the old man spoke with a cough.

The voice was distant and soft, as if Cletis were listening from the top of the hill above Abish's house. He could sense a being near him, but all seemed detached and confusing.

"You've taken all my strength from me. A noble fight, indeed. But then, I would expect nothing less from a son of mine." He reached down, grabbed a handful of hair from the top of Cletis's head and yanked upwards.

Cletis felt no pain.

"You chose not to kill me, so I will pay you the same respect . . . for now. But when I depart this place, you will be left here to rot within this chapter of frozen Time. You, the man you call your father, and Abish. You will see what it is like to be locked away with no hope of escape."

He crossed to the porch and studied the fallen box near the steps. He kept a careful distance from it and turned his attention to the handful of strawberry blond hairs pulled from his son's head. He spread them on the palm of his hand, closed his fingers around them again, and shutting his eyes in deep concentration, began the gradual transformation.

Cletis's eyes opened slightly, seeing, yet not seeing.

Wormlike, the man's old carcass shifted and pulled mysteriously, contracting and tightening as it gradually assumed its new and preferred identity. The supernatural process progressed steadily as the body of the Changeling bent and twisted and moaned with the eerie alteration. Layer by layer, the dark and decaying shell of the wretched old man was replaced by the form of the young boy—Cletis, Torlock—the chosen child who now controlled the magic of the ancient box.

Cletis's mind bravely struggled to command his physical strengths to action and continue the battle, but his body was now unable to cooperate. The pain and exhaustion, and now the final blast of the Lightfire, left him on the brink of death. Within the realm of this murky, mental landscape, Cletis roamed as if lost in a fog. Though he sought a way to escape the darkness that enveloped him—a way to rise and renew the battle—he could not, as if forced to wander aimlessly within the confines of his own clouded subconscious world.

His mission had failed. *He* had failed. The prophecy would be fulfilled in favor of the Traveler. The vile old man would renew his life through the powers of the box and re-create another world of evil and destruction. Cletis would die on this canal bank, and his father and Abish would live out the remainder of their lives within this dominion of frozen Time and die a dreadful death of thirst and starvation. Abish would never see her home and family again. Time, as Cletis, his friends and his family knew it, would be stopped forever, and there was nothing Cletis could do about it now.

All was wrong.

All was lost.

Yet within his dark mind he staggered on.

Delicately, even in his supposed failure, the encouraging words of his grandmother Teagan echoed through the abyss of his mind. At least he thought he heard her. He wasn't sure what was real or if he was even alive. But he wanted to hear. He tried to hear. Again the voice came—like a whisper or a feeling, and with her faint pleadings, her image took shape before him. Like a lamp in the midnight blackness, she knelt gracefully at his feet.

"You are a savior to our family, dear Torlock," she repeated, looking into his eyes.

Cletis felt he had heard those words before but couldn't remember where.

"What you will do for us will save our daughter . . . and countless others . . . and only you can do it." She studied his wracked and broken body. Her hand reached to his face and stroked the line of his jaw. "We will always be grateful to you."

Then, like a breath, she was gone.

Despite her words of encouragement, still the vapory fog shrouded Cletis's beaten, exhausted mind. Trapped within this heavy veil of darkness, he continued the struggle to find strength, to find life.

I want to hope. I'm tryin' to hope.

Though Teagan's words compelled him onward, still only shadowy night surrounded him.

Then there came another soft cry of concern. Again it was faint, yet audible.

"Cletis! Cletis!"

No, it's two voices. Two voices . . . speaking the same words.

They came floating and spiritlike. His mother, Anna, stood before him, and at her side, the young Abish. Like Teagan, they were delicate and airy, possessing an otherworldly glow that dispelled the gloom surrounding him. Anna and Abish held hands, unified in the message they bore.

"You have been so brave, Cletis." Anna spoke first, lovingly, pleadingly. "But now is the time, my son. You must force yourself to open your eyes. Take strength from us. Voice the words written in the box!"

The young Abish spoke next, through tear-filled eyes. "You have been so selfless, Torlock, my courageous son. But you must fight on! Open your eyes now. Find the strength. You are our only hope. No one else can do this!"

Cletis lifted an arm toward them, but their images faded.

Yet despite his shadowy confusion, his exhaustion, their yearnings penetrated his soul. *Only I can do this . . . I have to do this . . . Find it . . .*

Like surfacing from the gelatin waters of the canal, Cletis pushed through the darkness of near-death. He forced himself to concentrate on light, life and consciousness.

His eyelids opened slowly.

Though the forest twilight still surrounded him, he gradually recognized the porch at the back of Abish's house and the screen door he had fixed two weeks ago. He smelled the dust that settled around him and the green wood that smoldered on the far side of the canal. He tasted the water in his mouth and felt the cool of the stream on his legs and feet. He remembered the explosion that sent him flying into the canal. He remembered struggling to rise from the syrupy waters and gasping for life-sustaining air. Yet as his mind focused and his vision cleared, he felt again the agony of near death. It was more than he could bear.

Fight it! Stay awake! Keep your eyes open! he commanded himself. Battling the pain, he focused on the old home in front of him.

Near the porch steps, only a few feet from where Cletis lay, there stood a boy dressed in a Sperry's Cards and Coins baseball uniform. His back was to Cletis as he stepped toward the box, which still lay on the ground where Cletis had last seen it. The person bent down, lifted the box, and pulled it closer to his face. Cautiously he opened the lid and looked into the ancient relic. He turned slightly toward Cletis, revealing the cunning smile that betrayed the innocence of his profile.

Through eyes that struggled to see, Cletis looked up at a boy, who was in all respects his mirror image. The person before him was an exact replica of him—Cletis Dungarvan.

It's the Traveler, Cletis realized, fighting to remain alert. *It's him. The box recognizes him.*

The boy who held the box whispered something. Suddenly the relic began to glow with a red light that reflected on his face. He bowed his head forward into the box and inhaled deeply—as if breathing into his soul some rare, unique power. His eyes closed and his head pushed slowly backward.

Though Cletis could barely concentrate through the pain, he knew exactly what was happening. It was the dreaded rebirth of the Changeling. This was the dawn of the Traveler's second life.

Cletis remembered Mahon's words: "With the box opened in front of him . . . command the powers . . . say the words."

Cletis struggled to speak. His mouth moved slightly, but no sound came out. There was simply no strength. Dazed and exhausted, he watched the Traveler supernaturally morph, bend, and shift before him, and there was nothing he could do to prevent it.

Unable to battle the fatigue and pain that tormented him, Cletis's eyes closed again. As they did, once more the images of his caring mothers entered his mind.

"Cletis, you must find the strength! Soon it will be finished!" Anna spoke softly.

"Open your eyes, Cletis. You must say the words while the box is still open in front of him," added the young Abish.

Mahon and Teagan appeared behind them, followed by Garth, Elston, Pauly, and Timmy. Their silent, yet concerned, expressions all urged Cletis to muster the fortitude to finish the conflict.

Cletis fought to rally any remaining strength in his broken body. Deep within his soul he felt the urgency of his task. *No one else can do this . . . Gotta find it in me . . .* Cletis's heavy eyes opened feebly again.

The Changeling process was complete, yet the powerful, young Traveler who now stood next to the porch steps was seemingly unmindful of the dying boy behind him. Again he raised the open box to his face, and inhaling deeply through his nose, he continued to absorb the power of the red brilliance. His blond braid now hung down his back, and the black leather he wore fit snugly upon his muscular frame.

Close by, Cletis lay weakly watching, attempting to think, to whisper. *I can't let him win,* Cletis commanded himself. *I can't!*

The feeling came gradually—the soft, comforting sensation that spoke peace to his battered soul. Though he lay motionlessly, this flow of quiet calm seemed to pulse through every fiber of his being, energizing his broken frame. He felt his hair stand on end as a renewing power surged through him. Cletis weakly took a shallow, silent breath. Then, exerting all the effort he could rally, a fragile, yet life-altering, whisper sounded.

"Time that gave doth now his gift confound."

Hearing the words, the Traveler instantly looked up from the box and turned toward Cletis. His dark, empty eyes suddenly filled with horror. In the same split second, the dust-filled air exploded with a red radiance. Instinctively Cletis closed his eyes, not knowing what to expect. A deafening blast resounded around him, as if a bolt of lightning had struck the earth only inches from where he lay. With the impact, the ground jerked beneath him, jarring Cletis's pain-ridden body. He gasped with the agony of the sudden movement.

Then silence. It all happened in a breath.

Cletis heard something fall.

Slowly, cautiously, he opened his eyes. Dust and debris from the explosion filled the air around him and settled over the earth where he lay. The Traveler was gone. The box, several feet away, now leaned against the bottom porch step, directly below the screen door. He studied the old relic for a moment. For all Cletis cared, it could stay there forever. Despite his desire to hop to his feet and jump and cheer, Cletis groaned and closed his eyes again. His world faded into silent darkness.

CHAPTER 23

WELCOME HOME

To Abish it seemed that three or four hours passed before she saw any movement. Her eyes had been glued to the blue orb during the entire period of time. She had seen the flash of red light and the blue explosion that followed it, and then she had seen Cletis's eyes slowly close. Though there had been an immediate sense of relief and joy in having witnessed the boy's success and in having seen the Traveler vanish in the red light, she now felt an overwhelming motherly urge to care for and nurture the injured, brave boy. But that was impossible at the moment.

Finally she saw his legs move slightly and his head lift off the ground. He appeared to look about him briefly, as if searching for something or someone, or trying to remember where he was. Within seconds, he wearily laid his head back down on the dirt. Again he was still, as if resting and gathering strength. She reached her hand through the blue shell that enveloped Garth and squeezed his wrist.

"He's moving, Garth," she said anxiously. "He's moving."

Garth looked on silently, weakly smiling at what he saw.

Again Cletis's legs shifted, and he feebly lifted his head. He pulled his left arm in to his side and, sliding it underneath him, attempted to rise. But the effort was too great for his strength, and with a grimace of pain, he collapsed back to the earth. Again he rested. Then in a second attempt, he steadily pushed himself up off the ground and leaned back into a kneeling position. There he paused several seconds. Wincing in pain, he reached over with his left hand to support his broken right arm. Then, appearing to exert all his strength, he staggered to his feet. Finding his balance, he stood in place for a moment. He then faced the box that rested next to the step and, unsteadily, stepped toward it.

Abish and Garth looked on affectionately as Cletis studied the opened box at his feet. Then haltingly, he reached down, picked it up, and closed the lid. Like a newborn colt finding its balance on wobbly legs, Cletis finally stood with the box in hand. Though he faltered against the screens of the porch, a blue light surged around him. In a moment, he was gone.

Abish squeezed Garth's hand again. "I think he's coming." She arose instantly and turned toward the center of the room, preparing to meet the radiant energy of the conduit and, if needed, bear up her suffering son.

Seconds passed, but the conduit light didn't appear.

"Abish," Garth whispered.

She turned back to him. He was studying the blue orb that revealed Cletis's location. She stepped back to the bed and eyed the image that moved within the ball of light. To her surprise, she saw that her weak and wounded son now stood on the baseball diamond next to his good friend Elston.

Cletis bent over Elston's quiet body. "Everything will be okay, buddy," he whispered through gritted teeth. "Everything's gonna be fine."

He looked out toward third base, where Timmy had stood. Particles and dust lay scattered all around the bag. Cletis teetered slightly but regained his balance. His eyes drifted over to second base, where Pauly had once taken his lead with the pitch. He too was still gone. It was all a horrible nightmare from which Cletis was determined to wake.

Bowing his head, he coughed feebly and gasped with the searing pain in his upper right arm. "I'm gonna make this right, guys. I promise," he moaned.

Still holding the box in his left hand, Cletis looked over at the baseball that lay near home plate. Unsteadily he stepped toward it, and pausing above the ball, he studied it curiously.

He lowered himself to his knees, and setting the box next to him on the dirt, he lifted the lid. Cautiously he picked up the ball, rolled it in the fingers of his left hand, and placed it inside the box. He closed the lid and paused a moment to catch his breath. With his right arm cradled on his lap, he suddenly and fearfully turned toward the Canterbury dugout. No one sat on the upside-down seed bucket at the top of the steps. The Traveler was gone. The man was no more. The team and parents would realize that soon enough, and the real Mr. Martin, if there was one, would appear somewhere in the neighborhood, with an odd memory lapse of the last week or so.

The blue light of the conduit softly gathered around him. Cletis knew that soon there would be peace.

Abish squeezed Garth's hand and again turned expectantly toward the middle of the hospital room. Instantly the radiance of the conduit filled the space around them, and Cletis appeared within the energy field. He floated softly to the ground and staggered forward. Abish, careful to avoid bumping his broken arm, wrapped her strong, wide hand around his waist and pulled him to her side. He collapsed against her shoulder, and as she felt his wounded and broken frame against her, she could no longer restrain her tender emotions. She bowed her cheek onto his head and kissed his hair and ear, and lovingly wept over him.

Garth, watching from the bed, allowed a tear to slip down his cheek and onto the pillow under him. There before him stood his valiant Cletis—battle-worn, pale, broken, and exhausted, yet victorious.

Cletis was covered from head to waist by a filthy layer of dust and debris. His uniform was slimy and muddy from top to bottom and blood-soaked on his neckline and right shoulder. Streams of dried blood caked his matted hair above and behind both ears. His arms and legs still wore the signs of earlier bleeding from his numerous falls. The outside portion of his right sleeve was cooked to a black crisp, and where it had been completely burned away, the opening in the fabric revealed the painfully charred flesh scorched by the Lightfire. Above the burn, his uniform fortunately covered the broken bone that twisted nauseatingly up and through his skin just below his shoulder.

Abish led him to the chair by the side of Garth's bed, but Cletis chose not to sit.

"Mom came to me," he whispered, looking down on his father. "And Abish. They both came to me." Flinching with pain, he reached through the blue shield. "I don't wanna ever do that again," he added faintly, taking his father's hand. Cletis faltered once more, tipping to his left. Immediately Abish wrapped an arm around his waist and held him steady.

"Go take care of yourself," Garth whispered. "Take Abish. Do what you have to do. I'll be here, waiting."

Cletis nodded and then looked up to Abish. He studied her green eyes.

"Hold me in the conduit," he requested. "I'm not feelin' so good."

She looked down on him and smiled through her tears.

The blue light of the conduit gradually gathered around the two of them, and as Garth watched from his bed, Cletis and Abish disappeared.

Safely within the amazing magic of a Traveler's conduit, despite his pain, Cletis sensed that the final moments of Abish's lengthy voyage were at long last before her. Gratefully he allowed Abish to hold him upright. He slumped against her, barely able to stand.

"Are you scared?" he whispered.

"Shhh . . . I'm not thinking of that right now," she answered. "We've got to get you well, and then I'll think about my homecoming." She paused. "I'm happy to stand here and hold the brave boy who risked his life to rescue an odd, old woman like me. You are the valiant grandson, now broken and bleeding, delivering his mother back to her dear parents. We'll get you taken care of, and then we'll celebrate."

Cletis only coughed and moaned.

At last the energy field materialized within the grand lodge. Only two people greeted them. Mahon and Teagan stood near the three large, center pillars in reverent, yet anxious, anticipation and looked up at the glowing conduit. He knew that this noble couple, with their other-worldly understanding of the present, the future, and the nature of Time Travel, were fully aware that their daughter's demanding journey across the centuries and back again was finally at an end. To them, only eleven years had passed. To Abish, nearly a thousand. Mahon and Teagan waited as Abish and Cletis floated softly to the ground.

Mahon rushed to Cletis, took the box from his hands, and helped Abish hold him in place. He handed the box to Teagan, and then studied Cletis's body, inspecting his wounds. The old man could see that the boy was in shock and rapidly slipping into unconsciousness.

"Cletis, listen to me," Mahon said abruptly, patting Cletis's cheek. "You are a Changeling now. Heal yourself. It is in your power."

Cletis, startled by the man's words and actions, looked up at him through dazed and blurred vision. "I can?" he whispered back to the old man.

"Yes!"

"How?"

"I don't know exactly, but you must force yourself to concentrate on the greatest pain," Mahon explained, grabbing Cletis above the waist to steady him. "Take your thoughts there. Go to it in your mind and repair it. It is within your power to do so."

Confused by the instruction and completely exhausted, still Cletis haltingly turned his thoughts inward and concentrated on the pain that was ever-present throughout his body. Suddenly he felt a surge of power in his mind similar to the sensation that flowed through him when the Traveler first taught him to Change. He focused on the feeling and found that it could be moved according to his thought. Weak as he was, he drove the feeling downward through his head and neck and into his right shoulder. Gradually a picture came to his mind, revealing the damage. An awareness of his internal, physical make-up was instantly before him, and he clearly visualized muscles and veins, bones and flesh. He mentally entered his right shoulder and saw the broken bone that speared upward through the skin of his arm. The sight of it from the inside, though at first nauseating, promptly turned fascinating. He focused the surging power directly into the break and felt the lower bone pull backward down into his arm. From his mind's eye, he observed the step-by-step process as the ragged ends of the broken bone bonded into their proper place and knitted perfectly together again. Where once punctured by the sharp and jagged bone, muscle and flesh now gathered and mended around the wound. Blood vessels, severed and bleeding from the break, melded together perfectly and resumed their normal function. Though the course was somewhat painful to Cletis, it was nothing compared to what he *had* been feeling.

Abish, Mahon, and Teagan studied his shoulder as Cletis worked the healing process. The mound below the uniform sleeve shifted and lowered until no sign of the break could be seen. Cletis's eyes opened for a moment, as if in surprise, and then quickly closed again.

He moved mentally down his right arm and came next to the burn. Concentrating on the pain, he directed the surge of power into the center of the dark and oozing wound. His flow of thought penetrated the injury, and he suddenly felt a kind of tickling sensation as the skin cells seemingly began to rejuvenate and the flow of blood brought renewed life to the charred flesh.

Again his eyes opened. With the elimination of the pain came renewed strength. "I'm doing it!" he called out groggily, facing the trio. "It's like I'm inside myself making it happen and watching it happen!"

He closed his eyes again. Once more he focused on the power within and directed it down through his arms and legs. He concentrated on the healing process and, one by one, located the tiny openings in his flesh. In each spot, he directed the skin to close and mend. Instantly the sting and tenderness of the numerous tiny slashes came to an end. Though the dried blood remained smeared on the skin of his hands, arms, and legs, the cuts that once covered him were completely repaired.

He looked back up at Abish, Mahon, and Teagan and smiled with new energy.

"What about the cuts on your head behind your ears?" asked Abish, touching his head gently.

"Oh, yeah . . . " He lifted his fingers to the area and went again into his mind. Finding the surge of energy, he guided it into his scalp. The repairing process began quickly once more. Cletis watched from within as the flesh cleansed itself and mended together. Within moments, the deep and open gashes above both ears were completely healed.

Cletis sighed and dropped his hands to his sides. He eyed the three people in front of him, but before he could open his mouth to express his thanks, Mahon spoke.

"But there are certain things *you* cannot repair," he stated, rising and placing a hand on Cletis's head.

The agonizing pain of the broken arm and the burn together had easily covered the throbbing in his head, so much so that he had almost forgotten it. Now with the pain of the other injuries absent, he felt the pounding again.

"What you have is not a headache," Mahon explained. "It is the placement of evil within the bounds of a pure mind." He placed his fingertips on Cletis's forehead and closed his eyes. Upon whispering words that Cletis couldn't understand, a sense of calming peace instantly flowed into his head, and the throbbing came abruptly to an end.

Mahon lowered his hand. "Do you remember the mind of the Traveler?" he asked.

Cletis eyed him curiously, trying to recall the haunting images that had come with the Changing. But he could not. He remembered what had happened in those moments with the Traveler, but the specific details of the dark visions now escaped him.

"Good," replied Mahon, as if Cletis had just given him the response he desired.

Mahon then stepped back, and the four of them stood silently for a moment, considering the wonder of the events that had finally brought them to this point in time. Teagan placed the box on the ground and turned to Abish. Without speaking, she opened her arms wide. Like a tiny, injured child who longed for her mother's comforting embrace, Abish stepped forward. Teagan's arms enveloped the strange, odd body, while Mahon stood in next to them. With his long, thin arms, he gently encircled the two women. For several moments they stood together, weeping and swaying as they held one another.

Abish's shoulders rose and fell with her sobs, yet she extended a hand toward Cletis. He took it and was drawn caringly into the circle, wrapped under Abish's wide, heavy arm and pulled tightly to her side.

When the embrace broke, Mahon spoke.

"You have passed the test, Abish," he declared, eyeing her proudly. "Padar's prophecy is fulfilled. You have proven your faithfulness to the family and your desire to again guard the sacred Powers that are ours. And your wisdom and keen judgment have taught and prepared a new Traveler. Abish of Dungarvan, daughter of Teagan, you are now greater than us all."

He knelt before her and kissed her bulbous, puffy hand. Teagan followed suit, kneeling gracefully next to her husband.

"No, don't do this," pleaded Abish hoarsely, reaching forward and pulling them both to their feet again. "I will never be your superior, nor do I want to be." They stood proudly as Abish hugged Cletis next to her and kissed the top of his head. "The battle was Cletis's alone. I did nothing at that time but watch and pray and admire his courage." She looked down at the boy. "After a thousand years, he is again peacefully in my arms. Without him, I wouldn't be here."

"But there are still things to be done, Cletis, aren't there," Mahon spoke. "There is still work to do."

Cletis smiled and nodded, thinking about home and the park and the game and all the loose ends that needed to be taken care of.

But most of all he thought of Abish. He studied the old man's eyes. "Will Abish be Changed into the other Abish now?"

Mahon paused a moment, looked at Teagan, and then glanced back to Abish and Cletis. He took a deep breath and folded his hands behind his back. For several seconds he stood in silence.

"I have no power to Change Abish back to her old self," he finally replied.

Cletis eyed Mahon with instant bewilderment. He felt Abish lean against him, as if she had just received a heavy and painful blow.

"You mean you can't Change her back?" Cletis felt a sudden confused panic sweep over him.

Mahon walked to Teagan and wrapped an arm around her. "I am sorry. A Changeling altered her, and she must be returned to her former self through the powers of a Changeling. There is only one that I know of who now possesses such a miraculous ability."

Cletis thought about his words for a moment and then suddenly gulped. His eyes opened wider, and his jaw dropped. He noticed that both Teagan and Mahon were looking directly at *him*. He eyed them anxiously as the words sunk in. Cletis felt Abish's gaze turn toward him. He looked up into her green eyes and considered the pocked, old face that studied him so hopefully.

"Me?" he asked, turning back to Mahon. "*I'm* supposed to Change her back?" The question had been on Cletis's mind even in the hospital room when he asked Abish who had Changed her in the first place and who was there when it had happened. He had wondered whether this man *Padar*, the father of Ian, was a Changeling too. Cletis had realized that if Padar were now dead and gone, and if Ian lost the battle in which he and Cletis were engaged, there would be no Changeling to take Abish through the transformation. He now knew why Mahon had so strongly emphasized the learning of the Changeling power.

"You now have that gift and knowledge," answered Mahon. "In fact, you are the only one."

Teagan stepped forward and pulled several strands of long auburn hair from a pocket of her robe. She took Cletis's hand in hers and placed the hairs on his palm and closed his fingers around them. "You will need these. It is all of her original self that I possess, and I have closely guarded them purposely for this day. The task is yours, my dear grandson."

Cletis looked down at the hairs in his hand and then back up to Mahon and Teagan. "But I've only Changed *myself* into someone else. I've only done it to *me*. I've never Changed another person. How am I supposed to do it?"

"Do you remember what you did with Ian when you became him?"

Cletis remembered placing his hands on the man's shoulders, over the hourglass marks.

"But he Changed *me* into *him*. I'm Changing Abish back into *her old* self."

"If I understand how the power can work, what you will need to do is a mixture of what Ian did to you and what you did when you Changed into Abish. As you hold Abish's hair, allow her image to flow through you."

Cletis concentrated a moment, trying to remember the details of how everything took place in that time of Changing with the old Traveler. He turned to Abish, who stood watching him anxiously. *I'm her only hope,* he thought. *I guess I can do this. I guess I have to do this!*

Cletis allowed the blue light of the conduit to gather around him and Abish. "I don't know if I need this," he said, looking up into the energy field that encompassed them. "But when I Changed into the Traveler and there were two of us, it was inside a conduit—so maybe it helps. I really don't know."

Abish stepped closer to Cletis. It was her second time in the conduit, and she still seemed uncomfortable being there. He held the strands of her hair in his hand and looked across into her green eyes. He tried to reassure her with a simple, awkward smile. But, on the contrary, it was her funny smile that calmed him.

He took a deep breath. "I know this is kinda strange," Cletis spoke, "but you gotta be touching the marks on my shoulders. At least that's what I did with . . ." Cletis couldn't bring himself to speak the man's name. "That's what I did when *he* taught me. You need to put both hands on the hourglass marks."

She pushed her large hands up through the baggy sleeves of his baseball uniform, and placed her hands on the hourglass marks on his shoulders. With her touch, Cletis felt the familiar surge of power—as if the marks were alive and eager to assist in another important work. Abish seemed to feel it too, for her eyes suddenly widened with surprise.

"You ready?" Cletis asked, swallowing.

"I think so."

He studied her a moment, looking close-up into the face of the old hag he had grown to find so charming. The closeness reminded him of their first meeting on her back porch when he turned on the light, met her face-to-face, and yelped in fear.

"I'm thinking the same thing," she winked, planting a quick kiss on his forehead. "I guess I've done this before," she whispered. "But it was so long ago, I don't remember anything about it."

Cletis closed his eyes in concentration and squeezed the strands of auburn hair he held in his hand. Abish gasped as she felt a sudden surge of power pass into her hands. The stirring must have been much stronger than the slight tingling she first felt, for she lifted her fingers away from the marks.

"Just keep your hands there," Cletis spoke reassuringly without opening his eyes. "If you take 'em off, it'll break the flow and nothin'll happen."

She pressed her hands obediently back onto the marks. The conduit suddenly hummed with vigorous energy. Abish watched with wonder as the force brightened, lifting both of them off the ground.

"It'll be okay," Cletis spoke confidently. "I've felt all this before."

Mahon wrapped an arm around Teagan as Cletis and Abish rose within the conduit.

Immediately the image of the young Abish burst into Cletis's mind. She stood beautifully dressed in the traditional white and gray robes that resembled the clothing worn by Mahon and Teagan. Her beautiful hair dropped lightly over the hood of her robe that hung loosely about her shoulders. She walked toward him, graceful and confident as she came. Suddenly her image was surrounded with radiance, as if captured, protected, and prepared for the next step of the Changeling process. Instinctively Cletis sent the image—as if bound in a shell of mental light—coursing down through his head, neck, and shoulders until it reached the hourglass marks where Abish had placed her hands. He marveled at how this Changeling process, though new to him, seemed to run its own natural course, progressing through each succeeding step and requiring little mental interference on his part.

When the image of Abish arrived at the hourglass mark, Cletis's shoulders instantly burned with an intense fire—not a fire of pain but of power. Unexpectedly the surge of energy thrust the vision-light through the hourglass marks and into Abish's hands. The jolt electrified her, sending the image of the younger Abish into every cell and fiber of her being. Cletis opened his eyes. He knew the transformation would begin instantly, and he wanted to watch the process.

Abish's eyes opened wide with surprise as the mental image of her real self and the surge of energy from Cletis's shoulders fired into her soul. Slowly the Changing process commenced. Cletis could tell that she was beginning to feel movement within her skeleton and internal organs. Her mouth opened with a gasp, and she looked down at her body as the bones, tendons, and muscles elongated and morphed, abandoning the familiar shape of the old woman and welcoming her former identity. Abish watched as the sagging flesh of the squat, corpulent body pulled and tightened around her. She gazed over at Cletis in wonder as the bones in her legs stretched several inches in height. The large mass of her shoulders and back, legs and arms, shrunk, constricted, and lightened, resuming anew, the graceful figure of the beautiful, young woman she had once been. As the process continued, her crop of wild, white-and-gray hair shimmered and quivered against the conduit's blue light as the hairs lifted, lengthened, and flowed, evolving into the healthy, shiny, auburn hair of her youth. Her neck craned back, and her body hummed internally with the transition. The puffy, wrinkled skin of her hands and arms, legs and feet, suddenly smoothed and softened and squeezed snugly around the elegant frame remarkably similar to that of her mother's. Her facial features and ears, once overgrown and mis-shapen, now pulled tightly on the skull that shifted beneath them. The skin around her eyes, nose, mouth, and chin altered and melded into the lovely, striking complexion and countenance of the young Abish. The burlap dress and the worn, baggy footwear of the old hag also gradually transitioned, evolving into the beautiful gray robes and the fine, leather boots Cletis envisioned. Through it all, her exquisite clear, green eyes remained unchanged.

When the Changeling process came to an end and the surge of energy diminished, Abish's hands dropped from the wide sleeves of Cletis's baseball shirt. She bent forward slightly, as if winded by the ordeal, but her eyes were wide with excitement. A mixture of uncertain joy and fear was etched on her beautiful, new face. The conduit gradually disappeared around them, the light faded, and the two of them floated to the ground. Cletis stepped away toward Mahon and Teagan, joining them in the silent celebration of Abish's rebirth.

At first, Abish remained motionless—seemingly awestruck by the transformation. Then she gradually began the process of discovery. Like a graceful swan testing its wings, she lifted her arms away from her. In astonishment she looked down upon herself, studying the form she had completely forgotten. She flexed her hands, arms, legs, and feet, as if testing their fresh, new movement and agility. Mesmerized by the lightness and perfection of her shape, she touched the soft smoothness of the skin on her face, neck, and hands. She gasped, and a happy smile filled her countenance. Seeing the beautiful hair that rested upon her shoulders, she reached up hesitantly and caressed it. In fascination, she lifted a handful and studied its color and soft, healthy texture. Silently joyful, she spread her arms wide, extended her fingers, inhaled deeply, and turned a graceful circle.

She faced her family again. Her chin quivered slightly, and her fingers went instantly to her lips. She looked to Cletis and stepped forward and touched his cheeks. A look of surprise suddenly filled her countenance, and her fingers lifted to her throat. She took a slow, deep breath. "Cletis," she finally said, as if testing a voice she had not heard in a thousand years. Upon hearing the light, lilting, tender tones that replaced the raspy croak she had heard for so long, her hands lifted again to her mouth. She gasped softly. Then, giddy with joy, she began to weep. "Cletis," she spoke again. "Torlock."

The happiness of the moment appeared to be more than she could bear. In tears, she dropped to her knees in front of the trio. "Oh, my," she whispered. "It has finally ended. . . . It is over." She bowed her head into her hands and sobbed.

Mahon and Teagan caringly lifted her back to her feet and wrapped their arms around her.

"Mother. Father. Mama. Papa," Abish voiced softly as they held her.

Finally she stepped away from their embrace, enfolded Cletis in her new and graceful arms, and pulled him tightly to her. "Oh, my son," she whispered through her tears. "You don't know what this means to me. We have fought our battles, and you have helped me, and now we are finally together again."

"Abish, your Powers are to be restored," stated Mahon, watching the pair. "We will do that now." In seeming anticipation of his words, Teagan stood in next to Mahon and pulled her hood up over her shiny, white hair. Cletis stepped back as Abish's parents raised their hands and placed them just above her head. Cletis watched closely, wondering what magic or power he was about to witness. Abish smiled at him reassuringly and then closed her eyes in deep concentration.

"That the Light of Power may return to Abish of Dungarvan," declared Mahon solemnly.

A flame of blue light appeared instantly, just below Mahon and Teagan's hands and just above the crown of Abish's head. Cletis could see that it came from her parents' fingertips. The radiance expanded over Abish's head and face and then appeared to settle into her entire being. At once she took a breath, and her fingers opened and closed with the inflow of an old, familiar power.

The bestowal complete, Teagan eased her hood down onto her shoulders again and, with a smile, placed kisses on her daughter's cheeks. "May you use it wisely, Abish of Dungarvan," she whispered.

"May you use it wisely, Abish, Mother of Torlock," whispered Mahon, wiping the tears from Abish's cheeks.

Mahon then turned to Cletis. He squatted in front of him and brushed some of the dirt off Cletis's uniform. "My boy, there is still work to be done, as you well know. When all is accomplished in your time and place, come to us again, and we will celebrate Abish's and your homecoming privately and quietly . . . for, you see, there is a beloved, old woman who lives outside of our community, who must know nothing of your successful return. Do you know of whom I speak?"

Cletis looked over at Abish and then back to Mahon. He nodded his head.

Mahon turned to Abish. "I know that sounds unjust, my dear, but it must be."

Abish nodded understandingly. "You were successful."

Mahon faced Cletis and continued, "Go back to your father. He watches you even at this moment. Allow Abish to heal him."

Abish took a quick breath, realizing that such a power again existed within her. She stood behind Cletis, wrapped her arms over his chest, and pulled him back against her. Together they watched as Mahon lifted the box from the ground and extended it to Cletis.

He took it in his hands and instantly thought of Timmy and Pauly and the game that needed to be finished. And there was a ton of other questions that still had to be asked and answered.

"What about Time?" Cletis began. "And what about the game? How do I get things all started back up again? And what about the three people that . . . aren't there anymore?"

"The freezing of Time has placed you, Abish, and your father in an independent state," Mahon explained. "You have moved freely within that frozen state without disturbing any previous balance. After you have visited your father, you may place yourself in Time at whatever moment you wish. In choosing to move backward in Time, and placing yourselves at a moment just prior to the battle with the Traveler, you will save your friends from the evil he has done."

"But if I go back . . . if I go backward even a few minutes, will the Traveler be there?"

"No, he is gone. Wherever you decide to place yourselves in Time, Time will start anew from that moment. And only you, Cletis, can determine where and when Time's forward progress will begin. And since you, and Abish, and your father have progressed, step-by-step through frozen Time, you will not find a duplication of yourselves present in that specific moment and place where you choose to renew Time." He paused briefly. "Let me explain. Everyone else will be there as they were before, except you. You will enter the scene, and it will continue as it did in the past, until you do something to change what was happening. Certain things will remain unaltered—like what people said, or where they stood. And remember, what you are about to experience on the field of your game will *not* be as it was when the Traveler took you back to the town you called Belleville. There you saw your younger self. In that situation, two of you were present at the same time. When you go back to the *game*, you will not see another Cletis like you did before."

"So you're saying that if I choose to put us back somewhere near the end of the game, I won't see another Cletis standing there in the batter's box, frozen in time, with the bat in his hands?"

"That is right. You will not," he answered. "There will be only one Cletis. You. The power of your thoughts will place you exactly where you want to be. Take the box and open it. To start Time again, you must say the words that will appear on the bottom inside panel of the box. That is what Padar told us before his death. Words will be seen in the box. Recite them aloud."

"I hope they appear a little quicker this time," voiced Cletis, his mind still racing through a dozen questions. "What about me and my uniform?" he asked, looking down at the mess he wore. The outside of the right sleeve was burned half off and covered with dried blood. He was caked with mud, grass, dust, and smeared blood. "It's gonna be pretty weird if I am clean one second and then . . . poof . . . covered with all this the next."

Cletis turned back to Abish and looked up at her for advice.

Within moments, the ladies had dressed him in the clothing of the time, and the filthy uniform had been taken away for cleaning and mending. The dried blood and dirt was washed from Cletis's hair, face, and arms, and while he waited, Mahon brought him bread, boar meat, apples, and water. He placed them on a long, thin, wooden table in the corner of the lodge and then left Cletis to eat.

Again Cletis noticed the wooden box. It lay on the ground near the three poles, in the center of the lodge. He walked to it, lifted it up, and opened the lid. He removed the baseball, and stepping across to the table, he set the ball next to the fruit. He studied the inside bottom panel of the box. The words that were once etched inside had disappeared completely, and no new words were presently visible.

That's weird. How'd the old words vanish? They were burned into the wood, and now there's no sign of 'em.

While waiting in the lodge, Cletis mentally relived the details of the seventh inning. He paced the dirt in front of the table and planned out his strategy. He knew he was still at bat, and he remembered the circumstances—Timmy on third, Pauly on second, two outs . . . *But what was the count? Oh, well,* he thought, *I can just ask the umpire when I get there. But wait a sec . . . the first pitch was high, and the catcher stepped on my toes. The second pitch was low and outside, and the ump called it a strike. That was a lousy call.* Then he remembered the next pitch. *Yeah, it was the third pitch. That's the one I'm lookin' for. The catcher said, "Abish is dead." That was the pitch I wanted. The catcher's mitt didn't move an inch, and he caught it right over the middle of the plate. I hope I can put me back right at that moment. That way, it's just right before anything happens to Elston. And that way, Timmy, Pauly, and the Canterbury kid at shortstop will be okay.*

Mahon entered the lodge carrying a pile of folded clothing and a pair of boots. Quietly he placed them on the table. Behind him, the ladies entered, giggling as they came—as if they had just had the most exciting time together. Abish handed Cletis the cleaned, repaired uniform, and within moments, Cletis was back in his shirt and pants, and ready to go. The mend on the sleeve was a bit ragged, but that mattered little. In fact, in Cletis's mind, it would serve as an eternal reminder of the battle he fought in fulfilling the prophecy.

The moment came to bid farewell. Mahon stepped back to the table and gathered the clothing he had placed there. "You will need these for your father," he spoke, extending the bundle to Cletis. "After Abish heals him, he will have nothing to wear. His clothing there is frozen solid and heavy."

"Oh, yeah," Cletis agreed, taking the clothing. "Thanks."

Cletis placed the box on top of the clothing he held. With Abish at his side, he thought of his father in the hospital. The light of the conduit engulfed them again, and as Teagan and Mahon waved, Abish and Cletis were gone.

CHAPTER 24

THE GAME GOES ON

The blue of the conduit filled the hospital room, and a renewed and energetic Cletis looked down at his father. His dad rolled his head feebly toward the radiant light and smiled a greeting up at Cletis and Abish as they floated to the floor. But with the fading of the conduit's aura, the protective shield that enveloped Garth, as well as the orb of vision that floated above him, disappeared. Without the blue shell, Garth suddenly cringed in pain and closed his eyes.

Cletis set the clothing and the box on the green chair closest to the monitors, took Abish by the hand, and led her to the bedside.

"I watched everything," breathed Garth.

Without saying a word, Abish stepped forward and placed her hand gently over Garth's chest.

"I think we've met before," she whispered, leaning down to him. "But I'm trying to remember where."

A blue light surged from Abish's fingertips into Garth's chest. His body jerked and he took a quick breath. As the glow penetrated his body, the expressions of exhaustion and pain left his face. She held her hand over him for several seconds, watching his eyes as the infusion of light continued. He studied her face and hand curiously, as if he felt the electrifying flow penetrate not only his heart, but every organ, muscle and system of his body.

Finally, when the blue light faded, she slid her fingers up to his face and touched his cheek. "How do you feel?"

Garth pulled the oxygen mask from his face and slowly sat up. There he paused, as if inspecting himself. "Perfect," he stated. He watched her a moment, and then lifted his arm and carefully pulled the tubes and needles from his wrist and the back of his hand. "Won't be needin' these, I guess." He lifted the sheets and was about to swing his legs over the side of the bed when he remembered he was wearing only his hospital gown. Sheepishly he looked up at her.

"Thank you," he nodded, remaining where he was. "I'm not sure what you just did . . . but, uh . . . whatever it was, it worked."

"You're a Dungarvan," she stated matter-of-factly. "The same power is within *you*, hidden deeply away. One day, if you'd like, I will teach you how to find it and use it."

His eyebrows raised slightly, and he studied her.

"Dad," stated Cletis, breaking the silence and smiling mischievously. "Let me introduce you. This is Abish of Dungarvan, a close relative of mine."

"Uhhh . . . yeah," he answered, playing along. A nervous grin lifted one side of his mouth, and he sat up a bit straighter. "And a *distant* relative of *mine*, I suppose. Pleasure to meet you in person, ma'am," he swallowed.

"If I recall correctly," she whispered, "we *have* met before. It was at my home. You called me 'demented' and 'demonic'."

Garth reached up and rubbed his mouth and beard stubble. "I think I do remember that . . . vaguely. Well, I was . . . uh . . ."

She leaned toward him, took Garth's head in her hands, and planted a kiss firmly on his lips. After several seconds, she pulled away. "I forgive you. And I want to thank you for being such a wonderful father to this dear boy. He is brave and selfless, and he learned that from you."

Garth swallowed. "Well, he's had a mother that was a pretty good teacher too," he added modestly, still feeling the kiss. "*Two* mothers."

After a bit of an awkward pause, Cletis lifted Mahon's clothes off the green chair and placed them on his dad's lap. "Let's go. We got some business to finish!"

Garth eyed the clothes, frowned, and then looked up at Abish.

Within the conduit, Abish and Garth stood together in the robes and boots of the ancient Dungarvan family, and as the blue aura faded around them, and the pair drifted to the ground near the steps of the Sperry dugout, Cletis envisioned the medieval royalty of a by-gone century. For Garth, moving within the energy of the conduit was both frightening and amazing. Cletis smiled knowingly as he watched his father stand in wide-eyed silence from the moment the energy field materialized around them to the second his feet touched dirt on the baseball diamond.

Cletis held the ancient box under his left arm, and with Abish and his father at his side, he stepped forward and studied the host of frozen figures on the field.

"Timmy!" Cletis suddenly cried out. He darted across the diamond to where Timmy took his short lead off third base. The grass crunched under his feet as he went. "Dad! Abish! He's still here!"

Cletis jumped and danced around his little friend, until an accidental bump into a frozen Mr. Howard knocked Cletis to the dirt. Laughing, rising, and turning to second, Cletis spied Pauly standing in the base path with the Canterbury shortstop close behind him. "Pauly!!" Charging over to his outfield teammate, Cletis jumped in the air and yelled out again. "Pauly's still here too! Yeah! And even the shortstop! They're all here!! Nothing's happened to them! They're all okay!!"

Cletis, wanting additional evidence that he had brought them back to the exact right time, tossed a quick glance out at the scoreboard.

CANTERBURY 6, SPERRY'S CARDS 4.

"And the center field fence is still there too, and no grass is burned around it!" he called out, taking a few steps past second base. "And it says there's two outs and the count is one and one. Yep, we're right where we want to be!"

Cletis eyed Elston up the first base line and jogged past the mound and over to his friend. Hearing the crackle, Garth bent low to the grass and felt the sharp blades.

"This is beyond belief," he whispered. "Boy, no wonder Cletis was bleeding. These are like tiny needles stickin' up outta the ground."

Abish bent down next to him and rubbed her fingers carefully across the tops of the blades of grass.

"I knew all this would happen eventually," she sighed, "but I had no idea it would turn out this way."

They both rose together and headed up the first base line toward home plate. Cletis stood before them with a hand on Elston's back. Tenderly he patted the statue. "And Elston's still playin' up for the bunt," he called, looking back at his dad. "Looks like everything is right in place!"

When Garth and Abish joined Cletis, Garth put his hand out to touch Elston. For the first time, Garth experienced the rock-hard feel of a Time-frozen human being. Abish, too, placed her hand on Elston's solid frame.

"Weird, huh?" breathed Cletis.

"Unbelievable," sighed his father. "Beyond words."

Cletis grinned and looked Elston in the face. "See, I told you everything was gonna work out."

"No one will ever believe us, will they?" commented Garth, studying the unmoving human being in front of him.

"No, I don't think they will," answered Abish. "At least not in this day and age."

"If I figured this out right," Cletis continued, "I'm still up to bat right now . . . " Cletis moved thoughtfully toward the plate. The batter's box was empty, but Cletis's bat and helmet rested on the dirt near the catcher.

Still spooked, Cletis halted and peered over at the Canterbury dugout, searching for Martin. The seed bucket was still there, upside-down at the top of the steps. No one sat upon it. But in his mind's eye, Cletis saw the man watching him—watching him through those black and hollow eyes—spitting seed shells and smiling wickedly. Slowly he took several steps toward the Canterbury dugout, seemingly lost in dark and distant thoughts. For a long and silent minute he stood looking at the bucket.

Abish and Garth watched him closely, wondering what concerns and fears still warred in the young man's mind.

"Clete," called Garth, walking toward him. "You okay?"

Cletis finally nodded. He looked down at the box in his hands and turned and walked back toward home plate. He eyed the field as he approached the batter's box, studying again the positioning of the players. Near the plate, Cletis studied the catcher squatting in front of the ump.

"See this guy? He's a jerk." Cletis lifted his head toward the outfield and glared at the center and right fielders. "And those two guys out there. They're jerks too."

"But even your good friend Elston," reminded Abish, "did some pretty unsportsmanlike things, Clete. Maybe they were all under the Traveler's influence. Maybe he brought out the worst in them."

Cletis thought about that for a moment. He knew that Elston had never done a mean thing in his life—at least not for as long as *he* had known him. Maybe the same held true for the other guys too. Maybe they were all decent guys, just doing unexpectedly mean things under the spell of the Traveler.

Abish stepped closer to Cletis. Her arms were folded in front of her. Her graceful form seemed to float rather than walk.

"Cletis, there is something I need to say to you."

It was still amazing to Cletis to hear the calm and peaceful music of her new voice.

"You know those gifts we talked about with Elston? Hitting and fielding—when we were back at my house?" She touched the mended sleeve of his uniform. "Well, I didn't *give* you anything. You and Elston already had them in you. You simply discovered them. 'The orb shall be driven at his command,' was pretty much your own doing. You and Elston believed in me and in yourselves. You worked hard at it, and you made it happen. But it wasn't magic—at least as far as I know. It was your *own* efforts." Cletis eyed her thoughtfully. "So, anyway, I tell you all this because if you win this game, I want you to realize that it was done by your *own* abilities and not because of a supposed magic spell that never existed."

Cletis peered over at Elston. *Boy, it was like magic,* he thought. *We did things we had never done before. Could that have been in us all along, and we just needed to believe in ourselves to make it happen? Or did Padar have something to do with it?*

Abish looked back at the umpire. His right arm was frozen in the "strike" position, and the catcher below him held the ball—low and away—snuggly in his glove. "I think I know why you brought us back to this point in the game," she smiled. "The next pitch is coming right down the middle."

Cletis nodded, a slight grin formed on his lips. "Yep, he was cheatin', and I lost the pitch I wanted. So now I get a chance to play it, fair and square." He turned to his dad. "Is that wrong, Dad?"

"I personally think you deserve a fair chance at that pitch," Garth answered.

Abish turned her head back to the outfield, studied the fielders, and then tugged on Cletis's sleeve. "Okay then. Do what you know how to do."

Garth chuckled. "Let's see how this ol' ball game turns out."

Cletis held the wooden box in both hands and rocked it nervously up and down. He studied Garth and Abish as they stood in their ancient clothes. "Well, you'd better find someplace to watch, where it's not gonna look like you just appeared outta nowhere. I'll show you where."

Cletis pointed to a spot behind the Sperry dugout on the other side of the fence and up the right field line. It was the place, secluded under a stand of trees, where Cletis had appeared in the conduit just prior to the game. From there the entire field could be seen, but Garth and Abish would be hidden from the handful of Greenberg people who thought Garth was still in the hospital.

"Okay," called Garth as he and Abish walked off the field. "Time for some baseball magic."

Cletis nodded, and as he watched them walk away, he giggled out loud at their funny matching clothes and boots. *My dad, the plumber of Greenberg Junction, wearin' woolen robes a thousand years old. But I guess it's better than one of those open-back hospital gowns.*

Garth and Abish disappeared around the end of the dugout. Cletis took a deep breath and peered down at the box in his hands. *Well, let's get this game goin' again*, he told himself. *Except, I don't know what I'm doin'.* He opened the box, laid back the lid, and studied the bottom panel. Letters appeared slowly, glowing one by one, spelling out the message.

Cletis of Dungarvan, It's About Time.

Cletis studied the words curiously. "What? Is this what I'm supposed to say?" he voiced aloud, a bit bewildered by the phrase in the box. He looked up above him, into the twilight of the evening sky, as if the box writer were watching him. Suddenly the image of the man in the field came back to Cletis—the one who had watched Cletis and Elston and had appeared and disappeared so abruptly. *Padar,* thought Cletis. *That's who that was. It was Padar . . . my grandfather! It had to be! He's the one who arranged the magic to fit the prophecy . . . all the way down to the final phrase in the box.* He smiled up into the sky. *Thank you, Padar, wherever you are now.*

He looked out at Abish and his dad, who had just settled on the other side of the fence in shallow right field. His dad rested his arms on the railing on the top of the chainlink and then looked back at Cletis and nodded. Cletis peered down at the bat and helmet below him and then stepped over to the backstop. He squatted low to the ground and leaned against the fencing.

"Well, here goes."

He set the open box at the base of the backstop behind home plate, stepped back to the plate, and scooped up his bat and threw his helmet over his head. He adjusted himself in the batter's box, stared out at the pitcher, and taking a big breath, hollered, "CLETIS OF DUNGARVAN, IT'S ABOUT TIME!"

Motion and sounds and life were renewed instantly all around him.

"Stee-rike ONE!" bellowed the ump, punching the air with a right-handed fist.

"That was outside!" Cletis yelled back at him. *Yeah, that's what I said,* he remembered. *Just like that.*

"Young fellow, you wanna get tossed?" warned the ump.

Cletis stepped away from the plate and exhaled a long gust of air through puffed–out cheeks. He couldn't help smiling as he thought about how exciting it was to see people moving again. No one was frozen anymore. He adjusted his helmet, peered over at Elston, and gave him a big smile. Elston eyed him suspiciously and smiled faintly back at him. With a nod, Cletis looked down the third base line at Timmy, and then over to Pauly. Everyone was *moving*. Everyone was well.

The noises of the game were immediately loud and real. The Canterbury players and parents were calling and chattering and clapping. The Greenberg Junction crowd was cheering him on. Traffic, planes, birds—every sound was exciting.

Klu stood in the on-deck circle swinging his bat. "Here we go, Clete!" he called out. "A hit's a run! Maybe two runs! Gotta do it now!"

Cletis took in a long breath, as if sucking the happiness of the moment deep into his lungs. He glared down at the Canterbury catcher, who squatted again behind home plate. The boy stared up at him with a sly grin. Cletis exhaled, took a few practice swings, and turned to Mr. Howard for the signs.

I've gotta focus on the moment, Cletis demanded of himself. *Just play the moment.*

Mr. Howard simply clapped his hands and nodded his head. "Fire in the hole!" he hollered enthusiastically.

Cletis turned back to the plate and studied the outfield gaps— especially the one in right-center. *They're right where I want 'em.* He stepped back into the batter's box. *No matter where those guys are gonna be runnin' around, I'm puttin' this one to the right-center fence . . . over, if I can.*

When Cletis dug in at the plate, he felt his heart race with the thrill of the moment. Then the chant began again.

"Witchboy! Witchboy! Witchboy!"

The shifting infielders darted back and forth as the pitcher came set and eyed the plate. Taking signs from the catcher, he checked the runners on third and second, and then reared back, pushed forward off the rubber, and fired the ball home.

"Abish is dead," the catcher whispered.

Just what I wanted to hear. Here it comes. Basics. Remember the basics.

The pitch came in hard, fast, and straight down the middle. It floated in as big as a beach ball, and Cletis saw it clearly. *Squish the bug, drive the hips, extend the arms, and see the contact.* Attacking it, Cletis came around hard and felt the sweet, solid contact. CRACK! The right-center gap was the target, and the ball knew its destination. It shot into the darkening evening sky, like a sharp knife strategically slicing right field and center field straight down the middle.

As the Canterbury fielders raced after it, Cletis dropped his bat and took off. Again the action around him suddenly seemed to float by in slow motion. He approached first base, hearing the nearby cheers from Abish and Garth, but their voices seemed distant. He could hear the calls from the Sperry dugout and Mrs. Klu yelling from the stands. But the sounds—their exact words—were remote and muffled. His concentration was too keenly focused on what was happening in that precise moment to hear anything clearly.

To his left he could see that Pauly was turning the corner at third, which meant that Timmy, unless he had fallen between third and home, had already scored. *That's two runs*, Cletis figured as he reached the bag. *The game's tied at least.* He rounded first and watched the outfielders race into position, struggling to catch up to the ball that rocketed over them.

Half way to second, he saw the ball crash down on top of the fence bar and take a long bounce back into the field, toward the diamond. *There goes my home run*, Cletis commiserated as he charged around second base. *I guess I only got warning track power tonight.* The two fielders who reached the fence at about the same moment, slid to a halt, reversed direction, and chased the ball back toward the infield.

Sprinting to third, Cletis saw Mr. Howard's arm circling, sending him home to score. "GO! GO! GO!" he was shouting.

This is gonna be close, Cletis thought as he took a wide turn at third and headed for home.

Out of the corner of his eye, he saw one of the outfielders snatch the ball up from the grass and, with a crow's hop, fire it home. In front of him, Cletis saw the catcher squat low and prepare to take the throw. Pauly and Timmy both knelt on the opposite side of the plate, frantically waving their arms up and down, signaling for Cletis to slide. The big catcher knelt back on his haunches a good three feet up the line toward third, purposely blocking the plate and inviting the collision. Cletis knew that the tree-trunk catcher was almost twice his size, and he also knew that it was a rule that he had to slide in a situation like this or he'd be called "out."

He knows he's bigger than me, and he's playin' it smart.

Immediately the catcher's cheating, cruel words roared out in Cletis's mind. *"Abish is dead!"* With those words, Cletis relived the boy's cleats pressing rudely down on his toes. In his mind's eye, he saw the kid's cunning grin as he extended his hand down toward a fallen Cletis. "Sorry, witchboy," the big catcher had said.

With each step toward home, Cletis allowed his temper to surface. *But it's controlled right now, so that's okay,* he reasoned. *But this kid's got it comin', spell or no spell! So I gotta time my slide just right! Take him out if I can. This has got to be perfect.*

Teeth clenched and running at full speed, Cletis hit the dirt at the same moment the throw slapped into the catcher's mitt. In a cloud of dust, Cletis felt his rubber spikes hit the catcher's shin guards, and heard the catcher grunt with the force of the impact. The dirt flew around them, and the big kid fell backward, hit the ground with a thud, and sprawled across the plate. The ump continued to watch the play closely, but when he didn't make a call, Cletis realized that the catcher had never tagged him. At the same time, Cletis had not yet touched the plate. Out of the corner of his eye, Cletis watched the ball roll away from the catcher's glove toward the infield grass and saw the boy scramble after it. With Cletis's cleats still two feet short of the plate, he knew he had to move fast. In a flash, he sat up, rolled to his knees, dove forward on his chest, and stretched for the back edge of the plate. The catcher barehanded the ball in front of home and fell backward, searching for Cletis and trying to make the tag. The hands of both boys slapped the base at precisely the same moment. But the catcher's attempted tag was a good four inches away from Cletis's fingers, which now rested safely on the back point of home plate.

"HE'S THERE!" bellowed the ump, throwing his arms out to his sides like a heavyweight tightrope walker.

Instantly Cletis was on his feet jumping and cheering as Pauly, Timmy, and Klu surrounded him in the celebration. The Sperry bench emptied with a roar, and the teammates poured out onto the field and joined the circle, hollering and hugging and patting each other on their helmets and backs. In the stands, the Greenberg Junction parents were alive with energy and applause as they watched the rag-tag, sandlot team celebrate its well-earned victory. Mr. Howard jogged in from third, grinning and clapping. Abish and Garth cheered and applauded from the fence by the right field foul line as they watched the team holler and jump and dance in front of home plate.

The announcer's voice echoed across the field.

"Ladies and gentlemen, the Greater Metro Tournament comes to an end. Congratulations to Greenberg Junction. Tonight's final score: Canterbury Heights 6, Sperry's Cards 7. Coach Howard, we invite you to gather your players at home plate for the presentation of the trophies that will take place in just a few minutes. Thank you all for your support and attendance. Have a good night."

Another flock of roars and cheers lifted from the field into the calmness of the summer night as the parents in the stands added a final round of applause. Through the celebration, Cletis looked over to Elston, who now stood near the third base line, watching his buddies congratulate one another.

"Elston!" Cletis called to him, breaking free of the group and running across the infield.

Elston waited there sheepishly, as if wondering what Cletis would say after all the strange things that had happened before and during the game. When Cletis approached, Elston looked over to the Canterbury dugout behind him, seemingly concerned about what Coach Martin would do if he were seen talking with an "enemy" player. But the feisty coach was nowhere to be seen.

Covered with dust from his roll in the dirt at home plate, Cletis jogged up to his old buddy and extended his hand. "Nice game, Elston," he said with a smile.

Elston took his hand. "Yeah, nice game." He gave a quick nod toward right field. "Nice hit out there. Just about cleared the fence."

"Just about."

They shook hands for a moment, and then Cletis pulled him closer for a quick hug.

"Hey, man," started Elston, "sorry for all the dumb things that I've said and done in the past few days. Don't mean nothin' by 'em. I don't know what got into me."

"I think *I* do." Cletis patted his shoulder. It wasn't so solid this time. "But don't you worry. Call me. Maybe Dad'll let me ride my bike to your house. It'll only take me two or three hours."

Elston smiled at the thought. Suddenly the whole Greenberg Junction team gathered around him, shouting and cheering and patting their old buddy on the back, shoulders, and head.

Cletis quickly dodged away from the pack of celebrating friends, hustled to the backstop near the drinking fountain, picked up the wooden box, and raced down the right field line to Abish and his dad. There they waited patiently, watching him proudly as he jogged up to them.

"Nice hit, kid," spoke his dad, reaching over the four-foot fence and patting Cletis's shoulder.

"Thanks."

"You did it," added Abish. "We knew you could."

"Quite a collision at home," continued his father. "You okay?"

"Yeah, I'm fine. That kid was a bully. He needed to be plowed into."

"Well, looks like you played it hard and smart."

"Good form on that last swing," winked Abish.

Cletis studied the two of them for a moment. Though their clothing looked totally out of place for a baseball park, from where Cletis stood, the trees framed them handsomely against the darkening skies above. They looked perfect together.

"What?" questioned his dad, studying Cletis's goofy expression. "What's that look all about?"

"Uh . . . well . . . " stuttered Cletis. "I . . . I'm just thinkin' that they're gonna be running around wild in the hospital, trying to figure out where you are."

His dad smiled and looked up into the sky. "I'll just tell 'em my son had a championship game and I couldn't miss it. And that if they're not able to keep track of their patients, that's their problem."

"Well, we better start plannin' our stories, cuz I know some friends and neighbors who are gonna be askin' a ton of questions. So I think I need to get Abish to our house and get you back to the hospital."

"Can you do that okay?" asked his father.

"Yeah, as long as I find a private place to bring the conduit to me."

Suddenly, Rabbit sprinted up the base line toward the trio. Garth ducked away, hiding himself in the nearby trees. Abish, who had less to fear from seeing Cletis's friends, stood her ground.

"We're all headin' over to Klu's when we get home," Rabbit spouted. "But Mrs. Klu wondered if you needed a ride back to the hospital or a ride home."

"Oh . . . uh . . . thanks," stammered Cletis, trying to think. "Uh, yeah . . . I think a ride home would be great."

Rabbit turned to Abish and smiled.

"You played a super game," stated Abish, studying Rabbit's shiny black hair.

"Thank you," she answered, looking up into Abish's green eyes.

"They call you *Rabbit*?" Abish questioned.

"Yes, ma'am, but my real name is Roberta," she answered, still studying Abish's eyes.

"Well, you're smooth and graceful at shortstop. You've got soft hands and quick feet, and you look great out there."

"Thank you," she answered again. "Los ojos verdes . . . " she said distantly. "The eyes of the panther. You have beautiful eyes. There is a woman who lives near us—an old woman—whose eyes are exactly like yours. Beautiful, green eyes. They bring luck." She turned to Cletis. "I told them so. I told them the old lady's green eyes were lucky." She looked back again at Abish. "Your eyes too. You must have brought us luck tonight, ma'am." With those words, Rabbit bowed slightly and then dashed happily back toward the dugout.

Cletis took a breath and sighed. "Okay, let's get outta here. I'm not too good at makin' up truthful lies." He handed Abish the box, and in a second he was over the fence and standing at her side.

"What about the trophy ceremony?" she asked, looking back at the field. "You're not going to miss that are you?"

"No, getting you two back where you need to go should only take a few seconds, I hope."

"Then I'll watch it from home in the orb," she decided. "But to be truthful, I'm too happy to be worried about any questions." She combed his strawberry blond hair gently between her fingers.

They joined Garth in the shadows, and Cletis led them both into the depths of the pines, elms, and maples. Cletis was amazed at how suddenly the noise and light from the park were blocked out. For a moment the dark stillness reminded him of the hopelessness that enveloped him during those final moments of the battle with the Traveler. The gloom of the ugly memory sent a shudder through his whole being. He squeezed the softness of Abish's hand, and when she squeezed back, he instantly felt the comfort he needed. Though the new world of time travel and magical powers bewildered him, he was filled with a comfortable confidence that from now on his future would be blessed with the tender clarity of Abish's beautiful, green eyes; the continuous, never-failing stability of his father's strength and love; and the soft, blue glow of Dungarvan magic.

CHAPTER 25

COUSINS, PIGS AND THE BACK PORCH

The bustle and activity, the noises and smells of the village in which Mahon and Teagan lived astounded Cletis. It was like a pretend medieval festival where everyone dressed in authentic costumes of the day and lived the medieval life so that the visiting tourists could come and be entertained. But what Cletis experienced wasn't for tourists, and it wasn't pretend. This was the reality in which these people lived—a people who were the direct ancestors of his Dungarvan family. To Cletis, the village reminded him of the drawings in history books or the movies of England and Ireland that depicted gallant knights who roamed the hills and beautiful maidens with long hair who watched from castle windows.

While Cletis and Mahon meandered the village pathways, little children ran in and out of the huts and cabins around them, teasing, laughing, and playing. Laundry hung from ropes tied between trees and posts. Gardens full of flowers and vegetables grew behind the homes. Horses, sheep, cattle, and goats were corralled in the small barns and split-logged fences built between the quaint houses. The aroma of cooking meats and vegetables wafted round about the dwellings, and the soothing sounds of laughter, music, conversation, and work filled the air. The community was busy doing, making, living, sharing, thriving.

How Cletis wished Abish could join him and her father as they strolled. But inasmuch as Abish's return with Cletis was to be kept secret, she spent no time outdoors, unless Cletis transported her to places away from the town where she was far from people or traffic.

"One day, I'll bring Dad to this place," voiced Cletis, admiring the gray robes and the soft leather boots that Mahon and Teagan had given him. Though they weren't as comfortable as a T-shirt, jeans, and an old pair of sandals, he loved the earthy, natural feel they possessed. "I'd like him to see the village here and smell the sea and learn about the old side of the Dungarvan family."

"We're not old," advised Mahon, smiling. "We're the originals . . . the beginnings. And yet there were many before us too!"

Cletis smiled at the thought. Now, with his ability to move through time, young or old really didn't mean much anymore. He was beginning to understand that every person who walked the planet was on this same voyage called Life, basically riding the same currents but embarking and disembarking the ship at different times.

Cletis studied the hillside across the valley. Many of the trees were covered with white flowers. The weather was cool, and the gulls above them dipped and lifted, then disappeared toward the wide blue expanse over the spread of hills to the south.

"When I Changed into him," Cletis began, "I saw he was once good. In those last minutes, he could've killed me, but he didn't." Cletis looked up at Mahon.

"You're right. Ian was once good. When he was enclosed, or imprisoned, we visited him . . . *I* visited him. He was never humble. He never regretted his evil acts. He always threatened us, claiming we had stolen his powers. Even his father, in his old age, visited him."

"Padar?" asked Cletis.

"Yes, Padar. A powerful man and a good man, he was." Mahon scratched his beard in thought. "When Padar and I, as well as others, found that Ian would not change—that he would not soften—Padar spoke the prophecy. He had that gift. In order for the prophecy to be fulfilled, Abish would be tested, Ian would be tested, and you—the new Traveler—would be tested." He eyed the surprised, confused look that suddenly appeared on Cletis's face. "Yes, my son, *you.*"

Mahon looked out over the horizon. A soft breeze pushed against their faces as they walked. "You know that only a Traveler can bring to an end another Traveler's life before the rightful time . . . and that can only be done through the powers of the Traveler's box. Though you were young and vulnerable, the time was right. The magic in the box was created to recognize the pure, young man who would be its rightful owner. You were that boy. You were prepared for that role."

Cletis pondered his words. "What do you mean, 'prepared'?"

"Challenges. Trials. Setbacks. The awkward eye that you were born with. The ridicule of your peers. Your mother's untimely illness and death . . . Your loneliness. Through those tests, your heart became compassionate. Look at what you did for the Ketchums and Mr. Howard. And Abish. Very few people treated her as you did.

"A compassionate heart cultivates love," Mahon continued. "Why he didn't take your life at the very end is not known to us. Perhaps deep inside he genuinely respected you. *You* let him live when *you* could have destroyed him. Perhaps it was because of your birth or because of your courage or because of the love you possessed for your mothers. Yes, he could have destroyed you in those last moments. But he did not."

Mahon put a hand on Cletis's shoulder. "A mother's love protects a child with a far greater shield than armor. But when a young man, such as you, carries the immeasurable love of two mothers . . . oh my, he is near invincible!"

They walked thoughtfully onward, crossing over a small, wooden bridge on a pathway that led away from the village. Cletis looked down on the stream below, following its winding course through the lush dales and mounds that led to the sea. The caws of distant gulls carried on the soft breeze that brushed the grasses on both sides of the path ahead of them.

Then the dreadful thought came.

"Mahon! The ball! The baseball! Is it still in the lodge?"

"I don't know. It was there yesterday. Why do you ask?"

Cletis turned around and ran toward the bridge. "There should be two boys—both about five or six years old. They will take the ball to a bog—like a swamp. Is there any place like that around here?"

Mahon hurried along at his side. "I don't understand."

"In 1991—in my time—two boys'll be found in a bog somewhere

in southern Ireland. A place like this place! Their bodies'll be preserved in that bog, and they'll have a baseball with them. One of them'll stick it under his clothing. The searchers will find it with him. I read about it in a kind of book thing where they talk about discoveries and stuff like that. The only way a baseball could've gotten into their hands is through me! From the lodge! But if they have it now and they're playin' with it somewhere, it could mean that they'll end up stuck in a bog and die!"

Cletis and his grandfather reached the bridge, raced across the wooden planking, and hurried toward the village. Suddenly, Mahon stopped him, put a hand on Cletis's shoulder and, panting, looked into his eyes. "You think those two little boys will be from our village?"

"Can't be anyone else! One of 'em will have the medallion on a chain—you know, the bear and the scroll. They'll find it on him a thousand years from now. They both will die there in that bog, wherever it is!"

"Can you move to the lodge through the blue light?"

Cletis stopped. "Yes, I can."

"Then go and look for the ball," advised Mahon. "If it's gone, go to the north of the village. There is a dark pond about two miles away, following the large road that goes up into the hills. There are pits there where we have found the bones of large animals. The children know they are not to go there because the land is a swamp."

"But I thought you already knew about all this," questioned Cletis. "About the baseball and the boys and the bogs?"

"Maybe Padar knew of this, but I did not. Not all things have been made known to us. But if this has been made known to you, then we need to find the boys."

Cletis allowed the conduit to gather around him. "I'll go to the lodge, and then I'll go to Teagan. If I can't find the ball there, I'll go to the pond. Meet me there at that swamp!"

The energy of the conduit dematerialized in the center of the lodge, and Cletis came to the ground running. He raced to the table in the corner and searched through and around the remaining fruit and bowls and the wooden utensils that had been placed there since the last time he came. There was no sign of the baseball. He turned and raced around the walls of the lodge, scanning the ground and the crevasses between the standing timber walls and the three large middle poles that supported the roof. Still the ball was nowhere to be seen.

Cletis darted through the open door of the lodge and hurried across the pathway to the cabin where Abish and Teagan waited. He jumped the two stairs that led to the front door and frantically entered.

"Abish!" he called as he scooted by Teagan, who sat near the door.

"I'm here," Abish answered from an adjoining room.

Cletis hurried toward the sound of her voice with Teagan anxiously on his heels. Before he saw Abish, he began his explanation.

"Do you remember the tabloid—that newspaper that I bought back at home for initiation to get on the team? The one I put in Pauly's box with all the baseball stuff?"

She studied him curiously. "No, I don't think I do."

"It had an article about two boys that were found in Ireland—boys that were about a thousand years old by the time they found 'em—their bodies were like mummies because they had died in the bogs, and the bogs preserved their bodies. One of them supposedly had a baseball hidden under his shirt!"

Sensing the seriousness of Cletis's concern, Abish rose to her feet.

"Abish, I think those boys are from this village! I think they must live here somewhere, cuz I can't find the baseball I brought in the box yesterday! It's not in the lodge anymore!"

Teagan immediately stepped in next to Abish and nervously took her arm.

"I gotta find 'em," Cletis continued. "Mahon told me that there are swamps about two miles north of here where the kids aren't supposed to go. And it kinda sounds like it could be the bogs the archeologists were diggin' in, so I'm gonna go straight out there, and I'm gonna see if I can find 'em!"

"I can't leave here, Cletis," spoke Abish, sincerely. "No one is to see me."

"Where's Mahon?" questioned Teagan.

"He's up by the bridge! He might be comin' this way first, but he's gonna meet me up at that swamp. The boys were about five or six years old, I think. They were small."

"You go to the ponds, while I start searching for the boys," Teagan stated decisively. "We'll take care of things here, and I'll meet you there too."

"Abish, I know there's got to be more than one way to set this whole baseball prophecy thing in motion," Cletis spoke thoughtfully as the blue light gathered around him and lifted him off the ground. "What's done is done in the future, but I don't think I'm upsetting any Time balance if I try to get those two kids before they go into that swamp. I'll figure out somethin'." With his final words, he and the conduit vanished.

Cletis transported above the village. From his perspective, he could see the main road that led away to the north. He followed it the needed distance until he spotted the dark water that Mahon and Teagan spoke of. The area appeared to be the home of a massive swamp that surrounded a large, muddy pond.

There must be some oil or tar springs under all that, Cletis thought as he allowed himself to settle near a large tree close to the road. The moment he touched the grass-covered ground, he walked to higher earth where he could scan the edges of the immense swamp. Not a soul could be seen.

"Hey!" he called, listening anxiously for any sounds the boys might make. "Anybody here?" He wandered down the hillside until he hit level ground. The earth was soggy and sticky, and each step left a footprint two inches deep.

Suddenly the pungent, disgusting odor of death was in the air— like the smell of road-kill on the highway near Abish's house. Cletis looked around him, wondering where the stench came from. Finally he spotted the carcasses. To his right, about twenty feet away stuck in the mud, were the remains of three large pigs. They appeared to have been dead several days, and their stink was fierce.

Again Cletis scanned the area. "Anybody here?" he called again. Still only silence.

He skirted the north edge of the pond, trying to stay on dry land. As he searched the banks of the swamp, thick gray clouds gathered in the sky to the north. They appeared to be heading south toward the village. Cletis felt the breeze suddenly become a wind.

"Hey!" Cletis shouted. Tall reeds and grasses grew far out into the marsh, obscuring his view of much of the water. *The boys could be right under my nose, and I wouldn't even see 'em!*

Then he heard it. A child's voice.

"Where are you?" Cletis called out, racing in the direction of the sound. He hurried around the pond, attempting to stay away from the deep mud that would hinder his footing. "Keep talking to me! Say somethin'! I need to hear you!"

Again the soft cry came.

Cletis allowed the conduit to gather around him, wondering why he didn't think of using the gift earlier. He floated off the ground and moved out over the surface of the mud, searching the sludge and dark waters for the boys.

Finally, well-hidden behind tall reeds, he spotted the heads and arms of the two small children as they struggled desperately to remain above the surface of the gooey mud. Moving the conduit toward them, he could see they were crying desperately and slowly sinking into the black grave that engulfed them. To his astonishment, in the hand of one boy—the smaller of the two, a little blond child—was a slime-covered baseball.

Cletis considered the situation, trying to figure out the best way to pull the boys from the quagmire. *I know the Traveler pulled me up into the conduit, so I figure I can do the same thing with them*, Cletis reasoned as he directed the energy field closer to the boys.

He hovered over the head of the larger boy—a redheaded child who had sunk the deepest. But to Cletis's surprise, both boys looked up at him in fear, not knowing who or what he was. Instantly they cried and flailed all the more. As they struggled desperately to stay afloat, they sunk all the faster.

"Don't be afraid! Just grab my foot!" Cletis shouted as he floated above the redheaded boy. "Hurry!"

Instantly the little hands shot up through the conduit and eagerly latched on to Cletis's boot. Cletis attempted to lift the boy but found he was incapable of doing it. Try as he might, he couldn't budge the lad!

He's stuck in there too deep! When the Traveler pulled me up into the conduit, there was nothin' pullin' me back the other way or holdin' me down!

Cletis shot a glance over at the other crying boy. He could see that his shoulders were sinking deeper into the blackness around him. "Don't move or you're just gonna go down faster!" Cletis yelled, hoping the boys would calm a bit. It didn't work.

Can I drop the conduit into something solid? questioned Cletis. *Can I put it into the ground? Or into water or mud?* Cletis's thoughts raced as he tried to figure a way to extract the boys from the black slime. *I gotta do somethin' quick, or they're gonna sink outta sight!*

Cletis allowed the conduit to dissolve around him, and he dropped into the mud next to the redheaded boy. The boy's flailing shoulders were already below the surface, and his eyes bulged in panic as his chin touched the gooey mire. With Cletis now at his side, the boy grabbed the woolen robe, pulled himself close, and clung to Cletis. With the extra weight now dragging Cletis down, he knew he had to act fast. In an attempt to keep the boy's head above the brown liquid, Cletis placed his hands under the boy's arms, and lifted him upwards. Though the child was instantly able to breathe freely, Cletis sunk all the faster. With intense concentration, Cletis gathered the conduit about him.

I hope this works, he thought desperately, *cuz if it doesn't, we're both goin' down!*

The process was a bit slower than usual, but gradually the blue light enveloped the two of them. As Cletis held the boy tightly within the whirling energy, suddenly they were freed from the swamp and over dry ground. Yet, upon seeing the mud slowly gather into the gaping hole where other boy was last seen, the smaller child shrieked in fear, imagining himself left all alone to face a dark and murky death in the bowels of the bog.

On higher ground north of the swamp the conduit reappeared. It floated softly to the earth and dissolved, dropping not only Cletis and the redheaded boy to the earth, but emptying the gallons of oily mud caught in the energy field. As the sludge oozed down the hill back toward the swamp, the boy came to his knees crying and coughing and pointing out at the pond.

"Stay right here," Cletis pleaded with him, pulling off the outer woolen robe he wore and dropping it next to him. The lad sat down weakly and cried, wiping mud from his mouth and chin. "I'm goin' back for your friend," Cletis stated, touching the boy on the shoulder and looking into his face.

"He's my brother," the boy wept, looking out over the swamp.

Instantly the conduit gathered again around Cletis, and as he eyed the area where the boy floundered, with a thought, he was above the child, guiding the conduit down into the quagmire directly over and around the boy. Only his head and hands remained above the surface now, yet he still gripped the baseball. His neck craned back, the little boy frantically fought to keep the mud from reaching his mouth.

Without the robe to cover him, the coldness of the sludge took Cletis's breath away. Instantly he wrapped his arms under the boy's chest and lifted his head above the surface of the mud. The child gasped for air, crying with fright. Again, in the effort to hold the boy, Cletis sunk rapidly into the sludge. When he felt the mire touch the bottom of his chin, Cletis panicked .... And with the panic, instantly the blue conduit was gone.

Concentrate on the conduit! Keep the kid's face above the surface!

But the kicking and jerking of the frightened boy made the process all the more difficult. The dark liquid rose above Cletis's chin and covered his bottom lip. He strained to breathe and fought to summon the conduit. But in the grip of such tense circumstances, his mind was unable to focus. A moment before the dark liquid covered his mouth and nose, Cletis took a last, deep breath. As he sunk into the murky black slime, he fought to command the powers of the conduit. Despite his efforts to remain afloat, he felt the eerie sludge close in over the top of his head and sink into his nose and ears. Instantly, his world went black and silent.

The little boy is under too!! Concentrate on the conduit! I've got to get us out of here!

"NO!" came a distant and muffled cry. The pad of rapid footsteps upon the mud came softly into Cletis's ears. "NO!" Again the cry was heard. It was a desperate scream, followed by anguished sobs.

With a slight hum, the blue conduit appeared above and behind the weeping boy. It released its cargo, spilling a stream of black liquid and two boys onto the ground below. Cletis and the smaller lad landed and rolled, both coughing and spurting and trying to catch a lungful of fresh air. The redheaded boy raced back to his brother and lovingly wiped the mud from his face, mouth, and ears. Cletis sputtered and slowly came to his feet. His eyes burned and watered with the sting of the mud. Through blurred vision, he watched the two boys as they hugged and cried and clung to each other. To Cletis's utter astonishment, still, the tinier of the two gripped the muddy baseball, as if it were a treasure of greater value than life itself.

When the boys finally breathed freely, they turned to Cletis and measured him curiously. He was completely covered, from head to boot, with black, sticky mud, and he continued to cough, shake his head, blow his nose, and do all that he could to free himself from the slime that caked him inside and out.

"There is a stream."

The redheaded boy pointed to the north. He spoke in the same lilting accent of Mahon and Teagan. Both muddy children stood, took Cletis by the hands, and directed him up the rise.

About fifty yards above the swamp, a small stream of clear water tumbled down the hillside. It was partially covered from view by the tall grasses that grew heartily on its banks. But the boys were familiar with its location and features, for they led Cletis to a tiny dam on level ground, where the stream was deep enough for the three to immerse themselves.

Despite the biting coldness of the water, Cletis and the boys welcomed the cleansing current of the little pool. Within moments most of the mud had washed away, leaving behind only the traces of the swamp's tarry, black oil that now stuck to their clothing, hands, and faces like small chunks of chewed-up, black licorice. As he rubbed the mud from his face and arms, and allowed the chilly stream to course over him, Cletis noticed that the two boys, still in the water with him, were studying the baseball—holding it up to the light of the cloudy sky, dunking it under the water, and rolling it in their fingers. The older boy turned to Cletis, and when he noticed that Cletis was watching them, bowed his head apologetically.

"We found it in the lodge, and we brought it up here to play with it." He nodded toward his little brother, who now listened intently. "Donal and me—I'm Eamon—we knew no one would be here, because we are forbidden to come here. I threw this . . ." He held it up, searching for a word. " . . . this *orb* too hard, and it hit a rock and bounced far into the swamp. Donal went in after it, and when he was stuck, I went in to help him."

Cletis nodded, sensing that both of them could have easily become archeological treasures. He studied them, trying to guess their ages. Eamon looked to be six or seven years old; Donal, near five. The younger boy had light blond hair and a herd of freckles across his nose and cheeks. He spoke very little but smiled beautifully.

"I guess you could call it an orb, but its real n-name is a *baseball*," Cletis explained through chattering teeth. He laid his head back against a mossy, rounded rock, and drilled a finger into his ear, still trying to clean out the sticky mud. The boys watched him curiously. "But I need that one," Cletis added, pointing to the ball in the little boy's hand. "I'll b-bring you others."

The wind shifted abruptly, and Cletis caught a whiff again of the stinking, dead pigs. He dipped his whole body, once more, into the freezing water, and came up gasping, shaking his head from one side to the other.

"Come with me," Cletis announced, spitting and rising from the water. He stepped onto the grassy bank and rinsed his soggy boots once again. Emptying the brown water from them, he pulled them over his feet. The two boys did the same. Within moments, the drenched trio sloshed their way down the hill toward the dreadful stench.

"They were our father's," announced Eamon as he stood with Donal and Cletis over the dead pigs. Eamon wrapped his arm protectively around his shivering little brother. "We d-don't know why they died. Father was herding them over there." He pointed up the road to a grassy hill. "And suddenly these three fell to their knees and buckled over dead. So f-father dragged them here to the swamp to let them sink."

Cletis studied the pigs a moment and then turned back to the boys. *Maybe this was Padar's final piece of magic.*

"What I'm going to do is very important, but I need you to keep it a secret for me. If you p-promise not to tell, then I won't tell Chief Mahon you took his orb."

The boys' eyes widened with fright. "This is the Bear's?" questioned Eamon. "This orb is M-Mahon's?"

When Cletis nodded, Donal turned to Eamon. "Perhaps Grandfather will let us play with it."

"We should have asked him first," responded Eamon, guiltily.

Cletis eyed them curiously. "Wait a second . . . Chief Mahon is your grandfather?" he questioned.

The two boys shivered and nodded. "Yes. Our f-father is his oldest son," added Eamon, respectfully.

Cletis leaned back a moment, pondering. *Oh, my gosh . . . Abish has a brother, and I don't know anything about him. Which makes these guys my cousins! Eamon and Donal are my cousins!*

"Do you have an aunt named Abish?" Cletis continued, wondering if the boys knew of her existence.

"My father speaks of a sister," answered Eamon, "but we don't know her. She left the village before we were born."

Cletis thought for a moment, allowing the weight of their words to settle on his heart. He now studied the two boys in an entirely different light. "Listen to me carefully. It is important that I bury the orb," continued Cletis, holding up the ball. "And I must bury it in a very special and different way." He took Donal by the hand and pulled him forward and squatted before him. He looked into the boy's light blue eyes and his innocent, trusting face. Instantly Cletis noticed the chain that hung around Donal's neck. At the bottom of the chain dangled the round, silver pendant that would be mentioned in the tabloid article a thousand years from now—the pendant that carried the engraved image of a bear, a robed man, and the floating open scroll.

The sign of the Dungarvans under Chief Mahon. That's what they'll see. Then this is the right place, and these are the right boys. And we'll leave the future as it should be, but we'll improve the past. Both sides'll be happy.

He pulled Donal over to the side of the dead pig that lay closest to them. "Eamon," Cletis called back. "Come over here near us and watch. Cuz what I'm gonna do with him, I'm gonna do with you too."

Trembling, the boy obeyed and trotted over next to his brother.

Cletis yanked off his wet shirt, squatted down again, and placed his fingertips on the pig carcass. He then pressed Donal's hand over the Traveler's mark on his right shoulder and closed his eyes in concentration. Instantly Donal's image materialized in Cletis's mind, and the Changeling powers coursed through his being. Cletis felt his hair stand on end with the energized current. Donal jumped slightly, feeling the strange force that suddenly flowed from the mark on the shoulder of the magical boy. He looked back at his brother and smiled excitedly.

Instantly Cletis felt the surge stream down his arm and hand. As the power arced from his fingertips into the pig, the Changing process began. *This is different transforming something that is dead,* Cletis reasoned as he struggled to force the Changeling energy into the lifeless sow. Yet as he focused and concentrated, he heard both boys gasp. *Something must be happening,* Cletis told himself. Opening his eyes, he watched as the bones within the pig's body rippled with movement. The muscles, skin, and structure of the animal slowly came to life, morphing and bending, step-by-step assuming the shape of the young boy whose image filled Cletis's mind. The head and facial features of the creature shifted and pulled like a rubber mask, gradually taking on the likeness of little Donal.

Eamon laughed giddily and jumped in the air with excitement as he watched the pig's feet stretch and widen, transforming into a human likeness. The legs of the animal melded and churned and squeaked until they became an exact replica of the arms and legs of the tiny blond brother. Eamon watched as the fur and fibers that covered the animal's reeking body, lengthened and pulled and multiplied, finally assuming the weave and texture of the clothing and boots worn by Donal.

As the process came to an end, an exact replica of the little boy lay lifelessly in the shallows of the swamp, next to the other two pigs. Even the chain that hung upon Donal's neck was duplicated precisely.

"Thanks, Donal," stated Cletis, releasing the child's hand and glancing across at the handiwork of the Changeling powers. "Now, Eamon, it's your turn."

The big brother strode forward, looked down at Donal with a smile, and clasped Cletis's hand. Still shivering under his wet clothing, he turned to his little brother. "Does it hurt?" he asked, preparing for pain.

Donal shook his head. "It feels warm," came the soft answer.

Cletis stepped to the second pig and took Eamon's hand. He pressed it on the hourglass mark on the front of his shoulder and squatted down by the stinking animal. Cletis placed his fingers on the rotting carcass, closed his eyes in concentration, and again allowed the Changeling process to begin. Gradually the power flowed anew through Cletis's outstretched hands. Instantly the dead pig began to morph, stretch, moan, and mold. Within moments the bloated pink animal was transformed into an exact likeness of the redheaded brother, Eamon. The two little boys laughed out loud and jumped with excitement as they looked upon their lifeless twin brothers created from the dead pigs.

"Now," shivered Cletis, smiling at their reactions and rising over the two replicated little boys, "I n-need the baseball." Obediently Donal extended it to Cletis. "Remember, I'm gonna bring you more of these, if you want."

Donal smiled through chattering teeth and nodded up at him.

Cletis bent down and pushed the ball under the arm and clothing of Eamon's replica.

"One more thing," stated Cletis, turning back to the boys and suddenly feeling responsible for them. "You gotta know that those two forms—those bodies there that you see—they're not people. They are pigs. Dead pigs. Dead pigs that I Changed. Okay? They're not alive. You understand? You wanna touch 'em to make sure?"

The boys' eyes blazed with excitement, and they stepped forward, bent down, and prodded and tapped the two forms, giggling with wonder as they did.

"Remember, this is our secret. Okay?"

Again the boys nodded. When he was certain that the ball was securely in place, Cletis arose and summoned the conduit to gather around him. The little boys continued to watch with open mouths and fixed stares as Cletis called upon his inborn powers. Then, attempting something new, Cletis stepped away from the energy field. Even without him inside the swirling cylinder, it remained functioning, as if awaiting his orders. With a gentle wave of his hand, he guided the conduit over the two lifeless replicas of Eamon and Donal, and then widened the radiant, blue field to include the remaining pig.

"Let's get rid of that stinky thing too," Cletis announced.

As the blue light hovered above, the three bodies lifted away from the mud that bound them and floated up into the conduit. Cletis then directed the energy field out over the middle of the boggy swamp, halted the conduit, and lowered the lifeless forms to the surface of the mud. With a nod of his head, the conduit instantly disappeared, and the figures settled gradually into the sludge. From the bank near the road, Cletis, Donal, and Eamon watched the pond swallow the carcasses. A muddy bubble lifted and bulged where the bodies had sunk. It thinned gradually and burst with a satisfied belch, as if the dark, thick swamp had just swallowed a tasty meal.

"There," stated Cletis, wrapping an arm around each boy. "All the pieces are in place. The prophecy is fulfilled." They looked up at him, still trembling with cold. Despite their puzzled expressions, Cletis kept talking . . . to the pond, to the valley, to the world. "It's all done. Now I can go home and play some ball, and now *she* can rest." He chuckled lightly. "'Time that gave doth now his gift confound.' It's all come full circle here, eh?"

Cletis picked up his muddy robe and led the boys to the dry road on higher ground.

"Let's go get some clean clothes on," Cletis announced as the trio walked southwards toward the village. The wind still swooped past them, toying with their wet hair as they walked. The billowy, white-and-gray clouds continued to gather in the darkening skies above them. In the distance ahead—out toward the village—a flock of gulls paid no attention to the oncoming storm. Happily they rode the air currents, lifting and dropping playfully, and cawing with light laughter.

"There is an old lady that lives near your village," Cletis commented as they walked. "An old and ugly lady. Do you know of her or where she lives?"

Eamon looked up at Cletis. "Do you mean the hag that lives by the sea?" he questioned.

"Maybe," answered Cletis, thoughtfully.

"Some of the older boys in the village say she is a witch and that she has lived there for eleven winters," explained Eamon. "Some go to her house at night and watch her secretly."

Cletis lifted his head thoughtfully and looked toward the sea. He pulled both boys closer to his sides. "I know that old woman. And she's a friend of mine. Yes, she's ugly, but she's not a witch. Her heart's as good and as big as Chief Mahon's. She's as kind and gentle as your grandmother, Teagan." The two boys looked curiously up into Cletis's face. "Will you be nice to her?" he continued. "Will you do that? Will you treat her just like you'd treat your grandmother?"

The boys shook with cold, but nodded obediently.

The grasses on the hills bowed gracefully as the breeze skimmed over the top of them. The white flowers on the trees across the valley represented a promise of sweet harvest yet to come. Cletis pondered the simple beauties and the tender mercies that surrounded him. Then suddenly the Feeling came again, filling his being with energy and comfort and gratitude—as if someone who knew much more than he, someone who was always watching, was saying, "Well done, Cletis of Dungarvan."

Garth, Cletis, and Abish had been on the field, tossing a ball back and forth, hitting some flies to one another and taking advantage of the pleasant evening. But now Cletis watched from center field as Garth and Abish took another infield breather, sat down on the splinter-ridden dugout bench, and just talked. Cletis smiled, sliced his glove through a fog of gnats that hovered above his head, and watched a distant jet plane paint a white stripe across the blue heavens. On the outskirts of town the seven o'clock train announced its evening arrival into Greenberg Junction.

From where he stood, he watched Abish smile and laugh, and he wondered what old joke his dad had just told her or what plumbing task he had solved today that made for a funny story. *Dad, just get the job done!* He wanted to walk right up to them and tell them the obvious. But trying to maintain a level head, he felt it wise to keep his distance and his silence. *Dad says they got a lot to figure out.* He watched Abish laugh and lean in against his dad. *Abish sure looks different in jeans, sandals, and a regular shirt.* Cletis turned around toward his house, admiring the tickseed flowers that grew in yellow patches across the field behind the diamond.

"It doesn't take no Time Traveler to know what's gonna happen in the future here, Dad," Cletis whispered aloud. "And you've had three days to think about it."

Cletis peered off thoughtfully in the direction of Abish's old house. Again he pictured it in his mind, with all its weird and unique characteristics—the baseball room, the library, the blown-out bedroom, and the creaky back porch with the chimes. He pondered a moment, reliving the events that had taken place in and around that rundown old cottage. In his mind's eye, he saw the old woman—the dear old hag he had come to know. Ugly as she was, she was there in his memories, and he studied her odd features tenderly—her puffy hands, her baggy boots, her round face, her grizzled hair, and her emerald eyes. And as he thought about her—the feared witch of Greenberg Junction—he realized that he had grown deeply fond of that old woman.

As if being drawn to the place, he dropped his mitt where he stood, wandered away from the ball diamond, and started the half-mile walk to the hill that overlooked the canal and the broken dwelling. He knew he could use the conduit to transport himself there, but this gentle evening was made for walking and thinking, and he wanted to retrace the familiar path he had trodden so many times before.

For some strange reason, he longed to see the old woman—the old Abish—the squat, ugly, misshapen lady who had nurtured him through the entire ordeal of the prophecy. *Why? Why do I want to see* her *again? Abish is right back there behind me.* He fought against a funny urge to turn back to Abish and his dad. Instead he kept his eyes focused on the forest far ahead. His pace quickened, and he began to jog and then run.

Within minutes Cletis stood panting at the top of the hill, overlooking Abish's property. The damage around the place and in the forest, done by the Traveler during the frozen moments of Time, had been erased. But the old hole in the back wall still remained, yawning up at him. If he listened closely, he could hear her in his memory calling out to him for help from the canal. Drawn to the place, he began the short descent to the vacant home.

At the base of the hill, he jumped the stream easily and stood for a moment eyeing the house. Instantly the details of the final conflict with the Traveler rushed through his mind. The memories, so fresh and painful, brought tears to his eyes. *But that's not why I came here,* he reminded himself. He pushed the dreadful thoughts from the stage of his mind and focused instead on the sweet recollections of the old Abish. He crossed the dirt area behind the house, made his way past the gaping hole in the wall, and walked over to the porch. He pulled open the screen door, stepped up onto the wooden flooring, and paused for a moment. Abish's chair was there. Empty. Abish's house was before him. Empty.

He lowered himself onto the wooden cane-back chair, where he had often seen the old lady sit. The chair creaked under him as he settled onto it. Through the screens that surrounded him he looked out at the trees on the hillside behind the house. *In all her lonely thoughts she used to sit here.* The crickets chirped soothingly from the shrubs and overgrowth that surrounded the home. The waters of the canal gurgled a calming tune as they passed. *This is where she sat . . . wondering if she would ever see her family again . . . wondering if she would ever* have *a family again. No one came to visit her. She was all alone. A thousand years she faced that . . .* He looked up into the canopy of the trees across the canal. *Why? Why would she do that?*

He studied the screen door he had fixed a little over two weeks ago. He remembered how she had watched him as he worked, and how her eyes lit up when she found out he was Garth Dungarvan's boy. Cletis pondered that moment, trying to put some mental puzzle pieces together. *She was wondering if her test was finally comin' to an end, wasn't she. She was thinkin' that it just might be over. She was wonderin', if after all those years, she was finally gonna be able to see her family again. She carried the curse of that Changing all those years . . . and she never knew what happened to her little boy.*

Cletis leaned back in the old chair and balanced on two legs. He studied the boxes that were scattered on the porch in front of him. *I never really knew how she was doin' down deep inside. I never asked her. No one ever asked her.*

He sat several minutes, lost in his thoughts, listening to the lapping of the canal and the occasional chirp of a bird that flitted by. Despite the serenity that surrounded him, he was uneasy inside. He looked out at the forest on the hill and studied the tossing leaves of the maples that reflected the final rays of the day's sunlight.

"Cletis!" came his father's voice from the top of the hill. "Are you down there?"

Cletis remained silent a moment. "Yeah," he finally answered just loud enough to be heard. He wasn't ready to stop the flow of thoughts that coursed through his mind.

He heard branches and twigs snapping, and knew they were coming. At the base of the hill, they both jumped the canal and quietly approached, seemingly aware of Cletis's meditation. It was the first time Abish had been back to the place since Garth's hospitalization. It was the first time visiting the old home in the person of the new, real Abish.

They both stepped close to the back porch and spotted Cletis sitting in Abish's cane-back chair. Abish opened the screen and stepped up next to Cletis, while Garth held the door open and looked on. Despite their presence, Cletis sat silently, still far away in thought, pondering the ideas that flooded his mind.

"Are you all right, Cletis?" Abish finally whispered, kneeling in front of him and leaning back onto her heels.

He stared at her a moment, studying the features of the new woman. Yet her eyes were the same. *Look at her eyes*, he told himself. *The eyes are Abish.* He smiled at her. *It's weird how our roles have switched around. When the box disappeared, and I came here to her, she was sitting in this chair, and I was the one kneeling on the floor.*

"I'm trying to figure it all out, Abish," he began, attempting to organize his thoughts. "And you tell me if I'm right or wrong." He turned to his dad. "And you tell me too, Dad, cuz you know about this stuff." He took a breath and looked again out at the leaves of the maples. "I came here because somethin's missin' in me, and I couldn't figure out what it was . . . but I felt this was the place to come to, to find my answers."

Abish studied him, and settled her hands on his knees.

"First of all," he continued, " . . . and I'm just gonna say it, cuz I don't know any other way around it." He bowed and then looked up again. "I didn't really get to say good-bye to the old woman who used to live here. *That* Abish. And I wanted to. Things were all happenin' so fast when she had to go . . ." He dropped his focus from the trees and stared directly into her eyes. His vision blurred a bit, and he blinked hard against the forming tears. "So if . . . if you ever see her," he whispered, "will you . . . um . . . tell her . . . tell her good-bye for me?"

She smiled up at him.

"Second," Cletis started again, clearing his throat. "I didn't really know what she had gone through, and I still don't know now and don't think I ever *will* really know. I don't even understand what it's like to live fifteen years, let alone a thousand." He gazed at her for a moment, trying to see a bit deeper into her green eyes—maybe trying to find the old Abish. "But to live those thousand years without people around to help her, or without someone to say somethin' nice to her now and again, or without someone to touch her hand, or eat dinner with . . ." He paused and swallowed. "That's way past what I can understand." He rubbed his fingers across his chin, steadying his lips.

"And third—and this I think is maybe the answer to the second part . . . at least in my thinkin'—I believe the whole reason for this test and the prophecy . . . the *baseball box prophecy*, I guess you could call it . . . was to teach her to love so that she could teach *me* how to love the way *she* loved, and so that I could understand even better the love that my mom, Anna, had for me." He looked up at his father and then back to Abish. His hand lifted to his cheek, and he wiped away a descending tear. "Cuz I didn't really understand some of that until I Changed into you and until the real dark times when I was over there in the mud by the canal." He pointed to the place behind his dad. "That's when I felt it all the most . . . so that I could learn that *that* kind of love that I felt *then* is what . . . kinda holds everything together . . . and that there's nothing that can take its place." He sniffed and rubbed his eyes, feeling a bit sheepish about showing his emotions so honestly in front of the two of them. "I guess that's all."

Abish smiled up at him fondly.

"Whoever heard of such thoughts coming from the mind of a twelve-year-old?" She pondered a moment, then looked up at Garth and back to Cletis. "Well . . . you told me to tell you if you were right or wrong," she began. "My dear, brave boy, you are partly right, and you are partly wrong. To me, the purpose of the test, and the whole *baseball box prophecy* as you called it, was to teach me to love as my son loved—selflessly, heroically, fearlessly." She took his hands. "The hardest part of my test, by far—above all the loneliness and tears and empty years—was to see my son . . . one who had never done anything to deserve to be placed in such danger, fight my battle for me, risk his life, and come close to death so that I could . . ." Momentarily she was silent. She squeezed his hand reassuringly. "My son not only courageously fought that battle, but he prevailed because of his extraordinary ability to love and feel love." She studied Cletis's face, allowing her tears to drop onto her cheeks. "For a mother, there is no greater reward than that.

"And for a mother," she continued, smiling up at him, "it was worth the thousand-year wait." She knelt up straight, wiped away her tears, then leaned forward and kissed his cheeks. "Thank you, Cletis of Dungarvan," she whispered. "Thank you."

They studied one another for a quiet moment. Then, gracefully, Abish came to her feet and took Cletis by the hands. She pulled him up to her, wrapped her arms around him, and drew him close to her. "What a treasure you are, my son." She pressed her cheek down upon his strawberry blond hair. "And I will tell you this," she whispered above her ear. "If I happen to see your old friend—the one who used to live here—I will tell her of your kind words, and I will give her your love . . . though I think she has already felt it deeply." She kissed his forehead.

The evening breeze suddenly tossed the metal chimes above them. The happy tones of the hollow tubes seemed to announce a welcome to the new Abish. She looked up at the cylinders as if they were her old friends.

"Those chimes have invited many a boy to this back porch," she said with a wink, looking down at Cletis. "Who would have guessed that they would have called my only son, through centuries of time, to this very place?" Cletis looked up at the little chimes and smiled at the memories.

Abish pushed a box out of her way and stepped toward the back door. "Well, gentlemen, thank you for coming over this evening. You've seen the beautiful exterior," she teased, looking out at the dirt, the weeds, the canal, and the broken wall. "Would you like a tour of the interior palace?"

"We would," chuckled Garth. "Cletis knows the place, but I don't."

"There's a special room I'll show you," she spoke, winking at Cletis, "that I think you'll appreciate." With that, she turned, opened the rickety old back door, and entered the house.

Cletis paused a moment. He looked back at the screen door behind him, then up to the chimes that swayed in the breeze. His dad, who had stepped past him to the back door, waited at the threshold. Cletis reached up, tapped the chimes for old time's sake, and watched them dance and sing as they swung back and forth.

"This place is a dump, Dad," Cletis whispered, turning past the tattered array of old boxes. "I don't know how she ever lived here."

"Well, if it didn't look like a haunted house," his father answered, "it wouldn't have attracted boys like you."

With a nod, Cletis stepped up next to his dad and paused in the doorway. Unexpectedly another thought struck him. He panicked. "Abish!" he called, "Is that little pile of dust still on the fireplace rocks next to those other baseball cards?"

There was a momentary silence as Cletis awaited an answer. "Yes, it is," came the reply from within.

"Uh . . . that one will be our secret, okay?"

"Okay. But don't worry, I have four more of that card!"

Cletis gasped and closed his eyes in disbelief. His dad gazed down at him through a puzzled frown. Cletis smiled up at his dad, cleared his throat, and entered the house.

The moment he stepped into the rickety old hallway, the sweet scent of vanilla tickled his nose. He stopped, taking a second to explore the familiar fragrance. He had smelled it in her house and in his a dozen times over the past two weeks. But suddenly the vanilla took on a new and meaningful significance. Now the fragrance was sort of a connection between the present and the past—a kind of time-bridge linking the old Abish and the new, and the roots and branches of one gigantic Dungarvan family tree. Yet with newfound gifts and understanding, he realized that the past and present were now one and the same . . . as were his two families.

"You okay?" questioned his father, placing his hands on Cletis's shoulders.

"Yeah . . . yeah, I'm okay . . . pretty much, I guess." Cletis looked up at his dad. His tone turned suddenly impatient. "It's just that there's one question that needs to be asked."

"Yeah?"

"Yeah . . . and Abish will know the answer. I'm sure she will."

"Well then, you'd better ask her."

Cletis frowned up at him. "No, Dad, *you* better ask her."

His father eyed him curiously.

With the chimes still dancing behind them, Cletis took his dad by the arm and led him down the dilapidated, vanilla-scented hallway.

The End

Acknowledgements

Special thanks to teachers and classes who bravely sat through the preliminary readings of a living, changing document. Neresa Nielsen, Michelle Fredericks, Sonya Pearson, and Elaine Brough, you're wonderful! Thanks, too, to those of you who were willing to sludge through initial rough drafts. Your selflessness provided critical feedback. Tom Hughes, Kevin Krough, Kim Stinger and family, Krista El Bakri and family, Jentzen Newbold, Carol Childers, Bill Prows, Cynthia Hiatt, Julia Belleau, Bev Qualheim, Sona Gourgouris, David Newbold, and M4, please receive my heartfelt gratitude. Vaughn and Cecelia Benson, you were with me from screenplay to novel. I can't thank you enough. And Katie, my daughter and my editor—you kept me straight, concise, and ellipsisically correct.

About the Author

Actor and author Bruce Newbold has guest-starred, co-starred, and appeared in television programs such as *Hill Street Blues, L.A. Law, Touched by an Angel, Highway to Heaven, Tour of Duty, Major Dad, Everwood,* and *Father Dowling Mysteries.* He has also worked in such films as *Bonneville; The Executioner's Song; A More Perfect Union; Perfect Murder, Perfect Town; Silk Hope; Only a Stonecutter;* and the Disney TV movies *Pixel Perfect* and *The Poof Point.*

His one-man dramatization depicting the life and ministry of Jesus Christ, *In Him Was Life,* has been performed on stages in the United States and England.

In 1997, Newbold accompanied the sesquicentennial Oregon Trail/Mormon Trail Wagon Train, writing and hosting the fourteen-part documentary, entitled *Legacy West.* He was later commissioned by Deseret Book Publishing Company to write the experiences of the adventure. The book, *In Our Father's Footsteps,* was published in 1998.

The Baseball Box Prophecy is based on one of three screenplays Newbold optioned in the Hollywood market.

Bruce Newbold and his family live in Utah.

Hearthsong

For speaking engagements, or to contact
Hearthsong Entertainment,
or the author, please email:
brucenewbold@thebaseballboxprophecy.com.

TheBaseballBoxProphecy.com website design by M4.